1.31198

AUG 2007

FEB12

DATE D

D0874528

MAR 13 19

MAY 1   Trial Ba

813.52   1.31198

March, William
    Trial balance

15.95

Horseshoe Bend Regional Library
DADEVILLE, ALABAMA

THIS BOOK PROVIDED BY
ALABAMA PUBLIC LIBRARY SERVICE

The Library of Alabama Classics,

reprint editions of works important

to the history, literature, and culture of

Alabama, is dedicated to the memory of

Rucker Agee

whose pioneering work in the fields

of Alabama history and historical geography

continues to be the standard of

scholarly achievement.

Trial Balance

The Collected Short Stories of

William March

With an Introduction by

Rosemary M. Canfield-Reisman

131198 ✓

The University of Alabama Press

Tuscaloosa and London

Copyright 1929, 1930, 1931, 1932, 1933, 1934, 1935,
1936, 1937, 1938, 1939, 1940, 1943, 1944, 1945, by
William March

Originally published by Harcourt, Brace and Company

Introduction Copyright 1987 by
The University of Alabama Press
Tuscaloosa, Alabama 35487

All rights reserved
Manufactured in the United States of America

LIBRARY OF CONGRESS CATALOGING-IN-PUBLICATION DATA

MARCH, WILLIAM, 1893–1954.
    TRIAL BALANCE.

    (THE LIBRARY OF ALABAMA CLASSICS)
    I. TITLE. II. SERIES.
    PS3505.A53157T7 1987   813'.52   87-5900
    ISBN 0-8173-0372-3 (PBK. : ALK. PAPER)

TO

FINLEY *and* LUCILLE

CONTENTS

ACKNOWLEDGMENTS

Acknowledgment is made to the following magazines in which some of these stories first appeared: *Accent, Alabama Rammer-Jammer, American Prefaces,* the *Atlantic Monthly, Coronet, Encore, Esquire, Forum and Century, Good Housekeeping, Harper's Bazaar,* the *Harvard Wake, Kansas Magazine, Literary America, Mademoiselle,* the *Midland, New Mexico Quarterly Review,* the *New Republic, Pagany, Prairie Schooner, Red Book Magazine, Rocky Mountain Review, Scribner's Magazine, Story,* the *Tanager,* the *University Review,* the *Yale Review.*

INTRODUCTION

ROSEMARY M. CANFIELD-REISMAN

His novels are out of print. His short stories are omitted from most anthologies of Southern literature. In the current *Oxford Companion to English Literature*, which gives Mississippi's Faulkner almost a column, his name does not appear. Even in Louisiana State University's encyclopedic *History of Southern Literature*, he merits only four sentences in a section on "popular fiction," calling him a "male modernist" without "peculiarly Southern characteristics."[1] To the general public, he may be remembered as the man who wrote the story of a successful young murderess in the film *The Bad Seed*. Yet two years after his death, Alistair Cooke called him "one of the most underrated of contemporary American writers of fiction."[2] The literary world did not agree. While Yoknapatawpha County became a geographical reality to most of the world, Pearl County was unknown. Except for an edition of his fables produced by The University of Alabama Press in 1960, he went out of print. Except by his family and some Alabama literary historians, he seemed to have been forgotten.

Yet students of Alabama literature continue to believe that William March is probably the most important writer that this state has produced, as well as a major figure in the Southern Renascence.[3] There are signs that Cooke's cry in the wilderness may at last be heeded. In 1984, the definitive biography of March was published, *The Two Worlds of William March*, a brilliant work by the British scholar Roy S. Simmonds, who picked up the research where the Canadian critic Lawrence William Jones had left it at his untimely death. In 1986, March's Pearl County story "Not Worthy of a Wentworth" was featured in Philip D. Beidler's much-needed collection *The Art of Fiction in the Heart of Dixie: An Anthology of Alabama Writers*. The same year, March's native Mobile celebrated a week-long "Salute to William March," drawing together family, friends, and scholars for reminiscence and discussion. Finally, with the publication of this volume,

March's short stories will once again be generally available, and readers can determine for themselves how well these stories stand the test of time. On rereading March's novels and stories, I have been struck by his Southernness, a quality which has not generally been stressed. Even his defender Alistair Cooke insisted that the Southern details, while accurate, were incidental, because March's Southern settings were really no more than backdrops for his analysis of human nature. For Cooke, March's strength was that he was not a local colorist. Certainly one can respond to March's war stories without noticing whether a doomed soldier remembers Christmas in Alabama or in Kansas. Only a close reader will associate the Peabody Hotel in "The Shoe Drummer" with Memphis or notice that the boy in "A Snowstorm in the Alps" comes from Reedyville, March's fictitious south Alabama county seat, to New York and his death. Even when the setting is specifically and undeniably Southern, from diet to dialect, as in the three Pearl County novels and a dozen or so short stories, March, like Faulkner, transcends locality in his delineation of human nature. Yet in March, as in Faulkner, one sees a peculiarly Southern sensibility, a sensibility which infuses all of his work, whatever the setting. Born in a society which remembers its lost causes and its negated ideals, which has taken refuge in the seeming security of family, class, and religious certainties, which, under siege, has attacked its own nonconformists or retreated into narcissism, March could hardly have escaped its influence. Whether he writes of fascism in Germany or alienation in New York, he has the vantage point of a Southerner. As a result, he is neither less modern nor less universal, but perhaps simply more perceptive.

William Edward Campbell, who was to write under the pseudonym of William March, was born September 18, 1883, in Mobile, Alabama.[4] His mother's family claimed descent from a son of the Earl of March and a Lady Elizabeth Bacon, and William's own maternal grandfather was a prominent Mobilian. His father, John Leonard Campbell, was of Scottish descent, orphaned, and relatively uneducated. When he met Susan March, he was captain of a scow based in Mobile. After his marriage, he became a timber estimator in the forests of Escambia County in the Florida Panhandle and in Covington County, Alabama. The pay was not enough to provide anything but the bare necessities for the rapidly growing family— eleven children in twenty-two years—and the frequent moves of the Campbells prevented the children from obtaining proper schooling. An intelligent boy, William was no stranger to dreams of a better life. Ma-

rooned in Lockhart, Alabama, which was to be the Hodgetown of his
fictitious county, William had no high school to attend. Instead, he worked
as a clerk in a lumber company office. A year later, he escaped to Mobile,
where he worked in a law office and attended business school. Finding that
Valparaiso University in Indiana would offer him a high school course of
study, he attended for a year, obtaining the necessary diploma, with which
he entered the University of Alabama law school. After a year, he left for
lack of funds, and although he hoped to return, William Campbell was to
have no more formal education. He had already learned a great deal about
life as a poor boy in the rural South.

In 1916, William Campbell moved to New York, where he lived and
worked until the First World War broke out. In the Marine Corps,
Campbell had the combat experiences which he dramatized in his first
novel, *Company K*. He received three decorations for his courage. However, his initial idealism turned to a consciousness of betrayal. Campbell
was soon convinced that war, like religion, was a fraud perpetrated by
society, which encouraged man's natural cruelty and destroyed the
innocent.

Returning to Mobile after the war, Campbell was involved in the
founding of the Waterman Steamship Corporation, for which he worked
until 1937, establishing offices in Memphis, New York, and Hamburg,
and finally resigning in London, when the income derived from his successful business ventures would permit him to do so.

Meanwhile, Campbell had begun to write short stories, originally as an
antidote to boredom, when a duodenal ulcer limited his social life in New
York. Soon his stories were being published, beginning with "The Holly
Wreath" in December 1929 and "The Little Wife" the following month.
Of the three pseudonyms Campbell had used in submitting stories for
publication, "William March" seemed luckiest. Thus was born William
March, the writer.

By the time he retired from Waterman, William March (Campbell)
had published three novels: *Company K* (1933), a collection of first-person
sketches by members of a Marine company in the First World War; *Come
In at the Door* (1934), the story of a young Alabama boy who is responsible
for the lynching of a black; and *The Tallons* (1936), also set in Pearl
(Covington) County, Alabama, which in this work becomes the locale of a
love triangle resulting in the murder of one brother by another.

The three later novels were *The Looking-Glass* (1943), a study of narcissistic Reedyville citizens, too preoccupied with their own problems to help a poor boy whose father is dying; *October Island* (1952), an often comic account of mutual misunderstanding between natives and missionaries; and the most famous of his works, *The Bad Seed* (1954), which was adapted by Maxwell Anderson for Broadway and later made into a Warner Brothers film.

In addition to the many stories published separately in magazines or in anthologies, three short story collections were published during March's lifetime. *The Little Wife and Other Stories* (1935) included fourteen stories written between 1928 and 1933. All of these stories were later included in *Trial Balance*. In 1939, *Some Like Them Short* was published. Nineteen of the twenty stories in that collection are also included in *Trial Balance;* only "Nine Prisoners" is omitted, and its omission is a logical decision, since it formed the central incident in the novel *Company K*. When *Trial Balance* was published in 1945, readers could trace the progress of March's work from 1928 to 1944, with the assurance that the author himself had supervised the collection.

Although he was a highly successful businessman, March was also an extremely sensitive human being. It was not only the recollections of combat that haunted him. Roy Simmonds quotes William March's younger brother Peter: " 'He was always angry. He had a lot of rebellion in him. It was possibly a reaction to life in general, life in the South—not specifically his war experiences.' "[5] The anger March felt in response to class and race injustice in the South, for example, was no different from his anger at big city indifference and snobbishness in New York or at heartlessness anywhere else. As his story "Personal Letter" indicates, he was deeply troubled by what he saw during his two years in Nazi Germany, representing the institutionalization of cruelty and prejudice under the guise of patriotism. At any rate, March had a mild nervous breakdown and intensive analysis when he returned to England, and at the end of ten year's residence in New York after his resignation from Waterman, he had a severe breakdown. Brought by friends to south Alabama, March slowly recovered, while he lived first at the famous Grand Hotel at Point Clear and then at several locations in Mobile. Three years later, in 1950, he moved to the French Quarter in New Orleans, where he remained, writing and collecting paintings, until his death on May 15, 1954.

It is not surprising that life in the South has produced such anger in writers like March. Nor should the anger be attributed only to the perception of racial bigotry. It must be remembered that the South is the only section of the United States which has been defeated and occupied, with resulting economic deprivation. The Lost Cause was close to March, whose own paternal grandfather and numerous great-uncles had died in the Civil War. The general deprivation which ensued affected many families, not only the orphaned John Leonard Campbell, who as a result of the war was not able to receive the education which could have kept his own off-spring out of poverty. Yet for many in the South, along with the immediate economic effects of the War came disillusionment, a conviction not only that the outcome had not been worth the losses, but that the Cause itself, perceived as a crusade for freedom, was not what it pretended to be. Given his environment, one can understand the frequency with which March deals with disillusionment. In his own war, for example, March once again saw a crusade for freedom turned into futile butchery. The soda-jerk in "To the Rear," dying from the effects of gas, illustrates the theme:

> He began to think, against his will, of many things: of his enlistment, his eagerness, his romantic thoughts concerning noble deaths and imperishable ideas. Then, in justification of himself, he tried to recall one noble thing that he had seen or done since his enlistment, but he could remember nothing except pain, filth, and servile degradation.

In "George and Charlie," young Charlie Banks moves to Mobile, where he becomes a friend of practical, conservative George Owens. From his youth, Charlie has been an idealist. As a child visiting in Reedyville, he gave his savings to a beggar; later, working in Memphis, he protested discrimination and lost his job. At first, George rejects Charlie's revolutionary suggestions for the elimination of capitalism, child labor, the "'filth and disease and unhappiness'" of the slums, even poverty itself. After he has been fired for his radical talk, Charlie moves away, but his ideas linger. George marries and succeeds, but he cannot forget Charlie, and in his spare time, he pursues Charlie's ideas in the library. When Charlie reappears, George is delighted, but when he discovers that Charlie has given up his cause, George is shocked. Ten years in prison for a bomb he did not throw have cured Charlie of his idealism. Bitter, fearful, insecure, Charlie is now interested only in "'playing ball with the winning team.'" As the story ends, George, too, feels a sense of loss; although he would not have committed himself to the idealism which surely would have cost him his comfortable life in "his comfortable home," he wishes that Charlie had not changed. In some ways, the soda-jerk's discovery that society has sent him to battle against a phantom evil is less tragic than Charlie's abandonment of the fight against real evil.

Most March stories conclude with the perception of loss—loss of a cause, of an ideal, of a dream, of a life. One of the bitterest is "Miss Daisy." The title character is Daisy Burton, the gentle, crippled Presbyterian Sunday School teacher who is generally considered to be "the best practicing Christian" in Reedyville. Her kindness and her courage inspire love in nine-year-old Harry Piggott, and when she is injured, Harry visits her. Unfortunately, in her feverish delirium, Miss Daisy reveals her hatred of life, of God, and of humanity, which, quoting Caligula, she says that she would gladly exterminate. Because he had both idealized and loved her, the seeming embodiment of the Christian faith which she professed, Harry is horrified. When he backs away from motherly Mrs. Porterfield, who is attempting to comfort him, the gesture is symbolic, for as the story ends, Harry resolves, "'Nobody will ever fool me again! . . . Nobody will ever fool me again as long as I live!'"

In other stories, characters must face the fact that a dream, a personal goal, is lost forever, and with it, the motivation for living. Thus in "A Shop in St. Louis, Missouri," the Reedyville woman, Mattie Tatum, denies herself all but the most basic necessities for five long years so that she can open a dress shop in St. Louis, chosen because it is "the only large city she had ever seen." When her mother gets cancer, Mattie refuses to spend her savings for an operation which, the doctor indicates, would have given Mrs. Tatum only a few months more, at best. After her mother's death, however, Mattie is chained by guilt. Unable to escape, she spends her savings on a monument for her mother, thus relinquishing the dream which her mother's illness effectively destroyed and therefore also relinquishing her life.

Frequently March's characters are trapped in youth by their sexual drives, then doomed to years of regret. In "The Arrogant Shoat," the country girl Rancey Catonhead is ecstatic to be living in Reedyville, the greatest metropolis that she can envision; she is ambitious for a life in the circus, once she finishes training her pet pig. However, one kiss from Len Williams causes her to give up her dream and even her pig in order to get married. Only in old age does Rancey, now herself grown piglike, decide that her marriage and her motherhood have been a waste of her life. Vainly she wishes that she had run away with her shoat, and his foolish little performance, as he was taken away in his cage, becomes symbolic of her own meaningless and limited life. Happy in his own romantic illusion of their marriage, Len assures the mourners after Rancey's death that they had a " 'sweet, full life together.' " If she was a silly, performing pig, Len is a boastful guinea cock, crowing over what he believes to be his achievement.

Although he does not share the traditional romantic Southern view of womanhood, March is aware of its influence. One of his finest Reedyville characters, appearing repeatedly in his fiction, is Mrs. Joe Cotton, "Grand Mobilizer of the Christian Gladiators and Secretary of the Reedyville Society for the Fostering of Temperance and the Eradication of Vice," as she is described at the beginning of the short story "Woolen Drawers," which reveals the secret of her seeming chastity. Evidently when she worked at a hotel in Atlanta, the then Alice Ochs supplemented her earnings with gifts from her men "friends," thoroughly enjoying the sense of power which she felt as she aroused and satisfied their passions without herself being emotionally affected. A pair of woolen drawers changes her life. Because Alice has a cold, her roommate persuades her to wear the shapeless undergarments on her first date with the traveling salesman Joe Cotton. Not wishing to reveal her ugly drawers, Alice rejects Joe's advances, thus convincing him of her invincible virtue. The result might have come from a nineteenth-century Southern novel:

For a moment he regarded her simply; then he knelt before her and raised the hem of her skirt to his lips.

"I don't deserve your forgiveness, Miss Alice," he said in a choking voice. "I don't deserve it."

After Joe leaves Atlanta, he deluges Alice with letters pleading for forgiveness, expressing his need for " 'the sweet and tender love of a good woman' " and culminating in a proposal. After their marriage, Alice's disinterest in sex only further convinces Joe of her purity, and in the traditional pattern, he reveres his wife, now highly involved in religious and moral causes, and relieves himself with whores, to whom he sings Alice's praises. Both Joe and Alice have realized their dreams. He believes that he is married to a good woman, and she knows that she has attained power over Joe and, indeed, over the entire Reedyville community, which is subject to her because it accepts the Southern myth of womanhood. March sums up his own attitude in the fable "The Pious Mantis" when he describes the prayers of the female insect, just before "she turned meekly and chewed off her mate's head," which proves that "there is no creature more cruel in her heart than a pious woman."[6]

As far as the promiscuous woman is concerned, March's feelings are more ambivalent. In "The Female of the Fruit Fly," first published, interestingly, in *Mademoiselle*, a biologist's description of the insect which, once aroused, copulates indiscriminately could as well be applied to his runaway wife, who habitually indulges herself, then returns to make her husband's life miserable. On the other hand, March is sympathetic to Reedyville's most famous whore, Honey Boutwell, who is run out of town by Mrs. Joe Cotton, only to become famous and wealthy as a popular singer. In his novel *The Looking-Glass*, March comments that Honey's strength lies in her refusal to feel guilt, which prevented her from being the victim of society. Her standards were her own, not those imposed by Reedyville.

Although Honey Boutwell might have reason to feel grateful to Mrs. Cotton and her friends for driving her out of Reedyville, not everyone who disobeys the local moral laws escapes so easily. In "Happy Jack," Mrs. Cotton has only to announce that a white widow and a black man are living together as man and wife to effect his castration in the name of "American womanhood" and Southern decency. The local printer, Jack Sutton, objects in words which reflect March's viewpoint:

> "I do claim that they, as individuals, have a right to lead any moral life that suits them. If you people do not approve of the life they lead, then you, as individuals, have an equal right to have nothing to do with them."

However, the division of opinion in Reedyville is only as to whether the black man or the white woman should have been punished. It is this intolerance of dissent that finally drives Jack into madness.

March's anger at the narrowness, bigotry, and oppression which he recognizes as characteristic of Southern society is intensified by his appreciation of the natural beauty and great charm of his native area. Jack Sutton chose to live in Reedyville because, viewed from a troop-train, it looked like Paradise:

To the left of the siding was a cottage flanked by crêpe-myrtles cut back to make a hedge, now in full bloom, with blossoms scattered on the grass. In the night, spiders had spun webs over the hedge, which had caught and held dew, and as Jack watched, the sun came up between two trees, slanting the cabin with its light and turning the drenched webs into fire. Then a cow bell sounded from a field a long way off and a bird repeated, three times, a single note that was incredibly liquid and moving.

March's most lyrical passages describe the countryside recalled from his youth in south Alabama, indicating that March felt the sense of place so common to Southerners. He is sensitive to the slow tempo of Southern life, the talk on the front porch, the laughter. Thus "The Borax Bottle" begins with two of his favorite characters, Dr. and Mrs. Kent, spending Sunday afternoon in traditional Southern fashion:

That Sunday afternoon we sat on the shady, east porch of the Kent bungalow and gossiped, but with no real interest, about the people of Reedyville. Finally Mrs. Kent shook back her bracelets, picked up a palmetto fan and waved it lanquidly beneath her nose, her white, fluffy hair lifting upward in the breeze. "I don't know when we've had such a hot spell," she said in a resigned voice, "or one that's lasted so long, either."

Obviously March's anger derives not from a hatred of the South, but from the fact that he loves it too well, so well that, like Jack Sutton, he expects its people to live up to its loveliness, that, like the intelligent, well-educated black, Baptiste, in *Come in at the Door*, he is drawn back to the South both in memory and in actuality. It is significant that after his severe breakdown in 1947, March himself came home to be healed.

Unfortunately, the Southern sense of family and community can paralyze an individual who, unlike Honey Boutwell, is not able to resist their pressures. It is interesting that in "He Sits There All Day Long," set in the North, the son feels intense guilt because he has not been able to care for his father, but it is a personal emotion, not one induced by society, which indeed removes his father. In "A Shop in St. Louis, Missouri," Mattie Tatum not only gives up her dream as a self-inflicted punishment for what she feels was a lack of filial devotion, but she also expresses her sorrow publicly by building a monument to her mother's memory. The difference between the two stories, in many ways so similar, indicates how well

March comprehends the dark side of those Southern bonds which can be so comforting.

Family demands, too, often negate the dreams of individuals. March's "Not Worthy of a Wentworth" tells the tragic story of a woman whose family could never approve of the prospective husbands she found. While Carrie Wentworth simply needed a man who needed her, her family wished her to marry someone of her own social level. Thus by enforcing what the family and the community see as a rigid caste system, the Wentworths force Carrie into second childhood at sixty-two, pathetic as she plays with dolls which replace the children she was never permitted to have.

The pressures of place, family, and community, supported by a moral and religious structure which does not permit dissent, are difficult to resist. Generally it is outsiders and outcasts who challenge the social norms of March's Alabama, but because they are not native community leaders, these dissenters cannot convince the community that it is wrong. Thus Jack Sutton's closest friend makes a typical comment when Jack objects to the castration of the black man: " 'You don't belong to the town, Jack, and you can't understand our viewpoint.' " Then Jack is warned to drop the subject because " 'You can't do any good, and you'll only get yourself in trouble.' " In March's work there is a scarcity of upper-class liberals like Harper Lee's Atticus Finch, and those who do exist, like the well-meaning Kents, tend rather to comment privately upon the activities of people like Mrs. Joe Cotton than to lead a public crusade against them. Because there is no effective dissent within the community, the outlook for the oppressed seems almost hopeless. Thus in "Runagate Niggers," the system of black peonage is stopped only after an outsider reports it to the Federal Government. Then, of course, the entire community is shocked by the arrest of a landowner and the deputy sheriff, who are seen as totally justified in refusing to let a black family leave town. In a comment which expresses the community's outrage at the abridgement of *their* freedom, Birdie says, " 'For two cents I'd move out of this country and go some place where people still enjoy liberty. That's how disgusted I am with this here country.' "

At the end of *A Looking-Glass*, March gathers those who have triumphed over Reedyville. It is significant that all of them have had to leave the South in order to live their own lives and to attain success. However, the irrepressible Honey Boutwell shames Reedyville in one of March's funniest stories, "A Memorial to the Slain," told with delight by Mrs. Kent. By appealing to Reedyville's community spirit, easy patriotism, and greed, Honey traps it into accepting her gift of a statue in honor of the war dead, particularly her brother Breck, who had been noted for his sexual accomplishments before he became Reedyville's much-decorated hero. When the statue is unveiled, the community is shocked to see that Breck is completely naked and very lifelike. With comments about "the pure womanhood of Reedyville" and verses of "Stand Up, Stand Up for Jesus," the moral-religious faction agitates, at last removing the offending member with a mallet and a cold chisel. Although the statue is then removed for "repairs" and conveniently remains in a shed, Honey's victory cannot be questioned. Among other things, she has managed to divide opinion in a town which ordinarily has only one view on a subject. Even the anti-vice group could not deny the fame of the sculptor, and a large segment of Reedyville is too amused to disapprove. In fact, many hope the rumor is true that Breck Boutwell's missing organ is now used as a paperweight by Mrs. Joe Cotton.

Throughout his work, March shows his impatience with the smug assumptions of those who, themselves financially and socially secure, have no empathy with others. The narcissism of the socially and politically elite is the theme of the novel which many consider his best, *The Looking-Glass*, as well as of stories in *Trial Balance* such as "Senator Upjohn," "A Short History of England," and "Personal Letter." Set in New York, in London, and in Hamburg, these stories make it clear that March did not limit his social criticism to the South. However, the caste system of the South made it easy to ignore the sufferings of those on a lower social level simply because it was supported by the conviction that change would mean anarchy, and having experienced anarchy after the Civil War, Southerners could cite history to make their point. It is this contentment with the world as it is which makes quite logical the admonishment of the poor, old white woman in "Tune the Old Cow Died To" or the tenants in "Runagate Niggers" that they should be grateful for what they have, rather than hoping for more.

Although March cannot accept the Christian faith, which itself as institutionalized seems to encourage the crucifixion of the helpless, he does place his hope for the world in a transformation of the human spirit. To March, evil is the betrayal of trust, the crushing of dreams, the destruction of beauty. Even the good women of Williston are sympathetic with Dirty Emma, who killed her husband not because of his brutality toward her, but because he wantonly destroyed her white hyacinth, which was "as clean and pretty as anything in this world can ever expect to be." The narrator's mother, who heard Emma's dying confession, sums up March's own sympathy with those who love beauty enough to defend it:

> "I've come to think of her [dirty Emma] as one of The Furies themselves, a creature dedicated to the avengeance [sic] of those subtle crimes against mankind which pass unnoticed—those most terrible crimes of all, since men, as individuals, are so often unaware that they have been wronged."

It is clear to any reader of March that he attributes a good many of the miseries of men to their involvements with women. Pious women, seductresses, unfaithful wives, liars, girls out for marriage, vain women, fools—all parade through March's pages, intentionally or unintentionally destroying men, with the help of the myth of womanhood. However, March sees the gift of nurturing which some women possess as one of the hopes of humanity. Remembering old Mrs. Foley, the cheerful grandmother who ran Hodgetown's boarding-house and made life endurable for her lodgers, Donald Ridley envies her:

> He saw her now with great clarity, and he understood, at last, that in reality she had been one of the fortunate people of the world—one of those who know why they were born and what their particular usefulness is to be . . . Mrs. Foley had known clearly what her work was. It was to wake up the world and wash its face, feed it, and get it to work on time. She had known from the beginning, and had accepted it.

Like the heroine of "Whistles," Mrs. Kent has known from the beginning, or at least from the time of the emergency described in "The Borax Bottle," what her mission in life is to be. Frankie Kent would need a practical wife "to keep him out of trouble," it was obvious, and she would solve his problem. In the stories in which the Kents appear, it should be pointed out, Dr. Kent seems to be pleased with the solution.

The short story in which March most clearly states what might be called his doctrine of the spiritually elect, "The First Sunset," was privately printed and distributed to his family and friends at the dark Christmas of

1940.[7] The legend of the Christ-figure, Surd, is told by Dr. Ehrlich, a refugee from the Nazis, to a young Reedyville boy, Albert Evans. After Surd's martyrdom, Dr. Ehrlich says, his dust dispersed throughout the world. Now and then it touches someone, and these are the people who " 'confirm with their lives or their works, each according to his particular talent, Surd's message of beauty and mercy and love,' " the people whose " 'mission is to lead the world from brutality and hate back to peace and dignity again.' " Male or female, these are the nurturers and the saviors of humanity.

Above all, William March was a Southern writer, shaped by the rich, complex, passionate environment in which he was reared. Perhaps because he responded so completely to Alabama's colorful people and breathtaking natural beauty, he was the more angered by its cruelty, hypocrisy, and repressiveness. Yet if March learned about evil during his childhood in Alabama, later expanding that dark vision to New York, to London, and to Nazi Hamburg, he also must have learned about good. It is in the Pearl County stories that the kindly nurturers appear. It is to Pearl County that the refugee from Nazi oppression comes for sanctuary. And it is a young Reedyville boy, moved by the refugee's story, who prays to be one of those who will lead mankind to compassion and peace.

NOTES TO THE INTRODUCTION

1. Anne Goodwyn Jones, "Gone with the Wind and Others: Popular Fiction, 1920–1950," in *The History of Southern Literature*, ed. Louis D. Rubin, Jr., et al. (Baton Rouge: Louisiana State University Press, 1985), p. 367.

2. "Introduction to William March," *A William March Omnibus* (New York: Rinehart, 1956), p. xi.

3. Philip D. Beidler, "Introduction· Alabama Flowering I," *The Art of Fiction in the Heart of Dixie: An Anthology of Alabama Writers*, ed. Philip D. Beidler (University, Ala.: University of Alabama Press, 1986), p. 101.

4. For biographical details, see Roy S. Simmonds, *The Two Worlds of William March* (University, Ala.: The University of Alabama Press, 1984).

5. Quoted in Simmonds, p. 157.

6. William March, *99 Fables*, ed. William T. Going (University, Ala.: University of Alabama Press, 1960), p. 189.

7. Simmonds, p. 159.

Trial Balance

THE LITTLE WIFE

JOE HINCKLEY selected a seat on the shady side of the train and carefully stowed away his traveling bag and his heavy, black catalogue case. It was unusually hot for early June. Outside, the heat waves shimmered and danced above the hot slag roadbed, and the muddy river that ran by the station was low between its red banks. "If it's as hot as this in June, it sure will be awful in August," he thought. He looked at his watch: two twenty-eight —the train was five minutes late in getting out. If he had known the two twenty-three was going to be late he might have had time to pack his sample trunk and get it to the station, but he couldn't have anticipated that, of course. He had had so little time after getting that telegram from Mrs. Thompkins—barely time to pack his bag and check out of the hotel. Joe loosened his belt and swabbed his neck with a limp handkerchief. "It don't matter so much about the trunk," he thought. "One of the boys at the hotel can express it to me, or I can pick it up on my way back."

Joe noticed that one end of his catalogue case protruded slightly. With his foot he shoved it farther under the seat. It was a battered black case, made strongly to withstand constant traveling and reinforced at its corners with heavy copper cleats. One of the handles had been broken and mended with newer leather. On the front of the case there had once been stamped in gilt the firm name of "Boykin & Rosen, Wholesale Hardware, Chattanooga, Tenn.," but time had long since worn away the gold lettering.

The telegram had upset Joe: it had come so suddenly, so unexpectedly. He felt vaguely that somebody was playing a joke on him. He felt confused and helpless. It was difficult to believe that Bessie was so desperately sick. He sat for a time staring at

3

his finger nails. Suddenly he remembered an appointment for four o'clock with the buyer for Snowdoun and Sims, and he rose quickly from his seat with some vague idea of telephoning or sending a message to explain his absence. Then he realized that the train was in motion. "I'll write him a letter when I get to Mobile," said Joe to himself; "he'll understand all right when I explain the circumstances. He won't blame me for breaking that date when I tell him about my wife being so sick." Joe sat down heavily in his seat and again looked at his hands.

Ahead of him two young girls were leaning out of the window and waving to their friends. Their eyes were shining and their cheeks were flushed and they were laughing with excitement at the prospect of going away.

Across the aisle sat a gaunt farm-woman. Her red-veined eyes protruded. Her neck was swollen with a goiter. In her arms she held a bouquet of red crêpe-myrtle, which was already wilting in the heat. Beside her she had placed her straw suitcase and several bulky paper-wrapped parcels. She gazed steadily out of the window as if afraid that someone would catch her eye and try to talk to her.

It was very hot in the coach. The small electric fan at the end of the car droned and wheezed sleepily but succeeded only in stirring up the hot air.

Joe took from his pocket the telegram that he had received from his mother-in-law and read it again: "J. G. Hinckley, American Hotel, Montgomery, Ala. Come home at once. Doctor says Bessie not expected live through day. Will wire again if necessary. It was a boy. Mother."

Joe's hands clenched suddenly and then relaxed. It had all happened so suddenly; he couldn't quite get it through his head, even yet. He had taken a buyer to lunch that day and they had laughed and talked and told each other stories. Then at two o'clock he had gone back to the hotel to freshen up and the clerk had reached into his box and taken out the key to his room and the telegram. The telegram had been waiting for him for two hours, the clerk said. Joe read it through twice and then looked at the address to make sure that the message was really for him. He hadn't understood: Bessie was getting along so nicely—she had had no trouble at all—and the baby was not expected for a month. He had arranged his itinerary so that he would be with her when the baby was born. They had gone over all that and had arranged everything. And now everything was upset . . . Then he thought: "I was out talking and laughing with that buyer and the telegram was waiting here all the time." That thought hurt him. He stood repeating stupidly: "I was out laughing and telling smutty stories and that telegram was here all the time."

Joe leaned his head against the red plush of the seat. He felt numb and very tired. At first the signature "Mother" had puzzled him. He couldn't understand what his mother would be doing in Mobile with Bessie; then he realized that it was Bessie's mother who had sent the telegram. He had never thought of Bessie's mother by any name except Mrs. Thompkins.

When he had married Bessie her mother had come to live with them as a matter of course. He was rather glad of that arrangement: he was really fond of the old lady in an impersonal sort of way. Then, too, it was pleasant for Bessie to have someone with her while he was on the road. His work made it impossible for him to get home oftener than every other week end; and many times it was difficult for him to get home that often, but he had always managed to make it, one way or another. He couldn't disappoint Bessie, no matter what happened. Their year of married life had been the happiest that he had ever known. And Bessie had been happy too. Suddenly he had a clear picture of her lying on their bed, her face white with suffering, and a quick panic gripped his heart. To reassure himself he whispered: "Those doctors don't know everything. She'll be all right. Mrs. Thompkins was just excited and frightened. Everything's going to be all right!"

Ahead of him a white-haired old gentleman opened his bag and took out a traveling cap. He had some difficulty in fastening the catch while holding his straw hat in his hand; but his wife, sitting with him, took the bag and fastened it at once. Then she took his hat and held it on her lap. The wife was reading a magazine. She did not look up from the magazine when she fastened the bag.

Down the aisle came the Negro porter. He had a telegram in his hand. When he reached the center of the coach he stopped and called out: "Telegram for Mr. J. G. Hinckley!" Joe let him call the name three times before he claimed the message. The porter explained that the telegram had been delivered to the train by a messenger from the American Hotel just as the train was getting under way. Joe gave the porter twenty-five cents for a tip and went back to his seat.

The country woman looked up for an instant and then turned her eyes away. The young girls giggled and whispered and looked boldly at Joe; and the old gentleman, after settling his cap firmly on his head, took a cigar from his case and went to the smoking-room.

Joe's throat felt tight, and he noticed that his hands were shaking. He wanted to put his head on the window sill, but he was afraid that people would think him sick and try to talk to him. He placed the unopened telegram on the seat beside him and stared at it for a long time. Then he re-read the first telegram very slowly. "It must be from Mrs. Thompkins, all right," he thought; "she said she'd wire again if—" Then he thought: "It may not be from Mrs. Thompkins at all; it may be from somebody else; it may be from Boykin and Rosen about that cancellation in Meridian. That's who it's from: it's from the House; it's not from Mrs. Thompkins at all!" He looked up quickly and saw that the two young girls had turned around and were watching him, making laughing remarks to each other behind their hands.

He arose from his seat feeling weak and slightly nauseated, the unopened telegram in his hand. He passed through several coaches until he reached the end of the train, and went out on the rear vestibule. He had a sudden wish to jump from the end of the train and run off into the woods, but a brakeman was there tinkering with a red lantern and Joe realized that such an act would look very strange. When the brakeman looked up and saw Joe's face, he put down his lantern and asked: "Are you feeling all right, mister?" Joe said, "Yes, I'm feeling all right; but it's a little hot, though." Finally the brakeman finished his job and left, and Joe was very glad of that. He wanted to be alone. He didn't want anybody around him.

The rails clicked rhythmically and the wilted countryside flew past. A little Negro girl . . . in a patched pink dress . . . ran down to the track . . . and waved her hand. A lame old country man . . . plowing in his stumpy field . . . pulled up his lazy mule . . . to stare at the passing train. The rails clattered and clicked and the train flew over the hot slag roadbed. "There's no need of going so fast," thought Joe, "we've got all the time in the world." He felt sick. In the polished metal of the car he caught a distorted glimpse of his face. It was white and terrified. He thought: "No wonder that brakeman asked me how I was feeling." Then he thought: "Do I look so bad that people can tell it?" That worried him. He didn't want people to notice him or to talk to him. There was nothing that anybody could say, after all.

He kept turning the telegram over in his hand, thinking: "I've got to open it now; I've got to open it and read it." Finally he said aloud: "It's not true! I don't believe it!" He repeated these words a number of times and then he said: "It's from the House about that cancellation in Meridian—it isn't from Mrs. Thompkins at all." Then he tore the unopened telegram into tiny bits and threw the pieces from the end of the train. A wind fluttered and shimmered the yellow fragments before they settled down lightly on the hard hot roadbed. He thought: "They look like a cloud of yellow butterflies dancing and settling that way." Immediately he felt better. He drew back his shoulders and sucked in lungsful of the country air. "Everything's all right!" he said. "I'm going home to see the little wife and everything's all right!" He laughed happily. He felt like a man who has just escaped some terrible calamity. When he could no longer see the scraps of paper on the track he went back to his seat humming a tune. He felt very gay and immensely relieved.

Joe reached his seat just as the conductor came through the train. He nodded pleasantly as he gave up his ticket.

"Don't let nobody talk you out of a free ride," he said.

"No chance of that, Cap," said the conductor.

Joe laughed with ringing heartiness and the conductor looked at him in surprise. Then he laughed a little himself. "You sure are in a good humor, considering how hot it is," he said.

"And why shouldn't I be in a good humor?" asked Joe. "I'm going home to see the little wife." Then he whispered, as if it were a great secret, "It's a boy!"

"That's fine; that's simply fine!" said the conductor. He put his papers and his tickets on the seat and shook Joe's hand heartily. Joe blushed and laughed again. Then, as the conductor moved off, he nudged Joe's ribs and said: "Give my regards to the madam."

"I sure will," said Joe happily.

Joe was sorry that the conductor couldn't stay longer. He felt an imperative need of talking to someone. He felt that he must talk about Bessie to someone. He looked around the car to see if there was anyone he knew. The two young girls smiled at him. Joe understood perfectly; they were just two nice kids going on a trip. Either one, alone, would never think of smiling at a strange man, but being together changed things entirely. That made it an exciting adventure—something to be laughed over and discussed later with their friends. Joe decided that he would go over and talk to them. He walked over casually and seated himself.

"Where are you girls going?" he asked.

"Don't you think that you have a great deal of nerve?" asked the black-eyed girl.

"Sure I have. I wouldn't be the best hardware salesman on the road if I didn't have lots of nerve," said Joe pleasantly.

Both of the girls laughed at that and Joe knew that everything was all right. He decided that the blue-eyed girl was the prettier of the two but the black-eyed girl had more snap.

"We're getting off at Flomaton," said the blue-eyed girl.

"We've been in school in Montgomery," said the black-eyed girl.

"We're going home for the summer vacation."

"And we want the world to know we're glad of it!"

Joe looked at them gravely. "Don't make a mistake, young ladies; get all the education you can—you'll regret it later on if you don't."

Both the girls started laughing. They put their arms around each other and laughed until tears came into their eyes. Joe laughed too, although he wondered what the joke was. After awhile the girls stopped laughing, but a sudden giggle from the blue-eyed girl set them off again, worse than before.

"This is awfully silly!" said the black-eyed girl.

"Please don't think us rude," gasped the blue-eyed girl.

"What's the joke?" asked Joe, who was really laughing as much as either of the girls.

"You sounded so—so—" explained the blue-eyed girl.

"So damned *fatherly!*" finished the black-eyed girl.

Then they went off into another whirlwind of mirth, laughing and hugging each other. The old lady across the aisle put down her magazine and started laughing too, but the woman with the goiter held her bouquet of crêpe-myrtle rigidly and stared out of the window.

Joe waited until the girls had exhausted themselves. Finally they wiped their eyes and opened their vanity cases to look at themselves in their mirrors and to repowder their noses. Then he said:

"Well, I guess I ought to sound fatherly; I just got a telegram saying that I was a proud parent."

That interested the young girls and they crowded him with questions; they wanted to know all about it. Joe felt very happy. As he started to talk he noticed that the old lady had been listening and that she had moved over in her seat in order to hear better. Joe felt friendly toward everybody. "Won't you come over and join us?" he asked.

"Yes, indeed," said the nice old lady, and Joe moved over and made a place for her.

"Now tell us all about it!" demanded the blue-eyed girl.

"You must be very happy," said the nice old lady.

"I sure am happy," said Joe. Then he added: "There's not a

whole lot to tell except that I got a telegram from Mrs. Thomp-kins—Mrs. Thompkins is my mother-in-law—saying that Bessie had given birth to a fine boy and that both of them were doing splendidly; the doctor said that he'd never seen anybody so well before, but of course my wife wanted me to be with her, and so I just dropped everything and here I am. You see Bessie and I have only been married for a year. We've been very happy. The only bad thing is that I don't get home very often; but it wouldn't do to have everything perfect in the world, would it? She sure is the finest little wife a man ever had. She don't com-plain at all about my being away so much. But some day we hope to have things different."

"There isn't anything nicer than a baby," said the blue-eyed girl.

"What are you going to name him?" asked the nice old lady.

"Well, Bessie wants to name him for me, but I can't see much sense in that. My first name's Joe and I think that's a little com-mon, don't you? But I'll leave the naming part up to Bessie. She can name him anything she wants to. She sure has been a fine little wife to me."

Then Joe started talking rapidly. He told in detail of the first time he had met Bessie. It had been in the home of Jack Barnes, one of the boys he had met on the road, and he had been in-vited over for dinner and a little stud poker later. Mrs. Barnes didn't play poker, so Bessie, who lived across the street, had been invited over to keep Mrs. Barnes company while the men played. He had liked Bessie at once, and the boys had kidded him about not keeping his mind on the game. He had never told anybody this before, but when the boys started kidding him he made up his mind not to look at Bessie again, as he didn't want her to think that he was fresh; but he couldn't stop looking at her, and every time he caught her eye she would smile in a sweet, friendly sort of way. Finally everybody noticed it and they started joking Bessie too, but she hadn't minded at all. He had lost fourteen dollars and fifty cents that night, but he had met Bessie. You couldn't call Bessie exactly beautiful but she was sweet and nice. Bessie was the sort of girl that any man would want to marry.

He told of their courtship. He quoted whole paragraphs from letters that she had written, to prove a particular point which he had brought up. Bessie hadn't liked him especially, not right at first, at any rate; of course she had liked him as a friend from the first but not in any serious way. There were one or two other fellows hanging around, too. Bessie had a great deal of attention; she could have gone out every night with a different man if she had wanted to. Being on the road all the time had been pretty much of a disadvantage. He didn't have an opportunity to see her often. Or maybe that was an advantage—anyway, he wrote her every day. Then, finally, they had become engaged. She hadn't even let him kiss her until then. He knew from the first that she would make a wonderful little wife, but he was still puzzled why a girl as superior as Bessie would want to marry him.

He talked on and on, rapidly—feverishly. He told how he had once determined not to get married at all, but that was before he had met Bessie. She had changed all that. . . . Two hours passed before he knew it. His audience was getting bored, but Joe didn't realize it.

Finally the old gentleman with the cap came back from the smoking room; and his wife, glad of a chance to get away, made her excuses and went over to sit with him. Joe smiled and nodded, but paused only a moment in his story. He was in the midst of a long description of Mrs. Thompkins. Mrs. Thompkins wasn't at all like the comic-supplement mother in-law. Quite the contrary. He didn't see how he and Bessie would get along without her. To show you the sort of woman she really was, she always took his side in any dispute—not that he and Bessie ever quarreled! Oh, no! But occasionally they had little friendly discussions, like all other married couples, and Mrs. Thompkins always took his side of the argument. That was unusual, wasn't it? Joe talked and talked and talked, totally unconscious of the passing of time.

Finally the train reached Flomaton, and the porter came to help the girls off with their bags. They were very glad to get away. They were getting a little nervous. There was something about Joe they couldn't understand. At first they had thought him just jolly and high spirited, but after a time they came to the conclusion that he must be a little drunk or, possibly, slightly demented. For the past hour they had been nudging each other significantly.

Joe helped them off the train and onto the station platform. Just as the train pulled out, the black-eyed girl waved her hand and said: "Give my love to Bessie and the son and heir," and the blue-eyed girl said: "Be sure and kiss the baby for me."

"I sure will," said Joe.

After the train had passed the girls looked at each other for a moment. Then they started laughing. Finally the black-eyed girl said: "Well, Bessie certainly has him roped and tied." The blue-eyed girl said: "Did you ever see anything like that in your life before?"

Joe went back to the coach. "Just a couple of nice kids," he thought to himself. He looked at his watch. It was five twenty-five. He was surprised. The time had passed very quickly. "It won't be long now before I'm in Mobile," he thought.

He went back to his seat, but he was restless. He decided that he would have a cigarette. He found three men in the smoker. One of them was an old man with a tuft of gray whiskers. His face was yellow and sunken, and blue veins stood out on his hands. He was chewing tobacco gravely and spitting into the brass cuspidor. The second man was large and flabby. When he laughed, his eyes disappeared entirely and his fat belly shook. His finger nails were swollen and his under lip hung down in a petulant droop. The third man was dark and nervous-looking. He had on his little finger a ring with a diamond much too large.

They were telling jokes and laughing when Joe came in. Joe wanted to talk to them about Bessie, but he couldn't bring her name up in such an atmosphere. Suddenly he thought: "I was laughing and telling smutty stories with that buyer in Montgomery, and the telegram was there all the time." His face contracted with pain. He crushed the thought from his mind. Quickly he threw away his cigarette and went back to his seat.

A bright-skinned waiter came through the train announcing the first call to dinner. At first Joe thought that he would have his dinner on the train, as that would break the monotony of the trip and help pass the time; but immediately he remembered that Mrs. Thompkins would have dinner for him at home—a specially prepared dinner with all of the things that he liked. "I'll wait till I get home," thought Joe. "I wouldn't disappoint Mrs. Thompkins and the little wife for the world after they went to all that trouble for me."

Again he felt that curious, compulsive need of talking about Bessie to someone. He had a feeling that as long as he talked about her, she would remain safe. He saw the old lady and her husband in their seat eating a lunch which they had brought with them and he decided to go over and talk with them. "Can I come over and talk to you folks?" asked Joe.

"Certainly, sir," said the old gentleman with the cap. Then, in order to make conversation he said: "My wife has been telling me that you are going home to see your new son."

"That's right," said Joe, "that's right." He started talking rapidly, hardly pausing for breath. The old lady looked at her husband reproachfully. "Now see what you started!" her glance seemed to say.

Joe talked of his wedding. It had been very quiet: Bessie was the sort of girl who didn't go in for a lot of show. There had been present only a few members of the family and one or two close friends. George Orcutt, who traveled with a line of rugs out of New York, had been his best man. Bessie was afraid that someone would try to play a joke on them: something like tying tin cans to the automobile that was to take them to the station, or marking their baggage with chalk. But everything had gone off smoothly. The Barneses had been at the wedding, of course: he had met Bessie in their home and they were such close neighbors that they couldn't overlook them; but almost nobody else, outside the family, was there.

Then he told of the honeymoon they had spent in New Orleans —all the places they had visited there and just what Bessie had thought and said about each one. He talked on and on and on.

He told of the first weeks of their married life and how happy they were. He told what a splendid cook Bessie was and what an excellent housekeeper, how much she had loved the home he had bought for her, and her delight when she knew that she was going to have a baby.

The old gentleman was staring at Joe in a puzzled manner. He was wondering if he hadn't better call the conductor, as it was his private opinion that Joe had a shot of cocaine in him. The old lady had folded her hands like a martyr. She continued to look at her husband with an I-told-you-so expression.

Joe had lost all idea of time. He talked on and on—rapidly, excitedly. He had gotten as far as Bessie's plans for the child's education when the porter touched him on the arm and told him that they were pulling into the station at Mobile. He came to himself with a start and looked at his watch: seven thirty-five! He didn't believe it possible that two hours had passed so quickly.

"It sure has been a pleasure talking to you folks," said Joe.

"Oh, that's all right," said the man with the cap.

Joe gave the porter a tip and stepped off the train jauntily. As he turned to pick up his bag, he saw that the woman with the goiter was staring at him. He walked over to the window that framed her gaunt face. "Good-bye, lady; I hope you have a nice trip." The woman answered: "The doctors said it wasn't no use operating on me. I waited too late." "Well, that's fine!—That sure is fine!" said Joe. He laughed gaily and waved his hand. Then he picked up his bag and his catalogue case and followed the people through the gate. The woman with the goiter stared at him until he was out of sight.

On the other side of the iron fence Joe saw Mrs. Thompkins. She was dressed all in black and she wore a black veil. Joe went over to her briskly, and Mrs. Thompkins put her arms around him and kissed him twice. "Poor Joe!" she said. Then she looked at his smiling, excited face with amazement. Joe noticed that her eyes were red and swollen.

"Didn't you get my telegram?" she asked. Joe wrinkled his brow in an effort to remember. Finally he said: "Oh, sure, I got it at the hotel."

"Did you get my second telegram?" insisted Mrs. Thompkins. She looked steadily into Joe's eyes. A feeling of terror swept over him. He knew that he could no longer lie to himself. He could no longer keep Bessie alive by talking about her. His face was suddenly twisted with pain and his jaw trembled like a child's. He leaned against the iron fence for support, and Mrs. Thompkins held his hand and said: "You can't give in. You got to be a man. You can't give in like that, Joe!"

Finally he said: "I didn't read your telegram. I didn't want to know that she was dead. I wanted to keep her alive a little longer." He sat down suddenly on an empty baggage truck and hid his face in his hands. He sat there for a long time while Mrs. Thompkins stood guard over him, her black veil trailing across his shoulder. Finally he asked: "What time did Bessie die?" His voice was tight and hard. It seemed to come from behind his teeth. Mrs. Thompkins answered, "She was dead when I sent the second telegram." Then, as if her own grief were of little importance, she pressed her hands together and said, "Poor Joe! Poor Joe!"

A man in a dirty uniform came up. "I'm sorry, mister, but you'll have to move. We got to use that truck."

Joe picked up his catalogue case and his bag and followed Mrs. Thompkins out of the station.

1928

THE HOLLY WREATH

*T*o the left of the village square, a dead mule lay on a manure heap. Its legs were stretched to the June sky and its glazed eyes, wide open and rolled backward, were like pieces of dirty mica. Its yellow teeth were bared in a snarl. From between its teeth there hung a swollen purple tongue, and over it flies crawled and disputed and lived amorously.

Corporal Reagan and his water detail stood silent and surveyed the wrecked village. After a moment they saw the well at which they were to fill their canteens. It was in the center of the ruined square. "They really put the bee on this place," said Bouton mildly. "They did for a fact." He turned, as if for confirmation, to Keeney—but Keeney said nothing at all.

Leaning against the wall, his chin held high and his helmet set rakishly on one side of his head, was a dead man. His left hand was pressed against a wound in his side, but blood had flowed through his fingers and onto his uniform. His right hand, which still clutched the well rope, had been flung wide in his pain and rested now on the stone lip of the trough that carried away the waste water.

"He looks like he might make a speech at any minute," said Corporal Reagan. Keeney turned his head away, but Bouton rubbed his chin and said that the man would have to be moved or he would be in their way when they were filling the canteens.

As the men stood there, a humming sound came to their ears, followed by the explosion of a shell. There was the faint neighing of flying steel and a series of soft, kissing sounds as the shrapnel struck at the end of the village. Bouton grew boastful. "If it's me they're after, they're wasting ammunition," he said.

"I don't mind shrapnel so much," said Charlie Keeney. "It's machine gun bullets that worry me. I don't like the way they whine about your ears. They remind me of a sick woman quarreling with somebody in the dark."

"The thing I hate most is not having your meals regular, or a good place to sleep," said Bouton. "I never think about getting hit. I'm too lucky to get hit, and know it."

The shelling lifted as suddenly as it had begun, and after a moment Reagan turned to his detail and said: "Let's fill these canteens and get out of here while we got the chance. Keeney, you get that dead man away from the well. Drag him behind that wall where he won't get hit again. I'll screw on the canteen tops and rack them up, and Bouton can draw up the water."

Keeney found it difficult to loosen the dead man's grasp on the rope, but he finally succeeded. He held the rigid corpse under the arms and walked backward. The heels of the dead man dragging over the square made two furrows in the dust and collected half-moons of straw and refuse. Before he was at the well again, Bouton had hauled up a bucket of water. Reagan passed the first canteens to Keeney, who held them in his hand and tilted the side of the bucket, but his arm shook so that the water spilled over his hand and ran down into the stone trough.

Reagan said: "Don't you know how to fill a canteen yet? Put it in the bucket and let it sink. There, you can fill three at one time that way."

"They didn't have wells in Brooklyn, where I lived," said Keeney sullenly.

"They didn't have them in Topeka, either," said Reagan, "but I've got sense enough to know how to fill a canteen."

Bouton saw a clash impending and hastened to prevent it. "Say, Reagan, is that the place you come from?" he asked.

"That's it. Topeka, Kansas. Why?" Then, after a pause, he added, "What part of the world do you come from, Bouton?"

"I come from Memphis, Tennessee. And I wish I was back there, is all I can say."

Reagan said, "That makes it even all around, because I sure wish this war was over and I was back home again. My mother and I are going to move out in the country, to her father's old place, when I get back. We're going to put in greenhouses and

grow for the Kansas City florists . . . Say, what's the matter
with Keeney? What's the matter, fellow? Are you sick or something?"

Keeney had slipped down and lay with his back against the
well. His face was white and his hands trembled. "I never had
my hands on a dead man before," he said after a time.

"All right," said Reagan. "All right. Take it easy."

"It was the way he looked at me when I tried to open his
hand, and when I left him back of the wall he—"

Reagan said, "Why don't you just sit there until you feel
better? Bouton and I will finish the canteens."

Keeney got up unsteadily. "No, thanks, Reagan. I'll do my
part too. I'm not a baby, you know."

When the last canteen had been filled and placed on the
notched sticks, shells were flying overhead and exploding with
great rocking blasts on the Lucy-le-Bocage road. Suddenly they
were jarred almost off their feet by a heavy explosion, followed
by a series of blasts which seemed to increase in intensity. Later,
two other men with canteen sticks appeared at the far end of the
village. They ran toward the square, looking back now and then
over their shoulders. One of the men had a small wound in his
cheek which he wiped with a blue handkerchief. The new men
came up to the well and stood there, a little out of breath.

"They got an ammunition train on the Lucy road," said the
man with the wound. "We couldn't get through that way, so
we had to circle around those farm houses and across a field to
the right." The new detail commenced filling their canteens, and
Reagan said: "Do you think we can make it down the road? Or
is the shelling too bad there?"

"You can't get through," said the second man. "No."

The wounded man said, "Listen! Go to the end of the town
and strike out to the right until you come to a field with rocks
in it, and then you'll see two farm houses. So if you do that, and
turn to the right again, you'll come out on the road behind the
barrage."

Reagan and his detail picked their way across the square and
through the littered main street of the wrecked village. Pres-

ently they came to a lane which led into a field of flowering mustard. They came to the end of the field, but they did not see the ruined farms; instead, there was another field in front of them in which poppies were growing, a field wider than the first one and studded with large boulders. Reagan was somewhat worried. "I don't believe that fellow knew what he was talking about," he said slowly.

"Maybe we haven't gone far enough," said Bouton. "He said the field had rocks in it, remember?"

When the party was halfway across the second field there came suddenly the staccato tapping of a machine gun and a hundred bullets sang through the poppies and struck the ground at their feet. Before the gunner could get their range, they were safe behind a wide boulder, deeply rooted in the green field. They lay huddled and silent as the machine gun bullets chipped the solid rock over their heads in sudden rushes which sounded like the shrill, irregular breathing of a man suffering with asthma.

"How long will we have to stay here?" asked Keeney.

"Until it gets too dark for the gunners to spot us, I guess."

"But it won't be dark before ten o'clock. Do you mean we've got to stay here listening to those machine gun bullets all that time."

Bouton said, "Anyway, I'd rather be resting here in peace than digging trenches for lazy Frogs."

They lay in silence after that, each occupied with his own thoughts. It was Reagan who spoke first. "Say, this is Wednesday, isn't it?"

"It's Wednesday. Yes. But what difference does that make?" Bouton slid down and rested his head against his helmet.

"Nothing, except my mother always writes me a letter on Wednesday." Reagan unloosened his ammunition belt and unhooked his tunic at the throat.

"What time is it back home now?"

"You mean in Memphis?"

"Where else would I mean?"

Reagan calculated a moment. "It ought to be a little after ten, the same as it is in Topeka." Then, without warning, Bouton began to slap his thigh and laugh. He lay with his arm over his eyes, chuckling at intervals. "I was just thinking," he explained, "about what was going on in Memphis right now. My old man is sitting on the porch with his shoes off. Mamma is over next door visiting the Shoemakers, and Maudie—that's my little sister —is practicing her piano lesson. Maudie Bouton is the worst God-damned piano player in the State of Tennessee, but you better not tell the old man that."

Keeney drew his lips down scornfully and turned his head away, but Reagan closed his eyes and thought of his own home. He visualized his mother seated at her desk writing to him. He saw her finish the letter and gather the pages together. She folded them into an envelope and placed it on the hall tree beside her hat, her school papers and the old black handbag with the broken catch. She set her alarm clock to ring at half-past seven and puttered about the house for a time, locking doors and seeing that everything was safe for the night. He saw her comb out her hair and plait it into a scant, gray braid. A wave of tenderness came over him. He opened his eyes and smiled dreamily.

"It will be pretty nice when we get home, won't it?"

"It sure will," said Bouton. "It will for a fact."

Keeney faced them, his mouth twisted more than ever. "You two make me sick," he said; "mooning among your souvenirs like shop girls."

Bouton looked up in surprise and rubbed his stubble of a beard. People like Keeney were beyond him, and there was no sense in his trying to understand them.

The men stretched themselves out, and after an hour Bouton was asleep and snoring softly, his lips alternately pursed and relaxed; but Reagan, feeling his responsibility as a corporal, particularly since Bouton and Keeney were both new men, replacement troops who had only recently joined the company, fought down his drowsiness and kept on the alert. Keeney lay flat on his belly, his face cupped in his hands. Each time the gunners raked the rock with their fire and he heard the bullets striking the rock and ricocheting into the air with a high, querulous note, he trembled and pressed his face against his bent arm.

Reagan said softly, "Keeney! Keeney! Don't let it worry you so much. They can't get at you here." "That's got nothing to do with it. I'm not afraid of getting killed." "Then what's the matter with you?" "It's those machine gun bullets. I can't stand the sound they make." After a long silence Keeney spoke again: "How long have we been here, Reagan?"

But Reagan's answer was lost in a rain of bullets which struck the rock and whizzed upward. Bouton turned over and sat up. He glanced at Keeney. Keeney was trembling more violently now, and was sucking in his breath with a monotonous, hissing noise. "Listen," said Bouton. "You better stop that foolishness. Do you want to end up in a strait-jacket?"

Keeney did not answer. He lay trembling and making sobbing noises for a long time; then, suddenly, he sat up against the rock and reached for his rack of canteens. "I can't stand this any longer!" he shouted. "I'm going to run! I can't stand this quarreling in the dark, I tell you!" He stood upright and swung his canteens across his shoulders; then he lunged forward and ran awkwardly, the canteens swaying and clinking to his stride.

There came a sharp splutter from the machine guns and a quick rush of bullets. Jets of water gushed from the filled canteens and shone for an instant crystal clear in the afternoon light. Then Keeney stopped and threw the canteens from him with a wide, convulsive gesture. He began zigzagging crazily from side to side and running in sudden broken circles. He turned squarely and faced the gunners. A curtain of blood ran down his face. The sound of the bullets whipping his body was like the sound of a rug being beaten with a muffled stick. He lifted his arms to the gunners. "Don't! Don't!" he screamed. Finally he toppled over in the field, thrashing about like an animal and uprooting with his dying hands great bunches of poppies and wheat. At length he stiffened, contorted with pain, his head almost touching his feet, his uniform stained with his wasted blood.

Reagan stared at the twisted body for a long time. The red blood on the green uniform reminded him of something that he had once seen, but the impression was faint and elusive and would not come clearly into consciousness. He shut his eyes and turned his head away, but he could not shut out the sight of Keeney lying dead in the wheat.

Finally it occurred to him: Keeney in death looked like a huge, badly made holly wreath. After a time he called softly, "Bouton! What does Keeney remind you of?" He knew that Bouton would not understand, but he felt the need of talking to somebody.

Bouton gave the matter careful thought. "He looks like a dead Frenchman," he said at length. "They generally die curled up that way."

After that Reagan lay in silence and looked at the dead body. . . . A holly wreath . . . It started him thinking of his home and Christmas time and his mother. He unbuttoned his shirt and let the afternoon breeze blow against his throat. A faraway look came into his eyes. He glanced at the sun and judged that it was about half past six . . . A holly wreath . . . It would be half-past twelve in Kansas. He wondered what his mother was doing at that moment. In his mind's eye he pictured her room, every piece of old furniture with its lifetime of associations: the arm-chair where she read or sewed or corrected the school papers of her pupils; his father's picture in crayon, enlarged and hanging in a gilt frame on the wall . . . He would write his mother more often. It must be lonely living by herself that way.

He turned on his back and stared at the sky. He thought of the farm which he and his mother were going to have as soon as he got home. Gradually his thoughts became more broken and formless and he drifted into a dreamy, borderline state between sleep and waking.

There came to him then a clear picture of his mother asleep, one arm resting on her breast, the other under her pillow. He smiled at the well-remembered posture and held the picture before him for a time. All at once he saw his mother wake and sit up in bed, her eyes wide with fear. She turned on her night light and looked at the clock, and Reagan noticed that her hands were trembling. Finally she got out of bed and found her house slippers and the faded bathrobe with the yellow tassels. She sat down weakly in her armchair, as if overcome with emotion, and pressed her palms against her temples. It was a characteristic gesture and unconsciously her son copied it. He turned restively; he raised his own hands and pressed them against his temples, exactly the way his mother had done it. He noticed then that she was crying.

"Don't cry like that, Mother," he whispered. Then he saw her rise and walk to the open window, and the room blurred and melted away, and there appeared only his mother's face, magnified like a close-up in the movies. He could see the terror in her eyes and the way the loose skin under her throat trembled. She held onto the window sill for support and her lips moved silently.

Reagan rolled over on his side. He opened his eyes and said dreamily: "What did you say, Bouton?" But Bouton was fast asleep again. Once more Reagan lay on his back and looked at the sky. "I must have been dreaming," he thought, "but I was sure I heard somebody calling me."

His eyes closed drowsily, and again he had that overpowering wish to sleep. He wondered what had frightened his mother so badly, and when he had seen that peculiar look on her face before. Suddenly he remembered: It was the Christmas after his father had died and his mother had taken him to her father's farm to spend the holidays. His mother had been sad and she had cried a great deal, but Grandfather and Aunt Martha and Uncle Henry had been kind and understanding and had done what they could to cheer her up.

Aunt Martha was a big woman with soft brown eyes and reddened hands. She wore a black silk shirtwaist sewed over with glistening jet which caught the lamplight and threw it back. It gave her the appearance of being made of metal from the waist up. It had snowed the day before and the rolling, Kansas countryside was white and still. That morning Uncle Henry had got out of the sleigh and had taken him and his mother to gather evergreens and red berries.

When they had returned to his grandfather's house, his mother and Aunt Martha had taken the evergreens and red berries and woven them into wreaths which they tied with red bows and hung in all the windows. Aunt Martha told him that people put holly wreaths in their windows at Christmas so that folks passing down the road would know that they were happy.

Aunt Martha and his mother talked about old times and wove the wreaths exactly. They laughed and pretended that Jimmy was really helping them. Uncle Henry sat by the stove reading a newspaper, and Grandfather was by the window in his special chair. At intervals Uncle Henry would take his pipe from between his teeth and read them an item of local news or a funny story; and every few minutes Aunt Martha would put down her thread and scissors and run into the kitchen to look at her dinner . . . How good it smells!

And now the wreaths are all finished and Mother is cleaning her hands and winding up her ball of twine.

"Let me hang the wreaths, Mother."

"No, Jimmy. You're too small. You'll fall and hurt yourself."

Uncle Henry is putting down his paper and stretching himself. "Oh, let the boy hang them if he wants to. You can't baby him all his life, Cora."

"But, Henry, he's only five. He'll hurt himself."

"Oh, nonsense," says Uncle Henry.

And now Uncle Henry is drawing up a chair from the kitchen and placing a soap-box on the seat to make it higher. He lifts Jimmy high in his arms and swings him to the top of the pile. Jimmy is excited. He wonders if he will ever be as big and strong as Uncle Henry.

Jimmy knows that they are watching him, so he is hanging the first wreath with care, balancing it evenly on the nail. Now he has turned and is facing his audience. "See, Mother, I didn't fall. I didn't hurt myself at all."

Uncle Henry is slapping his leg. "That's the way I like to hear my boy talk," he says quickly.

Jimmy throws out his chest and swaggers a little. And at that moment he loses his balance; the chair is swaying backward and the box has slipped from under his feet. The next thing is his mother's frightened face bending over him. Her eyes are wide with fear and the muscles in her throat are throbbing. Aunt Martha is bathing his temple which is still bleeding a little.

"Jimmy! Jimmy!" his mother is saying over and over. . . .

Reagan opened his eyes with a start and sat bolt upright against the rock. High overhead a shell passed with a faint, boring sound, but he did not hear. He was still at his grandfather's farm with his mother and Aunt Martha bending over him, and Uncle Henry, contrite and shamefaced, holding a basin of water and a bottle of arnica.

"Don't worry, Mother," he says. "Everything's all right."

"Oh, my poor baby!"

"It didn't hurt a bit, I tell you."

"Jimmy! Jimmy!"

Suddenly Reagan stood upright above the rock which protected him. "See, I'm all right, Mother. I'm not hurt at all. I'll hang the other wreaths, too!" He laughed suddenly, the late sunlight gleaming against his young teeth.

There came a quick tapping from the German gun and a rush of bullets, and Reagan swayed and fell forward to the rock that rose to meet his smile. When Bouton awoke he found him lying sprawled across the rock, his limp arms half circling it. He was still smiling, but the stone had broken his teeth and bruised his mouth.

When it was quite dark, Bouton shouldered the three sticks and retraced his steps through the fields and down the long lane until he came again to the wrecked square in the ruined town. It was very late when he reached his company. "We lost our way coming back," he explained. "Keeney got killed. So did Reagan."

1928

THE AMERICAN DISEUR

*T*HE DOOR opened and Corporal Colley came into the room with a message for Doc Stokes, gunnery sergeant of the second platoon. "Captain Boyce wants Eddie LaBella to report with full equipment in half an hour," he said.

Joe Birmingham lifted his thin, alert face. "What's the matter with Eddie?" he asked quickly. "The old man's not sending him to officers' training school, is he?"

"That's the idea," said Colley. "That's exactly what he's figuring on doing." He stood sprawled in the doorway, blocking the morning light, and began rolling a cigarette.

"All right," said Sergeant Stokes. "You've spoke your piece. Get out! We don't want you hanging around this billet." But the clerk continued to shape his cigarette with exquisite care. Then, leisurely, he struck a match, turned and walked away.

The men of the platoon crowded around LaBella, offering their sympathy and cursing the stupidity of Captain Boyce, but Sergeant Stokes sat kicking his heels against the sides of his wooden bunk, his face puzzled and sullen. Captain Boyce's opinion of officers' training schools was well known in the company. It was known, too, that he always sent to such schools the poorest soldiers in his company. It was a good way to get rid of them, he argued. They never got their bars, of course, and the standard of the company was raised by sending them away. "That's a fine trick to play on a nice guy like Eddie," he thought. "That's a fine trick to play on a man."

"Don't let it bother you, LaBella," said Overstreet. "What do you care what the old man thinks?"

LaBella smiled in a superior manner. "I don't," he said loftily. "I don't value his opinion in the slightest." Then he paused, shrugged his shoulders and smiled. "How can he understand an artist like myself?" he asked humorously. "How could he be expected to appreciate a man of my talents?" Overstreet laughed in his tremulous, penetrating voice. "That's the way to take it, Eddie," he said.

LaBella was undoubtedly a man of many talents but unfortunately none of them was of a military nature. Before his enlistment he had been the male member of the team of LaBella and Belle. In his act he had sung a duet with his partner, the blonde Miss Belle, and had played a half-dozen musical instruments while she was changing for the eccentric dance with which they closed. But the thing that had made the act a headliner was LaBella's impersonation of the season's celebrities. LaBella knew this quite well and characteristically made no secret of his knowledge.

"When it comes to putting over an impersonation there's nobody in show business can touch little Eddie, the American diseur," he would say. And Miss Belle would open wide her lovely eyes and answer: "Yeah? And who was telling you that?"

LaBella's place in his company was an unusual one, but it was recognized and firmly established. When he was called out with his platoon on a wiring party or a trench building detail, nobody expected him to do any actual work. The other men did that gladly while LaBella sat by and entertained them with songs and anecdotes from a storehouse which seemed inexhaustible. Sometimes at night in a dugout he would make up sketches and act them out for his comrades: A French soldier dying in a shell-hole, confused and pitiable, questioning and revaluing the things he had been taught to believe; two shopgirls discussing their love affairs at the height of a bargain sale; an old man on his way to the poorhouse talking endlessly of his past gentility. But the men liked best his less subtle efforts. His version of a scene between Captain Boyce, noted for his prim neatness, and an amorous village wench was, in the minds of his comrades, quite perfect.

In that sketch Captain Boyce was torn between desire for the lady and horror at the fact that her neck was not strictly clean. Captain Boyce's French was no better than the lady's English, and they kept talking at cross-purposes. LaBella would stand in

one spot and speak in the Captain's precise, clipped voice; then
he would jump to another spot for the lady's endearments. There
were several endings to the story, but Sergeant Stokes liked best
the one in which Captain Boyce with disheveled hair and trembling hands repulsed the lady at last because he feared he would
wrinkle his uniform if he embraced her.

There was also the story of the fat colonel who galloped up
and down the road on his horse, shouting at the soldiers for
straggling. "You men ought to be in old ladies' homes!" LaBella
would say in a thin, toothless voice. "Look at me! I'm not tired!"
Eddie glared at his audience, sure of his laugh. All at once he
was on his hands and knees and became the Colonel's horse. His
back slumped. His legs splayed out. He turned his head and
looked back at an imaginary colonel who sat too heavily and
embodied in one tired neigh all the reproach of which the equine
heart is capable.

Sergeant Stokes could never hear the story of the colonel and
his horse often enough. He would lie on his bunk and roar with
delight. "God damn you, Eddie!" he would gasp, beating the
sides of the dugout with his fists. "God damn your time, kid!"

The men would continue to laugh and applaud and ask for an
encore, but LaBella would shake his head. In his heart he was
contemptuous of an audience pleased with such slapstick. One
felt that he was about to say: "Thanks very much. It's always a
pleasure to play this theater, I assure you." When at last the applause had died away, Doc Stokes would look up and say: "How
about singing 'Uncle Bud,' Eddie?"

"Not tonight, Doc. I'm a little tired."

Stokes would get up from his bunk and walk over to LaBella.
LaBella would try to escape, but Doc would catch him by the
arms and shake him affectionately. "A-w-w come on!—You'll
sing it for me, won't you, kid?" And Eddie would laugh and
shove Doc's face away with his open palm, or reach down suddenly and pull up the tail of his shirt. "All right, Doc," he would
say. "If you want to hear it, that means I'm going to sing it."

Sergeant Stokes was an old-timer. He had already done three
hitches and he was still under thirty. Captain Boyce considered

him the best non-com in the regiment and meant to have him commissioned at the first opportunity. When LaBella had first come into the platoon, from a replacement battalion, Stokes had asked with heavy sarcasm: "Say, you ain't the vaudeville Eddie LaBella by any chance?"

"Why, yes," said Eddie. "That's me."

"Well, I'll be damned," said Stokes. "I've seen your act a dozen times. You've got it all over anybody else I ever saw." He added in an amazed voice, "I never figured I'd meet up with you in person, though."

"Well," said Eddie, "here I am."

Immediately the men became friends, and although LaBella often laughed secretly at Stokes' guileless, uncomplicated mind, and ridiculed him behind his back, he really admired his strength, his leadership and his resourcefulness under fire; nor was he blind to the benefits arising from Stokes' patronage. But Stokes' feelings toward LaBella were not so complex: He simply regarded him as a person so superior to himself, or to the other men of the company, that his inability to drill or hold a bayonet properly or build a fire-step seemed quite natural. In fact, he would have been somehow disillusioned if LaBella had been able to do such ordinary, practical things. And so Stokes was very much upset when he got the message from Captain Boyce. Eddie saw that at once. It took most of the sting out of the insult.

Eddie said: "What the hell! I don't really care!" Then, later: "I suppose he's right at that, Doc."

"Like hell he's right. You're not the worst soldier in this outfit."

"Who would you say was, then?" asked LaBella in an amused voice.

Stokes thought ponderously. "There are a lot of them worse than you are, kid."

LaBella walked over and sat beside Stokes on his bunk. "If it wasn't for leaving you, Doc, I'd be glad to get away from the outfit," he said quietly.

"Aw, nuts!" said Stokes happily. "Aw, nuts on that, Eddie!"

LaBella smiled quietly to himself. "Doc is as simple as a child," he thought. "I can twist him around my finger. I can make him do anything I say."

When LaBella had at last made up his heavy marching order, Stokes walked with him to the company office. He was waiting there when LaBella came out again, and for a kilometer or two the men walked silently down the white road. Finally Doc burst out angrily, "If you hadn't been so dumb, this wouldn't have happened!" LaBella looked at him quickly, then he lowered his head. "Yes, Doc, I know. I'm just no good, I guess." There had been an indication of a break in his voice and he liked the effect. He tried it again: "I'm just no good, I guess."

"Who said you were no good?" asked Stokes sullenly. He stopped in the road and began kicking at a stone. "If they don't treat you right at that school, let me know." Eddie nodded. "All right; I'll let you know."

Doc stood looking at his boots. "Did you mean what you said about hating to leave me?"

"Yes," said LaBella. "Yes, I meant that."

"Maybe I'll see you sometime on the outside, after the war's over," said Stokes. But before LaBella could answer, he stuck out his hand. "Well, I'll leave you here."

"Good-bye, Doc. I won't forget you. Take care of yourself."

"Sure, kid. I'll take care of myself. You do the same."

Stokes turned and walked rapidly down the white, dusty road. For a moment LaBella watched him and then suddenly a strange feeling of shame came over him. He began to run toward the retreating figure. "Doc—wait!" he called. "Doc!"

But Stokes shook his head, raised his arms high in the air and would not turn around. LaBella stood silent, watching him until he had passed over the hill and out of sight.

A few hours later Sergeant Stokes sent his platoon out for bayonet practice and came alone into the deserted billet. He decided to take his pistol apart and clean it thoroughly. After a time one of the company buglers came into the room. He was weak with laughter. Then Stokes heard two men outside his window whispering and laughing. A door banged and from the billet adjoining there came the sound of loud laughter. There seemed to be whispering and laughter all down the village street. Stokes looked up sullenly. "Say, Music, what's the joke?" he asked.

The bugler raised his head from his blanket. His round eyes were set in a round face and his round mouth seemed planned by nature to fit neatly over the lips of a trumpet. "Get this, Sergeant; it's rich!" he said. "The Colonel decided to make some officers from the line, so he sent around an order for the best man in each company, see? Well, the skipper slipped up this time. He didn't even read the order; he thought it was just another officers' training school, and he sent Eddie LaBella. Well, when Eddie got up to Regimental, they swore him in as a lieutenant, and they're sending him back to the company. Did you ever hear anything richer?"

"All right," said Stokes. "Don't say anything more about it. Keep your shirt on. Don't talk to anybody about what you know."

But Stokes' warning was useless. The news had spread immediately. The men talked of nothing else that afternoon. After supper they were still laughing at the mistake which Captain Boyce had made when the door to the billet opened and Lieutenant LaBella himself entered. He was very excited. "Say, take a look at your new commanding officer," he said. He started telling them the story, impersonating, in turn, Captain Boyce, the colonel, and the staff officers at Regimental Headquarters. A few of the new men laughed uncertainly, but LaBella missed Stokes' voice. He was surprised at that; he redoubled his efforts. But Stokes sat staring at the floor and seemed embarrassed. Suddenly LaBella realized that Stokes for some reason was ashamed of him. He was puzzled. He went over to him.

"What's the matter, Doc?" he asked. Stokes avoided his eyes. He rose to his feet and stood at attention stiffly. Eddie laughed and dug him in the ribs, then he pulled out Doc's shirt-tail in the old familiar way. The men turned their heads away, pretending that they had not seen. LaBella quit laughing. "What the hell have I done, Doc?" he asked in a puzzled voice.

Stokes' face was red. "You're a lieutenant, Mr. LaBella."

"Sure I am. That's the whole point of the story. What of it?"

Stokes remained silent.

At that moment the door opened and Captain Boyce appeared. Instantly the men came to attention. Captain Boyce surveyed them for a moment. He smiled genially. "Carry on!" he said. The men relaxed. LaBella felt a strange rush of blood. For a moment it was difficult for him to breathe. He turned and spoke to Stokes crisply: "I think you understand my orders, Sergeant. See that they are carried out exactly."

"Yes, sir," said Stokes.

Captain Boyce spoke to LaBella as a brother officer and an equal. "I see you've already taken charge of your platoon," he said. "That's the ticket; that's fine." He turned to the men and made a concise speech concerning the advantage of making company officers from the line. He was convinced that the men would be glad to serve under Lieutenant LaBella. He talked of the necessity for discipline and obedience. At last he turned to LaBella, resting his arm across his shoulders. "I'll show you your new quarters, if you're going my way," he said pleasantly.

For awhile the men walked in silence down the village street, then LaBella began to laugh. "I guess you'll explain to Regimental tomorrow about that mistake, won't you?" Captain Boyce looked up mildly, and lied with a straight face. "My dear boy," he said, "there has been no mistake."

"You really meant to commission me then?"

"Of course I did. What's so remarkable in that?"

LaBella again had that tingling rush of blood to his head. His throat felt tight and it was difficult for him to catch his breath. He stopped in the muddy street, inflated his chest and saluted Captain Boyce stiffly. Later, in his new quarters, he looked at himself in his mirror for a long time, straightening his uniform and smoothing his hair. "How did I get the impression I wasn't a good soldier?" he thought. "I must be pretty damned good, after all, or Boyce wouldn't have commissioned me."

Six days later Lieutenant LaBella called on Captain Boyce. Captain Boyce was writing letters on blue stationery and he seemed annoyed at the interruption. LaBella looked at him miserably. "Get me out of this, Captain," he began.

"What's the matter with you?"

"Everybody's laughing at me."

"Yes?" said Captain Boyce.

"I didn't want to be an officer and you know it. I'm no good, and everybody is laughing at me."

Captain Boyce turned and put down his pen. "Well, what if they are?"

"Everywhere I go, people laugh at me. That story has got all over the regiment. Everybody knows it and makes fun of me behind my back. How can I command a platoon when nobody takes me seriously?"

Captain Boyce remained silent, a thoughtful look in his eyes. "Of course, I get excited and make mistakes," said LaBella. "When I stand up before the men I feel like a fool. I forget everything I ever knew. I get excited and give the wrong commands, and Stokes corrects me. He does that with pleasure, you may be sure. He wanted to be an officer himself, and he's sore at me for beating him out. I understand that. I know what's going on in his mind. Then everybody smiles and when they get back to their billets they lay on their bunks and laugh at me." LaBella paused. His arms dropped to his sides.

Captain Boyce spoke slowly: "What do you expect me to do about it? Do you want me to send around an order that any man caught laughing at you is to be court-martialed?"

LaBella stared steadily at his shoes. "I thought you might explain about my commission being a mistake, and get it canceled. That's what I really had in mind."

"Please don't be absurd," said Captain Boyce coldly. After a moment he added more kindly: "You're just self-conscious and you imagine these things."

"I'm not imagining things," said LaBella. "I know what I'm talking about, all right." Captain Boyce smiled doubtfully. "I tell you I know they're all laughing at me. Night after night I've stood outside the billets and listened to the men laughing at me."

Captain Boyce stared at him, a peculiar look on his face. LaBella flushed. "I had a right to do that. I had a right to know what the men are saying about me." Boyce sat in silence for a time. "I think you need a rest; I'll try to arrange leave for you," he said. He turned to the table and picked up his pen. LaBella started for the door and Captain Boyce called over his shoulder: "Don't pay any attention to the men and they'll soon forget all about it." LaBella hesitated, his hand on the latch, but Boyce had commenced writing again. LaBella closed the door and walked toward his quarters.

His way led past the galley where a line of men had formed, mess gear in hand, waiting for their suppers. At the end of the line stood two new men. As LaBella passed, one of the men leaned forward and whispered to his companion, and they both laughed. LaBella hurried past. Then he stopped, turned suddenly and came back to the men. He caught the first man by the shoulders and turned him around.

"By God, this has got to stop!" he shouted. The men stared in surprise, their mouths open.

"It doesn't make any difference *how* I got my commission; it doesn't make any difference how rotten I am. I'm an officer, and I'm entitled to respect." The whole line had turned. The cooks stopped dishing out the food. "What this platoon needs is discipline, and I'm going to see that it gets it!"

Stokes came up quickly. "Them men wasn't laughing at you," he said quietly. LaBella looked at him furiously. "You know all about it, do you?"

"Don't act this way, Lieutenant," whispered Stokes. "Don't for Christ sake!"

LaBella tried to smile. He succeeded only in showing his teeth. "What I said about discipline goes for you, too, Stokes!" Stokes remained silent. LaBella started to walk away, but when he had gone a few steps, he turned again. "Report to me in my quarters in ten minutes," he said.

Sergeant Stokes reported to him there promptly on time. LaBella started talking at once. He talked for a long time and Sergeant Stokes stood at attention, his helmet gripped tightly in his hand. LaBella talked rapidly. He did not realize that his voice had become shrill. He stopped talking as suddenly as he had begun. Stokes seemed very hurt. There was a puzzled look on his round, childlike face.

"You got me all wrong," he said. He repeated it over and over.

LaBella laughed shortly. "Don't lie to me. Do you think I don't know you're sore because I was commissioned by accident, when Captain Boyce really meant to commission you instead?"

Stokes looked down unhappily and shook his head. "I'm not sore at you," he said. "That thought never entered my mind."

LaBella turned to light a cigarette, but his hand trembled so the match went out. He threw the cigarette away. "I'm wise to you," he said. "You've done everything you could to ridicule me and turn the men against me. That's the thing that hurts me the most—your petty, God-damned jealousy!"

Suddenly Stokes came over to him and took him by the arms. "You're wrong there. I'd be the last man in the world to hurt you." LaBella's face relaxed. He seemed anxious to be convinced. Stokes continued talking. "You're wrong about me laughing at you, Eddie. I haven't done that, and I haven't let anybody else do it when I was around. Why, I told my platoon last night what I'd do personally to the next man I caught laughing at you."

LaBella jerked himself away. He walked to the far end of the room and faced the wall. He spoke gently. "That was most generous of you, I'm sure."

Stokes smiled happily. "I said: 'Eddie LaBella can't soldier to save his life and never will. He knows that as well as you do. But even at that he's better than any one of you bastards that laugh at him.' I said: 'The thing to do is try to help him and not make things harder.'"

"Get out of here!" said LaBella in a voice scarcely audible.

"But, Eddie—"

LaBella turned. His face was white and drawn. His mouth was twisted. "I said get out of here!"

When Stokes had gone, LaBella lay on his bed for a long time. At last he got up and began pacing the floor. "I'll show them who I am," he said. He began placing chairs together to form an even row. Then he mounted the chairs and walked back and forth across their seats. Gradually a far-away look came into his eyes. "I'm standing on the edge of a trench," he said. "Below me are my enlisted men. Shells are falling all about. The men are amazed at my bravery." Then he held his head sidewise, as if listening.

"God, but Lieutenant LaBella has got guts!" I heard that distinctly, but I won't let anybody know. "Lieutenant LaBella is the finest officer in the Marine Corps." A new man said that. I pretend that I didn't hear.

"Why does the Lieutenant expose himself so recklessly?"

"He's obtaining information on the enemy's position."

"It looks like he'd be afraid to expose himself that way!"

"What! Lieutenant LaBella afraid? S-a-a-y, the Lieutenant doesn't know the meaning of the word fear."

Everybody is looking at me with admiration, even Doc Stokes. I'm a better soldier than he is. He wouldn't have the courage to do this. Nobody would have courage enough to do this but me. I walk up and down. The shelling is getting heavier. That one was close. The men are frightened. I tell them not to be afraid. I encourage them by my example. It's an officer's duty to encourage his men. I am the perfect officer. The men know that. Another close one! The shelling is terrific now. I'm staggering. What is that sharp pain? I'm badly wounded. I'm swaying forward. I'm falling into the trench. There's a thin stream of blood running down my temple, but otherwise I'm not at all marred. My left arm is resting back of my head. My right knee is raised gracefully. Stokes is holding me in his arms. There are tears in his eyes.

"This is my fault," he says. "I drove you to your death, Lieutenant. Oh, can you ever forgive me?"

"I have forgiven you freely," I say. Then breathing becomes

difficult for me. "Those batteries are to the left, behind a clump of trees," I gasp. The men stand around me solemnly. They have taken off their helmets.

"Lieutenant LaBella is going to die."

"This will be a great loss to the entire Corps."

"There'll never be another officer as fine as Lieutenant La-Bella!"

I close my eyes. I am dead. Captain Boyce is coming down the trench. He stands before me with bowed head. He is crying without shame. "The heart of a gallant officer is stilled forever." He chokes. The men turn away to hide their emotion. "I'll see that LaBella gets the Medal of Honor for this!"

LaBella stepped to the floor. He extinguished his candle and lay fully clothed on his bed. When he awoke someone was standing beside him. In the gray light of morning he recognized Corporal Colley, the company clerk. Colley looked sullen and sleepy. "The company moved up to the front last night," he explained. "The skipper said you and I were to stay back with the kitchens and join the company when they came out again."

Later, an old French woman, her head tied up in a towel, came into the billet to make his bed. She seemed surprised at finding LaBella there. She talked excitedly, with many gestures, pointing at the road which led from the town. "All right! All right!" said LaBella. The woman watched him suspiciously while he made up his bedding roll and fastened it with a strap. He said: "I'm no God-damned good, so they left me back with the cooks."

The woman had understood only one word. "God damn! God damn!" she repeated. She rolled her eyes roguishly. "Shocking!" she said.

Corporal Colley was somewhat annoyed at LaBella's presence. He had planned spending the time sprawled comfortably on his blankets, a bottle of cognac at his side, but the presence of an officer prevented that. He sat staring out of the window at a girl raking a rubbish heap. As the girl bent over, her short skirt pulled up in the back and showed her thick, peasant legs. There was a stretch of skin above her knee with a red mark around it where her garter had bitten in too deeply.

Most of the time LaBella sat in silence, but occasionally he spoke of the trivial happenings in the company or wondered how the boys were getting along at the front. At noon Colley went to the kitchens for his dinner. He brought back food for LaBella. He brought back, also, cigarettes and a bottle of sour white wine.

Later in the afternoon a runner from Divisional Headquarters brought a note for Lieutenant LaBella. Some of the staff officers were having a party that night and they requested the honor of Lieutenant LaBella's presence, wondering if he would not come prepared to sing some of his comic songs, or, possibly, to give a few of his justly famous impersonations.

LaBella tore the note into tiny pieces. "What do they think I am?" he demanded furiously. Then he turned to the bored runner. "Tell them I am an officer and a gentleman, the same as themselves, and not a damned clown!" he shouted. "Tell them that with my compliments! Tell them that I won't forget this insult!" He walked up and down the narrow room, talking loudly to himself and waving the bottle of wine over his head. "My place is in the line with my platoon!" he said excitedly. "My place is with my men!" Suddenly he became more calm. "They can't put a thing like this over on me," he said. "I'm going to the front and join the company!"

Colley looked up quickly. He started to speak but changed his mind. Then he seated himself at the field desk and began working again on a muster-roll.

That night Lieutenant LaBella hailed a muleskinner going to the front with supplies. Hours later he located his company. The men had taken a position in a network of old trenches, and behind them lay the abandoned town of Pont-a-Mousson. LaBella had cut a small stick, and as he came down the trench he twirled it jauntily. It was daybreak and the company was marshaled against the sides of the trenches for the morning stand-to. A heavy mist lay like smoke above the duck-boards and beads of moisture dripped from the sides of the trenches. Where the trenches crossed the mist swayed in long streamers that trembled and undulated and touched each other for an instant.

LaBella came up to Sergeant Stokes. "I've come to take over my platoon," he said. At that moment there came a sudden hiss and a quick explosion a few yards beyond the trench. Then the shells fell rapidly.

"They been throwing one-pounders on that place off and on all night," said Stokes.

"Has anybody tried to locate their batteries?" asked LaBella crisply.

"No, sir. It's too foggy to see anything yet."

"I'll go up and locate those batteries."

"I wouldn't do that. It's pretty risky with all that shelling going on."

LaBella laughed loudly. He started climbing the trench at the spot where the shelling seemed heaviest. The men turned from their positions to look at him. LaBella had a feeling of exultation. "I'll show them who I am," he thought. "I'll show them I'm no clown to be laughed at."

But when he had crawled over the edge of the trench, the shelling stopped as quickly as it had begun. LaBella stood for a moment irresolute, then he twirled his stick and swaggered up and down the parapet of the trench. His chest was inflated. His chin was up. He waited for the shelling to begin again, but no shells came.

Stokes came and stood below him, his face anxious and worried. "You'd better come down, Mr. LaBella; they might start shelling there any time." LaBella laughed contemptuously. He paced up and down, twirling his stick. The men were silent. They were all staring at him. "In just a minute they'll start shelling again," he thought. He stood still and erect, his body plainly outlined against the sky. "Here I am, hit me with a thousand shells!" he whispered. The only sound was a sniper's stray bullet which passed high overhead.

"Do you want me to come up there with you?" asked Stokes anxiously.

LaBella stared at him for a moment, his lips twisted. "I don't expect such sacrifices from my men!" he said grandly. He resumed his walk, but he was less sure of himself. "They ought to start shelling again any minute now," he thought. There was no sound from the German batteries. Farther down the trench Wilbur Davey could be heard crushing walnuts against his helmet. LaBella became alarmed. "Why don't they start shelling?" he thought. Suddenly he stood quite still. The wind came out of his chest. His chin came down. "For Christ sake," he thought. "Start shelling!" He stood there foolishly on the side of the trench, his jaw trembling.

Then Overstreet began to laugh in his tremulous, penetrating voice. He tried to muffle it, but he did not succeed. Instantly the whole line was laughing. The men lay with their backs to the trench and roared. LaBella raised his hands impotently and passed them over his face. He took two steps forward and two steps backward, paused for a moment and stared at his comrades, his face twisted with hatred, turned in the direction of the abandoned town, and began to run. Where he had stood the low-lying mist eddied and swirled and settled down slowly.

All this happened in August. In October LaBella was picked up in Paris by military police, charged with desertion, and placed under arrest.

1929

A SNOWSTORM IN THE ALPS

So the day came finally when Joe told his friends good-bye and boarded the train for New York. The next morning he got to talking with a lady whose hands were covered with diamond rings and who had big blobs of jade hanging from her ears. When he told her his destination the lady said that she, too, lived in New York, but that she had been visiting her sister for the past two weeks. She spoke of her sister's opulence and the way everybody in Montgomery looked up to the family; she showed Joe a snapshot of her sister and her brother-in-law and their children; she talked about herself and her own family and how they had prospered. "Would you believe it?" she said proudly. "But not one word of English could I speak ten years ago."

Joe was surprised. "You sure speak fine now."

"Oh, yes—sure!" agreed the lady, and after a few moments she began questioning Joe about himself. "What kind of work do you want to do when you get to New York?"

Joe said: "I'm going to get a job with a big corporation and work right up to the top." He told her about Reedyville and his friends there, and how he hated leaving the place, in a way. As he talked of his ambition and his ideals his face flushed and he gazed into the distance with wide eyes. Presently he stopped talking. He raised his chin slowly, his nostrils trembling with eagerness and two fine, vertical lines appeared between his brows.

When the train pulled into the station the lady came over to Joe's seat to bid him good-bye. Joe shook hands with her and tried to thank her for her kindness, but she would never let him finish a sentence. She kept shrugging her shoulders and moving her hands back and forth in the air. The diamond rings flashed, the jade earrings swung in steady circles. "Now you be a good

boy," she said; "and don't you get in no trouble." She started
back to her seat but returned at once. "Come and see us sometime," she added.

"Yes, ma'am, I sure will," said Joe. He was pleased to have
made a friend so quickly. Of course he couldn't call on the lady
until she told him her name and gave him her address, and he
stood waiting for that information. She seemed on the point of
telling him, but changed her mind. She laughed awkwardly.
"Come see us any time," she said. She adjusted her hat, gripped
her handbag and pushed and elbowed her way through the line
of passengers waiting to get off. Joe stood watching her through
the window. "Maybe she didn't give me her address because
she figured I wouldn't make good and would try to borrow
money off her," he thought. He was filled suddenly with shame.

The landlady said the room was five dollars a week and never
vacant long. Joe took it. The next morning he set out to look
for work. Twenty days later he was still looking. There were
exactly thirty-five cents in his pocket and another week's rent
was due the next day.

He spent that night sitting on a bench in Madison Square. He
did not attempt to lie down; that seemed, somehow, a shameful
thing to do. Then, too, he feared that somebody from Reedyville might pass through the square and see him. He could never
live through a humiliation like that, he knew, so he sat bolt upright on the bench and after a time he got to talking with a boy
about his age who sat on a bench across the way. The new boy
came from Indiana and his story was almost exactly like Joe's.
They were both impressed at the strange coincidence. It made
them friends at once. So Joe talked about Reedyville and the
other boy, who said his name was Harry, told Joe about Evans-
ville. Harry was pretty hungry too but he said he didn't mind
because he knew that everything was going to come out all right
in the end. Harry said the trouble with people was that they
lacked faith in each other. Joe noticed that Harry was wearing
on his vest a gold pin with a brilliant in it. He asked him why
he didn't sell the pin and get something to eat but Harry said
the pin had been presented to him by the Reverend Culpepper

for not missing Sunday school a single time in five years and of course he wouldn't want to part with it.

The next day Joe tried even harder than ever to find work, but he came at night, tired and hungry, to sit again in the square. He looked carefully over the benches, but Harry was not there. "Maybe he'll show up later," he thought. As Joe sat on his bench he noticed a distinguished old gentleman who had walked past him several times. Joe glanced at him admiringly and thought that he would like to resemble that old gentleman some day. Then he became conscious that the old gentleman had paused and was regarding him steadily, and Joe lowered his eyes, as he didn't want to be thought lacking in manners. But apparently the gentleman hadn't thought that at all, because he circled the path again and then returned and sat down on Joe's bench. In a few minutes they were talking together.

The gentleman asked Joe a number of questions in a kindly, sympathetic way and Joe told him his entire story, except that he couldn't bring himself to say that he hadn't eaten for two days. After they had talked for a few minutes the old gentleman introduced himself as a Mr. Bondy. It seemed that Mr. Bondy liked to talk to young men—it kept him from getting old, he said. Later Mr. Bondy asked Joe to be his guest at dinner. Joe was afraid his clothes wouldn't be good enough but Mr. Bondy said clothes didn't matter at all.

During the meal Mr. Bondy kept up a lively flow of conversation and told a number of funny stories. Joe laughed at all the stories but in his heart he was shocked at such words coming from Mr. Bondy; it didn't seem right for a fine, dignified old gentleman to talk about those things.

They came out of the restaurant at last and turned west, and after they had walked for a few blocks Mr. Bondy stopped in surprise before a fine apartment house. He said he lived in that house. He hadn't realized they were walking toward his apartment. That showed what *habit* would do to a man! He laughed. However, since they were there, Joe might as well come up and have a drink with him.

Joe had never seen anything half so fine as Mr. Bondy's apartment, but he was particularly impressed by the valet who came in to serve the drinks. Joe thought he looked like a bad actor; and oddly enough Mr. Bondy seemed to read his thoughts, for he told Joe the valet had killed a man or so in his time. Joe said he would be afraid to have a man like that around the house, but Mr. Bondy said Steve was very gentle and affectionate, if he liked you; and of course he liked Mr. Bondy very much. "I'm telling you all this," said Mr. Bondy in a hard, nervous voice, "in case you think you can pull something and get away with it!" Joe stared without in the least understanding. "Oh, come now," said Mr. Bondy, "you're not half as dumb as you're trying to make me believe!"

Presently Mr. Bondy started asking Joe direct questions about himself. He wanted to know if Joe had a girl back in Reedyville and if he really loved her. So Joe told Mr. Bondy about Maudie Wilkinson and while you couldn't exactly call her his girl they *did* think a whole lot of each other.

Mr. Bondy talked on and on that way. Finally he took a ten-dollar bill from his pocket and put it in Joe's palm. Joe didn't know what to do. Finally he said he would accept the loan only with the understanding that he was to pay it back just as soon as he got a job.

Mr. Bondy commenced laughing in a high voice. Joe laughed too. He didn't quite know what the joke was but he didn't want anybody to think him stupid. A little later he rose to go. Mr. Bondy accompanied him to the elevator and warned him to be more careful about talking to strange people, particularly in parks. Joe thought that was peculiar advice, coming from Mr. Bondy: If he hadn't talked to strangers in parks he never in the world would have met such a fine old gentleman.

"Mr. Bondy sure is a prince," thought Joe; "they don't make them any better than he is, and that's a fact!" He decided to walk back to the square to see if Harry had returned. He thought: "Harry sure will be surprised when I tell him about Mr. Bondy and show him the money he lent us." But when he reached the square, Harry was not there.

Two days later Joe stopped before a lunchroom. A woman had just put a sign in the window reading "Busboy Wanted."

Joe wasn't sure what a busboy was. The words reminded him of a Christmas card he had once seen: a picture of an English inn before which had stopped a coach full of people. A young boy in a leather apron was assisting the innkeeper in unloading the baggage of the laughing guests. Joe went in quickly and a few minutes later he was at work. The job paid fifteen dollars a week with meals and Mrs. Glab, the proprietress, told him if he made good as a busboy she would promote him to counterman at the first vacancy. The countermen got twenty dollars a week but they were a shiftless lot according to Mrs. Glab. Mrs. Glab was some sort of a foreigner, Joe thought, but he wasn't sure just what.

The Bellfontaine Lunch had on its window a half-moon sign bearing the legend: "Ladies Invited," although few responded to its invitation. Its patrons were mostly sweaty workmen in soiled clothes or pale-looking clerks. On the floor was a layer of sawdust which was renewed once a week. Running half the length of the narrow room was a counter and behind it there were framed lists of the daily bill of fare. This list rarely varied. It began with "Vegetable Soup 15¢" down through "Eggs Any Style 25¢" to end with "Lamb or Beef Stew 30¢." Against the wall was a row of chairs each with a right arm like the angry claw of a fiddler crab.

A month or so later one of the countermen got drunk on gin and talked insultingly to Mrs. Glab. No man should say such things to a woman, not even to Mrs. Glab. Joe told the counterman that, but Mrs. Glab said for him to mind his own business and that she knew how to handle people like that. And Mrs. Glab was right. She answered abuse with abuse more vivid. She went to the cash register and flung the counterman's wages on the floor. She followed him on to the sidewalk and stood waving her arms and shaking her fists and screaming insults at him until he was out of hearing. The cop on the corner rubbed his big belly and laughed uproariously and after a moment Mrs. Glab began laughing too.

That was the way Joe got to be a counterman. Mrs. Glab said, though, that she couldn't raise his wages immediately as business was bad right then, and anyway she wanted to see first what sort of counterman he was going to be. Joe reminded her of her promise but Mrs. Glab said maybe he wasn't as good a busboy as she thought; anyway, even if he was that was no sign he would make a good *counterman*. Mrs. Glab had her doubts about the whole matter. She thought it would be better, after all, to call up the agency and get a regular counterman. Joe was sure he could do the work all right and at last she consented to let him try with the understanding that his wages weren't to be raised until he had made good. And so Joe got his promotion after all.

There were two other countermen besides Joe. One of them was named Charlie and he was about fifty years old. He had a ragged gray mustache and he never seemed entirely clean. He spoke in an apologetic voice and he was very anxious to please everybody. Charlie was afraid of anything with a sharp edge, but he was particularly afraid of knives. One end of the glass serving counter had been broken away, leaving a jagged edge exposed, and Charlie would never go near that edge of the counter if he could avoid it. The cooks and the other countermen used to frighten Charlie by picking up knives and pretending they were going to cut him. One afternoon he became so frightened that he went out of his head and locked himself in the Gents' Toilet and it was a long time before they could make him stop screaming.

Fred, the other counterman, said Charlie was entirely different when he was drunk for then he laughed and told jokes and talked about the fine women he had slept with in his time. Fred thought his stories about the women were a lot of lies. He didn't believe that any woman, at least not one who had any respect for herself, would fall for a dirty old bastard like Charlie.

Fred was not surprised, however, at his own success with women. They were always calling him up at the restaurant and Mrs. Glab didn't object so long as they called up during the slack hours. But she kept warning him to be careful with those girls: one of them was going to make trouble for him yet. Fred scoffed at the idea. "Did you ever hear of a dame making trouble for anybody whose pay was only twenty bucks a week?" he asked. "Christ," he said. "Christ almighty. Get wise to yourself."

One night Fred asked Joe to go on a party with him. His girl had a friend and she wanted Fred to bring along another boy and make it a party. So Joe freshened up and he and Fred met the girls at ten o'clock at the corner of Eighth Avenue and Twenty-third Street. Fred's girl was named Gloria. Joe's girl was named Peggy.

Gloria said the first round of drinks was on her and Fred said, "Oh, all right, if that's the way you feel about it." After several drinks Peggy took off her hat and lay back in Joe's arms. Gloria was talking about a man who had tried to frame her and get her railroaded on a vice charge and what she hadn't called him didn't bear repeating. She went into exact detail as to just what she had told him, but Fred kept interrupting her by putting his arms around her waist and kissing her. Gloria responded to his kisses with clenched fists and tautened body, but when each kiss was ended she would take up her story at the exact place where she had broken off and continue talking in a matter-of-fact voice.

After a time Joe felt himself getting drunk. He wanted to kiss Peggy the way Fred was kissing Gloria. She lay there against his breast, her yellow hair touching his lips. There was about her the heavy odor of perfume. His throat felt dry and his heart began to beat rapidly. He wanted to press his mouth against Peggy's red lips and to cup with his hands her young, beautifully modeled breasts, but he couldn't bring himself to do it before all those people. He lifted his head slowly, his nostrils trembled and between his brows there came the two fine, vertical lines.

Gloria laughed triumphantly. "I been trying to think all night what Joe reminded me of and when he looked up in that serious way I just thought of it. He reminds me of a big dog." Again she laughed. "There's a picture in my room called 'A Snowstorm in the Alps,' and in this picture there's one of those Sainbernnuds with a barrel fastened around his neck, and this dog is laying down, see? And across his paws is laying a little girl with curly yellow hair. I been trying all night to think what Joe reminded me of, and when he lifted his head in that slow way and frowned he was a dead ringer for that Sainbernnud."

Peggy sat upright and reached for her hat. She adjusted it with furious, unsteady fingers.

"What's the matter, Peg?" asked Gloria quickly.

"I'm going home," said Peggy. She closed her compact with a click. Fred's eyes narrowed. "Say, if you don't like this party you can get the hell out of here!" he said.

Joe wanted to know what Peggy had got sore about all of a sudden and Gloria said it was because Joe hadn't seemed to like her. Peggy wasn't used to having people high-hat her and Gloria didn't blame her, when you came right down to it, for feeling insulted at the way Joe had acted. Joe apologized for spoiling the party but Fred said not to bother about that. He said he used to be just as big a hick as Joe. He said it wouldn't be long before Joe got on to things and was as wise as he was.

One afternoon Joe and Charlie were busy polishing silver when Charlie put down his rag and began to make a peculiar whimpering sound. He walked to the end of the counter where the glass was broken and before anybody knew what he intended doing he sawed his neck back and forth across the sharp, jagged edge of the glass until the veins in his throat were severed. It took a long time to clean up the mess that Charlie had made, but when things were tidied up again Mrs. Glab called the agency. They sent her a heavy-set, stupid boy named Emil. Emil was always laughing at nothing at all and he put extra things on people's plates. Mrs. Glab had to speak to him about it repeatedly.

Fred kept telling Joe he was a fool to work for fifteen dollars a week and let Mrs. Glab put anything like that over on him. So one day Joe asked Mrs. Glab for the raise she had promised him. Mrs. Glab told him how hard things were right then and what a time she had making expenses. She said she wanted to tell Joe something, if he would swear not to tell anybody: she was figuring on buying a bigger restaurant in a better location and she wanted him to come with her to the new place, but right now things were tight. She couldn't talk that way to Fred or Emil, she said, but then she didn't feel toward them as she felt toward Joe. Joe said all right just raise him when she felt able to do it and Mrs. Glab said she certainly would as she considered Joe the best counterman she ever had working for her. This pleased Joe a great deal.

A few months later Fred got a little Italian girl in trouble and her father came around to the restaurant to see Fred. Fred promised to marry the girl, but after the father had gone, he turned to Joe indignantly: "Me marry a wop whore? Say, the old man don't think I got much self-respect, does he?" That afternoon he asked Mrs. Glab for his pay. He said he thought he'd skip over to Philly until the thing blew over.

Mrs. Glab called up the agency and the new counterman was named Mac. He had a pimply face and black sideburns and he wore a ring with a red stone in it.

One night when Joe had been working at the Bellfontaine Lunch for a little over a year a man came in just at closing time. Mrs. Glab was counting the receipts for the day, piling the bills in neat stacks. It was Joe's night on and there was nobody in the restaurant except himself, Mrs. Glab and the cook. The man seemed nervous. He kept looking at the door as if he expected somebody.

"What'll it be?" asked Joe.

The man looked around. "Give me some bacon and eggs and a cup of coffee."

Joe repeated the order to the cook. He drew a cup of coffee and set it on the counter. He noticed that the man was still watching the door. "Here you are, mister!" he said. The man started and faced Joe for the first time squarely. Joe was sure he had seen that face some place but he couldn't remember where. The man lowered his eyes and fumbled at the coffee cup and before Joe realized what was happening he found himself looking into the barrel of a pistol. Then he saw that another man had come into the restaurant. This man also had a pistol in his hand. The second man went over to Mrs. Glab.

Mrs. Glab's face was pasty. Up went her hands. Her lips moved but no sound came from them.

"Say, you can't do that!" said Joe. He took a step forward.

"Stay where you are, you fool!" said the second man.

"Don't move, Joe!" said Mrs. Glab. Her voice was pitched an octave too high.

Joe felt a sudden, unreasoning anger. He raised his head sharply and every thought and every impression faded from his mind, except the knowledge that property which he should be guarding was threatened. Without plan and without reason he walked forward toward the cash register, his jaw set and stubborn. There was a sharp report and he twisted and fell to the floor and the first man stood over him emptying a revolver into his body. Joe saw that the man's face was working like the sullen face of a small boy who had been unjustly punished. It was then he remembered where he had seen that face before. "Why, Harry!" he said in surprise.

Then Harry's face went away and Joe lay on his back, his head against the cashier's cage, and watched his blood flow across the floor and into a cup-like depression in the tiles. The depression filled quickly. There was a layer of sawdust floating on the blood. Mrs. Glab was on her knees, lifting him up. She said: "You shouldn't of moved, Joe. You ought to of had more sense than to move."

But Joe did not hear her. He had a feeling that some force was lifting his body from the floor and that in a moment he would lurch forward and float away. The thought frightened him. He threw out his arms and grasped the cashier's cage, raising himself slowly from the floor. Sweat came in beads upon his forehead and his chin began to tremble. He swayed again to the soiled floor and his face pressed flat against the sawdust. He made a bubbling noise with his mouth, thrust his buttocks into the air and turned on his back. A shudder passed over him. He raised his head slowly and the two fine, vertical lines came between his brows. Then he collapsed suddenly. His eyes rolled upward. His fists clenched and straightened slowly. His jaws relaxed and fell open.

1930

HORSESHOE BEND
LIBRARY
DADEVILLE, AL

THE SHOE DRUMMER

I'M GLAD she suggested walking up, rather than waiting for the elevator. I don't want any publicity in this little affair. Married women are responsible for most of the front-page stories. Husband out of town, eh? Well, they've been known to come home unexpectedly. Wouldn't I be in one fine mess then? She's taking out her key and opening the door. All right! All right! Go on in and have a look around.

"Well, how do you like the layout? Let me take off my hat and I'll fix you a drink. No, you sit down on that sofa. That's right, way back. Make yourself comfortable, and don't be afraid of hurting the furniture; it's all paid for."

Well, I needn't be ashamed to sleep here, it's a pretty nice place, but I don't like those dolls with their cloth legs tied in knots, though. They give me the creeps. Living-room, bedroom, kitchenette and bath. I'll find out about the bedroom later. It's my natural setting. Johnnie Holliday, shoe drummer. The Bedroom King. Oh, I'll see the bedroom all right. Here she is again. Well, let's get going.

"What are you so quiet about, Jack?"

"Was I quiet? Maybe I was thinking what a sweet little wren you are."

"Kidder! You don't mind my calling you Jack, do you?"

"I'll be sore if you don't."

"And I want you to call me Vera."

"Vera! It's a beautiful name, but not so beautiful as you."

She's squeezing my hand and pressing it to her heart. What a comedian I am. This is elementary stuff. And I want you to call me Vera. That little-girl voice isn't your type. I warn you: If you turn kittenish I'm going to bolt. By God I'll bolt. Why did I pick you up, anyway? It was the news of Amy's marriage

51

that upset me, I suppose. God damn old lady Nixon; why couldn't she mind her own business?

"Well, how about that drink? What'll it be? We got gin, Scotch and some aged corn. Or would you rather have a bottle of beer to start off with? All right, you just sit tight while I fix you up. I won't be gone a minute."

Vera has sense enough to keep the lights toned down; the dimmer the lights, the better she looks. Lord, but she's an old battle-ax, she is: hennaed hair and pouches and diamond-shaped wrinkles on the back of her neck. What could her husband have seen in her? Maybe she was prettier when he married her. A Civil War romance, no doubt.

So this is the bedroom? Well, all it needs is a ceiling mirror and a brewery calendar with naked women riding on kegs of beer. How can a decent man sleep in such a room? I wonder what sort of a room Fred and Amy are sleeping in tonight? Well, I wish you and Fred all the happiness in the world. I'll take my medicine standing up. How do you like that laugh clown, laugh! effect? Little Johnnie Holliday and his painted smile that hides a broken heart. What the hell do I care? I've got the laugh on Fred, at that: I had her first. If Fred wanted one of my cast-off women why didn't he tell me? I could have fixed him up with a better one than Amy. Oh, why did I have to run into the Nixons of all people in the world? Why, John Holliday, who'd ever expect to run into you in a hotel lobby this way? Oh, I'm up here visiting my sister for a few weeks. I've got some news for you: Amy Martin and Fred Rausch got married last week. You didn't know that? Well, it looks like Amy would have sent you an announcement, at least, after you went together so long.

"Here's a drink that Vera fixed her Jackie with her own little hands. That's the way I like to see a man drink his liquor: down the hatch with one swallow. Have another one? You can't walk on one leg you know. You don't talk much, do you? Well, it don't matter. A good-looking man like you don't have to be a interesting conversationalist. I bet you have a date every night with a different woman. Ha, ha, ha! Well, here's to our better acquaintance!"

This isn't going to be as bad as I thought. Vera isn't so bad. She's beginning to feel her drinks a little. I think I'll have another.

"What do you say to another one, Vera?"

"Sure, help yourself. Do you want the same thing this time or would you rather have some Scotch? We got some good gin if you'd rather have that."

"I'll stick to the corn."

"I'll have one with you. Say, don't put so much in mine. More ginger ale and less corn. I could tell when I saw you in the hotel lobby that what you needed was a couple of good shots. There's nothing like it when you're feeling blue. I knew you were feeling blue the minute I saw you walk into the writing room. I said to myself: 'There's a fellow that feels blue,' and I hoped you'd come over and talk to me because I was feeling blue too. Not that I make a habit of talking to strange men, but I knew you were feeling blue too. Is that mine, Jack? Well, here's looking at you. Say, cheer up, can't you?"

She's leaning against me again. What do you expect me to do? Take you in my arms and shower you with kisses? Not yet. Not on four drinks, madam. I'm afraid you overestimate your charms. We've got lots of time. I haven't anything to do until nine o'clock tomorrow morning and your husband won't be home for two days. Don't crowd me. Everything in time.

"You're a sweet little girl, and I'm pretty lucky, I guess."

"Go on with that stuff, don't try to kid a kidder. How 'bout another one, baby? That's right. I can tell a regular when I sees, pardon me, see him. Make it the same, Jackie dear. You know I'm getting a edge on. How 'bout you? You got no kick at all. Make yours bigger. Am I talking too loud? Well, here's a million years! What you thinking about, honey? Tell Vera what you thinking about."

"I was just thinking what a lucky fellow your husband is. You've been married just a short time I suppose?"

"You're wrong there. George and I have been married for

fifteen years. Of course I was nothing but a baby at the time.
Where did I meet George? Oh, I met him when I was working
at the glove counter at Carson's. George was selling lingerie
then and he used to stop at my counter and buy gloves for his
girl friend. He'd make me try them on because he said his girl
friend had hands just like mine. Oh, he said a lot of silly things
about how pretty my hands was and so I got to liking him
finally. He wasn't fresh like most of the fellows you meet but
was a thorough gentleman in every particular. I was crazy about
him by that time and so when he asked me to marry him I did it.
I didn't know what I do now. I was just an innocent girl in
those days. Oh, what's the use? A man like you wouldn't understand George; but nobody can say anything against him to me
and get away with it. Am I talking too loud? You're not like
George at all, but you're nice too. Oh, let's have another drink."

By God, her hands are beautiful; I hadn't noticed them before. Well, she's due a break. I knew I'd get Amy off my mind
when I'd had a few drinks.

"Here's your drink, Jack. Say, I'm getting drunk, baby. Gee
but you're nice; you're the nicest man I've met in a long time
but you're too cold. Refined men are always cold at first, though.
I like refined people and I was brought up to be refined myself.
You don't believe that; you think I'm a bad woman. Yes, you do,
I know you do. You don't respect me at all. What right have
you got to think insulting things about me? Who the hell are
you, anyway? I don't care if I am crying. I'll cry as much as I
God-damned please. Now what do you think of that? You've
just sat here for the last hour like you was better than anybody
else and thought insulting things about me."

She's right, I ought to be ashamed of myself. Poor little lonely
girl. I do like her a lot. I'm putting my arm around her and I'm
caressing her cheek. She's still crying a little. I should kiss her,
I suppose.

"You really respect me? Honest to God, do you, sweetheart?
Of course you'd say now you respect me. You really respect me?
Then kiss me, honey. Hold me closer in your arms and kiss me!
No, no, no! Don't do that! What do you think I am? I thought

you said you respected me? Listen, Jack! Jack! Let's have another drink. Please don't do that, Jack. Listen, dear, let me up
or I'll be angry. I want to fix another drink. There, you've
mussed me all up and you've torn the strap of my brassière. Oh,
don't worry about it, baby. To hell with the strap. Let's have
some gin and orange juice this time. I'll go fix it. No, don't
come with me. Make yourself comfortable and don't worry
about the old strap any more."

What happened to me all of a sudden? Lord, but that was a
rotten thing to do. I'll have another drink while she's gone.
That's peculiar; my hands are trembling and my heart is beating
too rapidly. I should have my heart examined. I'm nervous and
jumpy. I've been feeling strange for the past few months. I ought
to see a doctor. Sometimes I think that nothing around me is
real; that the people walking on the sidewalks aren't real people
at all; they are tailors' dummies worked by machinery. They
frighten me and I want to spring into the air and fly away. I
feel as if I were going to faint at such times. I wonder what is
the matter with me? I haven't felt really well since that scene
with Amy, almost two years ago. Probably I should have my
heart examined. Maybe I'm going crazy. I'm excited. I shouldn't
have treated Vera like that. I didn't mean to hurt her feelings.
I'll apologize again. Poor lonesome little girl. Why the hell
doesn't the old bitch come back? She needn't think she can treat
me this way. She knows what's coming off, although she's not
the sort that would pick up just any kind of a man. She liked
me at once. She said she did. She's a sweet, gentle little woman.
But of course you couldn't be seen with her publicly. I'm restless. I'll turn on the radio. There's Vera at last. She's putting
down the drinks. I wonder if she can dance.

"Do you want to dance, Vera?"

"Sure I do. Let's pull back these rugs. We won't disturb nobody. It's early yet."

She's in my arms. What a beautiful waltz. I'm closing my
eyes. She dances beautifully. Amy danced like that. Amy, Amy,
why did you do that? Why couldn't you have waited? We
could have straightened things out later. She is standing on her

toes and is kissing me. My head is whirling and my heart is pounding again. I'm holding her close to me. I'm kissing her throat and her golden hair. We're walking over to the couch. This isn't Amy. Well, what if it isn't? Who the hell cares? I'm a little drunk but I know what I'm doing. It's all right. I don't care. Why not?

Well, that's that. There's no use in my staying here any longer. I ought to be getting back to the hotel; I've got a hard day's work ahead of me tomorrow. I'll finish my drink and make my excuses and leave.

"Here's your drink, baby. Gee, the ice has all melted. No wonder at that, though, standing near you. How's that? Ha, ha, ha! I sure had you sized up wrong. Nothing cold about you; I'll say there's not! That's right, dear, drink it all."

For Christ's sake shut up, can't you? What a filthy little swine I am. I'm sick at my stomach. Oh, well, it doesn't matter, I suppose. I don't know whether I can stand up or not. I'll feel better after a while. I'll get up and go in a few minutes but I want to rest now. Amy, Amy my darling, I want you to know that I'm ashamed of myself.

"That's right, Jack, stretch all the way out and let me lie beside you. Put your arms around me. There, like that. Do you like to have me stroke your hair? George is crazy about my hands. He used to come to the glove counter where I worked, but I told you all that, didn't I? Of course I told you all that. I remember it perfectly. I'm not that drunk. George is a good man and he takes care of me well, but he acts funny in some ways; the way he acts about my hands, I mean. He's not a man in the way that you are. Do you understand what I'm trying to say, honey? He's always wanting me to keep my hands covered up when there are people around. He thinks it's disgusting for me not to have them covered up before people. He's been like that ever since we married, but he's getting worse it seems to me. I don't understand him at all, but I love him. You don't believe that, but I do love him."

"Are you tired? All right, let's go to bed and get some sleep.

Just go in the bedroom, baby; I'll fix your clothes on a hanger for you and I'll get breakfast while you shave and take your shower in the morning. I'll love cooking breakfast for you. Either side of the bed suits me. That's right. Now close your eyes and go to sleep, and I'll be with you just as soon as I can straighten up a little bit. Gee, but you're tired. I believe you're asleep already. My sweet baby!"

I'm tired; Christ, but I'm tired. I'm depressed and I'm disgusted with myself. I don't know how I feel. I'm dizzy and the room is swaying a little. I'd like to get up and start running over house-tops and never stop again. Why did I run into old lady Nixon of all people in the world? It was the news about Amy marrying Fred Rausch that upset me. I hate her. I try and I try but I can't get her off my brain. I feel that somebody had burned her name on my brain with a hot poker. I can see it plainly: the "A" and the "Y" are very heavy but the "M" is scrawled out like a child's writing.

How very strange, says the doctor performing an autopsy on me: this man has the name Amy burned on his brain. Oh, that's nothing, says his assistant, my Aunt Jennie had a hen that laid an egg with God is Love on it. I wonder how many men have slept in this bed before me? Dozens, probably, and dozens more will sleep in it after she's forgotten me. Oh, yes, she'll forget me all right. Amy forgot me and she really loved me once. She promised that she would love me always. Always. How droll. How God-damned droll. I hate her. I wish she were this woman here. I'd like to humiliate her as she humiliated me. Oh, why did she have to say those things? It's true Mother never liked her—she was right about that.

I remember the talk Mother had with me as plainly as if it had just happened. . . . Since you've met this girl you've for-gotten all those nearest and dearest to you, Son; and then she put her face down in her hands and I could see her crying. Poor Mother, what a sad life you've had. I didn't know what to say; it hurt me to see her so unhappy. I told her that she was mistaken but she only pressed my hand and said over and over: She is unworthy of you, Son. I could feel her tears on my hand. I can feel them now. Promise me that you will forget this unworthy girl. But I couldn't promise that. I told her I would try, but I didn't really mean it. I thought I could straighten it out. Then Mother said: This will kill me, but I don't want you to reproach yourself in any way. I've lived my life and I'm old and worthless. I won't stand in your way. I didn't sleep at all that night. I kept going over and over the scene, trying to find a way out. And then the next morning Mother went to see Amy. Why did Amy have to say those things to her? Oh, God, wipe the whole thing out of my mind. I want to forget it.

Amy called me up that afternoon and I went to see her at once. I won't go over that again. I'm determined that I won't go over that again. Quit thinking about it; think of something else quickly. I will quit thinking about it. I can't quit thinking about it. I can't. I went to see her and she said that she loved me and was still willing to marry me, but I must promise to break completely with my mother. How could I do that? I told her I couldn't promise that and she was furious. She said those things about my mother: all lies; lies. I will not go over that again. It hurts me too badly to go over it. I won't, I tell you, I won't. Dear God, don't make me go over that again; it hurts too badly. Let me forget it. Wipe it out of my mind. She said my mother had a mind like a sewer. Don't let me remember that, please. She said the Board of Health should fumigate our house and that the whole family should be soaked in the dipping vat for diseased cattle. She said— No, I won't remember that; that's going a little too far. I won't remember that, I tell you. Make me forget it, dear God. Please. She said many things: all lies; lies. I didn't say anything at all. I was frozen. I just stared at her.

She was wearing a green dress that day and she had on a string of gold beads. I can see her now. I can see the shape of her mouth. The way she held her head. Her lovely throat. Stop it. Stop it. Stop it. I'm exhausted. Why do I keep going over it? Why does my brain keep racing this way? Am I going crazy? They say when you think you're going crazy you never are and vice versa. *And* vice versa. A lady came into a department store and said to the clerk: I see that dark tan shoes with light tan tops and vice versa are popular this season; so the clerk showed her some and she said, Yes, these are dark tan bottoms with light tan tops but I don't see any vice versa on them. Then the clerk said: That, Madame, is French for "three straps." Ha, ha, ha. I'm laughing merrily. You've got to play up to the buyers to sell them, but I hate that vice versa joke. Vice versa, indeed. Vice . . .

What a vicious creature I am. I'm steeped in vice and vice versa. I ought to be fumigated for lying with this old bat's arms around me. Now really, I won't stay all night, Madame. You can hardly expect me to stay all night for a few simple drinks and my breakfast. I'll say that to her and then I'll put on my clothes and go back to the hotel. She knows that I'm awake. She's holding me tighter. What a comedian I am. No, Madame —positively no. . . . Oh, very well if you insist; after all I suppose one must be as polite as possible when a guest in a lady's bed.

I don't understand myself at all. Women of this sort repel me and yet I'm helpless with them. Why do they run after me so? Of course I'm unusually good-looking and people take you at your face value I suppose. If this old hen knew how she repels me she wouldn't be kissing me so. She'll tell her friends tomorrow what a wonderful fellow I am. She'll spin this night out for a week and then the next time George is out of town she'll pick up another little traveling salesman to tide her over. There are men paid for such things, but that's in Europe, of course. Amy had German blood from her mother's side of the family. What of it? She means nothing to me. I wish she were this woman here. I'd like to humiliate her. I'd like to pay her back for making me suffer.

I remember the picnic at Walker's Lake. That was before I went on the road. We wandered off from the others and sat down under a dogwood tree. She had on a tan dress with darker tan trimmings and tan shoes and stockings and vice versa. How dainty and cool she looked. She had taken off her hat and let her yellow hair hang down. How beautiful she was. We lay against a mossy log. We were very happy. I don't know yet how it happened. Amy had cut a little switch and kept tickling my ears with it and laughing when I tried to catch it. I laughed too. Then I tried to take the switch from her. I put my arms around her to get it and I felt her warm body against mine. I felt her heart beating against mine. I felt her sweet breath on my cheek. I felt holy and uplifted. I took her in my arms and kissed her like this. Like this. And then it happened. I kissed her like this. Again and again.

"Vera loves to have you kiss her that way."

Kissed her again and again. And everything is melting into ecstasy. They lied to me. You haven't forgotten me. Nothing shall ever part us again. I love you. I want to die in your arms, Amy. I want to be annihilated at this instant.

"What a silly girl Vera was to say you was cold."

I'm very tired. I want to go to sleep. I just want to go to sleep now. Rock-a-bye, baby, in the tree-top. Don't leave me, Amy. Stay with me, darling. Nothing can ever hurt you with me. I'm almost asleep. Almost asleep. How pleasant it is to sink miles down into sleep. I can hear someone laughing in the street, but very faintly. I can hear a train whistle, but very faintly. I'm so tired and so happy. I'm drifting down, down into a sweet darkness. I wish I never had to wake up again. Stay with me, Amy. Must sleep now. Must sleep. Must . . .

What are all these people doing here? It's a picnic of course. I must find Amy. We came together. She has on a brown dress and the sun is shining through her lovely hair. Amy! Amy! Where are you, dear? She doesn't answer. Everyone is hurrying and I'm rowing as hard as I can but I can't move the boat from the dock. You frightened me, dear. I thought I had lost you. It isn't Amy. It's an old woman who sits in a rocking chair and cries. Never mention her name again. This girl is unworthy of you. And the funny little man with the pistols goes skipping over the surface of the lake. There's scum on the lake. People use it for dipping purposes, only it isn't a lake after all: it's the

shore of the ocean and an open-air restaurant. I am alone. Never
have I been so alone. So terribly alone. Don't cry like that; it
isn't manly. I'm alone and lost. I run from group to group but
they close together and won't let me in. I am looking for something. I ask people but they laugh at me and give me different
directions. They confuse me. An old woman wants me to stay
with her, but I won't do it. She smells of creosote. Amy! Amy!
. . . I hear the echo of my voice. Amy! Amy! . . . I have lost
her. People are laughing and pointing at me.

Everybody has a plate filled with food. The men and women
are all exchanging plates and walking off toward the little wood.
I'm so alone. Don't cry like that. There's Amy sitting on a throne
surrounded by many men. They are asking her to exchange her
plate for theirs, but she laughs and shakes her head. How lovely
she is with her hair gleaming in the sunlight. I'm in the crowd
fighting my way through. I offer my plate to Amy. She steps
down from her throne and gives me her own plate in exchange.

A chair is rocking, rocking, although nobody is sitting in it.
Rocking back and forth. Rocking back and forth. The plate has
been dashed from my hands and lies on the ground broken.
This girl is unworthy of you. Don't cry like that; it isn't manly
to cry like that. There are plenty of other women in the world.
There's an old battle-ax with dyed red hair and pouched eyes.
She's guarded by a dragon named George who has a hundred
beautiful hands and who thinks she's a fairy princess. That's
funny. It's so funny I'm crying. The dragon is waking up. He's
looking at me. Leave me alone, dragon. I didn't hurt your bed.
He's coming toward me. His hands are squeezing my throat.
He's breathing fire in my face. Don't kill me, dragon. Don't
destroy me. I'm helpless. I can't move. I can't breathe.

"What's the matter, baby? Were you having bad dreams?"

Who's shaking me? Is the hotel on fire? . . . I'm not at the
hotel. I'm with a woman who picked me up in the lobby. I'm in
her apartment.

"Didn't your supper agree with you, honey? You were groaning and crying in your sleep."

Her husband is out of town. He won't be back until day after tomorrow. God, how rotten I'm going to feel tomorrow. Why did I do a thing of this sort. I wish I could die. I wish I could forget everything. I can't go on facing things any longer. . . . There's that dragon again. He's looking at me suspiciously. The little man is shaking the door and trying to get in. They ought to have that lock fixed. It's hard to open. Maybe the key doesn't fit. Help me. Save me. She's shaking me again. She's breathing like a frightened animal. The lock is turning. The little man has on a derby hat. He's her husband. His name is George. She lied to me. I'm tricked.

"Jack, what's the matter? You've been acting funny! Are you sick? Jack! Listen, baby!"

He's coming in. He's turning on the lights. He's at the bedroom door. Oh, God, I wish the earth could open and swallow me. How my head aches. My heart is pounding. My mouth is dry. What a coward I am. I'm trembling. And this woman here; she's frozen with fear. He can see us. He's standing there as if he were petrified. Well, you see what's going on; say something, can't you?

"Jack, listen! What are you scared of? There's nothing there, darling!"

He doesn't know what to do. He can't believe it. It's too sudden for him. He's been destroyed and he just stands there staring. He's going to turn on that cluster of bright lights. Don't do that. Spare me that. I'll do anything you say to make it right, but don't turn on those lights. I don't want to look at myself. I don't want to look at you. I don't want to look at this woman here. I don't want—

"Jack! For God's sake!"

What a funny little man he is. He's taking off his hat and is hanging it in the closet. At a time like this. I've ruined his life. I've wrecked his world. I'd like to tell him that I'm sorry. Should I say: "Good evening, sir, I've just wrecked your world—I hope you don't mind?" I'm looking at the woman. Her hair is hanging in her eyes. Her mouth is open like an idiot's. There's saliva in the corners of it. She has pulled the cover up over her breasts but her thighs are bare. She doesn't know that. Why doesn't somebody tell the woman that she's exposing herself? She's paralyzed with fear. Her own life is wrecked too. Everybody's life is wrecked. Why doesn't the man say something? He's trying to understand this thing, but he can't. It happened too suddenly for him.

I can't stand facing things any longer. Not any longer. What am I laughing for? The woman thinks I'm crazy, but I'm not crazy. When you think you're crazy you never are and vice versa. They print divorce news in the society column along with the social diseases. That clerk at the Peabody Hotel is named Post. He just stands there staring. This woman that he thinks he's in love with is unworthy of him and he's just discovered it. I'm laughing again. I wish I could die. I felt then that I was falling. I'm sick at my stomach and my legs feel weak. I'm afraid that I'm going to vomit. I don't want to live any longer. Why doesn't the man shoot me instead of standing there blinking his eyes? Hit me over the head and finish me up. Put me out of my misery, that's the kindest thing to do. Don't let me suffer this way. You wouldn't let a dog suffer this way. I can't go on facing things any longer. Finish me up with a stone.

I almost fell again. Things are wavering and getting unreal. I could jump into the air and float away if I wanted to. I feel hysterical. I want to shout and cry. I want to sing. I can't keep still much longer. I've kept quiet all my life and now I can't keep quiet much longer. I'm laughing again. Those aren't real people, you fool; they're wax figures worked by strings. The female figure is getting out of bed. Good Lord, she's naked. What grotesques they both are. They're supposed to be husband and wife. They're constructed with wonderful care, but distorted a little for the sake of comedy, of course. The husband is sitting down. What a tragic face. I'm glad I came to the theater tonight, because I was worried and I had something on my mind. Or was that a year ago? It doesn't matter. I'm laughing out loud. Be quiet. Be quiet. You're annoying the other guests. I can't stop. I . . .

What happened to me then? I almost fell. I'm being hurled in space. Faster and faster. This darkness terrifies me. Black sickening senses down terrified stairs of drowned men rotting through whirling spaces. Lights snapping tortuously through whirling white faces gazing in wonder through frozen tear glances. Rhythmically turning through whirling black spaces. Whirling in nausea; turning in pain. Whirling rhythmically; turning rhythmically. Faster in rhythm; faster in rhythm. Faster. Faster. There's the sun and the moon. Help me. Save me. I'll be dashed to pieces. I'll be annihilated . . . Don't . . . Don't . . .

I'm crushed to pieces. Something sticky is running into my eyes. I've fallen and cut my head. This is death: this is the reality of death. White burning bright lightness with eyesocket aching and throbbing when tired brain erases oaths that nobody heeds. Burning white aching horror. Shout. Scream. An octagon-shaped oath is a marital obligation on a hotel register if there are no better rooms available but a bathroom for dipping purposes and dim lights to hide one's guilt are really essential. Turn out those lights, bell boy, or you'll get no tip from me. They shine through me. They illuminate my brain. Don't look at the things that are written there, ladies and gentlemen. You'll be shocked. You'll be nauseated. You'll be convalesced in agonized convulsions of goldenglow with the sunlight gleaming through your hair and you really are the only woman that I have ever loved. Amy.

Who is it screaming that way? He ought to be stopped. It's unmanly. You can't break me on the rack. You shan't treat me that way. Amy is responsible for this. She wants to destroy me, but she can't. Nothing can destroy me. I'm master of the sun and the moon and the stars. Mother, Mother, don't let them destroy me. Who is it shouting and talking? Am I doing that? Why not? I'll shout as much as I please. I've never talked before but I'll talk now. I'll never stop talking. I'll talk forever. You are all against me; you want to destroy me, but you can't.

I'll destroy the universe. This is the moon that I have in my hands. I'm dashing it into space. It shatters with the tinkle of glass. The moon is made of glass. Who is that naked woman running about and wringing her hands? She's frightened. She never before saw the moon destroyed. This is the sun. I'm hurling it to nothingness. What a wonderful sensation. I'm destroying the world piece by piece and thoroughly. Piece by piece. Hurling. Tearing. Breaking. Splintering. To bits. To fragments.

I want a room and bath with bacon and eggs and a wife of my own, or is this a table d'hôte and has everything been properly fumigated. If it isn't fumigated I won't live here. I have my orders from the Board of Health. Does that old hag go with the room? I don't want her; take her out. This is a lovely honeymoon for a man. For God's sake, don't let her touch me. Amy, let me alone, can't you? Can't you let me rest? I'm dead now. Can't you let me rest even when I'm dead? I must spend the night with her. I won't do it. I won't. Help. Save me. She's trying to destroy me. They all want to crucify me. I can't stop shouting. I never want to stop shouting. I want to tell everything now.

Won't somebody turn off the faucet? Where's the key to the dipping vat? I'm going to drown my mother. I've wanted to do that a thousand times and now I'm going to do it. A girl who is unworthy of me wants me to do it. Don't struggle so hard, Mother. I don't want to reproach myself afterward. It won't be hard. Don't resist me so. Just keep your head under and don't struggle. That will only make it longer. You are old and worthless and I hate you. I've hated you for a long time, my sweet darling. I've hated you for such a long time. This is hideous; I can't go through with it. How she moans and struggles. I must. I can't have Amy otherwise that unworthy girl. Stay with me otherwise, you unworthy girl. Don't leave me. I'll kill her thoroughly, dear. I'm holding her head under. She's struggling, but I won't relent. I must make a good job of this. I've been weak all my life. I'll be firm now. She's struggling, but very faintly. She's stopped. She's still. It's over. It's done. I've killed her. She's floating face upward in the dipping vat. Her hennaed hair is trailing straight down in the water and her lips are moving. Her beautiful hands are quiet. I'm not to reproach myself. I've killed her, Amy; for you, dear; for your sweet sake.

Where did those people come from? They weren't here when the marionette show started. Get out, you fools; this is my room.

But wait: those children with their legs tied in knots can't get out. If you want to keep your children at home you must tie their legs in knots and then they won't run away. But you must start very young when their bones are tender and why doesn't somebody untie the knots in the legs of the poor children and then I will be free. Then I can walk out of this room like a man. I can like a man I can and be free. Free free then. I'll be free; free free why can't you see I can't go on any longer like this. Can't any longer. Can't. . . .

And those men in uniforms armed with clubs? Walking toward me so slowly. They're mad because I killed my dear mother. It's none of their business. Get back, you God-damned swine. Don't put your filthy hands on me. You're unclean. Your fingernails are soiled. You haven't been in the dipping vat. I haven't done anything except kill my mother and that's no crime, is it? I'm not to reproach myself. I'm backing away slowly. They can't fool me. They want to crucify me.

Don't think you can take me like that. I won't stand for it. I'm in a corner. I won't let them touch me. I won't be tortured. I won't be crucified. I've just destroyed the universe, do you hear? I've stood all that I can stand. I can't stand any more. I am Christ but you must not crucify me. Get away, you publicans. Don't touch me. Don't—

I'm fighting. Fighting. Struggling. Biting. You cowards, fight fairly. You swine—you God-damned swine. Let me loose. I'm kicking. I'm tearing. I'm biting. Struggling furiously. Why do you want to crucify me?

I'm exhausted. They have me down. Don't hit me again. Take that sponge away from my nose. That's chloroform. You can't fool me. It's chloroform. "Mother! Mother, they're going to chloroform me! Take it away, I tell you! Take it away!" . . . I'm smothering. . . . I'm whirling in space. . . . Whirling in space. . . . "Don't crucify me! . . . Don't crucify me! . . . Don't crucify me! . . . Don't—"

1930

MIST ON THE MEADOW

*W*HEN Brother Hightower came at last from the twilight of the pine grove he saw before him a meadowland, filled with flowers—saffron and pink, bell-shaped and shaped like stars —lying damp and cool in the late afternoon and flowing richly to meet a line of cypresses that fringed the lagoon and marked where the marsh began. It had been dark among the trees, but the meadowland swam in a light fluid and amber that blurred the outline of the cabin before him and softened the harshness of the clay plastered against its sides. The cabin was built of hewn logs that had weathered brown, and was set squarely in the midst of the meadow. At its back, a sagged chimney of sticks and red mud threw smoke into the air in a thin, curving stream.

Brother Hightower reined up his pony and removed his feet from the stirrups. "That must be the Gentry place," he thought. Before him stretched the meadow and the marsh, but to his left the land rose to irregular bluffs of red clay which hung like a shelf above the eastern edge of the lagoon.

He stretched his bony legs and turned to survey the cabin more carefully. Then he settled again to the saddle and began to think of himself and his mission. He thought of the sinfulness of the world, of the viciousness of men and of the souls he had somehow saved in his itinerant preaching years, and his heart flooded with a feeling of humility and power. He raised his arms to heaven and his eyes rolled upward. "Lord! Lord!" he moaned. "Make me worthy to serve in Thy vineyard!" His face became distorted and he twisted with pain.

As he prayed, there came from across the meadow the voice of a man calling his pigs, and the answering sound of swine welcoming and disputing their supper. Hightower had dropped his reins, and the pony, with lowered mouth, wandered at will and cropped the grass eagerly. Presently the preacher removed his clerical hat and wiped the moisture from his forehead and his hands. Then he took up the reins again and guided his pony toward the cabin.

As he drew nearer, the squeals of the swine came louder to his ears, and he could distinguish easily the words the man was using: "Hey, there—Emma! Git outen that trough! Whoever learnt you manners? What would folks say, now, if they seen you actin' thataway?" Brother Hightower frowned at the joyousness in the man's voice. He halted his pony and dismounted stiffly. Before him was a sty, in which milled a dozen fat pigs, and a man who was feeding them slops and mash from a tin bucket. The man was dressed in a brown shirt and faded overalls, grotesquely patched with colored scraps which had also faded. His sparse red beard curled upward at the ends, and his head was entirely bald. He wore no shoes. His voice was affectionate, and he laughed continuously at the antics of his pigs.

"Git away, Emma, I tell you—give old Charley a chance. He ain't had a mouthful!" With his bare foot he shoved her away from the trough with a tolerant, loving gesture. "I declare: that Emma's the *hongriest* sow ever I seen!" Again he laughed happily.

Brother Hightower cleared his throat sharply and said: "Good evening, and God be with you all." His voice was deep, with a rich, trembling intensity.

"Good evenin', preacher," the man said mildly.

"Is this the Gentry place?"

"Yes, preacher. I'm Jim Gentry."

"I allowed you was Jim Gentry. I'm the Reverend Hightower, the humblest of God's servants, and I'm on my way to hold a revival for the folks on Pigeon River."

Gentry walked to the edge of the pen and held out his hand. "I'm glad to make your acquaintance, preacher. I've heerd folks a-talking 'bout you. I've heerd it said Christ Jesus stood before you one time, honorin' and raisin' you up above all men."

Hightower bowed his head. "You have heard truly, brother. It was Him that gave me the wrath to make sinners quail and forsake their lusts. It was Him that gave me the power to heal the sick and a hand to cast out devils." Jim shifted his weight nervously and drew back, and with his bare, horny feet he stroked the backs of his swine.

Suddenly he turned and faced the cabin. "Exa!" he called loudly.

A woman appeared in the door. She was a tall woman, taller than her husband and almost of a height with Hightower himself. Between her decaying teeth was a sweet-gum brush which she chewed with a thoughtful, automatic insistence. Her eyes were pale under their bleached brows and blue veins stood out in her wrists. When she saw the stranger she drew back suspiciously, but her husband's voice reassured her.

"This here's the Reverend Hightower on his way to preach a revival at Pigeon River."

The name had a magic effect on Exa. She came down the steps quickly and approached the two men. "You don't come none too soon. The folks at Pigeon River are ungodly, I've heerd it said." She gazed at Hightower fiercely with her pale eyes, and Hightower stared back, his own eyes dark and dilated with emotion. "Ungodly and sinful, Sister Gentry," he whispered. "Singing songs and dancing and lusting after flesh."

Exa spoke to her husband: "This is a holy man, Jim." But Gentry laughed foolishly and turned to finish feeding his pigs. Exa spoke again to the preacher: "We'll be proud to have you stay with us a spell. We hain't got much, but what we have is yours withouten even askin'."

"You are kind thoughted, Sister Gentry, but I aim to pass on my way at daybreak. There's work in the Vineyard of the Lord and the reapers are few." Exa nodded her head in complete understanding. "Come into the house, preacher; supper'll be ready right soon. Jim'll take care of your pony." Hightower turned then and followed her into the house.

The cabin consisted of two rooms and a lean-to. There were no lamps, but a blaze of pine knots lighted the room and cast great shadows against the walls. Hightower removed his hat and his black, tight-fitting coat, and Exa brought him water from the stove and poured it into a basin. When he had finished his wash and had combed out his damp, black hair, supper was being placed on the table. He seated himself at once and commenced a blessing, but almost immediately he was interrupted by sudden laughter and the sound of chains being shaken. He uncovered his eyes and gazed at the burlap curtains which screened the entrance to the lean-to, but he did not pause in his prayer. As he watched, there came to his ears a sound like the popping of a cork and a hiss such as some fabulous snake might make. Exa half turned in her chair, but her eyes remained downcast and devout. Again there came the rattling of a chain, angry and more insistent, and presently the hissing changed into an irritable and impotent chatter. Brother Hightower brought to an end his blessing and raised his head. He looked enquiringly at Jim.

"That's *Tolly*," said Jim proudly; "that's my boy, Tolly!"

Exa was on her feet instantly. "Oh, my po' baby—did its ma go and forget it? Did its ma clean forget little Tolly's supper? Now that's a shame; that's what I call a mean shame!" As she talked, she piled victuals on a tin plate, and presently she brushed the curtains aside and went to her son. The querulous chattering ceased at once. There was now the sound of lips being smacked and food swallowed sensuously. Occasionally Exa's voice was heard whispering some endearing phrase: "Eat it all, honey—greens is *good* for Mamma's baby."

Gentry dragged one foot across the floor slowly. Then he looked down at his plate, as if to hide the pride in his eyes: "Tolly's the beatenest boy you ever seen," he said. "There ain't nobody like him in the county. They just lost the pattern after they finished makin' old Tolly!" Then he leaned back in his chair and chuckled at some old recollection.

Brother Hightower frowned and shook his head. "But chains, Brother Gentry . . ." he began; "to put one of God's creatures in chains . . ." His voice thinned out into silence.

"Oh, pshaw!" said Gentry; "that don't mean nothing; Exa don't mean no harm by chainin' him up, but she can't be a-watchin' him every minute, after she done put clean clothes onto him, and iffen she didn't chain him up, Tolly'd just liable as not go get in the pen and wallow with the hogs."

Hightower looked up in surprise. "Will he do a thing like that?" he asked in an uncertain voice. Then an expression of distaste came over his face. "Wallowing with hogs!" he repeated; "wallow in filth with hogs!"

"Sholy," said Jim; "sholy. Now what all's wrong with that?" Then he began to speak earnestly. "They're good clean hogs; them hogs is the best in this county; they're registered stock; I guess them hogs is better blooded by a whole passel than you or me, preacher. It's their nature to wallow, and Tolly's nature to wallow, and I always say to Exa, if they don't mind Tolly in their pen, then Tolly ain't got no call to mind them."

Hightower shoved his plate away with a sudden gesture of disgust. He rose from his seat and walked to the fire, kicking at a log that protruded from the hearth and giving life suddenly to the shadows that seemed painted against the wall. But Jim continued talking in his soft, contented voice.

"He looks right cute there in the pen with them pigs, and him so covered with mud that nobody could say for sure what was hog and what was Tolly. That boy Tolly," he continued, "he sure is one case, now! He sure is the very beatenest one! But he's a real good boy and nobody can say different. He never meddled nobody's business and he never caused sorrow in his life. Sometimes of a morning he picks flowers in the medder or watches a humming bird all day, but then sometimes he goes to sleep against a cypress knee in the cool of the lagoon." Then Jim began to laugh louder and slap his leg. "That boy Tolly!" he repeated proudly, "he sure is one case!"

The curtains parted and Exa came again into the room and seated herself at the table. Hightower made a deep, sympathetic noise in his throat. "I'm sorry for you, Sister Gentry, in your trouble." Exa bowed her head and looked down at her hands. There was a long silence and then Jim glanced at his wife timidly, turning at length to the preacher for support. "There was a young fellow through here last fall, come to teach school at

Liveoak. He said we ought to send Tolly to the 'sylum. Said he might get cured iffen we done that."

Exa's eyes narrowed and her bleached brows became dangerous, as if the subject were a sore one. She rose from the table and walked backward slowly. "Nobody can take Tolly and lock him in a dungeon for a lunatic!" she said. She stretched her arms across the opening to the lean-to, and stared fiercely at the two men, as if her husband's words had somehow put in motion forces which would take the boy away. Brother Hightower walked toward her, his voice sweet with sympathy. "There, now, Sister Gentry! Nobody's going to take the boy away. Brother Jim spoke without thinking. He's an earthy man and he knows not the yearning of the spirit nor the ways of God; but no man could be heartless enough to put God's own handiwork in an evil place of atheists and infidels where prayers are never heard and where His sacred word is flouted and scorned." He placed his arms protectingly around Exa's shoulders and guided her back to the table. "Sister Gentry, God has placed a heavy cross on you and yours, but rejoice and be exceedingly glad! For He punishes them that He cherishes, and you are His very dearly loved. Rejoice, sister, and kiss the hand that chastens you! Rejoice and be glad!"

Exa looked up pleadingly. "Preacher, what ails Tolly?"

Hightower walked across the room rapidly, his black hair tossing excitedly to his stride. Then he turned and faced the woman. His eyes were dilated and his hands were trembling. "Your son is possessed of a devil!" he whispered. There was a note of exultation in his voice. "Your son is possessed of a very terrible devil!" he repeated.

"Aw, shucks, preacher," said Jim mildly.

When the meal was finished at length and Exa had cleared the table, a sweet mist was rising off the lagoon and a moon rode high above the trees. The pine grove lay quiet and dark to the north and the meadowland was an enchanted and a lovely place. The men had walked onto the porch and sat smoking their pipes. Hightower was talking of his conversion and Exa, washing her dishes, could hear his deep voice plainly.

"It happened nigh to dark, when I was plowing in the field. There come a sound of wings about my ears and I seen the air was filled with angels. They roosted in the trees and sat white on the rails of the fence, singing a hymn of praise. I fell to my knees, knowing well the sinful life I had led. 'Lord! Lord!' I said. 'Wash me with blood, and make me as white as wool.' I buried my face in the dirt and waited for death to take me, but something lifted me up, and Christ Jesus stood before me. I put my hands over my eyes, being unable to bear the sight of His glory, and swayed my head from side to side, moaning. 'Spread My glory to all men, and preach My gospel to every nation!' He said. 'Halleluiah! Halleluiah!' sang the angels in voices as sweet and as high as a trumpet note.

" 'How can I preach for You?' I cried out; 'I, an unlettered man who cannot read Thy holy word!' 'Doubt not, for thou canst really do these things!' He said in a voice of thunder. 'No, Lord,' I answered, 'I never had no schooling and not one word can I read.'

"Christ Jesus raised His loving arm and I seen that He had a whip of scorpions. He brought it down across my shoulders time and time again. 'It is written that My house shall be a house of prayer, and ye doubt that I am the Son of God come to save the world from sin!' . . . And me crouching between the rows of young corn, baring my breast to the whip and saying: 'Do with me what you will, gentle Lord. Beat me! Make me the lowliest of Thy slaves and I shall love Thee dearly! Rend me limb from limb, if that be Thy sweet wish!' And when they found me my mouth was cut and bleeding and my teeth was broke and there were great bruises on my back and chest to show where the whip had been."

For a moment there was silence, oppressive and brooding, and then Hightower began speaking again: "That night when I returned, word passed amongst the neighbor folk and they come to look at me, and to marvel, and I told them what they longed to hear. When a great crowd had collected, we walked down the road until we come to the settlement, and there, in the presence of them all, I called for a Bible and read aloud the Gospel according to St. Mark. And when the people who had known me all their lives seen that I could really read, they fell upon their knees, fearing, and I baptized them in the river and received them into the church of God. Then when it was dawn we walked down the road again, singing hymns of praise and waving green branches."

Exa put down her dishcloth and stood silent in the room. The fire was dying into embers but the moonlight streamed brightly through the open window and the door. Her husband's voice, soft and apologetic, came to her ears. "I can't read none, neither."

"Praise God for that, Brother Gentry! When God wants to give a man the gift of tongues or the gift of print He will signify His wish, as He done with me. And every book except God's sacred Word should be burnt in flames." There was another long silence, so long that Exa feared the preacher would not speak again, but presently he continued.

"That morning as I walked the road with my disciples praising God and waving branches, I worked a miracle. A nigger come running down from his cabin by the creek, toting a little black girl whose legs were twisted and withered away. I put my hand on the child, who had never walked a step, and commanded that she rise up. And right away she rose up from the road and ran skipping and laughing through the fields. And when my disciples seen that they fell on their knees and kissed my dusty feet, but I said: 'Verily, verily, praise not me, but render thanks to my Father in Heaven, for I am not as mighty as He.' "

There was a silence between the two men. Jim Gentry pulled upon his pipe with a faint hissing sound, but Brother Hightower stared across the meadowland, his eyes dreaming and drawn upward. "For I am not as mighty as He," he repeated sadly.

Exa's voice sounded suddenly from the doorway. "Can you cast the devil out of Tolly, preacher?" Her nostrils were quivering with excitement and her white eyebrows were drawn together. Hightower drew on his pipe deeply while Exa waited with clenched fists for his answer. "I have cast out devils," he said warily; "I have cast out many devils, Sister Gentry."

Jim Gentry got up from the steps and stood with his toes

pressed into the soft loam of a flower bed. "Now, Exa—you all let Tolly alone, can't you?"

But Exa continued to stare at the preacher. "Can you cast the devil out of Tolly?" Her fists were pressed against her breasts and she was breathing heavily.

Brother Hightower stretched out his hands and bowed his head. "I can if it be the will of God, Sister Exa."

"Now you all let Tolly alone, I tell you. He's not a-botherin' nobody."

But Exa and Brother Hightower paid no attention to Gentry. They were staring at each other again with parted lips and furious, exalted eyes; and presently Exa went into the house and unchained her son.

Tolly was undersized and sallow and no thought held his features together or gave his face significance. His forehead bulged above his eyes and his jaw lay relaxed and toneless beneath his parted lips. He walked to the edge of the porch and held out his arms. "Fire! Fire!" he said eagerly.

"No, honey, that ain't fire—that's just the *moon!*"

"Tolly's got as much sense as you or me," said Jim; "Tolly's got as much sense as anybody, iffen he wanted to use it." Hightower shook his head vigorously. "It's the devils in him that call out for the fire!" he said.

Jim looked helplessly from the exalted face of his wife to the more exalted face of the preacher. A feeling of resentment came over him, but it passed almost immediately. He could never defy anyone as powerful as Brother Hightower and he knew it. "Po' little Tolly!" he said sadly; "po' little Tolly!"

Exa seated herself and Tolly sat beside her, resting his meaningless face against her shoulder. Hightower regarded them carefully. "How old is the boy?" he asked. "He's going on twenty, preacher, but small for his age, as you see." Exa smoothed back her son's coarse, hemp-like hair and stroked his cheek with her hand.

Suddenly Hightower spoke directly to the boy. "Tolly, look at me, son!" But Tolly paid no attention. "Tolly! Listen to Brother Hightower; he's going to make you well again." Exa had risen to her feet, lifting the boy in her strong arms. Hightower had also risen, and presently he came over to the boy and placed his hands upon his forehead. Tolly hissed and spat and his face wrinkled with terror. "Tolly, ain't you 'shamed!" said Exa reproachfully.

"Don't blame the boy, sister; it's the devils in him that done that." He caught Tolly by the arms and held him firmly, and Tolly became very excited. He struggled and spat and tried to free himself. He began to chatter excitedly and later to make low, pleading noises; but Hightower held him tightly. "This is going to be an uncommon hard devil to rout, Sister Gentry," he said; "it might be best to chain the boy up while I pray."

"What makes you all keep a-pesterin' Tolly so?" asked Jim querulously. "He ain't done nuthin' to you."

Exa gave her husband a glance of scorn. Then she picked up the loose ends of the chain that circled her son's waist and snapped them through two bent spikes driven into the logs of the cabin. Tolly looked from one face to the other quickly. He drew close to the wall and clung there in terror, but Hightower pursued him relentlessly. He lifted the boy's face and gazed at him with deep, yearning eyes.

"Devil, come forth!" he whispered. Tolly began to laugh foolishly and to shuffle his feet, but he could not draw his eyes away from the preacher's eyes. Hightower swayed his head back and forth with a slow, steady motion and Tolly's head swayed with him. "Come forth, devil, from this soul! . . ."

For a moment there was silence. Then a crane called shrilly from over the marsh and the swine, dreaming in their wallow, grunted twice and turned nervously.

Presently Hightower fell to his knees and began to pray in a deep, rich voice. He lay on the floor praying, his eyes distended and his hands splayed widely. Finally he rose to his full height and placed his palms against Tolly's cheeks. Tolly did not resist him now. He lay passive against the logs of the cabin, glancing from his mother to the preacher in terror. Hightower lifted his eyes to heaven. The muscles of his face twitched, his jaw was set and he talked cloudily through locked teeth. "Grant me this miracle, Lord!" he whispered. "This miracle you done once with your own sweet hands!" Then he forced back the boy's head until their eyes almost met and cried in a loud voice: "Come forth, devils, and depart from this boy!" Tolly began to tremble more violently. He rattled his chains and beat his head against the wall.

At that moment the pigs awoke and made a low, worried sound. They rose heavily and huddled together against the farthest wall of the sty, grunting in uncertain protest. Then they broke their grouping and trotted apprehensively around the pen, coming together, at last, in the center of the sty, to stand there, waiting, making a vague grunting noise.

Jim touched the preacher on his arm in mild protest. "Why don't you all go inside and shet the door?" he asked. "My pigs is getting upset with all this racket a-goin' on. Them's blooded, high-strung pigs, preacher, and they can't stand this to-do."

But Brother Hightower did not even hear him. His voice was becoming stronger and more exultant. Again he lifted Tolly's head, and again he gazed deeply into his shrinking eyes. "Come forth, devils!" he demanded. "Come forth and enter yon filthy swine!" A strange echoing sound came from Tolly's throat. He clutched the side of the cabin for support, clung for a moment, and fell sharply to the floor.

Instantly the pigs began to squeal in terror, lunging furiously against the sides of the pen. At the sound of their distress, Jim Gentry sprang from the porch and ran to the pen and stood trying to quiet his pigs with soft, loving words, but they paid no heed to him at all; they continued to squeal and hurl themselves against the sides of the sty until at last its walls gave way against their weight. Then the released swine ran across the meadow to the east, in the direction of the bluffs, milling and whirling in broken, furious circles and tearing each other with their teeth; and when they reached the bluffs they continued to whirl, and a moment later their bodies were silhouetted against the moon as they pitched over the edge and into the water below.

Brother Hightower stood in silence, his body rigid, his eyes flaming. Then he turned and faced Exa, praying rapidly, and

Tolly rolling on the floor. "I have performed the miracle of the swine," he whispered, as if awed by his own power. "Bear ye witness," he said; "bear ye witness to my holiness!"

At the preacher's words, Tolly crept eagerly to him, kissing his hands and embracing his long legs. His face, which had once been meaningless and content, was now meaningless and frightened. "Save me!" he screamed over and over. "Save me from eternal torment!" Then his face began to twitch and his body jerked spasmodically as Jim Gentry unsnapped the chains that held him to the wall, and carried him into the house. "Po' little Tolly," he said; "po' little boy! If ere a man can show me where you're bettered withouten your devils, I'll give that man a pretty." Then he looked sadly across the meadow and closed the door to the cabin.

For the wind was changing and the mist that had hung above the marsh began to thrust furtive arms between the trunks of the trees, and to spread over the surface of the lagoon. From the lagoon the mist moved across the meadow with a slow, imperceptible motion, obliterating bushes and outhouses and familiar landmarks. Soon the pine grove and the bluffs would be lost under a covering overwhelming and impalpable; soon the horizon would be wiped away and the land blotted up completely, and nothing in all the world would remain except Tolly rattling his chains and Brother Hightower, with raised, enigmatic arms, praying harshly before the cabin.

1930

THE WOOD NYMPH

*W*HEN the new guest arrived at the inn, Mrs. Siegert had made it a point to introduce herself. "You're Miss Innis, aren't you?" she asked; but Miss Innis only stared at her. "Oh, yes," she said presently. Her voice was tiny and it trembled like the voice of a little girl embarrassed by her elders.

"I'm Mrs. Addie Siegert," that lady continued. "I come to the inn every season. Now you may tell me all about yourself."

Miss Innis stood regarding her with round, uncertain eyes. She said: "Oh, I did hope I wouldn't have to meet any *people* here!" She seemed on the verge of tears, her jaw trembling a little.

"Well, really," said Mrs. Siegert in a strange, baffled voice. "Well, really, Miss Innis!"

But this afternoon Mrs. Siegert was on the sunny side of the porch rocking excitedly and explaining Miss Innis to her circle. "But wait!" she pleaded; "I haven't told you the strangest part of all."

"You mean what she said about being a wood nymph?" asked Mrs. Corning.

Mrs. Siegert nodded. "Her exact words were, 'I don't want to meet people because I'm a wood nymph, and I won't have anything in common with people.' Those were her exact words. I pledge you my honor."

Eloise Gore made a warning sound: "Sh-h-h! Here she comes now!"

Miss Innis came onto the porch and looked about her with a rapt, vacant stare. She was wearing army breeches with spiral puttees that afternoon. Her feet were shod in stoutly soled boots and a man's felt hat rode high upon her unbobbed, graying hair. Her thighs were high and wide in the khaki uniform and her

79

bosom curved extravagantly. Slowly her eyes came back to the
porch. She ran down the long steps and skipped across the lawn.
"You see?" said Mrs. Siegert hysterically.

"Be careful, Addie!" said Mrs. Corning. "She'll hear you!"

But there was little chance that Miss Innis would hear the
people who discussed her eccentricities, for there were more
important matters on her mind, and she was thinking, at that
moment, of the pool. She had come upon it on the day she
arrived at the inn, and since then she had spent most of her time
seated at its rim and looking into the water.

The pool was tranquil and black and it lay below a waterfall,
to the left of a basswood tree. Three of its sides were covered
with close growing shrubs. When there was no breeze the leaves
of the shrubs hung lacquered and deeply green, but when a
breeze blew, they lifted upward and flashed their undersides to
the sun. The sight of the leaves trembling in waves of silver, or
silver-gray, was very beautiful to Miss Innis, but more beautiful
than anything, she thought, was the shingle of sand that bounded
the eastern side of the water.

Miss Innis never tired of looking at the pool. Occasionally she
would get up from her seat under the basswood tree and lie upon
the sand, scooping a palmful of the black water and holding it
close to her eyes. But in the sunlight the water was not dark any
more; it was as clear as crystal, and that fact invariably disturbed
her. She would hold the water in her hand a long time before
pouring it back into the pool, striving at such moments to see
the exact instant when its clearness became black again.

Afterwards she would lie upon her back, puzzled, and think
why that should be so. Her eyebrows would come together and
her lips would pucker up, and at such moments she looked like
a confused little girl, prematurely aged, who would never be
able to do her sums correctly.

This afternoon she watched a pair of birds who hung suspended above the water and fanned the air so rapidly with their
tiny wings that they seemed without movement at all. Then,
suddenly, as if upon some imperceptible signal, they would fall
downward and skim the surface of the water, and rise again, in

an effortless curve, without so much as wetting the tips of their crimson, vibrating tails.

Miss Innis watched the birds for a long time. "It seems such a simple thing to do," she thought. "You just let yourself go, and fall downward, and then, when you have almost touched the pool, you spring up again." She wondered if she could master the trick if she watched the birds closely enough. "Of course I could dive from the top of a tree," she said out loud. "That part is simple enough. It's hanging suspended and then springing back afterwards that's really hard, I imagine." She smiled vaguely and closed her eyes.

"If you try it, you'll only get wet."

The soft, purring voice came from behind her, but Miss Innis was not startled at all, because even before the voice answered her, she had known that he was there, and even before she opened her eyes, she knew how he would look.

The boy was dressed in brown overalls and a shirt which had once been pink. His teeth were white against the golden brown of his skin and his hair was a deep red. When Miss Innis had collected her wits, she spoke to the boy.

"Are you a human being?"

"Certainly *not!*"

"I beg your pardon. I didn't mean to be offensive."

"Well, how would you like it if I thought *you* were a human being?"

"I never thought about it that way before," said Miss Innis.

The boy lay on the sand and began building a house, shaping the substance with caressing, experienced fingers. Miss Innis laughed suddenly, and she found it impossible to stop. She was disappointed that the boy did not share her knowledge or join her laughter, but he seemed devoid of either subtlety or humor, and at last she saw that he was growing angry at her merriment. He destroyed the sand house and got up, brushing his clothes.

Miss Innis was beside him at once. "Please don't go away," she pleaded. "I wasn't laughing at you *personally*. It was something else."

"How long have you been a wood nymph, anyway?" he asked suspiciously.

"Not long," she said humbly. "Any errors I make are errors of the mind, not the heart."

"I don't even know what you're talking about."

"It doesn't matter," said Miss Innis, shrugging her shoulders. "It doesn't really matter, does it?"

"What's your name?" asked the boy.

"Miss Innis, of course."

"What's your first name?"

"Oh, wouldn't you like to know *that?*" answered Miss Innis, laughing archly. "Oh, wouldn't you like to *know!*" she repeated, throwing provocative glances over her shoulder.

Then, suddenly, her mood changed. She sat beside the boy and spoke earnestly. "I was only joking. I don't mind telling you my name. It's Gertrude."

"You're a mortal woman," he said.

He stretched out on the sand again, his arms spread wide, one knee slightly raised. "How perfect he is," thought Miss Innis. "He's so perfect he ought to be covered with short, silken fur." Aloud she said, "A long time ago someone I loved called me Trudy, but I liked to have him call me that."

The boy yawned, turned on his side and rippled the pool with his finger.

Miss Innis began to cry shrilly. "Don't pretend!" she said. "You know very well that it's too terrible to think about. 'Don't put your hands on me again,' I said. Then he began to curse me, and everybody in the white house came out of their doors and stood looking at me in pity. I covered up my ears and ran away as fast as I could."

Miss Innis stopped crying and said: "Oh, well, let's not think about it any more." Then, after a moment: "Shall I dance for you?" and without waiting for his reply she sprang up and began to skip about. She held her arms out and waved them up and down; she stooped and gathered handfuls of the water, flinging it into the air and laughing with abandoned gaiety. She pretended that she had a veil in her hands, which, at her pleasure, floated above her head or trailed the earth at her feet. She would whirl dizzily for a moment and then sink to the ground, arching her back and distending her fingers. When she was tired, she came again and sat with her back to the basswood tree.

The boy said: "You are a mortal woman."

"Yes."

"I am the thing you have always wanted."

"Yes," said Miss Innis. "Yes."

She came over to the boy and put her arms around him. She drew his head down to her shoulder and rocked him gently. A feeling of peace came over her. She felt that she was on the verge of an experience deeper and more sensuous than sleep. She was sinking down, endlessly, from one void to deeper and more delicate voids beneath. She closed her eyes and abandoned herself to her sensations. And so they rested for a long time. "Kiss me," she said. "I am a human woman."

When Miss Innis opened her eyes later on and looked about her she was surprised to see that the afternoon had passed. The sun had already set, but the wood floated in a light as golden and as heavy as honey. She had the feeling that she rested on the bottom of a sea in which trees, blurred and indistinct, were growing. She felt, if she willed it, that she could raise her arms and splash the air; that she could spring upward, without effort, if she willed it, and float in the light, and that it would bear her weight.

Then she got up and walked across the sand, her lover's arm about her, her head resting against his shoulder. There were red markings on the surface of the pool, and the shrubs which grew close to its brink were reflected reversed and still from a depth which was limitless.

But when they reached the pool and she felt the cold water swirling about her feet, she drew back and asked her lover a question. At his answer, she smiled and stepped forward, and immediately the pool closed over her head.

She rose to the surface and began to struggle furiously and to strike out with her hands, and she found herself, somehow, in shallow water again. She crawled out upon the sand and

stood there incredulous. Beneath her she could see the boy swimming strongly, his body flashing through the water. Then he rose
to the surface and held out his arms to her, standing knee-deep
in the water, awaiting her.

Miss Innis stared, her mouth opened wide with terror, for he
stood revealed to her at last, and in that final, syrupy haze of
twilight, his face sucked inward with a slow, gaseous sound and
fell away. There were no lips now for her to kiss and no lan-
guorous eyes to look at her beauty. She stood paralyzed before
these things, and then she turned and ran blindly, tearing her
clothes on brambles, stumbling over logs and falling headlong
into shallow ravines.

Once in her room, she locked the door and took off her wet
clothes. She pulled back the covers of her bed and lay there
trembling. "No! No!" she said over and over. "I won't do it!
I won't go there again!"

But even as she spoke, she knew in her heart that she lied to
herself. "No! No!" she said desperately. "It's too terrible. I'll
leave this place tonight and never come back. I won't do it."

She turned on her back and cried softly so that the other
people at the inn could not hear her. "There's something strange
the matter with me," she said. "I'm not really well. I'm not well,
at all."

1930

TO THE REAR

*T*HE COMPANY was going to the rear for ten days and the men were in high spirits. They sat waiting for the relief troops to arrive, their packs rolled and their equipment stacked.

Lying flat on one of the wire bunks in the dugout was a boy with an eager, undeveloped face, and weak eyes which were habitually narrowed against sunlight. His ears crinkled and bent forward like the leaf of a geranium and his shoulders were high and thin with the sparseness of immaturity. He was Private Ernest Lunham, and before his enlistment he had worked as a soda-jerker in a drug store in Erie, Pa. He was coughing steadily into a soiled handkerchief, his face the color of biscuit dough dusted with ashes. At intervals he would shiver, as if cold, and then he would catch his breath with a surprised, wheezing sound. He had been gassed that afternoon while he and Private Overstreet were gathering firewood for the officers' dugout.

Jimmy Reagan, corporal of the squad, came over to him: "What did the doctor say, Ernie? Why didn't he send you to the hospital?"

Lunham sat up and stared around him, as if unable to remember exactly where he was. Then he began to talk: "When I went in the sick bay, the doctor looked me over and listened to my heart. 'So you claim you got gassed?' he asked in an amused voice. 'Yes, sir,' I said. 'How do you explain that when the Germans haven't thrown over any gas for a week?' 'I don't know,' I said. 'I'll tell you how you got gassed,' said the doctor, 'you dipped a cigarette in iodine and smoked it. Did you think I'd fall for anything like that?' I didn't say anything—it wasn't any use to say anything."

Lunham lay back on the wire bunk, as if exhausted, and breathed heavily. There were red splotches coming on the backs of his hands and on his forearms. His weak eyes pained him. It was with difficulty that he held them open.

"*That's* a bright son of a bitch for you!" said Joe Birmingham. "Why didn't you ask him where you'd get a cigarette to put iodine on?"

"I didn't say anything at all," said Lunham, "I just came on out."

Corporal Reagan called Buckner, LaBella and Davey and they whispered quietly. Then he conferred with Birmingham and Overstreet. At last he approached the bunk where Lunham lay.

"You don't have to worry about carrying the clip bags or taking your turn on the *chauchat*," he said. "You don't have to carry anything but your pack."

Max Tolan, the last member of the squad, came off watch and entered the dugout. He was a powerful man, with a nose that flattened to a triangle and nostrils that splayed widely. His lips were thick and calm; they seemed made of a substance somewhat harder and somewhat less flexible than flesh. For a moment he stared at Lunham quietly. Then, somehow, his lips managed to open. "He don't have to carry even that. I'll carry his pack for him," he said.

A little later Lloyd Buckner approached the bed, a package in his hand: "Here are some malted milk tablets I've been saving. You'd better eat them, Ernie—they'll do you good."

Lunham nodded his head, but he did not speak. He wanted more than anything to thank Buckner and Max Tolan and the rest of the men for their kindness, but he was afraid he would start crying and make a fool of himself if he tried to say anything.

At six o'clock the relief troops came and the men moved in single file down the communication trenches that let to the rear.

The trenches widened after awhile and became less deep. On either side were the charred remnants of a grove of trees. Many of the trees had been uprooted in past barrages and lay flat on the ground; many, with dead limbs trailing the parent stem, had split asunder in the shelling, or snapped halfway up their trunks; but a few of the trees, sapless and black, stood upright in the field, inflexible now in the March wind. The terrain hereabouts was pitted with great shell-holes from which the roots of the fallen trees protruded dry and seasoned.

Overstreet became very excited. "That's the place where Ernie got gassed!" he said. The squad stared about them curiously. "That's the very place," continued Overstreet. "I wanted to go farther back, around Mandray Farm, for the wood; but Ernie thought this would be as good a place as any; so I said all right, it suited me if it suited him."

Overstreet hunched his shoulders and scratched his armpits. He started whistling *La Golondrina* through his teeth. He was a stocky lad, with a neck so short and a chest so thick and rounded that people were surprised, upon regarding him closely, to discover that he was not a hunchback. His teeth were infantile and irregular and they grew together in a V shape. His voice, a counter-tenor, was high with a quality of tremulous, penetrating sweetness in it.

"How did Lunham happen to get gassed?" asked Buckner.

"Well, it was this way," said Overstreet. "Ernie thought the dry roots in the shell-holes would make good firewood, so he jumped down and began chopping them off. I sat outside and took the roots that he handed up and cut them small enough for the dugout stove." Overstreet was conscious that the whole squad was listening to him attentively. "Well, sir, while we were working there, a French soldier came running toward us. He was waving his arms about and shouting. You know how these Frogs act?" Overstreet turned to his companions. "Sure!" they said. "Well, I put down my ax and I said to Ernie: 'What's wrong with him, do you suppose?' And Ernie said: 'Maybe he's sore because we're taking firewood!' Ain't that right, Ernie?" Overstreet said suddenly. Lunham nodded his head but he did not answer; he was saving his breath for the long march.

"Well," continued Overstreet, "when the Frenchman reached us, he began to talk excitedly and make gestures, but Ernie and me didn't know what it was all about; so finally this Frenchman catches hold of Ernie's arms and tries to drag him out of the shell-hole; but Ernie gives him a shove in the chest and the

Frenchman falls backward into a mud puddle. Ernie and me were laughing like everything by that time, but the Frog kept staring at us in a peculiar way. Finally he seemed to see the joke, because he began laughing too. He made a low bow to Ernie and me and as he turned to go, he blew us each a kiss.''

The communicating trench was only waist-high now and the men could see the barren fields that stretched interminably on either side. It was seven o'clock, but it was not entirely dark. Then, after a time, the trenches ended in a road that was roofed carefully with a framework of wire netting, over which burlap sacking, painted brown and green, had been thrown.

"What happened after the Frenchman left?" asked Wilbur Davey.

Overstreet, feeling his importance as a narrator, waited a moment before resuming. "Well, Ernie went on cutting roots and I went on chopping them up; but after awhile he said to me: 'Say, Al, did that monkeymeat at dinner make you sick?' and I said, 'No, why?' 'Nothing,' said Ernie, 'except I keep tasting it.' Then, about five minutes later, he said to me: 'Al, I'm beginning to feel funny.' 'What's the matter with you?' I asked. 'I don't know,' said Ernie. 'I'm going to heave, I think.' I looked down and saw that he had dropped his ax and was leaning against the side of the hole. His face had got gray and his forehead and his lips were sweating like he had a fever. 'You better come up here and lay down,' I said; but he didn't answer me. 'Listen, Ernie,' I said, 'come on up here with me!' "

Overstreet paused a moment. "When Ernie didn't answer me, I jumped down and lifted him out of the hole. He tried to stand up, but he couldn't make it. Then he fell down and began to heave. Well, as we lay there, who should come back but the French soldier. He had a civilian with him this time who spoke English. He told us that the terrain around Verdun had been shelled so many times that the ground was full of old gas. It was dangerous to dig in shell-holes, he said, because a man could be gassed before he knew what was happening to him."

Overstreet laughed in his high, tremulous voice. "The joke sure was on Ernie and me. There he was heaving at the top of his voice; and all I could think of to say was: 'We're much obliged to you fellows for telling us.' "

The camouflaged strip ended at last and the troops came out on the Verdun road. Darkness had settled, and the faces of the men were no longer visible. Joe Birmingham was talking about his hoped-for leave. Birmingham was bright-eyed and sudden with an alert, intelligent face. His straight hair, parted in the middle, hung upon his forehead like yellow curtains imperfectly drawn. His teeth were strong and brilliantly white, and as he talked he moved his hands with quick, nervous gestures. He could read print that was not too difficult and he could sign his name to the payroll, but that was about all.

"And when I get to Paris, the first thing I do will be to round up a dozen of the best looking ladies in town: four blondes, four brunettes and four red heads."

"I wouldn't be caught short if I were you; I wouldn't economize on women that way!"

Joe paid no attention to Overstreet. "One of the blondes is going to be dressed in purple silk and have violet perfume on her. The best looking brunette is going to wear a red dress with pearls sewed down the front of it and be scented up with carnation. The red heads will all wear green dresses and Jockey Club and have lace on their drawers."

"How about a blonde flavored with vanilla for me?" laughed LaBella.

"I'll take a red head," said Lloyd Buckner, "but she'll have to wash off the Jockey Club."

Reagan spoke then: "Don't let them kid you, Joe. If there's anybody in this squad who's particular, it hasn't been brought to my attention."

"Oh, we'll come to your party all right," interposed LaBella; "you can bank on all of us accepting."

Birmingham gave him a friendly shove. "You will like hell come to my party!—If one of my girls got a look at you dirty bums they'd—they'd—" Birmingham paused, groping for the appropriate word.

"Swoon?" suggested Buckner helpfully.

Birmingham looked up mildly: "For Christ sake, Buck! Don't you ever get that off your mind?"

Reagan smiled a little, but Buckner and LaBella began to shout with laughter. Sergeant Stokes came toward them angrily. "What's going on here?" he demanded; "do you want the Germans to start shelling this road?" LaBella interrupted him. "All right, Doc; all right," he said quietly.

Lunham walked in silence. He was standing the hike better than he had thought possible. He looked at his pack, riding high on Tolan's shoulders, and at Tolan walking firmly, with no sign of fatigue. It was white of Max to carry the extra pack, particularly since his feet blistered easily, as everyone knew, and long marches were difficult for him. "The fellows sure have been white to me," whispered Lunham softly to himself. He began to feel feverish and from time to time he took a mouthful of water from his canteen.

The men continued to laugh and joke, but they were careful not to raise their voices. Then, after a time, when their muscles were cramped and tired with the burdens they carried, they became silent, one by one, and settled down in earnest for the long march.

The road bent again and ran north and east, and a late moon rose slowly behind a burned farm-house. To the west Very lights and colored flares were ascending, hanging motionless for a time and then drifting toward nothingness with a hesitant, languid motion. There came a sound resembling iron wheels jolting over a bridge of unnailed, wooden planks; there was a constant flash of guns along the horizon and the muffled sound of exploding shells.

Birmingham unbuttoned his cartridge belt. "Give 'em hell!" he said excitedly. "I wish I was with you to give the bastards hell!"

"Do you think we're really going back for a rest?" asked Davey.

"That's the information they're putting out."

Tolan made a gesture of disbelief with his heavy, wooden lips. "That's all bunk about getting a rest."

Eddie LaBella spoke up: "We're getting a rest, all right—in a dirty town with a dozen manure piles and one cafe."

"It might be all right at that," said Birmingham. "Some of these Frog women ain't bad!" He brushed his yellow hair out of his eyes and licked his lips in an exaggerated, sensual way. "Baby! I'll say they're not bad!" Lloyd Buckner stared at him with sudden unconcealed distaste. He seemed on the point of saying something but changed his mind. He turned his head away.

"The next time they have a war they'll have to come after me with a machine gun," said Reagan laughingly.

"Some of these Frog women ain't bad," insisted Birmingham. "I'll bet we have just as good a time as we had in Chatillon. I'll bet—"

Buckner whispered something to LaBella behind his hand. Labella laughed and in turn whispered to Reagan; but Reagan shook his head. "Let him say it!" said Birmingham. "What do I care what he says?"

The early exuberance of the men had disappeared. They were tired now and becoming irritable. Lunham, walking painfully, realized that. He took no part in the conversation. His nausea had returned and he clutched at his belly. "I won't heave again," he kept repeating miserably. "I'll put my mind on something else! I won't heave again!" He hugged his thin ribs with his elbows and rocked back and forth beside the road. Then he began to retch shrilly. He slipped to the side of the road and pressed his face into a heap of dead leaves that had drifted against a log. When his nausea had passed he felt somewhat stronger. He rose to his feet and stood there swaying. He tried to laugh. "There went Buck's malted milk tablets!" he gasped.

The moon had detached itself from the burned farm-house and swung now swollen and yellow and low in the sky. The sound of the iron wheels became fainter and at last a turn in the road hid the flashes of the guns from view.

"How long have we been on the road, Jimmy?"

Reagan looked at his watch. "A little better than five hours," he said.

The road rose gradually. The men were feeling the march in earnest now. They shifted their packs and strapped them higher on their shoulders. A rhythmic whirring of motors was heard overhead. Then the sound of the motors ceased and across the face of the setting moon the bombing plane floated and listened. Sergeant Stokes came running down the road. "Fall out in the fields and lie down!" He stood there swearing excitedly at the men who were slow in obeying: "Don't bunch up like sheep! Spread out and lie down!"

The men stared up at the plane drifting silently above them. "He's got guts flying so low on a bright night," said LaBella. At that moment there came the sharp, quick bark of an anti-aircraft gun, and two flashlights began to play crosswise in the sky. "They'll never get him," said Reagan, "they're firing too high."

Birmingham lifted his quick, excited face. "Shoot hell out of him!" he said. He moved his hands excitedly and bared his white, perfect teeth: "Give the bastard hell!"

The plane with motors whirring again was zigzagging up the sky, the gunners firing impotently. In a moment he was lost in the clouds and the guns became silent again, but the flashlights moved across the sky for a long time, crossing each other and uncrossing with a jerking, mathematical precision.

"They let him get away," wailed Birmingham. "I could shoot that good with a rifle. Christ! They let him get away!"

Buckner could hide his dislike no longer. "You're quite a little fire-eater when you're safe behind the lines, aren't you?"

Birmingham looked up resentfully. "I've stood enough of your cracks! Who the hell are you, anyway? You act like you were Jesus Christ or somebody!"

Before Buckner could answer, Reagan stopped him. Buckner spat in the road. "I can't help it, Jimmy. I've got a belly full of that common little swine and he might as well know it."

"Who the hell are you?" shouted Birmingham excitedly. "I don't see no bars on your shoulders!"

Overstreet began to laugh in his high, penetrating voice: "That's the idea, Joe. Don't let him get away with that stuff."

"What I said goes for you, too!" said Buckner coldly.

LaBella narrowed his eyes and pursed out his lips, as if deny-ing beforehand the malice in his words. "At least Buckner can read and write. He didn't have to get the drill corporal to recite General Orders out loud until he memorized them."

Birmingham's alert little face twisted suddenly. He was eternally conscious of his illiteracy and ashamed of it.

Wilbur Davey, who spoke rarely, spoke now. "That was a dirty crack to make, LaBella."

Reagan turned, his customary good nature gone. "Pipe down, all of you, or I'll report the whole squad when we get in." But the men paid little attention to him. They continued to quarrel for a long time.

Presently the column turned from the main road and took a road to the left. The ground was rising sharply now, and the hills of Verdun were imminent and threatening ahead. Lunham raised his canteen and drank the last of his water; and as he returned the canteen to its cover and adjusted his belt, he noticed that Tolan had begun to limp. A feeling of despair came over him. In terror he leaned forward and touched Tolan's arm. "We'll get paid when we get to the rear, Max, and I got four months coming." Tolan turned, a slight frown on his primitive features, but he did not answer. "I won't forget about you carrying my pack," he continued, "you can be sure of that." But Tolan continued to limp painfully, giving no sign that he heard. "I won't forget about you being so white, Max. We'll go out pay night and spend every franc of that money." Lunham paused, his face frightened and abject. "What do you say, Max? What do you say to that?" Tolan regarded him in silence, steadily. His round blue eyes were interested and bright. Then he sighed and shook his head doubtfully.

The company was falling out beside an abandoned village and a young officer, on horseback, came clattering down the road. "There's running water in the wash house to the left of the square, if you want to fill your canteens," he said, as if he were reading from a book. It was apparent that speaking to men made him nervous and self-conscious. Overstreet made a derisive, sucking sound with his lips and repeated a strong phrase. The young officer's blush could almost be felt. He ignored the remark and a moment later he could be heard delivering his message farther down the line.

Tolan had swung Lunham's pack to the ground and sat regarding it stolidly. "Honest to God! Max, we'll spend every franc of that money. We'll have a fine time, all right!" Tolan seemed to be turning the matter over in his mind. His heavy lips opened once or twice, but no words came from them. Then he picked up the pack and laid it regretfully in front of Lunham. "My feet hurt too bad," he said.

The load on Lunham's shoulders was a hand, heavy and insistent, to tug at his breath and draw him gradually backward. His heart began to pump alarmingly and the veins in his neck were taut and swollen. "Christ! Christ!" he gasped.

After that he lost all feeling of time, all idea of direction and all sense of individual identity. He was aware only of feet moving over the surface of the road in an irregular pattern and of men quarreling continuously. He seemed detached and no longer a part of his surroundings, and gradually he possessed the power to stand outside his body and to survey himself and his companions impersonally. There was Reagan shuffling doggedly, his dreamy, impractical eyes tired and serious; there was Max Tolan with ankles turned outward, flinching each time his feet touched the road; LaBella, cheap and flashy, his theatrical prettiness caked with dirt and streaked with sweat. He saw Overstreet, his triangular mouth open and his infantile teeth displayed; and Lloyd Buckner's predatory, deeply curved nose thrust forward, his light eyes cold and sullen. Only Davey walked with dignity and only Birmingham's wiry body seemed impervious to the weight he carried, or the steady tug of the miles.

Without warning Lunham staggered and lurched forward. Somebody shoved him into his proper place. He righted himself with difficulty, confused, uncertain. "My mouth tastes salty," he said in a frightened voice. Reagan regarded him closely. "You've started bleeding," he said. Lunham pressed the back of his hand against his mouth and then withdrew it. "You're bleeding, all right," said Buckner. The feet of the men were hardly clearing the roadbed. They shuffled in a monotonous rhythm while the moon hung low in the sky, and from the east there came the smell of fresh water.

"Why can't he take his turn carrying the clip bags?"

"He's sick, Eddie. You wouldn't ask him to do that when he's sick." Reagan's voice seemed to come from a great distance.

Davey made one of his rare speeches: "I guess he's not much sicker than anybody else."

"If he was gassed, why didn't they send him to a hospital?"

The knowledge that his comrades were discussing him gradually penetrated Lunham's consciousness. He realized now that they had·been talking about him for a long time. Birmingham laughed: "He might fool us, but he didn't fool that doctor at the sick bay none. They're wise to those old gags."

The road curved to the right and circled the base of a hill. The young liaison officer came galloping down the road again. The moon had set and there was an indefinite feeling of daybreak in the air. "Fall out for fifteen minutes before you start climbing the hill," he said. He repeated the order firmly. If the men tried to razz him this time, they'd find out very quickly who he was. But the men remained silent, perversely ignoring him. They fell to the ground gratefully. Tolan took off his shoes and began to pour water on his blistered feet. Davey was already asleep and snoring softly, but Birmingham and Buckner continued their quarrel.

Lunham lay on his back and stared at the sky turning faintly gray toward the east. An imperative drowsiness was overpowering him, but some impulse made him struggle against it. With eyes closed and lips half parted, his thin face and wilting ears seemed doubly immature and pathetic.

The men were talking again, their voices coming from a distance, remote and blurred. "Why can't Lunham take his turn on the clip bags?" LaBella's voice was flat and toneless. And Overstreet, petulant: "By God, he's no sicker than anybody else!" There came a thud on the earth beside him and Lunham knew that the clip bags lay before him. He began to laugh. "I never heard anything so silly," he thought; "I can't lift those bags, let alone carry them up the hill."

He turned on his face and pressed his body against the cool, damp earth. The feel of the soil against his cheek steadied him and gave him strength and gradually the cloudiness that had obscured his mind disappeared. He was conscious of his body paining him unbearably. He drew up his arms and pressed his hands against his burning lungs. He began to think, against his will, of many things: of his enlistment, his eagerness, his romantic thoughts concerning noble deaths and imperishable ideas. Then, in justification of himself, he tried to recall one noble thing that he had seen or done since his enlistment, but he could remember nothing except pain, filth and servile degradation. "By God, they sold me out!" he thought. "The things they told me were not true." He lay trembling at his discovery, his eyes closed, his lips opening and shutting silently. An unbearable sense of disgust came over him. He reached for the rifle that lay beside him, surprised to realize that the thought had been in his mind for a long time, and stood bending forward clumsily, his mouth swaying above the barrel as he tried patiently to spring the trigger with his foot.

Joe Birmingham was coming toward him shouting a warning. "Look out! Look out!" he cried. The two men struggling for the rifle stumbled back and forth beside the road. The entire squad was on its feet now, but it was Wilbur Davey who wrenched the rifle from Lunham's weak hands and flung it into the valley below them. He slapped Lunham sharply on both cheeks. He said: "What are you trying to pull off? Do you want to get court-martialed?"

Lunham had fallen to the road and lay with his face pressed into the dirt, but the men paid no further attention to him. "Oh, Christ! Oh, Christ almighty!" he said in a weak, childish voice.

The first light, new and hard, came over the tops of the hills and cast strange shadows on the faces of the men. In a farmyard somewhere a cock crew, and below in the valley mist hung above the fields. Word came down the line for the men to fall in. They rose stiffly and put on their equipment. Lunham did not rise. He lay limp and relaxed, his arms outstretched; and as he lay there he could hear his comrades climbing the hill; he heard their hard breathing and their grumbling voices; he heard the irregular shuffle of their feet, the clink of a canteen and the creaking of a leather strap. But after awhile even these sounds became faint and vanished, and he was alone.

Presently a peasant woman carrying a wicker basket strapped to her back and leading a she-goat with a distended udder, paused on her way to market and stood regarding Lunham with uncertainty. The she-goat, feeling the rope slacken, approached cautiously and nibbled his uniform, twitching her sensitive muzzle and baring her yellow teeth, but the woman jerked the cord and the goat moved away. Lunham turned and lifted his head heavily. He was still bleeding—a thin, insistent stream which would not stop—and where his mouth had rested there was a pool of blood which the earth had not entirely absorbed.

From her basket the woman took a metal cup and got down upon her knees, the she-goat spreading her hind-quarters obediently. When the cup was full, the woman lifted Lunham's head and held it to his lips, but the milk was tepid, with a rank smell, and after he had swallowed a portion of it, he rose suddenly to his knees and swayed dizzily from side to side, his face white and dead, his hands splayed like the claws of a hawk. Then he tried desperately to stand upright, but his knees collapsed under him and he fell flat on his face and vomited with a hoarse, screaming sound.

The woman stretched out her arms and raised them slowly sidewise with a gesture singularly frustrate and moving; and as she raised her arms the handle of the cup turned on her finger and the milk ran over its edge and spilled into the road. But Lunham lay stretched on his back, his face and hands covered with sweat, his thin body trembling.

"Let me alone," he said. "Let me alone for Christ's sake."

The woman had risen and stood regarding him with placid, compassionate eyes. She shook her head sadly. "*Je ne comprends pas!*" she said.

In the valley a farm-boy shouted to his team, a dog barked on a high, pure note and a flock of rooks, circling with slowness, dropped silently into a field.

1930

MISS DAISY

THAT afternoon Mrs. McArthur, my Sunday school teacher, came to see Aunt Juliet. I was getting too big to be in her class any longer, and she thought I should be promoted to the Intermediate Section. "I surely will hate to lose Harry," she said; "he's a good boy, Miss Piggott, in a lot of ways, and he don't give me near so much trouble as some of the others; I'll sure hate to lose him, and that's a fact; but he's just getting too big."

I was out in the backyard, playing with Leo, when Mrs. Mc-Arthur came to see Aunt Juliet, but they called me in after a little while. Aunt Juliet must have been expecting company that afternoon, for she had on her black silk shirtwaist and skirt, and her hair was parted so that the gray streak didn't show at all. She had a gold chain around her neck, with my grandmother's watch on the end of it. You could hear the watch ticking, but you couldn't see it, because it was tucked behind a leather belt that she always wore. From where I was sitting, I could see my hands in the glittering belt; they were fat and blown up, and not like my hands at all. I began to move about and try to see how much of myself I could make the belt show at one time, but Aunt Juliet stopped me.

"For pity sake, Harry! Can't you sit still more than two minutes without twisting all over the place? You're worse than a worm in hot ashes."

"If you think *Harry's* bad, you ought to see *some* of them!" said Mrs. McArthur, but she laughed when she said it, though.

I sat up straight in the chair again, but I didn't say anything. Mrs. McArthur had a square flat face. She always wore gold earrings that went all the way through her ears and fastened with a screw on the other side. The earrings were very heavy, and they pulled the bottoms of her ears down. I thought her face looked like a map of the United States with Florida on both sides.

"Don't you want to be promoted to the Intermediate Section?" asked Mrs. McArthur after a while.

"No, ma'am," I said.

"Why, I'd be ashamed," said Aunt Juliet, "a big boy like you, going on nine years old and still in the Infant Section."

"Now, Harry," said Mrs. McArthur, "you'll like it better in the Intermediate Section."

When Aunt Juliet called me in, Leo and I had been playing Indians on the warpath and we were just getting ready to attack the settlers' wagons. Leo thought he'd better go on home, but I begged him to wait and he said he would, if I didn't stay inside too long.

"All right, Mrs. McArthur," I said; "I don't mind going in the Intermediate Section."

Mrs. McArthur thought a moment and then she spoke to Aunt Juliet. "Maybe he'd like it in Miss Burton's class. Don't you think you'd like it in Miss Burton's class, Harry?"

"I don't care," I said.

"All right, then," said Mrs. McArthur. "If it suits you, Miss Piggott, I'll speak to Miss Burton on my way home and see if she's got room for Harry."

"Is it *Daisy* Burton you're speaking of?" asked Aunt Juliet.

"Yes," said Mrs. McArthur. "She lives with the widow Findley on Cherokee Street."

"I used to know her," said Aunt Juliet, "and I'll be proud to have Harry in her class. She's a fine type of Christian woman."

Mrs. McArthur nodded her head. "She's all of that and more. Mr. McArthur and I were talking just the other night about whom we considered the best practicing Christian we knew, and we both agreed it was Daisy Burton."

"Well, she's a fine woman," said Aunt Juliet, "and I don't know anybody who's had a harder life than she has, either."

After a while Mrs. McArthur got up to leave, but when I went back to look for Leo I found that he had gone home.

A lot of people thought it funny that Aunt Juliet sent me to the Presbyterian Sunday school, when all the other Piggotts were Methodists, but before I came to Reedyville to live, my mother had taken me to the Presbyterian church, that being her church, and Aunt Juliet didn't think it right for me to change, now that my mother was dead. So on Sundays Uncle Carter used to hitch up the surrey and drive me to the Presbyterian church first; then he would go back and get Aunt Juliet and Aunt Emmaline, and drive them to the Methodist church.

I liked living with my uncle and aunts. They were very good to me. Aunt Juliet was the oldest, Uncle Carter was next, then came my father, and Aunt Emmaline was the youngest of the Piggotts. My father's name was Herbert, but I could never get used to hearing my kin people call him that, as my mother had always called him Mr. Piggott. When Aunt Juliet would say to Uncle Carter: "Do you remember the time Herbert bought a goat from a little colored boy and Papa made him take it right back?" or, "It's not surprising Harry don't like okra: Herbert wouldn't eat it either, no matter how Mamma fixed it!" I always thought they were talking about somebody else.

That afternoon I kept thinking maybe Leo had got mad because Aunt Juliet had called me in, and after supper I said: "Aunt Juliet, can I go over and see Leo Zerback for a little while?" Aunt Juliet said yes, she guessed so, but to be back before eight o'clock, because she intended going to bed early.

Mrs. Zerback had had snow pudding for dessert that night, and she gave Leo and me what was left over, and we went out on the back porch to eat it. After a while Mrs. Zerback came out and sat with us. She was a big fat woman and she wore calico wrappers all the time. She laughed in a loud way and slapped her leg like a man.

"Well, Harry," she said, "I saw old Mrs. McArthur going to visit your house today; I'll bet you've been misbehaving in Sunday school."

"Oh, no, ma'am, I haven't!" I said. "But she's going to promote me to Miss Daisy Burton's class in the Intermediate Section."

"Well, you couldn't find a better teacher than Daisy Burton," said Mrs. Zerback seriously. "A finer woman never lived—I've always said it, and I'll say it again. Why, when my washer-woman's daughter was sick last winter, it was Daisy who sat up with her night after night, like she was her own sister, instead of a stranger, and if anybody should ask me, Daisy was the sickest of the two."

Mr. Zerback came out on the porch in his stocking-feet and brought a pitcher of lemonade and a plate of oatmeal cookies with pecans in them. "How do, Harry," he said. "Everybody well at home?"

"Yes, sir," I said. "Everybody's all right."

Mrs. Zerback was still thinking about Miss Burton. She nodded her head a couple of times. "She's what I call a real, earnest Christian, and this would be a better town if there were more like her in it."

"Who are you talking about, Lorena?" asked Mr. Zerback.

"I'm talking about Daisy Burton, that's who."

"Oh, sure," he said, as if he ought to have known all along whom she was talking about.

"When Leo grows up, I hope he marries a girl one half as sweet and good as Daisy," said Mrs. Zerback.

"I'm not going to marry anybody," said Leo.

Mrs. Zerback began to laugh and slap her leg. "I'll bet you do, though," she said. "I'll bet you marry the first little snip that comes switching down Oak Street."

The next day was Sunday, and Mrs. McArthur took me in and introduced me to my new teacher. "This is Harry Piggott, the boy I was telling you about," she said.

"Welcome to our class, Harry!" said Miss Burton in a cheerful voice. Miss Daisy was a dried-up, little, gray-headed woman, about fifty years old. One of her legs was shorter than the other, and she had to use crutches to walk. Her eyes were light blue and they looked like they were going to water any minute. Her lips were always turned up at the corners in a gentle smile. As she stood there talking to me, she balanced herself on one crutch and kept patting my head and rubbing my cheeks and hugging me around the neck. Her voice was very soft and sweet. It sounded like pigeons under the eaves of a barn.

That Sunday the lesson was about God telling Abraham to take his son Isaac and sacrifice him as a burnt offering, but Miss Daisy stopped when she came to the place where Abraham raises the knife to slay his son, which is just before the Voice of God comes in. She said she didn't like such subjects, and she didn't think they should be taught in Sunday school. So instead of the regular lesson that day, she gave us a talk. It was almost like a sermon, except that she kept looking into our eyes, squeezing our hands and patting our cheeks as she talked. "Hate is *de*-structive," said Miss Daisy; "but love is *con*-structive." She told us how terrible it was to hurt dumb animals and how badly the mother bird felt when she came to the nest and found it robbed. "Oh, if we could only love things, instead of hating them, what a better world it would be!" she said. I made up my mind that I would never shoot at cats with my air rifle or rob another bird's nest as long as I lived. When Miss Daisy's talk was over, we all stood up and recited the class pledge: "I will love God and my fellow men with all my heart and with all my soul, and I will do no act that will bring pain to others." I thought to myself: "Miss Daisy certainly is the best woman in the world."

"Well, Harry," she said, when the lesson was over, "do you think you're going to like it with us?"

"Yes, ma'am," I said.

A boy named Albert Gran spoke up: "Harry got in the class just in time to go to the picnic."

"Oh, so he did!" said Miss Daisy; "we're having it a week from next Wednesday at James' Lake, and we extend you a very hearty invitation to attend, don't we, boys?" The boys in the class said yes, they did.

When Sunday school was over and we were waiting for church to begin, I asked a boy named Tommy Van Bergen about the picnic. He said Miss Daisy had one every July. She hired a wagon and a driver from Moore's Livery Stable and had the wagon filled with straw. Then the class drove out into the country somewhere and spent the day. Tommy had been the year before and he said everybody had had a fine time.

Tommy was the biggest boy in the class. He was almost thirteen. We sat down on the church steps and he told me a lot about Miss Daisy. She took in sewing for a living and was very poor. Mrs. Findley gave her a room free for helping with the housework, but Miss Daisy had to pay her own board. Mrs. Findley had a daughter named Sadie who was only twelve years old, but was already in the third class in High School. Everybody said she knew more than any teacher in town. I had never met Sadie Findley, but I had heard a lot about her. Leo Zerback's mother was always saying to him: "I'd be ashamed not to know the multiplication tables farther than the fours when little Sadie Findley is almost through geometry . . ."

"What makes Miss Daisy lame, Tommy?" I asked.

Tommy said he thought everybody in town knew that: When Miss Daisy was a young girl her sweetheart got her in trouble and then ran away with a beautiful bareback rider; so Miss Daisy had tried to hide her shame by throwing herself under the hoofs of a runaway horse. I wanted to ask Tommy what sort of trouble it was her sweetheart got her in, but I didn't say anything at all.

We always had fried chicken and charlotte russe for dinner on Sundays. It was hot in the dining room, but nobody seemed to care much. We had company to dinner: Cousin Katie and Cousin Ella Kendrick, who ran a truck farm near Morgantown, had driven over to spend the afternoon. They were big, sunburned women with rough hands, and they never talked about anything except tomato worms and how dear fertilizers were getting to be. Aunt Juliet made a great fuss over them, but I knew that she was really ashamed of them and that was the reason she invited them so often. Of course Mr. Charlie Hemmes was present too. He and Aunt Emmaline had been keeping company for five years, and he was like one of the family. He came every Sunday for dinner and spent the day.

Mr. Hemmes was tall and pale. He wore high starched collars and eyeglasses that hooked around one ear with a fine gold chain. I always had an idea that his head wasn't fastened on his neck at all, but was only balanced on top of his collar like an egg in an egg cup. That Sunday I got to thinking how funny it would be if his head should roll off his collar and break on the floor, and I started laughing.

"For Heaven's sake, what is Harry always giggling about?" asked Aunt Emmaline.

"Don't notice him," said Aunt Juliet. "If you notice him, you'll encourage him to act worse."

Uncle Carter reached under the table and patted my knee. He winked at me so that nobody else saw it. Everything was quiet for a little while and then Mr. Hemmes spoke to me: "Well, young man, I trust you liked your new Sunday school teacher."

"Yes, sir," I said. "Yes, sir, I did like her."

"Miss Burton is a most remarkable lady, I understand," said Mr. Hemmes.

Uncle Carter put down his knife and spoke to us all. "Dr. Atwood gave a talk to the Big Brothers' Council last week. His subject was 'Fortitude in Facing Life's Problems,' and he used Miss Daisy Burton as an example. Of course, he didn't mention her by name; he referred to her as a 'courageous little saint who lives on Cherokee Street,' but everybody knew who he was talking about. He said he had operated on her twelve times altogether, and he just didn't see how she kept going. She was in constant pain, day and night, he said; but people didn't realize that because she was always so sweet and cheerful. Every time he operated on her he was sure she would never come out of it alive, but she always did; and she came out smiling and without a word of complaint. He said he just didn't see how she stood the pain and that she should be an example to us all in meeting Life's adversities."

I had never heard Uncle Carter speak so much at one time. He had finished serving the plates and everybody began to eat.

"What complaint is Miss Burton afflicted with?" asked Mr. Hemmes. Mr. Hemmes taught English in High School.

I spoke up then: "Her sweetheart got her in trouble and then ran away with a circus rider, and Miss Daisy threw herself under the hoofs of a runaway horse to hide her shame."

Aunt Juliet put down her fork and looked at me with her mouth open, but Aunt Emmaline rolled her eyes at Mr. Hemmes and they both blushed and laughed a little.

"Harry Piggott!" said Aunt Juliet; "where did you hear such a thing?"

"One of the boys told me," I said.

"Who was it?" asked Aunt Juliet. It was Tommy Van Bergen, of course, but I pretended I couldn't remember. "Well, whoever it was, he ought to have his mouth washed out with soap," said Aunt Juliet. It was then that I found out what Tommy had told me was a lie, and that Miss Daisy really had tuberculosis of the hip. She had had it since she was a little girl.

When dinner was over, I told Aunt Juliet about the picnic and she said, "Well, I don't know whether a boy who talks like you do should go or not."

"Where are you going to have the picnic?" asked Cousin Ella. So I told them all about it. We had all eaten too much dinner and everybody was feeling drowsy. Cousin Katie kept talking about how a new kind of cutworm was killing her cabbages right and left, and Cousin Ella would say, whenever she stopped for a moment: "It just looks like it's one thing or another all the time!" Aunt Juliet was listening politely, but I knew she wanted to go back to her room and take off her corsets and put her wrapper on. "Tsch! Tsch!" she kept saying absently.

Aunt Emmaline and Mr. Hemmes had gone into the parlor and she was playing the piano while he sang. "Charlie Hemmes's got a real sweet tenor voice," said Cousin Katie sleepily. Aunt Juliet put her hand under her patent leather belt and loosened it a little. "He's a good, steady young man, too," she said.

"Mr. Hemmes ought to make a good match for Emmaline," said Cousin Ella. Aunt Juliet smiled and nodded her head. "We all think so," she said in a whisper.

"Aunt Juliet, can I go over and play with Leo?" I asked.

"Not on Sunday, Harry."

"Aunt Juliet—please!"

"Oh, let him go," said Cousin Katie, laughingly; "little boys don't like to stay indoors."

"Well, I don't know . . ." said Aunt Juliet. "I'm as broad-minded as the next one, but the Zerbacks are Catholics, and it don't seem right for Harry to be over there on a Sunday. If it was a weekday, I wouldn't say a word."

On the morning of the picnic Aunt Juliet woke me early, and at half past seven the wagon came by and I got in. Miss Daisy was sitting in the middle of the straw, with the boys grouped around her, and she seemed very gay. The lunch baskets were all piled up on the seat beside Zilk, the colored man who drove for the livery stable. Sitting next to Miss Daisy was a little girl with a long neck and teeth that stuck out. Miss Daisy said: "This is little Sadie Findley. She's going to help with the lunch and share our day." Sadie said: "Oh, how do you do?" in a drawling way and Ed Barron mocked her behind her back. Sadie turned to see what the boys were laughing at, but Ed's face was straight by then. Sadie Findley looked like she was always expecting somebody to ask her to bound Kentucky or to tell them the capital of Vermont.

I started to crawl in the back of the wagon, but Miss Daisy said for me to come sit by her. Everybody laughed at that, and so did Miss Daisy, and then she waved her hand and said in a gay voice: "Don't anybody listen—I've got a secret to tell Harry!" This is what she whispered in my ear: "I wanted you to sit by me because I like you better than the others!" A warm feeling that kept getting warmer came over me. "I like you, too, Miss Daisy!" I whispered back.

We had a fine time at the picnic. We went swimming in the morning, but Miss Daisy made Zilk sit on the bank and watch the whole time. Sadie sat under a tree, reading a book, and Miss Daisy hopped about on her crutches, fixing lunch. After lunch, Tommy Van Bergen jumped a half-grown rabbit, and all of us ran after him, but the rabbit went into a hollow log. Albert Gran said the best way to get him out was to make a fire inside the log, but Zilk said he knew a better way than that. He cut a forked stick from a willow tree and trimmed off the leaves and branches. Then he sharpened the forks until the points were like needles. He said the way to do it was to stick the sharp forks into the rabbit's hide and then twist it around and pull him out. Miss Daisy saw us dancing around the log and begging Zilk to let us be the one to pull out the rabbit, and she came hopping toward us on her crutches as fast as she could. "I'd be ashamed to torture a poor defenseless animal!" she said. "Oh, I'd be ashamed . . ." Then her crutch slipped and she fell down to the ground. Zilk helped her up again and Sadie handed her her crutches.

"You are a nasty lot of little boys," said Sadie, "and you ought to be—" But Miss Daisy reached out and put her finger on Sadie's lips, not letting her finish. "Don't say such things, Sadie!" she said gently. "Don't say such terrible things!"

We all helped Miss Daisy back to the spot where she had placed her pillows. A little later Zilk hitched up the team, and it was time to start home. Miss Daisy didn't say anything at all coming home. She had hurt her hip when she fell and her face was white. She lay stretched out on the straw, with her eyes closed, and she tried to smile. I kept wishing that she wouldn't try to smile that way. I sat close to her and she rested her head in my lap. The warm feeling kept coming over me and all at once I got very tight inside. I leaned over and pretended to tie my shoe, and when nobody was looking, I kissed Miss Daisy without her asking me to do it. Miss Daisy opened her eyes and smiled at me. Then she put her hand under the straw and held my hand and I knew that I loved her more than anybody in the world.

Mrs. Findley taught our class that next Sunday. She said Miss Daisy had been feverish ever since she got back from the picnic, but she hoped to be out again by next week. Dr. Atwood had been to see her several times, and he had decided another operation was necessary, but it could wait until the weather got cooler. So I told Aunt Juliet about Miss Daisy being sick and asked if I could go see her that afternoon and take her some flowers. Aunt Juliet said she thought that would be a nice thing to do. She also said I could take Miss Daisy a bottle of her best scuppernong wine. "Be sure and remember, now," she said; "a small glass before meals and a small glass upon retiring."

I knocked at Mrs. Findley's door and Sadie opened it. She took the flowers and put them in water. Mrs. Findley came in and thanked me for the wine; she was sure it would do Miss Daisy a world of good.

"Would you like to go up to Miss Daisy's room and see her?" she asked. Then, without waiting for me to say anything she spoke to Sadie: "Take Harry up to see Miss Daisy."

The room was bare except for a washstand and a bowl and pitcher painted with purple morning-glories, and some religious pictures on the wall. Miss Daisy was lying in bed when we came in. Her lids were closed and I thought she was asleep. She looked very weak and helpless. I wanted to put my arms around her, the way I used to put them around my mother when she was sick, and tell her not to worry, because she was sure to be well again before long. I felt a peculiar feeling in my throat, and I was afraid I was going to cry. I hadn't cried where anybody could see me for a long time. I walked over to the window and turned my back. "Please get well again, Miss Daisy," I whispered.

After awhile she turned on her back and opened her eyes. "This is Harry Piggott," said Sadie in a loud voice; "he brought you these pretty flowers." At first Miss Daisy didn't say anything, then she began to laugh and talk to herself. "She's out of her head again," said Sadie; "she doesn't even recognize us."

We drew our chairs close to the bed and listened to what Miss Daisy was saying. "They're going to operate on me again, and I can't stand it! I can't go through that pain again!" Her voice got so low we couldn't hear what she was saying, but tears kept running down her cheeks, and Sadie wiped them away with her handkerchief. Then she opened her eyes wide and looked about her, making a motion to show that she wanted to sit up. Sadie and I fixed the pillows behind her back and she seemed to realize for the first time that we were there.

She began to laugh sweetly. "Oh, you pathetic little fools," she said, "to sit there and feel sorry for me! You think you'll escape, don't you?" She turned her head away and closed her eyes. "Go away!" she said. "Go away! I hate the sight of you both!"

Then her voice became stronger and suddenly she began to curse and revile the Scriptures. She said she didn't believe in a future life, and the only thing that made her believe in God was the fact that He had tortured His own son on a cross. She talked that way for a long time. I felt my blood getting cold and my scalp began to prickle. If she had been screaming or making a loud noise, it wouldn't have been so bad, but she wasn't. She was talking in the low, sweet voice she used when she spoke to her class. Her lips were turned up in a gentle smile and if you were not listening carefully you would have thought she was reciting the class pledge instead of the words she was saying.

Sadie sat in a chair by the window and turned the leaves of a book. "Miss Daisy's delirious," she said.

Miss Daisy continued to talk. She said she hated everybody in town, but people were too stupid to know that. She wished a big fire would burn up the world or that a tornado would come and wipe out the whole human race. She said that only Nero could understand how she really felt because she, too, wished that the world had but one neck and that she could sever it with an ax.

"Nero didn't wish that," said Sadie in triumph. "That remark is generally attributed to the Emperor Caligula."

I got up from my chair and backed out of the room. I ran down the stairs and stood trying to open the latch on the door. Mrs. Findley came up and opened it for me. "Why, what's the matter, Harry?" she asked. "You're as white as a sheet." I didn't say anything at all. I just ran down the walk.

When I got to the old Porterfield place, I crawled behind the hedge and lay there for a long time. I kept thinking of the things Miss Daisy had said, but I thought most about her wishing the world had only one neck. I thought of the neck of the world as being the size of the molasses barrel in Mr. McArthur's store, and every time I closed my eyes, I could see Miss Daisy smiling sweetly and talking about love while she chopped at the neck with a bloody ax. Then I started to tremble. I tried to stop but I couldn't.

Old Mrs. Porterfield and her son Mr. Edward were coming across the lawn. I hoped they wouldn't see me, but they did, and they came over to where I was lying. "What's the matter, sonny?" asked Mr. Edward. "You got a chill?" I didn't say anything at all.

Old Mrs. Porterfield got down on her knees and lifted me up. "Now! Now!" she said. "You tell me all about it." She put her arms about me and tried to draw me to her, but before I knew what I was doing, I pulled away so hard that her glasses came off and she sat down in a flower-bed. Then I backed away from them, under the hedge.

"Nobody will ever fool me again!" I thought. "Nobody will fool me again as long as I live!"

1930

A SHOP IN ST. LOUIS, MISSOURI

OLD MRS. TATUM was often secretly amused at her daughter's lack of either imagination or humor, and she was, as often, pained at the contemplation of her barren, plodding life. "Mattie's the most curious girl ever you seen," she would confide to the widow Findley, across the intervening fence. "It's just work, work, work, with Mattie, all the time."

She had wanted Mattie to marry, like other girls, and have a family of her own, but Mattie had other and very definite plans for her future; or, rather, she had a single plan, a single idea, and everything she thought, said or did centered about it. The idea had come to her during her second year at the Beehive Store, after she had overheard a conversation between Mrs. Dunwoody and old Mrs. Wentworth, both of whom had traveled widely, and seen the world. Mrs. Dunwoody had said: "Mattie Tatum is too good to be working in a little town like Reedyville; she ought to have her own shop in New York or Chicago." And Mrs. Wentworth had answered: "I've never seen anybody with such an instinct for clothes. It sounds like an exaggeration, I know, but in my opinion there isn't a designer in Paris with half her natural ability."

And Mattie had knelt concealed, silent behind the counter, a smudge of dirt on her cheeks, her dull eyes suddenly bright. All that day she remembered the conversation she had overheard, and then she came to a decision. "I *will* have a shop of my own!" she said suddenly. "I'll save my money, and open a shop in St. Louis, Missouri!" (When she was a little girl her parents had taken her to St. Louis on a visit. It was the only large city she had ever seen.)

Mattie Tatum was a calm, unimaginative woman with an oily face and teeth that were never entirely covered by her lips.

It was strange that one who did so much to make others beautiful should take no interest in her own appearance, but she was satisfied to remain a frumpish old maid who looked even older than her thirty-one years. She lived with her mother in a cottage on Cherokee Street, and her life was a narrow one with few companions and few pleasures. Occasionally she went to a movie, or a church social, with Katie Prestwood, her assistant at the store, but mostly she spent her evenings working on extra sewing or reading the current fashion magazines. She would pore over these magazines for a long time, examining photographs of actresses and society women in the rotogravure sections of the Sunday newspapers, stopping, occasionally, to speak to her mother. "That model ought to look good on Clarine Palmiller," she would say critically; "that is, with the waist-line raised an inch, and the skirt not quite so full."

Old Mrs. Tatum would agree hastily, and then there would be silence again. She was awed by her daughter's prominence in the community, and she would never, under any conditions, have disputed her. Then, too, she had not been well for the past year and she found it difficult to concentrate on anything that did not concern her ailments.

After Mattie had made up her mind, she thought of nothing except her shop and how to make it possible. She had only to close her eyes to see the shop plainly, her name, "Madame Tatum —Gowns," in bold gold-leaf on the window. With her usual thoroughness, she went into the matter from every angle, and she decided that she could not venture from Reedyville until she had at least three thousand dollars at her disposal.

And so she began saving her money with a methodical ferocity which startled her easy-going mother. She begrudged herself everything except the barest necessities of life. She took extra sewing at night: pleated shirts and fine, hand-made underwear for Mr. Kenworthy, Mr. Edward and Mr. Joseph Porterfield, and other gentlemen of the town. She even discharged the family washerwoman and did the work herself, bending over her tubs until two or three o'clock in the morning. But in spite of her thrift, her ceaseless pinching, the accumulation of her capital had not been an easy task. Then, after five years of working and planning, she saw a possibility of fulfilling her wish, and as her shop drew closer to reality, she could think of nothing else. Behind her calm, bulging forehead, her brain raced with excitement. At night she would lie awake for hours planning her shop, settling this or that detail. "Just think," she would whisper, "only a few months more and I'll leave this place forever." She would hug herself with excitement, and her tongue would make a caressing noise against the roof of her mouth.

She was thinking of her shop one night in October as she walked quickly down Cherokee Street toward her home, and ran up the steps. The house was dark. The kitchen stove was cold, and there was no sign of supper. She lit a lamp and looked about her. Then, suddenly she discovered her mother lying sprawled on the back porch, her head resting on the doorsill, the armful of wood she had been carrying scattered about her. She was groaning feebly, apparently in great pain. Mattie lifted her mother and carried her into the house. She said: "I'm going to call Dr. Lawrence this time, no matter what you say."

"I don't need a doctor, baby. I'll be all right."

Mattie became provoked. "I'm not going to have you suffering like this any longer. There's not any sense in it." She went into the hall, where the telephone hung, and picked up the receiver. Mrs. Tatum, who could hear her through the open door, began to groan and twist her head about. When Mattie returned to her mother's bedroom, she had taken off her hat and her coat. "Dr. Lawrence wants you to come to his office tomorrow morning. He's going to make a full examination," she said.

"There ain't no sense in that, Mattie; it's just wasting time and money." But Mattie did not bother to answer. She was busy removing her mother's clothes and slipping a nightgown over her shoulders. Mrs. Tatum began to whimper. "Suppose he says there's something real bad the matter with me. Suppose he says that." She pressed her face against her daughter and began to cry softly. "If there's something real *bad* the matter, I don't want to know it!" Then she added: "Don't make me go see that doctor! Please don't make me go!"

"Now, Mamma," said Mattie patiently. "Now, Mamma."

Dr. Lawrence had been in Reedyville only a short time. His methods were modern and impersonal, and he brought with him a considerable amount of laboratory equipment. When the examination was over, he called Mattie on the telephone, and she came to take her mother home. "Is Mamma bad off?" she asked. Dr. Lawrence nodded his head. "Yes," he said. "Very bad indeed, Miss Tatum."

Mattie stood, removing her shabby gloves. "Oh, I see," she said. "I see what you mean." Then, after a long time, she spoke quietly: "But there must be something you can do. There must be something you can do to *help* Mamma." And Dr. Lawrence answered: "An operation might prolong her life for a few months, but even that's doubtful, now." He glanced appraisingly at Mattie's run-down shoes, her worn coat and her faded hat. Mattie noted his glance and understood the thought back of it. A suspicious, defensive expression came over her face. "How much would it cost to have an operation?" she asked in a frightened voice.

"It would be expensive, I'm afraid, in the long run," said Dr. Lawrence. "You'd have to take her to New Orleans or Mobile."

Mattie sat down quickly, and linked her fingers together. So this was the way it was going to be. "Oh, I might have known something like this would happen," she thought bitterly. "I might have known." The muscles in her cheeks began to twitch, and her lips drew back suddenly from her long teeth.

"Would three thousand dollars be enough?" she asked.

"Yes," said Dr. Lawrence; "yes, I think so."

That night Mattie could not sleep. As she lay in bed, she tried to think of her mother's suffering and that she was soon to die, but that seemed relatively unimportant compared with the fact that her plans were now hopelessly disarranged. She would never be able to leave Reedyville! She would never have a shop in St. Louis! She adjusted her pillow, and lay there staring into the dark. Then a feeling of resentment came over her. "It's not right for me to go on sacrificing myself all the time," she thought. "I worked harder than a nigger for that money, and now I'm right back where I started from!" She lay awake for a long time, turning her problems over and over in her mind, but at last she got up and went to her mother.

"Mamma . . ." she began.

"What is it, baby?"

"I want you to have an operation."

An unaccustomed feeling of tenderness came over her. She put her arms around her mother and kissed her time and time again. Mrs. Tatum, unused to any show of affection, looked up at her daughter, flattered and somewhat embarrassed, and smoothed her limp, finely spun hair. "We haven't got money for operations, Mattie."

"We have, too; we got that money I saved."

"No, daughter," said Mrs. Tatum. "You got your heart set on a shop in St. Louis, Missouri, and I want you to go on with your plans."

Mattie bent down and kissed her mother. "It's sweet of you to be always thinking about me, but that money is yours, if you want it."

Mrs. Tatum sighed. "Just do whatever you think is right, Mattie," she said.

"No! No!" said Mattie in a frightened voice. "*You* say, Mamma! *You* say what to do!"

But Mrs. Tatum lay back on her pillow, her hands patient and waiting, her face tired with her monotonous years. She said: "I don't care. It don't make no difference to me one way or the other."

Mattie went back and lay on her bed. Toward daylight she fell into a troubled sleep in which she dreamed that she ran down a field, flying with outstretched arms over hedges and rivers and ravines. But when she reached the railroad station, her trunk came open and all her belongings spilled onto the floor. Everybody laughed at her shoddy equipment and pointed their fingers, and afterwards she could never make her things fit back into the trunk, try as she would. Mattie felt nervous and apprehensive because the train was approaching and she was not ready. The wheels of the train made a strange, rushing sound that steadily got louder. "Mattie Tatum! Mattie Tatum!" they said. "Oh, help me! Help me!" said Mattie to the people. "The train's coming and I'll be left." But nobody would help her. They stood there laughing and making remarks behind their hands until a waiter in a white jacket came out of the station ringing a bell.

Mattie got up and looked at her watch. It was six o'clock and somebody was ringing the doorbell. She tiptoed to the door and opened it. Miss Amelia Upchurch, one of their neighbors, stood before her. "I heard your ma was sick," she said. "I thought I'd better come over and help out. I said to myself right away, 'Poor Mattie can't work all day and take care of her ma too!'"

She was a wrinkled, heavy-lidded old woman who was never known to visit the well or the happy. Tragedy arrived and there at her elbow was Miss Amelia, a sour, snuffling old creature with a talent for sorrow. She stepped over the doorsill and walked into the room on her stiff, half-flexed legs. She took off her hat with its stuffed, moulting old bird, and hung her coat carefully on the hall tree. "You go get dressed before you take cold, Mattie. I know what to do for the old lady."

Mattie went back to her room. She unbraided her long hair and brushed it slowly. For a moment she had forgotten her problem but it came back to her intensified. Twice she stopped and the brush hung limply by her side. She thought: "This is a hard, mean world, and if you want to get anywhere you've got to be hard, too. Why should I give that money to Mamma for an operation?"

Outside she heard Miss Amelia rattling the lid of the stove as she went about preparing breakfast. Her mother was now awake. She coughed and called to Mattie in a frightened, querulous voice. "Look at Mr. Palmiller and Mr. Hardaway. Look at the two Howard boys, or anybody else who ever amounted to anything. They wouldn't hesitate a minute!"

At that instant Mattie put down her brush. The line of her jaw set defensively and a harsh light came into her eyes. "Well,

I'm going to be as hard as the next one!" she said. "I'm going to St. Louis, Missouri, just like I planned to do."

Mrs. Tatum's death came earlier than the doctor had expected. It happened on a cold, rainy afternoon, six weeks exactly from the day Dr. Lawrence had made his examination. Everybody commented on how well Mattie was taking her mother's death. She went about the house putting things in order, neither helping nor hindering Miss Amelia in her plans for the funeral. Her calmness continued while she was being driven to Magnolia Cemetery, and through the sermon which Brother Saul Butler offered at the grave-side. She stood there quietly, aware only of the acid smell of new cloth that clung to her hastily sewn mourning dress and the black veil that draped her shoulders. Her mother's death and burial seemed an impersonal thing which concerned her not at all. But when the last prayer had been said, and the quartette commenced their song in slow, reverent voices, a strange change came over Mattie. "Why that's Mamma's favorite hymn!" she thought. Suddenly she seemed unable to breathe. She lifted her veil and fixed it over the brim of her hat. Her face was white, and she noticed that her hands were trembling. She began to move her feet about nervously. She clutched her fists together. "I won't give in!" she said. "I won't think about Mamma. I'll think about something else! I'm going to be just as hard as the next one!" She wished that the quartette would stop singing, but they went on and on. She lowered her veil again and clutched her hands together. "I *won't!*" she said between her teeth. "I won't give in!"

But something inside her, over which she had no control, seemed to lift her and push her forward. She fell to her knees in the wet clay and swayed her head from side to side. "Mamma! Mamma!" she cried in terror. "Mamma! Don't hold it against me!"

A group of neighbors came over and lifted her up and Mrs. Willis Overton held her protectingly. But Mattie pulled away from them, flinging her arms about. "Don't touch me!" she said in a shrill voice; "I'm not fit for decent people to touch." Without warning, she rushed forward and would have thrown herself into the open grave with her mother. She said over and over: "Take it, Mamma! Take it! I don't want it! Honestly, I don't want a penny of it!"

Later she had a recollection of being driven home seated between the Reverend Butler and Mrs. Overton; of Dr. Lawrence bending over her bed, giving her medicine to quiet her, and of the excited hum of neighbors in the room adjoining. Then she slept.

She awoke in the night. Her heart was pounding against her breast and there was a feeling of suffocation in her throat. She sat up in bed and lit the lamp beside her. She got up, unaware of the cold, and walked to her dressing-table, examining herself in the mirror; but the sight of her long, sallow face terrified her. "You're the meanest woman in the world," she said. "You really are." Then she covered her face with her hands and cried.

She lay on her bed again, her face pressed deep into a pillow. When she thought of her mother lying out in the cold rain, a sense of pain which was almost unbearable, came over her, and she thought that she, herself, was going to die. She remembered the hard life her mother had led, and how nobody had really appreciated her. And now that life was over, and she would be forgotten. "Oh! Oh!" said Mattie. "Oh! Oh! Oh!" Her mind was in a turmoil. She was unable to think coherently, but she was sure of two things: She would never leave Reedyville as long as she lived, and she would not use for herself one penny of the money she had saved. The idea of a shop in St. Louis seemed unbelievable to her now.

At first she thought that she would take her money from the bank and burn it. (She felt that only after the money was destroyed could she free herself from guilt.) But as she lay on her bed thinking of Magnolia Cemetery and its poor, undignified graves decorated with shells and bits of colored glass, another idea came to her: She would erect a monument to her mother's memory with the money. She sat up in bed quickly, surprised that the idea had not come to her before. She looked at her watch and saw that it was a little past five o'clock. She would go to Mobile on the 6:22 and select the monument herself. She began to dress rapidly, putting on her mourning robe and pinning the black veil to her hat.

The monument arrived at last and was set up in the cemetery. It was made of white marble, and on it were carved two angels with expressionless faces. One of the angels stood upright and held a lily in her hand, as if undecided where to put it down, while the other figure, the bottoms of her feet upturned, knelt in an attitude of prayer. The monument dominated with its magnificence one entire corner of the cemetery, and made more trivial the graves that surrounded it. When it was new and bright, the people of Reedyville often came, merely to admire its perfection, but before the year was out it had become blackened by smoke from the Porterfield Foundry and Pattern Com pany, and fouled by the droppings of sparrows. Every Sunday and every holiday Mattie Tatum comes to sit by the monument. She is a middle-aged woman now. Her hair is thinning and has become gray, and her cheeks have pulled away from the bones of her face and droop downward in long triangles of puckered flesh. When she thinks how happy she used to be, sitting quietly in the lamplight with her mother, a feeling of despair which is almost unbearable comes over her. Her lips draw back in pain, the muscles in her throat twitch and tighten and her hands flutter upward and rest against her cheeks. Then she lowers her veil and wills not to remember, and after a time her face is expressionless again and her hands quiet.

She sits by the grave a long time. Occasionally she destroys a weed which has found foothold on the mound, and occasionally she gets up without reason and bends above her mother, picking up in her trembling hands the dead leaves which drift in eternally from the oaks of Wentworth Grove. "Don't hold it against me, Mamma! Don't hold it against me!" she whispers over and over, her stringy old neck bending low above her mother, her hands pressed tightly against her dry and shriveled breasts.

1931

GEORGE AND CHARLIE

GEORGE OWENS was a quiet, methodical young man who always hung his towels up to dry before throwing them into the laundry hamper and who paid his bill regularly each Saturday night. In a word, he was an ideal lodger, and Mrs. Maddern often wished there were more like him in the world. George was twenty-two years old in those days. He was red-faced and plump, with short arms and legs and mild brown eyes, and he worked for the Acme Building Supplies Corporation, a concern that manufactured roofing tiles and other building material.

One day Mrs. Maddern told him that her nephew was coming to town to work in the traffic department of the Excelsior Cotton Mills and had written asking to stay with her. But, unfortunately, every room in the house was filled just at that time, and, since George had such a big room, she wondered if he would share it with her nephew until something else turned up. George preferred being alone. He was taking a course in Business Administration that winter by mail and he disliked having the routine of his life disturbed, but he didn't know what to say to Mrs. Maddern without hurting her feelings. "If you don't like the arrangement after you meet Charlie, just say so," she kept repeating; "because if it's not entirely satisfactory to you, I don't want you to share your room for a minute." George nodded his head. "All right, Mrs. Maddern— Just do what you want to." Mrs. Maddern said, "That's right nice of you, George, and I appreciate it. I appreciate it in more ways than one, because I think a sound young man like you will have a good influence on Charlie. He's a sweet boy, at heart, but he hasn't acted right in the past, and he's caused his mother many a tear and heartache."

Charlie, it seemed, had revolutionary ideas which were always getting him in trouble. "He had a fine job in Memphis," said

Mrs. Maddern; "as fine a job as any boy only twenty years old could ask for, but he got into an argument, and lost it. It was something about a colored man drinking water out of the same glass that white people used. I don't know the straight of it, but Charlie defended the colored man's action and said a lot of things he shouldn't have said and the result was he lost his position."

"Well," said George, "I should think he *would* lose his job under those conditions."

That night Charlie Banks arrived and Mrs. Maddern introduced the boys. Charlie was somewhat above middle height. He wore his hair brushed straight back and plastered to his skull; he had a large, high-bridged nose with a cleft in the tip of it; his chest was slightly sunken and his shoulders hunched forward; his hips were so flat and undeveloped that one wondered how his trousers remained in place. At first the boys were very polite, each anxious not to obtrude on the privacy of the other, but after dinner, when they felt they knew each other better, they began to exchange their views of life. It was two o'clock before they finally went to bed.

In the office the next morning, George discussed his new roommate with Isabel Leary, one of the stenographers. Isabel admired George a great deal and listened attentively to everything he said. "This fellow I'm telling you about is a socialist, or something," said George. "He thinks nobody should own property except the State. He says the desire to own property is the basis of injustice."

"Why, I never heard anything so silly," said Isabel.

"That's what I told him, too," said George. "I said: 'Ideas like that aren't sound; they won't work out, in practice.'"

"Why don't you tell Mrs. Maddern, frankly, you don't like the arrangement and ask her to move him?"

George waited a moment before replying, turning the matter over in his mind. "Oh, I don't know," he said slowly. "I like talking to him, in a way. I like to hear what other people think."

All that day George remembered the new ideas that Charlie had put in his head and thought of arguments to prove their unsoundness. Toward closing time, he found himself looking forward to talking with Charlie again, and after supper that night they took up their conversation where they had left off the night before.

"You never saw such a lot of dumb-bells as there are at the Excelsior," said Charlie. "All they think about is going to the movies, and all they read is the Official Railway Guide and the Consolidated Freight Classification Tariff. Mr. Whitfield, he's the boss, has a picture of his wife and three kids on his desk. They look like they'd just stuffed themselves with roast beef and mashed potatoes and were ready to go to sleep for the winter. That'll give you some idea of *him*, I guess!"

"Why, what's wrong with having a picture of your family on your desk?" asked George in surprise.

Charlie shook his head: "If you don't see for yourself, there's no sense in me trying to tell you."

George kept turning the matter over in his slow mind. "I'm damned if I see anything wrong with that; I think it's a very nice thing to do."

"All right!" said Charlie. "All right! Have it your own way!"

The arguments continued nightly. George thought them very stimulating and looked forward more and more to his evenings with Charlie. As the weeks went by the boys fell into the habit of taking long walks at night before going to bed. Often these walks took them along the river front and through the poorer sections of the town. At such times Charlie would stare with distaste at the unpainted shacks huddling together beside the railroad tracks and a strange look would come into his eyes. "A few years from now and this sort of thing will be impossible," he would say. "All this filth and disease and unhappiness will be wiped out."

"I know, I know," said George patiently. "But what can you do about it? How can you improve it?"

"The State," began Charlie in an excited voice; "some day the State—"

"Now, Charlie," said George, "don't start about the State again. Don't start that all over." He began to laugh good-naturedly, trying to elbow Charlie off into the gutter. But Charlie grabbed his arms and the two boys struggled, laughingly, on the brink of the shallow ditch. "It stands to reason everybody can't be wrong about things except you," said George.

"All right! All right!" said Charlie. "Have it your own way."

The winter passed rapidly. Then one day Charlie lost his job. Some of the things he had said got back to Mr. Whitfield, and Mr. Whitfield had him up on the carpet. Charlie was contemptuous and defiant. "Sure I said it!" he answered. "I said there ought to be a law against you working children in the mills. Sure I said it! And I'll say it again!" Then he launched into a long speech in which capitalism, injustice and his government of the future were inextricably mixed. Mr. Whitfield sat in amazement, staring at him, his lips opening and shutting without making any sound. His face was white with anger and it was only by remembering what Christ would do, if confronted by a similar situation, that he prevented himself from striking Charlie across his insolent, immature face. Finally Mr. Whitfield's lips were able to form words. Then suddenly he lost control of himself and began to shout: "Get out of my office you—you Goddamned little anarchist! Get out! We don't want people like you in our organization!"

Charlie repeated the whole conversation to George that night, and George shook his head helplessly. "You just can't get away with that sort of thing. You can't go around saying what you really think. People won't stand for it. You ought to know that, by this time, Charlie."

A passionate look came into Charlie's eyes. "I'll say what I think just as long as there is injustice in the world!" he said. He walked to the window and began lowering and raising the shade. Then he spoke quietly in a voice from which all arrogance had gone: "I can't bear the sight of people living in unhappiness and ignorance. I don't ask anything for myself, George; I haven't got an ax to grind. I don't even care what happens to me afterwards. Of course, what I think and what I say may not make any difference, one way or the other, but, by God! I'm going to keep thinking and talking and nobody can stop me!" Then Charlie turned abruptly and began packing his trunk. At that moment a peculiar feeling came over George. He had begun, suddenly, to see Charlie from a new angle. There was a curious tightness in his breast and throat. He wanted to say something that would make Charlie realize his changed viewpoint. He walked over and took him by the arms. "Charlie—" he began. But Charlie stopped him. "All right, you damned old capitalist!" he said laughingly. "Go ahead! Tell me I'm a fool. I don't care. Have it your own way!"

Suddenly he shoved George on the bed and began beating him with a pillow. The boys shouted with laughter. They rolled across the bed and on to the floor and began pummeling each other.

The door opened and Mrs. Maddern entered. "This is no time to be skylarking, Charlie," she said sadly. "Haven't you any sense of responsibility at all? I'm sure I don't know what your poor mother is going to say when I tell her you're in trouble again." The boys arose and began straightening their clothes, self-conscious and somewhat ashamed at their outburst of animal spirits.

"Well, crying won't do any good," said Charlie. Mrs. Maddern shook her head and sighed, the jet ornaments on her bosom heaving up and down to the rhythm of her emotion. "What are you going to do now?" she asked.

"I don't know, exactly," said Charlie; "but I'm going some place where people have a little intelligence, you can be sure of that!"

"Poor Charlie!" said Mrs. Maddern. Then she began to laugh, in spite of herself, at his absurdity.

After Charlie had gone, George found time hanging heavily on his hands. He took up his course in Business Administration again, but he could not interest himself in it. He felt ill at ease and dissatisfied. He found himself thinking about Charlie almost constantly and wondering what Charlie would do or say under certain conditions. In reading editorials or listening to political speeches, he would often think: "That's very well put, and it sounds all right, if you don't know, but I'll bet Charlie Banks could shoot his argument full of holes in about two minutes." He recalled some of the books from which Charlie used to quote and one day he took out a library card and commenced going there regularly, bringing home armfuls of books on abstruse subjects which he read patiently two or three times, and which he did not entirely understand.

One day he asked Isabel Leary for a date. There was an excursion down the bay that night and Isabel suggested that they go. The moon was bright and the boat slipped through the water, leaving in its path long angles of yellow foam. Suddenly George had a sense of desolation that almost overwhelmed him. He put his arm around Isabel's waist and drew her to him, and Isabel shivered and lay eagerly in his arms. Later he tried to talk about Charlie and his ideal city, but Isabel heard little that he said. She lay quietly and planned her wedding.

After his marriage the months slipped by placidly for George, one so precisely like the next that he scarcely realized how quickly they were going. He had made it a point to call on Mrs. Maddern every Sunday afternoon, and she received him in her tiny, over-furnished parlor. Mrs. Maddern had never accepted the modern style in dress. For Sundays she still wore a black silk costume that smelled of camphor, with a high collar, reinforced by whale-bone, and a skirt that touched the floor. She would sit in her rocking-chair and stretch her shapeless legs to the fire and at such times George could see the pucker across her ankles that indicated the terminus of her woolen drawers. During the afternoon Mrs. Maddern would serve fruit-cake and elder blossom wine. She would tell George about her latest symptoms and the difficulties of running a boarding house for unappreciative people and George, in turn, talked about Isabel, who was expecting her second baby shortly. But they both knew that Charlie Banks was the bond that held them together and in the end their conversation invariably turned to him.

"I don't know where he gets his crazy ideas, I'm sure," she would say, "but even as a little boy he was like that. I remember one summer when he was about ten years old. There was scarlet fever in Reedyville that year and my sister sent him down to visit me until it died down. Mr. Maddern was alive in those days. He took a liking to the boy and was always giving him money to spend. Charlie wanted a catcher's mask and glove and he was saving to buy them. Well, after a time he had enough money saved up and Mr. Maddern and I took him down town to buy it, but as we passed the square, he saw an old blind man who was playing a mouth-organ and, before we could stop him, Charlie took his money and put it in the beggar's cup. Mr. Maddern was really provoked with him that time, I remember."

George leaned forward eagerly. "That sounds just like Charlie," he exclaimed. Then, after a moment, he added somewhat self-consciously, "You know, Mrs. Maddern, we didn't really appreciate Charlie when he was here, but I've been reading and thinking a lot since he left and the more I do, the more I keep wondering why we are here on earth. Where are we going? What are we working and struggling for, anyway?"

"It's not for us to think about those things, George."

George continued: "You and I don't matter. We live our lives and die and it doesn't make much difference one way or the other. But people like Charlie are different; they shove the world along and make it a better place to live in."

"Well, I don't know," said Mrs. Maddern doubtfully. "All I ask of Charlie is that he act like everybody else. I hate to say it, but it has always seemed a little common, to me, for a person to be always talking about poor people and injustice." She sighed deeply, the jet ornaments on her bosom moving upward and reflecting the firelight. George looked at her quickly. Then he realized, in a flash, that Mrs. Maddern, of late, had begun to irritate him. "She doesn't understand Charlie at all," he thought. "She hasn't got the slightest idea of what Charlie is struggling for."

The next Sunday afternoon he did not go to see her, and finally his visits ceased altogether. Mrs. Maddern was hurt at his neglect. She said she wanted to apologize if she had done anything to offend him, but George said it wasn't that at all; he was going to the library on Sunday afternoons now, and that took up most of his time. Isabel found these studious habits exasperating, but, on the whole, she was satisfied with the choice she had made. George was a good husband and a good father and he provided for her and their children adequately. He had been promoted three times since their marriage and he was now head of the auditing department, a substantial position, Isabel felt, for a man only thirty-five years old.

Then one morning Charlie Banks returned. George was overjoyed at seeing his friend again, but his first impression was that Charlie looked sick and down and out. There was a long scar on his cheek, another across his forehead, and the bridge of his nose had been flattened. He had a whipped, hangdog expression, and he could not look anyone in the eye. They sat in silence for a few minutes, thinking of the past.

Finally Charlie spoke: "I guess I might as well tell you, and get it over with. Then if you don't want to know me any longer, just say so." He lowered his eyes, as if ashamed of the confession he was to make.

"I won't feel that way, no matter what you tell me," said George.

Charlie spoke rapidly. "Don't be too sure about that. Wait till I tell you; I've been in the penitentiary for the past ten years."

George reached out and touched his arm. "That doesn't make any difference to me, and you know it."

Charlie turned his head away, overcome by emotion. "I was innocent! I swear to Christ I was innocent!" His voice was low, but it was trembling. George came over to him and caught him by the shoulders. "There now, Charlie," he said. "There now, kid!"

But Charlie did not even hear him. His hands were locked together and he moved about in his chair. "They wouldn't let me sleep. They kept shoving me around and calling me filthy names. But I hadn't thrown that bomb, and I wouldn't say I had. They twisted my arms and beat me with nightsticks. Then a big cop knocked me down and commenced kicking me in the ribs and in the face. I couldn't stand it any longer. They made me say I did it, do you understand? They made me, Charlie Banks, say it!" Charlie began to tremble violently. He put his head down upon the desk and cried silently, his thin shoulders jerking back and forth. "Don't think about it any more," said George. "Don't think about it, Charlie. It's all past and done now."

"I want to start all over," said Charlie. "I've learned my lesson, and all I want now is another chance. I guess I got what was coming to me. I'll mow lawns. I'll carry out slops. I'll do anything." His voice had become humble and his manner cringing.

"Don't talk like that!" said George sharply.

Charlie began to laugh. When he laughed the scar on his face reddened and gave him an unpleasant expression. "What's wrong with that sort of talk?" he asked.

That night George told Isabel about Charlie's return. He thought it would be nice to have him over to Sunday dinner. Isabel did not like Charlie Banks; she felt that he had imposed on George and that he had been a bad influence in his life, but she consented, finally. She felt it was not fair to deprive her husband of Charlie's friendship, if it meant so much to him.

Charlie arrived promptly at noon. He was very pleasant and self-effacing, and he made a particular effort to be agreeable to Isabel, complimenting her on her cooking and admiring her home. Isabel was delighted with him. She talked on and on about the small gossip of the neighborhood and the radio programs she was interested in. She talked of the children, repeating all the bright things they had said, and Charlie listened eagerly to the details of her placid, uneventful life.

It was late afternoon when he rose to leave. George rose also. He said he would go with him as far as the drug store and buy a cigar. After the men had walked in silence for a few minutes, George said timidly, "You don't know how I missed you when you were gone. I didn't have anybody to talk to."

"Is that right?" said Charlie in a matter-of-fact voice.

George laughed in a self-deprecatory way. "I often think what a fool I must have seemed in the old days. I don't see how you put up with me, Charlie! But I've been reading and studying since I saw you. I think we have more in common now."

Charlie did not answer, but an expression of fear came over his face as George continued earnestly: "Do you remember you once said life didn't have any meaning for a man with courage enough to look at the facts? And I laughed and made fun of you for saying it?—Well, I understand, now, what you meant. It hasn't any significance at all." He paused a moment, a puzzled expression on his round, stupid face. "What's it all about, Charlie? Where are we going? What do we get out of it?"

Charlie shrugged his shoulders, as if annoyed at George's simplicity. Then he began to laugh harshly, the scar on his face turning red. "You've got no kick coming. You've got a good job and a good home, haven't you? What else do you expect?"

George looked at him in surprise. "You've changed, Charlie," he said mildly. "You're not at all like you used to be." They had reached the drug store and Charlie stood still on the sidewalk. It was January and dusk came early. Behind them the sun was low in the sky, and, as they stood there, the lights in the drug store were turned on.

"Sure I've changed," said Charlie; "I've got wise to myself." The lights from the store cut a dim triangle through the late afternoon and fell across the faces of the men. There was a purple shadow where the bridge of Charlie's nose had once been. "Do you think I was sent to jail because anybody believed I was really guilty?" continued Charlie. "If you do, get that idea out of your head. I was on the wrong side of the fence, that's all! Well, from now on I'm playing ball with the winning team, and I don't care which team it is."

George said: "Charlie! Charlie! Don't talk like that!" Charlie was surprised at the emotion in his voice. "Say, what's the matter with you, anyway?" he asked. Then he began to laugh. "You've changed some yourself. I always thought of you as being on the right side, along with the people that sent me up."

George closed his eyes, but he did not answer.

"While I was in jail," Charlie continued, "I kept thinking about you. I said to myself a thousand times: 'George Owens has the right idea. He tried to tell me what a fool I was and where I was headed, but I wouldn't listen to him. Oh, no! I thought I knew it all!'"

"Don't throw that up to me now," said George quietly, "I don't think that way any more." Then he added: "There's so much sadness and injustice in the world. There are so many things that ought to be remedied."

"All right," said Charlie, "you remedy them. You try it awhile."

George spoke earnestly: "I can't stand up to people, and you know it. I don't think quickly, the way you do, and when I try to express my views, I get confused and begin to stammer. You're the man to do it, Charlie. You can't go back on me now."

Suddenly Charlie's fists clenched, his lips drew back from his teeth and a look of mingled hatred and cunning came into his eyes. "I'm playing ball with the winning team!" he repeated stubbornly. At that moment George knew that he no longer had anything in common with Charlie Banks. He turned without a word and walked away.

But Charlie was coming behind him, running sidewise and catching at the sleeve of his coat. His face was frightened now, and his manner cringing. "Don't get sore at me, George," he pleaded. "You're the only friend I've got in the world. Don't get sore at me." George stood still again and leaned against a telephone pole. Charlie caught the lapels of his coat with both hands and stared down at the pavement. "You won't tell anybody I was in jail, will you, George? You wouldn't do a dirty thing like that, would you?"

"I won't tell anybody," said George.

"I don't want the cops here to know I got a record," said Charlie. "You don't know what they can do to you. You don't understand."

"I won't tell anybody."

Charlie began to tremble. "I don't ask much," he said. "All I want is a job and a chance to start all over again. That's not being unreasonable, is it? That's not asking much."

"No," said George. "That's not asking much."

Quietly he removed Charlie's hands, turned and walked toward his home. When he arrived, Isabel was giving the children their supper. She called brightly from the kitchen, "I'll have to apologize for what I said about your friend, Mr. Banks. I've never seen such an improvement in anybody in my life." George looked at her in amazement, but he realized she was quite serious. "How stupid Isabel is," he thought; "how stupid everything is!" Then he walked onto the porch and sat on the steps. He had forgotten his cigar, after all, but he got out his pipe and began filling it slowly.

The sun had set and there was a fine, purple haze in the air. Far away he heard the whistle of a steamer coming up the channel and the steady mooing of the tugs that accompanied her. He lit his pipe carefully, shielding the flame with his palm. A breeze was blowing up from the Gulf, bringing with it a smell of salt air, tar and ripening bananas. He remembered a twilight, years ago, when he and Charlie, tired from one of their walks, had sat on a bale of cotton and watched the yellow river flow into the bay. The scene came back to him vividly. Someone had been burning marsh grass, that time, and the glare was reflected in the sky and in the shallow bayous to the east. He remembered, too, the sound of a concertina, muted and indistinct, from a Spanish bark anchored in the stream, and how clumps of dead hyacinths, their purple blossoms soaked with oil, kept floating past. Then Charlie had begun talking of his city of the future where everyone lived together in understanding and love and where hunger, hatred and unhappiness were not known. Again he saw the look of rapt eagerness in Charlie's eyes, and the way he kept moving his hands back and forth, as if he were writing words on the air. Then he, George, had risen and come over to him. "What you say sounds all right, Charlie," he had said, "but it's not practical. Everybody can't be wrong but you."

Inside Isabel was putting the children to bed, humming a tune. Presently she came to the door. "Put on your overcoat, George," she said; "you'll take cold in the night air." George nodded his head.

"All right," he said; "all right."

He knocked out his pipe and sat staring at his hands. "Maybe if I'd encouraged Charlie, and not laughed at him. Maybe if I'd done that . . ." Then a strange, excited feeling came over him and he stood upright, trembling. There was something profound that he wanted to say, and for a moment he felt that he

was about to put in one sentence all the beauty and all the brutality of the world, but in the end words eluded him, and he leaned
against a post, tired and deflated.

Isabel was speaking to him again from the living room.
"George! Put on your coat if you're going to sit out there.
You'll take cold."

But he did not answer his wife this time. He walked to the
door and stood there irresolute, his hand fumbling for the knob,
a puzzled expression on his round, child-like face. "I wish I'd
never met Charlie Banks!" he said. He turned, entered his comfortable house, and closed the door behind him. "Charlie!
Charlie!" he whispered to himself. "Charlie, what made you
change so?"

1931

WOOLEN DRAWERS

*M*RS. JOE COTTON, Grand Mobilizer of the Christian Gladiators and Secretary of the Reedyville Society for the Fostering of Temperance and the Eradication of Vice, was the terror of small bootleggers and poolroom keepers, and she had tracked down and prosecuted more than one frightened prostitute who had drifted into town. She was a large, solidly built woman, with fine, black eyes and wide shoulders, and when she walked around Court House Square with her swinging stride, glancing keenly from side to side, she was a handsome woman in spite of her forty-five years.

Before her marriage she was known as Alice Ochs and she had worked at the cigar counter of a commercial hotel in Atlanta. Naturally, she had a great many friends both among traveling salesmen who came regularly to the hotel and strangers in town for a few days. These men were generally bored and lonely and many of them would come over to Alice's counter and talk to her, drawn by her black hair, pink cheeks and sparkling, jet-like eyes. (It was because of her rustic prettiness and her ability to attract men that she had been selected for the position she now held, a fact which Alice knew quite well.)

Alice was proud of her good looks and proud, too, of the fact that she was always dressed in the latest style. She had a contempt for dowdy women and she often told her roommate, a woman named Trix McAllister, that she didn't blame men for being untrue to their wives when she considered what most wives looked like after a few years.

It is doubtful, however, if Alice could have made such an excellent appearance on the salary the hotel paid her, but fortunately her men friends were always giving her presents of clothing, jewelry or even money after an evening spent in her company. After her brief and indiscriminate affairs, there was no sense of shame to harass her, nor was there any feeling of guilt in her mind; on the contrary, the fact that she had created powerful emotions in others and had, herself, remained entirely unaffected gave her a consciousness of superiority to her lovers. As the man lay in her arms, exhausted for the time being, Alice would kiss his lips and his eyelids in a gentle, contemptuous manner, and a feeling of power would come over her.

For awhile Alice's life moved calmly, and then one day in January, 1907, there occurred a series of trivial events which affected her entire existence. The weather, which had been mild and spring-like, changed suddenly, and Alice contracted a chest cold. The night before Trix McAllister had rubbed her with a mixture of turpentine and mutton-suet, and Alice felt considerably better the next morning. The girls arose somewhat later than usual and Alice began to dress hurriedly.

Trix watched her in surprise. "Alice Ochs!" she said. "You don't mean to tell me that you're not going to wear any more clothes than that! Why, with your cold, you'll have pneumonia before night!" Alice continued to dress. "Don't worry about me, Trix. I'll be perfectly warm. Don't worry about me at all." (Alice was fond of Trix, a woman a good deal older than herself who was always trying to mother her.)

But Trix laughed in a half-provoked way and shook her head. She went into the next room and began rummaging in her trunk. In a few minutes she returned carrying across her arm a suit of shapeless, fleece-lined underwear which had belonged to her husband during his lifetime. "You put this on, and don't be so stubborn," she said. "Nobody's going to see it. Nobody's going to know one way or the other."

Alice protested vehemently. She took a great deal of pride in her personal appearance and she was particularly proud of her beautiful, handmade underwear. She had found that men always admired elaborate underwear—her embroidered corset-covers and heavily starched petticoats—scented with violet sachet powder and decorated with cherry-colored ribbons.

Alice glanced at the grayish, rust-stained union-suit which lay

across Trix's arm and contrasted it with the pair of cambric
drawers she had laid out to wear that day, with their yards of
cream-colored lace and insertion, through which she was running
pink and blue ribbon; and the sight of the woolen underwear,
its clumsy buttons, its shapeless square seat and baggy knees,
made her shudder with distaste.

"No, Trix," she said firmly. "I'll be perfectly all right as I am.
Don't you worry about me."

But Trix was insistent and Alice after much protesting put on
the woolen drawers. Afterwards, she went to work as usual. She
chatted with her customers and rolled poker-dice with them for
cigars or coupons. Among Alice's friends was a man named
Joseph L. Cotton who traveled for a textile house and who,
when calling upon a new account, opened the conversation by
saying: "My name's Cotton and I sell cotton *piece* goods!" Then
he would laugh in a friendly way and show his fine teeth. Joe
had blonde hair which was very curly. He liked to think that
he knew a great deal about life, but in reality he was very simple.

He was in Atlanta that day, and, as usual, he came up to
Alice's counter to talk to her and to joke her about being too
proud to have a date with a plain drummer like himself. (He
had wanted to go out with her several times in the past, but
Alice had always had something better to do.) This afternoon
Joe also asked for a date and finally, to his surprise, Alice gave
him one. They planned having dinner together and going later
to the theater.

The evening passed pleasantly enough, and after the theater
was over, Joe suggested that Alice come with him to his room.
Alice consented as a matter of course. When they were in his
room, Joe locked the door and winked mysteriously. "We don't
have to worry about the house detective," he said, "because he
happens to be a personal friend of mine."

"All right, Mr. Fixer," said Alice languidly. She lighted a
cigarette and inhaled deeply, her head thrown back. Joe's blue
eyes became bright and excited. He took Alice in his arms, kissing her throat and her lips, and they sat for a time embracing and
murmuring words of love. At last Joe moved to the bed and

began unlacing his shoes. Alice picked up her cigarette, which was still burning, and drew another puff of smoke through her lungs. The smoke irritated her throat and she coughed slightly.

"I'd better let Trix rub my chest with mutton-suet again," she thought vaguely. Then she sat up straight in the chair, her languid manner gone. She had remembered just in time about the woolen union-suit which Trix had persuaded her to wear. For a moment she became panic-stricken. She knew she would die of humiliation if any man caught her wearing those baggy, woolen drawers. The very thought of such a thing filled her with shame, and she blushed. She got up quickly and put on her hat.

Joe walked to her in his stocking-feet. "What's the matter, Alice?" he asked in surprise. Alice put her hand on his arm. "I've had a very pleasant evening indeed, Mr. Croxton," she said, "but I think I'd better go on home now. Be sure and look me up again the next time you come to Atlanta."

"So that's the sort of game you play?" said Joe in a hard voice. "Well, let me tell you something, sister: you can't pull that stuff on me and get away with it!"

"I don't know what you mean, I'm sure," said Alice.

"All right, then," said Joe. "I'll show you pretty quick what I mean."

He took her by the arms and threw her roughly upon the bed, and held her there. Alice struggled to free herself. She was surprised at Joe's strength, and had not expected him to behave in any such manner. As she struggled to free herself from his hands her brain was working with rapidity. Then, all at once, she ceased to struggle and lay beside him crying softly. After she stopped resisting him, Joe kissed her once or twice in a sullen, hangdog way and then he sat up beside her on the bed, outlining the pattern in the carpet with his toe.

"You think you're pretty wise, don't you?" he asked. "Well, by God, you can't put anything like that over on me. It may work all right with guys who haven't been around much, but it won't work with me."

Alice buried her face in her hands. "You don't understand,

Mr. Croxton," she said. "I'm not the sort of girl you think I am at all." Joe made a laughing sound.

"Oh, I don't blame you for thinking those things," said Alice. "I'll admit you have a perfect right to think what you did about me."

Joe looked at her in a puzzled manner, unable to make up his mind.

"I wanted to have a good time like other girls and I thought I could do what they do," she went on. "Other girls have always said that a man wouldn't like you until you did things like that, and I did so want *you* to like me, Mr. Croxton."

Joe looked at her uncomfortably. He wanted to say: "My name isn't Croxton; it's *Cotton*," but he remained silent.

Alice was crying in earnest now. Slowly she raised her head and looked at Joe appealingly. She had known, of course, that he was completely defeated now, and that she could go home unmolested when she chose; but she was surprised to notice there were tears also in Joe's eyes, and that his lips were trembling like a little boy's. For a moment he regarded her simply; then he knelt before her and raised the hem of her skirt to his lips.

"I don't deserve your forgiveness, Miss Alice," he said in a choking voice. "I don't deserve it."

"Now, Mr. Croxton," said Alice nervously, "everybody makes mistakes, I guess."

When she repeated the story to Trix that night the girls laughed until they were exhausted. Trix lay on her bed and slapped at the counterpane helplessly. "I don't see how you stood it without laughing in his face, Alice! Honest to God, I don't," she gasped.

"I *had* to keep a straight face," said Alice; "but when he got down on his knees, I thought I was going to split." She raised her arms upward, put on her nightgown and yawned: "Well, I'll never see that sap again, I hope," she said.

The next day Alice received a letter from Joe by special messenger. He was leaving for Chattanooga that morning he said, and he wanted to apologize again. He went over and over the same ground for ten closely written pages, affirming and reaffirm-

ing Alice's beauty of soul and pleading that she forgive him in
time for the stupid mistake he had made.

"It is hard for a girl of your innocence to understand a man
of the world like me," wrote Joe; "but I've been on the road
for a long time and I've met so many women of the 'other kind'
that I have become hard and lost my ideals. Last night you
showed me how far I had drifted. But now," he continued, "I
have reached the point where I need the sweet and tender love
of a good woman. Oh, Alice! Help me to renew my faith in
womankind!" At first Alice didn't know what to make of the
letter, but finally she showed it to Trix, and they had another
good laugh at Joe's expense.

Early the next morning another letter arrived from Joe. It was
much like the first one, being devoted entirely to Alice's purity
and Joe's unworthiness. Alice read the letter two or three times,
a thoughtful look on her face. For some reason she did not want
to share this letter with Trix, from whom she had no secrets as
a rule; but Trix seeing it on Alice's dressing-table, picked it up
and began reading it out loud, making laughing remarks at Joe's
stupidity.

Alice felt a sudden, uncalculated anger against Trix. She took
the letter out of her hand and put it away without a word.
After that a letter came from Joe each morning. These letters
were impressing Alice against her will.

At the end of the first week she answered Joe's letters, a detail which she failed to reveal to Trix, and after that she fell
naturally into the habit of writing him daily. She gave up smoking cigarettes because Joe asked her to; she began dressing more
modestly because Joe liked modest women; and she gave up
entirely her dates with other men. And so things went for a few
months and then Alice Ochs became Mrs. Joseph L. Cotton
and moved with her husband to Reedyville, where he had lived
as a boy, and where he had rented a home for his bride.

Once in Reedyville, with her early life behind her, Alice
Cotton drifted without effort into the church life of the town.
Joe and his kinsmen were Methodists, so Alice became a member of that denomination too. At first Joe was afraid his wife
would be bored in Reedyville, after the exciting life she had led,

and that she would find the narrow, religious routine of the town confining, but such was far from being the case. Alice, who had never in her life received religious training, took to it instinctively, knowing that she had at length found her true vocation. As she sat in church listening to the hymns and the thundering, denunciatory sermons, she kept thinking: "This is what I really wanted. Why have I missed it in the past?" Often she was sorry that she was not a Catholic, so that she might have become a nun and dedicated her whole existence to religious worship.

During the second year of their married life, when her husband was home on one occasion, Alice locked her bedroom door against his advances and told him that that sort of relationship was over forever between them. Such a relationship was permissible only for the purpose of bringing souls into the world, she said; and it was apparent, now, that God did not see fit to bless their union with children. Joe did not agree with his wife's views, but he continued to love her patiently, hoping that her new mood would pass.

It never did, of course, and as the years went by, Joe Cotton spent more and more of his time on the road. He rarely visited Reedyville any more. During the week when he was busy he seldom thought of women, but often on a Sunday in a strange town he became lonely and picked up some girl on the street and took her to his room. At such times Joe would send out for a bottle of gin and he and the woman would drink until they were tipsy. Then he would begin to talk about his wife.

"I married an angel," he would say. "I married the best woman in the world." He would cry maudlin tears and his companion would embrace him and call him a poor boy and everything would run smoothly until they began to haggle over the amount of money he was to pay for the privilege of having his comforter spend the night with him.

Occasionally reports of Joe's goings-on got back to Reedyville and reached his wife's ears. She would sigh patiently and roll her eyes upward when people told her such things, but in reality she didn't care in the least what her husband did on the road. Gradually she took more and more interest in her church work and in time she joined Mr. Palmiller's interdenominational temperance and vice society, becoming its most efficient and belligerent member, crusading against cigarette smoking, drinking, and the sexual relationship. For the first time her life was perfect and complete. She was happy in her new work and she believed that God and His angels noticed everything she accomplished for good, and often spoke of it among themselves.

The temperance and vice society met each Monday evening, generally in the directors' room of the Palmiller State Bank. Mrs. Cotton, as secretary, always came early with her minutes and records and reports. She would seat herself at Mr. Palmiller's elbow and arrange his papers for him or fill his glass with water. Later, there would be old Miss Emmaline Maybanks sitting in a wicker chair, flanked by Mr. Baker Rice and Mrs. Daniel O'Leary.

One night after the regular business meeting had been attended to, Sister Joe Cotton began to talk about the things that went on at Mattress May's sporting house on New April Avenue, and how the night clerk at the Magnolia Hotel sent out for girls when his guests requested such attentions. There were a series of shocked exclamations and demands for more exact details. So Sister Cotton told them what they wanted to hear, omitting nothing. When she had finished, Miss Eulalie Prescott banged her cane on the floor and leaned forward eagerly.

"How did you find out so much, Sister Cotton?" she asked. "How did you happen to hear about these shocking things?"

Sister Cotton smiled firmly. "It's my duty as a Christian woman to know what's going on in this town," she said. "I don't know how I do it. I just seem to be able to sit down and figure out what bad women are going to do. You might call it a kind of talent, I guess—like playing the piano by ear."

Mr. Palmiller rose and offered a prayer in which he thanked God for having given to Alice Cotton her unparalleled understanding of sin and her great power to detect and confound sinners. This virtue, according to Mr. Palmiller, was as important in its way as the power to do good, or the necessity for practicing brotherhood and love.

1931

HAPPY JACK

*T*HE MERCHANTS PRINTING COMPANY faced Court House Square, and when work was slack, Jack Sutton, the proprietor, would sit back in a chair, his feet upon his littered desk, and smile at the people who passed his window. He was a small man with nervous hands, a jutting, deeply curved nose, and a round chin, delicately modeled, which did not seem to fit the rest of his face. After awhile, his friends would drop in, one by one, to talk. Jack was fond of people and he set great store by his friends. Secretly, he was pleased at his popularity in the town. Not even his peculiar views affected his standing. Everybody liked him, and joked with him, in spite of the fact that they thought him somewhat impractical, if not actually eccentric.

For example, a group would be discussing an actress or a society woman mentioned in the papers as having smoked a cigarette in a public place, and Jack would become excited and lean forward eagerly. "What's wrong with that, if she *wanted* to do it? I can't for the life of me see how smoking cigarettes has anything to do with her morals."

Mr. Palmiller spoke then, in his quick, waspish voice. "Would you want *your* wife, or daughter, to smoke a cigarette?" "Why, sure," said Jack; "that is if I had a wife or daughter."

"I'd hate to think what would become of the world if everybody felt like you do," said Ira Cunningham, shaking his head.

Then Jack would begin to laugh, the lines in his cheeks deepening. "Now, Ira, I'm not as bad as all that!" he would protest good-naturedly. After a moment, he would say more seriously: "Of course I can see your viewpoint, too, but I think you're wrong; you're looking at this thing the wrong way."

Then Willis Overton would speak up. "Jack doesn't really mean what he says; he's just talking to be different."

"But I do mean it!" said Jack earnestly. "I do mean it, Willis!"

Then everybody would laugh, and shake their heads. "Folks may think that way where you came from," said Ira Cunningham heavily, "but people here wouldn't stand for such things. No, sir, they wouldn't stand for such goings-on a minute!"

Later, when Jack had gone to Mrs. Findley's boarding-house, where he lived, he would think of these conversations. Then he would smile tolerantly. "These people are all right," he would think. "They pretend to be hard, and all that, but down underneath they are kind and charitable. I'm not fooled by what they say."

And so several years passed. The printing shop was prospering, and Jack felt that he was now a definite part of the town. Then one night a shocking thing happened.

Three miles from town, on the Valley City Road, a widow named Pierce ran a small farm. Her husband had been dead for some years, and, since that time, she had living on the place a Negro man called "Driver," who took care of the heavy farm work. The farm was isolated, and nobody paid much attention to the widow Pierce and her farm-hand until Mrs. Joe Cotton, in the course of her home missionary work, discovered that Driver and Mrs. Pierce were living together as man and wife.

There was considerable excitement when Mrs. Cotton made her report public, and the next night a committee of masked men called at the Pierce farm. There were eight men in the party, but they selected Ira Cunningham their spokesman, and the other men hid behind trees and bushes.

Ira walked up the steps and knocked on the door. Mrs. Pierce opened it a little. "I want to see your nigger, Driver," he said.

"What do you want to see him about?"

"I want to see him about training me a bird-dog for next fall."

"He ain't in here," said Mrs. Pierce.

"He's here, all right," said Ira. Then he turned and spoke to the men concealed outside. "Come on in; he's here all right."

The eight men pushed into the room and Driver stood there leaning against the back door, too frightened to run. His clean overalls were patched at both knees with squares of a darker material. The patches were crudely sewn, with no two of the stitches the same length, as if done by someone whose sight was failing. His shoulders were jerking and his jaw trembled. Sam Whittemore walked over and hit him in the face. Driver's head banged against the wall, but he made no effort to protect himself.

Mrs. Pierce began to throw herself about, but Bob Jowder and a man named Ellis shoved her into a closet and turned the key. She thrashed about on the floor and beat the partition with her fists. "I know the names of every one of you!" she screamed. "If you hurt Driver, I'll have you all arrested! I will! I'll have you all arrested, so help me God!" But the men paid no attention to her. They closed in on Driver, dragging him down the steps in the direction of the barn; and there, by the light of a lantern, a sack stuffed in his mouth to muffle his cries, the man named Ellis castrated him with a bone-handled pocket knife.

Before the eight men returned, late that night, the town somehow knew what had happened, and were talking about it in excited groups. But Jack Sutton did not hear of it until breakfast the next morning. One of his fellow boarders, Creary Berdine, had the exact details. Finally Mrs. Findley spoke up: "It's too bad that the law couldn't have taken its course, but Driver got just what was coming to him, I suppose." Then she spoke loudly so that the colored cook could hear her: "I hope this will be a lesson to the other Negroes in this town."

Jack sat there with a puzzled look on his face. "But why?" he asked. "Whose business was it? What difference did it make?"

Old Mrs. D'Alembert got up and threw down her napkin. "I won't stay to hear American womanhood insulted," she said. "I won't listen to it!" She looked at Jack furiously, tears of rage in her eyes.

"But I don't see?" said Jack. "I'm not insulting anybody." But Mrs. D'Alembert withdrew from the room, banging the door behind her.

Then everybody laughed, but Mrs. Findley spoke to Jack, gravely. "We know you're only talking in fun, but you shouldn't tease poor old Mrs. D'Alembert that way, Mr. Sutton. You owe her an apology. You really do!"

Jack shook his head helplessly but he did not say anything.

All that morning the matter remained in his mind, troubling him. At noon he went over to the Farmers National Bank to talk to Willis Overton, whom he considered his closest friend. "I'll admit it sounds pretty bad to an outsider," said Willis, "but what else could people do, in a case of this sort? You can't let a white woman live with a nigger that way!" "Why not, if it's what they both want?" asked Jack. "Well," said Willis, "it sets a bad example, I suppose." Jack's face became red with anger. He got up suddenly and overturned a chair. Then he sat down again, and looked at the floor.

Willis Overton was folding paper into squares, a distressed expression on his face. "You don't belong to the town, Jack, and you can't understand our viewpoint," he said. Then, as Jack Sutton rose to go, he came over to him and caught him by the arm. "Listen, Jack," he said, "you can say anything to me that you want to, but don't talk the way you have before other people. You can't do any good, and you'll only get yourself in trouble."

But Jack paid little attention to his friend's advice. All that day and for days following he talked of nothing except the affair at the Pierce farm. The more he talked about it, the more it seemed to oppress him. He stopped strangers on the street, going over his arguments again and again. Finally he wrote an article reviewing the affair, in which he defended the right of Mrs. Pierce and Driver to live together as man and wife, if they, as individuals, chose to do so. They hurt nobody, he declared, and nobody had a right to interfere or sit in judgment.

"The fact that Driver was a Negro, and Mrs. Pierce a white woman, has nothing to do with the situation," he wrote. "I am not going into that phase of the matter at all. I would feel as strongly about it if they were both white or if they were both black. That is not my point. But I do claim that they, as individuals, have a right to lead any moral life that suits them. If you people do not approve of the life they lead, then you, as individuals, have an equal right to have nothing to do with them. That is sound and simple. That, at least, is understandable. But for a mob to go out there and mutilate a human being who could

not even defend himself, is unbelievable among people who call
themselves civilized."

Sutton took considerable pains with his article, and when it
was finished, he read it with a feeling of triumph. "When people
read my arguments, they'll see the matter in a different light," he
thought. "They'll be ashamed of themselves, then. You may be
sure of that." Later Jack printed the article on his press and sent
a copy of it to every resident in the county.

At the end of the week a farmer named Jim Prouty came to
see Jack. Jim was about fifty years old. He wore high starched
collars without a necktie, and when he was a boy his left eye
had been blinded by a blow from a stone. Jim sat down and took
from his pocket a copy of Jack's pamphlet, tapping it, for em-
phasis, against his knee. He came to the point at once: "I wanted
to come by and shake hands with you, Mr. Sutton," he said,
"because I believe you're a straight thinker, and I wanted to
tell you I believe what you say is right."

Jack leaned forward impulsively, in his old manner. His eyes
were interested and eager again. To himself he kept saying: "I
knew it! I knew people would see this thing, once they had it
put before them in the right way!"

"Yes, sir," continued Jim, "you've got the right slant. I've
knowed Driver for more than twenty-five years, and there wasn't
a better nigger in Pearl County. He wasn't to blame. I guess any
nigger would have done the same thing, if a white woman give
him the chance."

Jim blinked his blind eye, over which a dirty, phlegm-like
film had formed. "Yes, sir, any nigger would have acted the
same way, I guess, and, like you said, that mob shouldn't have
harmed him none." For a moment Jim sat silent. Then he nodded
his head a couple of times. "What the boys *should* of done," he
added, "what they *should* of done, when they went to the farm
that night, was to take a big needle and a piece of copper wire
and sew up that sorry Pierce woman. That's what they *should*
of done, I guess!" Then, before Jack could say anything in reply,
Jim walked out of the office, mounted his saddle mule and rode

off down the road, the sun beating on his white collar, the hooves of his mule kicking sand into the air.

When he had gone, Jack Sutton sat motionless; then, on a sudden impulse, he went to his door and bolted it, as if the town frightened him, and he wanted to shut it out. After that he lowered the shades in his office and sat in semi-darkness for a long time.

Later he got up and walked away from the town. When he had gone about three miles, he turned off from the road, through an abandoned field, and went toward the creek that fed James Lake. It was late in June and the air was very still; the sunlight beat down on the old field, leaving a shimmer above it. Beside him the creek moved quietly, and in the bay trees that grew thickly, birds chirped. Jack lay on his side and held his hand in the water, feeling its coolness. His head felt hot and tight and he trembled at quick intervals. Then, for some reason, he remembered why he had come to Reedyville to live, why he had picked it above all places. Suddenly he felt foolish, and he began to laugh at himself mockingly. He was glad now that he had never told the story to anybody, not even to Willis Overton; but when he had been a young man, during the Spanish American War, he had found himself, along with many other soldiers, on a troop-train bound for New Orleans. On the third day of the trip he had awakened to realize that the train was no longer in motion. He sat up and rubbed his eyes. All about him were men sleeping heavily, their arms and legs thrown wide, and there was, in the coach, an odor of cigarette smoke, breath, and perspiration so sharp that he could almost taste the stale odor on his tongue.

In disgust, he put on his clothes, walked to the end of the train, and looked about him. To the left of the siding was a cottage flanked by crêpe-myrtles cut back to make a hedge, now in full bloom, with blossoms scattered on the grass. In the night, spiders had spun webs over the hedge, which had caught and held dew, and as Jack watched, the sun came up between two trees, slanting the cabin with its light and turning the drenched webs into fire. Then a cow bell sounded from a field a long way off and a bird repeated, three times, a single note that was incredibly liquid and moving.

At that instant the place had taken on a meaning beyond the scattered blossoms, the blazing cobwebs or the slow note of the bird. An eager look came into his eyes. "Everything is so quiet," he had whispered; "everything is so quiet, newly washed and beautiful." Then he had stretched his arms wide and held them out to something which he did not understand and had thought: "Some day I'm coming back to this place. This is where I want to spend my life."

As Jack remembered his gesture, he began to curse and to laugh harshly. Before him, at the edge of the old field, two mice came and looked at him, twitching their whiskers. Then he stood upright, but the sense of terror which had made him walk into the country came over him again more sharply. His knees felt weak, suddenly, and he lay down again by the stream, breaking up twigs and throwing them into the current.

But when the sun was low in the sky, he got up, feeling stronger, and more calm, and bathed his face in the stream. Then he brushed off his clothes, turned and walked toward Mrs. Findley's boarding-house. It was late when he reached it, and supper was almost over, but he seated himself, with the other boarders, and began to eat. Then immediately he put down his fork and laughed loudly, his eyes crinkled into a tight line.

"Well," said Mrs. Findley, "tell us the joke, so we can laugh too." But Jack did not answer. His nose was drawn down and white, and his round chin began to tremble. "Tell us the joke," Mrs. Findley urged. "Tell us the joke, Mr. Sutton." Jack did not hear them. His voice had become hysterical and shrill, and tears ran down his cheeks.

Mrs. Findley became alarmed. "Mr. Sutton!" she said sharply; and then, again: "Mr. Sutton!" Creary Berdine and Harry D'Alembert came over and shook Jack's shoulders. At their touch, he slid from his seat and fell to the floor, and lay with his face pressed into Mrs. Findley's red and green rug.

An hour later they had undressed him and put him to bed. They tied his arms and legs with clothes-line and bound him to the bed with trunk straps. All that night and all the following day Jack continued to laugh. "I see what you mean!" he shouted, over and over, "but I'm the only one who really understands what you're driving at! You've got the right slant on things, and I'm glad to make your acquaintance!" Then he would fling himself upward, trying to free his hands and legs, the iron bed making a thumping noise against the floor. At length he would lie back and begin laughing again. "A needle and a piece of wire was all you needed!" he would say. Then he would start laughing again.

A crowd of people gathered in front of Mrs. Findley's gate, and she went out and asked them to move on. "It's Mr. Jack Sutton," she explained. "We don't know what it is, yet, but it's some sort of fever. You'd better not stop. It may be catching."

Bob Kirkland listened to the unending laughter for a moment and spoke up: "I don't care if I do catch it, if it makes me feel as happy as Jack!" he said. Later on his answer was repeated many times, and the nickname caught on at once. The whole town discussed Happy Jack Sutton and his strange sickness. Then, three days later, he stopped laughing as suddenly as he had begun. But he seemed to have shriveled during his sickness. His face was pasty, his lips were drawn back from his teeth and the lines in his cheeks had deepened. On the afternoon he returned to his shop, a committee of his old friends dropped in to congratulate him on his recovery, but Jack would not see them. He stood locked in his office and spoke through the door. "Get out of here!" he said, "get out and don't ever come back—any of you!" Then his lips drew tight, and he bared his teeth. His head shook back and forth in a caricature of mirth, but no sound came.

That week he moved from Mrs. Findley's boarding-house, and slept on a cot in the back of the shop, eating his meals at the Deerhorn Cafe when it occurred to him that he was hungry. He began to avoid everyone he had known, and he would even stare at people with such a look of cold contempt that they were uneasy. Soon the people of the town began, in turn, to avoid him, and they would draw away, apprehensively, at his approach.

His business fell away rapidly, and soon there was no work for him at all. Six months after his sickness his equipment was seized under an attachment and sold at sheriff's sale. Jack stood there indifferently. He was penniless. He had no place to turn and no way to earn a living for himself.

An old friend of his, Adolph Moore, came over to him. "Where are you going to live, Jack?" he asked. Jack did not answer. He shrugged his shoulders and turned away. Something about his frail, drooping figure touched Adolph. "I tell you what, Jack," he said. "I got a room fixed up over my livery stable. It ain't much to look at, but you can stay there, if you want to. I can pay you a little," continued Adolph, "for helping with the horses and watching the place at night. It won't be much, but it'll be better than nothing, I guess, until you get on your feet again." Jack did not look up. He stood thinking. Then he nodded his head, turned, and followed Adolph Moore.

The room was dark, and during rainy weather it leaked. At one end was a small iron stove, its legs resting on four cans of packed sand. Above the stove was a pine shelf containing a can of condensed milk, a sugar bowl with a tin spoon protruding, and a bottle of catsup which had begun to ferment.

And so a new life began for Jack. He would work for hours, drawing a curry-comb across the flanks of the horses until they were like satin, watching the wrinkles of delight that ran behind his stroke. In time each horse came to have for him a distinct individuality, and when nobody was around, he would sit on a box facing the stalls and talk to them. Often he would tell them about the time he stood at the end of the troop-train and watched the sunrise and the blazing cobwebs. "As the train moved away," he would say, "an old man with a hoe on his shoulder was crossing the tracks, making a swishing noise as he brushed through the grass. I stood there waving my arms and shouting at him; but the old man was deaf, and at first he did not understand what I wanted to know. Then the train began to move faster, but the old man ran after it, his hoe jerking up and down, his hand cupped to his ear. 'Hey? Hey?' he kept saying in a cracked voice. At last he understood what I wanted to know. 'Reedyville!' he shouted. 'This town is *Reedyville!*' Then he sat down on the track and wiped his face and neck with a handkerchief."

Jack would laugh his soundless laugh, his eyes shut, his face twisted. He would rock back and forth on the box while his whole body trembled to his silent mirth. When he had finished, he would begin to cry angrily. "One of these days I'm going to tell this town what I think of it!" he would say. "You just wait. I'll tell them yet. You'll see!" But the horses would make a whinnying sound and look at him with their soft eyes, nuzzling his cheeks with their lips.

Occasionally, when the regular drivers were busy, Jack would be called to take a traveling salesman to Morgan City or Hodgetown, but this happened rarely. His sullen manner and scowling face alarmed such strangers, and they generally preferred waiting until one of the regular drivers returned. Then, too, he had grown incredibly tattered with the years. His finger nails and ears were caked with dirt and there was about him a strong odor of the stables. He was never asked to drive any of the local people; they would not have risked their lives with him. They considered him a madman, and were of the opinion that he should be locked up.

"I saw that Happy Jack on Oak Street today," Mrs. George Wheeler would say to her Wednesday afternoon Rook Club. "I had to hold my nose, he smelled so bad! He was walking along with his lips moving, but when he saw me, he stopped and looked at me in a way that made my blood run cold! Then he stopped, and began to laugh without making any sound. His face was twisted up until he looked like a monkey."

"Something ought to be done about him," said Emmaline Hemmes; "I don't know what this town is coming to. He ought to be put in an institution!" Then the ladies would put down their cards and discuss Happy Jack for a long time.

But Jack cared little what people thought of him. As the years passed, he went into town less and less, and finally he did not leave the stable at all, except when he had to buy food for himself. He would come into McArthur's grocery regularly at five o'clock of an afternoon, holding in his hand a slip on which was written his list of groceries, and wait silently until Mr. Mc-Arthur, or his clerk, Chester Penny, took the order. He always spent his money in unusual amounts, such as eleven cents' worth of flour, eight cents' worth of molasses, or six cents' worth of kerosene. If there were other customers present when he entered the store, they would move away and glance at him out of the corners of their eyes.

Then, later, as he walked down the street, his purchases clasped to his breast, people would step to one side of the narrow, wooden sidewalk, giving him the right of way. Often he was pointed out to strangers: "That's Happy Jack Sutton," they would say. "He had a fever fifteen years ago, and he hasn't been right since."

And so the years passed, and there was Jack Sutton, an old man with a stooped back, spindling legs and gray hair that hung soiled and matted to his shoulders. It would have been hard to recognize in this feeble creature the young soldier who stood at the end of a train, more than thirty years before, with eager eyes and uplifted arms. A new generation had grown up in the town since that time. They knew nothing of his early life. They remembered him only as a village character, a furious old man with bleary eyes and teeth rotted and broken with decay. Indeed, Jack's teeth had troubled him for a long time. Often at night they ached so badly that he could not sleep. At such times he lay in bed making a sound that resembled the whinnying of the horses in their stalls below. At last an old Negro man named Zilk, who hung around the stables, offered to pull Jack's teeth, and one night, when he was in special pain, he consented. Afterwards he lay on his bed, a soiled rag pressed against his gums. Then, on the second afternoon, he went to McArthur's grocery, to buy corn meal and milk to make gruel.

It had rained steadily that day and a misty rain was still falling as Jack walked down Lipscomb Street, stepping over puddles of water that stood undrained in the street, the few coins he possessed clutched in his palm. Then he turned into Oak Street and approached the store. When he entered, the other customers drew back in fear. But almost immediately a gasp of surprise went up, and everybody began to nudge his neighbor and whisper behind his hand. They looked at each other in a puzzled manner, uncertain if this man were really Happy Jack. For the loss of his teeth had made a startling change in Sutton's appearance. His nose was pinched at its roots and bent downward, and his face foreshortened and folded back, and as he stood there, grasping the counter for support, his body weak and breathless, even the dullest person could see that Happy Jack was not a dark figure to be feared; he was only an old man with vacant gums and a deflated face who could harm no one.

Chester Penny, Mr. McArthur's red-headed clerk, wrapped up Jack's parcels, and placed them before him. Then, from a bin behind the counter, he scooped a handful of Brazil nuts and placed them in Jack's open palm, along with his change. He winked knowingly at his other customers. "Hey, Happy Jack," he said, "crack these nuts, and you can have 'em!" Chet held his sides and laughed explosively at his joke, and everybody laughed with him. Jack stood looking from face to face, surprised, unprepared for this new attitude. Then, quickly, he flung the nuts at the clerk's head. But everybody laughed more than ever at that. They doubled up with laughter, shaking their fingers at him and clucking their lips as if they were talking to a child. "Tsch! Tsch! That's no way to act, Happy!" they said. "That's no way to act!"

Jack picked up his purchases and walked from the store. A crowd of half-grown boys and men had formed outside. "Hey! What's your rush, Happy!" they said. "Where you think you're going, anyway?" Then the crowd blocked his path, surrounding him, and began pushing him about and pulling his beard and his long, matted hair. One of the boys kicked his heels in the air and began to bleat like a goat "H-a-a-ppy J-a-a-ck!" he said. "H-a-a-ppy J-a-a-ck!"

"Look out!" said Chet Penny from the doorway, "look out he don't *bite* you!"

Jack stood with his back to the store, examining each face as if he wanted to fix it in his mind forever. The crowd became larger and the sidewalk was blocked. People from adjoining stores peered from their windows, or stood in the street, to watch the fun, as Jack, his body shaking, his jaws working, backed slowly away. But when he reached the edge of the wooden walk, somebody stuck out a foot, and somebody gave him a push, and Jack tripped and fell into a puddle of water. He lay on his back in the mud, his purchases scattered about him, the meal sack broken and spilling slowly, the milk mixing with the mud and giving it a rich coloring.

Then he stood on his unsteady legs and faced his tormentors. His wet clothing adhered to his body, outlining its frailty, and particles of mud smeared his face and clung to his beard.

"And so I says, 'Crack these nuts,'" repeated Chet Penny from the doorway, laughing again at his joke. "I says, 'Crack these nuts and you can have 'em!'"

Willis Overton, an old man with a neat white beard, was pushing his way through the crowd. "Don't!" he said in a kindly, protesting voice. "Don't tease him! Don't tease the crazy old man!"

Jack turned then and stared incuriously at Willis, as if he had never seen him before, at the yapping, excited faces that surrounded him, at the town itself. Suddenly his lips began to move. "I'm not crazy," he said; "I wish to God I was crazy!" Then he stood erect, squared his bent shoulders. "Now is the time," he thought; "now is the time to tell these people what I think of them!" He opened his jaws and began to talk rapidly, but with his teeth gone, and his cheeks sucked in, his voice came out of his throat cracked and reedy, like a cheap whistle, hissing against his gums with a lisping sound, and the things he was saying, which he had thought profound as he lay in the dark room over the stable, seemed absurd now, even to himself.

He quit talking as suddenly as he had begun and stood there in silence, his chin working patiently to touch the tip of his nose, his arms hanging limply from his shoulders. He raised his arms and pushed at the air, as if to repudiate the town and what it stood for; then his face twisted up and his eyes closed; his lips trembled, sucked in, and puckered out slowly, as if he awaited a kiss.

The boy who could bleat like a goat began again to kick his heels in the air. Then everybody began to laugh and bleat like a goat, their voices rolling in confused volume over the roof tops, toward the sky. "H-a-a-ppy Jack!" they shouted. "H-a-a-a-ppy J-a-a-ck!"

1931

HE SITS THERE ALL DAY LONG

I STOOD with my cap in my hand while the superintendent bawled me out. "What's all this about passing floors with an empty car?" he asked. "Now get this in your head: the tenants of this building pay for first-class elevator service, and they've got a right to expect it!" I just looked down at the floor; I didn't have any comeback.

"The starter says he's had a dozen kicks about you in the past few days. He says you don't pay any attention to his signals."

"I guess he's right," I said. "I haven't got a leg to stand on."

Mr. Donovan looked in his black book. "You been with us a year now and you've given good service in the past. What's come over you, anyway?"

I didn't say anything to that. What could I say?

"You act like you got something on your mind worrying you," said Mr. Donovan. "I don't want to ride you if you're feeling sick. What's the matter with you?"

"I don't know," I said.

I couldn't tell him about the old man and how I see that look in his eyes all the time. I couldn't do that. He'd think I was crazy myself. I couldn't tell him that every time I get to thinking about the old man, and how he sits there all day long looking out of the window, I feel light and funny and forget where I am and want to cry and bang my head against the elevator wall. I couldn't tell Mr. Donovan a thing like that, now could I?

God damn that settlement house woman! Why couldn't she mind her own business? Why couldn't she stay on Park Avenue where she belonged and play with her Pekingese dogs and not come around bothering other people? What business was it of hers if it suited Mamma and me to take care of the old man?

What kick did she have coming? But oh, no! She had to come sticking her nose in. I blame her for the whole thing, that's what! I blame her. . . . No, I guess I'm more to blame than anybody else; I had no business letting them talk me into it. I should have stuck by the old man no matter what happened. I'm going to tell you the whole story. You'll see then what I mean; you'll agree that I'm the one to blame. Maybe you can tell me what I ought to do.

It all happened six months ago when the old man took sick one morning. He had just passed his fifty-second birthday. That's not really old. Why, I carry up in my car every day men that are at least sixty-five or seventy years old and they are as spry and pink-cheeked as you please, but of course they haven't worked hard all their lives. That makes a difference, all right. The old man had to work like a slave for the little he got. Well, about a week before his birthday Mamma and me decided we'd give him a party and have everybody bring him a present and wish him a long life and all that. My sister Viola and Al, her husband, came over from Elizabeth with their three kids that night. My oldest sister Evelyn and her husband came down also. Mamma had cooked up a good supper, with all the dishes the old man liked, and everybody laughed and had a good time. Well, say—he was sure tickled when he tumbled to what was coming off. "Gee!" he said, "whoever in the world thought of giving an old man like me a birthday party, now?" "It was Danny's idea, I'll bet," he said later. "Yes," said Mamma, "Danny was the one that thought of it first."

After supper some people from upstairs came down. They were wops and one of them could play anything you called for on his accordion. I stayed out in the kitchen and opened bottles of beer. I didn't want anybody to go away thirsty. After awhile everybody got warmed up good, so Al started a buck-and-wing, but Viola made him stop. "Sit down, Al," she hollered, "and nobody won't know you're drunk!" "Yeah?" said Al, "I'll show you who's drunk!" Then his feet slipped and he sat down on the floor. Well, he took it good-natured. He laughed like everything.

Then things got quieter and the old man began to talk about the time he crossed from Ireland in a sailing vessel. Everybody sat around respectful and asked questions when he stopped talking for a minute. Finally he asked the accordion player to play a song named "The Harp That Once Through Tara's Halls," but the wop didn't know that piece, he said. He played one called "You're the Cream in My Coffee," instead.

Well, about eleven o'clock Viola's kids got sleepy, so she and Al had to take them home. Then everybody went home because the old man had to get up in the morning early and Mamma began to put the place in order again. The old man made out he was pie-eyed and staggered a little and I began to clown and pretend I was a cop putting him under arrest. Before I knew what was coming off he put his arms around me and pulled me to him. "You're a good boy, Danny," he said, "and I want you to know I wouldn't ask for a better son." He said that to me—honest to Christ he did! Nobody asked him to say it. He wouldn't say a thing like that unless he meant it, would he? And then for me to do what I did when he was sick and down and out. Oh, Jesus! It don't seem possible that anybody could be that low! It really don't!

I'm glad we gave him that birthday party, though. He talked about it for a month afterwards. I remember just a few days before he had that attack he was talking about how Viola's youngest boy, Freddy, picked up a glass of beer belonging to the accordion player and drank half of it before anybody could stop him. When the old man thought of that he began to chuckle. "That's a great youngster of Viola's," he said. "He's going to take after his granddaddy."

"Well," said Mamma, laughing, too, "little good that'll do the poor lad."

And then that morning he took sick. It happened suddenly. The old lady had got up and gave him his breakfast and was fixing his lunch-box when he made a gagging noise and blew bubbles out of his mouth. Then he stood up and tried to tear off his collar. I was up and almost dressed by then and when the old lady hollered, I came running. We picked him up and laid

him on the bed. He had begun to stiffen up some and his mouth
was bleeding where he had hit it against the edge of the table
when he fell. I took off his shoes and his pants and opened his
undershirt. The hair on his chest was turning gray in patches
and his hands lay on the bed palms upward with his fingers
bent in. His finger nails were thick like they were made out of
metal. They were caked halfway down with dirt and stained
with oil. I tried to straighten out his fingers, but I couldn't do
it. Then his face began to turn gray, and his eyes rolled backward.

He lay that way for two months and four days without speaking and without moving his head. Then he seemed to get some
better, and the doctor said he could sit up. So we fixed him a
chair by the window, and he would sit there all day long, not
moving. If you turned his head one way, he would look that
way until you moved it in another direction. The old lady would
come in every few minutes to see that he was all right. She
was afraid he might have another attack and fall out of the chair,
so she couldn't leave him for long.

Well, the doctor bills and the medicine came to a tidy sum.
Oh, sure; you've got to expect that. It took about all we had
saved. Things got pretty bad for us, I'll admit that. With the
old man's pay envelope stopped, it was hard trying to come
out even at the end of the week. I only make twenty bucks and
that don't go far, as you know, with a sick man to take care of.
We couldn't expect any help from Viola or Evvie. They were
willing to do what they could, but after all they're married and
got families of their own to think about. At last we were down
to rock bottom. We didn't know what to do or which way to
turn. Then one morning a woman at the A&P store told Mamma
about that charity organization, and she talked it over with me.
"Nothing doing," I said. "We'll pay our own way. We don't
ask charity from anybody."

"Where's the rent money to come from, and who's going to
pay the electric light man when he comes around for his?"
Mamma asked.

"Maybe I can get a job working part time at night," I said. "We're bound to think of some way."

"If I didn't have him to look out for, I might get cleaning work in an office building," she said. "That would help out until times got better."

"Get that idea off your mind," I said. "I guess I'm head of this family now, and I won't have you scrubbing up after other people. I'll think of something if we can hold out a little longer."

Well, things went on like that for a couple of days and then Mamma went to the organization. That night when I got home the Park Avenue dame was sitting there. It didn't take but a minute for me to see how things were working. I spoke to her politely, but I told her I thought she'd better be going on home, because she had made a mistake. "We're not taking charity," I said. "We're much obliged to you, and all that, but you've come to the wrong house."

"I told you he was going to act like this," said Mamma. "I told you so." Then she turned to me. "You talk that way because you're young and full of pride, Danny," she said. "Wait until you're as old as I am and see how much pride you have." Then she began to cry. She said I'd hurt her feelings in front of the charity woman. "God knows," she said, "this is a bitter pill for me to swallow, Danny, but what else can we do? There's just $1.74 in the whole house, and the rent not paid, with the gas sure to be shut off if we don't do something."

I didn't know what to say. I sat down and tried to think of something, but I couldn't. There were one or two women standing in the hall, at our door, listening. I walked over to the door. "Get the hell away from here," I said, "and mind your own business." I slammed the door in their faces, and went into the kitchen and sat down. The charity woman came in and sat down beside me and took my hand in hers. "I'm your friend, Danny," she said. "I want you to think of me as your friend."

"Yeah?" I said.

"Losing your temper won't help matters any," she said. "That won't solve your problems."

I sat there without saying anything.

"Your mother tells me that you're only nineteen years old," she said.

"I'll be twenty in October," I said.

The lady shook her head. "You're too young to try to carry a burden like this. It's too big a load to put on your shoulders. Our organization wants to help worthy cases like you and your mother." I sat there thinking for a few minutes. "All right," I said. "What do you want me to do?"

"Nothing at all," said the lady. "All we ask is that you go on working the best you can and not interfere with the plans your mother and I have made."

"Yeah?" I said. "What plans have you got?"

"Well, in the first place," she said, "we can get your mother work over on the Avenue in a bachelor's apartment. It's hard work, I know, but she's a strong woman, and she's willing to do it. She can earn ten or fifteen dollars a week that way. That'll make all the difference in the world, you'll find."

"Oh, sure," I said. "We thought of that ourselves. That's a fine scheme. But who's going to take care of him while she's away working? Do you want him to fall out of his chair and break his neck, or have another spell with nobody to look out for him?"

The lady took both my hands in hers and held them again. "Now, Danny," she said, "what I'm going to say will hurt you, I know, but we've talked it over and it's the only thing to do. Your father will be better off in an institution."

I took my hands away and sat looking at her. "Say, you're not really figuring on a thing like that?" I asked. "You're not figuring on doing a thing like that to him?"

"It's the only way out," said the lady. "He'll have the proper care and medical attention there. It's the best thing to do."

I got up from my seat. "No," I said. "No." Then Mamma, hearing me talk loud again, came in the kitchen and they both began to work on me. It wasn't fair to Mamma, the lady said, to be tied hand and foot all day. And it wasn't fair to the old man to deprive him of the care and attention which we couldn't give him at home. It wasn't as if he understood things, she said. His mind was completely gone; he was like a little baby; but with care and attention, he might get well again. The charity lady talked that way for a long time while Mamma sat and wrung her hands and said I was insulting her before the lady. I wouldn't listen to them any more. "No," I said. "No."

But the next day it was the same thing all over again. I went on that way for several nights, and then I gave in. I shouldn't have done it; I know that now. But what could I do? I didn't have anybody to talk to. I didn't know which way to turn. The lady said everything was nice at the asylum and that Mamma and me could come over and visit him regular and see for ourselves that he was being treated right. I began to feel very tired after a while. They had me all mixed up. "All right," I said. "All right, then."

I went back to the room. The old man's head had slipped down on the back of his chair. His mouth was half open. I wiped off his face with a towel, and looked in his eyes. They were blue like flowers in a florist shop, but there wasn't any expression in them at all. It was like he was dead and waiting for the undertaker to come. I began to think of what the lady said about him being like a child again. I thought of a lot of things.

Then I took the last dollar we had and went to the speakeasy on the corner and bought a bottle of gin. I stood in a doorway across the street until the social lady came out and got in her car and drove away. When she had gone, I went upstairs and Mamma and me sat in the kitchen drinking. After a while Mamma began to cry again. "I know you think I'm a heartless woman," she said. "I know you blame me for all this. You'll hold it in your heart to your dying day."

"I don't blame you for anything," I said.

"Yes, you do, Danny," she said. "You'll hold it in your heart against me. You know you will. God knows, I tried," she said. "I tried to do the very best I knew how. I defy the Holy Virgin and all the saints in heaven to say I didn't try."

"I know you done what you thought was right," I said. "I know that, Mamma."

But Mamma sat shaking her head. "It won't be bad at all in

the asylum," she said. "The lady says there are lots of green trees all around it. You remember how he liked trees, and how he was always talking about Ireland, and how sweet and green everything was there?"

"All right," I said, "but don't talk about it any more."

Mamma wouldn't stop talking. She poured out another drink from the bottle. "The attendants all wear fresh white uniforms. They don't even let you say the word lunatic there; they refer to them as 'patients' and they take them out for a walk twice every day."

I got up and went into the next room, shutting the door. But Mamma went on and on. I could hear her talking to herself and crying even after I had gone to bed. I thought the gin would make me sleep, but it didn't. I kept remembering one Sunday when I was a little boy, and how the old man took me to Coney for the day. We ate hot dogs and corn on the cob and went in all the side shows. In the afternoon, we went swimming. Gee, we had a good time that Sunday! I went to sleep coming home on the subway and the old man carried me all the way from the station in his arms. The next morning when I woke up I thought I was still at Coney. I kept saying, "Let's go ride on the roller-coaster again!" The old man laughed and laughed. I remembered, too, the time when I was playing ball in Hudson Street with some kids and that truck hit me, breaking my arm, and how the old man sat up with me night after night whittling a boat which he put in a glass bottle for me. Everybody else in the house was asleep except me and the old man. I kept turning about in bed and getting the sheets all knotted up when I remembered those things. "There ought to be some way for us to keep him at home," I thought over and over, but I couldn't think of any way to do it.

That was two weeks ago. Last Saturday the charity lady had all the papers fixed up and signed proper and they came and took him away. I went along with him to see that everything was all right. The old man didn't move an eyelash during the ride. He just sat there, with me holding him up. After awhile, we got to the asylum and it was time for me to go back home and leave him. I went over to tell him good-bye. Then a funny thing happened. I can't be sure of it, even now, but when I took hold of his hand, his eyes seemed to turn in their sockets, his mouth opened and closed a couple of times, and his lids came down slowly. For a second I thought I was going to keel over. The next thing I knew the door had shut and I was outside.

I sat on the steps thinking for awhile. Then I walked down to the office of the head doctor and explained about the old man. I told him the old man was just sick, and not crazy, as they thought. I told him we'd all made a mistake and I was ready to take him back home with me. But the doctor wouldn't even listen when I tried to tell him about the look on the old man's face. "You can see your father any regular visiting day," he kept saying. "No," I said. "No. I'm going to take him home with me." But I couldn't get him out. It takes money and lawyers to do that. What could I do? Answer me that—what could I do?"

Coming back on the ferry I kept seeing that look in his face. "By God, they can't treat me this way!" I thought. "Who do they think they are, to get away with a thing like that? I've got influential friends. There's an old gentleman named Mr. Molloy who rides in my car every day. He always says, 'Good morning,' and 'Good night, Danny,' and asks how I'm feeling. He's rich and he owns a lot of things. I'll bet he owns that asylum, too. I'll bet those doctors would feel pretty cheap if he went over with me on visiting day and said to the head man: 'What the hell are you trying to pull on my friend, Danny? Now, you let this boy take his old man back home, like he wants to, and if I hear any more out of you, I'll fire the whole outfit of you!' "

How do those doctors know the old man is crazy? How can they say what goes on in his mind? Suppose he's got just as much sense as you or me, but can't talk or express himself? Suppose he was trying to let me know that when he moved his lips and closed his eyes. . . . Think of that! What a sweet idea he must have of people right now! What do you suppose he's thinking of right this minute? All right, then, I'll tell you: He's thinking how he worked hard all his life trying to raise a family decently and to pay the rent and buy groceries. And what did he get out of it? Nothing! He's thinking: "It was all right when I got my pay envelope regular. It was all swell then and they pretended to think a lot of me and gave me birthday parties; but the minute I was down and out, and not able to work for them any longer, they put me in this place with a bunch of crazy people." That's what he's thinking about, and he's right.

He's thinking: "I never expected a lot from the rest of the world, but I wouldn't have thought this of Danny. I believed he was different and really cared something about me; but Danny's just a dirty little rat, after all. He's got his hand out like everybody else, I guess!"

"Oh, Christ! Can't you see how it is? Can't you see why I get confused and mixed up and want to bump my head against the side of my car when I think of the old man, and how he sits there all day long with his hands lying loose in his lap? But I know what I'm going to do. I'm going over to see him next Sunday. I'm going to explain the whole thing to him and make him understand how it happened. "Don't you worry," I'm going to say. "I'll get you out of this place; I'm going to take you back home very soon. You'll get well in no time and we'll all be happy again. Don't you worry; leave it all to me. I got influential friends working on your case and we'll have you out of this place before you know it. You just leave everything to old Danny! Don't you worry at all!" That's what I'm going to tell him.

1931

THIS HEAVY LOAD

*I*T WAS a dilapidated brick house, with sagging balconies and rusty, iron grill-work. Mrs. Southworth, the landlady, who was intended by nature to be a bos'n on some sailing vessel, but who, by mistake, had become a woman instead, showed me her vacant room and stood with her hands folded under her apron, her iron jaw clamped down. "All right, find fault with it, and see what happens to you, my fine sailor man!" I imagined her thinking. But when I told her the room would suit very well, and paid her for a week in advance, she became more cordial.

Later she invited me downstairs for a drink. We had three together, and by that time we were excellent friends. She began to tell me about the other people in the house: Across the hall from my room lived a man named Downey, and Mrs. South-worth didn't quite know what to do about him. He hadn't paid her a cent of rent for the past two weeks, since he lost his job, and why she let him stay on was a mystery to her! Only there was something about him, something she couldn't quite under-stand. But what he ate, or how he managed to keep alive, was something she couldn't figure out. He spent all his time sitting by his window, carving on a block of wood, or looking at the river, deep in thought. "If it was *you*, now," she continued, "I'd have you out in the street, bag and baggage, before you knew it, but *this* fellow . . ." She paused and shook her head, as if puzzled.

That night I saw Downey for the first time. He came out of his room as I was coming up the stairs, a paper parcel in his hand from which minute shavings were spilling. His skin was porcelain-like in its dry brittleness, and his eyes were sunken. The lines in his cheeks and in his forehead were so deep they seemed cut there with a knife. When I passed him on the stairs, he stopped and held on to the banisters for support. Then I spoke to him, and he looked up quickly and stared into my eyes; and I understood why even a realist as hard and as unimaginative as Mrs. Southworth couldn't throw him out. There was the same eagerness in his eyes that you see occasionally in the eyes of a dog mourning for his lost master. I looked at the lined face and his full, sensuous mouth for a moment. I said: "I understand we are neighbors. I've just taken the room across the hall until my ship is ready. I'll be glad to have you come in and talk to me sometime."

"Thanks very much," he said gravely. That's all there was; he didn't commit himself one way or the other. As I went to my room, I saw him still standing there by the banisters watching me. A few nights later he did come to my room. He sat in my one chair, without movement. He seemed even frailer and more exhausted than when I first saw him. I took out a bottle of whiskey from my bag and offered him a drink. He shook his head. "There's no answer in that," he said; "there's no comfort there."

"Well, maybe not," I replied; "but it'll warm up your belly nicely."

Then, somehow, I began to talk to him about my early life. I talked simply, without pose or affectation. For some reason I put myself out to please him. He listened gravely, sympathetically. When I had finished, he in turn began to talk about himself. He came of well-to-do people, I think. At any rate he had gone to college and had got his degree. The next year he returned to his hometown and married the girl he had loved since boyhood. Then war had been declared and he wanted to enlist. There had been a scene with his wife when he signed up at the recruiting station: He was married with a wife and two babies to look out for; there was no reason for him going to France. Leave that to men without obligations! But he had gone anyway. He didn't know why; he simply knew that he must go. He had come through the fighting without injury; or rather he came through without bodily injury, but what he had experienced and what he had seen shocked him profoundly. He must have been an idealistic, highly emotional man with little actual knowledge of the world.

He did not tell me all this in its proper sequence, of course. It came out by fragments which I pieced together in my mind later on. As he talked I kept looking at his strange face and tried to find a word or a phrase which would describe it, but I could not. "Austerely sensual," was as close as I could come, but that, I realized, was pompous and high-flown; and it was not quite what I wanted, anyway. But Downey was talking again in his somewhat hoarse and somewhat hesitant voice.

"When I got back home, I felt that the end of the world had come, and that I was left alive by accident," he was saying. "I kept thinking that all the time. I had been sure, once, of what was evil and what was good, but I knew, now, that those things were only words, meaningless in themselves and taking significance from other words equally meaningless and equally subject to change. I was lost in a strange world that frightened me."

As Downey talked, I could imagine his efforts to readjust himself. He had hoped when he was discharged that a return to normal life would solve his problems, but he found very soon that that was impossible. He had nothing in common with his wife any more; the deep sense of understanding which had existed between them was gone. He began actually to hate her for what he considered her smug sense of right and wrong, her constant talk of religion. He got so he couldn't stand the sight of his children either. An overpowering feeling of restlessness came over him.

One night his wife got him to go to church with her. It was the first time he had been in a church since he had enlisted. He sat in his pew, slightly sickened, not believing any man could be as harsh and as stupid as the minister seemed. Then he got up, walked out of the church and went back home. When his wife arrived half an hour later she found him in their living-room swinging an ax, smashing the furniture to bits. That same night Downey went to a friend of his, a lawyer, deeded everything he owned to his wife and children and left town.

As Downey told me his story, all jumbled up and not in its

proper order, as I'm telling it to you, his voice was without emotion, and his body was quiet. Occasionally he moved his hand backward and forward on the arm of the chair, and occasionally he wet his full, sensual lips. Then suddenly he lowered his eyes. We sat there in silence, neither looking at the other. I offered him a cigarette, which he took. From the way he sucked it into his lungs I knew it was the first smoke he had had for a long time. I thought it better neither to offer comment on what he had told me, nor to ask him to continue. A few minutes later he got up and went back to his room.

After that, Downey came to see me often. He never talked so freely as he had the first time, but in the next week he did tell me a great deal about himself: After he had left his wife (he had never seen her since, and he had no wish to see either her or his children), he had gone to Chicago and had got a job as motorman on a streetcar. At night he went to the public libraries and took out books, books on philosophy and religion mostly, but he could find nothing in them that he wanted. Then —Downey thought this himself—he became slightly insane. He began writing obscene pamphlets in which he proved that there was no God; that there could be no God. Later on, he went to New York and worked in a restaurant as a dishwasher. At night he read or wrote his rambling, profane pamphlets. Occasionally he would talk to late-comers in the restaurant, trying to convince them, as he had convinced himself, that the skies were empty. But the taxi-drivers or the workmen to whom he talked laughed at him and tapped their foreheads.

From New York he drifted to Philadelphia, where he remained for a few weeks. But his restlessness came over him again. He had been in Omaha, New Orleans, Detroit, Denver, St. Louis, Kansas City and Seattle within a short time, but he remembered nothing of those places except the various furnished rooms he had lived in, and even they, because of their lack of individuality, had gradually merged in his mind into one composite room. Many times he could not find work, and more often than not he was hungry, but something inside him impelled him constantly forward. He did not know what he was seeking, or even that he was seeking anything. He simply knew when the impulse came over him that he must get away.

As he talked in my room, he could not remember the names of some of the cities where he had been. He would refer, often, to places as "where the man in the United Cigar store had a gold tooth in front," or, "where the landlady was in mourning for her daughter," identifying an entire community with one of its members.

As the years went by, he found it more and more difficult to get work. Then, too, he had started to drink pretty heavily. In Cleveland, Ohio, he met a waitress and they lived together for a time—not more than a month or so, I gathered—but he had left her, too. She had really loved him, he was sure, and he might have been happy with her, but when the urge to run away came over him he could not resist it.

Later, in Detroit, a man in a rooming-house started him using drugs, and after that his descent had been swift. He had quit reading. He had quit thinking. He worked when he could get work and stole or begged when he couldn't. There was nothing that he hadn't done, he told me, no degradation that he hadn't experienced. He told me these things quietly, without self-consciousness and without shame, as if he were speaking clinically about another person whom we both understood.

The drugs-and-drinking period had lasted about three years, he thought, and then one morning in Frisco, in an agony of disgust with himself, he had signed as a seaman on a sailing vessel. His going to sea was not premeditated. He did it on impulse, without thought. He felt, dimly, that he might find in a foreign country what he had looked for and been unable to find in America. He did not find it, of course, but the trip improved his health, and when he returned to the United States, six months later, his desire for drugs had left him. After that he had gone to sea regularly for a few years, but he rarely made two voyages in the same steamer.

Then, finally, he had been unable to get a ship at all, but he managed to keep himself alive by doing odd jobs around the docks. Later he got a job as delivery boy for a grocery store. It was while he was so employed that he came to live in Mrs. Southworth's dingy rooming-house, about a month before I met him.

He told me all this over a period of days.

"What is it you want?" I asked. "What are you looking for?"

"I don't know," he said. "I wish to God I did know. If I knew that, I could lay down this heavy load and rest."

We sat smoking quietly. We had come to the point where we would sit quiet together for long periods. "Where did you learn wood-carving?" I asked casually. He looked at me, but he did not answer. "Mrs. Southworth told me that you were carving a block of wood," I continued, "and of course I saw you taking out those shavings that night."

His lips opened and he seemed on the point of telling me something, but he changed his mind. "I'll be going now," he said. When he reached the door he turned and came back to me: "You're not offended, are you?"

"Of course, I'm not," I answered; "why, of course, I'm not." Then he went out. "He'll tell me about the carving later, when he is ready to do it," I decided. I was correct, for sure enough he did tell me. My ship was out of drydock by that time and was going on loading-berth the next day. It was my last night in Mrs. Southworth's establishment, and my bag was almost packed when Downey rapped on my door. It was January, and the weather was cold. Outside a mist-like rain was falling. The wind flung the chill rain against my window in intermittent rushes, like the brushing of leaves.

I opened the door and Downey entered. I stood gaping, amazed at the change that had come over him. His step was brisk and his eyes were shining. He seemed to have dropped his sickness, his hunger and his despair like a shabby coat. There was a buoyancy, a joyousness about him that I could not understand, and which I was not prepared for. When he came into my room, his shoulders were straight and there was color in his lined, haggard face. He kept moving about and touching things with a surprised delight. His clothes were soaked, and I could see the raindrops clinging to his frail neck and chest, but he seemed unaware of the cold, as if there were something within that warmed him. He sat back in my chair and laughed deeply, the contented laugh of a happy man—it was the most restful sound I have ever heard—and began to talk slowly, trying to find words simple enough to describe his happiness. He raised his hands and brought the blunt tips of his fingers together.

"I have found what I have been seeking!" he said. "I have put down my load!"

For awhile he talked incoherently, but gradually I began to follow his sentences, and piece out his story. It was while working as a delivery boy for the grocery store, before I met him, that he had picked up a block of wood. He had been taking a walk along the bay front that Sunday afternoon, and he saw the block on the dirty beach, just out of reach of the tide. The wood was a golden brown color, and unlike any wood he had ever seen. Apparently it had grown in a far country and had been thrown overboard from some ship by a sailor. When Downey picked up the block and turned it over and over in his hands, he saw that the wood was strangely grained, and, as he examined it, he thought he could detect in its looped and whirled surface the outline of a head. When he discovered that, he sat down and began to trace with the blade of his pocketknife the figure in the wood.

He sat flat on the dirty sand, the block resting between his legs, and worked slowly. Before him was the bay and a small beach littered with driftwood, tin cans and grapefruit rinds, while behind him, somewhere in the distance, a switch engine was spotting cars of freight for a steamer working overtime. The rhythmical bumping of the cars as the engine hit them and shoved them forward, came muffled and uncertain, and more and more indistinct, until, at last, the sound lost its meaning for Downey and became the booming of surf a long way off. And as he continued to work, the dirty beach disappeared also, and another and an older scene superimposed itself. This is the way Downey described the change to me:

"As I sat there carving on the block, I thought of myself not as a middle-aged delivery boy for a cheap grocery store, but as

a naked brown man who had crawled out of the protection of
his jungle for the first time to stare in amazement at the sea.
Behind me stretched hot, misty swamps with purple and red
flowers, larger than a man's head, swinging like bells from the
trees. Birds, colored unbelievably, were screaming always on
one persistent note, flapping back and forth between the ancient
trees, or resting, balanced on the swinging lianas, their wings half
flushed and ready for flight. Ferns grew as tall as cliffs, and there
was a rich mist hanging over everything. And as I sat there
looking into that jungle, a strange thing happened to me. I lost
all sense of time and space and even of my own identity. I seemed
so completely a part of the background I visioned. I could see
my own body sitting there—a little, patient, brown man, making
a god from a piece of curiously grained wood.

"Later, when it became dark, I returned to my room, carrying the block with me, stroking it with my hands. I had become
obsessed with the block; so much so that on the following morning, when it was time to go to the grocery store, I found that
I could not. I really made an effort to go out of the room and
leave the figure which was taking shape under my hands, but it
was impossible."

That had been three weeks ago and since then Downey had
worked patiently. He knew nothing of wood-carving, he told
me, and he had no tools to work with except his knife and a
crude scraper which he had made out of a safety razor blade.

At first Downey had been somewhat ashamed of what he
was doing, but as he continued to work the idea gradually took
a firm hold on him. "Why shouldn't I make a god of my own?"
he asked. "Why not? I could not accept the gods of other people." His eyes closed and his lips pressed forward with a faint
quiver, as if recently touched, in love, by other and unseen lips.
"What was there absurd about that?" he asked. He sat in his
dark room hour after hour carving and whispering to himself.
"I am creating a god of compassion and tenderness. I am not
making him all-wise or all-just or all-powerful. I am creating
an eager god who loves joy, laughter and dancing; not cruelty,
not bloodshed. 'Sing!' he says. 'Sing and love and dance, for the

world is a beautiful place and life is something strange which passes quickly!' "

Downey continued to talk, a slight, self-deprecatory smile on his lips. I did not interrupt him. There was nothing that I could say, after all. Suddenly he got up and raised his arms above his head in a gesture of complete adoration.

"Today I completed the figure and polished it with oil until it shone like a rich lamp in my room. I stood there looking at it. It was not a very good carving, but I had made it, I alone, and I loved it! Then I began to feel half ashamed because it had taken such a hold on my thoughts. I put the figure on the table in my room, and stood aside to examine it critically, with half-closed eyes; but before I understood what was happening, I found myself on my knees before it, my head thrown back, my hands pressed together, rocking from side to side. Words came tumbling out of me, words which I had not used for a long time: 'Lord! Lord!' I prayed. 'Heal me! Save me! Make me whole!'

"Then an essence flowed through my body. I could feel it moving about in my veins, washing me clean. I could feel tight things, buried in my body for a long time, being loosened and untied by the essence and smoothed flat again. My flesh tingled with a new life. Then, as the essence surged back and forth through me, like a river, all grief, disgust and shame were washed away, and a feeling of rest such as I had never before known came over me. I knelt before the figure for a long time, at peace, my heart swelling with joy and love as if it would burst through my side."

Downey got up and walked to my window and stared for a time at the river, seen indistinctly through the rain. It was still blowing, and gusts of wind swept the rain against my window with a faint sound, like thrown sand. He stood there, silent, watching the rain swirling over the river, watching the lines of black smoke from factories breaking under the force of the wind and coming together again. Then, after awhile, he began to talk in his joyous, new voice:

"A long time afterwards, I got up from my knees and went

out and walked in the rain. I had forgotten how beautiful red brick could be, or the way wet asphalt reflected in a shallower world the things that surrounded it. I wanted to touch everything with my hands: the red bricks, the iron posts, the rough bark of trees. I wanted to feel everything, see everything, and hear everything again. And so I walked in the streets for hours, surprised that the world was so much lovelier than I had thought it; watching the way a tree bent against the wind, the shape of a cloud scurrying across the sky, or raindrops congealing and dripping slowly from the end of a green blind. Somewhere during my walk a woman came to a window and said to someone else within: 'Get the blue; blue wears longer.'

"As I walked the streets, I kept turning those words over and over in my mind. To me they possessed a beauty not of this world, a significance beyond the stretch of our dull senses." Downey laughed joyously and pressed his hands together. "Do you understand what I'm trying to tell you?" he asked.

"Yes," I said.

He was silent for a moment and then he continued: "Later on, I saw a man walking toward me. He was an old Negro, and he carried a sack filled with junk slung across his shoulders. I went over to him, to help him with his load, but he pulled away, as if I meant to rob him. I had wanted to tell him about my new happiness, and to share it with him, but when he pulled away, I saw how wrong I was. That was the mistake people had always made. I knew, then, that I must never show my god to anybody or even speak his name to another."

Again Downey walked in my small room. "I'm so happy," he said; "so perfectly happy. Nothing can ever touch me again. Nothing! Pain, hunger, old age, death—they're meaningless words, now! They're nothing to me at all!" Then he lifted his enraptured eyes and stared into the sky at a vision which I could not follow.

I got up and began to finish my packing, looking occasionally at Downey standing by the window, watching his exalted face. And I knew, then, for the first time that man is not yet a completed thing; that he is only part of other things which he cannot

name and which he but dimly understands. He must have a
master if he is to have peace, and if he loses one, he will not
rest until he has found another. He talks eternally about freedom,
but he can never be free, for he is a frail, lost creature, too weak
as yet to walk unaided.

I closed my seabag and snapped the lock, saddened all at once
because these things were true.

1931

MR. EDWARDS' BLACK EYE

*W*HEN Mr. Edwards, Sales Manager of the Goliath Feather and Trinket Company, returned home from his spring visit to the trade, he reported at once to the President of his company, Mr. Shaddock. It was not quite ten o'clock in the morning, but already Mr. Shaddock's soft, corrugated paunch was littered with pipe ashes and the chewed fragments of toothpick; and when he saw Mr. Edwards standing there beside his desk, he laughed suddenly and leaned back in his swivel chair, the bits of toothpick bouncing up and down to the rhythm of his mirth.

"Who hung the shiner on you, Earle?" he asked. "What was the fellow's name, and how did you happen to get in an argument?"

Mr. Edwards seemed determined to ignore his black eye, for he said casually: "Mr. Shaddock, I finished up my trip in New York City, like we planned. I made some new contacts there that ought to be valuable later on, but I think we better stop doing business with the Three Novelteers. I don't seem to have the same degree of confidence in their manager, Milton Holzheimer, that I used to have."

"Tell me about it later on," said Mr. Shaddock. "What I want to know right now is who hung the shiner on you."

Mr. Edwards was silent for a moment, then he sighed, touched his bruise, and spoke in a soft, resigned voice. "Well, you see, Mr. Shaddock, it was this way," he said. "Milton Holzheimer asked me to dinner one night, and I said I'd like to take in this Greenwich Village you hear so much about; so he took me to a place he knew. It was in a basement, and there was a little dance floor in the middle. At the back there was a bar where you could get what you wanted to drink." He paused and stared at his shoes, his round, innocent face pink with embarrassment.

"Don't stop at this point, Earle! What happened later?"

"This restaurant catered to all sorts of peculiar-looking people, Mr. Shaddock, but I guess you know how I am. I say when you're in another man's town, you might as well take things the way they are and not ask questions; so Milton and I had dinner and three or four drinks. We had just finished coffee and were getting ready to light our cigars when I saw two girls get up from their table and start dancing together. One of those girls was mighty pretty to look at, Mr. Shaddock!"

"I see now," said Mr. Shaddock. "Everything is falling into place."

"Mr. Shaddock," said Earle earnestly, "when two girls dance together in public, what does it mean?"

"It means they want a couple of the boys to come to their rescue and cut in on them, and that's what usually happens, too, if they're not *too* homely."

"That's what I said to Milton Holzheimer, Mr. Shaddock. I said they wanted somebody to cut in on them, and I aimed to be the one that did it this time. But Milton just raised his eyebrows and looked at me in a funny way."

"You said one of the girls was pretty. What was the other one like, Earle?"

"Mr. Shaddock, that other girl was big and sort of rangy, and she didn't take any pride at all in her appearance. She had a bartender haircut, and she wore a man's coat. When she walked, she swaggered like she owned the place."

"That's the way it generally is," said Mr. Shaddock, nodding wisely. "Find me a real pretty girl, and I'll find you her homely friend not a block away."

"Anyway, when I suggested to Milton that he and I cut in, and he didn't take kindly to the suggestion, I said that if he wanted the pretty one, I'd take the other, and we could swap over next time. Milton only shook his head, though, and said, 'Take my advice and don't interfere in situations of this kind.'"

Mr. Shaddock filled his pipe and said: "I know; you didn't pay any attention to him. You went over to these girls, stopped them and asked the pretty one to dance. Then you turned and said to the big girl, 'But don't you feel slighted. I'll be back for you next time.'"

"It was something of that sort, Mr. Shaddock. Maybe not the exact words, but you got the general idea. So this big, burly girl stuck out her jaw and told me to mind my own business. 'If you wanted a girl, why didn't you bring one with you?' she said."

"I see the whole thing," said Mr. Shaddock. "You kept insisting, and so the ladies called the bouncer, and he gave you the black eye. Correct me if I'm wrong."

"You're way off, Mr. Shaddock. It wasn't the bouncer that hit me. It was the lady herself that did it. First, she pushed on my chest and said, 'Go on! Mind your own business, can't you!' But I didn't like to be put off that way, not with everybody looking at me and snickering, so I slipped my arm around the little girl's waist and said, 'Come on! Let's dance this one!' And just about that time, the big girl landed a sock on my jaw."

"What was the pretty girl doing all that time?"

"Mr. Shaddock, I hate to say it, but when the big one jumped me, the pretty girl laughed like the whole thing was very amusing and said, 'Hit him again, Tommy! Hit him harder next time!'"

"Another thing I never liked is women that call themselves by men's names," said Mr. Shaddock. "I never considered it attractive."

"So the big girl hauls off and socks me a couple of times more, like her friend suggested. She did it so quick that I must have been caught off balance. Anyway, I fell over a table where people were sitting and hit my head. That's what really knocked me out. I don't believe any woman could hit me hard enough to knock me out, so it must have been the bump on the table that did it."

"I never liked to have women hit me," said Mr. Shaddock. "I don't approve of it."

"Well, I guess that's about all there is to the story," said Earle, "but I hope you won't spread it around the office, Mr. Shaddock. I told you because I felt you had a right to know, and anyway Milton Holzheimer is sure to mention it to you sooner or later."

"If it had been me that got socked," said Mr. Shaddock, "I'd have socked the lady right back. I'd have taught her a little lesson."

"No, Mr. Shaddock, I don't blame the lady at all in this instance. Of course I did at first, particularly when Milton took me home in a cab and laughed at me all the way, like the thing was a joke. But later on I got to thinking, and now I see the error of my ways. You see, I'd always heard that New York was sort of loose when it came to morality. That was my mistake, and I'm man enough to admit it. My intentions toward the young lady were honorable, I can assure you; but her companion didn't know that; and so I say she had every right to protect her little friend, and that I got what was coming to me."

Mr. Shaddock nodded gravely. "Maybe the girls were sisters," he said. "Maybe the big one had promised her mother that she'd look out for her little sister."

"Yes, sir," said Earle, hanging his head. "I think maybe you've hit on the real solution. The more I think about it now, the more clearly I see how bad I acted. It's a hard thing to say, but I realize now that the girl who socked me has more real reverence for womanhood than I do."

He lifted his head and stared miserably out of the window, his face and neck turning red. There was a silence, and then Mr. Shaddock swung forward in his chair, shuffled the papers before him, and said: "That's all water over the dam, Earle. . . . Now, tell me about the Midtown Novelty and Paper people. They're into us plenty, and I've been holding up their last shipment until I could get a report from you on their financial set-up."

1932

UPON THE DULL EARTH DWELLING

*H*E SHOVED through the gates an instant before the guards closed them and men were unmooring the ferry as he stepped aboard. He pressed forward toward her bow and stood there. Behind him, on the shore that he was leaving, lights were being turned off in buildings; before him was New Jersey, seen dimly through smoke. The ferry cut a precise angle athwart the dirty river, in which floated pieces of waxed paper and bits of broken wood. The mist penetrated the texture of his worn overcoat and he was suddenly cold. He folded his arms across his chest. He raised his head and looked at the sky. Above him, against the diffused last light of the sun, a sea gull, with hard, knowing eyes, turned sidewise and circled with exact grace.

He dreaded going home. There was going to be another scene with Jeanette; that was inevitable. He had a picture of her sullen, angry face and remembered the full flavor of her bitterness. Unconsciously he pressed backward, crowding the people behind him. It had all started that morning at breakfast. The children had finished and had gone into the next room to get ready for school when the telephone rang. Jeanette answered it. When she returned to the table, the sullen look was in her eyes. "It was Belle Payne. She called up to say Fred's had another raise from his firm. They've made him assistant manager now."

"Well," said Roy, "I think that's fine. It's a good break for Fred."

"You think it's fine, do you?" answered Jeanette. She got up and walked to the stove and poured herself a cup of coffee. "You sit there and think it's fine," she continued, as if the sentence held some obscure meaning. "Well, why don't you get a raise sometime?"

"Fred's in a business that's making money," said Roy. "You don't hear of anybody in the freight brokerage business making money, though."

Jeanette sat down at the table and shoved back her plate. "Always an excuse! Always something!"

"I'm lucky to have a job at all with things the way they are."

"You're afraid of everything," said Jeanette. "You're afraid of your own shadow."

"I'm not afraid for myself," said Roy. "It's you and the children I'm afraid for." Jeanette shook back the strands of hair that fell into her eyes and rested her rough, manlike hands on the table before her. Slowly her face got red. "Always an excuse," she said. "Always something."

Roy sat there for a moment, hurt before his wife's scorn, ashamed of his own inadequacy. Then some of Jen's indignation communicated itself to him. "By God, you're right!" he said. "I won't stand it any longer! I'll see old Reddick first thing this morning and make him give me more money!" He got up briskly and walked to the door. Jeanette walked with him and stood holding his coat. "Hurry up," she said; "you'll miss the 8:30 ferry."

But now as Roy stood at the bow of the boat watching the slow patterns of the gull he regretted his promise. He had regretted it even before he reached his office that morning. Suppose instead of giving him a raise the old man should tell him to look for another position? What would they do then? The more he thought about it the more frightened he became. By ten o'clock the idea had become preposterous; at twelve o'clock he was thankful he had any job at all.

As the ferry reached the Jersey shore and bumped into its berth he began to feel humble and slightly ashamed of himself. When he and Jeanette had married they had planned many things: a house of their own in the suburbs; good schools for the children, when they came along; long automobile trips over week-ends. But he knew now that none of those things would ever be possible for them.

The guards unsnapped the chains and opened the gates and

the people behind him shoved him forward on to the dock. He stood there for a moment perplexed and unhappy, jostled by the crowd, then he walked through the station and climbed aboard a waiting streetcar.

When he reached home Jeanette was putting supper on the table. The children were sitting around the lamp studying their lessons. There were three Newberry children. Junior, the eldest, was eleven. Then came Harriet, who was eight. The baby of the family was Silvia. She was three, and she was her father's delight. She was a plain child with limp, finely spun hair and round, wide-opened eyes. But to Roy she was beautiful. The two elder children looked up without curiosity when he entered and then returned to their books, but Silvia ran toward him, flinging her arms about his legs and dancing up and down in her excitement. He picked her up and held her tightly, their cheeks pressed together.

"O-o-o! Gee!" said Silvia. "You tickle, pop!"

Jeanette came in with a dish in her hand and began arranging the table. "Supper'll be ready in a minute," she said.

As Roy watched her, remembering the pretty, animated girl she had once been, a feeling of tenderness came over him. He put Silvia down and walked toward her, touching her hand with clumsy affection. But Jeanette drew away from him.

"Hurry and get washed up," she said impatiently. "You're late now."

The children were already seated at the table when he returned. Jeanette began to dish out the food and Roy remembered suddenly about the raise. He had forgotten it for a moment. He looked into his wife's eyes, but he could read nothing there. "Maybe she's forgotten all about it," he thought; "maybe she didn't take me seriously." But almost immediately he knew that she had not forgotten. Without raising her eyes she spoke through tight lips: "Did you take care of that matter we talked about this morning?"

Roy looked significantly at the children. "We'll talk about that later," he said quietly. His appetite had somehow disappeared. He made an effort at eating, but he could not. Silvia put down her spoon and looked at him. "What's the matter, pop? You're not eating supper."

"I'm not hungry, sweetheart."

Later he sat under the light with Silvia sitting on his lap, her head resting against his shoulder, while he turned the pages of an illustrated magazine and explained the pictures to her. On the other side of the table Jeanette was sewing on school dresses for Harriet. She peered at the cloth with her nearsighted eyes. A moment later she put up her hand, shielding her face from the light.

"You ought to get your glasses fixed," said Roy. "There's no sense in straining your eyes that way."

"Where would I get the money for new glasses?" asked Jeanette bitterly. "You don't think the man is going to give them to me, do you?"

"I think we can get them fixed, all right."

"It's all very well for you to say that," said Jeanette. "You can always suggest something to buy, but you can't ever say where the money's coming from, I notice." She turned away, her lips drawn down. For a time they sat silent and then Jeanette got up. "Come on, Junior! You and Harriet both! It's time for you to go to bed. If you haven't learned your lessons by now you never will."

Silvia was already asleep against her father's shoulder. In her dreams she raised one hand and placed it against his mouth. He pressed his lips forward, kissing her open palm, and Silvia smiled a little. Her eyelids fluttered and she sighed and relaxed into deeper unconsciousness. Roy lowered her to his lap, away from the light, and looked at her young, delicate face. At first they had not wanted Silvia. She had been unexpected and she had upset their plans; now her father could not contemplate an existence without her. Jeanette had wanted to name her Agatha, for an aunt who might be expected to do something for them later on, but Roy would not listen to it. He had insisted without explanation that the baby be called Silvia and in the end he had had his way. He had never told this to anyone, but when

he and Jeanette were courting they had gone one night to a
vaudeville show. Late in the program a woman in black velvet
had come on the stage. She was very famous, according to the
program. She sang a few arias in a contralto voice, and then, as
an encore, she had stood in the center of the stage and had sung,
very simply and without accompaniment:

> Who is Silvia? What is she
> That all our swains commend her?
> Holy, fair and wise is she,
> The Heavens such grace did lend her . . .

At her words Roy had closed his eyes. The theater and the
crowds faded away and he saw a cool glen pied with sunlight
in which youths and maidens rested or sang songs. Where the
glen opened, a field of green oats began; beyond that stood a
pavilion of silk, and in it a princess lay sleeping. Then Roy saw
himself among the swains. He was dressed in a golden doublet
and crimson tights and he wore shoes of pure silver. He saw
himself approach the couch and stare in wonder at the princess
who looked so strangely like Jeanette. With his eyes still closed
he had reached out at that moment and taken Jeanette's hand and
held it. It was then that he knew for certain that there was a
common destiny for him and Jen which they could never escape.

As he thought of these old things he smiled to himself and
rocked Silvia back and forth. He touched her limp hair, and a
feeling of tenderness came over him. Silvia must always be happy
and sweet and beautiful. Her life must be rich in beauty and
love. She was so gentle and so lovely.

He started to hum under his breath.

> Then to Silvia let us sing
> For Silvia is exceling;
> She excels each mortal thing
> Upon the dull earth dwelling . . .

When Jeanette returned to the room he was still humming.
He got up at once and put Silvia's limp form into his wife's
arms. But Jen set her down on the floor and shook her until

her eyes opened. "You're getting too big to be treated like a baby any longer. Now you go to bed, miss!"

Silvia rubbed her sleepy eyes. A smile came on her lips. "Good night, pop!" She looked at her father with sweet, shallow eyes, colored like oak leaves.

"Good night, sweetheart! Good night! Good night!"

Roy sat rustling his paper, reading a paragraph here and there. He was still turning the pages when his wife re-entered the room. She sat down opposite him. "Well," said Jeanette. "Did you get your raise?"

"No," said Roy.

Jeanette put her hands on the arms of her chair. "They treat you like a dog, if you had sense enough to realize it! You work and slave and what do we get out of it?" She began to smile with her tight, furious lips.

"So he wouldn't give it to you," she continued. "He begrudged you that, did he? There he is living in luxury, and we're starving to death." Jeanette's face became redder. "I'd like to tell him what I think of him!" she said. "I'd like to tell him where to get off!" Her voice was getting steadily louder. Then, in the middle of a sentence, she became silent. She got up and walked heavy-footed toward the telephone and began turning the leaves of the directory.

"What are you going to do, Jen?"

"I'm going to call up Mr. Reddick and tell him what I think of him. I'm going to have that satisfaction if it's the last thing I ever do in this world!"

Roy came up to her quickly. "No," he said. "No."

He caught her by the arms, but she struggled in his grip. "I'm going to tell him! I'm going to speak my little piece for once."

Roy released her. He looked down at the floor, a shamed expression on his face. "I didn't ask him for a raise," he said. "I didn't do it."

Jeanette stared in amazement, her mouth open. Roy continued rapidly. "Suppose I'd asked him and he'd told me to look for another job? You don't know how hard times are right now. You don't realize how many men are out of work, Jen."

But Jeanette interrupted him. "You didn't ask him?" she repeated incredulously. "He stands there and says he didn't even *ask* him!"

"Now, Jen. Now, Jen."

"You're a fine one to call yourself a man! You're a fine one to be the head of a family!"

"Now, Jen!" he said.

"You didn't even ask for a raise! Oh, no. You'd rather let your wife work her fingers to the bone!"

"Jeanette, please!" he said. "The children can hear you."

"Let them hear me; it won't be any news to them. They know what sort of a man you are." He took her by the shoulders, trying to quiet her, but at his touch she began to cry and throw her arms about.

"Jeanette, don't—" he whispered.

Outside he heard a door slam and then stealthy footfalls. That meant the people across the hall were listening again. Almost immediately the tenants upstairs began to beat on their water pipes. But Jeanette paid no attention to these interruptions. She went on and on and on, her voice trembling and hysterical.

Roy's face twisted and his eyebrows drew together. "I'm doing the very best that I know how," he said.

He put on his hat and his threadbare overcoat and opened the door. In the hall there was a group of neighbors who had been listening to the scene. Roy looked at them for a moment, his face white, his hands trembling. He walked quickly down the steps. In the unlighted doorway a girl with cheap furs was leaning against a young sailor, their lips pressed together as if they never meant to take them away. Farther down the street the lights of an all-night lunchroom shone out on the sidewalk. A streetcar without passengers went clanging past.

Roy buttoned his overcoat and shoved his hands more deeply into his pockets. He walked a long time aimlessly, unaware of where he was going, but finally he came to the cut through which the railroad tracks ran. Below him the station was dimly lighted. On the platform were two men and a woman waiting for trains. They stood there dejectedly, yawning at intervals.

When Roy saw a train approaching, he slid down the bank upon impulse and walked toward the tracks. "It'll be over in a second," he thought. "There can't be much pain. It'll happen too quickly." He closed his eyes, set his jaw, and tried to step forward in front of the train. But something held him and he could not do it. He walked up the stairs and over the bridge which led to the street.

Presently he saw a door open and two men came reeling out. Without any definite plan he entered and went up to the bar. The place was almost deserted. He put fifty cents on the counter before him and ordered whisky. He drank it quickly, shuddering a little. Then he drank two more. The whisky settled his stomach and in a few minutes he felt warmth flow through his body.

He began to feel exhilarated and talkative. He invited the bartender to join him in a drink.

"What line are you in?" asked the bartender.

"I'm in the freight brokerage business."

"That's a good business if it's worked right."

"There's not much in it now, though," said Roy. "It's all shot to pieces."

"It's the same with my business," said the bartender, nodding his head. "It's all shot, too. We don't get the fine class of people we used to, no more." Roy did not answer. "Let's have another drink!" he said a moment later. His tongue was already getting a little thick.

"Put up your money," said the bartender. "This one's on the house."

"All right," said Roy. "The next one will be on me." He raised his glass. "Here's to better times and happier days!" The bartender touched his glass. "Okay!" he answered.

A new customer came in and the bartender left Roy to serve him. The new customer and the bartender seemed to be good friends. The bartender called him Sam in a familiar manner. Sam began a funny story. When he had finished Roy threw back his head and laughed loudly.

"Say, that's an old one!" said the bartender, laughing also. "Get an earful of this one!"

He, too, told a story and then everybody had drinks all around. Roy felt better than he had in months. He began to boast slightly, to talk of his work at the office. The bartender listened politely, but Sam became restive. "Don't talk shop, old man!" he said. "It isn't good form. You must really do something about your manners." Then he said, laughing thickly: "I'll buy another drink. Who has any objections to offer to that?"

"I have," said Roy. "It's my turn to buy." But Sam was insistent. A hurt look came into his face. "What's the matter with my money?" he demanded. "Do you think my money's no good?"

"I'll tell you boys the best way to work that," said the bartender tactfully. "Sam, you buy this gentleman's drink, and this gentleman buys your drink!"

"That's the way to work it," said Roy. Then he added in a puzzled manner: "But who buys your drink?"

"I'm taking a rain check," said the bartender.

Sam came over and put his arm around Roy's waist, swaying back and forth unsteadily on his legs. "What's your name?" he asked.

"Roy Newberry."

Sam turned and addressed the bartender: "I want to apologize to Mr. Newberry for hurting his feelings. I wouldn't do that for the world with a fence around it."

"We know that, Sam," said the bartender gently. "This gentleman's not insulted."

"Yes, he is," said Sam. He put his head on the counter and began to cry softly. "You all think my money's no good!" he said over and over.

"Come on, Sam!" said Roy. "Come on. Buy me all the drinks you want to!" His head was reeling and he began to lose, at intervals, a sense of his identity, or a consciousness of where he was. He had his drink with Sam, returning the courtesy a few minutes later. The bartender bought another drink and it was Roy's turn again. But when he reached for his glass he stumbled and almost fell. He held himself upright by grasping the edge of the bar and squinted his eyes. The bartender's face seemed twisted out of shape and his features melted and ran together. "If a man works hard for his family, it's not right to blame him if—if . . ." He held on to the bar, swaying back and forth. His words were flat and without resonance. He had a feeling that he, himself, was not talking; that somebody behind him was saying the words he heard.

"Oh, for Christ's sake!" said Sam. "Can't you think about anything else?"

"If a man tries the best he can," continued Roy; "if he does the very best he knows how . . ." He looked about him vaguely. "If he does that, he shouldn't be—he shouldn't be—" He withdrew his hands from the rail and stood upright, and almost immediately the bar began to spin. The next thing he knew the bartender was bending over him, slapping him smartly on the cheeks. Roy opened his eyes. Sam had gone and the bartender was yawning.

"It's three o'clock," said the bartender. "We're closing up."

"I don't care," said Roy. "Go ahead and close."

But the bartender and another man, whom he had not previously seen, jerked him upward, and in a moment he felt cold air in his face. "You better go on home to the missus," said the bartender.

"I'll bet she gives you hell!" said the second man, laughing.

"All right," said Roy.

The cold air steadied him somewhat, but he was still not entirely sure of his directions. He staggered about for a long time, and then, finally, he found himself facing the all-night lunchstand which indicated the beginning of his block. A few minutes later he opened the street door and climbed the stairs, holding on for support. He found the key, at last, and came into the living room and began taking off his shoes; but the effort was too much for him and he fell onto the couch.

He was still resting that way when Jeanette came into the room and began to shake him. "It's seven-thirty," she said. "You'd better get up and eat your breakfast or you'll be late for work." Roy turned over and opened his eyes. Somebody had removed his coat and shoes during the night and covered him with a blanket. He sat up on the sofa, feeling sick and miserable, and rubbed his hands over his face. He tried to stand up, but the room began to spin and his stomach lurched upward and turned over. He walked to the bathroom and closed the door. His face was gray and he was trembling when he came out. He lay stretched on the sofa again and Jeanette washed his face with wet towels, smoothing back his hair.

"Poor boy!" she said. "Poor boy! How do you manage to put up with me?" Then she added softly, as if the admission cost her a great deal: "I want you to know that I don't blame you in the least. I don't know what makes me act the way I do."

Roy thought: "Oh, Jesus Christ, I wish I could die."

1932

THE ARROGANT SHOAT

*W*HEN Rancey Catonhead was a fine, strapping girl of eighteen, her Aunt Lucy Hargrove, who lived in a brick house in Reedyville, came down with a spell of break-bone fever. Aunt Lucy had no children of her own. She lived alone with Uncle Henry, a good man, in many ways, but one totally incapable of taking care of a sick wife. What was more natural, then, than the letter he wrote his sister-in-law asking if Rancey could visit them during her aunt's convalescence?

Rancey was very excited over the letter. She wanted very much to go to Reedyville, of which she had often heard. She danced about in her thick-soled, man's shoes, her sunbonnet thrown back and hanging down her shoulders. "Let me go, Ma!" she pleaded. "I'll take the best keer in the world of Aunt Lucy. I never yet been nowheres, and you know it!"

Mrs. Catonhead was rinsing a mess of collard greens when Rancey read the letter to her. She lifted a leaf in her hand, against the sunlight, and pinched off a damaged spot with her stained thumb and forefinger. "We'll see," she answered. "We'll see what your poppa says."

And so, a few days later, Rancey's few possessions were washed, starched, and carefully mended. Len Williams, her father's farmhand, made a chest of seasoned poplar for the journey. Since the chest was for Rancey, he took considerable pride in his work. He planed and tinted the wood, and then studded the chest with an intricate design in brass and copper nails. Mrs. Catonhead packed the box, kissed her daughter quickly, and off Rancey went to Reedyville.

It was the first time in her life that she had been more than a mile or two from the farm on which she had been born. Len Williams had hitched up the farm wagon. He drove her to the

191

railhead, and saw her safely on the train. He brushed off a seat for her and arranged the box as a foot rest; then he stood in silence. Rancey had hardly spoken during the drive to the railhead. She did not speak now, but continued to look at her folded hands, as became a young girl embarking on a journey. But when the conductor called "All aboard!" she glanced up shyly and smiled at Len; and Len bent forward and kissed her ineptly on the chin. Then he ran out of the coach and stood red and embarrassed on the platform. Rancey saw him through her window. "The nerve of Len insultin' me that-a-way!" she thought happily.

Aunt Lucy was much better than Rancey's mother had expected, but the fever had left her weak. Uncle Henry said it was only a question of keeping her cheered up until she got her strength back.

Aunt Lucy was a huge woman with the unbelievable breasts that sculptors carve on heroic figures. She lay propped with pillows, a lace cap covering her thin, grayish hair.

"Well," she said. "So you're Debby's oldest girl?"

"Yes'm," said Rancey; "guess I am."

"Land sakes!" said Aunt Lucy, laughing in spite of herself, "don't you know for certain?"

Rancey laughed too, and after that she and her aunt were good friends.

Aunt Lucy had married well. Her brick house, with its fine furnishings, was a constant wonder to Rancey. On an easel in the parlor was a picture of a church set upon a lonely moor. Lying all over the moor was snow, which the artist had represented by bits of mother-of-pearl glued to the canvas; and above the church was a round moon, many times the size of what a moon should be. Back of the picture, on a shelf, rested a small kerosene lamp. One night as a surprise Aunt Lucy lighted the lamp for Rancey, and in the darkened room the moon shone out brightly from the canvas; peaceful light streamed through the church windows. The snow in the foreground sparkled and gleamed like opals. Rancey thought the picture was the most marvelous thing she had ever seen. "Oh!" she said in a rapt, unbelieving voice. "Oh! . . . Aunt Lucy!"

"It's a real nice picture," said Aunt Lucy, striving to hide the pride in her voice. "There's not another one like it in Reedyville, I guess."

But as wonderful as Aunt Lucy's house was, Rancey marveled even more at the eccentricities of the fine ladies of Reedyville. She had never before seen anything like them. There was one proud lady in particular who carried a long-haired dog, and who had a nigger boy to walk behind her carrying a red sunshade. Rancey had never imagined anything so impressive.

Before Rancey came to Reedyville, a circus had been there; its posters were still clinging to fences and barns. Rancey, from her aunt's shuttered windows, could see these posters plastered to the fences opposite. She could see men and women dressed in tights flying through the air and grasping one another's hands. Then there were lines of elephants walking sedately behind each other, with strange, dark men astride their necks. There were striped tigers with mouths like red caves. But the picture that interested Rancey most of all was posted against Moore's Livery Stable. It showed a tall, stout lady with yellow bangs, before whom waltzed a young pig. The pig waltzed solemnly, elegantly, as if aware of his importance and proud of the gold chain around his neck. Below the picture were the words: "Mlle. Marie and her pet: The world's most intelligent pig."

Rancey would stand before Moore's Stable and look at that picture by the hour. Even when she thought about it at night, she would become excited. "I bet I could train me a pig, too, iffen I put my mind to it, and iffen I had ere a pig to train," she would think.

She talked about the lady with her accomplished pet so much that one day Uncle Henry brought home a tiny Berkshire pig for her. When he had seen it in a farmer's wagon before Court House Square, he had thought immediately of Rancey, and what she had said about wanting a pig of her own to train, and the farmer had sold him the pig at once.

And so the weeks passed pleasantly. Aunt Lucy was almost well once more. She was walking about her house now, and commencing to take an interest in things again. Rancey had grown fond of her. Then there came a letter from her mother saying they needed her at home on the farm to help with the younger children. Rancey hated to leave Reedyville, but, as Aunt Lucy said, she could come see them again sometime; so Rancey again starched and ironed her belongings, and packed them neatly into the poplar chest.

She slipped back into her old life without effort. Cotton picking was coming on, and she had little time to remember the things she had seen in Reedyville. The little Berkshire pig throve with Rancey's devotion, and grew quickly into a fine, arrogant shoat. He was so tame that he followed Rancey everywhere, and it was almost impossible to keep him out of the house. She taught him to stand on his hind legs and turn around clumsily. Rancey called it round-dancing, and even her mother laughed at that. Often she tried to tell her mother about the picture with the lamp behind it and about Mlle. Marie, and her trained friend, but her mother never had time to listen to any story to its end.

But if her mother was too busy to listen, Cliff Catonhead was always an audience. He was still in checked-aprons, the youngest of the children, and he was Rancey's especial care. She would walk with him, during the hazy fall afternoons, to the footbridge that spanned the *bogue*, the shoat trotting behind them. Then Cliff would sit wide-eyed while Rancey made the pig stand up on his hind legs, his forefeet bending delicately at their joints, and turn round and round, as if he never meant to stop.

"I'm a-goin' to get me a job in a circus," she would say; "and I'll wear spangles. I'll wear me some pink tights, too! Let them that don't like it say their say; what do I keer!" And Cliff, always silent, would stare at her with his solemn, sweet eyes, and thrust his thumb into his mouth.

Sometimes Len Williams, who never let her out of his sight for very long, would come down to the footbridge and peer under at them. Often he would see Rancey sitting quietly sewing, the shoat uprooting the earth at her feet, with Cliff asleep against her breast. One day he too sat down beside her. He bent his lips until they rested against her strong, young neck, and before Rancey knew it, she threw her arms around him. "I don't keer whether I travel with a circus or not," she said; "I don't keer ere a bit about travelin' with a circus!" At her words the shoat turned and squealed. Then, from force of habit, he rose on his legs and circled time after time; but Rancey could not see her shoat, because her face was pressed against Len Williams' over-alls.

That night Len asked Mr. Catonhead for Rancey. Len was a good man; he saved his money and he was buying a place of his own in the north end of the county. Nobody could rightfully object to him, so old man Catonhead said they could marry in October, after the cotton had been ginned, for all of him; but the trouble was, he didn't have any money for wedding dresses, and Rancey would have to get along with what she wore for Sunday. He would give his consent to the wedding, and throw in his blessing to boot, but that was about all he could do with things the way they were. This shamed Rancey a great deal. She thought over the matter for several days, trying to solve her difficulties, and then she came to a conclusion. The shoat had grown enormously fat and sleek under her care. She would sell him at market and buy a proper wedding dress with the money. She had to get rid of the shoat anyway; she couldn't keep him forever. A married woman would have a house to look after.

That fall she and Len married, and for a few years she was too busy in her new home, helping Len with the farm, and taking care of the Williams children, which came, for a time, as regu-larly as the years themselves, to think much about her old home, or to grieve over leaving it. She thought of herself as a matron, settled for life. But when she was thirty years old, her father died. Rancey went back to the farm for the funeral. She thought her mother looked old and peaked, and the place had changed. She, herself, felt changed also, and out of place, and she was anxious the whole time to get back to her own family.

Then, a few years afterward, her mother also died. Both she and Len went that time. They left the children at home. That same year her brother Cliff married one of the Cornells girls. Just think of little Cliff married! It made Rancey want to laugh.

Why, Cliff was only a baby when she left home, and now little Cliff was a man, getting married! Well! The thought of Cliff's marriage brought back, somehow, memories of her shoat, and she got out the pink ribbon which he had worn when he was small, and which she had carefully folded away at the bottom of her poplar chest. "Oh, well," she thought, "he brought a good price at market, anyway!"

And so the years slipped by. It was surprising how quickly they passed. Here is Rancey Williams with grown children, with a boy old enough to be wanting to enlist in the army and fight Germans. That struck Rancey as funny. There were several German families in the county, now. She remembered one old man in particular who wore a pair of light blue pants and who played on a horn. And little Len wanted to go shoot Germans! She had to laugh at the absurdity of people.

The next year Millie, her oldest daughter, wanted to marry. She had picked out a man named Jim McLeod. He wasn't the sort of man Rancey would pick to marry, but if Millie had her mind set on it—

Millie had her mind set on that one thing. "But, Millie, you're so young to be a-gettin' married!" said Rancey.

"I'm older than you were when you got married," said Millie.

There was no getting around that. There wasn't anything more for Rancey to say. A few days later she opened the poplar chest and took out her wedding dress. She went to Millie with a smile, the dress across her arm. "I'm a-goin' to wear my wedding dress at *your* wedding, Millie," she said proudly.

"Oh," said Millie. Then, after a moment, she added reproachfully, "But, Mamma . . ."

The smile left Rancey's lips. She felt her spirits droop. "What's the matter with it, Millie?" she asked.

Millie sought for words: "But, Mamma, don't you see? It's all out of style. People don't wear clothes like that any more."

So that was it. Millie was only worrying about her old mother. She wanted her mother to look as well as anyone else at the wedding. But little Rancey cared what folks thought, or whether or not they laughed at her. Let them laugh! There was little enough fun in the world anyway! "Don't you worry, Millie," she said. "I won't keer ere a bit if folks laugh fit to bust."

Millie looked at her in silence, irritated at her stupidity. "But, Mamma! Be sensible! Of course I don't care what you wear, but Jim's folks will be there, too, and they're particular."

Rancey thought a moment before nodding her head. "All right, Millie; it won't make no difference to me. I want you to have your wedding like you want it, honey." She went back to the porch and looked at the dress in the morning light. It was out of style, there was no getting around that, and the silk had lost some of its luster, and was beginning to crack where it had been folded so long. Then, for some reason, Millie and her earnestness struck her as funny. She began to laugh. She folded the dress back into the box and wrapped tissue paper around it.

After Millie and Jim married, they went to live in Morgantown, but twenty-five miles didn't seem such a distance any more. People got about quicker. There were automobiles everywhere, now.

More years passed. Things were easier on the farm. There wasn't so much work to be done. Rancey started putting on weight about that time. She had once been proud of her small waist and her fine body, but somehow it didn't matter now how fat she got. She would stand before her mirror and look at herself. Her neck was thick and reddened and there were rolls of fat across her shoulders. Her throat flowed to her breast in great corrugated ridges. "If Millie Marie had a-looked like me, nobody could a-told which was the *pig*," she thought. Then she would go sit on the porch and rock and watch the road. The county was getting more densely settled. New people were coming in all the time, and the old settlers were dying off or moving out. It was surprising how many people passed up and down the road in a day.

Millie, to her mother's surprise, seemed bent on carrying on the family tradition for fecundity. There was always a baby at the McLeod house. They were prospering, too. Rancey would rock and rock and think of them, a tender smile on her lips. At night she tried to spend her time sewing, but she discovered that her eyes were not so good as they used to be. She had to call Marie, her second daughter, to stop her housework and come thread the needle. When she made a dressing-sacque for herself one night out of the wrong side of the flowered goods, she was very provoked. The children laughed at her for her mistake, and she was hurt. That night she cried for the first time in years. It wasn't the way she had cried when they told her about little Len being killed in a foreign land—that time people heard her crying as far away as Tarleton's store—but quietly and hopelessly. It was all so senseless. There was no reason for her crying that way.

The next week Len took her to Morgantown to visit Millie and Jim, and while there an oculist fitted her with glasses. Her teeth were getting bad; they hurt her a great deal. But Rancey had made up her mind that she would never sit in a dentist's chair, no matter what happened. The idea terrified her. Len had all his teeth pulled out and a plate fitted that trip. Both Millie and Jim spoke to each other about how stubborn Rancey was getting as she grew older.

It was about that time that Rancey began talking to the children about her wonderful trip to Reedyville, and what a fine house Aunt Lucy and Uncle Henry had lived in. She talked of the strange ways of the city ladies, with their white hands and their fine manners, and of a ruby ring which Aunt Lucy had worn on her finger. She mentioned the wonderful picture her Aunt Lucy had had, with snow made out of pearls; but mostly she talked of the shoat that she had raised on a bottle and taught to round-dance.

"I sold my shoat, though," she said. "Yes, sir, I sold him! When they taken him away, he tried to stand up in the crate and do the steps I'd learned him, a-squealing all the time, but the crate was too small for him and he kept bumping his head and falling down. He kept squealing and waltzing and knocking his head until the man had drove out of sight down the road. Then I run behind the branch and hid in a thicket of gall berries until your gramper come down and made me go up to the house." Suddenly

Rancey began to laugh. "Law," she said. "Law! What a skittery girl I must a-been!"

But somehow the children didn't seem interested in her trip. They would listen politely enough, but when she had finished talking, they would go away quietly. It wasn't any fun telling about things if folks didn't ask questions! But Rancey excused them: They were young, and there were so many other things to occupy their minds.

One spring day Rancey complained of a pain in her stomach. She had felt the pain off and on for some months, but she hadn't said anything about it. A woman of her age couldn't expect to be without some sort of ailment; it would pass off. But the pain got worse as the weeks went on, and that spring day she told Len about it. Len insisted on taking her to Morgantown to see a doctor. She resisted, ridiculing the idea that anything serious could be wrong with her, but in the end she gave in.

The doctor was young and brisk. There was about him a clean smell of scented soap and carbolic acid. She was suddenly ashamed of her fat old belly. She wanted to tell him that she had once had a fine figure and had been considered pretty, but she realized the doctor wouldn't care one way or the other. After the doctor had finished his examination he stood thinking for a time. He prescribed some medicine which stopped most of the pain. So Rancey went back home with Len, but she couldn't get out of bed any more. Everybody was very kind. The neighbors used to send in little things for her to eat, or stop Marie or one of the other children and ask about her, but often Rancey did not know this, because the medicine the doctor had given her made her drowsy. Sometimes, however, in spite of the drugs her mind was alert and she would sit up and look about her, completely conscious, completely aware of her surroundings. She was in such a condition one Sunday afternoon when Sarah Tarleton, a friend of many years, called.

"You must hurry and get well, Rancey. You got so much to live for."

"I'm a sour and a disappointed woman," said Rancey. "Death can't come too soon for me."

"You must think of Len and the children," continued Sarah in her exact, stilted voice. "Len is a good, steady man, and your children all turned out a credit."

"Len's a man like any other; and as far as the children go, I don't see where it makes ere a bit of difference whether they were born or not. My whole life was throwed away."

"No woman who has made a home and brought up eight children has wasted her life," observed Miss Sarah sententiously.

"Janie Barrascale raised fourteen. Who cares? I wish now I'd a-taken my shoat and run off to a circus, like I started to."

One night Rancey died in her sleep. Millie and Jim came as quickly as they could. Len sat on the front porch the next morning smoking his pipe and feeling lost and uncomfortable. The fact that he wasn't working made it seem like a Sunday. Rancey's death wasn't exactly a shock. They had all been expecting it for a long time. Millie came out on the steps and sat down beside her younger brothers and sisters. Her father and Marie were talking about Rancey's good traits. Marie started crying again, and Millie couldn't help crying too, try as she would not to.

All that morning Len rocked back and forth on the porch in his chair, his mottled, sparse neck stretched forward like the neck of a guinea cock. "She made me a good, contented wife," he kept saying to the people who came on the porch to sit beside him and offer comfort. "We had a sweet, full life together."

1932

THE EAGER MECHANIC

THE STREET had once been a good one, but time had long since destroyed its gentility. It was lined now with chain-stores, filling stations and cheap hotels. But a few of the fine houses remained as they had been, and it was on the porch of such a house that the old man sat on sunny mornings.

He was so old and so shrunken that it was difficult to tell at first if he was a man or a woman. He sat in a huge chair, his body wrapped in a shawl, and closed his eyes wearily, as if he had seen enough of the world and would shut out the little that remained.

Occasionally he would raise his arm in a weak, petulant gesture and knock off the woolen cap which he wore, and at such times a fringe of stained, yellowish hair stood up on the back of his head. The shawl and the stubborn, upstanding hair gave him the appearance of a sick dancer wearing an amber comb. Then, almost immediately, a tall woman would appear from the depths of the house and stand above him patiently. She would pick up the cap and put it upon his head again, her teeth bared in a strong, professional smile, and talk with simple words, in a raised voice, as if she were speaking to a child. When she had rearranged his shawl and his cap, she would go back into the house and leave him alone in the April sunlight.

Sometimes he would lift his head and watch sparrows quarreling in the eaves above him, or trace with his dry forefinger the shadows thrown by the iron grill-work, but in the end he would lean forward and rest his chin on the banisters and watch the young mechanic who worked in the garage across the street.

The mechanic was young and eager. He wore uniforms which showed off his strong legs and his vigorous thighs. There were usually smudges of grease on his cheeks and hands. For a long

time the old man had watched him at work running from car
to car as if walking were too slow for him. He whistled a great
deal and occasionally he even sang fragments of popular songs
in a voice persistently off key. When there was no work to be
done, he would wrestle with the other mechanics. Sometimes,
when he thought he was unobserved, he would turn handsprings
in the vacant lot which adjoined the garage. At first the old man
had been vaguely annoyed by these antics. "The young fool!
The young fool! The young fool!" he would whisper to himself
angrily.

And then, one morning, the young mechanic had come across
the street and spoken to him, and the old man had answered in
his thin voice. The young mechanic had stood there talking of
his work, of how well the station was doing and his chances for
a raise very soon. He spoke of having a garage of his own some
day, but that, of course, was in the remote distance. When he
had finished, the old man, in turn, began to talk. He spoke with
acrid, slyly chosen words, but the flavor of his bitterness was
lost on the young man who stood there grinning widely, as if
vastly amused, his arms resting against the iron fence that separated them.

The next day he came again to talk to the old man, whom he
now considered his friend. He ran across the street waving his
hand for no reason at all and chuckling to himself. The old man
shuddered suddenly and pulled his shawl closer. He said: "You
seem very happy this morning."

"Sure, I'm happy!" said the mechanic. "Why shouldn't I be?
I've got a good job and I make good money, don't I?" Then he
began to drag his finger across the iron fence. "Say, I'll let you
in on a secret," he said. "I'm going to get married this summer.
But don't tell any of the other boys about it yet. I don't want
them kidding me."

The old man leaned back, a hard, amused light in his eyes.
"I'll try not to talk indiscreetly," he said, his lips drawn back
into a bloodless line. "I'll try to keep your secret."

"Oh, sure," said the young mechanic. "I knew I could trust
you not to talk."

The old man looked up and down the shabby street, and then his eyes returned to the mechanic, regarding him contemptuously for a moment before he spoke. "You expect to be very happy in your marriage, I imagine. Nothing will happen to you, as it does to other people, of course. Your life will flow evenly and sweetly."

"Why, sure," said the mechanic in a surprised voice. "Why, sure. That's right."

Suddenly the old man felt as if he were going to cry. He closed his eyes and leaned forward, lifting his battered face to the sunlight. "I'm old, so very old," he thought. "I've lived too long. I've seen too much and I've experienced too much. When I listen, I can hear men building the coffin which will soon hold me; when I smell, I am conscious of the decay that will lie in the black earth where I, too, shall lie; when I close my eyes, I have a little of the blackness which will shut away this beautiful world forever."

He raised his thin arm and held it before him, moving it slowly back and forth, and a wavering shadow came against the brick wall beside him. He watched the shadow for awhile, fascinated by it, conscious that the mechanic was still standing eagerly before him, talking about furniture, rent, and desirable locations.

Then fury came over the man because he was old and because the mechanic was young and so eager. His lips puffed out and his face began to twitch. And then, almost immediately, he thought: "I'll tell him what awaits him! I'll find words to pierce even his stupidity!" For a moment he sat with eyes closed, thinking of the words he was to say, shaping them cunningly. He sat that way for a long time.

Above him, in the eaves of the house, a sparrow began to tread his hen, and the old man turned to watch them. They rolled over and over in the gutter, chirping and ruffling their brown feathers. Then they tumbled straight down, striking the iron grill-work, agitating the coral vine, until they reached the lawn, still locked together, and trembled there, their heads drawn close to their bodies, their feathers blown up to twice their

normal size. They lifted their beaks to heaven and shivered, utter-
ing all the time shrill, ecstatic cries.

When the sparrows had flown away, the old man raised his
arm again, and again the uncertain shadow came on the wall
beside him. He thought, "Sooner or later nothing is of any importance. At the end nothing is more important than the shadow
of my arm against this wall!" Then he turned to the young man
standing before him. The mechanic had thrown back his head
and was smiling. His eyes were brown and untroubled and his
white teeth glistened in the sunlight. He stood there eagerly, as
if he awaited words of wisdom.

At last the old man spoke from the depths of his bitterness,
through bloodless, wry lips: "I should like to be present at the
happy event. You must send me an invitation to your wedding."

"Sure I will!" said the mechanic happily. "You didn't think
I'd forget you, did you?"

1932

A SUM IN ADDITION

C OLLINS said: "Sure there's a corkscrew in there. You'll find it chained to the wall. All hotels have 'em." And Menefee answered from the bathroom: "Well, there's not one in *here*. Look for yourselves if you boys don't believe me."

"That's a fine way to treat drummers," said Red Smith. "I'll write and complain to the management." He got up and stretched himself. "I'll look in the closet," he said. "Maybe I'll find something to open it with in there."

Menefee came back into the room and put the unopened bottle on the dresser, his head drawn backward and turned at an angle, his eyes squinting up. He ground out the cigarette that had been burning between his relaxed lips. "You boys keep your pants on," he said; "I'll go down and borrow a corkscrew off a bell-hop." He put on his coat and went into the hall, closing the door behind him.

Collins sat back and rested his legs on the vacant chair, looking lazily over his shoulder at Red Smith. Red was pulling out drawers noisily, or standing tiptoe to peer at shelves just above his head. Then he stopped, picked up something and came into the room with it. It was a sheet of hotel stationery covered with writing and it had been crumpled into a ball and thrown into the closet.

Red opened the sheet and smoothed it flat, and when he had read it, he passed it to Collins, a peculiar look on his face. "Read this, Wade," he said.

Collins read slowly, the paper held close to his eyes. At the right of the sheet, and commencing it, was the following entry: "Cash on hand $17.45."

Then, to the left, were the following entries:

```
Expenses babyies funerel (about) ............$148.00
Wifes hospital bill (about) ..................   65.00
Owe to grocery store .....................      28.17
Back Rent (2 mo.—make it 3) ...............     127.25
Incidentals ...............................      25.00
                                              ————
                                             $394.42
```

A little farther down the paper were the following words: "Will borrow four hundred dollars from Mr. Sellwood." This sentence was repeated, like an exercise in penmanship, over and over, until the paper was filled with it. At first the words were written boldly, heavily, and there were places where the pen had broken through the paper behind the determination of the writer; but as the writing progressed, the man seemed less sure of himself, as if his courage and his certainty were fading away. The sentences were more perfect here, with an occasional mended letter; they were written more slowly, as if each letter were pondered. The last sentence was not finished at all. It dwindled thinly into wavering illegibility.

Collins had read the thing through and sat with it in his hands. He said sympathetically: "Tough! Tough!" then added: "He knew he couldn't work it out. He knew he was fooling himself; so he crumpled up the paper and threw it in the closet."

Red Smith sat down, resting his elbows on his knees, his bright, coppery hair shining in the light. Suddenly he had a picture of a shabby little man sitting in this same cheap hotel room, going over his problem, over and over, and finding no answer to it. Finally he said: "Don't you suppose Mr. Sellwood let him have the four hundred bucks after all? Why not?"

Collins sighed, the masonic emblem resting on his fat stomach rising with his breath. He spoke mockingly: "Of course not, Little Sunshine. Of course not! Maybe our friend went to *see* Mr. Sellwood all right, but Mr. Sellwood said that times were hard right then and he had a lot of expenses of his own. I guess that's about the way it worked out."

Red lifted his alert face. "I think you're wrong, Wade, I think everything worked out all right."

But Collins shook his head. "Not a chance, young fellow!" he said. "Not a chance!"

Red replied: "Just the same, I think Mr. Sellwood let him have the four hundred bucks. He was an old friend of the family, you see. Then he got a good job for this fellow that paid more money, and this fellow came back home almost running. He came up the steps three at the time to tell his wife. Everything worked out fine for them after that."

"Maybe he met Santa Claus on the way home," said Wade heavily, "and old Santa slipped the money in his stocking." Then he said more seriously: "The fellow who wrote that is sitting in some other cheap hotel tonight still figuring, and still trying to find an answer, but he won't, because there isn't any answer for him to find."

The door opened then and Menefee stood before them, a corkscrew in his hand. "Everything's okay," he said. "Everything's all set."

"We'll leave it to Menefee," said Red Smith. "Give him the writing, Wade, and let's see what he thinks."

Collins passed over the paper and Menefee examined it carefully, as if he did not understand it, before he looked at the two men, puzzled a little.

"What's it all about? This don't make sense to me."

Collins shook his head. "Good old Menefee. Trust him."

Red laughed a little and said earnestly: "Don't you see the point, Menefee?"

Menefee read the thing through again, turned the paper over and examined the writing once more. "I'm damned if I do," he said helplessly. Then a moment later he added triumphantly: "Oh, sure, sure, I see the point now! Sure I do. It's added up wrong."

Red Smith looked at Collins and they both laughed. "It *is* added up wrong!" said Menefee, indignant and a little hurt. "Eight and five are thirteen and eight are twenty-one . . . seven makes twenty-eight, and five thirty-three—not thirty-four, like it is here."

But Collins and Red Smith continued to laugh and to shake their heads.

"All right," said Menefee. "I'm dumb; I admit it." He pulled in his lips and spoke in a high, quavering voice: "Come on, boys; let your poor old grandmother in on the joke!" He picked up the bottle and poured three drinks into three tumblers, grumbling a little to himself. "I never saw such superior bastards in all my life as you two are," he said.

1932

PERSONAL LETTER

Hamburg, Germany,
December 17th, 1932.

DEAR MR. TYLER:

I wrote you a long, official letter last week and forwarded same via the S.S. *Manhattan*. That letter, which should be in your hands by the time you receive this, contained information you wanted regarding berthing facilities, pilotage in and out, tug hire, stevedoring costs, etc., etc. If I failed to cover any point that you had in mind, or if any part of my report is not detailed enough, please let me know, and I'll remedy the situation promptly.

As you will remember, you also asked me to drop you a line under private cover regarding my personal impression of this country, and that is what I would like to do in this letter. I have thought a good deal about the best way to accomplish this, and have come to the conclusion that the easiest way to do it is to simply recount a little incident which happened the other night in a cafe.

First, let me say again that the agents you have in mind for representing us here are very efficient and have co-operated with me at all times. Herr Voelker, director of the agency, has been especially helpful. He is an intelligent and highly educated man. A few nights ago, he asked me to have dinner with him and attend the opera later, which I did. After that, he suggested we take in a beer cafe that he knew of, and so we went there, too. This place was pretty well filled up when we arrived, mostly with men in storm trooper uniforms. I won't explain who they are, as I covered that point in my first letter under the heading of Political Situation and Future Outlook, to which I refer you.

Well, Herr Voelker and I went to the basement bar and

ordered our drinks, talking together all the time. We were speaking in English and discussing business matters and things in general, and at first I didn't notice that a group of these storm troopers had closed around us, shutting us off from the others at the bar.

To make a long story short, the leader of the group touched me on the shoulder and told me that I was in Germany now, and that while I was in Germany I would speak German or nothing at all. Most of these North Germans speak English very well indeed, since they have eight years of it in school, and so, naturally, this fellow spoke English, too.

I twisted around and looked these boys over, but they only held their backs stiffer, threw out their chests and frowned, just like something out of the opera I'd just seen. I still couldn't believe I'd heard correctly, and so I said, "Were you speaking to me?" And this leader answered in a voice which trembled with anger, "I repeat for the last time. When you are in Germany, you are to speak German. If you cannot speak German, you are to remain silent. Is that clear? We will endure no further insults from foreigners."

By that time I was sure it was some sort of a gag which Herr Voelker and the boys had cooked up for me. You know the sort of thing I mean, don't you? Like the time at the Traffic Association dinner when they played that joke on Oscar Wilcoxon. If you remember now, a girl with a baby in her arms burst into the dining-room just before the speeches began. She asked if there was a man present named Oscar Wilcoxon, and when the master of ceremonies said that there was, she demanded that he marry her, like he had promised to do, and give a name to his child.

Everybody was in on the stunt except Oscar himself, and it got a lot of laughs. Oscar kept trying to explain that somebody else must have been using his name illegally, because he'd never seen the young lady before in his life; but this girl had been carefully coached in her part, and the more Oscar tried to explain matters, the worse things got. I kept thinking to myself at the time that if anybody pulled a trick like that on me, I'd fall right in with the gag and say yes, I was the father of the baby all right, but I couldn't be sure about the mother because it was always so dark in the alley back of the pickle works where we met.

Well, when the storm trooper said what he did about not speaking English in Germany, I wanted to laugh, it struck me as so comical, but I didn't. I'd already decided to play it their way and pretend to take the whole thing seriously. So I kept a straight face and said, "You gentlemen would like others to believe that you are real Germans, but you are not real Germans at all. If a real German heard what you have just said, he'd cover his face with shame."

I waited a moment and then added, "If you were real Germans, like you pretend to be, you'd realize that since I'm not a German, but an American, that I'm not as bright as you are. You'd know that Americans haven't got your culture, and that we haven't had your natural advantages. Americans think slowly," I said. "They don't master languages the way you do." Then I sighed and turned back to Herr Voelker, as if the subject was ended, as far as I was concerned.

The storm troopers seemed nonplused at my attitude, and they went into a huddle at one end of the bar. My German isn't the best in the world, but I could understand most of what they said without any trouble. The gist of it was that I was right, and that they were wrong; that even though I was a foreigner, I had the true philosophy. Well, I let them talk it over for a while, and then suddenly I wheeled around and gave them the other barrel. "A true German doesn't expect the same perfection from inferior people that he expects from himself," I said. "I thought that was something everybody knew by this time."

I said all this in a quick, stern voice, Mr. Tyler, and the troopers straightened up and stood at attention while I gave them a thorough dressing down. At the end of my speech, I said, "So you see? If you were true Germans, and believed in your mission, you wouldn't humiliate me before my friends. Oh, no, you wouldn't do that at all! Instead, you'd come to me as a teacher and say, 'Let me instruct you in our beautiful language! Let me explain to you our wonderful way of life!'" I waited a moment and then said sadly, "No. No, you are not true Germans. You only pretend to be. And now go away please before I lose the last of my illusions."

I nudged Herr Voelker with my elbow and winked behind my hand, but he only raised his eyes and stared at me over the edge of his glass. By that time there were tears in the eyes of the leader of the troopers. He apologized to me in great detail. He wanted to buy me a drink, to prove that everything was all right, but I thought I'd keep the thing going a little longer, and played hard to butter up. Finally, I did let him buy me a drink, and then I bought him one in return. I thought, then, that the joke would break, and the laughter and the explanations come, but that didn't happen, and I began to feel a little uneasy.

Not long afterwards, Herr Voelker and I got up to leave. When we were outside, Herr Voelker said he was sorry such an unpleasant incident had occurred, and that he would have prevented it if he had been able to do so. He said he thought I had acted with rare presence of mind in being frank and aboveboard with the storm troopers, instead of trying to lie my way out of the situation. I was so astonished that I stood still on the pavement and said, "Did you think I meant what I said? An intelligent, educated man like yourself? Did you really believe I was in earnest?"

And, before God, Mr. Tyler, Herr Voelker drew himself up haughtily and said, "Why shouldn't I think you meant it? Every point you made was logical and entirely true."

Mr. Tyler, I've often read in books about an icy hand which clutched at somebody-or-other's heart. I never before took the words seriously, thinking it was just a phrase that writers used, but now I know that it's a true expression. That's exactly the way I felt as I walked along with Herr Voelker until we reached the taxi rank on the corner, and I got into a cab alone, and went back to my hotel.

Now, maybe there isn't anything important in the incident, but I think there is. There's something going on beneath the surface here as sure as you're a foot high. I don't quite know what it is so far, but I do know that it's something horrible.

This turned out to be a long letter, didn't it? I suppose you'll be receiving it during the Christmas holidays, so let me take this opportunity of wishing you a happy Christmas and a prosperous New Year. People here celebrate Christmas in a big way. They gather together in groups, sing songs about the Christ child, and weep over the loved ones who are far away. It is the season of love, goodwill, and the renewal of old affections, or so Herr Voelker tells me. He invited me, as a special compliment, to spend the day in the bosom of his own family, so I could see first hand what a German Christmas is really like; but I expressed my regrets, and said that business obligations made it necessary for me to be in Paris on that day. To tell you the truth, Mr. Tyler, everybody here frightens me a little—they are all so full of sentiment and fury.

With best regards, and again wishing you the compliments of the season, I remain,

Sincerely yours,

ROBERT B. McINTOSH.

1932

THE PATTERN THAT GULLS
WEAVE

*T*HE MAID opened the door and Fräulein Gieseke came into the reception hall. The ladies were upstairs awaiting their lessons, she said, and Fräulein was to join them in the library when she had taken off her wraps. Fräulein Gieseke nodded her head briskly in her professional manner. She was a tall, somewhat stout woman with a puckered mouth and blue eyes which were a little faded.

She looked about the room and sighed, raising her wide, soft bosom upwards as if she wore a girdle of iron. "Such bad taste," she thought. "So *much* of everything."

She stood waiting until the maid had gone away. She did not like to exhibit her peculiarities to others, if she could avoid doing so, but it was difficult for Fräulein Gieseke to get in motion, once she had stopped. There was a complete ceremonial through which she must go. First she had to close her eyes and stand perfectly still; then she must raise her hands, as if she were a child unused to standing alone, and balance herself exactly. Almost immediately she would sway forward and then backward for a time or two before her feet began to move with irregular, jerking steps. But when this ceremonial had been completed to the last detail, the mincing gait disappeared and she strode forward with steps which were long and sure.

Once she had stood outside a room and heard two of her pupils discussing her peculiarity. "She reminds me of a Christmas toy that you wind up with a key," said one.

"I know," answered the other gaily; "I know just what you mean: something that rattles and jerks and walks toward you on a table!"

And Fräulein Gieseke had stood blushing for shame, but in her heart she knew that the description was just. "They are only young, silly girls," she said to herself. "They don't mean to be unkind." Then she had thought: "There's so much rudeness in the world these days; so little consideration for the feelings of others. I'm sure people were not like that when I was a girl."

But today she mounted the stairs energetically, her step becoming more and more sure. She came into the library smiling. The three young ladies and their mother were awaiting her, grouped about a large table. "This afternoon we must speak only in German!" she said enthusiastically. She raised her finger in humorous warning and shook it at the young ladies. "Only German this afternoon!" she repeated. "Only German!"

The young ladies and their mother looked at one another in alarm; then they glanced down at their open books, their brows puckered in an effort to understand the meaning of the words printed there.

Fräulein Gieseke settled back comfortably in her chair. "Today we will take a trip into the country, *nicht?* And will talk about the many beautiful things we see about us? It is summer and we are walking down a country lane. Birds are singing in the trees and everything is green and very beautiful." She turned to the middle daughter: "And now, Fräulein Marjorie, will you begin, please?"

The young lady lifted her book higher, pouted her red lips and read slowly. After a moment she stopped. "I don't understand about the dative," she said; "what is the dative case, Fräulein?"

Fräulein Gieseke said: "We won't trouble to learn too much grammar at first. Later, yes; but for the first lessons we will build our vocabularies."

"We don't have a dative case in English," said the eldest of the young ladies.

"Oh, yes, yes!" said Fräulein Gieseke. "It is understood, even though not expressed as such. It is the case of the indirect object."

The mother looked up and shook her head in firm, pleasant

denial. "My daughter is quite right," she said, settling the point forever. "There is no dative in English."

"*Bitte*," said Fräulein Gieseke, turning to the youngest daughter. "*Bitte*, will you continue, Fräulein Claire?"

When the hour was over, Fräulein Gieseke put on her wraps and the maid opened the door for her, and she stood for a moment in the doorway adjusting her overshoes. The sky was gray and overcast and there was a fine, cold rain falling. Before her stretched the Alster, misty and unreal. At its edges thin ice had formed and had been broken into irregular blocks with serrated edges. Fräulein Gieseke walked toward the railing and stood there quietly.

Across the lake lights were coming on, but they shone blurred and indistinct through the grayness of the mist-like rain. Without reason a feeling of sadness came over her. She tried to shake it off, to resume her professional, energetic manner, but she could not. She suddenly felt very helpless and very much alone.

"When I was a young girl, things were so different," she said.

Below her the swans were gliding slowly, sullenly, their long throats drawn backward, between the floating pieces of ice; and over them, against the sky, gulls were flying. The hungry gulls wheeled and turned, huddled together in a huge ball, flying inward and outward, upward and downward, intent and silent, their sharp, bright eyes scanning the water for food, their gray wings beating against the gray sky.

Fräulein Gieseke watched them for a time, wishing that she had brought bread for their hungry beaks, and as she stood there quietly, unconscious of the fine, mist-like rain, seeing only the predatory gulls and the sullen swans beneath them, she felt weary and old and without purpose.

Then the quietness of the place was broken. To her left a boy with ragged clothing and a sick, white face stood under a tree, his cap held in his thin outstretched hand, and began to sing. He knew but one song and he sang it over and over, holding out his cap to the people who passed.

But nobody paid any attention to the singer. They hurried past quickly to their individual destinations, sure of themselves, sure of where they were going and what they were to do.

Presently no one passed at all, but the boy sang on and on in his thin, sweet voice; the same song over and over.

All at once Fräulein Gieseke had a strange, unreasoning feeling of anger against the singer. She went over to him. She opened her pocketbook and fumbled for the money which she had earned that afternoon, dropping it piece by piece into the damp, shabby cap. She spoke with quiet fury to the boy: "Have you no pride? Do you think they care? Do you think they will listen to you? Have you no pride at all?" But the boy stared at her incuriously with calm, remote eyes and went on with his song.

The woman continued in a scolding voice: "You're sick! You shouldn't be out in this weather! You should be home in bed taking care of yourself!" She stopped, her anger vanished, and she stood looking at the damp earth. "You really *should* wear warmer clothing," she said in a helpless voice. "You must go home at once and change." But the boy continued his slow, melancholy song in a voice a little hoarse and a little off key and would not look at her again.

Fräulein Gieseke turned and stood balancing herself with her spread hands, as if she were a ballet dancer about to rise on the tips of her toes. Her body swayed backward and forward a little and in a moment she walked away mincingly with irregular, jerking steps.

Beside her, the swans, the beautiful, helpless swans, blew out their feathers disdainfully and glided among the broken ice, and over her head the famished gulls wheeled and turned endlessly. The gulls flew upward and downward, inward and outward, whirling and circling eternally with wings which never touched, over and over in the same pattern, seeking food. It was as if each gull had an invisible, colored thread in its beak and was weaving a tapestry against heaven, a design too delicate and too subtly colored for eyes to see, but which would, one day, pull down the skies with its accumulated weight.

Fräulein Gieseke buttoned her sensible, shabby coat more closely about her neck. "Food—" she said contemptuously. "Food—" But she could not finish the sentence.

1933

THE FIRST DIME

*C*HARLIE huddled in the doorway, protected somewhat from the tugging wind; but when he saw the old lady approaching with her dog, he squared his shoulders and walked toward her with something of his old carelessness. He whispered: "It'll be easier, the first time, to ask an old dame. It won't be so shameful." The old woman stopped and peered over her nose-glasses at Charlie, surveying his wrecked shoes, his dirty and reddened hands, his unshaved face. The terrier bitch stretched forward, dancing in the cold, and sniffed his trousers, making a whining sound.

All at once Charlie's jauntiness vanished. The set speech which he had rehearsed in the doorway went out of his mind. He spoke rapidly in his terror: This was the first time he had ever begged. She must believe that, for God's sake. He wasn't a bum. He'd had a good job until just a few months ago. This was the first time, and he hadn't eaten for almost two days. He was a man with self-respect and she must believe that. It was important. She must believe that, for God's sake.

The old woman had opened her bag. She dropped a dime into his palm.

Later Charlie sat on a bench in Washington Square, clutching the coin tightly, crushing with his heels clods of soiled and brittle snow. In a little while he would get up and buy something hot for his gnawing belly, but first he must sit here a little longer and adjust himself to shame. He rested his face against the iciness of the iron bench, hoping that nobody could guess his degradation by looking at him. He thought: "I never had anything in my life except a little self-respect, and I haven't even got that now. I sold out pretty cheap, I guess."

1934

THE TOY BANK

*A*RTHUR's birthdays were exciting events largely because his grandfather sent him a present on that day, something unusual, and not to be anticipated like the toy his mother bought for him, or the single handkerchief, with his name, Arthur Kent, worked in one corner, which came each year from Aunt Lida in Tennessee; but this year the gift from his grandfather had not arrived, and it was already afternoon and he had been six years old for almost a whole day.

It was spring and he went into the back yard and sat under the china-berry tree that grew there like a giant umbrella. Even if Grandfather had forgotten him, or thought him too big for presents any more, it was something which he must accept, as he accepted all the incomprehensible doings of grown folks. Before him, on the beaten, grassless earth which lay like a circle in the tree's shade, Argentine ants were crawling in an implacable circle, their heads lowered as if smelling the earth for guidance, their long bodies sucked sharply at the waist, as if drawn taut, with thread, into two exact ovals.

Arthur leaned against the tree and closed his eyes. His birthday this year had been unsatisfactory as a whole, for his father had been away for almost a year, and there had been no toys at all from his mother, only sensible things which he needed, such as stockings and a new cap. Above him the china-berry tree was loaded with tiny, lavender flowers, but they were already a little past their full bloom, already shriveled a little and crisped at the tips of their minute petals; and bees flew in and out making a drowsy, comforting sound. From the house came his mother's voice, summoning him:

"Arthur? . . . You, Arthur?"

Her voice, when she called him this way, was always uncertain, rising on the last syllable of his name as if she asked a question, as if she pondered his reality. He got up and went to her.

"I want you to run down to the grocery for me," she said. "Here! I've written out a list of things to get. Then go to the butcher shop and ask Mr. Long to give you a pound of stew-meat." All at once she became gay. "When you've done that, you may stop at the drugstore and ask them to send a pint of ice cream at six o'clock."

Arthur's eyes opened wide. "Chocolate or strawberry?"

"Whichever you decide. It's your birthday and we'll have a celebration."

She laughed and touched his head, but almost at once her laughter died, her gaiety vanished. She was counting the coins again and frowning, annoyed and helpless before their inadequacy. "We won't have the ice cream after all," she said. "We'll have it another time."

"But you promised," said Arthur. "You promised; you know you did!"

"We'll have it another time, Arthur. There'll be lots of other times."

Arthur put on his new cap and went out of the door, a puzzled look on his round face. Why had his mother promised the treat and then gone back on her word? He sighed. It was incomprehensible, and there was no sense in trying to figure it out. He must simply accept it as a thing which grown people did, a thing which he could not understand.

He was busy with these thoughts when he returned to the house. His mother saw him and came out to the gate to meet him. She said that the postman had called during his absence and that the present from his grandfather had arrived, after all. It was a toy bank made of iron and trimmed with nickel. It was shaped like an old-fashioned safe and rested solidly on four small legs. Arthur held the present in his hands feeling its weight, excited and slightly disappointed.

"What is it?" he asked. "What is it good for?"

"Why, it's a bank. It's for saving money. I think it's very nice, don't you?" She laughed bitterly. "Very nice, and in extremely good taste, too. Oh, very appropriate!"

The front of the bank could be opened like the door of a vault, and the key which unlocked it was looped through one of the bank's handles with a pink ribbon. Arthur inserted the key and turned the lock. The door swung open and two crisp, one-dollar bills, folded with a piece of notepaper, dropped to the floor. His mother picked up the note and read the message which his grandfather had written:

My dear Grandson:

You are getting old enough to learn thrift and about the value of money. You will find soon enough that it is the only thing you can rely upon in this world, and if you have it you will be independent of everything and everybody. I hope this small gift will be the nucleus of your future fortune, and I wish you a very happy birthday.

Your obedient servant,

John M. Kent.

At that instant the bank became very precious to Arthur. He had not understood the letter entirely, but he felt that his grandfather had given him a talisman against his uncertainty and terror. There were so many things to be afraid of: his father's long and mysterious absence from home, his mother's shabbiness, her worry and her sudden fits of crying. But most of all the toy bank was a thing to protect himself and his mother against the world which lay all about them, the menacing world that his mother knew but of which she did not speak.

Arthur locked the two bills inside his bank and carried the key on its ribbon around his neck. When he shook the bank and listened he could hear the rustling the notes made as they brushed against the iron sides of the cage; and then, one day, he had an idea: he would take the bills and change them into small coins, and each night before he went to bed he would drop one of the coins through the slit in the bank's top. When he told his mother of the plan, she smiled and nodded, and that afternoon the grocer changed the money for him. He went later to the butcher and the druggist, reducing the coins to smaller and smaller amounts, and by nightfall he had forty nickels in his pocket. One of these he dropped into the bank immediately; the others he put into a tobacco tin and hid them under his shirts and underwear.

Each night after he had said his prayers and his mother had gone away, he took a single coin from the tobacco tin and dropped it into the metal bank, listening to the clinking sound it made as it struck the side of the cage. Gradually the bank became heavier and heavier, until, at last, the final coin was deposited. It was then that Arthur gave the key to his mother to keep, as if he feared that he would lose it, or that he might be tempted to open the door and spend the money he had saved; and every night before he went to bed he would lift the bank from its position on the mantelpiece and feel its weight, listening to the sliding sound the coins made as they shifted from side to side at his whim.

Sometimes he would take the bank in his hands and hold it for comfort as he sat in the shade of the china-berry tree. It was late June now and the sun was hot. The tree was covered with small, hard berries, greener than young grass and as lustrous and as polished as emeralds. At his feet the unresting ants passed patiently in their unending circle, or radiated at angles toward the weeds that smothered the garden. Arthur turned the bank over and over in his hot hands. He closed his eyes. He would start school next fall; then, in no time at all, he too would get a job like the grocer's boy; but he would put all the money he earned in his bank, and when it was full he would ask his grandfather to send him another and a larger one.

One day it seemed to him that the bank was lighter. He told his fear to his mother. She smiled and kissed him.

Arthur said: "But it *is* lighter. Here, take it yourself, and you'll see!"

His mother answered, "I think it's just the same. You're six months older than you were when the bank came and you are getting to be such a big, strong boy that it only *seems* lighter."

Then Arthur went away, not quite satisfied, but accepting

what his mother told him as something beyond his reason; and when a few days later the bank was alarmingly lighter, so much so that anybody could tell the difference at once, he said nothing at all. That night he lay in bed thinking, and all the terrors which the bank had quieted came back to him. The next day the bank did not shake at all, no coins rattled against the sides or slid with a comforting, rustling sound over each other when he tilted the bank sidewise.

His mother said: "The coins are stuck together, that's why they don't clink any more. It often happens." She smiled and bent down to kiss him, but Arthur pulled away from her and went outside. He watched his mother from the porch until he saw her go into the kitchen, make a fire in the wood-stove and start preparations for supper; then he tiptoed into the house and entered his mother's bedroom. He found her purse where she kept it hidden in her bureau drawer, and in a pocket was the key to his bank, the pink ribbon, a little soiled and faded now, still dangling. He walked into his own room and lifted the bank from the mantel; but even before the miniature, vault-like door had swung all the way back, he saw that the bank was empty. He stood there for a while holding the bank in his hands. He had known all the time that he would find the bank empty and that his mother had lied to him, but there had been an unreasoning hope that the actual opening of the bank would prove him wrong. He stood holding the bank stupidly, his mouth slightly opened, his eyes frowning; then he made a quick, shrill sound and hurled the bank against the wall.

Almost at once his mother stood in the doorway watching him. She had been wiping a cup, and she still held it half concealed in a dishcloth. When she saw the opened bank a shamed look came over her face.

"Arthur," she said pleadingly. "Arthur, listen to me!"

Arthur said, "You took it! You took it! I trusted you and you took it!" He threw himself upon the floor and pressed his face against the uncarpeted boards. He repeated over and over: "You took it! You know you took it!" He turned on his back and held his hands over his eyes. "Why didn't you ask me for it? I would have given it to you."

His mother put down the cup carefully as if, in her poverty, she was afraid, even at this moment, that a thing as precious as a cup might be broken. She got down upon her knees and tried to comfort him, but he would not let her touch him. She sat back on her haunches and regarded him, and when she spoke at last her voice was unexpectedly bitter:

"Who are you to condemn me? How can you know what I've been through?"

She cried harshly, her thin hands pressed against her cheeks. "Do you think I *wanted* to take your money? Do you think I'd have done it if I hadn't been at the end of my rope? Do you think that badly of me?"

But she saw that he was too preoccupied with his own grief to hear her or to understand what she was saying. She got up, picked up the cup and the dishrag and went out of the room, closing the door behind her. A long time later, after he had exhausted himself, Arthur, too, went out. He sat again under his tree and stared at the familiar and toiling ants. He broke a stick from the tree and held it across the circle in which the ants ceaselessly moved, and the line halted in dismay, touching with their feelers this uncalculated impediment to industry. One large ant, bolder than the rest, began to crawl over the stick, but Arthur lifted the twig and held the ant suspended vertically in mid-air. The ant climbed slowly to the top, and when it found nothing further to grasp it reared upward and explored the vacancy of space with its forefeet, balanced exactly at its black, wasp-like waist; then Arthur reversed the stick and the ant drew the two smooth cylinders of its body together, turned, and finding new purchase, patiently began the ascent again. He was still playing with the twig and the ant when his mother came to the back door and called in her timid, questioning voice:

"Arthur? . . . You, Arthur? Come eat your supper."

But Arthur would not answer his mother at first. He sat rigidly under the tree, his eyes fixed on the earth. "She took it," he repeated over and over. "I trusted her, and she took it." His mind could go no farther than that.

"Arthur?" she called again. "Arthur, where are you?"

Her voice was anxious and she waited for his reply. Suddenly the boy got up in terror and ran toward his mother through the thick weeds. She met him at the steps. She sat down and took him in her arms, smoothing his hair while he cried against her breast. He had accepted what his mother had done although he did not understand it, and he had forgiven her, but he knew, dimly, that while neither of them would ever mention the toy bank again, it would lie between them like a barrier as long as they both lived.

1934

SENATOR UPJOHN

*T*HE WAITING ROOM of the employment agency was cold. The floor was sprinkled with cigarette stubs which had burned out and scarred the floor. The manager, a man with a mouth like a shellhole, sat making notes. Outside, in Sixth Avenue, a radio was broadcasting a New Year's message from Senator Upjohn to his constituents: "This is the richest country in natural resources on the face of the earth and I tell you, my unseen friends, we must not lose faith." His rich voice was cut off, blurred by a truck.

The manager beckoned languidly and the man indicated went to him. He said he had been an actor, a bookkeeper, a salesman. He'd had experience as a stationary engineer. He would do anything. The manager wasn't impressed. He seemed worn out with ineffectual people. He spoke: "How old are you, Kennedy?" Kennedy said: "Thirty-five," but his voice was cautious. There was no conviction in it.

The senator continued: "We must put our shoulders to the wheel in the true American spirit of faith and fair play."

The manager laughed contemptuously: "What the hell you handing me? *Fifty-five* is closer. Did you think I wouldn't spot that dyed hair?" Kennedy closed his eyes. "I had to do something. They won't take a man as old as me." The manager said, drawing pictures on his pad: "Well, is that my fault?"

Senator Upjohn, intoxicated with the beauty of his own voice, was continuing, emotion agitating his words: "I assure you, my friends, there is enough for all; there is food and work for all."

1934

THE LAST MEETING

JOHN came into the dingy, outmoded restaurant and waited
for a moment until his eyes became adjusted to the semi-
darkness of the place. He raised his thin face and stared steadily
above the heads of the dispirited people who sat before him eating their luncheons. After a moment his glance rested on the
vacant table set in an alcove, and he noted with relief that it was
screened somewhat by the palm that stood beside it, a spurious
affair of paper and hemp which sprouted from dusty moss as
false as its own raveling fronds. He went to the table and sat
down, grateful all at once for the slight privacy which the alcove
and the disintegrating shrub afforded. He took off his hat and
his gloves and placed them on the chair beside him. That, he
thought quickly, would force his father to sit opposite him;
there would be the width of the table between them, at least.

A middle-aged waitress, as faded as the background against
which she moved, came up to serve him. She brushed crumbs
and cigarette ash into her tray with a fretful, preoccupied gesture and spread a napkin over the stains that other diners had
left behind them on the cloth. When she had finished, she fetched
a bill-of-fare from a near-by table and put it before him. She
stood looking at him incuriously with eyes which had once been
fine.

"I'm waiting for a guest. I won't order until he comes."

The waitress nodded and filled his glass with water. Then she
walked in heavy-footed silence and sat on a bench near the entry
to the pantry. Another waitress bearing a tray of empty dishes
passed and they spoke to each other, laughed briefly, and then
turned their heads away.

John looked at his watch once more. It was five minutes past
one, and already his father was late, but the thought consoled

him a little and he smiled bleakly. "Why should I expect him to be on time, or to do what he says?" he thought. "I imagine he's changed very little in the past five years." He turned his head at an angle and looked at the door, conscious of the muffled, hammerlike sound of leather heels beating against the boardwalk. But he heard these things dimly, as if from another world, for he was at this moment concerned mostly with his own resentment.

His father had a colossal cheek to force himself on him this way! That was the sheerest cheek, and no mistake about it, after the way he had behaved in the past! There was nothing his father had not done in the old days to shame them all, and it was because of him that John had left home just as quickly as he was able to make a living for himself. Since that time he had endured things, he felt, merely for the sake of his mother and his sisters: the arrogant demands for money which he could not afford, the drafts on his bank account which pride, at first, had made him honor, but which necessity had, at length, forced him to protest. Recently there was the embarrassing matter of the check which the bank manager had questioned and which John had explained.

"But this is so obviously *not* your signature, Mr. Coates. It isn't even an effective attempt. It's plain to anybody that this is a bungling forgery." The official had stopped on an annoyed, ascending note as if he had meant to end his sentence with the words, "my good fellow," but had thought better of it. John had looked coldly at the manager, thinking, "I'd be obliged if you wouldn't patronize me quite so obviously, because I'm an English gentleman, the same as yourself, or at least you have no way of *knowing* that I'm not." He got up, hooked his umbrella over his forearm, and drew on his gloves, smiling with frigid amusement. "I'm afraid I must disagree with you, Sir Robert. That bungling forgery, as you describe it, is my signature, and I'll be obliged if you'll debit my account with the ten pounds."

John shook his head, remembering this recent scene, and glanced again at his watch. It was a quarter past one, and he decided that he would not wait much longer. When his father had telephoned from the railway station that morning, explaining that he had just got in, he had felt a quick, depressed sensation in his stomach and his one thought had been that he must keep his father away from his office and his friends at all costs. He had been panic-stricken for a moment, not quite knowing what to do, and he was surprised at the exactly right note of heartiness he put into his voice when he did answer.

"How long will you be in town, Father? You must have lunch with me, at least! Shall I come to the station to meet you, or do you think you can find your way about?"

And his father had explained in his light, mocking voice which somehow gave the impression that he smacked his lips daintily over his words as if they were tangible things to be tasted: "I know my way about quite well, Mercutio. I lived here as a young man, long before I married your mother or before you were born. You didn't know that, I take it."

"No," said John. "No, I didn't know that."

There had been a moment of silence in which John sat drawing the profile of a man with exaggerated sideburns. He framed his picture in a triangle as precise as he could make it. "Is there any particular reason for your trip, Father? Is it on business?" He drew a circle about the triangle and then obliterated his sketch with four quick, brutal lines.

"No. No, it hasn't anything to do with business, except in a remote way. I merely wanted to visit the place again, to see some of the old friends I remember." There was a short silence and in a moment his father added, "I have been sick, as your mother probably wrote you. I have been quite sick."

It was then that the older man suggested lunch at Ravino's and John agreed hastily before his father reconsidered his choice. He knew of the place vaguely as being close to the boardwalk in the more down-at-the-heel end of the town, but he had never been in it. At any rate, he was not likely to meet any of his friends there, and for that he was grateful; but he was puzzled, nevertheless, that a man of his father's florid tastes should have chosen such an obscure place.

He rested his elbows on the cloth before him and cupped his thin, aristocratic face in his hands. He closed his eyes for a few seconds, but opened them with nervous prescience at the exact instant his father came through the door with aged jauntiness and stood posed inside the room as though he had expected a burst of applause. John pushed back his chair and stood up, thinking, "How he has changed since I saw him last!" But he made no sign of recognition. Then their eyes met across the room and his father came rapidly toward him, his hand stretched forward as if this were a thought-out entrance in one of his for-· gotten, romantic plays. He was, John noted, wearing a soft, pale green hat which was years too young for him, and his light top-coat was too pronounced both in its cut and in its checked lavender-and-fawn pattern.

"Well, this is really very nice! You're looking very well, Mercutio. I'm glad to see you."

John said: "I wish you wouldn't call me that, Father. I don't use the name any more. I've taken the name John since I left home."

"There's nothing wrong with the name Mercutio. It's a very distinguished one, as a matter of fact."

"Possibly so, Father; but I don't like it, I'm afraid."

"I've played the role hundreds of times. It's a very good name, and very unusual."

"I find it slightly absurd, I'm afraid."

He sat down again, smiling with the correct shade of cordiality at the coffee stains on the cloth which the waitress had failed to hide.

"Oh, very well. Very well." The older man hung up his hat and coat and sat opposite his son while he removed his lemon-colored gloves. He stuffed them into the pocket of his topcoat and rested his hands on the cloth. John moved his eyes and examined his father's hands, noting dispassionately that they were as brittle and bloodless as cracked porcelain, and of the same yellowish white; that the nails were swollen a little and the tips of his fingers were blue. It was then he knew that his father was going to die, that before long he would be free of him for-ever. He looked up from the table, thinking these things, and read the framed signs that hung on the wall: Ravino's Still Hocks; Ravino's Dry Amontillado Very Choice; Ravino's Sparkling

Moselles for All Occasions—his lips moving slowly to form the words. When he spoke, his voice was calm, devoid of all emotion.

"How did you amuse yourself this morning, Father? I hope you found something interesting to do."

"I walked about looking at the old places I remembered, but they've torn so many of them down."

"Yes. Yes. That's quite true."

The petulant waitress came toward them and waited while they ordered their luncheons. She adjusted another napkin on the table and filled the two glasses to their brims, her free hand resting professionally on her hips. When she had finished, she bent forward and switched on the lamp that stood on the table, and instantly the older man's face emerged sharply from the blurring duskiness of the alcove. It was then that John saw that his father's hair and eyebrows had been dyed a hard, brittle black, and that against his parchment skin there were spread two unmistakable, fanlike reaches of theatrical rouge.

"I went this morning to call on some of the old friends I remembered, but they're mostly dead now. The ones who are alive didn't seem to place me." He laughed with disbelief. "I didn't think the people here would ever forget me, a small place like this. I played three summers here in repertory, and I was something of a sensation. I tell you, my boy, I packed them in. Things were much different in those days! I was known as Cyril Mullaney then, but my manager made me take my own name when I made my first appearance in London."

Cyril sighed, leaned back in his chair and glanced up at the waitress. He sat up straight and examined her more closely, his eyes half closed. He had seen her before somewhere, he was sure of that, but he could not quite remember the occasion. He shrugged his shoulders and dismissed the matter from his mind. "Yes," he continued, "this place has changed since my day. When I was a young man, Ravino's was the exclusive place to go to, but look at it now! Everybody came here in those days, all the fashionable people. There were private dining-rooms upstairs where we held our parties. It was all very gay."

They selected their food while the heavy-footed waitress noted their orders on a pad. She returned almost at once and put the food on the table before them, and again Cyril looked at her speculatively. He raised his finger and stroked his lip with the mannered, graceful gesture that he had used in so many of his old successes.

"I've known you at some time in my life," he said positively. "I can't place you now, but it must have been many years ago."

The waitress, whose vocabulary had of late been modeled after the American movies she had seen, threw back her head and spoke from the corner of her mouth. "Sure you have. Sure. So what?"

"I remember now," said Cyril. "It all comes back to me. It was the last season I played here. You wrote me a note and met me at the stage door. You had a girl friend, and I brought along a man from the company named Arthur Holden. I was called Cyril Mullaney in those days, don't you remember? We came to this very place for supper." He laughed with delight, his porcelain cheeks stretched tightly across the bones of his face.

The waitress turned and stared. "So what?" she repeated sullenly. "So what, big shot?"

"I even recall your name," continued Cyril proudly. "It's Annie Wheatley."

John leaned back in his chair, so that his face was more completely screened by the dusty palm. "It isn't necessary for him to talk so loudly," he thought. "He's grotesque enough as it is."

The waitress said: "I never saw you in my life before, and what's more if you don't take your hand off my knee I'll call a police officer." She looked contemptuously at the old man, and then turned to John, seeing his embarrassment. "Scram, big shot!" she said. "Scram!" She laughed disdainfully and winked, as if she and John shared a common secret. All at once Cyril became very gay. It wasn't possible for her to have forgotten him. She must remember him. His pictures had been in all the papers and on the boards before the theater. He had had dozens of letters from his female admirers, just as he had received the note from her.

The waitress drew back. "Scram!" she said. "Scram!" She

walked away, disappearing into the obscurity of the service
pantry.

"She hasn't forgotten me!" said Cyril. "She remembers me
very well." He lifted his dying hands again, and again he turned
the turquoise-and-silver ring on his finger.

"Have you been sick long, Father?"

"She remembers me very well, you can be sure of that."

"Did the doctors say what the trouble is?"

"A doctor's concern is to frighten you so badly that you'll
pay his outrageous bills, Mercutio."

"Did your doctor succeed in frightening *you* that badly,
Father?"

"No," said Cyril in delight. "No, I can't say that he did."

There was a long silence between them while they ate, but at
last Cyril spoke again: "Being sick so long has left me short of
funds. It's only temporary, of course, until I get an engagement
for the summer." And John, chewing steadily, looked up and
nodded. His father was coming into the open now. They were
getting down to the real reason for his visit. But his father need
expect nothing from him this time; he refused to be bled any
more.

The waitress came out of the pantry with her friend, a woman
as frayed as herself. They stood whispering together while the
waitress touched her hair and her cheeks and nodded her head
to indicate the direction in which her friend was to look. It was
as if she said: "Yes, he's really got rouge on! There! There, back
of the palm. You can't see him very well from here!"

The second woman picked up a handful of silver and walked
carelessly, too carelessly, in the direction of the alcove. She
stopped at a near-by table and began to rearrange it. She raised
her eyes in anticipation of what she would see, but she got no
farther than John's cold stare fixed steadily upon her face. She
lowered her head, gathered up her silver in confusion, and retreated.

All at once John felt an unaccustomed fury within himself.
He beckoned to the waitress who had served them and who still
stood by the door awaiting her friend's incredulous corroboration

of what she had just been told. She started to turn, but he
crooked his finger imperiously and she came toward the alcove.

"This fork that you gave me is dirty," he began in his cold,
passionless voice. "You can see that it hasn't been cleaned
properly."

She took the fork and examined it, turning it over and over in
her hands, not quite knowing what to say. "I don't clean the
forks," she said at length. "I'll tell them about it in the kitchen."

John smiled steadily, "You don't clean your fingernails either,
it seems, but that, I take it, is a matter of personal choice, Miss
Wheatley."

The woman's neck turned red. She glanced quickly at her
soiled hands and as quickly put them behind her back.

"I don't know the class of people who come here as a rule,"
said John. "Possibly they don't mind. I'm afraid that I find it
slightly—" he paused and smiled again, weighing his words—
"slightly nauseating," he said at last.

"Yes, sir."

Cyril had stopped eating and was looking from his son to the
waitress as if not quite understanding what was taking place.

"You are Miss Wheatley?" said John.

"Yes, sir."

"You may give me the check, please."

He took the slip and folded it into squares. "The gentleman to
whom you were so rude is my father, if that interests you."

Then he got up and helped his father with his coat, proud that
no sign of his fury escaped to the watching world. Cyril looked
at his son's grave face and at once his own face became grave,
as if he could adjust himself instantly to the atmosphere about
him, could be depended upon to fall immediately into any situation and read his lines appropriately, even though he had not
known what had gone before.

When he had settled with the cashier, John held the door for
his father and followed him to the pavement outside. He was, on
the whole, pleased with his handling of the waitress and with
the manner in which he had put her at once in her place. He had
been cool, dispassionate, and completely master of his hands,

his voice, and his face, and that thought would have, on another occasion, pleased him; at the moment, the problem of his father, and what he had better do with him, negatived his satisfaction.

Cyril reached out suddenly and took his son's arm, and John stiffened slightly at the touch, but he lifted his head and smiled his steady, uncompromising smile as they walked along the promenade, talking of things which they both knew to be of no importance, the penetrant breeze from the sea lifting Cyril's coat and swirling it about his knees. After a moment John glanced at his father and then turned his head, for in the sunlight the dyed hair and eyebrows were fiercely revealed, and the spread rouge stood out like crimson patches on yellow cloth. He wondered, then, just what his father demanded of him this time and how long he purposed staying. He was willing to do his duty within reasonable limits, but his personal life, he felt, was his own and he had no idea of sharing it with his father or of introducing him to his friends. Making a place for himself in the stolid, unfriendly town had not been easy, but he had succeeded at last by the unaltering force of his character, and he was accepted now. He would not have that new security jeopardized.

They turned after a moment and went into a small park. They sat together on a bench and watched the sea flashing with silver in the chill April sunlight. They had exhausted their protective talk and they were both silent for a time, neither quite knowing what to say. Again John glanced at his father, and again he turned his head away. He would let the future take care of itself, he decided. He would sit here for a decent interval and then go about his business and dismiss the whole matter from his mind. Perhaps it had been a mistake to see his father in the first place. He would not make that mistake a second time. Certainly he would refuse his father the money he would, inevitably, ask.

Cyril, as if understanding his son's thoughts, began to talk again, his eyes fixed on the sea with a desperate craftiness. "I'm disappointed with my trip on the whole, Mercutio. It has been quite disappointing. My expenses have been very high of late." He turned the turquoise ring on his finger and added, "My sickness, of course . . . I had thought to raise the money among my old friends here, but it seems not." He drew his coat about his thin body and shivered with distaste, as if at some humiliating memory.

"I'm sending home all the money that I can possibly afford. I keep very little for myself."

"Yes, yes, Mercutio. I'm not denying that. But I'm used to so many things, and I can't give them up now. It's different with you."

"There's one thing, at least, that you must give up," said John, smiling fixedly. "You must give up signing my name to checks. That is forgery, as you know."

"You take these things too seriously," said Cyril. "I knew you'd send me the money. It wasn't forgery, really. I merely signed the check with your name to save time."

"Yes," said John. "Yes, I know."

"If I could raise twenty pounds, I think I'd call the visit off and go back home tonight," said Cyril wearily. "The whole thing has been a bitter disappointment."

"I'm sorry, but I haven't twenty pounds, Father."

Again there was a long silence, and then Cyril, as if trying a new attack, began to talk about the daughter who had married the year before and moved to Bristol, while John listened uneasily, suspicious of his father's sudden interest in her welfare. It appeared that the family rarely heard from her, and it seemed as if she were trying to forget that they existed, or that she was ashamed of them now. He had been thinking before his illness of visiting her, to assure himself that she was quite happy in her new home and that her husband treated her with consideration, for he knew her pride, and if her marriage was not successful she would never say a word about it, being much like himself in that respect. At any rate, he would like to make sure.

"There's no necessity for that, Father. I hear from her regularly. She wrote me last week. She's quite happy."

Cyril raised his hand and stroked his lips with his forefinger, his eyes narrowed in shrewdness. "I'd like very much to read her letter," he said after a long pause. "I'd like to assure myself first-hand." John said, "I'm afraid I haven't the letter with me. I left it in my desk at the office"; but almost before the words were off his tongue he knew that he had blundered.

"Shall we go to your office together and get it?" said Cyril gently. "It will give me a chance, as well, to see where you work, and to meet your employers."

John shook his head quickly, lifted his umbrella, and began jabbing at the pebbles in the path. "Why do I permit him this power over me?" he thought. "I'm a grown man. He couldn't exploit me this way unless I permitted it." He held the umbrella against his legs and furled the silk more tightly with his cold hands. When he had finished he fastened the snap and looked steadily out to sea, knowing himself defeated. It would be better, he said at last, if he went alone for the letter, and if his father waited for him there in the park. The office was being decorated, and everything was in confusion. He got up and straightened his necktie, calculating how much money he could possibly spare, wondering if his father would be content with less than the twenty pounds that he demanded. "I'll take a taxi," he said. "I'll be back very soon." He turned and walked away, afraid that Cyril might overrule the plan, but his father sighed, leaned back against the bench, and began to rotate the silver-and-turquoise ring on his finger.

When he reached his desk, John counted the money that remained in his pockets and examined his bank balance again, although he knew to the shilling the amount he possessed. He shook his head helplessly. He would have to ask the cashier for another advance, no matter how greatly he disliked doing so. He concluded his arrangements at length, and wrote Cyril a note: "Dear Father: I am enclosing eighteen pounds. It is all I have at the moment. I hope that you have had an enjoyable trip. Please give the family my regards when you see them tomorrow." He blotted the sheet on which he had written his message, folded it exactly over the notes, and slipped it into the envelope containing his sister's letter. Then he buttoned his topcoat, glanced at himself in the mirror above the washstand, and went out of his office.

His father was sitting on the bench where he had left him, but he got up expectantly at John's approach and braced himself against the seat, swaying slightly. John handed him the envelope, and Cyril, feeling its added bulk, smiled and nodded in approval, his parchment skin pulled so tightly over the bones of his face that he seemed to be a dead man revived for an occasion of gaiety after years in his grave rather than one who was only now going to death after a long and happy life.

"The waitress's name was Blanche Wheatley; not Annie. The girl she brought along for Holden was named Annie."

"Yes," said John.

"You were very rude to her, Mercutio. Unnecessarily rude."

"Yes," said John.

Cyril had become very animated, very arrogant now that he was in funds again. He excitedly shaped the new jade green hat more becomingly to his head, half turned toward the town, and glanced longingly at two girls who passed arm-in-arm down the promenade.

John said: "I'm afraid that I must be getting back to work. I'll say good-bye now."

"You mustn't blame me too bitterly later on," said Cyril; "you mustn't expect me to change at my age."

John said: "No. No, of course not."

He watched while his father turned from the small park and passed on to the promenade, hesitated, and then walked in the direction that the girls had taken, his fingers touching and re-touching his new hat, his silver ring, and his dyed mustache, as though he thought himself still the actor of romantic roles to whom a world of women wrote their amorous, pleading notes. Then all at once his father's retreating figure trembled and shattered before John's eyes, and he knew, then, that the defenses he had built up so laboriously in the past years had failed him at last, and without warning, and that he was stretched again on the rack of old issues which could never be settled for him in this world. He turned and walked toward the bandstand, his eyes unfocused against the blurred and wavering sea, his hands closed so tightly that he could feel the bite of his nails against his flesh.

He would be all right in a minute or so, but he was, he thought scornfully, behaving at this moment precisely like the emotional French, who weep and embrace in the streets. He was a man with no more dignity than those Americans who call noisily to acquaintances across dining-room floors.

"Father! Father!" he said.

He hooked his umbrella over his forearm, raised his thin, delicately chiseled face, and closed his eyes. He pressed his hands against his face and willed not to remember. "Father! Father!" he said. And then a long time later: "Father!"

1936

BILL'S EYES

*T*HE NURSE came into the room where Bill sat and glanced around to assure herself that everything was in readiness for the doctor. They weren't used to such famous men in hospitals of this sort, and she was afraid each time he came to see Bill that the doctor would ask some question which she could not answer, some technical thing which she had learned in her probationary days and had promptly forgotten, such as, "Define lymph, Miss Connors, and state briefly the purpose it serves in the economy of the body."

She dragged her forefinger over the table, examined it critically for smudges, and looked briskly about her for a dustcloth. Since there was none, she lifted her uniform above her knees and held it away from her body while she wiped the table clean with her underskirt. She was conscious of the exposure of her thighs, and she turned her head slowly and looked at Bill. He was a strong, thickset man with a muscular neck and a chest so solid that it seemed molded from the metals with which he had once worked. He was, she judged, about twenty-five. The fact that such a young, full-blooded man could neither see the charms that she exhibited nor react to them, because of his blindness, as a man should, excited her and she began to talk nervously:

"Well, I guess you'll be glad to get this all over with. I guess you'll be glad to know for certain, one way or the other."

"I know now," said Bill. "I'm not worrying. There's no doubt in my mind now, and there never was."

"I must say you've been a good patient. You haven't been upset like most of them are."

"Why should I worry?" asked Bill. "I got the breaks this time, if ever a man did. If there ever was a lucky man it's me, if you know what I mean. I was lucky to have that big-time doctor operate on me for nothing just because my wife wrote and asked him to." He laughed contentedly. "Christ! Christ, but I got the breaks! From the way he's treated me, you'd think I was a millionaire or the President of the United States or something."

"That's a fact," said Miss Connors thoughtfully. "He's a fine man." She noticed that she still held her uniform above her knees and dropped it suddenly, smoothing her skirt with her palms.

"What's he like?" asked Bill.

"Wait!" she said. "You've waited a long time now, and if you wait a little longer maybe you'll be able to see what he looks like for yourself."

"I'll be able to see all right, when he takes these bandages off," said Bill. "Don't make any mistake about that. There's no question of maybe. I'll be able to see all right."

"You're optimistic," said the nurse. "You're not downhearted. I'll say that for you."

Bill said: "What have I got to worry about? This sort of operation made him famous, didn't it? If he can't make me see again, who can?"

"That's right," said the nurse. "What you say is true."

Bill laughed tolerantly at her doubts. "They bring people to him from all over the world, don't they? You told me that yourself, sister! Well, what do you think they do it for? For the sea voyage?"

"That's right," said the nurse. "You got me there. I don't want to be a wet blanket. I just said *maybe*."

"You didn't have to tell me what a fine man he is," said Bill after a long silence. He chuckled, reached out and tried to catch hold of Miss Connors' hand, but she laughed and stepped aside. "Don't you think I knew that myself?" he continued. "I knew he was a fine man the minute he came into the hospital and spoke to me. I knew—" Then he stopped, leaned back in his chair and rubbed the back of one hand with the fingers of the other. He had stopped speaking, he felt, just in time to prevent his sounding ridiculous. There was no point in explaining to Miss Connors, or anybody else, just how he felt in his heart about the doctor, or of his gratitude to him. There was no sense in talking about those things.

Miss Connors went to the table and rearranged the bouquet of asters which Bill's wife had brought for him the day before, narrowing her eyes and holding her face away from the flowers critically. She stopped all at once and straightened up.

"Listen!" she said. "That's him now."

"Yes," said Bill.

Miss Connors went to the door and opened it. "Well, doctor, your patient is all ready and waiting for you." She backed away, thinking of the questions that a man of such eminence could ask if he really put his mind to it. "I'll be outside in the corridor," she went on. "If you want me, I'll be waiting."

The doctor came to where Bill sat and looked at him professionally, but he did not speak at once. He went to the window and drew the dark, heavy curtains. He was a small, plump man with a high, domed forehead whose hands were so limp, so undecided in their movements that it seemed impossible for them to perform the delicate operations that they did. His eyes were mild, dark blue and deeply compassionate.

"We were just talking about you before you came in," said Bill. "The nurse and me, I mean. I was trying to get her to tell me what you look like."

The doctor pulled up a chair and sat facing his patient. "I hope she gave a good report. I hope she wasn't too hard on me."

"She didn't say," said Bill. "It wasn't necessary. I know what you look like without being told."

"Tell me your idea and I'll tell you how right you are." He moved to the table, switched on a light and twisted the bulb until it was shaded to his satisfaction.

"That's easy," said Bill. "You're a dignified man with snow-white hair, and I see you about a head taller than any man I ever met. Then you've got deep brown eyes that are kind most of the time but can blaze up and look all the way through a man if you think he's got any meanness in him, because meanness is the one thing you can't stand, not having any of it in you."

The doctor touched his mild, compassionate eyes with the

tips of his fingers. "You're a long way off," he said laughingly.
"You're miles off this time, Bill." He switched off the shaded
light on the table, adjusted a reflector about his neck and turned
back to his patient, entirely professional again.

"The room is in complete darkness now," he said. "Later on,
I'll let the light in gradually until your eyes get used to it. I
generally explain that to my patients so they won't be afraid
at first."

"Christ!" said Bill scornfully, "did you think I didn't trust
you? Christ! I've got too much faith in you to be afraid."

"I'm going to take off the bandages now, if you're ready."

"Okay!" said Bill. "I'm not worrying any."

"Suppose you tell me about your accident while I work,"
said the doctor after a pause. "It'll keep your mind occupied
and besides I never did understand the straight of it."

"There's not much to tell," said Bill. "I'm married and I've
got three kids, like my wife told you in her letter, so I knew I
had to work hard to keep my job. They were laying off men
at the plant every day, but I said it mustn't happen to me. I
kept saying to myself that I had to work hard and take chances,
being a man with responsibilities. I kept saying that I mustn't
get laid off, no matter what happened."

"Keep your hands down, Bill," said the doctor mildly. "Talk
as much as you want to, but keep your hands in your lap."

"I guess I overdone it," continued Bill. "I guess I took too
many chances after all. Then that drill broke into about a dozen
pieces and blinded me, but I didn't know what had happened
to me at first. Well, you know the rest, Doc."

"That was tough," said the doctor. He sighed soundlessly and
shook his head. "That was tough luck."

"What I am going to say may sound silly," said Bill; "but I
want to say it once and get it off my chest, because there's
nothing I'm not willing to do for a man like you, and I've
thought about it a lot. Now here's what I want to say just one
time: If you ever want me for anything, all you got to do is to
say the word and I'll drop everything and come running, no

matter where I am. And when I say anything, I mean *anything*, including my life. I just wanted to say it one time."

"I appreciate that," said the doctor, "and I know you really mean it."

"I just wanted to say it once," said Bill.

There was a moment's silence and then the doctor spoke cautiously: "Everything that could be done for a man was done for you, Bill, and there's no reason to think the operation was unsuccessful. But sometimes it doesn't work, no matter how hard we try."

"I'm not worrying about that," said Bill quietly, "because I've got faith. I know, just as sure as I know I'm sitting here, that when you take off the bandages I'll be looking into your face."

"You might be disappointed," said the doctor slowly. "You'd better take that possibility into consideration. Don't get your hopes too high."

"I was only kidding," said Bill. "It don't make any real difference to me what you look like. I was kidding about what I said." He laughed again. "Forget it," he said. "Forget it."

The doctor's small, delicate hands rested against his knees. He leaned forward a little and peered into his patient's face. His eyes had become accustomed to the darkness and he could distinguish Bill's individual features plainly. He turned on the small, shaded light, shielding it with his palm. He sighed, shook his head and rubbed his hands against his forehead with a thoughtful movement.

"Have you got some kids at home, too?" asked Bill.

The doctor went to the window. He pulled gently on the cord and the thick curtains parted and slid back soundlessly. "I have three little girls," he said.

The autumn sunlight came strongly into the room and lay in a bright wedge across the floor, touching Bill's hands, his rough, uplifted face, and the wall beyond.

"Well, now, that's funny. I've got three little boys. Can you beat that?"

"It's what they call a coincidence," said the doctor.

He came back to the chair and stood between Bill and the

sunlight. "You can raise your hands now, if you want to," he said wearily.

Bill lifted his hairy, oil-stained hands and rested them against his temples. He spoke with surprise.

"The bandages are off now, ain't they, Doc?"

"Yes."

The doctor shook his head and moved to one side, and again the strong sunlight fell on Bill's broad, good-natured Slavic face.

"I don't mind telling you, now that I got my eyesight back," said Bill, "that I've been kidding about not being afraid. I've been scared to death most of the time, Doc, but I guess you knew that too. That's why I'm acting like a kid today, I guess. It's the relief of having it over and knowing that I can see again. . . . You can turn on the lights any time you want to. I'm ready."

The doctor did not answer.

"My old lady was in to see me yesterday," continued Bill. "She said they're holding my job for me at the plant. I said to tell 'em I'd be there to claim it on Monday morning. I'll be glad to get back to work again."

The doctor was still silent and Bill, fearing that he had sounded ungrateful, added quickly: "I've had a fine rest these last weeks, and everybody has been damned good to me, but I want to get back to work now, Doc. I'm a family man and I've got responsibilities. My wife and kids would starve to death without me there to take care of them, and I can't afford to waste too much time. You know how it is with your own work, I guess."

The doctor went to the door, and spoke gently. "Nurse! Nurse, you'd better come in now."

She entered at once, went to the table, and stood beside the vase of asters. She looked up after a moment and examined Bill's face. He seemed entirely different with the bandages removed, and younger, even, than she had thought. His eyes were round, incorruptibly innocent and of an odd shade of clear, childlike hazel. They softened, somehow, his blunt hands, his massive chin and his thick, upstanding hair. They changed his entire face, she thought, and she realized that if she had not seen them she would never have really understood his character, nor would she have had the least idea of how he appeared to the people who knew him before his accident. As she watched him, thinking these things, he smiled again, pursed out his lips and turned his head in the doctor's direction.

"What's the matter with you?" he asked jokingly. "What are you waiting for? You're not looking for a tin cup and a bundle of pencils to hand me, are you?" He laughed again. "Come on, Doc," he said. "Don't keep me in suspense. You can't expect me to know what you look like until you turn on the lights, now can you?"

The doctor did not answer.

Bill threw out his arms and yawned contentedly, moved in his chair and almost succeeded in facing the nurse who still stood beside the table. He smiled and winked humorously at the vacant wall, a yard to the left of where Miss Connors waited.

The doctor spoke. "I'm about five feet, eight inches tall," he began in his hesitant, compassionate voice. "I weigh around a hundred and seventy-five pounds, so you can imagine how paunchy I'm getting to be. I'll be fifty-two years old next spring, and I'm getting bald. I've got on a gray suit and tan shoes." He paused a moment, as if to verify his next statement. "I'm wearing a blue necktie today," he continued; "a dark blue necktie with white dots in it."

1936

GERALDETTE

*T*HERE was about her that quality of aloofness seen in women who have tired, at length, of the exhibition of their charms, and it was this characteristic, no doubt, which accounted for the story that she had been an actress before her marriage, a story which persisted even after everybody knew, in reality, that she was a teacher in the grade schools of Hutchens when Clyde Harper met her on one of his business trips and married her.

While nobody in town, not even Mrs. Cora Forsythe, had any specific charges to bring against her, it was obvious that the people of Williston didn't quite approve of Geraldette. Perhaps it was her Christian name and the fact that she pronounced it, not as would be expected, with the accent on the first syllable, but on the second: Ger*ald*ette. But as if understanding the slight distrust of the town, and determining to defeat it, Geraldette never talked about herself or her past life. She had no close friends and for recreation she sat mostly on her side porch in the afternoons, or under the lamp in her living-room at night, and did needle-work. Her house adjoined our own, and old Mrs. Paul Cobb, who called to see my mother one afternoon to get her recipe for making lye-hominy, paused on her way home and stood half in, half out, of our front door. She glanced significantly at the Harpers' house and spoke:

"Anybody but Geraldette would get lonesome with her husband gone half the time. It looks like she'd go out more, or mix more, anyway."

Grady and I moved off the steps, where we had been pasting stamps in our albums, and sat beneath the porch, feeling the coolness of the brick supports against our backs. We were ten years old at the time and we had no secrets from each other. We had pledged our friendship forever.

247

"She seems to take an interest in housework and sewing," said my mother.

"I don't for the life of me know what she does with all that Battenburg and Mexican drawn-work after she finishes with it," continued Mrs. Cobb. "Land and water, it looks like the house would be cluttered full of it by this time!" She lowered her voice warningly. "Sh-h-h!" she said. "Here comes Geraldette now." She waited a moment. "Good evening, Mrs. Harper," she said. "What are you working on this time?"

(It was typical that, although everybody called her Gerald*ette* when speaking about her, she was invariably addressed to her face by her married name.)

Geraldette waited a long time before answering, as if time were of no importance to her. She raised her arms, when she had arranged her chair to her satisfaction and had settled herself in it, and exhibited an oblong of thin cloth. "I'm making a table runner and a set of doilies," she said. She turned her chair so that she half faced the wall, lifted her sewing basket and began to work, the long, thin piece of cloth lying across her knees and touching the spot of sunlight on the floor. There was, between her brows, a spot which was always slightly reddened, a small, pea-shaped bump which rose rhythmically and subsided without ever coming to a head, without actually turning into anything so definite as a pimple.

My mother and Mrs. Cobb came onto our own porch and sat in chairs. "How long is Clyde gone for, this time?" asked Mrs. Cobb.

Geraldette lifted her finger and touched the spot between her brows. "Clyde got back this noon," she said. "He had a big dinner and he's lying down resting."

"Well," said Mrs. Cobb, "I hope he had a good trip, because if he don't sell the lumber, there ain't much sense in the boys at the mill making it, now is there?"

Then Mrs. Cobb and my mother, who were settled in their rockers for the afternoon, began to talk of the news of the town, and Grady and I, out of sight below them, listened to what they said. Geraldette listened, too, for they politely kept their voices loud enough to include her in the conversation, if she cared to take part; but she said nothing at all unless asked a direct question. She merely sat rocking in her chair, consulting her pattern at intervals and at intervals touching the reddened spot between her brows.

The talk that afternoon was mostly about Sam Palfrey and what a remarkable man he was, all things considered. He had recently come to Williston to clerk in the commissary and never had anybody so quickly left the imprint of his personality on the town. He had, almost before he got his trunk unpacked, set about organizing a baseball league among the men of the different departments of the plant, and under his sponsorship the teams played after supper, and on Saturday afternoons, in the park between the planer mill and the Negro quarters. He took a Sunday school class of girls and taught them enthusiastically, although it was seen at once that his scriptural knowledge was less, if anything, than that of his pupils. Mr. Palfrey was not religious, he was merely friendly, and if his class learned little about the Bible, it did have a great deal of fun listening to his reminiscences and laughing at his jokes.

He invariably arrived in the Sunday school room breathless and a little late, after the announcements and preliminary prayers had been got through, and sat on the last bench, his thick, brown hair parted precisely in the middle and held down with pomade. He smiled, nodded and looked about him quickly, verifying that his little girls were all there and were ready to assemble about him when the bell rang and classes began. He need not have worried, for each of the fifteen little girls whom he taught was in love with him, and nothing could have induced any one of them to miss a single instant of his presence.

"Sam Palfrey's talking now of getting up a club for putting on plays," said old Mrs. Cobb. "I never saw the beat of that man for get-up-and-git. He's already got eighteen or twenty people on his list of members." She raised her voice, bringing Geraldette into the conversation once more. "But I expect Mrs. Harper knows more about that than I do," she continued in a light, apologetic voice. "I expect she was among the first asked."

"Whatever in the world will Sam Palfrey think up next?" asked my mother mildly.

"I haven't been asked," said Geraldette. "I don't even know him."

"You haven't *met* him yet?" asked my mother in astonishment. "Then you're the only person in Williston who hasn't." She rubbed her palm over the broken place on the arm of the wicker chair. She smiled tolerantly and shook her head. "I don't see how you managed to *escape*. He just came up to me in the butcher shop and introduced himself."

"Why, she don't even *know* him yet!" said Mrs. Cobb in amused despair, but speaking straight in the direction of the velvet-bean vines. "Why, I'd a-thought you and him would be among the first to meet in this town; I'd a-thought that you two would have met right off, somehow, because you got so many interests in common."

Geraldette raised her shoulders languidly and touched the reddened spot between her eyes. She held the pose thoughtfully, as if listening to some sound within her house, unheard by the others. "Clyde's up and walking about," she said. "We must have waked him talking so loud."

Clyde Harper came onto the porch and stood beside his wife, his eyes blinking in the sunlight. He straightened his tie and smoothed down his disheveled hair. He was a small man, with dainty hands and feet. His full, sensual mouth was tightly compressed, and his nostrils lifted and fell with his breath, like the lid of a pot which is worried at its edges by steam. He bent over his wife and kissed her forehead, whispering something in her ear. Geraldette got up at once and went into the house, and Clyde, who was by nature even more silent than his wife, stood talking to my mother and Mrs. Cobb; but he seemed embarrassed and ill at ease, as if the mere effort of speech took too much out of him. "I can never find anything, once I lay it down," he said, "but Geraldette will put her hand on it in no time."

Geraldette returned to the porch and handed him his order book and pencil, sat again in her chair and continued her sewing. Clyde opened the book and examined it studiously, his wide,

thin nostrils expanding and sinking under the repressed intensity
of his breath, as if he hoped to find some sentence there which
he could repeat and which would cover the embarrassment of
his departure. He shut the book finally and said: "I'm going to
the office now. I'll be back in time for supper."

When he had gone, the talk turned again to Mr. Palfrey. It
seemed, during the next weeks, that the town talked of little else,
for the play which his committee had selected—it was called "A
Wife's Ordeal"—was taking shape under his coaching, and the
whole town was interested. It was produced at last in the Knights
of Pythias hall, and it was a great success. It was played on a
Friday night, I remember, because the next day was Saturday
and Grady and I were going fishing for the last time before
school started. We had spent the afternoon digging wiggler-
worms for bait and had put them, in a can sprinkled with earth,
in our woodshed for safekeeping. Since we were both going to
Mr. Palfrey's play, and were to get up at daybreak the next
morning, Grady was spending the night with me.

At the last minute two of Mr. Palfrey's actors got stage fright
and refused to go on, but fortunately they both had small parts
which Mr. Palfrey could play also without conflicting with the
principal male role which he had finally accepted after it was
found that it could not be adequately filled otherwise. The evening, as it turned out, was entirely his, and nobody begrudged
him his success; but oddly enough it was his interpretation of one
of the small, abandoned parts—that of an old grandmother who
sat by the fire in the second act—which amazed the people most.

"I've seen shows in regular city theaters," said Mrs. Alf Hen-
derson over and over, "and among the best, too; but never have I
seen anything to touch Sam Palfrey as that poor old lady, heart-
broken over her granddaughter's fatal misstep."

Grady and I left at once. The last thing we saw was Mr.
Palfrey standing among his admirers, the pinkish make-up still on
his face, and looking very dashing in his velveteen jacket and
knee breeches which the costume committee had made for him
out of an old pair of wine-colored curtains. He kept moving
backwards, as if to escape his admirers, laughing with deprecia-

tion, raising his hands outward and disclaiming any credit whatever for the success of the show. We went home through the alley, but stopped for a moment at Geraldette's gate, for there, beneath her lamp, and beside the open window, she sat and worked with slow, mechanical efficiency on a sofa pillow.

"I guess everybody in town was there except Geraldette," said Grady. "It looks like she don't care for anything but sewing."

I didn't answer until I was in bed beside him and had blown out the lamp. "Clyde left on another trip yesterday. I guess Geraldette thought it wouldn't look right to go to the show with him out of town."

We went to sleep at once, but Grady woke me suddenly in the night. He had dreamed that all the worms had crawled out and got away, and he wondered if I had thought to put a piece of wood or a brick over the top of the can. I had not. I had merely set the dirt-filled can on a rafter and left it there. I didn't believe the worms would get out, but Grady insisted that he had read that somewhere in a magazine. We got up after a time and dressed. We tiptoed down the stairs, yawning behind our hands. I looked at the clock in the hall. It was ten minutes past two.

We walked, Indian fashion, close to the board fence which separated our house from the Harpers', but before we reached the shed we stopped at the same instant and looked at each other, for we had both heard a crunching step on the Harpers' gravel walk. Silently we pulled ourselves upward and peered over the dividing fence, and in the faint light we saw Geraldette standing against her back door. She seemed to have on nothing except her nightgown and slippers, and as we stared she rolled her head languidly against the door and yawned. We knew at once that the man standing halfway down the walk was Sam Palfrey. Then Geraldette whispered something which we couldn't catch and came down the steps toward him. They met in the shadow of the japonica bush and clung to each other passionately for a minute or two, their bodies locked, their lips pressed together.

When we were in bed again, Grady spoke: "Clyde's got Indian blood in him, they say. If he ever finds out what's going on, he'll kill Sam Palfrey as sure as you're born."

I said: "We got to swear never to tell what we saw tonight. Never as long as we live."

"Go get the Bible," said Grady. "We'll swear on that."

We took our oaths with our hands resting on the Book. "How did they ever manage to get acquainted?" I asked after a moment. "How did Sam Palfrey manage to meet her? That's what I can't figure out."

We lay back against our pillows and pulled the sheets up to our chins. We were excited and a little solemn at our knowledge, but most of all we were proud of Mr. Palfrey. It seemed to us then that there was no difficulty which he could not surmount, and we were happy, somehow, that we belonged to the same sex as his own. That next afternoon Geraldette came onto her porch at the usual time, dragging her rocker behind her. When she had seated herself, and got her sewing basket arranged, I went to the dividing fence and peered over.

"What are you making this time, Mrs. Harper?"

She held up her work, but she didn't answer at once. Finally she said: "I'm crocheting a sort of head doily for one of the parlor chairs. I don't know what the regular name for it is."

"It don't look so comfortable, does it?"

My mother, hearing our voices, came to the window and spoke to me. "Don't pester Mrs. Harper, son. Can't you see she's busy?"

"One of these days," said Geraldette, "when I get more time to myself, I'm going to make a knotted bedspread. I always wanted to make one and I believe I can do it."

"They're a lot of trouble to do," said my mother. "Mrs. Cobb's daughter started one last year, but she gave it up."

"I knew a lady back home in Hutchens who made one," said Geraldette. "She was offered twenty-five dollars for it."

"I imagine it was worth it, at that," said my mother.

"The material alone came to twenty-three dollars," said Geraldette, "not counting the work, and that was worth *something*."

She stopped, as if already she had talked too much, and lapsed again into her old, contemptuous lethargy. She rested her hands in her lap, raised them and touched the waning bump between her brows.

"You should have been present at 'A Wife's Ordeal' last night," said my mother sympathetically. "Sam Palfrey certainly made a name for himself with his good work. I never saw such a performance in all my life as the one he gave when he turned loose, finally, and just let himself go. You missed a treat, indeed, Mrs. Harper!"

"Did it go off well?" asked Geraldette idly.

I walked away in the direction of Grady's house, wanting to tell him of this conversation, but I remembered my oath. Not once during the following weeks did we speak of what we knew, but I got into the habit of lying in bed, long after the rest of the family were asleep, and listening for Mr. Palfrey's step on the gravel walk next door, wondering when Clyde would find out and when it would happen.

Then, to the amazement of the town, it did happen. Grady and I heard the details as soon as we were out of school. It seemed that Clyde had come into the commissary at about 1:35, pulled a pistol out of his pocket and had shot Sam Palfrey. Sam was selling a can of salmon to Mrs. Horton's colored cook at the time, and the force of the bullet had knocked him backward over a molasses barrel. This, the town thought, had saved his life, for Clyde's next two shots went high and did no damage. Then Mrs. Horton's cook began screaming: "He's done killed him! I know he's done killed him!" She threw the whole force of her black bulk against him, grabbed his arms and struggled with him until the other people in the store came up and disarmed him. Clyde shook his head at the people's questions and would not answer. He stood uncomfortably with his back against the counter, his full sensual lips pressed together, his nostrils lifting upward and falling with slow, passionate calmness. Later on they had taken Mr. Palfrey to Dr. Cromwell's office, where his wound had been dressed and the bleeding stopped, but they had decided to put him on Number 47 and to send him to Mobile for a regular operation. They had, therefore, taken him to the L. & N. station on a stretcher, so we learned, and that was where he now was.

When we had taken in these details Grady and I, without waiting to discuss the matter, turned and ran rapidly in the direction of the station. We approached from the rear, that being the shorter way, and the first person we saw was little Mamie Lou Giddings, one of the girls of Mr. Palfrey's Sunday school class. She had beaten us by a few seconds only and she stood, now, panting, against the steps of the freight depot, too breathless, even, to pull up her ribbed stockings, too torn with anguish to note that her tidily kept pencil-box had come unfastened and that erasers, pen points and stubs of colored crayon were spilling about her unlaced shoes. Then Ellie Childers and Blanche Forsythe arrived at the same moment, peered from behind a tank car on the siding and jointed Mamie Lou against the steps. The three little girls stood huddled together for comfort, but their eyes were averted with grief and they did not speak.

They had put Mr. Palfrey in the white people's waiting room and his stretcher, with its soiled, grayish blanket, was placed diagonally between the stationhouse stove and the woodbox. Neil Arrowmake, the station agent, was on guard at the door, keeping back the curious people. Grady and I worked our way through the crowd and peered in. Sam groaned, rolled his head from side to side and lifted upward on his elbows. When he saw us standing there, with our wide-opened mouths, he spoke to Neil. He wanted to talk to us, he said, since we were young boys with our whole lives before us. He wanted to give us the good advice which he, himself, had never received. The men at the door shoved us forward and we went sheepishly toward the stretcher. We stood above Mr. Palfrey and listened while he talked in a contrite voice.

He wanted his plight to be an object lesson, he said; he wanted us to realize that there was no happiness in violating the commandments of God and the laws of man, and if we profited by his mistakes, then his pain was not wasted; there was a point, in that event, to his present suffering which would make it endurable. All at once I knew that Mr. Palfrey wasn't shot very badly and that he'd soon be well again.

Grady, who had not even been listening to him, squatted down on the floor. "How did Clyde manage to find out about you and Geraldette?" he asked softly. I knelt on the other side of the stretcher and before we knew it, we were telling him what we had seen on the night of the play, of our oath and how we had not once spoken of the matter since, not even to ourselves. Mr. Palfrey, overcome for a moment at such loyalty, reached out and took our hands in his own. We were, he said, true friends.

The people outside, thinking that we were praying together, shuffled their feet and took off their hats. After a moment Mr. Palfrey answered Grady's question, but his manner to us had changed now, for he had accepted us as equals and fellow-conspirators. He winked cautiously behind his hand and beckoned us to bend closer over his cot. He did not have the faintest idea, he said, how Clyde had found out; possibly Geraldette knew, but he hadn't seen her since the shooting, and it wasn't likely that he would ever see her again with things the way they were. It was a pity, for naturally he would always wonder.

He asked us then to move his stretcher so that his body was turned away from the people in the doorway, and when he was certain that they could no longer see his face, he raised his eyebrows and laughed. He stuck the tip of his tongue between his teeth and winked humorously as if to say: "I can play these penitent parts if people expect it, but they aren't my choice. My natural bent is for gay, romantic roles or light comedy." He moved his hands about, sighed voluptuously and spoke in so soft, so quick a voice that we had to bend close to catch what he was saying.

"You'd never believe, just to look at her, what a fine figure she's got," he said rapturously. "I've seen a good many in my time, and I know what I'm talking about." There was a misty, swimming expression in his eyes. "By God! she was a well-made woman," he said. He stopped suddenly, overcome with the memory of Geraldette's beauty, but a moment later he began to speak again, to catalogue more methodically her charms, as if he had wanted to talk to some appreciative person about these things for a long time, for already, even before her husband's bullet was safely out of his flesh, she had become one of his reminiscences. Before he had finished the train pulled into the station and stopped and the men came into the waiting room and picked up the stretcher.

By that time Mr. Palfrey's entire Sunday school class had assembled to see him off. They stood grouped together against the steps of the freight depot, crying silently and twisting their dresses, their eyes fixed on the ground, but when the men carried Mr. Palfrey to the baggage car and lifted the stretcher high in the air, the fifteen little girls could control their grief no longer. They threw their arms about each other and cried loudly, for no matter what their elders might say later on about Mr. Palfrey, and no matter what individual punishments awaited them for this, their public behavior, they loved him still, and they did not care at this moment who knew it. He had repudiated them, they felt, and had left them abandoned and ashamed, but their betrayal was collective and not individual, and they would bear it collectively, taking comfort from one another. They climbed upon the platform so that they could see him to the last, their slates and geographies clasped to their immature chests.

"Good-bye, Mr. Palfrey!" they called in their shrill, anguished voices. "Good-bye! Good-bye! Good-bye!"

I stood by the tracks as the train pulled out of the station, passed over the trestle and blew, at length, for the crossing at Ewell. I had meant to ask Mr. Palfrey a question, but I had had no opportunity after he began to talk about Geraldette. The thing that troubled me was how he had managed to meet her in the first place. He couldn't have gone up to her in the butcher shop and introduced himself as he had with my mother, for she would have merely looked at him a moment, smiled her vague, indifferent smile, moved away and have forgotten him the next instant. Had she written him a letter and made an appointment? Had they known each other before they both came to Williston? Had he simply gone to her house, knocked on the door and entered? It was probable that I would never know now.

I expected the family would want to know where I had been so long, but when I got home nobody said anything to me. Old Mrs. Cobb and her daughter Helen had come to call on my mother and they were just seating themselves comfortably when I came in and hung up my cap. The purpose of her visit, Mrs. Cobb explained, was to give my mother the recipe for May haw jelly which she had promised last summer. The thing had slipped her mind until that very afternoon, but when she recalled it, she and Helen had just hurried over as they were, without bothering to dress. She knew my mother would be anxious to have the recipe at once, for it would come in handy next May when haws were ripe once more in the swamps.

I found out more information from Mrs. Cobb and Helen. They had taken Clyde to the lockup for safekeeping, until they could get Mr. Palfrey out of town safely, but there would be no charges against him and no doubt he would be released any minute now. He had refused to say anything when they questioned him, but the town was buzzing with excitement over the affair and they knew, without being told, that a man shoots another one, without obvious provocation, for one reason only. Nobody had seen Geraldette since morning, and the shades were still drawn on both sides of the house.

Mrs. Cobb placed her chair by the window and pulled back the curtains, peering out at the Harpers' house. "I'd be scared out of seven years' growth if I was in *her* shoes," she said. "God alone knows what a man like Clyde will do to her when he comes home."

Helen said: "They got no right to let Clyde out at all. A man like that! Going about shooting people!"

Then, as they talked, the side door opened and Geraldette came onto her porch, dragging the rocker behind her. She arranged her sewing at her feet, spread the material on which she was working over her lap and looked for a moment up and down the street, but languidly and without interest, as if, already, she had digested the situation and had dismissed it from her

mind as of no further importance. Slowly she raised her hand
and touched the diminishing bump between her brows, smiled
her aloof, enigmatic smile and began to work.

"She's started on her knotted bedspread," said my mother in
awe. "She said she was going to make one when she had more
time on her hands."

1936

SWEET, WHO WAS THE
ARMORER'S MAID

ON SATURDAY nights, when their work for the week is done, the charwomen gather in the steamy basement of the building awaiting their pay. Occasionally they speak of corridors or of difficult baseboards which they have scrubbed in their time, but mostly they sit in silence, their stiff hands curved against their pinned-up skirts, until the manageress comes to check their buckets and mops and to give them the money they have earned. Then they open their envelopes and count the shillings, the half-crowns and the small notes with trembling fingers. Later on, three of the charwomen, Lilian Mitchell, Ella the American, and the German woman Hennie, go to The Queen's Coin, Joe Mallet's public house, for their evening of pleasure.

Joe's pub is conspicuous for its drabness even in its neighborhood of dirt and listless rain. In the daytime, when loaded lorries from the dock rumble past and almost brush the sides of the buildings that line the narrow street, the sign above the door trembles with its wall, and even the glasses behind the bar vibrate. But in spite of its dreariness, The Queen's Coin has a distinction of its own, a uniqueness which has set it apart, for there is a legend that Elizabeth, the Queen of England, once stopped there on a summer afternoon and ordered a mug of ale.

When she had finished, she tossed a silver coin in payment, but it fell short, hit the railing edgewise and rolled off among the tables and the empty casks. After she had ridden away, the publican, his barmaid, his wife, and the customers who had stood gaping against the wall came to life and began to search feverishly for the lost piece of silver. At the end of exactly forty-two minutes it was found in the adjoining room, standing upright against the leg of one of the benches. The incident has now

260

passed into the web of English tradition, for on each anniversary of that day the original situation and search is duplicated and the publican, his wife, his barmaid and the patrons who have gathered for the ceremony get down earnestly upon their knees, thrust their rumps into the air and seek for the coin which had already been found more than three hundred years ago.

But the three old women do not go to The Queen's Coin because of its traditions or its historical significance. Their preference for it is due entirely to the fact that they consider Joe Mallet, the present lessee, their particular patron. Once, years before, when Lilian Mitchell was a celebrated beauty at the height of her splendor, Joe, as an errand boy, had brought flowers to her from her admirers. Once she had incredibly given him ten shillings and had told him to buy mittens for his reddened hands and stockings for his thin, gangling legs. He had never mentioned the incident, nor had he identified himself, but, because of his memory, he gave Lilian and her friends free drinks when they had no money and let them sit in his warm public house and talk of their past.

One Saturday night the three wrecked beauties went to The Queen's Coin and entered in single file. They glanced incuriously at Joe's two barmaids, chaste, blonde women who seemed carved from twin blocks of wood and then gilded badly. Sam, the waiter, wiped his forearms on the towel he wore tucked through his belt, came up at once and spoke to them.

"Coo!" he said. He turned and winked at the twin barmaids, but they paid not the slightest attention to him. "Coo!" he repeated. "Coo! It's narsty wevver we're 'aving. Proper *narsty wevver* it is, not 'arf!"

The old beauties walked through the smoke-filled room and sat at their table in the back. The little thieves and the petty thugs who lined the bar turned at the sound of their hoarse, old women's voices and looked at them a moment, turned their backs and went on with their conversations. Sam came up with the bottle of gin which they invariably bought on these occasions.

Ella, being an American, and for that reason considered more practical than the others, figured the cost of the bottle, divided

by three and collected from her companions. When the trans-
action was completed and the money had been counted against
Sam's purplish palm, he filled the glasses. Then the old women
clutched their drinks in gnarled fingers, with acorn-swollen nails,
and raised three bloated, work-cracked fists, drinking their gin
at a single gulp. Almost immediately they felt it flaming through
their veins, deadening the present, bringing back the past. Again
they drank from filled glasses, and again they felt the fierce
impact of the alcohol. They sighed and leaned back against their
chairs. This was the moment for which they had worked all
week. Their tongues were loosened at last. They could talk
again of the old times, the beautiful days that were lost forever.

Lilian put down her empty glass, an expression of sadness in
her face. "I never thought I'd come to this," she said. "I never
thought I'd end this way." She shivered a little. She was a shapeless woman, with legs slashed across by swollen veins and lips that
resembled relaxed bacon-rinds. Her teeth were yellow, broken
and decayed. Her nose was pulpy and soiled and threaded
throughout with purplish veins. Not one feature gave any hint
of the beauty that Joe alone remembered now, the beauty that
had made her famous in her generation.

Hennie nodded her head. "*Ja! Ja!*" she said. "*Immer so. Immer
so.*" She lifted her glass invitingly and put it down, a dreamy
look in her eyes as if she listened to a waltz.

"Things would have been different with me, too," said Ella,
"only my boy got in trouble in Cleveland." Then she added
fiercely: "They framed him, the dirty scuts! They framed him,
that's what they done!" She wiped her lips on the back of her
hand. "Cleveland is a town in Ohio," she added. "It's the town
I come from."

Lilian continued: "Robbie Markham was mad over me, as I
told you. Everybody in Mayfair knew about it. Robbie gave me
the necklace I was telling you about. He put it around my throat
one night and fastened the catch. Afterwards he kissed me back
of my ear and said, 'Your neck is like the whitest marble.'"
Lilian smiled roguishly and touched the place that her sweetheart had once kissed, but her neck was foul, now, and fallen to

pieces. It was patterned, criss-cross, with wrinkles, like the diamond-patched back of a snake. She filled her glass again.

"A fellow in Milwaukee gave me a diamond ring one time," said Ella, "but the next morning he said I stole it offen him while he was drunk, and I had to give it back." She paused a moment, sipped her gin daintily and then continued: "Milwaukee is in the state of Wisconsin. It's a nice town. They made beer there in them days. Maybe they do yet. How do I know?"

Hennie drank her gin slowly, shuddering each time she swallowed. "*Ja*," she said, smiling vaguely. "*Ja, ja, ja.*" For no apparent reason she began to laugh to herself. "*Immer so*," she said. "*Immer so.*"

"Robbie used to come to my house to see me, but never when Mr. Ryder was there," said Lilian. "I laughed and told him to forget me, but he took my hands in his and kissed them reverently until I made him stop. 'You're so lovely and unsoiled,' he said. 'You're like an English rose in a hedgerow.'"

She leaned back against the wall, her hair hanging about her face in grayish folds, and as she sat there remembering her triumphs, she kept pushing the falling hair from off her face. A feeling of sadness came over her. Robbie had taught her everything: how to speak, how to dress, how to carry her head. He had brought her the right books to read, had told her the right gossip about the right people and she had never questioned his advice. He had been more like a schoolmaster than a lover, and she had memorized the poems that he had marked as important at the moment, had rehearsed diligently the amusing anecdotes which he had, himself, written for her. And she did not remember, now, what had happened to him at last. It was all so long ago.

"When I was playing in burlesque," said Ella, "I got featured billing. They billed me as Ella DeVoe, the Nineteenth Century Venus. That was in Chicago, in the big state of Illinois."

The two blonde barmaids turned their heads at the same instant, as if their long teamwork together had made it impossible for them to function separately, and looked blankly at the bloated, garrulous old women, examining for an instant the mottled flesh which hung pendulous from their withering jaws.

They raised their eyebrows, touched their gilded hair and turned back to their customers with the same stiff movement of their torsos, their reaching teeth half bared in faint, well-bred cordiality.

Lilian sat with her hands relaxed in her lap, her eyes far away, a slight smile on her lips. "One afternoon I went to walk in the park with my dogs. It was snowing, I remember, but there was no wind to blow it into your face. It fell straight down, without any sound. Then I saw Mr. Ryder coming toward me. We met and walked together through the park. 'Now, Mr. Ryder,' I said, 'you're making a great deal out of nothing. Robbie doesn't mean anything to me at all, and you know it.' 'I notice, nevertheless, that you're wearing his jewelry,' he said. 'You must give him back his presents. I won't have you taking things from other men!'"

Several strangers had come into the bar and had lined up, and Joe, himself, was serving them. The three old women looked at the newcomers for an instant, and then, as if upon signal, looked down again.

Ella said: "In Atlanta, Georgia, fellows would come into the house and ask for me by name. Real spenders they was, not tightwads like they have these days. 'Where's little Ella tonight?' they'd say to the Madame. 'She's a dandy!' they'd say; 'she sure is a good kid!' Many's the time I've made fifty or seventy-five bucks in a night. But that was in Frisco. 'She's a sweet baby,' they'd say."

Lilian was not listening. "When Mr. Ryder said what he did, I looked up and smiled at him. He was a handsome man. There are no men like him any more, no real gentlemen. He loved me and he spent money like water, but he had a wife in Scotland and two daughters in school on the Continent somewhere. 'You must give up this half-baked poet,' he said. 'Give him back his presents!' The snow was falling all about us. The dogs were covered with snow. They kept shaking themselves and looking at us with sad eyes. When they shook off the snow the bells on their harness tinkled. I felt happy all of a sudden. Then I saw a beggarwoman walking toward us through the snow. I took off the necklace and dropped it into her cup. 'Take it, you pitiful old thing,' I said. 'Take it! Take it!' "

The doors pushed forward and three water-front women entered with their sailors. The women were young and exuberant with full, rouged mouths and black, beaded lashes. They were, already, a little tipsy, and they swayed across the room with noisy good-nature, crowding themselves at the table to the right. When they were seated with their men, one of the girls tilted back her chair and laughed loudly.

Ella said: "Mind your manners, Miss!" She straightened her hat and pulled her chair closer to the table. "Mind your manners!" she repeated fiercely, but under her breath, as if she addressed her known world and knew the futility of protest.

"When Mr. Ryder left me at my door, I went upstairs to dress, and I found Robbie waiting for me. He had brought a new book, a volume of poems written by a Mr. Swinburne, a friend of his whom he admired greatly and who was fashionable at the time. He had marked the passages that he wanted me to memorize, and he read them aloud to me while I dressed." Lilian closed her eyes and smiled, reliving her happy past. "I even remember a part of the poems to this day," she said. She bent closer to her companions, to make herself heard above the merriment of the sailors and their girls, and recited slowly, her lips smiling a little, her brows drawn together:—

> "Meseemeth I heard cry and groan
> That sweet, who was the armorer's maid,
> For her lost youth did make sore moan
> And right upon this wise she said:
> 'Ah, fierce old age with foul bald head,
> To slay fair things thou art over fain,
> Who holdeth me? Who? Would God I were dead;
> Would God I were well dead and slain!' "

She lifted her head proudly at her feat of memory, and the folds of sagged flesh which hung pendent and dead from her cheeks, and the wrecked line which had once been her throat, trembled to her pride. She knew that neither Ella nor Hennie had been listening to her; that they were not concerned with such transitory things as poems. They were, she knew, thinking of their own triumphs instead, but she did not care. She was not really speaking to them, after all.

"New Orleans was the place in the old days," said Ella. "*There* was the town for real spenders and for good times! Men weren't tightwads, the way they are now." She straightened, turned and looked angrily at the young woman whose chair pressed hers, whose voice drowned out her own. "Mind your manners, Miss," she repeated sullenly, the words coming from her lax, toothless mouth with a blurred lisp.

The three old women sat-silent for a time, staring with patient exasperation at the noisy table to their right and then glancing down at their own work-cracked hands. They finished their bottle and looked at each other significantly. They rose, pushed back their chairs and straightened their clothing, for their evening was spoiled and there was no sense, now, in trying to prolong it. They walked with grave unsteadiness to the door while the gilded, spinsterish barmaids stared at their retreating backs with the dispassionate calmness of primitive woodwork. A moment later they were on the pavement outside, swaying there, leaning against the side of the building for support.

In the street to the left were pushcarts pulled up to the curb, and housewives milled about and jostled one another under the harsh, revealing flares. They pulled their shawls more closely about their shoulders, pinching the vegetables and the pale fruit, turning over the shoddy material spread before them and examining it thriftily before they spent their sixpences. From the river there came a liquid, washing sound and the sharp smell of minor putrefaction. A peddler, trundling his barrow, was approaching. When he saw the three swaying, undecided old women, he stopped his cart and showed the cheap lace and stockings that he sold, holding them spread on his forearm.

Lilian rubbed her roughened hands over her face. "That night I wore a gown of mousseline peau de soie, fitted to the figure, which Mr. Ryder had bought for me in Paris. Across the upper ruffle of the bodice, and down the side of one panel, was a flock of black swallows in full flight." She leaned against the wall and lifted her pouched face to the glare of the gaslights. She was talking too loudly, she felt, a thing which Robbie had so often warned her about, but she was unable to stop now.

The peddler, who did not understand English very well, looked at her a moment and then, patiently, began to repack his wares. Two soldiers on leave and a workman stopped, stared at the old women and laughed.

Lilian began to throw her arms about with stiff, grotesque gestures. "When I came out of my boudoir, Robbie Markham put down the book of poems. He looked at me a moment in wonder and said: 'A man could die for you and not regret it!' He took my hands and kissed the tip of each finger. 'These little, white hands,' he said. 'So lovely. So helpless.' He took me in his arms and held me. He said, 'You're like a pink rose with the dew on it.'"

A police constable came over slowly. "What's the matter 'ere?" he asked. He turned to Ella and permitted himself a pleasantry. He said: "You'd better take this rosebud back to the conservatory, Miss, before I do my duty and run her in for disturbing the peace."

A man in a plaid cap grinned toothlessly under the gas flares and spoke: "Are you sure it was a *rose* he called you, Grandma?"

The three old beauties swayed, righted themselves and passed unsteadily between the avenue of flares, walking in single file on the outer edges of their feet with the springless, mechanical gait of old people whose bones have settled to habitual rhythms, their elbows drawn close to their flanks as if there were still mops trailing behind them, their taut arms straight down as if they bore without release the totaled weight of all the scouring water they had ever lifted.

"The scuts!" said Ella fiercely. "The dirty scuts! They frame you, that's what the police do to you. Even in this country they frame you!" She shoved the straggling hair out of her eyes. "The scuts!" she repeated. "The bloody scuts!"

But Lilian was speaking again, her head nodding to her words: "Between the panels, the skirt was powdered with gold and decorated with bows of white satin antique, with a fringe of gold. The sleeves were gold powdered mousseline and the flounces were of plain mousseline edged with d'Anencon lace, four inches deep."

"*Ja*," said Hennie in a high, delighted voice. "*Ja! Ja! Ja!*" But her words were not meant for Lilian, nor for any living thing in this world. She spoke, instead, to the man who stood forever at her elbow, the dead man who walked beside her wherever she went. She cupped her hands over her shapeless belly, nodding her head with the timed jerkiness of an ingenious toy. "*Ja!*" she continued eagerly. "*Ja! Ja!*" her face yielding and yet coquettish, her voice soft and delighted.

1936

THE LISTENING POST

*T*HEY stood there at the listening post and looked outward across the land, their rifles resting against their relaxed bodies, their elbows leaning on the parapet before them. Morning was not far away, but there was no sign of light breaking against the sky; there was, as yet, only a dimming of stars already diminished, and the moon that lay close to the horizon gave, now, an unpolished and an ashen glow.

Johnnie sighed and shifted his weight. A wind had sprung up and he lifted his head and breathed deeply, as if he would smell out the spring before its first sign appeared. He spoke after a moment, his words muted against his cupped palm, his voice soft and sibilant.

"It's already springtime in Alabama," he said. "Redbud is out in the swamps at this moment and the willows back of the Brennan place are as green as can be." He picked up his rifle and rubbed his hand against its stock. "The azaleas in Mrs. Sam Tyson's front yard are in full bloom."

Alan nodded his head. "Yes," he said absently. "Yes."

"I lived in town, like I told you last night," continued Johnnie, "but I knew the Brennan boys well. I used to go out there pretty near every Saturday. When the clump of willows started to turn green, we knew it would soon be time to go swimming again. One of the Brennan boys—he was just my age—was named Dave. He enlisted the same time I did. In fact, five of us quit high school in our senior year to enlist together. Well, Dave Brennan was one of them."

Alan unbuttoned his tunic and let the fresh air of morning blow against his neck. Before him, in the space between the listening post and the enemy trenches, were the bodies of men killed in a raid earlier that night. The men lay stiff and sprawling, their bodies outlined in the light of the thin, late risen moon.

Johnnie said: "Everybody laughed when they heard Dave Brennan had enlisted. They said they couldn't think of anybody who'd make a worse soldier. Dave could never stand to see anything suffer, and even the sight of blood made him sick. When they butchered at the farm, Dave used to go stay in town with Arthur Scales until it was all over."

Alan straightened a little, staring again at the bodies of the men before him, wondering who they were and what they had been in life, and as he watched, he saw a column of mist moving detached and ghostlike across the field. He took off his helmet and put it beside his elbows on the parapet, but his eyes remained fixed on the moving column of mist. All at once he began to feel quiet and strange. "It might almost be a man," he thought. "That column of mist looks like a man gliding about in a long, white robe."

Johnnie said: "Dave Brennan was a Catholic and he said he wanted to be a priest when he grew up. He was always nice to everybody, and people liked him, even if they did laugh at him when he enlisted to end all wars forever."

Alan nodded his head, not listening and yet hearing, somehow, the story that Johnnie told. With some impersonal and yet passionate part of his mind he weighed and sifted the story until he found, at length, its basic meaning; then, unconsciously, he began to weave the new meaning he had found into his own phantasies, keeping a part of Johnnie's story intact as he heard it, re-creating a part and resetting the whole against the background of the trenches, the barbed wire and the dead soldiers. He sighed and shifted his weight, following the slow-moving column of mist with his eyes. "It might even be Christ moving across the field," he thought. He rested his face in his palms, his eyes withdrawn and without expression.

"I often wonder what finally became of Dave Brennan," said Johnnie. "We all went through training camp together, but we got put in separate companies later on. The five of us tried to stick together, but we couldn't work it. Dave was the smallest of the five, and the most helpless. I wonder how he made out. He may be dead for all I know."

For a moment Christ stood quietly in the field, then He turned and walked toward the man who lay crying without sound against the earth. He was a very young man and as Christ stood above him he lifted his hands and pressed them against his face, his lips moving as if he repeated patiently a prayer which had neither beginning nor end. Then he opened his eyes and looked up and he saw Christ standing before him. He saw that the lips of Christ moved, too, in prayer, and that His eyes were wet with pity. The man, when he saw these things, drew back toward the shadows. He lifted his tunic and covered his torn body.

"Do not look at me, Christ," he said. "You cannot see my body and still love men. Do not look at me."

But Christ knelt beside the man and touched his wounds with slow, compassionate fingers. "I, too, despaired," He said. "I, too, despaired and cried toward evening."

To the north, where the line curved in a half-circle, a flare went up, floated for a time and fell; and in that interval Johnnie was silent, his eyes falling slowly with the falling light.

"There were five of us who enlisted together," he repeated. "We were good friends all our lives. We had a club when we were boys called 'The Faithful Five.'" He laughed softly, his lips kissing his own palm, at the memory which suddenly seemed absurd, now that he was twenty years old and a grown man. "Dave Brennan was one of the five. Another was Arthur Scales. He was the one Dave stayed with when they butchered at the farm. Arthur had a sister named Elsie who used to bake raisin cakes for our club when we met. She married Fred Huggins, cashier of the Farmers' and Drovers' Bank. They've got three children now."

Johnnie rubbed his thin face thoughtfully, collecting his thoughts. "Arthur wasn't religious like Dave Brennan," he said after a moment, "but they were good friends. We were all good friends, but Dave and Arthur were closer to each other than

the rest of us were. Arthur had a quick temper and when he
got mad he'd come at you with a stick or a knife or whatever
it was he had in his hand at the time. I remember once, when
we were about thirteen years old, that his old man gave him a
larruping with a buggy whip. The teacher in school had sent
Arthur home with a note. She said Arthur had tripped up another boy right before her eyes when they were marching into
the classroom and she thought he should be punished. She said—"

Johnnie broke off suddenly. "What are you looking at?" he
asked suspiciously. "I don't believe you've heard a word I've
been saying."

Alan said: "I'm listening to you, Johnnie, but I've been watching that patch of fog moving about." He waited a moment and
added: "What did Arthur's father do about the note?"

"He laughed at first," said Johnnie, "and took it as a joke. He
said if Arthur would apologize to the teacher, he'd let him off
this time. But Arthur hadn't tripped the boy and he wouldn't
apologize for something he hadn't done, so his old man got
madder and madder at his stubbornness and finally he whipped
him three times; but Arthur wouldn't give in, even then. At
sundown he came to the place near Opper's mill where we held
our meetings. He showed us the welts on his back and legs. He
had an old suitcase with him and he said he was going to run
away. He got mad all over while he talked and showed us the
welts, and all of a sudden he picked up a club and began to curse
again. He went over to a blackjack sapling and began beating
it to pieces."

*When He had closed Dave Brennan's eyes, Christ stood up and
turned. Then His face flamed with His anger and He strode toward the wire, toward the obscene man who was caught and
cursing there. The man thrashed about and beat at the wire with
his hands. His voice was shrill and his words struck the air with
the fury of stinging bees.*

*Christ towered at a great height above the man, His face ter-
rible in His anger, His words rumbling with the roll of thunder.
"Blasphemer!" He cried. He raised His arm as if He would strike*

the dying man. "Do you not fear My wrath?" He asked in His terrible voice, "or know that I will seal with fire your sacrilegious mouth?"

But the cursing man only laughed. "Seal my mouth," he said. "Seal it if you can."

He raised upward on the wire and lifted his head in the direction of Christ's voice. It was then Christ saw that the man's mouth had been shot away.

"We were all a little afraid of Arthur when he got into one of his rages," said Johnnie; "that is, all of us were afraid of him except Dave. It was Dave who went over to him that afternoon and took the club out of his hand. He said it would be better if Arthur would come back and talk things over with us, and sure enough Arthur did what he was told."

From the south and far away there came the clicking sound of machine guns, but it was so faint, so muffled, that it was hardly heard. There was silence after that.

"We used to talk about what we were going to be when we were men," said Johnnie. "Dave wanted to be a priest, like I already said. Arthur had decided to be a surgeon, and he was going to medical college as soon as he finished school. Cy Cameron and I had had the least trouble deciding. Cy wanted to be a farmer, just as his folks had always been, and I knew from the first that I was going to work in my father's shoe store at the right time. So you see Tom Fleming was the only one of the five who hadn't already made up his mind. Tom was always asking questions and he wanted to know the reason for everything. He got the best marks in school and Professor Morgan, who taught physics and chemistry, said he was a real scholar. . . . Well, Tom finally made up his mind the afternoon Arthur beat the blackjack to pieces with a club."

Alan said: "Why did he decide on that particular day, Johnnie?"

"It was like this," said Johnnie. "After Arthur came back and sat down, Tom Fleming began to talk as if the affair was as impersonal as a problem in geometry. He took a pencil and a

sheet of paper and drew a line down the middle of the page.
On one side he wrote all the reasons we could think of for
running away and on the other side he put all the reasons for
staying. He argued both sides of the question, and when he
had finished, he counted up the points scored and found that
Arthur would be almost two hundred per cent better off if he
made it up with his old man."

*But Christ would no longer listen to the impieties of Arthur
Scales. He walked to the east, away from the cursing man. He
stopped near the trenches of the enemy and waited. The third
man lay quietly, with no movement, no contortion of his body,
his gaze fixed against the fading moon. Christ said: "Peace!
Peace! I am the resurrection and the light."*

*The man turned his head and looked thoughtfully at Christ.
"It may be that You can tell me what I want to know," he said
after a moment. He began to reason and to ask questions, but
Christ stood confounded before him, shaking His head. "I do
not know these things," He whispered.*

Johnnie said: "After Tom Fleming had checked off all the reasons for going and for staying, Cy Cameron began to laugh. He
said that Tom ought to be a scientist, like Professor Morgan, since
he got more like him every day, and Tom nodded suddenly.
'That's what I'm going to be,' he said after a moment."

*"Then possibly you can tell me this," said the dying man,
"since a variant of the story I'm about to repeat is told also of
You and Your Father." . . . He narrowed his eyes, collecting
his thoughts: "In my company there was a man named Carl Reiter
who had been brought to America by his mother when he was
three years old. Carl was killed finally and it was said that he
had met his own father, whom he did not remember, of course,
and that they had shot each other. They were fighting on different sides, you see. Later on I heard the same sort of story
many times. Sometimes it was a pupil and an old schoolmaster,
sometimes it was two brothers who met accidentally; sometimes,
as in the case of Carl Reiter, it was father and son. The story
varied a great deal, but the idea was always the same. Once it was*

about a man detailed to shoot two women spies. He discovered afterwards that the women were really his mother and his sister."

But Christ twisted at His robe and shook His head helplessly.

"What I want to know is this," said the dying man. "Is there a connection between these legends and the desire that make men fight and kill each other? If there is a connection, what is it and why does it work in that particular way?"

Christ said: "I cannot answer your questions. I do not understand these things."

The dying man moved his head to its original position and again he looked at the stars. "Go away," he said patiently. "Go away, please."

Johnnie said: "Everybody called him Cy, but his name was really Philip. He was a cousin of the Brennan boys, and after his people died he came to live with them because he didn't have any other place to go. Cy was in the same grade at school with us, but he was two years older than Tom, Arthur, Dave and myself. He was a great deal bigger, too, and at fifteen he was stronger than most men. He had plenty of common sense, but he didn't take to books very well. We used to help him out or he never would have passed from grade to grade with us. Cy was always laughing and in a good humor, and no matter what people did to him, he never minded."

Christ turned from Tom Fleming and ran toward the west, where the last of the wounded men lay. The man to whom He hastened was very big. His eyes were pained and uncomprehending and his brown hands were held forward and curved as if they still grasped the handles of a plow. The man moved slowly from side to side, dying without noise, as an animal dies.

Johnnie said: "After Tom made up his mind to be a scientist like Professor Morgan, the five of us sat around talking for a while. Arthur admitted that going back home was the sensible thing to do, but if he did it, it meant that his old man would give him another hiding for running away. He got mad all over again and began to shout what he would do if his old man hit him again. Then Cy Cameron spoke seriously: 'I'll go home with you, if you want me to, Arthur,' he said. 'Maybe your old man will be willing to take it out on me this time. Maybe he'll be willing to let you off, if he knows I'm ready to take it instead.' "

"We all laughed at him, but Cy didn't mind at all. He kept smiling and saying good-naturedly: 'Well, what's so funny about that? I don't see anything funny about it.' "

Christ came rapidly toward Cy Cameron. In His haste He did not see the wire stretched low to the ground. He tripped and fell and lay flat against the earth, moaning a little; and when the dying man saw Christ in pain before him, he somehow forced his broken bones upright and walked forward. He stopped after a moment and swayed. He lifted Christ in his arms, holding Him against his wounded side, rocking Him gently as a child is rocked.

"*You have fallen,*" *he said in his soft voice.* "*You have fallen and hurt Your hands.*"

It had grown lighter, now, and it was possible to see the trenches of the enemy, five hundred yards away. The men. at the listening post lowered their heads until they were hidden behind the small parapet. They were silent, each busy with his own thoughts, and in that interval they heard the sergeant approaching with the men who were to relieve them, their feet making a thin noise against the duckboards.

Johnnie said: "At home the boys and girls meet at Eden's Drug Store on Sunday afternoons. Later on they pair off and go walking in the woods or sit around at one of the girls' houses laughing and singing songs."

Against the horizon there were lines of pink and yellow and red, and the small clouds, like bouquets of withered violets thrown against the sky, were touched from beneath with color. The men unfixed their bayonets as their relief drew nearer. They stepped from the ledge and flexed their muscles.

Johnnie said: "The fields are green at home now. The redgum trees are in full leaf in the woods." He paused a moment, rebuttoning his tunic. "God!" he said slowly. "God, I wish I was there again!"

1937

A SHORT HISTORY OF ENGLAND

PERSONALS

Lost and Found, 2/6 a line. Trade, 12/6 a line. Personals, 5 shillings a line.

Wednesday April 28th

"Oh, to be in England
Now that April's there . . ."
R. BROWNING
Inserted by Old Subscriber.

A STRUGGLE TO KEEP ALIVE. The mother of Edward, Paul, Winnie and John, all under nine years old, is ill with her unending struggle against poverty. Was once a waitress but ill health makes that impossible now. Husband out of work for many years. Will you help? 5 shillings will feed each child for a week. Send contributions to Royal Society for the Poor, Tottenham Court Road, W.1.

ALF. Have done nothing but worry since you left Sunday night. Thought you would write long ago. Please write. Will explain everything. FLORRIE.

CORONATION. A few choice seats still available. 25 at 6 guineas; 10 at 8 guineas. Private room with balcony (limited to 7 persons) 60 gns. Write quickly in order avoid disappointment. Box 976 this paper.

CORONATION. View Procession with clear eye. Applaud with steady hand. ALCOHOLISM treated in secret. Brochure on request. Horton's Institute, Banbury Road.

Thursday April 29

CORONATION PROCESSION. We have a secret for you. Some of the best seats still available. Finest locations at Marble Arch. Prices 6 to 10 gns. Higgs Travel and Planning Bureau, Old Bond St.

EX-SERVICE MAN implores work. Wife and family to support. Will do anything not criminal. Please write Box 434.

ALF. Am using the money you left for these messages. It is all I have. Please write. Children need you too. It is better we stick together no matter what comes. Am sorry for things I said last Sunday night. I did not mean them. I love you my sweetheart. FLORRIE.

OVERSEAS VISITORS. Take advantage of opportunity and improve your accents while visiting Coronation. Instructions in English given by lady of education; errors in deportment corrected by lady of title. Seven lessons for 10 gns. Box 930 this paper.

CORONATION. View historical spectacle with composure. You may smile, cough or laugh with complete confidence if you first use GRAY'S UNIVERSAL PLATE POWDER, knowing your teeth will not slide, slip, rock or pop out.

Friday April 30

ALF. My darling. My darling. Come home. Please come home. Relieve this remorse and agony of doubt. I did not mean what I said. I was only tired and worn out. It is not your fault that you cannot get work to do. Come back to me my darling. You tried the best you could. Let us be together at least. I love you with all my heart. FLORRIE.

CORONATION. Titled gentleman will let his four-room flat during Coronation Week. Oblique view of procession from roof. 200 guineas. (No Australians.) Applications addressed to Bingham & Ellis, solicitors, will be given gracious consideration.

CORONATION. Professional man will let his eight-room flat during Coronation Week. Ideal location facing direct line of march. Splendid view. Fee 100 gns. address H.T.Y. this paper.

Do you know that the death toll from tuberculosis alone is 26,000 people annually? Sunlight, proper housing and nourishing food will do much to end this frightful toll of human life. Are doing what we can with inadequate funds. Please send your contributions no matter how small to Secretary St. Editha's Hospital for the East End.

"Happy is England! I could be content
To see no other verdure than its own;
To feel no other breezes than are blown
Through its tall woods with high romances blent . . ."
                                        JOHN KEATS.
Inserted by Old Subscriber.

Saturday May 1
Unwanted plates and artificial teeth gratefully accepted and turned to use. Wellington Circus Dental Clinic.

ALF. Have been thinking things over since you left. I had not seen your viewpoint before. Was so worried and sick of poverty could only think of myself and children. I hadn't thought of you as being ashamed all the time. I did not mean it when I said if you were a man you'd find work to do. Many men are out of work through no fault of their own. Please come back and forgive. At least write a line and relieve this anxiety. FLORRIE.

DIAMOND TIARAS. Cartwright and Eddings, Ltd. Regent St., have superb selection to suit every pocket.

CORONATION. Wanted two desirable front position seats somewhere along route. Will pay up to 20 gns. for first-class accommodations. Address Box 429 this paper.

CORONATION SEATS. Best location along route. Exceptional accommodations. No overcrowding. Each person a separate chair. Every facility for COMFORT during waiting. Ambulances in attendance. View this historical and religious spectacle in comfort with no fear of fainting or being trampled upon. Cox and Boutwell, Piccadilly.

Sunday May 2

Young Gentleman of rank will consider acting as guide for Coronation visitors. English people preferred. Fees arranged. Write Box 865 this paper.

To OVERSEAS VISITORS. Distinguished county family will dispose of surplus paintings by lesser-known English portrait painters. Ideal opportunity for Americans and Australians. Address Box 836.

ALF. If you had seen these messages I know you would have written to relieve my anxiety. You must not do the rash thing you threatened. That is no way out. I am afraid to look in the paper for fear I will see you have. Please, please come back. I did not realize before how terrible it must be for a man to be idle against his will or how ashamed you were for what you could not help. If you cannot forgive me at least let me know that you haven't done yourself in. Please. Please. FLORRIE.

CORONATION. The Constable Ticket Agency controls the best sites on route. Some left in Pall Mall, Cockspur Street, Whitehall, Park Lane, Piccadilly, St. James St. and others. View this religious and historical spectacle in comfort and dignity. Running buffets. Comfort accommodations. Loud speakers at all addresses. Seats under 5 gns. already sold out.

JANIE doesn't mind the dirt, the squalor or the lack of sun. She is used to those things. Her father is dead and she lives with her aunt in a wretched hovel. Food was scarce enough when her aunt was able to get occasional work. It is almost nonexistent now. Will you spare 5/? It will feed her in luxury for a week. Royal Society for the Poor. Tottenham Court Road, W.1.

"Life is good, and joy runs high
Between English earth and sky:
Death is death; but we shall die
To the song on your bugles blown,
    England . . ."
                            W. E. HENLEY.
Old Subscriber

Monday May 3

DAPHNE. Would dearly love to meet Lord S. Will bring Reggie along too. Will make it a point to have a supply of CORONATION PEARL CORK TIPS, designed especially for this occasion. My dear! I wouldn't be *seen* smoking anything else! DIANA.

ALF. Please, please my darling, let me know that you are still alive. Went to church yesterday and prayed to God to keep you safe from harm. Read your old letters to me and mine to you in afternoon. We were so happy in those days. What could have changed us so? Am worried to death. Please write to me, my love. Just one word to let me know you are still safe. FLORRIE.

THE KING CHARLES CLUB expresses regret and apologizes to its resident members for the necessity of asking them to give up their accommodations during Coronation Week.

CORONATION PROCESSION. View in complete comfort from rooms of exclusive club with distinguished list of members. Rooms for parties a specialty. Finest view in London. 6 to 15 gns. inclusive of light luncheon. THE KING CHARLES CLUB.

FURS and evening gowns rented by day or by week. Confidential. Write Box 777 this paper.

CORONATION. Feel fit during Coronation Week. You can conduct your life with the dignity and timed regularity of the procession itself if you take Burlington's Liver Beans. Burlington Medicine & Food Company, Southampton Row W.C.2.

Tuesday May 4
ALF. Was sure would hear from you by today. Using last money insert this message. Will send children Aunt Phyl if she will take them in. I love you alone and always will. Am at my wits' end. Do not know what to do next. Have prayed that God will send me some sign of you today. Please write just one line to let me know you are still alive. FLORRIE.

CORONATION. Best seats Marble Arch. RUNNING BUFFET. Higgs Travel and Planning Bureau, Old Bond St.

CORONATION. Best seats Piccadilly neighborhood. UNOBSTRUCTED VIEW. Cox & Boutwell, Piccadilly Circus.

CORONATION. Best seats Whitehall. LOUD SPEAKERS. The Constable Ticket Agency, Whitehall.

CORONATION. Best Seats Pall Mall. COMFORT ACCOMMODATIONS. Montgomery & Norris, Agents. Pall Mall.

ON THE NIGHT OF APRIL 26 a poorly nourished man about thirty-five years old fell or threw himself before an oncoming bus near Hyde Park Corner. Anybody who saw the accident or who can identify the dead man please communicate with New Scotland Yard or telephone Whitehall 1212.

CORONATION. Preserve the solemn memory of this historical event for your children and grandchildren by purchasing mugs, ash trays, vases and other novelties appropriately designed for Coronation Week. Surprise your overseas friends with evidence of your good taste. Cook & Thompson Novelty Company can meet every demand. Catalogue on request.

"This happy breed of men, this little world,
This precious stone set in the silver sea,
Which serves it in the office of a wall,
Or as a moat defensive to a house,
Against the envy of less happier lands,
This blessed plot, this earth, this realm, this England."
                                        W. SHAKESPEARE
Inserted by Old Subscriber.

1937

TIME AND LEIGH BROTHERS

*E*ACH time that Mrs. Furness hired a new servant for her boarding-house she discovered anew what a bother Leigh Brothers really was. It was true that he paid his bill regularly and that he had been with her for a long time. He was neat enough, and he was undoubtedly quiet, and nobody could dispute the fact that he was on time for his meals; but these qualities of punctuality, dependability and consideration for others, admirable though they were when thought of as abstract virtues, became, somehow, repulsive and chilling in him, and he was, she felt, not quite human with his time schedules, his eccentricities of diet and his unending concern for his health.

"No, no," she said to the new waitress. "No, no, Liza. Not that way for Mr. Brothers. Mr. Brothers likes his water cooled a little but not cold. Cold water disagrees with him. You mustn't leave the ice in. Just put the ice in for a little while and then take it out."

She walked to her wide dining-room window and picked two leaves from her begonia plant. "Mr. Brothers is on a fruit-and-raw-vegetable diet at the moment," she continued. "He takes nothing cooked. Remember that. Nothing cooked. And even when he does take cooked food, you must never serve him anything fried."

"Not even *aigs?*" asked Liza, her voice thin and astonished.

Mrs. Furness lifted her face and rubbed the flesh that lay folded on her wrinkled, lantern jaw, resembling more than ever a perplexed bloodhound.

"Not even *eggs*," she said firmly.

The new waitress stood immobile beside Mr. Brothers' special table, her mouth opened a little, while Mrs. Furness went up the stairs. Then she walked into the kitchen and took the starched apron from the nail on which her predecessor had hung it that very morning. The cook was sitting at the service table, slicing apples, onions, raw carrots and bananas into a blue bowl.

"Here, gal!" she said. "Put Mr. Brothers' supper on the table."

It was then Liza knew that she could no longer control her emotions. She sat on the floor and rocked back and forth, one hand pressed flat against her mouth to muffle the sound of her overwhelming mirth.

"Gwiner bait me a trap wid a collard leaf," she said, slapping the floor helplessly with her free hand. "Gwiner bait me a trap, dat's what *I'se* gwiner do!"

The cook looked up at the kitchen clock and then sat on the stool to the left of the range. She pursed her thick lips and shook her head with the resigned sadness of one who has worried with Mr. Brothers' foibles of diet for a long time. "Wait, gal!" she said patiently. "You just wait!"

She began, then, to talk of Mr. Brothers and his peculiarities, and Liza, listening entranced, rolled her eyes at intervals and said, "U-u-u-h! How come?" her voice drawn thin and unbelieving at the quaint, child-like behavior of white folks.

Mr. Brothers, she learned almost immediately, had a fine job with the Porterfield Iron and Foundry Company and everybody said he'd go a lot higher if he wasn't so cranky and so careful about his health; and if Liza thought the diet of raw vegetables so amusing, she had much to learn. But the strangest thing of all, she said, was the way he measured each minute of his life by a schedule, a schedule which he wrote out at night before going to bed for his exact guidance the next day.

"Mr. Brothers has got him a gal, too," said the cook. "Her named Miss Dorine Willis and she teach school. He go to see her every Sunday night. He come home at half-past ten. No sooner, no later. Just half-past ten."

"Gwiner bait my trap wid a collard leaf," said Liza, rocking back and forth. "Dat's what I *sho* gwiner do."

At that moment they heard the firm, worried step of Mrs. Furness and they both began working again. Mrs. Furness spoke from the door: "It must be close to six o'clock. You better start fixing the ice tea, Liza."

The cook glanced out of the side window and sucked at her gums. "Hit already *is* six o'clock," she said. "Dere comes Mr. Brothers through the front gate."

The three women watched him as he fastened the latch with one quick, efficient movement and walked briskly up the brick walk. He was a medium-sized, well-setup man, and on his low, wide forehead his flaxen hair was parted in the middle and then brushed upward so that its tips resembled the crinkled wings of butterflies. His eyes were shrewd, gray and narrow.

When Mr. Brothers reached the steps he stopped, cleared his throat and spoke a few words to the Clayton Girls, the two spinsterish women who gave Mrs. Furness' establishment the note of gentility which she desired. Then he looked at his watch, went up the stairs and began to prepare himself for dinner.

His room was very neat. On the walls there were three framed mottoes and nothing else: Time Is Money; The Moving Finger Writes and Having Writ Moves On; This Golden Hour Once Past Can Never Be Recalled; and as Mr. Brothers stood for a moment seeing these familiar things, a sense of security came over him. He felt that he had earned his security through his own unceasing watchfulness. He glanced, then, at the daily schedule stuck in his mirror and he smiled and nodded, happy that another day had passed precisely as he had planned it. Every minute was accounted for in black and white. He had wasted nothing.

A moment later he lifted his eyes and examined his reflection in the glass.

His neck and chest had that proportionate, compact thickness, seen not in laborers but in sedentary men who love their own bodies and who have taken selected exercises over a period of years. His shoulders were unusually broad. He accentuated their width with the cut of his coat and with the tucked half-belt of cloth sewn across its back. From this belt pleats radiated upward from his waist to his shoulder blades and puffed outward, below his armpits, like an opening fan whenever he bent forward or raised his elbows.

Mr. Brothers permitted himself one indulgence during the day. After his evening meal he invariably went to Bland's Drug Store on Millwall Street and bought a cigar which he smoked on his walk back home. On this particular evening the Clayton Girls had already seated themselves in their rockers on the front porch when he came out of the dining-room door, their heads, in order that nothing might be missed, turned in opposite directions of the street. When they heard his step in the hall they twisted in their chairs and looked over their shoulders, lifting, like pigeons, their wide, virginal bosoms upward, as if they pressed too heavily on their digesting dinners.

"It's hot," said the elder Miss Clayton. "It's hot even for late June, I find."

"It'll be hotter than this in July," said Miss Leila Clayton. She began fanning herself with a paper fan.

But Mr. Brothers did not concern himself with these trivialities of conversation. He nodded, went briskly down the steps and opened the gate, and as he walked down the tree-lined street, he bowed to acquaintances, his eyes darting from one group to the next as if he sought to surprise some secret from them. These people who made no effort to conserve their vital energies, he thought, but wasted them with love, rage, avarice and ambition were unaware that—

His mind stopped at this point as it always did, and he was neither able to finish his thought nor to put into words the basic truth which, he felt, he understood and others did not. He shook his head with annoyance. At any rate, *ambition* had no place in his scheme of things! He squared his wide shoulders and breathed deeply. "Death loves a shining mark," he said to himself mysteriously. Let others do what they pleased; it was no concern of his.

These meditations on his own immunity, his separation from

the common lot, brought him peace, as they always did, and he came into the drug store with a feeling of well-being.

A man he had never seen before leaned against the counter talking with the cigar clerk. Mr. Brothers gave the stranger a sharp, inclusive glance, and at once he had an instinctive dislike for him. The man's character, he felt, was betrayed by his lounging posture, his relaxed shoulders, the careless way that he tied his necktie. He was probably a drummer from the Magnolia Hotel caught in town over night, since he was obviously the sort of man who would miscalculate his train schedule.

The stranger was talking when Leigh Brothers came into the store. "Yes, sir," he was saying, "today is my birthday. I'm forty years old, so my life is already more than half over. That's plain to anybody, I think. Of course, I still think of myself as a young man, but pretty soon I'll have to change that."

The clerk said: "You don't look forty. You don't look it, and that's a fact."

Leigh Brothers came up to the counter and selected his cigar in silence. He glanced appraisingly at the stranger from the corners of his eyes. The man looked his years, all right, and more, too. This was to be expected, for it was plain that he was a man who burned up his energies without thought and without thrift.

"I'm forty, all right," said the man. "There's no doubt there. And in ten years more I'll be fifty. Then give me another ten years and I'll be sixty. A man is old at sixty, you can't dispute that; at least I never heard of anybody of sixty who considered himself young." The stranger talked slowly, persuasively, a faint smile on his lips as if he were, even at that moment, making fun of himself.

Leigh Brothers took his change from the clerk and half turned from the counter, listening against his will to the stranger's words. The things the man was saying disturbed him. He tried to cut off the end of his cigar with his pocket knife, but he was not successful. He closed his eyes, his lips puckered up and he put the knife back into his pocket.

The clerk insisted stubbornly: "You don't look forty, though. You don't look it. That's all I can say."

Leigh Brothers turned so that his face was hidden from the clerk and the stranger. He thought: "What the man says may be true enough for him, but it doesn't apply to me because I've always lived sensibly and taken care of the body that Nature gave me." He dilated his muscles until he felt the warm, comforting pressure of his arms, thighs and belly against his clothing. At that instant he had a feeling of anger against the stranger. He wanted to say, "What business have you got here? If you don't like this town, why don't you get out? We can get along all right without your kind."

"Give me ten years after I'm sixty," continued the stranger in his soft, bantering voice, "and then I'll be seventy." He bent forward toward the cigar clerk. "Just think of that, sonny! Thirty years from tonight I'll be an old man of seventy. A man is lucky if he lives that long. After seventy it's just chance and sitting around waiting for the undertaker to nail you up in a box and put you underground for the worms to eat."

The clerk said: "I don't think about those things. That deep stuff is over my head."

The stranger laughed. "Oh, yes, you do," he said. "Everybody thinks about such things now and then. There's no man alive who hasn't pictured himself in a coffin or seen his body rotting underground."

Leigh Brothers took a match from the tray on the counter and tried to strike it, but his hands trembled so that he was not able to do it. He caught his rounded chin in his palm and pulled downward on it with a clutching, milking motion. Then he shook his head and went out of the store, the unlighted cigar still between his teeth, the unlighted match held tightly between his thumb and forefinger. He would listen no longer to the things the stranger was saying, nor would he recognize the fact that he, himself, was already forty-two, but as he walked the board sidewalk beneath the pungent, dusty oaks that lined Millwall Street, he began, against his will, to compute his own remaining years, as the stranger had computed his, counting them neatly against his spread and trembling fingers.

When he reached the watering trough in front of Burlson's

Feed and Grain Store he stopped and looked downward into the water, seeing at first only the reflection of his own frightened face. It was not entirely dark, and against the sides of the wooden trough, bitten away at its edges by the champing teeth of horses, he saw, a moment later, thin, apple-green fingers which lifted upward rhythmically and fell with the trembling of his knees against the boards to which they grew.

He turned at the sight and hurried down the street. He could no longer lie to himself; he could no longer delude himself, for he faced his enemy in the open for the first time, and he knew that there was no escape for him. Time was his enemy and he knew that now. He had denied it and he had hidden from it all his life. He had tried to master Time, to divorce it of its terror by dividing it, with his schedules, into units so small that he could control them and make them serve his own ends—and he had accomplished nothing.

Suddenly he took the cigar from between his teeth and threw it into the street. He made a quick, indrawn sound with his mouth. The Clayton Girls, on the porch before him, turned and lifted their bosoms upward at the sound, their rocking chairs motionless for a moment.

He felt that he would be safe, once he was in his bedroom with its magic mottoes, its schedules and its exercising apparatus, but when he lay at length on his bed and pressed his hands flat over his eyes, he felt no relief. Time was his enemy, he thought over and over. It was impersonal and without pity and it could not be appeased, no matter what he did or how he lived his life.

He opened his eyes and stared at the walls of his room, examining once more the meaningless mottoes. Outside his window locusts sang shrilly in the oak trees and there was a sharp smell of dishwater and mown grass in the air. He passed his hands over his body, the body which he had nourished, protected and loved so well, turning his head from side to side on his pillow. "No! No!" he said. "I won't agree to it. It's not fair. It's not just." He got up after awhile, not knowing precisely what he was going to do, and yet having made an important decision.

First, he got out the tin box that held his time schedules and began tearing them to pieces. The schedules were an exact record of almost his entire life. They were arranged for instant reference with the correct month and year written on each packet. They were to have been his defense, his guarantee of immunity, but he knew, now, that no matter how long he had served Time, or how carefully he had recorded his fidelity, his faithfulness would not help him at the end.

When he had torn the last schedule to bits and had scattered the pieces on the floor, he washed his face and stood staring into his mirror with despairing eyes. "No! No!" he said. "I don't agree! I don't consent! I refuse to have this thing happen to me!" But all at once he knew that Time stood implacably at his elbow, his hand raised to strike; and in the mirror he saw, at last, the terrifying picture that he could not face.

His legs would no longer support him and he sank to his knees, rocking back and forth. "I don't agree!" he said. "I refuse! I don't consent!" Then he collapsed suddenly from his waist and swayed forward until his head pressed against Mrs. Furness' hooked rug, his coat, below his armpits, puffing out like a fan. "Me too," he said at length through his dry lips. "Me too! Me too!"

The cook and Liza were still in the kitchen when Leigh Brothers came in and asked them to fix him some ham and eggs.

"Now?" asked the cook. She looked significantly at the clock and added: "You know you can't eat no fried food, Mr. Leigh!"

"I'm eating it from now on," he said. "From now on I'm going to act just like everybody else."

The cook was moving about sulkily with a skillet in her hand, grumbling a little under her breath, but Liza sat on her stool by the window and stared at Mr. Brothers without shame. She was only sixteen years old, and she was inexperienced, having just come to town from a farm the day before. Perhaps her critical standards were not entirely formed, but Mr. Leigh Brothers, it seemed to her, was real nice-looking—for a white man.

"When I finish," said Leigh Brothers, "I'm going to ask a certain lady to marry me. I'm going to have a full life from now on. I'm not going to miss anything."

The cook looked up, interested at last. She took two eggs and a slice of ham from the pantry and placed them before her on the service table. She stirred up her fire and began slicing bread. "That sort of sudden, ain't it?" she asked in a high voice. "Miz Furness always say when you git a sudden idea, you better sleep on it first."

Leigh Brothers shook his head. "I've been sleeping on ideas all my life," he said, "and I haven't had much fun. I want to change all that now. I want to get married."

Liza slid from her stool, her back braced against the wall, and rocked from side to side, one hand flat against her mouth. "Wh-e-e-e!" she said in her thin, soft voice. "Wh-e-e-e! Gwiner bait *my* trap wid a collard leaf!"

The cook said: "What you need now is blood-meat, Mr. Leigh. A man needs plenty blood-meat in his belly when he ask a woman."

"Wid a collard leaf," said Liza, rocking from side to side and slapping at the floor with her free hand. "Wid a collard leaf! Wid a collard leaf!"

All at once Leigh Brothers saw again the coffin-like watering trough and its encrusted bottom on which rested pale grains of oats, washed, no doubt, from the muzzles of horses. He had not seen them at first, in the dim light, but after a moment they had shone out, water-logged and yellow, their glint broken and wavering and washed upward to his eyes on the trembling water.

He lifted his head slowly and threw back his magnificent shoulders, but his exact mouth continued to tremble. He caught at his chin with his palm and pulled downward with a despairing, milking motion.

"Me too!" he thought over and over. "Me too!"

Leigh Brothers and Dorine Willis were married the next week and went to live on Myrtle Street, in the old Upshaw cottage. It seemed to the town that Leigh had completely changed with marriage. It made him more active, for one thing, and he no longer lived so much to himself. Indeed, he took an interest in everything that went on. He and Dorine went everywhere.

They knew everybody. She bore him a child the first year of their marriage. They have six children now, the eldest eighteen. "A man remains young through his children," he often says when addressing one of the civic clubs to which he belongs. "In a way, children are a kind of immortality."

Dorine is happy in her prosperity and she is proud of the importance of her husband, but she still does not know what it was that changed him so completely, nor why it was he asked her to marry him so suddenly after his years of indecision. In fact Leigh Brothers has, himself, almost forgotten.

But sometimes, at dusk, when he walks down Millwall Street and passes the old watering trough, or stands under the dusty oaks watching the Clayton Girls still rocking back and forth on Mrs. Furness' front porch, still lifting, like pigeons, their aged breasts above their digesting, identical dinners, a strange feeling comes over him, and he remembers again the untidy stranger and the words he said that night so long ago.

On such occasions his small, pathetic mouth puckers up. Quickly he lifts his hands and shoves back the unresisting air. "No! No!" he says over and over. "I don't agree! I'm not resigned! I refuse to have it happen to me!"

After a moment he closes his eyes and crushes the unbearable thought from his mind, takes off his hat and brushes back his white, butterfly curls. At such times he breathes eagerly and squares his still magnificent shoulders. Then he stares at his watch, nods and hurries away, anxious not to be late for his social engagement, or for the Committee Meeting of the Community Fund later on. He buttons his coat and shakes his head in despairing, angry denial, for the days pass so imperceptibly that a man can be tricked into thinking that they will never end, that by his thriftiness he can make them last forever.

"No! No!" he says. "I don't agree! I am not resigned!"

1937

NOT WORTHY OF A WENTWORTH

I HAD fallen into the habit of visiting Mrs. Kent on Wednesday afternoons, and it soon became an established fact that I was expected on that day. She received me on the wide porch which opened onto her garden, and while she fixed my tea and offered me the small, pecan cakes I liked so well, she told me of the town and its people.

On this particular Wednesday I looked idly at the garden while she talked, my eyes fixed on the fig trees banked against the whitewashed back fence. She followed my glance and nodded. "Figs will be ripe in another week at most," she said. "The trees are loaded this year." She put sugar in her own tea, then leaned back and said: "I'm glad the crop is going to be good, because Carrie Wentworth and her mother are so fond of them." She paused, then added in explanation, "You see, it's always been understood that the Wentworths have the figs from the branches on their side of the fence."

"The Wentworths?" I asked. "Who are the Wentworths? I don't think you've told me about them yet."

She stared at me with disbelief. "Do you mean to tell me that you've been in Reedyville for two whole months and haven't heard of the *Wentworths* yet?" She bent forward and patted my cheek gratefully. "You're such a comfort!" she said. "Imagine having somebody all to yourself who doesn't know the first thing about this place!"

"When I think of it," she continued after a moment, "I'm not surprised, after all, that you haven't heard of the Wentworths. They've lost their money and they've gone down a lot since my day. . . . Just ask your mother, when you write her, about old Mrs. Cora Wentworth and her daughter Caroline! She'll remember them all right. . . . When we were girls, your mother and I used to be awed pretty thoroughly at the Wentworth magnificence, and to wonder if we'd ever grow up to be as dainty and accomplished as Carrie." She stopped again, nodded her head and went on with her story, her voice cool and brisk.

The Wentworths, it appeared, had once been a numerous family with their relatives and their connections, but they had died off or moved out of the state until there were left now only the two women next door. Old Mrs. Wentworth before her marriage had been Cora Reedy, so her daughter Caroline was closely related by blood to the Porterfields, the Gowers, and the Claytons. On her father's side there were, beside the powerful Wentworths, the Howards, the Eades, and the Lankesters. It was thus obvious, if I would permit my hostess to be a trifle lush, that Carrie Wentworth was, in a manner of speaking, the unique vessel in which the most aristocratic blood of Alabama met and blended.

This fact was first pointed out by her great-uncle, old Mr. George Gower, during the family celebration which followed Carrie's christening, and the Wentworths, with his words, realized the gravity of their responsibility. When she was old enough to begin her education, Carrie had had a special governess for languages and painting, while her grandmother, old Mrs. Reedy herself, had taught her needlework and deportment. But Carrie had been in no way precocious, in spite of her distinguished ancestry. She learned what was expected of her as well as the average girl, and that was all.

My hostess gave me these preliminary facts with the offhand efficiency of a property manager arranging his set. She was silent for a few moments, recapitulating her facts to determine if anything essential had been left out. "Oh, yes," she said. "Carrie developed a nice soprano voice as a young girl and she took lessons on the harp." It seemed, during these years, that Carrie often played for family guests in the gilded, Wentworth drawing-room, but people were impressed less by her skill as a musician than by the fact that anybody as tiny as Carrie could play an instrument as formidable as the harp at all.

To summarize, Carrie as a young lady had been dainty, pretty and quite accomplished with her music, her water colors, her needlework and her languages, but then so had many of the other girls. It was her laugh more than anything else which made her so attractive. The laugh was clear and tinkling and it differed from the flat laughs of most people in that it leapt upward from note to note with the clear certainty of a coloratura soprano practicing a passage. "Everybody in Reedyville, but her family in particular, took it for granted that Carrie would make a brilliant marriage," said Mrs. Kent. "The only problem was, Where could a man be found who was worthy of her?"

When Carrie was about sixteen she was sent to a finishing school, where she specialized in voice and the harp. She came home that summer and the first thing she did was to fall in love. The boy's name was Herbert Thompson and he worked in a bank. Carrie used to meet him when she could at the old pavilion near James Lake, and Herbert told her all about himself and his plans for the future. He was ambitious, and he didn't expect to be a bookkeeper all his life. He was studying every night at home, and one day he expected to be an accountant or a bank examiner.

It was then Carrie realized that she didn't even know the multiplication tables very accurately, but she went to work at once and before the month was out she was halfway through the arithmetic Herbert had lent her. It was due to Carrie's sudden interest in mathematics that the Wentworths learned about the affair.

When questioned by her family, Carrie admitted that she and Herbert were going to marry just as soon as he was able to support a wife in *any* sort of style; and she thought her interest in arithmetic should be plain enough to anybody with ordinary, common sense. Her future husband was going to be an accountant, and she meant to help him achieve that ambition. It was true his more intricate problems would always be beyond her small, feminine mind, but in time she hoped to become so proficient under his guidance that she could handle most of the lesser, routine matters by herself, thus leaving him free for the important deals when they came up. Naturally they would have little to live on, particularly at first, but, when you came right down to it, who cared?

The Wentworths were shocked at Carrie's attitude, but they were sure nothing would come of the affair, since Carrie and her sweetheart were both so young. Anyway, old Mrs. Wentworth took her daughter abroad in the fall. They returned three years later, when Carrie was about nineteen or twenty. She spoke French, Italian and German fluently now, and she had picked up a working knowledge of Spanish. She made her formal debut in New Orleans that year and she was a great success, but the men she liked didn't come up to the standard the Wentworths had set for themselves, and the one or two that the family regarded as eligible made Carrie, as she expressed it, "sick."

"Carrie and her mother came back to Reedyville the following spring," continued Mrs. Kent. "I'll always remember Carrie sitting in her carriage one April evening about dusk. She was going to a party with one of her admirers from New Orleans who had come to visit her, and, as I gawped, she lifted her dainty, plump shoulders and laughed her famous, tinkling laugh. She had on a white satin gown, and she was wearing a blue velvet evening cloak with a high collar of white fur. I suppose the fur was some sort of fox; at any rate, I'd never seen anything so magnificent before, and it seemed to me that Carrie was exactly like one of the porcelain figurines which my mother kept locked in her parlor."

Mrs. Kent laughed softly. "I must have been about fourteen in those days and I was a big, lummox of a girl. When I got home that night I remember I cried for a solid hour merely because Caroline Wentworth was so dainty and so charming, and I wasn't. I remember Carrie's exact age that way too, because I asked my father to get me a velvet cloak with white fur and he laughed at me. I pointed out that Carrie Wentworth had one, and my mother said, 'Of course she has. She's eight years older than you.'

"What I didn't know at the time," continued Mrs. Kent, "was the fact that the cloak was a present to Carrie for giving up Herbert Thompson the second time. You see, when she got back from her season in New Orleans, she met Herbert at a party and fell in love with him all over again. The family was provoked, but they handled the situation with what most people considered a great deal of common sense. This time they tried to ridicule Carrie out of love."

There hadn't been much the matter with Herbert personally. The greatest objection the family had to him was the unalterable fact that his father openly shaved people in a barbershop at the corner of Magnolia and Broad streets. But Carrie had a mind of her own, and she insisted that she would marry Herbert Thompson and nobody else. She would be very glad to live in a room over the barbershop, among the mugs and old razors, as her family predicted; she would even lather the faces of her father-in-law's customers, as her uncle Ralph Porterfield humorously suggested. She stuck out her firm, Wentworth jaw. She was going to marry Herbert Thompson, she said, and the family might just as well make up its mind now, as later!

She gave in finally, just as everybody knew that she must, and went to visit relatives in Louisville for the season. It looked as though her people were right when they said she would forget Herbert, once she was in different surroundings, because before the year was out she was in love once more, this time with a watch-repairer named Samuel Maneth. The affair had been under way for some weeks before the cousins in Louisville found out about it and wrote back to Reedyville in alarm. Mrs. Wentworth and her mother, old Mrs. Reedy, went immediately to the rescue.

It wasn't that the Wentworths had any prejudice against Jews or anybody else, and it was all right for Mr. Maneth to marry whom he pleased, so long as it wasn't a Wentworth. Then, too, if a Jew did actually marry out of his own faith, it was only reasonable to expect him to have a considerable sum of money. But this little man didn't have a penny to his name beside his wages. He couldn't even hold a job very long.

All the family connections got together that time. The whole thing would be funny, they thought, if it weren't so exasperating, and Carrie's talent for falling in love with the wrong people was really getting to be a problem.

The family feelings weren't helped very much when Carrie attempted to justify herself, to make her position clear. Mr. Maneth was perfectly respectable, she explained, and she had met him when she took her watch to the jeweler's to be repaired. He was so thin and nervous, his hands were so cold and damp, that it was plain to anybody that what he needed was a faithful wife who would cook nourishing meals for him at proper intervals and to see that he dressed himself warmly and took better care of his health. He was not only a watch-repairer, Carrie explained, he was interested in social problems as well, and he was always addressing meetings after his working hours. Carrie had gone to several meetings with him. His mind was so brilliant, she explained, and his theories of right and wrong, particularly with regard to real property, so abstruse, that they were beyond her for the moment, but she could at least read books and learn, and while she never expected to approach him in the intellectual field, she could, at least, give him the sympathetic understanding and companionship which he needed so badly. Certainly she could take care of him, cook for him, wash his clothes if necessary, and raise his children.

At this point Carrie burst into tears, according to Mrs. Kent, and ran out of the room, while her family sat looking at each other in complete bewilderment, wondering from what strain Carrie had inherited her innate commonness. They shook their heads, for Carrie's attitude made it difficult to handle the matter. In the end Mr. Maneth solved the problem for them. Everybody was surprised, as they hadn't thought that he might have his pride, too. He returned Carrie's letters and wrote her a note saying that marriage for them was an impossibility.

Mrs. Kent raised her eyebrows humorously and passed me another pecan cake. "It might have been better all around if Carrie had either been more yielding or independent enough to break away from her family entirely," she said. "At any rate, she didn't do either. She simply drifted along, hoping that things would somehow right themselves. But in the meantime the girls she had known, the girls of her own age, were marrying right and left and starting families of their own, and there sat Carrie with her languages and her skill on the harp waiting for a man to come along who was good enough for her to marry."

The man who suited her family in every particular appeared when Carrie was about twenty-five, and his name, with what Mrs. Kent considered "an unprecedented example of poetic appropriateness" was Rex Ayleshire. He came from Louisiana and he was a distant connection of the Claytons'. He was handsome, witty, intelligent, and he had money; and what was more important, the Wentworth and Reedy families conceded freely that his family was even better than their own.

He was a lawyer who had come to Reedyville to settle the estate of a client, and when the family saw him, they knew that here was Carrie's husband sent to them by a divine providence. They sighed with gratitude when he fell in love with Carrie almost on sight. But Carrie, to their dismay, shook her head, laughed her tinkling laugh and said no. She admitted his obviously superior qualities, but the fact remained that he simply made her "tired."

Then, as if to consolidate her position and to end the family pressure, she fell in love right under Mr. Ayleshire's nose. This time it was a man named Charlie Malloch, a machinist. The whole town was laughing by this time, and they predicted that Carrie would turn up at the machine shop the next Monday morning in overalls, handing Charlie his tools when he needed them.

The family anxiety shifted quickly. It wasn't so much a question now as to whether Carrie could be induced to marry Rex, it was rather how she could be prevented from marrying Charlie. The result was that Rex went back to Louisiana and Carrie and her mother went to London for a visit.

Mrs. Kent lit another cigarette and leaned back in her chair. "Everybody was sure that Carrie would land an earl or a duke or something equally grand. Other American girls, with far less money, family or good looks, had done the same, but when they returned to Reedyville, Mrs. Wentworth told her friends with considerable disgust that Carrie refused to interest herself in her opportunities. She was through with Carrie, she said. She gave her up as hopeless.

"Oh, yes," said Mrs. Kent thoughtfully, "I must tell you this: When Carrie came back from England that time she was wearing exaggerated earrings and she smoked openly and rouged her cheeks and lips. Her clothes were too young for her, so everybody thought. She had taken to dotted swiss dresses, sashes and pink sunshades. She went everywhere in those days and her tinkling, gay laugh was heard a great deal. Her father died about that time, too, and it was found out that while the family was well-off, they didn't have nearly so much as people had thought. . . . Afterwards, with Carrie and her mother living alone, they quarreled more than ever."

But the worst quarrel of all took place when Carrie was in her middle thirties. It seemed that a Swiss baker had come to town and opened a pastry shop. He borrowed money from the bank to get started, and after a time he was doing reasonably well. Carrie, along with the other ladies of the town, used to patronize him. The man's name was Zuckmar, and he was Carrie's age or a little older. It wasn't long after she met him before Carrie began to take up cookery and to comb the town for family recipes, and Mr. Zuckmar started baking little cakes for her with her name outlined in colored icings.

Carrie left off her earrings, her sashes and her organdies and buckled down to the work of helping Mr. Zuckmar make a success of his shop. Before the summer was out he had asked her to marry him, and Carrie had cried for an hour on his shoulder and then consented. But she had learned caution, and she was determined that nobody should thwart her plans this time. She decided to keep their engagement secret until the store was paid for and they were operating free of debt. When this happened, they would simply go to Montgomery or Selma and get married, telling nobody until afterwards.

Indeed, Carrie and Mr. Zuckmar handled their affairs with such discretion that her family had no idea whatever of what was going on, so Mrs. Ralph Porterfield had a shock one Saturday morning when she took a short cut through the alley that ran behind the pastry shop and suddenly heard her niece's coloratura laugh on the other side of the high, board fence. She opened the gate and went in, and the thing she saw took her breath away:

There was Carrie Wentworth with her knees resting on a piece of sacking and her skirt pinned back over her waist. She had a scrubbing brush in her hand, and as she laughed and talked she scoured the kitchen of the pastry shop briskly with lye soap and water. Above her stood Mr. Zuckmar, who was also laughing. He had a spoonful of sticky cake-icing, and he was threatening to pour it down Carrie's back unless she gave him another kiss instantly. They were speaking Italian, so Mrs. Porterfield didn't know what they actually said, but their meaning was obvious enough when Carrie gave in laughingly and lifted her lips upward to his. At that moment Mrs. Porterfield backed out of the gate, not believing, even then, what she had seen.

Naturally the family was shocked at the idea of Carrie married to a pastry cook. Old Mrs. Philip Howard predicted that she would end up clerking in the store or even waiting on the tables, and Carrie forgot her caution for the moment and flared up in her old manner. She said that waiting on tables was precisely what she intended doing, because, after they were married, she and her husband were going to put in tables and sell ice cream and cold drinks. Mr. Zuckmar, she explained later in a more placating voice, was the sweetest, the most honorable and the most marvelous of men, and he was one of the very cleverest, too, once you got to know him, but he was a little helpless, like all men, and she couldn't give him up now, even if she wanted to, because she didn't know what would become of him if she wasn't there to aid him in his difficulties.

The family row that night was the worst in the history of the town, but Carrie refused to budge an inch this time, and Mr. Zuckmar couldn't be moved out of his phlegmatic, even-tempered calm. They might have succeeded, after all, except for two things: Carrie, naturally, didn't have one penny of her own, and Mr. Zuckmar was operating on borrowed money. When the family put the matter before Mr. Palmiller, of the Palmiller State Bank, he saw at once that a girl of Carrie's standing couldn't be permitted to disgrace her family the way she planned. He called his loan and forced the pastry cook out of business. A few days later a committee visited Mr. Zuckmar and suggested that he locate in some town in the West, where business conditions were better. . . . When she got Mr. Zuckmar's farewell note, Carrie began to cry shrilly. "My God!" she screamed over and over. "My God, can't you ever let me alone?"

After that Carrie didn't even bother to quarrel with her mother any more, and for a long time nobody saw her at all. But times were changing rapidly, and after a year or so nobody even thought of her very much, for already she belonged to the past. It was about this time that the Wentworth family had to sell their big house on Reedy Avenue, and move into the cottage whose back garden joined the garden of my hostess.

"And that," said Mrs. Kent, "is the monotonous history of Carrie Wentworth, on your thumbnail! I used to laugh at her, along with the rest of the town, but I don't any more. I understand her too well now." She sighed. "Poor Carrie! All she wanted was to marry a man who needed her, one she could love and serve faithfully. She was the most uncomplicated woman I ever knew." She stopped and laughed softly. "Poor Carrie," she repeated. "If she'd succeeded, she'd probably have bored her husband to death, and he'd have wanted to wring her neck a dozen times a day, but he'd never have given her up. Never as long as he lived. He would have loved her too much."

I sat silent for a moment, watching the shadow of the camphor tree touch the fence slowly and lengthen. Then, all at once, there came a sound of high, tinkling laughter from the Wentworth yard, laughter which leaped upward from note to note and died away. It was almost as if the crystals of a chandelier had been brushed unexpectedly by a passing hand.

"What is she like now?" I asked.

Mrs. Kent said, "Would you like to see her for yourself?" and when I nodded, she got up from her chair, and we walked down the steps and across the lawn. We reached the dividing fence and peered over.

Before us, a withered little girl sat under a pear tree playing with dolls. She was wearing a frock which ended above her knees, and her gray hair hung over her shoulders in thin, exact curls. Her legs were bare except for the pink socks which reached her ankles, and anchored over her ears were old fashioned, steel rimmed spectacles.

Mrs. Kent rapped on the fence to attract her attention and called, "Carrie! Oh, Carrie! Come here a minute."

Carrie looked up with her bright, eager eyes. She picked up an armful of her dolls and skipped to the fence. She stared at me with curiosity.

"How old are you, little girl?" I asked.

"I'm sixty-two," she said, "and my name is Caroline Wentworth." She held up the dolls for me to see.

"We came out to look at the figs," said Mrs. Kent. "They'll soon be ripe again. I know you'll be glad. You and your mother must take all you want."

From inside the house there came a voice surprisingly full and vigorous. "Carrie!" said the voice hoarsely. "Carrie, who are you talking to?"

Carrie said: "I can speak five languages. I can sing quite well. I can do embroidery."

"Carrie!" called the voice in terror. "Carrie! Carrie!"

Carrie said: "Yes, Mamma, I'm coming now." She started away and then came back to the dividing fence, her eyes roguish behind her spectacles.

"My name is Caroline Wentworth," she said gaily. "I can paint in water colors. I can play the harp."

She turned, then, and skipped up the gravel path, her dolls riding before her in her spread skirt, her gray, thin curls tossing up and down to her stride. She reached the door and faced us again. She waved her hand, laughed her high, tinkling laugh and went inside.

When she had gone, we stood quietly beside the whitewashed fence, the late sun touching our hands. It was Mrs. Kent who spoke first.

"I seem to be *bristling* with platitudes this afternoon," she said softly, "and I know how platitudes frighten young intellectuals from the city, but I never hear old Mrs. Wentworth call her daughter, nor see Carrie skip up the walk and into the house, without thinking that the Wentworth back door closes slowly on a whole generation, a period of time, an era which cannot live again." We turned from the fig trees and walked back to the wide, vine-shaded porch. "Yes," I said. "Yes."

1937

A MEMORIAL TO THE SLAIN

*A*T LEAST Reedyville is unusual in one way," I said. "There's no war memorial. How did you escape?"

My hostess, Mrs. Kent, leaned back in her chair and held a lace handkerchief to her eyes. Her shoulders shook with merriment. "Don't ask me to tell you *that* story, Clark," she begged. "After all, I do have my standards of reserve." She smoothed out her thin summer dress and looked at me mockingly. "Not that I wouldn't like to tell it," she continued, "because the affair of the war memorial is the most amusing thing that ever happened in this town."

For a moment she sat with her brows drawn together and then began:

"The story is a little involved, and I think I'd better tell you first about a girl named Honey Boutwell. She was run out of Reedyville by the same society that objected to the war memorial some years later, so the story ties in there, too. Anyway, Honey was our prize bad girl while she lasted, and she lived out near the canning factory. I can recall the Boutwell family very well indeed, since their mother used to do sewing for us by the day. I remember one of the boys—his name was Breckenridge—even better than I do Honey. By the way, you'd better keep Breck's name in mind, too, because he comes into the story later on. I suppose he's the hero. But let's stick to Honey Boutwell for the moment.

"Honey spent her time hanging around the Magnolia Hotel mostly, watching the drummers and waiting to be picked up; and before she was sixteen, she had already been mixed up in a scandal or two. In those days she used to wear her hair in what we called a Psyche knot, so you can realize how long ago it was. When she wasn't picketing the hotel, she was usually standing in the alley back of the old opera house waiting to talk to the actors. . . . You see, Honey considered herself an artist too, because she danced and sang songs at stag suppers. It was said that she also took off all her clothes for the gentlemen when they paid well enough, and it was this lack of formality, more than anything else, that made Mr. Palmiller and his vice society get after her so relentlessly, coming, as it did, on top of her unfortunate affair with old Mr. Howard. Unfortunate for old Mr. *Howard*, I mean."

Mrs. Kent smoothed back her gray, neatly waved hair. "In those days," she said, "nobody ever thought that dingy, hoarse-voiced little Honey Boutwell was going to be the only famous person that Reedyville ever produced, but that's the way it worked out. After she left town that night so hurriedly, to escape going to reform school, nobody heard of Honey for a long time. Then she turned up in Boston, of all unlikely places, mixed up in a murder. She must have been twenty in those days. Next she was singing on the stage in Paris, where she still is, so far as I know. The French say that she's a great artist. Maybe she is. Anyway, she's very celebrated, I understand."

Dr. Kent, hearing our voices, came out of the house and sat with us on the porch. He spoke to his wife: "Excuse me a minute, Cordie, but one of my patients from up Pearl River way brought me a hatful of turtle eggs. I gave them to Mamie and she's fixing them for supper."

Mrs. Kent smiled and went on with her story. "Have you got Honey all straight in your mind?" And when I nodded, she said: "All right; let's get on to her brother Breck. I can place Breck more easily than the other Boutwell boys because he was the one with an inverted thumb. You see, it grew backwards, toward his wrist, instead of straight up, as a thumb should."

"When she went out to work by the day, Mrs. Boutwell used to bring each new baby with her until it was weaned. I was studying Roman history during Breck's nursing period, and the first time I saw him, I picked him up and said: 'Why, he's just like the Emperor Elagabalus, isn't he?' Then Mrs. Boutwell took off her spectacles and sat at the sewing machine while I read the passage about Elagabalus out loud. She was proud of Breck after that, but disappointed, too, since the Roman emperor had both thumbs inverted, while Breck had only one."

"I told Mamie to simmer those turtle eggs in spiced sherry," said Dr. Kent. "I hope she doesn't spoil them. She says she knows how to do it."

"Don't worry, darling," said Mrs. Kent. "Mamie's a very good cook. They'll be exactly right." She smiled absently and went on with her story:

"When Breck grew up, his love life ran true to the Boutwell tradition, and from all accounts he should have been enough to keep Mr. Palmiller's vice society working every minute of their time, but the trouble was, they couldn't get anything on him: not one of his girls ever gave him away. I understand that when he wasn't making love and getting the little canning factory girls in trouble, he hung around Rowley's Pool Parlor, shot dice and bet on race horses.

"I hadn't seen Breck for a long time," continued Mrs. Kent, "until one day just before we got into the war. I was walking down Magnolia Street and there was Breck on a bench outside the pool parlor. I knew which one of the Boutwell boys he was when I got a look at his upside-down thumb. He had on a pale, fawn-colored suit that day, and a plaid cap, and in his lapel was a button which read: 'Let's Get Acquainted.' I suppose he must have noticed me looking at him, because the next thing I knew he was walking beside me, squeezing my arm.

" 'Hello, Peaches!' he whispered, 'let me be your cream!' "

Mrs. Kent's shoulders shook once more with merriment, and once more she pressed the lace handkerchief to her eyes. "I was so surprised, I couldn't say anything at all. I just stood there backed against the window of the Beehive Store with my mouth opened like an idiot's and watched Breck chew the stub of a toothpick. He was perfectly at ease. Across the street Professor Inman was giving a lesson in his studios. The piece being played was 'O Promise Me,' one of his favorite selections for the violin, and his pupil, I think, was little Charlie McMasters; but whoever the pupil was, he was earnest and he was putting in a lot of feeling.

"'Why, Breck Boutwell!' I said at last. 'Aren't you ashamed of yourself?'

"He smiled good-naturedly and rolled his eyes. 'All right, Cutie,' he said. 'There wasn't no harm in *asking*, was there?' Then, since he recognized me at last to be an old patron of the family, he added in explanation: 'I didn't mean to insult you none, Mrs. Kent, but I work on averages, like a baseball pitcher. You can't beat averages.'

"'No,' I said. 'No, I suppose you can't.'"

"I walked away to the obbligato of little Charlie McMasters' violin, trying my best not to keep step with

> O *prom*-ise me that *some*day you and I
> Will *take* our love to-*gether* to some sky . . .

but not succeeding. Well, that was the last time I ever saw Breck Boutwell."

Again Mrs. Kent leaned back in her chair and laughed deeply. "At any rate, we're getting a little closer to the war memorial," she said, "because I'm sure you guessed long ago that Breck was killed in the war. He was. It was at St. Mihiel, and to everybody's surprise he died quite heroically, with a couple of medals."

At that moment some friends went by and Mrs. Kent waved to them. When they had passed, she continued her story.

"All right! We've got all three sides sketched in. There's Honey, her brother Breck, and Mr. Palmiller's vice society. Hold on to them while I tell you about the campaign of the *Reedy-ville Courier;* it won't take long.

"In 1920 the editor of the *Courier* discovered that we didn't have a war memorial and it shamed him, he said. He took the matter up with the Legion Post and discovered that Breck Boutwell was the only man from our town who had been killed in the war. The editor would have preferred somebody from a good family, but Breck was better than nothing at all, and that week the *Courier* printed his picture and an account of his military career in the Marines, paying a good deal of attention to the two medals. In the same issue there was a long editorial pointing out the need for some appropriate memorial to our slain, and urging the formation of a committee.

"The next week a committee was actually organized, with Robert Porterfield as chairman, to raise money for the monument, and Mr. Palmiller and his society came out publicly as sponsors of the plan; but before the committee had a chance to get down to work in earnest, an unexpected thing happened: The *Courier* got a letter from Honey Boutwell, of all people. We learned something then that we hadn't known: Honey had never missed a single issue of the *Courier* since she left town, and she was still on its list of subscribers; so while we had often *wondered* about her, she had always *known* what we were doing from week to week.

"The letter really came from a firm of French lawyers, and it wasn't very long. Their client, the great *artiste*, Madame Honey Boutwell, had read of the plan to raise money for a monument, and she was willing to finance the whole thing herself in memory of her beloved brother, Breckenridge. She had already taken the liberty of discussing plans with the renowned sculptor, M. Paul Gagnon, and he would accept the commission because of his warm personal friendship for Madame Boutwell and because of his admiration of her as an artist. The only stipulations were, naturally, that the design be left entirely to M. Gagnon and Madame Boutwell and that the monument itself, when completed, be displayed in a dignified and prominent place in the town, a place worthy of the genius of its creator."

Mrs. Kent rubbed the arms of her chair and winked knowingly. She said: "The first thing Mr. Porterfield's committee did was to look up the sculptor, since they didn't have too much faith in Honey, and they didn't really believe that she associated with serious, substantial people. To their amazement they discovered that what the lawyers had said wasn't French exaggeration as they had suspected. It was all true. That settled it. It wiped out Honey's bad character almost overnight. If she associated with great men, they argued, men whose biographies were actually in encyclopedias in public libraries, then she had either changed for the better since she left Reedyville, or they had been mistaken about her in the first place.

"Mr. Palmiller and his society, who had objected at first to accepting anything from a woman they had been forced to run out of town, were won over one hundred per cent. They said it was plain, that Honey had repented at last, that there was good in her after all, and that it would not be Christian to prevent her doing this good and generous deed. So the committee accepted the gift formally, and in due course the statue arrived."

Dr. Kent took out his pipe and filled it. "And what a ruckus it stirred up when it did arrive!" he said softly.

"At that time, anybody in town would have defined a war memorial as 'one to three doughboys in leggin's and helmets, with extended bayonets,'" said Mrs. Kent; "but on the day the statue arrived the Memorial Committee, at least, knew that it wasn't always as simple as that. They had planned to put the thing in the center of Court House Square, the busiest place in town; but after one look, they began to doubt the wisdom of that.

"The *Courier* that week carried an article by Mr. Porterfield. He said that, after reflection, it had been decided that M. Gagnon's distinguished piece of work would show up to better advantage against a background of greenery, so the date of the unveiling was postponed until a proper site in Wentworth Park could be prepared. By that time we all knew something had gone wrong, but only the Committee knew what, and they wouldn't say.

"Well," continued Mrs. Kent, "the whole town was simply crazy with excitement, particularly when it was known that Mr. Porterfield had telephoned the Metropolitan Museum of Art in New York to find out if Paul Gagnon was really a respectable and reliable man. They wondered if there hadn't been some confusion in names, after all; but the gentleman from the Metropolitan said quite firmly that there was only one Gagnon and that there was no mistake, adding that the town should be immensely proud to have a piece of his work to exhibit."

Mrs. Kent clapped her hands with delight, like a little girl.

"Reedyville was simply crazy with curiosity, as I've already said, but we found out soon enough, on the day the statue was unveiled, and I'll never forget that day as long as I live."

"What was the statue like, for Heaven's sake, Miss Cordie?"

"Don't try to rush her, son," said Dr. Kent gently. "You won't make any progress that way."

"It went far beyond anything we had suspected!" said Mrs. Kent. "Oh, far beyond that! And it was plain why the Committee thought shrubbery more appropriate than the traffic of Court House Square. You see, the memorial was made of white marble, and it was quite orthodox in execution. In the background there was a female figure with draperies, scaled a little larger than reality. I suppose she represented Death or Mother Earth or something of that sort. The second figure, the one in the foreground, was male and life-size. The legs were rigid and firmly planted, and the body swayed backward a little from the hips. The arms were extended, and we saw at once that one thumb was inverted toward the wrist, instead of growing upward, and that the face was unmistakably the thin, intense face of a Boutwell."

"That sounds harmless enough," I said.

"Wait," said Mrs. Kent mockingly. "Wait until I tell you the rest." She leaned back in her chair again and pressed the handkerchief to her eyes. "You see the figure in the foreground, the figure of Breck Boutwell, which everybody had recognized at sight, was entirely naked and it was—" She stopped a moment and then went on: "It was entirely *complete!* It was the most uncompromisingly complete statue I've ever seen. M. Gagnon had been generous with both his time and his material, and nothing had been skimped."

Dr. Kent tamped his pipe lightly. "That piece of work almost wrecked this town," he said.

Mrs. Kent said: "It was something like meeting an acquaintance on the street when he didn't have his clothes on, the statue was so lifelike. Breck's eyes were half-closed and his head was inclined a little to the left, and as I peered past old Mrs. Clayton's shoulder, I could almost hear him sucking his toothpick stub and whispering, 'Hello, Peaches. Let me be your cream!' "

Mamie, the cook, appeared unexpectedly at the door. "Miss Cordie," she began, "them turtle eggs Dr. Frank brought home is swiveling round the edges and they done started to turn brown. They ain't acting right."

"That's what they're supposed to do," said Mrs. Kent. "Another half-hour on the stove won't hurt them." Then, when the cook had gone, she continued her story: "The invited audience at the unveiling took it politely enough, although I'll never forget the expression of baffled rage on Mr. Palmiller's face when he realized that he had sponsored this thing and that he had been tricked. Then everybody began to talk and to move away, leaving poor Breck Boutwell naked and abandoned in the middle of some rhododendron bushes." She sighed. "Poor Breck; I'll always remember him. He was the only man who ever insulted me."

Dr. Kent said: "It was averages, honey. Breck had three zeros and a decimal point in front of *you*." He winked and turned to me. "Why don't you stay to supper?" he asked suddenly. "If you haven't eaten fresh-water turtle eggs, you've got something to look forward to."

"Of course he's going to stay," said Mrs. Kent. "Of course he is!" She smiled, patted her husband's hand and went on with her story.

"News about the memorial got around in no time, and that afternoon a batch of girls from the canning factory came to see for themselves. There was already a crowd when they got there, but the girls elbowed their way through, laughing and making remarks. 'That's Breck Boutwell, all right,' they said critically. 'That's Breck Boutwell, and no mistake!' They stopped beside the rhododendron bushes and slapped each other on the back, screaming with mirth and pointing. 'Hi, there, Breck!' they shouted. 'Hi, there, kid!'

"That monument divided this town for a few months," said Dr. Kent. "I don't know what Honey expected out of it, but I, for one, think she got her money's worth."

Mrs. Kent said: "The town fell into three groups. One of

them, headed by Mr. Palmiller, was determined to have the memorial removed, Paul Gagnon or no Paul Gagnon, agreement with the French lawyers or no agreement. The second group, with Ella Doremus as spokesman, thought the work very beautiful—which it was—and considered its artistic value wiped out any local inferences, accidental or otherwise. The third party thought the whole affair a joke, and good publicity for the town. Feeling got very bitter in a few weeks, particularly after Mr. Palmiller and Sister Joe Cotton began to distribute leaflets."

Mamie came once more to the side door. "Miss Cordie," she began in a worried voice, "them turtle eggs *still* ain't doing right! I baste 'em and baste 'em, but they don't firm up inside!"

Mrs. Kent said: "Turtle eggs never do. Anyway, we're coming in very soon now. Have a little patience, Mamie."

"Yassum," said Mamie doubtfully. "Yassum."

"The funniest leaflet of all was signed by Mr. Palmiller himself," said Dr. Kent, "and I've always thought his closing lines, from the standpoint of an old romantic like myself, the most disheartening I've ever read. Here they are, as nearly as I can remember them: 'And so the womanhood of Reedyville must daily view this spectacle to their detriment, our pure womanhood, many of whom are mothers!' "

Mrs. Kent said: "And so things went on until one Sunday morning when Mr. Palmiller and his society took matters into their own hands. They met about daybreak in front of Breck's statue. There was a prayer and a verse of 'Stand Up, Stand Up for Jesus,' I understand, before Sister Cotton climbed on the pedestal, pulled a cold chisel out of her bosom and held it firmly while Mr. Palmiller swung his mallet and made Reedyville safe for both maidens and ladies already married."

"Afterwards," continued Mrs. Kent, "there was nothing left for the town to do except take Breck down for repairs. They've got him in a shed back of Moore's old livery stable, they say. He's been there for the past fifteen years."

"What became of Breck's—" I began and then stopped. "In other words, what happened to—"

"You mean," prompted Dr. Kent mildly, "what became of the *detached* part of the memorial? If you do, I'll have to admit that nobody really knows. Some say the vice society has it on file with their postal cards and obscene literature; others claim that Sister Joe Cotton uses it in her office as a paperweight."

At that moment, the screen door behind us creaked slowly and the three of us turned our heads at the same instant. We saw Mamie's serious face being pushed toward us through the widening crack. She wiped her perspiring arms on her apron and rolled her eyes upward. "Miss Cordie," she began desperately, "them eggs done started *poppin'*, now! They ain't gwiner hold out much longer!"

At that instant, and without warning, the three of us began to laugh like idiots. We leaned back in our chairs and rocked from side to side, while Mamie looked from one to the other with surprise and rubbed her lip.

I went over to Dr. Kent and took him by both forearms. "I never ate turtle eggs," I gasped. "How big are they? How do you do it?"

But this set Dr. Kent off worse than before. He got up, pulled away from me and leaned against a post. "They're the size of big marbles," he said helplessly, "and they've got soft skins." He circled the post with his arms and rested his cheek against it. "You break 'em against your teeth, like grapes!" he shouted hoarsely.

Mrs. Kent bent forward, with his words, and pressed her streaming eyes against her palms. "Set another place, Mamie," she whispered as if in pain. "Mr. McBride is staying for supper." She leaned back in her chair, relaxed and defenseless, her plump shoulders shaking.

Then Mamie, who had watched us with such perplexed dignity, doubled up suddenly against the screen door, her hands folded over her belly. She had not understood our laughter, but she was taking part in it against her will. She raised her body up and down from the waist, like a man doing exercises. "Lord God!" she cried in an ecstasy of mirth. "Lord God, have mercy on this crazy household!"

1937

TUNE THE OLD COW DIED TO

IT WAS still not dark when Cousin Dermott and the man from the slaughterhouse came back from the barn, and as they approached, Ella left her post beside the cypress vines and went into her kitchen. She had wanted to ask Cousin Dermott about his plans when the stranger arrived, just after supper, but she had not dared. Cousin Dermott had definite opinions on many subjects, and one of the things that displeased him was women who were always asking questions, or who interrupted a conversation between men; and Ella, realizing more and more each day the uncertainty of her position, the slender thread that bound her to this household, accepted his views with craven acquiescence.

Later, she heard the two men talking together as they came up the walk, and she went to her dishpan and began washing the supper dishes, stretching her head toward the open, unscreened window and trying to make out what they said; but when they were seated on the porch and she heard the rhythmic creaking of their rocking-chairs, she did a daring thing.

First, she rattled the dishpan to show that she was busily at work and not idling away her time; then she tiptoed to the door which opened onto the porch and stood with her ear to the crack; but the man from the slaughterhouse and Cousin Dermott were not talking about the cow at all. They were, to her surprise, talking about her instead.

The stranger knocked his pipe against the railing. "Who was the woman standing on the back gallery when we come up the walk a minute ago? I didn't know you had any women on the place, Mr. Archer."

Dermott waited before replying, as he always did, as if he examined a trap. "That's Ella," he said. "Ella's one of my wife's kinfolks, and she come to live with us, before my wife died, because there wasn't no other place for her to go. I didn't need her with my wife here to do the work, but afterwards Ella come in right handy."

The stranger nodded, but he did not answer. He yawned and looked idly at the tints of lemon and verbena pink laced in streamers against the sky. Both men knew they were only talking of unimportant things for a time before they started haggling over the cow.

"Ella was a good worker in her time," said Dermott, "but that was before she got the rheumatism so bad. She don't work so good now." He rubbed his thin face thoughtfully. "There ain't many more months left in Ella, I expect."

Ella started guiltily. She wondered how Cousin Dermott had found out about her rheumatism. She had tried to keep it a secret, and she thought that she had fooled him. Maybe he'd found the brick she heated at suppertime in the oven and took to bed with her to press against her aching back and shoulders. She moved a step from the door, her old breasts rising and falling with dismay.

The man from the slaughterhouse spat above the rail and let his eyes wander contemptuously over the small farm. Against the fence, near the pile of stacked stove-wood, the two sons who remained at home sat on a bench, their work for the day accomplished, and played with a clay-colored hound puppy.

"If I hadn't a-took Ella in," continued Cousin Dermott, his eyes fixed shrewdly on the stranger, "she'd a-gone to the county po' farm, I reckon."

"I'll give you six dollars in cash for her," said the slaughterhouse man suddenly. "I'll take her off your hands at that price, but it's my top offer. If I get that out of her hide and tallow I'll be lucky."

And Ella, listening by the door crack, raised one hand and pressed it quickly against her cheek, her heart beating in terror; but she realized almost at once that the stranger could not possibly be referring to her. Her hide and tallow had no value whatever. He was speaking, now, of the cow he had recently inspected, the old cow who had occasioned his visit, and the bargaining had begun more quickly than she had expected. "Land sakes!" she whispered under her breath. "Land sakes!"

Dermott said, "I won't let her go for a penny less than fifteen dollars. There's more'n twenty dollars' worth of sausage meat on her, not counting hide and tallow."

The stranger shook his head. "She's too old for sausage meat. Six dollars is my outside offer."

Ella turned from the door and went back to her dishpan. She rattled the cups and saucers and sang shrilly in her cracked, old-woman's voice, but she stopped after a few bars and brushed her gray hair from out her eyes. She knew the worst now. The thing she had dreaded was taking place at this instant: Cousin Dermott was actually selling the old cow, and the man from the slaughterhouse would take her away in his truck as soon as they struck a trade.

Presently Ella slipped out of the door, hoping that nobody would see her or question what she was doing, and went to the barn the long way, through the withered kitchen garden and around the clump of yaupon trees. Her neck was thrust forward and her eyes peered anxiously into the twilight, and as she walked as rapidly as she could manage with her old legs, she held one arm stretched forward for protection, like the feeling antenna of an insect.

The old cow was resting in her stall. Her head was lowered and her eyes half closed, and she brushed her back now and then with her threadbare tail; but when she heard Ella's familiar voice whispering to her from the doorway, she got up clumsily, bumping her rump against the stall.

"I'm sho' going to miss you," said Ella. "I just don't know how I'm going to make out with you gone. I won't have nothing but myself to talk to."

As she approached the stall, the cow turned, backed up and offered her hindquarters, from long habit, her legs spread invitingly. Then Ella fumbled for the milking stool and sat down, pulling gently on the old cow's teats.

The cow had not calved for a long time now, and her period of service was over, but this illusion of giving and receiving milk was a game which Ella and the cow played endlessly together, as if they sought to be polite to each other.

Ella said: "You po' old thing! You ain't got no idea at all what Cousin Dermott's going to do with you, now have you?"

She shifted the stool until she found an even surface for its legs, and continued:

"Cousin Dermott's a mean man in lots of ways. He won't have anything around the place that's outlived its use, he says."

The cow lifted her head and swallowed. She stretched her neck forward and blinked, and her tongue, like an oiled piston rod, slid languidly up each of her nostrils.

Ella rested her forehead against the flank of the old cow and began to cry. She wanted to explain how she felt about the poor-farm, but it was difficult for her. "It ain't that I'm a proud woman," she said. "It ain't that. It's just that nobody in our family ever *went* to the po' farm so far, and I don't aim to be the first. I can remember as a girl hearing my mother say, 'Ella, we had lots of trouble and we been cold and hongry more times than not, but nary one of the Howells ever seen the inside of the *po'* farm yet!'"

From the house she heard Cousin Dermott calling her name loudly and she jumped, one hand held against her heart. Then she patted the old cow quickly and went to the door. "I'm a-coming," she called out in her quavering voice. "I'm a-coming now, Cousin Dermott!" She went back to the house as fast as she could on her stumbling legs, wiping her eyes with her apron. Cousin Dermott didn't like women who cried. He had always said that he wouldn't have a woman of that sort about the place for three minutes.

When she reached the house, the two boys had joined their father and the stranger on the porch. Ella paused at the steps and spoke breathlessly in the direction of Dermott's rocking-chair. "I been down to the barn for a minute. The speckled hen's been acting funny. I thought I'd find her nest, maybe."

Then Dermott's voice came from the other end of the porch. "Warm up that coffee from supper," he said. "We'd all like a cup. If there ain't enough left over, make some fresh."

It was then Ella knew she had made a mistake. She had spoken to the buyer from the slaughterhouse and not to Dermott as she had intended. But it was the first time she'd ever known anybody who had dared to sit in Cousin Dermott's chair, and her mistake was, in a way, a natural one. She tried to carry off her error gaily, to conceal how bad her eyes had become since she broke her glasses three years ago. She laughed shrilly and straightened her back. "I'll have that coffee in no time at all," she said. She opened the kitchen door and went to the stove, throwing a stick of wood on the coals.

Her eyes had bothered her for a long time now, but they had been getting so much worse lately that she could hardly read the headlines of the weekly farm paper. There wasn't really much the matter with her eyes, she knew; it was only that she was getting old and near-sighted. Once she had talked to Mrs. Morkill, who lived about a mile down the road. Mrs. Morkill had just bought a new pair of spectacles from the mail-order house, and she had let Ella try them on as they stood talking by the gate. They had fit perfectly, and for the first time in years Ella had seen a face that stood out with its features distinct and separate from one another. She had turned her neck and had stared at the countryside in amazement, realizing all at once how much she had not been seeing.

"That style is No. 57-A," said Mrs. Morkill, "and you ought to get you a pair, too, Ella. Just order by number and tell them your age. They cost two eighty-nine, including a real nice case."

For days afterwards Ella had thought of nothing except the glasses, and wondered how to raise two dollars and eighty-nine cents. She had even thought of asking Dermott for the money, but she dismissed that idea at once. Dermott had no time for women who pampered themselves with eyeglasses and such truck. They were just trying to put on airs, he maintained, and he couldn't abide that sort. But then Cousin Dermott was only fifty, and his sight was perfect, and she, Ella, was already sixty-eight.

Dermott called from the porch: "Ella! Ain't that coffee ready?"

"It's ready right now," said Ella. She put the cups and the

spoons on the table and peered into the cupboard for the sugar bowl.

The younger son stretched himself and twisted the silken ear of the hound puppy around his forefinger. "If you all want to drink coffee, somebody better go find the *pot* for Cousin Ella," he said in his soft, lazy voice. "Cousin Ella's as blind as a bat."

The four men came into the kitchen and sat at the table. Dermott and the buyer from the slaughterhouse had stopped talking, so Ella knew that the trade had been completed. She stood beside the stove, humming a tune under her breath to indicate that she was not interested in them in the least, but anxious to know what they had decided, and what they intended doing next; but the men drank their coffee without talk, and when they had finished, they got up and went to the barn.

Ella left the table as it was and sat on the bench against the wall, bending forward to rest her arms and shoulders. Her rheumatism was bad tonight, what with the excitement about the cow and everything, and since she was alone now, there was no point in keeping up her pretense of being young and spry. Anyway, Cousin Dermott already knew about her rheumatism, so she might as well get the brick out of the oven and take it to bed with her openly. It was a relief, in a way, for him to know. She started for the stove but stopped halfway, her hands pressed against her cheeks in perplexity.

It might be that Dermott had been talking idly, and that his words were chance ones; it might be that he didn't care one way or the other about her rheumatism, but was laying a trap to catch her for something else, as he had done when she broke the water pitcher; it might be that he'd only *seen* the brick in the oven, figured out what she used it for, but didn't know for *sure*; it might even be that he'd guessed she was listening at the door, while he and the stranger talked, and was just having a little innocent fun.

She wanted to cry. Existence was so complex. It was so hard to know what was the right thing to do. She shook her head and walked about the room. "I'm a *deceivin'* old woman, Lord!"

she said; "but I don't want to go to that po' farm if I can help it."

Later on she went upstairs and into her room. She turned back the covers on her bed, lit the lamp and put it on the table beside her chair. She picked up her Bible and sat down. She could no longer read print, but she opened the Bible at random and ran her fingers across the page, repeating out loud passages that she remembered.

But she could not concentrate. The sale of the wornout old cow had frightened her more deeply than she realized. She closed her Bible after a moment and got up nervously, went downstairs again and stood in the dark, on the far side of the house. Her own room faced the lane, and she did not want to know when the men took the old cow to the waiting truck, nor to hear her low as she passed under the window. She tidied up her kitchen and put the coffeepot and the cups away in the cupboard. When she had finished, she came upstairs once more and wiped her table with a cloth. She opened her bureau drawers and rearranged her belongings. She went to the window and stood there, but she did not look out.

"It's not that I'm a proud woman," she said, "but n'ary one of the Howells ever went to the po' farm yet, and I'd be so ashamed all the time. If folks knowed I was at the po' farm, I'd be so ashamed all the time."

She turned and walked downstairs again and stood in perplexity with one hand pressed against her cheek, wondering why she had come to the kitchen in the first place. Then she straightened a chair against the wall, opened and closed the cupboard door twice and returned to her room. "Cousin Dermott ain't going to do it," she kept saying. "Dermott's a good, kind man in lots of ways."

Below, in the lane where the truck waited, Dermott turned to the man from the slaughterhouse and spoke slowly. He said: "You must get acquainted with a lot of folks, going about the county the way you do."

"I do," said the stranger. "I do for a fact."

Ella blew out her lamp and came to the window, hearing

the men's voices below in the lane. She held her breath and stretched her neck forward, but she could not make out their words. Then she turned, went to her washstand and poured water into her basin. At once she dumped the unused water into the slop-jar, took her towel from its hook and wiped her dry face and hands. She hung her towel up once more and walked about her room, picking up objects senselessly and then putting them down again. "There's nothing to be a-feared of," she kept repeating. "Cousin Dermott ain't going to do it, even if he did sell the old cow for hide and tallow."

She came back to her table at last and stood there, caught in her anxiety, her hands touching, in turn, her cheeks, her hair and her withered old breasts. A moment later she closed her eyes and began to sing, her voice shrill with terror:

> "Safe in the arms of Jesus,
> Safe on His gentle breast,
> There by his love o'ershaded
> Sweetly my soul shall rest . . ."

In the lane below the four men looked up at Ella's window, raising their heads at the same instant. The man from the slaughterhouse let down the runway and tugged at the rope that circled the old cow's neck.

"What's that funny noise coming from the house?" he asked.

"That's Cousin Ella," said the elder of Dermott's boys. "Cousin Ella goes on like that sometimes."

The stranger said: "Well, it sounds right smart like 'the tune the old cow died to,' now don't it?" He slapped the rump of the old animal beside him, to make the point of his joke more obvious.

The boys laughed with him in their shy, soft voices, glancing uncertainly at their father to see if he approved.

But Dermott had not even heard the man from the slaughterhouse. His eyes were narrowed and he stared up at Ella's window, listening to her thin, penetrating voice. He discovered, at that moment, that the one thing he could not abide was a woman who was always making a racket about the house. He turned to the man from the slaughterhouse and spoke:

"If you run across a strong woman that appreciates a nice home and one that ain't a-feared to work for her keep, let me know." Then he turned angrily to his younger son who lounged at that moment against the fence, the long, velvet ears of the puppy crushed gently in his palm.

"Quit playing with that hound and go help your brother at the truck!" he said. "We're po' folks here, and there ain't no place on this farm for anybody that don't earn his keep."

1937

NOT VERY—SUBTLE

*A*FTER she finished her conversation and put down the receiver, Hazel's first impulse was to 'phone Peg immediately and tell her that there was no need to hurry, but she realized at once that Peg was already on her way. Peg should arrive any minute now. She bit the end of her pencil and looked up at the clock, turned to the counter and took the telegram that the sleek-necked man had composed so laboriously before her eyes. She read it impersonally, counting the words from end to beginning with her tapping pencil:

> SOLD WAHTOGCO ON WINKETTES IDEA NOW WILL THEY BE SURPRISED BABIES.

The sleek-necked man put his elbows on the counter and took off his new, complacent spring hat. There was about him a rich odor of bay rum and brilliantine. "And did I have a job of calico to sew up *this* time," he said, rolling his prominent, fat eyes. "The boss said to me, 'Joey, you can't fix it. You're good, but you don't fix it this trip!' Well, it all goes to prove you can't know too much about alpacas." He laughed contentedly.

Hazel glanced in her rate-and-distance book. "Sixty-four cents," she said coldly. She took the money and made a few signs on the top of the telegram.

"What's the matter?" asked the sleek-necked man. "You act like you wasn't interested. What's the matter with me, anyway? Something wrong?"

Hazel lifted her pencil and tapped her cheek. "I'm afraid you're not very—*subtle*," she said languidly. She read the line as she had heard an actress read it not long before, with a pause of precisely two seconds between the final words. She turned from

325

the counter and sat at her desk. When she looked up, the man had taken the hint and was walking away, settling his coat.

"No, I'm not innerested," she said in the direction of his retreating back. "Nothing you got to say will innerest *me*, you big, sweet-smelling seal."

She sat quietly for a moment, wondering why it was that rich, attractive men never seemed to send telegrams. When she had taken this job, she had thought it would be such a good opportunity for meeting interesting people, but it hadn't worked out that way. . . . In the distance she could hear the low, aphrodisiac hum which rose from the fluid life of the hotel lobby and floated tantalizingly to her ears, but here, in this backwash, nothing exciting ever happened.

She picked up the receiver, at length, and telephoned the message to the operator who would transmit it to its destination, but before she had finished, she saw Peg approaching from the angle of the porter's desk. She beckoned to her, and Peg came into the office and stood beside the counter.

Hazel said: "Oh, gee, Peg! I gotta stick around here about a quarter-hour more. Mrs. Klugsmith—she's the relief girl—'phoned a minute ago and said she'd be late. Her mother's got worse or something."

"Oh, it don't matter," said Peg. "The feature don't go on till 2:25." She sat opposite her friend and glanced curiously about her. "Well, how do you like your new job, Hazel? Everybody at the office said to say 'hello.'" She bent forward and eased the rims of her snake-skin shoes. "I'm glad, in a way, your relief is late. It gives us a chance to talk where it's nice and quiet."

Hazel smiled bleakly. "It's nice and quiet *here*, all right," she said. "That's the trouble with this job. I never know what's going on, stuck here back of the porter's desk. It's not like I was out in the lobby where I could anyway see people and hear them talking to each other."

"I don't know," said Peg. "I like it quiet I guess."

"I know," said Hazel, "most anybody but me would like it here, I guess"; and then added: "I guess I got too much imagination and I'm too innerested in people and what goes on for my own good. Mamma is always saying, 'Hazel, your imagination and the way you're innerested in people and what goes on is going to be your ruin yet. I never saw a girl with so much imagination,' she says. 'You ought to be a writer and make money out of it.'"

Peg was not listening, having heard these things before, and when Hazel paused to catch her breath, she spoke quickly: "Here's something will make you sit up! Ivy Hughes has got her a boy friend at last. They're going to marry, or that's what *she* says, when this fellow gets him a steady job. Well, I almost laughed out loud when she was telling it in the Ladies' Room and I thought, 'It's not you this fellow wants to marry. It's your steady job he wants to marry.'"

Hazel made a motion of displeasure with her lips. "At her age! I think that's disgusting!" She raised her brows. "Miss Hughes isn't very—*subtle*, is she?"

Peg ignored the interruption. She continued to talk quickly: That dizzy girl in the filing room had copped her off a rich man and had quit work; Mrs. Biggers still came to get her husband at closing time, as if anybody else wanted him, the fat slob; Mr. Rowland called that blonde every afternoon at four, like he always did; Miss Connelly had a boil, but Peg hoped nobody would ask her *where*, because if they did, she'd have to say right out it was where Miss Connelly customarily sat down. . . .

Hazel said: "I gotta take care of a customer. Wait a minute." She took the proffered message and read through it:

UNLESS YOU DISCONTINUE REFERENCES IN ALL BROADCASTS TO LADIES MY FAMILY WILL SEEK SATISFACTION AM IN NO MOOD ARBITRATION WILL SUE FOR ONE AND ONE HALF MILLION DOLLARS THIS IS MY LAST WARNING.

Peg continued to talk softly: "Oh, yes! They've never done anything about that chimney on top of the candy factory and smoke comes in the window where the stenographers sit something awful. It already ruined that pink dress of mine you liked so much."

"How do you want to send this?" asked Hazel. "A day-letter?"

"Send it straight," said the man. He looked about him with his sick, inflamed eyes, his hand twitching. "I've stood all I can!" he said. "Do they think I'm made out of stone?"

Hazel counted the words, speaking at the same time to Peg. "Gee, Peg, it wasn't that pink organdy I liked so much? The one you had on when you met the movie actor, was it?"

"Listen," said the suffering man. "Listen to what they're saying about the ladies of my family and see if you blame me—"

"One dollar and sixty-four cents," said Hazel. She took the money and stared at him. "I'm afraid I'm not very innerested in what they said about the ladies of your family, see?" She gave him his change, patting her hair. "What do you think I am," she thought indignantly, "to be innerested in a nut like you who hasn't got the price of a haircut even? What do you think I am? A nut?"

"Yes," said Peg. "That was the one. It was the low-neck, pink organdy you liked so much."

Later, when the sick man had gone, Hazel sat again beside her friend. She spoke ruefully. "You know, Peg, you make me even more dissatisfied than ever with this job. It don't matter how cute I dress here, nobody ever sees me." She picked up the 'phone and transmitted the message to the operator.

"Speaking of clothes," said Peg, "get an earful of what Roy said last night. Roy said: 'When you going to start sewing on the wedding dress? When you going to stop playing the field and settle?'"

"He *didn't!*" said Hazel excitedly; and then, at once, "What did you say to him?"

"I said, 'When I settle it will be for a guy that really appreciates his good luck and shows it by making me presents like other girls get, and not one like you always criticizing and finding fault.'"

"The trouble with men is they haven't got fine feelings," said Hazel thoughtfully. "They haven't got imagination or fine feelings like we have. They're just not—*subtle!*" She nodded her head and continued. "I saw Eddie on Tuesday and we sat in the

park, and when I said for a joke I was going to take off my
shoes and stockings and go wading in the fountain, the way
Claudette Colbert would do it, he said I was crazy. Finally he
said all right go ahead and wade in the fountain, if I wanted to
get pinched so bad." Hazel shook her head commiseratingly and
pursed out her lips. "I wouldn't be tied down to a man like
Eddie. Eddie hasn't got a sense of humor like I have."

Peg looked admiringly at her friend. Nobody but Hazel would
have thought of such a cute thing to do. She laughed a little,
envy mixed with her admiration. In the office where they had
worked together it was Hazel who was always thinking up things
like that. It was the quality that made her so irresistible. Peg
took out her handkerchief and touched her eyes. "I declare,
Hazel," she said, "the man that marries you sure has got to have
a sense of humor."

Hazel looked down modestly, pleased with Peg's flattery. "He
sure *has*," she agreed. "If he hasn't, I'll never get married at all."

There was a girl standing at the far end of the counter and
Hazel got up to serve her. They talked briefly together while
Peg critically examined the stranger's shabby hat and coat. A
moment later she saw Hazel fluff out her shoulders as if repudiating responsibility for something; and when she came back to
the desk and sat down, Peg learned that the shabby, sick-looking
girl hadn't wanted to send a telegram at all. She had merely
wanted to know how to get to East 116th Street.

It seemed that she'd just got out of a hospital, and had come
to New York to meet her husband, or something, but he hadn't
shown up at the bus terminal, like he said he would. She didn't
have much money left, but the last address she had from her
husband was on East 116th Street, and she wanted to know
how to get there.

"And so," concluded Hazel, "she'd of spilled her whole life
story if I hadn't of stopped her; so I told her, 'Ask the porter if
you want some information. This is a telegraph office, and we
don't furnish information'; but what I *wanted* to say to her was,
'Don't tell me your troubles, Miss, because I got troubles of my
own.' "

Hazel laughed tolerantly and turned back to the counter. She served the two clients there rapidly. When she had finished, she put the telegrams on the desk, making her cryptic signs, while Peg continued to talk of the office and its affairs.

The switchboard operator almost got fired for listening in on Mr. Patchett's conversations; Mr. Wilfrey, the new partner, had lost a lot of dough in the market, and was he wild; Miss Nielson had finally got her desk moved into Mr. Patchett's office, and she was wearing a new set of furs, now that she and Mr. Patchett understood each other so well.

Hazel got up quickly and began putting on her coat. "Oh, gee, here comes Mrs. Klugsmith now," she said. She took out her case, powdered her face and realigned her lips. She was adjusting her hat when Mrs. Klugsmith came through the gate and was introduced to Peg. A moment later Mrs. Klugsmith sat in the chair that Hazel had just vacated, picked up the telephone and repeated the last two messages to the operator:

OPERATION SUCCESS DOCTOR SAYS SHE WILL BE WALKING EVERYWHERE INSIDE MONTH THANK GOD LOVE AND KISSES ADVISE COUSIN MAMIE AND MRS. GOLDFARB.

Peg said, "Oh, yes, I forgot to tell you that fresh elevator boy got canned finally. He said something insulting to a girl named Elsie Kelly that works on the 9th floor."

Mrs. Klugsmith continued to read with efficient distinctness, spelling the words the operator did not catch immediately:

COME TO NEW YORK FIRST TRAIN THEY'RE ALL HICKS HERE AND DON'T LET NOBODY TELL YOU DIFFERENT WILL SEND FARE IF INTERESTED.

Then Peg and Hazel, still talking together, their arms interlocked, went through the gate and approached the hotel lobby. When they reached the angle of the porter's desk, they stopped and stood quietly.

Peg said: "Mrs. Klugsmith looked like she's been crying. What's the matter with her mother?"

Hazel did not answer at once. She was thinking of other things.

She was looking straight before her, examining, with excited eyes, the lobby and its mixed life. Against each wall was a wide half-circle of chairs, and at this hour they were filled with what appeared, from a distance, to be a curved sequence of duplicate women, women whose eyes were fixed staringly forward in the unseeing vacuity of soldiers being decorated for bravery. The slim, identical legs of the women were crossed precisely alike, and each had the same handbag in the dip of her foreshortened lap.

Hazel turned back to her friend. "Mrs. Klugsmith?" she repeated absently. "Did you say something about Mrs. Klugsmith, Peg?" And then, remembering: "I don't know what's the matter with her mother. She told me once, but I wasn't particularly innerested and I forgot. I think, though, she said it was a cancer or something."

She looked again at the lobby. Men were walking knowingly up and down in front of the desk, or standing beside the potted palms, staring steadily at the slim, identical legs of the slim, identical women. Another group of men, and all millionaires, too, no doubt, stood beside the cigar counter and talked, the wordless sound of their voices rising and falling in a blurred, provocative rhythm.

All at once Hazel made a gesture with her arm in the direction of the telegraph office. She said: "You see what I mean, Peg? How hard it is for a girl with imagination to be cooped up in that place where nothing ever happens? It's all right for a settled woman like Mrs. Klugsmith, but for a girl like me, innerested in everybody, and what goes on, it's, it's—"

She broke off suddenly and raised her shoulders pathetically.

"Sure," said Peg soothingly. "Sure. I know how you must feel, Hazel!"

1937

RUNAGATE NIGGERS

*L*AFE ROCKETT's wife began talking as soon as Uncle Elbert arrived and eased himself into the wicker chair on the porch: "I don't know what this country's coming to, when they put law-abiding citizens like Lafe in jail for no reason!"

Uncle Elbert rocked, rubbed his chin and said: "If you want me to help Lafe out of his trouble, you'd better tell me what happened, Birdie."

"It really began last winter, Uncle Elbert, when Lafe put a nigger couple named Sam and Aphie to farm his cut-over land near Milden, and no niggers ever got better treatment from a white man than those two did. Lafe advanced 'em their vittles and rented 'em a mule, but from the first those two niggers was always complaining. They said the land was so pore and stumpy that nobody could make a crop on it without some fertilizer. Sam said the only thing that growed well on that land was the squash and collards that Aphie raised.

"Well, things went on like that, with them niggers complaining that they didn't have enough to live on, and Lafe advancing meal and sidemeat now and then, until the cotton they'd planted was forming bolls. Lafe used to ride out regular to look at the cotton, and even though it was pindling, because of them niggers being so worthless, he figgered the crop would just about pay for the vittles he'd laid out and the rent owing to him.

"Uncle Elbert, Lafe treated them niggers as fair as anybody could, but they was just no-account. This'll give you some idea: Last spring Aphie wanted a dog for company, so Lafe gave her a hound puppy. Well, sir, when Lafe seen that hound three months ago, he said the sight of it made him want to cry. It was nothing but skin and bones. He said he couldn't understand how anybody could treat a dog like that. Sam said the reason was because they hadn't had nothing to eat all summer, themselves, except collards and squash, and that a hound wouldn't eat squash or greens."

"I haven't got no use for folks that treat their dogs sorry," said Uncle Elbert. He shook his head.

"Things might have been all right," continued Birdie, "except for that rainy spell in September. It started just when the cotton was made and ready to be picked, and it lasted three weeks, nearabout. When it was over, Sam and Aphie's whole crop was soured and rotted in the bolls. After that, it looked like those two niggers was hanging around our kitchen all the time, begging for vittles. There wasn't much Lafe could do, but to show you how fair he acted, he said he'd let 'em stay on another year, if they found a way to feed themselves. By that time they'd have all the stumps out, and could make a better crop. He even said he might advance some fertilizer next spring if things worked out well."

Birdie laughed bitterly and wiped her mouth. "We found out later what a sly one that Aphie is, and how she was working behind Lafe's back all the time she was begging him for vittles. You see, Uncle Elbert, she had a sister cooking for some white folks in Chicago, so when Aphie got old Mrs. Todd to write a hard-luck letter to this here sister, she answered right off and sent what money she'd saved up, telling Sam and Aphie to come on to Chicago. That next day Mrs. Todd read the letter to Aphie and told her how to cash the money order.

"Well, Sam and Aphie must have had a guilty conscience, and when they ran away, they didn't go to Milden to cash that money order or take the train there, because they knowed Lafe would hear about it, sure, and stop 'em. Instead, they lit out one night to walk to Lippincott, twenty miles away. It might have worked, at that, except the Pritchett boy seen 'em on the road, figgered out what was going on and told Lafe. He also knowed about Aphie's letter, because Mrs. Todd was his aunt, so when Lafe found out about that, he did what anybody would: He wired the deputy sheriff at Lippincott to watch for two niggers carrying bundles and leading a hound and to hold them until he got there.

"Lafe said, when he got back from Lippincott, that he and the niggers and the sheriff all got to the depot about the same time. Sam and Aphie had already cashed the money order and were buying tickets when the sheriff put the handcuffs on 'em. It provoked Lafe right smart to see those niggers spending money they rightly owed him, so he lost his temper, like anybody would, and started hitting Sam and Aphie with a strap he happened to have with him at the time. But the story that he chained 'em to a tree when he got 'em home is a pure lie! He only *said* he'd do it, if they run off owing him money again, to show off before that woman at the depot.

"You see, Uncle Elbert, when the trouble started there was a young white woman standing on the platform who seen the whole thing, and when Lafe started hitting the niggers, she opened her camera and took pictures of it. She even followed the men back of the depot and talked with Lafe and the sheriff, laughing and joking. She asked Lafe how it happened, and he told her the whole story, just as I've told it to you; but the woman shook her head and said she didn't believe that part about sending the telegram. That was too smart to think of, she said, and she thought Lafe was making that part up.

"Well, sir, by that time she'd told her name and Lafe and the sheriff had told theirs, and they were all laughing and talking together in the friendliest way, so the sheriff took out the telegram and showed it to her, to prove Lafe was right. So this woman said she'd like to keep the telegram for a souvenir, and put it in her purse. The train pulled in about that time and the woman shook hands and got on board. . . . Well, like you've already guessed, she went straight to Washington and turned the photos and the telegram over to the Government, and yesterday two Federal men arrested Lafe and the deputy sheriff on a peonage charge, and took 'em to jail."

Lafe's wife was quiet for a moment, rocking back and forth. "I declare," she said bitterly. "I don't see how any white woman could go back on her own race that-a-way! I don't see how anybody could be so low-down!"

Uncle Elbert spat over the rail and wiped his chin slowly.

"I been figgering things over all yesterday and today," continued Birdie, "and the more I think, the more disgusted I am with this here country and the way things are run. Things have come to a pretty pass when a man can't catch his own runagate niggers!"

Uncle Elbert spoke thoughtfully: "Lafe got him a lawyer yet?"

Birdie said: "For two cents I'd move out of this country and go some place where people still enjoy liberty. That's how disgusted I am with this here country, and I don't much keer who knows it, either!"

1937

THE FEMALE OF THE FRUIT FLY

*H*E PAID the taxi-driver and came up the steps, glad that another lecture trip was over and that he would soon see his wife again. He fumbled for his latchkey and let himself into the hall. "Edie! Edie!" he called. He whistled the three muted notes which were a signal between them. "Edie! Why didn't you meet me at the station?"

There was no answer and he put his bags down, telling himself that there was, as yet, no cause for alarm. No doubt his wife had failed to get his telegram or had mistaken his train. The door at the end of the hall opened and Mrs. Peters, the cook, came out wiping her hands.

"Mrs. Farr isn't here," she said. "She left last night after she got your telegram. There's a letter for you upstairs. It's on the mantel."

He started up the stairs while the cook stood staring at him. She said: "Supper is ready any time now. I'll put it on the table when you come down, Professor."

"I take it," he began slowly, "that my wife won't be here tonight."

"She won't be here," said Mrs. Peters. "That's right. She took the seven o'clock train last night."

He went up the stairs and into the bedroom which he had shared with his wife. He saw the note at once. It was leaning against a vase, propped by an ashtray. When he had read it twice, he folded the note slowly and put it into his pocket.

He turned after a moment and began unpacking his bags. From the bottom of one bag he took out the present which he had brought home for his wife. It was a jade elephant with spread feet, whose neck lifted triumphantly in the air and whose trunk curved backward a little. The gift had been too expensive, really,

336

but he knew that Edie would like it for her collection, which marched before him on the mantel; so he had bought it anyway.

Later he washed his hands and face and went downstairs again. Mrs. Peters began at once to put supper on the table.

"I suppose everybody on the campus knows by this time."

"If they don't," said Mrs. Peters, "it's only because they're all blind and haven't got ordinary sense."

He sat at the table and unfolded his napkin. "In her note, my wife said she was leaving with a man named George Reilly. Do you know who he is? Did he live here in town?"

"Oh, I know him all right," said Mrs. Peters. She put both hands on her hips and shoved downward. "George Reilly runs that bar and grill on Green River Road. You know. The place where soldiers from the training camp hang out. But how she met him in the first place is a mystery to me."

Mrs. Peters hovered beside the table, unable, in her indignation, to go away. She began to talk rapidly: She had worked for many people in her day, both here, at the university, and in town, and she had made it a point in the past to keep her mouth shut about matters which didn't concern her. She thought the professor could truthfully bear her out in this, and he nodded his head absently.

She had thought she'd learned something about people, after all these years, but apparently she hadn't. She sighed and raised her arms outward. The affair wouldn't be so baffling to her if Mrs. Farr had been another sort of woman; but she had always seemed so intelligent and refined, a woman so content with her husband, her home and her circle of friends.

Dr. Farr bent over his food but he did not answer.

Mrs. Peters picked up the used dishes and backed toward the pantry door. "You asked a minute ago if I *knew* George Reilly. Yes, I know him well, because he grew up in this town, and there's one thing sure: He won't give her the love and care that you did. He won't even take care of her proper, and when the time comes, he'll walk off an' leave her, and that'll be the end of it."

She rested her back against the pantry door and said helplessly: "I just don't understand Mrs. Farr at all. A man like George Reilly shouldn't fool a four-year-old child." She pushed suddenly against the door with her back and sidled through to her kitchen, puffing a little.

Dr. Farr lifted his spoon and turned it in his palms, remembering the time he had first met his wife, and how he had fallen in love with her almost at sight. She had been very popular, and as he had sat that first afternoon turning a cocktail glass in his palms and listening to the blurred babble of voices about him, he had calculated his chances with her. He had concluded they were not good. Later, when he knew her better, and learned that she was engaged to a man in Chicago, he had thought that he had no chance at all. But he had persisted blindly and then, suddenly, she had married him one night, to the surprise of her family and himself.

Mrs. Peters came back with coffee. "We had good weather here while you were away," she said, "except on Tuesday. It rained all day last Tuesday."

When he finished his coffee, Dr. Farr got out his typewriter and sat at his desk. His vacation was over and the new term began the next day. He flipped the pages of his desk diary until he came to the page he sought and noted the first item: "Monday, 9:30 A.M.—Class Elementary Biology." He bent above the diary, his hand shading his eyes, thinking: "Why? Why didn't I insist on her going with me? Why did I leave her alone for two whole weeks?"

As a rule he started this particular term with a lecture on the significance of mutation. He opened his desk and searched for his last year's notes. When he found them, he started to type, but before he had finished a page he tore the sheet from the machine and inserted another. He had changed his mind. He rearranged his margins and began again, typing in capitals at the top of the new page: "Notes on the Theory of Sexual Selection."

Farther down the page he continued: "For a long time there has been a theory that the females of certain species tend to select as mates only the most active, the most brilliantly colored or the strongest males of their kind. This principle was first comprehensively stated by Charles Darwin, but it was disputed, even in Darwin's own day, and for a time it fell into disrepute. At the moment, the trend seems to favor it once more. Then let us examine briefly the facts on which this theory was built and see how consonant they are with facts which the investigations of our more brilliant, present-day scientists have brought to light."

He wrote methodically, his mind concentrated on the task before him. He could hear Mrs. Peters in the kitchen washing the dishes, still mumbling to herself. She came into the room at length, folded a cloth and put it away. Dr. Farr stopped his work and turned in his chair. "Would you say that George Reilly is better looking than I am?" he asked.

Mrs. Peters seemed a little surprised. "Why, no," she said after a moment. "No, I would not say that."

"Is he more intelligent, or stronger than I am? Is he better able to protect her?"

Mrs. Peters smiled for the first time that night. "Now, Dr. Farr," she began. "I've already told you the kind of man George is, and you know it."

He sat quietly for a time, his hands clasped around his knees. "You're a woman, the same as my wife," he said. "Maybe a woman's viewpoint is different from mine. Can you think of any reason she might have had for leaving me?"

Mrs. Peters pondered the question. "Maybe you're a little too sobersided for a young man," she said at length, "but that don't seem like reason enough to me." She shut the drawer and came closer to the desk. She seemed a little embarrassed. "You always seemed affectionate enough with her, Dr. Farr, and I, for one, would never take you for a cold man with anybody you really cared about, but sometimes—" she stopped, apparently unable to shape her words delicately enough . . . "but sometimes things are not right between a couple, if you know what I mean, no matter how loving they look to outsiders."

"Everything was all right between us," he said. "It was nothing like that."

Mrs. Peters sighed and went back to her work. A moment

later Dr. Farr began to type rapidly: "Now that we have discussed the evidence on which this theory rested originally, let
us examine as impartially the evidence against it, taking first for
our purpose, the newt.

"In its breeding season the male, ordinarily a dull brown color,
acquires stripes of yellow, orange or orange-red, and an imposing
crest whose purpose seems to be entirely decorative often grows
upon his back. With this equipment he goes in search of a
female, and when he has found one, he deposits near her a small
sack which contains his sperms. Then, wildly, he swims around
his female, displaying his crest, his coloration and his antic
charms to the best possible advantage; and if he succeeds in interesting her, she will go to his bundle and pick it up, thus ensur-
ing the continuation of her kind.

"Superficially this appears to support the theory that the
female through her sexual preferences determines the characteristics of some species, in that she will select as a partner only a
male handsome enough or vigorous enough to put her into a
receptive state; but let us look at things a little more closely.

"As scientists far more able than myself have pointed out, it
must often happen that several males come upon the same un-
stimulated female at the same time, and that they find themselves
all competing for her favor. Let us assume for the purpose of
this lecture that one of the males is of normal vigor but of ex-
ceptionally beautiful coloration; that another is vigorous enough
in his antics but is of ordinary coloration, and even lacks the
characteristic crest, while the third competitor has no mating
coloration at all and is so lethargic as hardly to be interested in
the female at all.

"Under these conditions it is reasonable to assume that after
the female has been put into a receptive state by one male, she
has no means whatever of distinguishing his sperm sack from the
sacks of his rivals. Thus it is likely that the brilliantly colored
male will be the one who stimulated her sufficiently, and as a
result of such stimulation that she will pick up the sack of the
dun-colored male who did not interest her at all.

"It is therefore apparent that the newt who succeeds through his courtship in putting the female of his kind into a willing state and the male with whose sperms she eventually fertilizes her eggs, are not necessarily the same."

He broke off and stared at the wall before him. He closed his eyes, trying to blot from his mind the face of his wife and her lover. There was little that he could do now, and there was no point in thinking too much. He lit a cigarette, his hands trembling. To him there had always been something childlike and appealing in his wife's sweet helplessness and he spoke aloud, as if already he defended her to the world. "It isn't as if she were a depraved woman," he said. "It isn't as if there were anything immoral about her. People will say that about her, but if they understood her as well as I do, they would know at once that it was not true."

The telephone rang, and he got up at once and went into the hall. He stood with his fingers beating on the surface of the small table, listening to the insistent ring which seemed, now, to fill the house with sound; then, without lifting the receiver, he came back to his desk, and after a moment the ringing ceased. Mrs. Peters came through the connecting door. "It's been ringing like that all day," she said. "I told them I didn't know where Mrs. Farr was, or what her plans were."

All at once Dr. Farr wanted to talk to somebody. He began slowly, his voice hesitant, while Mrs. Peters stood across the room and nodded her head at intervals.

This was not the first time his wife had left him. It had happened once before, three years ago. He had been teaching in another college at the time, and that was the reason he had left and come to this place. They hadn't exactly asked for his resignation, but after his wife returned to him, a few months later, he had found it necessary to leave, just the same. He closed his eyes again and lifted his hands, making a small, beating gesture against the air.

He must start looking for another job, he supposed, and the sooner the better, but he dreaded going through all that again. It was a pity, in a way, because he liked his work here and he liked the friends he had made.

Mrs. Peters gathered up the loose strands of her hair and tucked them under her hat. "Will you take her back this time, too?"

"I don't know."

"Then you'll take her back," she said. She went to the door and opened it. "I haven't told anybody what I know, and I don't intend to," she continued. "There'll be a lot said this time, too, but none of it will come from me." She closed the door, and after a moment Dr. Farr turned back to his typewriter.

He wrote: "In conclusion, there are those experiments which have been made with the common fruit fly. The male of this species, when courting the female, does so by alternately stretching out each of his wings, and after a short time union takes place. It has been demonstrated, in cases where the wings have been completely removed from the males, or only partially removed, that a longer period of courtship is necessary before the female responds, so it would seem incontestable that the male with an efficient wing spread is more attractive to the female of the fruit fly than one whose wings have been modified or removed entirely.

"But let us examine what happens, in actuality, when a female is given the opportunity to choose, after she has been stimulated, between a fully winged male, a partially winged male, and a male with no wings at all. In such cases, it has been found after repeated tests that the female shows no selective faculty whatever, that she will choose the partially winged male, or the male with no wings at all, just as often as she will choose the superior one, and that she will accept any male at all after the lapse of time characteristic of courtship with a fully winged male.

"It is thus obvious that when the female of the fruit fly has the opportunity to discriminate she cannot do so. She can only be stimulated by one male until she reaches her instinctive, willing state, and when she has reached that state she will submit to copulation, but the male of the fruit fly with whom she copulates is merely a matter of propinquity and chance."

Dr. Farr got up from his typewriter and walked about the room, his hands touching the objects about him nervously. Another sort of man, he felt, would get drunk, or curse, or even go after his wife and her lover with a gun, but he knew that he, himself, would never be able to achieve relief so simply.

He came back to his desk after a time and read his notes through, redrafting a sentence or changing a word here and there. He looked at his schedule for the next day. He was down for another lecture at eleven, but he would have time to prepare that in the morning. He shoved back his chair, feeling tired all at once; then he locked and bolted the door and went to his bedroom.

At once he saw the jade elephant, still resting on Edie's dressing-table where he had put it. He picked it up, and as he stood with his thumb caressing the smooth jade, he had an impulse to throw the ornament through the open window, into the shrubbery below. Instead, he went to the mantel and shifted the procession of elephants until the new statue was fitted into its proper place in the long, graduated line. He thought: "I am what I am, and Edie is what she is, and it isn't likely that either of us will ever change. That is unfortunate. That is really unfortunate."

Later, he undressed and lay in bed. He found his cigarettes after a moment and lit one, watching its tip brighten and die away against the darkness. He knew, then, that no matter what Edie did, or how greatly he despised her, as he did at this moment, when George tired of her, as the other man had, he would be waiting to take her back, just as Mrs. Peters had predicted.

He wondered bitterly why this should be, why he denied himself those luxuries of indignation which others knew. Another man would have considered himself irreparably wronged. He would have thought only of himself, feeling no responsibility toward her at all; and since he could comprehend no viewpoint except his own, he would have cursed her and washed his hands of her as a simple matter of principle, sure of the world's approval and of the expressed sympathy of his kind.

Then, slowly, he saw the basis of his bondage and acknowledged it to himself. "Yes, yes!" he said wearily. "But how could I do such things? How could I defend such a position for myself? . . . I understand her too deeply."

He crushed out his cigarette and turned on his back, his head pressed against the cup of his laced fingers, his eyes looking straight into darkness. . . . You were taught that understanding was an enriching thing, that it brought contentment and happiness to those who possessed it, and yet this was not always true. As often as not, understanding was a most cruel bond which tied the strong to the weak forever, and without pity.

He turned again, settling his pillow, staring at the line of elephants seen dimly on the mantel. At that moment he knew clearly what the remainder of his life was going to be, and he shuddered.

1937

THE FUNERAL

*W*HEN her little niece died, Mrs. Kirby went at once to her brother's house on Madison Street and took charge of things. She had made all the arrangements for the funeral herself, she had even selected the small, satin casket, and she stood, now, receiving late floral offerings and greetings the friends who came to offer their sympathy.

"It's very sad," she kept saying. "I can't believe it, even yet. Only a week ago and she was as well and strong as you or I. She took sick two days after her seventh birthday."

The bell rang again and she turned from her friends and opened the front door. It was then that she saw Reba, the cook's little girl. Reba stood beside the fence, a look of amazement on her scarred, black face. Her nappy hair had been plaited by her mother and tied with thread the Sunday before, but the thread was coming loose and the plaits, unraveled a little now, stood up on her skull like tiny lengths of frayed, black hemp. She was wearing a faded, print dress which the dead child had outgrown; but the dress was too small for Reba, as well, and beneath it her bare legs and a stretch of her lathlike, black thighs were visible.

Mrs. Kirby opened her mouth, as if to speak to the child, but she did not. She merely took the wreath from the delivery boy and went into the parlor where the coffin was. She put the flowers down, and when she came back to the hall, she saw that other friends had come. The new arrivals went at once and stood above the small, white casket. They were early, and after whispering together, they seated themselves at the far end of the room and waited for the funeral service to begin.

Mrs. Kirby came onto the porch once more, stopping beside the cypress vines. "Reba," she said, "you can't stand out here staring at people. Go play in the back yard."

"Yassum," said Reba. "Yassum." She moved from the fence regretfully, looking back over her shoulder. At that moment the florist's wagon turned the corner and stopped again, and the delivery boy came up the walk with another design. It was from the schoolchildren of the little girl's class this time. The design was almost as tall as Reba herself, and it showed two gates swinging outward, gates made of dampened moss into which flowers had been stuck. Above the opening gates, and supported by a rod, there floated a stuffed, white dove with outspread wings.

"Reba," said Mrs. Kirby patiently. "Reba, don't you hear me talking to you? Go back to the kitchen and stay with your mother."

Reba looked at her imploringly. "Yassum," she said meekly. "Yassum." But it was not possible for her to move from the fence. She turned her neck and her black, bullet-shaped head slowly, following the floral offering up the steps with her eyes and sighing when the door shut away its magnificence. Mrs. Kirby started to speak again, but changed her mind. She went to the kitchen where Cora, the cook, bent over her sink, scrubbing pots.

"You must tell your little girl to go away from the fence," she said. "She's standing there staring at everybody who comes in. I've told her to go away, but she won't mind me."

Cora looked up and wiped her lips on her sleeve. "Reba ain't got good sense," she said reproachfully. "You knows that. You knows Reba never did have good sense." She turned ponderously and reached for the thick switch which lay on the shelf above the woodbox. She went into the side yard and stood half screened by shrubbery. "Come away from that fence, gal!" she whispered fiercely. "Come away from that fence befo' I put another knot on your haid!"

"Yassum," said Reba meekly. "Yassum."

She backed warily away from her mother, making a wide half-circle, but when the clump of cypress trees and small crêpe-myrtles were between them, she turned and ran, throwing her legs out.

"Let me ketch you by that fence agin," said Cora. "Jes' let

me hear one mo' word about how you doin'!" She followed her daughter, shaking her switch, but Reba ran into the kitchen, picked up the scouring cloth and began washing the pots still left in the sink.

When the dishes were done, she went onto the back porch and stood beside the steps, remembering once more the remarkable things she had seen that day. She sat down by the window on an upturned scrubbing bucket and began plaiting the strands of an old mop with her black fingers. Then she got up quickly, having forgotten her mother's wrath, and went again to the side yard, but this time she did not go near the gate; instead, she sat in the swing that hung from the limb of a small sycamore tree.

The swing and the tree were partly surrounded by the half-circle of crêpe-myrtles and cypress saplings, and it would be difficult for Mrs. Kirby to see her there. She gripped the two ropes of the swing and propelled herself backward and forward, her head nodding rhythmically to the creaking of the ropes, one bare, skinny leg dragging in the dust.

Between gaps in the shrubbery, she caught occasional glimpses of the sidewalk. Many people were coming to the funeral now, and when she twisted sideways, and craned her neck, she could see them open the gate and walk on tiptoes up the gravel path. At length the minister turned in at the gate, and the funeral service was about to begin. The minister was dressed in black, and he was tall and solemn. His eyes, at once stern and forgiving, looked searchingly at the congregated people before he inclined his head a little, as if he gave his blessing to all alike.

Reba began swinging wildly, her head higher than the limb to which the swing was fastened, her black, out-thrust legs agitating the tops of the crêpe-myrtles. It was then she saw, above the tops of the shrubbery, that there was no longer room for visitors inside the house, and that latecomers stood on the porch outside. Beyond the gate, on the sidewalk, the classmates of the dead child waited, their backs pressed against the picket fence.

She swung back and forth furiously and laughed with a strange excitement which she did not understand. Then all at once she became quiet. She brought the swing to a standstill as quickly as she could, trailing one leg in the dust as a brake, and glanced fearfully from Mrs. Kirby to her mother.

Mrs. Kirby said: "You can't hear anything inside except that swing creaking back and forth, and it looks from the windows like a hurricane had hit the tops of those crêpe-myrtle bushes."

"Come away from that swing, gal!" said Cora angrily. "Come away, like I tell you!"

"Yassum," said Reba in her soft, meek voice. "Yassum."

She sidled cautiously away, and when she had the shrubbery between herself and her mother, she began to run. She ran as far as the old carriage-house; but she stopped there, grinning foolishly. "You see, Mrs. Kirby?" said Cora. "You see?"

When Mrs. Kirby had gone, Cora walked toward the carriage-house, but she stopped when she was almost there. "What make you pick a day like this to act so crazy?" she asked. "If it wasn't disrespectful to the daid, I'd whup you within an inch of your life." She went back to her work, pretending that she had forgotten about the swing, and a few moments later Reba came trotting up the path.

Cora seized her by the neck when she came in the door. "Now, Miss," she said triumphantly. "I got you now, and I ain't gwiner let you get away from me agin." She shoved her down onto the stool beside the stove and thrust a bowl into her hands. "Here, gal," she said. "Finish shelling them peas." She went into the pantry and began sifting flour on her breadboard. "Say something, Reba," she said. "Keep saying something so I'll know you ain't run off again."

"I don't know nothing to say."

"Say yassum. Keep saying yassum."

"Yassum," said Reba meekly.

She picked up the bowl and began shelling the peas, thinking once more of the funeral. It was the first time she had seen a funeral for white folks, and she had not imagined that anything could be so magnificent; but there was much that she did not understand, and as her mother walked from pantry to kitchen and back again, she considered these puzzling matters with her slow mind. A week ago the little girl who had died had merely been another child, like any other, but with death she had taken on a strange sort of importance; and people who had hardly known her, now crowded the house for the privilege of looking at her; they wept openly for her; they wore black in her honor; they sent her flowers.

It was then that Mrs. Kirby came into the kitchen and asked Cora if she wanted to see the little girl for the last time. Cora began to cry, wiping her eyes on her skirt. She rolled down her sleeves, put on a clean apron, and followed Mrs. Kirby into the hall; but she stopped in the doorway and spoke warningly: "Keep sitting on that stool until I get back, Reba," she said. "You move one inch off that stool and I'm going to put a knot on your haid. See if I don't!"

"Yassum," said Reba meekly. "Yassum."

She sat quietly for a time, trying to concentrate on the peas before her, but when somebody began to play on a fiddle, and somebody began to sing a white-folks' hymn which was both sad and comforting, she could hold out no longer. She put down the bowl and twisted her raveling plaits, rolling her black, bullet-shaped head from side to side. Then she got up from the stool and went through the back door. "Yassum," she said pleadingly in the direction her mother had taken. "Yassum."

When she turned the corner of the house, she saw that the hearse and the carriages for people to ride in to the cemetery had come. The hearse was drawn by white horses and they stood, now, shaking out their manes and biting at each other's necks. Reba took in these details quickly and then dropped to her hands and knees, following the line of shrubbery that circled the house. She crawled carefully, and when she reached the parlor window, she stretched her thin neck upward and peered in.

The first thing she saw was the coffin. It was set in the middle of the room. It was pure white and beautiful, and it was piled high with flowers. There were silver handles to the coffin, and streamers of white ribbons hung from its sides. She caught her breath with amazement. She stared with her mouth half open, her eyes wide with wonder.

The preacher stood beside the casket and comforted the weeping people. Then he turned and spoke to the parents of the dead child: The ways of God were not our ways, and it was not given to mortals to understand them. We could only bear our losses with fortitude, and this mother and this father must comfort themselves in the knowledge that their child was not dead in the real sense of the word, but that she awaited them in heaven.

Reba sighed and shifted her weight. She craned forward a little, and she saw her mother standing against the far wall. Cora's shoulders shook with her grief, and at intervals she lifted her apron and pressed it flat against her streaming eyes. All at once Reba sank back on her haunches, her face cupped in her palms. "Yassum," she said softly, drawing the word out interminably. "Yassum."

The service was over at last and men carried the coffin down the steps and put it into the waiting hearse, piling the flowers around it. Then, when the carriages were filled and the hearse moved away, Reba could remain hidden no longer. She went again to the fence and stared openly, dragging her feet in the dust. The procession was under way now, and as it moved off, the schoolchildren, who had waited so patiently, fell in behind the last carriage and marched solemnly.

The last carriage had disappeared around the corner when Reba felt her head jerked backward and heard her mother's voice. "Now, then!" Cora said. "Now, then, I'll settle with you, Miss!" She shoved her daughter forward until they reached the old carriage-house. Reba fell down and pressed her face into the dust. "Don't whup me," she begged. "I won't do it no more. Don't whup me, please, ma'am." But her mother brought the stick down over her cringing head and shoulders. "You gwiner mind me," she said. "From now on, you gwiner do what I tell you!"

The whipping was over at last and Cora started back to the house, but she stopped in the path. "They'll be back from the graveyard in a little while, and they'll be hungry. I got to get supper going," she said. Then she sighed despairingly and raised her arms outward. "What make you *do* the way you do, Reba?" she asked. "What make you provoke me the way you do?" She rolled down her sleeves. "I ain't a mean woman. Ever'body knows I ain't a mean woman."

"Yassum," said Reba.

"Go wash that blood off'n your haid," said Cora, "and then bring me in some stove-wood."

"Yassum," said Reba meekly. "Yassum."

She waited until her mother was in the kitchen and then she stood up, leaning against the door. She unbuttoned her dress and turned her head sideways, examining the bruises on her scarred back. She touched the bleeding place on her head and began to cry again. "Yassum," she said. "Yassum." She sank to the ground once more, her hands, with fingers interlocked, clutched between her thin, black knees. She rocked back and forth and made her foolish, intaken sound. "Yassum!" she said over and over. "Yassum! Yassum! Yassum!"

She got up after a while and carried in the wood for her mother, but when the box was filled, she went again to the side yard and stood at the gate. It was beginning to get dark, and already the small cypresses and the crêpe-myrtle bushes cast shadows against the house. Before her, on the gravel walk, were the heads of flowers, fixed by florist's wire to toothpicks, which had fallen from the mossy designs in which they had originally rested. Reba picked up the flowers and stuck them into her tightly plaited, nappy hair, until it looked, after a moment, as if she wore a white wreath on her head.

Afterwards she went to the swing and shoved herself backwards and forwards, thinking once more of the little white girl's funeral. At first it had seemed to her that the funeral could not have been more magnificent, but familiarity with its details made her, now, more critical; and as she swung back and forth, one leg dragging in the dust like a brake, she talked to herself:

"When I have *my* funeral," she said, "I'm gwiner have me a band, too. Gwiner have *all* white horses at my funeral, and folks gwiner send up sky rockets that night."

Then, slowly, she let the swing come to rest and sat quietly.

Something important had occurred to her and she was motionless for a time, her hands gripping the ropes of the swing. "Why, I can have a funeral, too, if I feel like it," she said in surprise. "Nothing to stop me from having a funeral as good as *anybody*, if I want to."

She swung back and forth slowly, pondering this idea, her toes almost reaching to the edge of the crêpe-myrtle bushes. It seemed to her at that moment that she had found out, unaided, a fact of great importance, a thing which should be known to everybody, but was not. She opened her eyes very wide. She threw back her bullet-shaped head, stretched her mouth and made her foolish, intaken sound. The thing she had discovered seemed so simple, so easy to arrange, that she wondered why everybody else didn't think of it too.

"Why, there ain't nothing to having a funeral," she said contemptuously. "I can have a funeral if *I* want to; ever'body can have a funeral if *they* want to." She swung more rapidly, her legs shooting up above the tops of the crêpe-myrtles. When she remembered again the words the preacher had spoken as he stood beside the white child's coffin that very afternoon, it did not seem sensible that anybody would want to live in a world as harsh as this one was when they could have, so easily, not only eternal happiness in heaven, but a magnificent funeral as well. She brought the swing to a stop and got up. She took the wooden seat from the swing and stood it carefully against the trunk of the tree.

She hesitated a moment, then, having made up her mind, she climbed the sycamore like a small, excited monkey, anxious to put her plan through before her mother or Mrs. Kirby found out what she was up to and stopped her. She straddled the limb to which the swing was fixed and unfastened the knots in the rope; she wound the rope around the limb until she had shortened it expertly to the length she needed, laughing all the time with pleasure and nodding her head in anticipation of her triumph.

Cora came onto the porch and called, "Reba? Reba, where you at? I want you to go to the meat market for me."

But Reba flattened against the tree. She held her breath while her mother continued to call, seeing again, in her mind's eye, the triumphant details of her approaching funeral. First, there were the white horses and the brass bands. The bands played slow, sad music continuously, and the proud horses, as if conscious of the importance of such an occasion, pawed at the ground and shook out their white, silken manes. Mrs. Kirby was dressed in black silk, and she pressed a lace handkerchief to her eyes. She stood at the front door to take the floral designs, explaining the details of Reba's death to the mayor of the town, the minister of the Baptist church and the unending stream of lesser people who crowded behind them.

"It's little Reba, this time," said Mrs. Kirby. "Yes, sir, it's little Reba, and we're all so upsot we just don't know *what* to do!" She began to cry again. "Looks like we don't get shut of one funeral in this house till we have another one, now does it?" She bowed her head submissively. "Yassum," she continued, as if answering a particular question, "Reba was a sweet child, and no two ways about it. I tell you *ever'*body gwiner miss Reba, and that's a fact!"

Cora called from the porch: "Reba! Reba, where you at? You better answer me, gal, if you know what's good for you!" She stood a moment on the steps as if debating a point, then she went toward the old carriage-house mumbling to herself angrily. When she was out of earshot, Reba spoke: "Yassum," she said in her small, meek voice. "Yassum, I hears you."

She stretched her neck and peered around the trunk of the tree, but when her mother reached the carriage-house and went inside, she bent down and caught up the dangling rope. Then she straddled the limb and inched forward cautiously. She stopped when she reached the middle of the limb and looked about her. She lifted the rope and wrapped it around her throat, tying a knot solidly at the side. "Yassum," she said, drawing the word out interminably. "Yassum."

Cora came away from the carriage-house and stopped beside the canna bed. "I knows you're hiding out some place," she said. "I knows as well as I'm standing here that you hear every word

I'm a-saying." She went back onto the porch and took a drink of water, throwing what was left in the dipper onto the ground with a faint splash.

But Reba sat quietly for a time, her black knees gripping the sycamore limb, looking about her slowly and listening to her mother's voice. At that instant she had a clear picture of Cora weeping over her coffin, just as she had wept over the coffin of the white child. "Reba! Reba, come back to us!" she said over and over, her face twisted with the force of her grief. "Don't leave us here to mourn, sweet little Reba! Don't leave us this-a-way, honey!"

Then Reba drew back her head and made her foolish, intaken sound. "Yassum," she said softly. "Yassum." Suddenly she lifted her arms and swayed forward. She unlocked her knees from the limb and fell eagerly, the rope pulling her up and jerking her head sideways. At once she lifted her lathlike arms and tried to grasp the limb above her head, but she could not; then she jerked her body convulsively and made a shrill, strangled noise while the rope spun outward in a circle.

Cora said: "I hear you, Miss. I hear you laughing and acting silly and provoking me!" She shook her shoulders angrily. "All right, stay where you is! You'll get hongry befo' long, and then I'll catch you!" She went inside and rattled the stove-lid, throwing in firewood. A few minutes later she came back to the porch and looked about her again.

"There ain't no way to get away from me, gal," she said. "You'd know that by now, if you had any sense." She looked straight at the clump of crêpe-myrtles which screened the swing from the house and raised her voice a little, as if she addressed personally the bundle which hung limp and strangled at the end of the still-vibrating rope. She said: "When I get supper cooked I'm gwiner come look for you; and when I look for you, I'm gwiner *find* you; and when I find you, I'm gwiner give you a whupping you'll *remember!*"

1937

A HAIRCUT IN TOULOUSE

As I sat in the lobby that afternoon noting the color and diversity of the Legionnaires' costumes, I saw Bob Decker for the first time since 1919. He was at the newsstand buying cigarettes. He turned after a moment and caught my eye. He came over at once, his hand stretched out.

After war was over, the Government had sent a number of men to the French universities. I had gone to the University of Toulouse, and it was there I had known Decker. We shook hands and he sat beside me on the sofa. We began to talk of old times.

He was dressed in gold-braided, black trousers, tight-fitting across the hips and calves, which flared out like large dinnerbells above his ankles. Around his waist was a wide, crimson sash. He wore a white silk blouse and a jacket of black velvet.

"I remember you by the name of Foxy," he said. "That's what we used to call you out at the barracks. Maybe I never knew your other name."

Then he told me about himself and what he'd done since we'd seen each other last. He'd gone back to California after he'd got out of the Army, married and got a job. He'd done very well, it seemed. He had a boy and a girl already old enough to be in high school. His youngest child, a girl, was with him this trip and he was, as he talked with me, waiting for his wife and his daughter to come downstairs.

The front of the snug-fitting, velvet jacket was frogged with gold braid and the sleeves and back were embroidered intricately. He wore a wide sombrero-like hat with a flat top. From the brim of the hat tiny bells swung, tinkling faintly when he moved his head. He pushed up the chin-strap, took off his sombrero and placed it on the sofa.

355

"Well, Foxy!" he said. "Imagine running into you like this!"

With his sombrero off, I saw that his hair was getting thin and that it was gray at the sides. His belly, in spite of the broad sash, pushed upward like a small balloon.

Decker laughed and slapped me on the knee. He said: "You were talking about Toulouse a minute ago. Now, that's funny, because I was thinking this morning about Toulouse and something funny that happened there." He lowered his voice. "I never told this story to anybody before, and I wouldn't even tell it to you except you were in Toulouse, too, when it happened, and know how the French are."

"Say," he continued, "do you remember that little barbershop out near the barracks?"

I said No, but that I'd like to hear the story, anyway.

"Well, it was this way," he began. "When I left my outfit, I said I was going to let my hair grow out so I could comb and brush it again. You remember, don't you, how they made us clip it short? Half an inch was the length we had to keep it, according to regulations. Well, my hair was getting pretty long even before I left the outfit in Germany, but I let it wait. I said I wouldn't have it cut again until it was long enough to part.

"So I waited a couple of weeks after I got to Toulouse and then one day I stopped at the barbershop I've already mentioned. I couldn't speak French and the barber couldn't speak English, but I pointed and made motions. Finally the barber went into the back of the shop and called his wife, and when she came out I said again what I wanted done. I wanted a haircut, I said, but I didn't want any taken off the top until it grew out more. I just wanted it trimmed some at the edges, and the clippers put on my neck.

"I kept making motions like I had clippers on my neck and then holding my hair down with my hands to show that I didn't want any taken off there; but Madame couldn't understand what I wanted either, so she went to the window and called the grocery man next door.

"Well, I went over the whole thing with the grocer and his wife, and finally the grocer thought he understood what I was driving at. He made an excited noise and came to the chair where I was. First he fluffed out my hair at the sides and back; then he stood away from the chair, lifted a lock of hair and wound it around his index finger, gesturing all the time with his other hand and talking to the barber.

"By that time the grocer's daughter and some other people had come in and sat in a row, like they were at church, but everybody relaxed and started to talk when the grocer got through explaining what it was I wanted. So then the barber opened up one of his drawers and took out a pair of curling tongs, talking to himself in the mirror like he was saying, 'Well, why didn't you *say* so instead of making motions that put me off?'

"I just sat there looking at him while he heated the curling tongs. I couldn't say anything because I didn't know for sure if he was going to use them on me or not. Then about a minute later I did know, because when the tongs were hot he came over to me and took a piece of my hair between his thumb and forefinger, ready to start."

Decker laughed apologetically and touched his head. He moved the sombrero back and forth on the sofa, making the little bells tinkle. "You can see for yourself," he said, "that my hair is a little curly; or anyway it looks like it was curled at one time, but that the curl had pretty near all come out. So I figured that's what the Frenchman thought. He thought I wanted it curled first and trimmed later."

Decker grinned and went on with his story. "I had a picture of what the boys at the barracks would do if I turned up with my hair curled like a Frenchman's, so I took the tongs out of the barber's hand and shook my head.

"But this little barber and his wife wouldn't take No for an answer. They kept smiling and saying Yes, and finally the grocer and his family and the neighbors started saying Yes, too." Decker turned to me for support. "You know how the French are about a thing like that? Well, things went on that way for a time with me saying No and the French barber and his friends saying Yes.

"Then the barber's wife had an idea. She spoke to her husband

and the neighbors and then went out of the door saying something I took for, 'Don't go away, because I know just what you want!' And so I sat in the chair awhile longer, and sure enough the barber's wife came right back. She had been running and she was out of breath. She had something in a package when she came in and she handed it to her husband.

"So this little barber opened up the parcel and I saw that his wife had gone down the street somewhere and borrowed a pair of *pearl-handled* curling tongs. I never figured that out, but I guess she thought I was kicking because the other pair wasn't good enough.

" 'No, no!' I said. 'Just put the clippers on the back and leave it long on top like it is. That's all I want. I don't want my hair curled.'

"But I couldn't make any impression on that French barber. He just smiled and nodded to his neighbors, and when I finished talking he only shrugged his shoulders and said something I took to be, 'Well, these are the best curling tongs in this neighborhood. They'll have to do.'

"So I gave up then. There was too much against me. I figured I might as well let him go ahead and curl my hair if he wanted to so badly. If it looked too bad afterwards, I figured I could slick it down with vaseline or something before I went back to the barracks.

"He did a good job, I must say that, while his wife and the neighbors crowded around and made admiring noises. Finally when he was through, he put the clippers on my neck and trimmed my hair at the edges like I wanted it done in the first place. Then he handed me a mirror to look at myself in.

"The first thing I thought was, 'By God! This can't be me!' But it was, all right. You see my hair was fixed in curls all over my head and the barber had brushed it up at the back and pulled it out at the sides in some way I'd never seen before."

Decker broke off suddenly. "Say, Foxy, did you ever see one of those French postal cards with a young man leaning on a table and writing a letter to his sweetheart? Or just sitting with his chin in his hand looking up at the moon? Well, that's what

I looked like. I swear I looked just like something you see on a French postal card. I wouldn't have believed it was in me if I hadn't seen it with my own eyes."

He looked down in sudden embarrassment and slid the sombrero back and forth across the sofa, making the little bells tinkle. Slowly his neck and face turned red. He raised his eyes after a moment and grinned. "Now, here's the funniest part," he said presently. "When I looked in the mirror I didn't feel silly, like I thought I would, and I didn't feel ashamed. I *liked* it the way the barber had fixed me. I don't know how the little barber did it, but he brought out something in me that I didn't even know was there before, and, as I just said, I *liked* myself that way.

"So then I said to myself, 'All right, I'm going to leave it this way. I'm free, white and twenty-one, and I'll wear my hair curled, by damn, or any way I please, if I *like* it! It's nobody's business but my own how I wear my hair!' I thought.

"Then I thought: 'I'll go back to the barracks like I am now and if anybody's got any objections, I'll take a poke at his nose.' But when I thought things over, I knew it wouldn't be as easy as that. All would happen would be that the boys would razz the pants off me, not one of the boys, but all of them; and they'd keep it up as long as I stayed in Toulouse. I knew then that I was whipped, because you can't go around poking the noses of people who aren't even sore at you, now can you? If you tried it they'd only hold your arms and laugh all the more.

"So I stood there thinking about these things and looking at the curls the French barber had put on my head. I knew I'd never get 'em out with vaseline or anything else in time to go back to the barracks, so I knew what I had to do. So I went to the shelf and picked up the clippers, stood before the mirror and cut a path down the middle of my head about an inch wide. After that there wasn't anything for the barber to do but finish the job I'd started and clip my head all over.

"Madame, the barber's wife, almost fell out of her chair when I ran the clippers across my head, and the grocer's daughter began to cry. The others just opened their mouths and looked at me. I wanted to tell everybody why I had to do it, but I couldn't. Anyway, it was all over in a few minutes and when the barber was through clipping my head, I paid what I owed and went back to the barracks. But all the time I kept saying to myself, 'I'm free, white and twenty-one, by God!' and then something else in me kept answering, 'Yeah, you're so free you can't even have your *hair* cut the way you want to!' "

Decker outlined the pattern in the rug with his toe and laughed self-consciously. He said: "I'll bet to this day that those French people still think Americans are the craziest people in the world." Then he straightened up, looked above my head and got up quickly. He put on his sombrero and drew his stomach muscles taut, sucking his small, balloonlike belly under his sash again. "Here's my old lady now," he said. "I want you to meet her and my little girl."

A stout woman accompanied by a child about twelve came over. Decker said: "Agnes, I want you to meet an old Army friend of mine I just ran into. We fought the battle of Toulouse, France, together." Then he turned to me. "Foxy, this is my wife and my youngest daughter, Phyllis."

Mrs. Decker reached up and adjusted the gold cord that held the sombrero anchored under her husband's chin, moving it backward a little. "You mustn't judge Bob by the way he looks now," she said. "He's just skylarking now, but for the rest of the year he'll be as sober a citizen as you'll find." Then she added: "All the boys from his Post are dressed just like he is, and besides this is such a big town nobody knows who you are anyway, do they?"

She turned to her husband. "It's getting cooler outside," she said. "If you're going out with Phyllis and me you better put something over what you got on. You'll freeze."

"I'll be all right," he said. "Don't worry about me."

The little girl spoke for the first time. She had edged away a little and it was plain that she was slightly ashamed of her father. "Don't you think Daddy looks *silly* dressed that way?" she asked.

Decker looked quickly at the child and for a moment the

expression in his eyes must have been the same as it was when he picked up the French barber's clippers; but it passed almost at once and he smiled, reached out and put one arm about his daughter's waist. He drew the child to him affectionately, her embarrassed face resting against his silken flank, the top of her head flush with the lowest button on his tight-fitting, gold-embroidered jacket. He stroked her cheek with his finger and spoke mildly:

"Don't you suppose Daddy knows that as well as you do?" he said.

1937

WHISTLES

$\mathcal{T}$HE OTHER night Mr. Ridley saw a play in which a whistle offstage was the principal actor. The scene was a small factory town, and each time anything happened to a character, the whistle blew steadily, muted at first, but getting louder as the disaster it announced became more and more apparent. The play and the blowing of the whistles stirred old memories which his mind at first could not recall, but as he walked slowly home, with the crowds of Times Square jostling him, the past came back with such vividness that it was almost as if that one phase of his life was not remembered at all, but re-created and existing beside his life of the present.

He was twelve years old again, and again he lived in Hodgetown, Alabama. He saw the old place in all its details—the way the town was laid out, the yellow, frame houses of the workmen, the company office, and the sawmill itself, with men hurrying home from work, their shoulders covered with sawdust. He saw faces and repeated names which he had not remembered for years, but mostly he thought of old Mrs. Foley and the things she told him about whistles.

She was past sixty when he first had met her, and as he turned east on 42nd Street, he remembered why she had gone to Hodgetown in the first place.

The mill superintendent had had a good deal of trouble with the running of the company boarding-house. It was a two-story frame building which housed the workmen who had no families of their own, and the superintendent hadn't found anyone who could run it satisfactorily. Then he got a letter from Mrs. Foley. She said she'd heard about the trouble with the boarding-house, and she thought she could take hold and run it right. She was a widow, she explained, and her children had grown up and married. She had two grandchildren she was raising, but she found time hanging heavy on her hands. She'd never run a boarding-house before, but she'd lived in sawmill towns since she was born, and she was sure she could make out. In desperation, the super-intendent wrote her to come down and take charge.

Everybody in Hodgetown had wondered what Mrs. Foley would be like. They expected a big, rawboned woman with a hard face and an undershot jaw, but she was nothing like that. Instead, she was somewhat dried up and timid. Her sandy, grayish hair was thinning now, and on top of her head there was a bald spot about the size of a silver dollar. She got off the local one afternoon in April with her grandchildren—a boy of fifteen and a girl of twelve. The boy was named Fletch and about five years before he had had an accident while playing with some dynamite caps which he had found. There was nothing left of his right hand now except a thumb, which seemed, standing alone, twice the length a thumb should be. The girl was more like her grand-mother, or what her grandmother had been. She was plump and sandy-haired, and she laughed at everything you said to her, no matter what it was.

When Mrs. Foley had got her baggage and her family safely off the train, she said, first thing, that the boarding-house would have to be scrubbed. She asked the superintendent to send her two strong men from the mill next morning, and he promised. Then she went off to take official possession.

The workmen came next morning at six, and Mrs. Foley started at once to dismantle the rooms. She went about with her head tied in a towel, a can of kerosene in her hand, supervising the workmen, and when the men had finished the heavy work in each room, she scrubbed the floors and walls and even the ceilings with lye soap and hot water.

Mr. Ridley's family had lived across the street, only a few doors away, and Mr. Ridley himself, who was a young boy in those days, had gone over to watch.

When Mrs. Foley saw him standing there, she turned and spoke ingratiatingly, "What's your name, little boy?"

"Donald Ridley."

"Oh, so you're the doctor's little boy?"

"Yes, ma'am."

"Well, Donald," she said after a moment, "why don't you take your good clothes off and work, too? You can help Fletch and Ada scour baseboards." She handed him a brush. "I got to run down and see about dinner pretty soon," she said. "The big whistle's due to blow in an hour and thirty-five minutes."

That was how he got to know Fletch, and Fletch told him that morning about his accident with the dynamite, while Ada scrubbed on her hands and knees, looking up at them, and laughing at each pause in the story as if she had never heard it before and considered it enormously amusing.

After a while Mrs. Foley came back to see how things were going. "We'll leave the heavy work for the men," she said. "All we'll do is to sort of clean up behind *them*. We ought to be about half through at supper-time, and before the big whistle blows tomorrow night, I bet there won't be a speck of dirt on these here premises."

For a minute or so there was only the sound of the four brushes against the woodwork, and then Mrs. Foley spoke again. "I'm going to give all three of you children a genuine pretty for helping out so good. See if I don't."

The first whistle, awakening the town, came at five o'clock in the morning. In the winter-time it was completely dark then. Sometimes when his father was returning from a sick call, Donald would wake up before the first whistle went. If there was a light in Mrs. Foley's window, he did not have to look at the clock, but would get up and dress, for he knew that soon the big whistle on the sawmill would sound, and that with its first booming, steamboatlike blast she would be knocking on the lodgers' doors and seeing that they did not go back to sleep.

Then, exactly at 5:15, she would have breakfast on the tables. At ten minutes to six she would start the men off on their way to work. Sometimes she'd start a man a little earlier. "You better leave five minutes before the rest, Mr. Maybridge," she'd say, "because you'll never get there by six if you don't. You know how slow you are." Or: "You boys quit joking Charlie Gorman about how much he eats. He may take a long time at table and leave the house later than you do, but he'll be down at the stackers working before the rest of you get as far as the lath mill."

Then, when she was alone with the littered breakfast tables, she'd roll up her sleeves and go to work. Later she'd leave Ada in charge and go shopping for food. Sometimes she'd go to the neighboring farms in search of fresh vegetables, but at ten o'clock, no matter where she was or what she had to attend to, she'd turn and say: "I've got to get my dinner started now. The big whistle is going to blow in two hours, or nearabout."

She ran the boarding-house for five years, and things went smoothly under her management. Then she took sick. Mr. Ridley remembered the day well. He was almost a member of the Foley establishment by that time, he was over there so much. His father had gone to see her professionally, and when he came home he told Donald that what Mrs. Foley had been having for the past months were heart attacks, and that she'd have to take things easy.

Donald went to the boarding-house and sat by Mrs. Foley's bed. "Well, I never heard such foolishness," she said. "Your father says I got to stay in bed for a month at least. It's easy enough for him to say stay in bed, but who's going to run things with me in bed, I'd like to know? Why, it must be almost time for the twelve-o'clock whistle now, and I got to get up." She raised herself on one elbow and looked at Donald for advice. "You're a smart boy, Donnie," she said. "You got lots of book-sense. What do you think?"

"I think you ought to do what my father says."

She lay back again, only half convinced. "Ada is a good manager," she said doubtfully. "It's true Ada can manage almost as well as I can, but there's a lot of things she don't know about yet. I'm having smothered steak today, and there's tomato gravy with it. Well, sir, that would be all right except George Patmore can't eat tomatoes in no shape or form. They upset his stomach so bad that he ain't a bit of good for two or three days afterwards."

Mr. Ridley said: "You just rest. I'll tell Mr. Patmore not to eat any of the tomato gravy."

"Oh, George Patmore will eat the tomato gravy," she said. "You may be sure of that. Nothing you or anybody else could say would stop him. George'll eat anything that's passed him, whether it makes him sick or not. Now, if I was just up and about, I'd fix some special gravy that *looked* like the other but didn't have tomatoes in it, and then he'd never know he'd missed anything. That's the way I worked it last Wednesday."

She broke off suddenly. "Well, now, I *know* I got to get up!" she said. "Joe Yates has got to shave this noontime sure, and that's all there is to it. I just remembered that this is a Wednesday, too, and it's the night Joe's girl over on Calumet Street comes to eat supper with him. He won't shave unless you make him, and his girl told me the other day that if he didn't take to shaving more regular, she was going to up and quit him." She sat up in bed again. "I got to get up, because Joe won't shave unless somebody like me stands over him the whole time and coaxes him."

She threw back the bedclothing suddenly and said: "Hand me my shoes, Donnie. I'll get up for a little while and start things to running smoothly."

She got up and tried to walk across the floor, but she could not make it. Mr. Ridley helped her back into bed, and he sat beside her again. "Well, sir!" she said in surprise. "Well, sir!"

Her spell of faintness had frightened her, and she rested quietly against her pillow and closed her eyes. She was silent for a long time, but when her heart had quieted down she began to talk of her early years, as if she realized at last that her life was over and she sought to find some common denominator for her days.

"You know, Donnie," she began, "I was born in a little sawmill town. It was a place called Shearn's Mill, and the first thing I remember very good was when I was a little girl, not more than five years old, helping my mother get the menfolks off in the morning.

"They didn't have a whistle at Shearn's Mill. A watchman used to come out in the morning and beat a piece of tin to wake up the hands. Then Mamma and me would get breakfast and see that Papa and the boys ate proper and washed theirselves good."

She talked slowly, recalling each detail of her past: "Papa was a restless man and kept moving us about from one place to another. I'll bet there's not a sawmill town in this part of the state that we didn't live in at one time or another. Things went on like that until I married.

"My husband was a millwright, and we started housekeeping in a place called Ivy Pond. It was a sawmill town, too, and the only difference to me was I had only one man to cook for instead of a passel. I remember Ivy Pond so good because they had a deep-pitched whistle that used to get stuck about twice a week, and when it did it just kept blowing away until some of the men climbed on top of the mill and fixed it.

"Then after we left Ivy Pond, we went to a place called Motley. The whistle at Motley had a sharp, sour tone, and it nearabout put my teeth on edge to listen to it. I never could abide the whistle at Motley, but then they didn't have many whistles in those days that sounded as fine as the ones we got right here in Hodgetown."

She lay back, caressing the bald spot on her crown. "You know, Donnie, I never thought much about it before, but when I look back, the thing I remember best about places I lived in is the kind of whistle there was on top of the mill."

A moment later the Hodgetown planer sounded its blast, and then the lathmill whistle and the whistle atop the sawmill went together.

Mrs. Foley said, "I spent my life answering whistles, but this is one time I can't do it."

Mr. Ridley told her: "You'll be up again in a few days. Don't worry about it."

"I don't know about that, Donnie," she said. She laughed triumphantly, holding her sides. "But I'll bet when I die and they lay me to rest, Gabriel's trumpet will turn out to be just another sawmill whistle," she said proudly. She nodded her head a couple of times and added: "That's just the way it's going to be, and I want to serve notice right here and now that if it is, I'm not a-going to get up out of my grave."

Ada came in to see if her grandmother wanted anything. She'd be in again as soon as she got the men fed and back to work, she said, but right at the moment she was busy fixing some special gravy for Mr. George Patmore, one without tomatoes.

Then Mrs. Foley laughed in spite of the pain it caused her, and pressed her hand against her heart. "Well, I never!" she said. "Well, I never, for a fact!"

In those days Mr. Ridley was reading a great deal, and he was pondering for the first time the great issues of existence. What Mrs. Foley told him about her life, and the forces which had regulated it, made a deep impression on him. With his new knowledge, his new insight, he thought of her as a pitiful, ignorant old woman whose life had been spent in senseless bondage to whistles.

He hinted at these things one afternoon, but she looked at him in complete amazement. "Now, whoever put such ideas in your head?" she asked. "Why, I'd say offhand that I had a full, happy life." She became more serious. "I worked hard doing what I wanted to do, and I know now that I really accomplished something. I married and raised a big family that turned out as well as average. Now, what else could I have been?" She rubbed the bald spot on her head thoughtfully and then went on: "I'm thinking that you're the one who's mixed up about things, Donnie —not me."

Mr. Ridley went to see her almost every afternoon during her sickness, and she told him much of her early life, but the more she said, the more she affirmed her contentment with her lot, the deeper his sense of her personal tragedy became, until, at length, she was the fixed symbol in his mind of all injustice.

He had tried once or twice to explain her plight to her, choosing his words as delicately as he knew how; to show her how sad and how wasted her life had been.

"What are you going to do with your life, Donnie?" she asked mildly.

"I don't know," he said. "That is, I don't know definitely yet; but there's so much oppression and injustice in the world, and I want to do something about it."

"Why don't you be a doctor like your father?" she asked. "There's a good way to help people, if that's what you want to do."

"I don't know," he said. "That's all right in its way, but it's too small. I want to do bigger things than that."

She smiled suddenly with amusement and made a clucking sound with her lips. "You don't want to do anything for the good of people," she said. "You just want to sit around and talk about it."

But seeing the hurt, serious expression on his face, she reached out and touched his hand. "I know you're well up in your books," she said, "but you haven't got much common sense for a boy going on seventeen, have you, Donnie?"

She died a few weeks later, and they arranged to bury her in the Hodgetown cemetery. Mr. Ridley, walking home that night after he had seen the play with the whistle offstage, recalled the funeral of twenty years ago in all its details.

The funeral had been on a Sunday afternoon, with the mill shut down and the men not working, so almost everybody in town had gone. There had been a hearse and a few carriages for the family. The rest of Hodgetown had walked to the graveyard. The funeral had formed at the boarding-house and had passed down Hiawatha Street, the full length of the town. Then, when the procession approached the railroad cut and the steps which led to the planer mill, everybody saw old Mr. Stamford standing on top of a boxcar in the cut watching the funeral come down the street.

He was an old man, about the age of Mrs. Foley. He had boarded with her until his widowed daughter came to Hodgetown to take care of him, and he and Mrs. Foley had been friends.

The old man seemed greatly affected by the death of his friend, and he took off his hat and bent his head as the hearse came nearer. He looked about him undecidedly for a moment, as if he wanted to do something for her to show his respect, to make some appropriate gesture. Then, as if suddenly knowing precisely what to do, he climbed down the side of the boxcar, ran up the steps and went into the powerhouse. A moment later the whistle on the planer began to sound—thin, insistent, wailing.

Almost at once the watchman at the lathmill, hearing the planer whistle and interpreting it correctly, began to sound the whistle there, and before the procession turned off Hiawatha Street into the road that led to the graveyard, the big whistle on top of the sawmill went, too, with its full, booming blast.

The whistles kept blowing during the march to the cemetery, and even during the services at the graveside they could be heard, while Mr. Ridley stood there wondering how anybody could be so insensitive or so cruel as to blow the whistles over a poor, dead old woman whose life had been nothing more than a long series of whistles, and who was entitled now to her rest. It seemed brutal and inhuman to him. He wanted to protest, but he realized that nobody would understand what he had to say.

The whistles still blew at intervals while the empty hearse and the carriages returned to Hodgetown. They stopped blowing in the order in which they had originally begun—the planer first, then the lathmill, and finally the big whistle on top of the sawmill.

He had thought about Mrs. Foley and her funeral for the remainder of that summer. In the fall he had gone away to school and gradually he had forgotten her. He hadn't thought of her at all in years until this particular night—the night when he heard the whistle offstage.

He went into his apartment, his mind still busy with the past, but he did not turn on his light. He sat in the dark smoking a cigarette and again the past came back to him with such vividness that the details of his early life seemed not so much remembered as experienced again in their entirety. Then, as he sat there smoking, he suddenly saw old Mrs. Foley's life in another light. He understood at last why her friend the watchman blew the whistle at her funeral and why that was the one gesture for him to have made, the one compliment. He saw her now with great clarity, and he understood, at last, that in reality she had been one of the fortunate people of the world—one of those who know why they were born and what their particular usefulness is to be.

He wondered, then, what his own usefulness was, for what unique purpose he had been created. He discovered that he did not know, that few people ever know; but Mrs. Foley had known clearly what her work was. It was to wake up the world and wash its face, feed it, and get it to work on time. She had known from the beginning, and had accepted it.

He wondered if his own benign but vastly superior attitude toward others, his earnest efforts to rescue those who did not want to be rescued, to save those who did not even know that they were lost, were not a little juvenile, a little presumptuous.

1937

CINDERELLA'S SLIPPER

*H*E WAS the Mr. Hollings of the law firm of Wetherall, Byrne, Hollings and Lipman; not yet so experienced, politically, as his immediate senior, C. Ralph Byrne, nor so well connected as old Mr. Wetherall with his endless settlements of estates and his trusteeships for rich old women, but he had gone a long way for a man thirty-five years old who had started without influence or money. He had succeeded through the force of his determined ability, and as he came into the outer office and saw again his name, Mr. Vernon L. Hollings, in gold lettering on his private door, he felt a sense of satisfaction, knowing that this reality marked one of the goals he had set for himself.

He stood at the switchboard, inside the railed-off enclosure, and took off his gloves. Before him was the stenographers' room, and he saw at once that Miss Cavallo's place had been filled. He drew his gloves through his palms three times and went to the drinking fountain, bent over, and pressed the button that threw a small stream of water into his mouth. From the drinking fountain, he could see the new girl more plainly, and the first thing he noticed about her were her feet. She was wearing, probably for the first time, a pair of black, patent-leather slippers whose gleaming newness stood out all the more against the background of her general shabbiness. Her shabbiness was not a thing that you could identify definitely, it was more generalized; but you knew at once, no matter how unimaginative you were, that she had had no new clothes, with the exception of the bright slippers, for a long time.

He turned from the fountain and went toward his private offices. His secretary, Miss Link, was on the 'phone when he came in. She covered the mouthpiece with her palm. "It's the executive council of the Non-Partisan Church League," she said.

"They want you to speak at their dinner tonight. Senator Swathmore was to have done it, but he got sick at the last minute."

He smiled and nodded, and Miss Link turned back to the 'phone. "Mr. Hollings just came in," she said, "and he'll be very happy to be with you. Let me have the address and the time, please."

Hollings went into his inner office. He was about to push the button for Miss Link when old Mr. Wetherall, the senior partner, came in and sat down in the wide chair by the window.

"Well, Verne," he began genially, "I got the goods on you this time. I saw you admiring the little number who took over Miss Cavallo's job." He laughed heartily. "When you went to get a drink of water, you weren't fooling *me*, my lad! I knew it wasn't a drink of water you had on your mind."

He was a man in his middle sixties with white hair and a full, sensual mouth. He had been famous for his love affairs in his day, and he still treated the jet-trimmed old ladies, who were both his clients and his contemporaries, with heavy, male coquettishness.

Hollings took off his reading glasses and leaned back in his chair. He smiled and nodded his head. He had learned, long ago, that falling at once into the mood of others was the surest method of having your own way in the long run. "You caught me this time, Mr. Wetherall," he said amiably, "so I won't try to fix up an alibi."

Mr. Wetherall laughed again, pleased with himself, and pulled at his white waistcoat. He rolled his eyes suggestively. "You didn't know it, Verne, but I was behind you all the time, and I thought: 'Verne always was a sly dog with women, one of the sly ones, and keeps them all guessing; but this time I've got the goods on him.'"

Verne sat looking at his senior, smiling ruefully and nodding, but his mind was far away. He thought again of the new girl, of the patent leather slippers which seemed so out of place in her generalized, genteel shabbiness, and he wanted to laugh. Possibly she had bought the slippers with her last money when she got this job, her old ones being too far gone to serve any more.

When Mr. Wetherall got up and went back to his own office, Hollings rang for Miss Link. She came at once with her book, and she made a slight face at the door through which Mr. Wetherall had passed. She turned back to Mr. Hollings and they both shook their heads and laughed. She was in love with him and she had been for a long time, but then so were all the other girls in the office. She had no hope of having him for her own. She had given that up long ago. He was a man, she felt, who would belong to no particular woman, but to the world. There was something about him at times that made her think of a character in history, and underneath his courteous, smiling tolerance she felt a fierce driving force which made him alien and a little terrifying.

He picked up the pile of letters and went through them, his mind working with the sureness and the rapidity which Miss Link had always admired. Between letters he stopped, looked into Miss Link's eyes and smiled his slow, ingratiating smile.

"Mr. Wetherall," he said lightly, as if answering the question which had been in her mind when she came in, "seems quite smitten with the new girl who took Miss Cavallo's place."

Miss Link put down her pencil. "At his age!" she began indignantly; then seeing the faint, ironic smile about his eyes, she too had smiled.

"Who is she, anyway?" he asked.

And Miss Link told him what she knew. She was a Miss Purdy and the managing clerk had just hired her. This was her first job, but she had good recommendations and the shorthand school said she was going to be expert with a little more experience.

"Poor kid," said Verne. "She looks frightened to death, doesn't she?"

When Mr. Hollings was in this sort of mood, when he showed the tenderer side of his character, Miss Link found it difficult to hide her devotion.

She got up when the dictation was over. She stopped by the door, her hand on the knob. "Oh, by the way," she began suddenly. "We were talking yesterday about that new reform party.

Well, I told them you'd see their committee this afternoon at 3:15."

He nodded, thanked her, and turned back to his work, but his mind was no longer on it, and he kept thinking against his will of Miss Purdy. He wondered what her first name was, and for a moment he was tempted to call Miss Link back and ask her, but he realized that that would be too revealing. He would find out in time, anyway. He could wait.

He met Charlie Byrne, one of the other partners, when he was returning from lunch. They got out of the elevator together and came down the corridor.

"Say, what's all this about your running for office?" Byrne asked. Then, without waiting for a reply, he went on: "I'll say one thing, and it's this: You're a wonder. You're one in a million. One of the organizers of the party lived next door to me out in Sandford Hills, and he told me that they'd been checking up on you for a month. They even talked to maids and elevator boys at your place, but they didn't turn up a thing. They've just about come to the conclusion that you're God's gift to the party." He became more serious. "Say, fellow," he said, "do you know that half the women in this town cut your pictures out of the papers and frame them?"

They paused inside the door, beside the switchboard. To the left the stenographers were busily at work and Hollings looked again at Miss Purdy, his eyes focused on her trim ankles and her glistening, new slippers. Her feet were so dainty, he thought, so ridiculously small for this clumsy age.

Then he went into his office and plunged once more into his work. He was still busy when the committee called. They explained the purposes of their party and the support that was behind them. A good many people were sick of the conditions in town, they said, and if Mr. Hollings would consent to run on an independent ticket, he could depend on their organization 100 per cent. They had looked him up and had come to the conclusion that he was the one man who could be put in. His speech-making, his wide social life, and his public stand against vice in the past had made him more prominent, possibly, than he realized.

Hollings listened politely. He was quite aware of his growing political importance. Did these people take him for a fool? Did they think he wasted his evenings addressing silly clubs because he liked doing it?

"Of course we realize that your law practice is important," said one of the gentlemen. "It's asking a great deal of you when we ask you to give it up. But then you can do so much good."

Mr. Hollings inclined his head, but he did not speak. It was true his law practice was very profitable, more so, possibly, than these people imagined, but it was not an end in itself; it was merely a stepping-stone to the thing that he wanted more, and that was power. He would have what he wanted some day, but he knew it was not yet time. He said finally: "I'd be defeated this year, and so would anybody else you supported; but two years from now it should be a different story."

He went to the door with the committee and stood chatting with them beside the drinking fountain. Over their heads he could see Miss Purdy still typing away, her blonde hair brushed out of her eyes and anchored back of her ears with clips. She looked very tender and very young. He followed the line of her body with his eyes and saw, then, that she had taken off one of her shoes. He wanted to smile. She was probably quite conscious of the daintiness of her feet, and, in her vanity, she had bought the new shoes a size too small. He wondered what she had done with the missing shoe. He shifted his position a little and moved his head slowly. He saw after a moment that she had hidden it behind her wastebasket. No doubt she thought that the basket hid both the shoe and her stockinged foot from the outer office.

When the committee had gone, Mr. Hollings went over to Miss Purdy and spoke casually. "Take a memorandum for me, please," he began. "I'm afraid I'll forget it if I don't make a record now."

She looked up at the sound of his voice, and when she saw who it was, she became a little confused. She picked up her book, moved her chair back, and, in her nervousness, she brushed her pencils onto the floor. He bent over and picked them up, smiling reassuringly at her. "Just take it onto the machine," he said quietly. "It's very short."

He began to dictate slowly, and when he had finished, Miss Purdy took the typed note from her machine and handed it to him. He thanked her and smiled his slow, ingratiating smile; but when he was seated again at his desk, he rolled the memorandum into a ball and stuck it into his pocket. His throat was dry with excitement. His hands felt cold all at once, and he pressed them together. He noticed that his hands were trembling a little.

Miss Link brought him his letters at half past four, reminding him that he must leave earlier than usual if he expected to change his clothes and get to dinner on time. There was nothing else for the day, she explained, except routine matters which she could handle herself. If anything important came up before closing time, she'd call him at his apartment.

He put on his coat and hat and went with Miss Link into her smaller, adjoining office. He opened her door, and as he stood there drawing on his gloves, he noticed that there was a slight commotion in the stenographers' room. Miss Link went at once to see what it was, and he stood beside the door watching her. When she came back she was shaking her head at the absurdity of the situation she had discovered.

"It's about Miss Purdy's shoe," she said. "One of Mr. Wetherall's old ladies was in to see him about an hour ago, and she brought a terrier puppy with her. The puppy was running about the office like mad. Well, one of Miss Purdy's shoes is missing— she said she took it off for a minute to ease her foot—and it seems the dog must have picked it up and hid it somewhere about the office, or took it home with him."

Mr. Hollings buttoned his overcoat slowly. "Well," he said laughingly, "that *is* a crisis, isn't it?"

"It's more serious than you think," said Miss Link. "Miss Purdy hasn't got another pair of shoes to her name, probably. And how is she going to get home tonight? She can't go down the street with one shoe off and one on."

Mr. Hollings thought once more of Miss Purdy and again he

had that warm, tender sense of beauty which made him feel as if he were going to start trembling again. He took out his wallet quickly. "Poor child!" he said softly; and then, "Find out what size she wears and get her another pair before closing time." He handed Miss Link a ten dollar note. "Don't let her know where the money came from," he said. "It would probably embarrass her."

Miss Link said: "I'll tell her that Mr. Wetherall's client found the shoe in her automobile and called up to ask me to replace it." She took the money and stood watching him as he passed through the office and out of the door. There were not many men in the world as fine as Mr. Hollings, she thought. If there were more like him, this would be a happy place to live in, indeed.

He took a taxi downstairs and was driven to his apartment. He stepped into the elevator and looked at his watch. It was only a quarter past five, and he had plenty of time to take his bath and dress. His valet, hearing a key in the lock, came into the living-room as Mr. Hollings entered. Miss Link had 'phoned earlier in the afternoon, he said, and he had already laid out Mr. Hollings' evening clothes. He came a step closer, as if to take his employer's hat and coat, but Mr. Hollings shook his head and went into the small room which served as a study, and which he kept locked. He stood for a moment listening at the door while the valet moved about the living-room outside, and when everything was quiet once more, he put his hand into his coat pocket and took out Miss Purdy's lost shoe.

He sat beside his desk and held the shoe in his hand, stroking its glazed, black surface with his fingers; then, after a moment, he went to the closet, which he also kept locked, and opened it; and there, on a shelf before his eyes, were the other shoes that he had loved, the shoes which had preceded Miss Purdy's.

They were all women's shoes except one, and all black, as Miss Purdy's shoe was black, except one. The single, masculine shoe, the alien one, was light tan, and it sat, like some great shoe of shoes, guarding the small, feminine flock about it.

He had seen the tan shoe and its mate, freshly polished, outside the door of a hotel room early one morning, and he had taken it. He did not know why, because he had never before been interested in men's shoes; but this particular shoe had taken his fancy anyway, possibly because of its newness, its old-fashioned last, and the glazed brightness of its almost lemon color. It was a high-topped, countryman's shoe with wide toes. There were eyelets half way up, and beyond that were a series of metal hasps into which the crossed strings fit neatly. He hadn't seen a shoe like that in years, and he had picked it up upon impulse, stuck it under his coat, and hurried back to his own room. Later he had put a twenty-dollar bill in an envelope and stuck it into the remaining shoe. He was not a thief.

He heard his valet coming back to tell him that his bath was ready, and he shut the closet quickly and locked it. He came into his bedroom and undressed, thinking again of the committee who had called upon him that day. They knew very little about him, indeed, if they thought that he would be content with an office as trivial as the one they had offered him. He had considered it at all only because the office would serve as an entering wedge to his larger ambitions. Naturally, he had not told this to the committee, but his interest was not so much in enforcing the inadequate laws already in existence, as in passing other and more drastic laws, laws which would protect people more completely from their own disgusting and inherent desires.

When he had finished his bath and had dressed, he came into his study once more, and once more he unlocked the closet. He took Miss Purdy's shoe tenderly in his two hands, as if it were some small, terrified bird, and bent above it, rubbing his cheek against its gleaming surface.

It seemed incomprehensible to him, at that moment, that another man would embrace a mass of flesh, stuffed with digesting food, when there were shoes to be loved, shoes as impersonal and as beautiful as the one he now held against his lips; and yet there were: in fact, you couldn't go to the theater or to the movies, or even walk in a public park, without seeing men and women locked in each other's arms, their lips pressed together.

He lifted his head, his eyes burning with the pure, fierce light of a crusader. A shoe was also flesh, in a way, he thought; but it was flesh with the disgusting things taken out. He drew his lips down quickly. There was something terrifying and something pathetic in the intensity of his disgust. He resembled, at that moment, nothing so much as one of the handsomer, early Christian martyrs.

He put the shoe back on the shelf at last and turned from the closet. It was unfortunate that he had to go to the dinner, but he would get away as quickly as possible; he would spend a long, happy evening with the shoe, after all.

He went to the door and stood there regretfully with one hand on the knob. In his mind's eye he saw the slipper sitting with a sweet placidity on its shelf, awaiting his return like a faithful wife. Again he had a feeling of quick, warm excitement and he felt for a moment as if his flesh had somehow liquefied and was dripping slowly from his bones. He leaned against the door for support, his blood pounding in his ears, his breath coming with difficulty through his half-open mouth. He recovered in a moment, turned and blew a kiss to the slipper.

"Good-bye, my love! . . . My love!" he said passionately. "Good-bye, my love! . . . Good-bye for a little while!"

1937

THE FIRST SUNSET

*W*HEN Albert Evans was six years old, his mother took him to spend the afternoon with Mrs. Langkabel, a school friend of hers. Mrs. Langkabel, a widow, ran a truck farm about ten miles from Reedyville. She was on the lookout for her guests, and when she saw their automobile turn in from the road that day, she hurried to the gate to meet them. A tall man with a brown, wrinkled face walked behind her.

After she had greeted her friend, Mrs. Langkabel introduced the old man. "Katie," she said, "I want you to meet my cousin from the old country. He wasn't here the last time you came out for a visit."

The old man said: "I am Dr. Albert Ehrlich. Emma forgot to tell you my name, didn't she?" His English was perfect, but he spoke it with a slight foreign accent.

Mrs. Evans laughed gaily. "Well, now that *I've* just met an Albert," she said, "let me introduce one to you, Dr. Ehrlich." She indicated the boy who stood beside her. "I mean by that, I want you to meet my *son* Albert."

The old man and the boy looked at each other and then shook hands. The fact that they both had the same first name made them friends at once, and while the two women laughed and talked together about old times, the doctor showed his namesake around the farm. Late in the afternoon they went to gather eggs, and coming back, they sat on the kitchen steps and watched the sun go down behind an oak thicket.

Inside the house Mrs. Langkabel and Mrs. Evans were still talking, and Albert could hear their voices plainly. "Mamma was born in the old country, too," said Mrs. Langkabel. "You remember her, don't you, Katie? How we used to laugh behind her back at the way she spoke English? Well, Dr. Ehrlich is her first cousin, and she was always talking about him when she was still alive. She was so proud of him later on, and they used to write to each other. So I asked him to come live with me because of Mamma."

Albert looked curiously at the old man, but he realized that his friend had not even heard Mrs. Langkabel's words. His mind was far away, and his eyes were fixed on the setting sun. Then, suddenly, he spoke:

"Did you ever hear the story of the first sunset?"

"No, sir," said Albert. "No, sir, I never did."

"Dr. Ehrlich is well known in his own country, I imagine," said Mrs. Evans. "Such a distinguished-looking man. Such nice manners."

"He's well known the world over," said Mrs. Langkabel. "It's more than you think, Katie. And why shouldn't he be? He devoted his whole life to the good of others."

The doctor lifted his chin a little, nodded thoughtfully and began his story: "All this happened a long time ago, Albert—long before Christ was born, and even before our own God was known about—but once upon a time there was a land something like our own, except that it wasn't round the way our world is, but was shaped more like a big mill wheel with two flat sides.

"The underside of the wheel was on the ocean," continued the old man, "so of course the upper side faced the sky; and it was here, in this region, that the old, pagan gods lived. The gods had many fine palaces to live in, but the most magnificent of all was on the sun. Early in the morning the sun-palace would come up over the eastern edge of the wheel, just as it does over our world today, my little Albert, and would begin its trip across the sky. It was the source of all light and all heat, and the wheel-people knew this quite well; so when they saw that the palace had appeared again, they would come out of their holes in the rocks, stare upward and make their cruel, bloody sacrifices.

"All day long the wheel-people had the sun to warm them and give them light, but when it had traveled all the way across the sky and had reached the western rim of the wheel, it went off into unknown lands, and the wheel was dark and cold again until it returned."

Dr. Ehrlich paused a moment, smiled and looked down at his namesake, who sat on the step just below him. Then he bent forward timidly, as if he wanted to put his arm about the boy, but, as if remembering something, he sat up straight again and continued his story:

"Life on the earth-wheel was a terrible experience," he said. "The people there were cold and miserable all the time, and there was never enough to eat. It was a bleak, rocky land that they lived on, and there was not much around them except the ocean, the sky and the wide salt marshes.

"It would seem that the common misery of the wheel-people would draw them together, wouldn't it, Albert? . . . Sadly, it did not work out that way, because they were unforgiving and cruel to one another and they were forever fighting among themselves. It was the only thing they knew."

"What did the wheel-people look like, Dr. Ehrlich?"

The old doctor thought a moment, his lips pursed slightly. "They had thick, clumsy bodies," he began, "and their backs didn't straighten all the way up, as ours do. They had long arms and short, twisted legs; they had coarse, yellow hair and their mouths were half-open all the time.

"And so things went on like this for ages and ages, and then a strange little boy was born among the wheel-people, and our story really begins. At first the boy seemed like the rest of his kind, but there was something inside him that made him very different from them. You see, Albert, this peculiar little boy didn't believe in the cruelty and bloodshed which he saw every day, and he said so when he was old enough to express himself; but when he tried to talk about the things which he *did* believe in, such as justice and kindness and mercy, the people didn't know what he meant. They had never even heard of those things before.

"If he had been only a little different," continued the old man, "they would have killed him outright, no doubt, and forgotten all about him; but as it was, they were afraid of him, and they thought that he was the servant of some powerful devil, so they only drove him out of the tribe with rocks and clubs and left him back of the marshes to die of cold and hunger."

Albert moved up to the step beside the doctor and looked steadily into his eyes. "What was the boy's name?" he asked.

"It was Surd. Do you think it fits the story all right?"

"Yes, sir," said Albert.

Dr. Ehrlich got up and went to the shelf where a bucket of water stood. He drank slowly, as if pondering his next words, his sunburned throat rising and falling as he swallowed. In the silence Albert heard his mother and Mrs. Langkabel talking again:

"Cousin Albert looks real well now; yes, Katie. It's being out in the sun and the open air so much. But you should have seen him when he first came. So pale and sick-looking then. So thin and peaked. I guess, though, that came from being in prison so long."

"My heavens!" said Mrs. Evans in a shocked voice. "Did they really put him in prison?"

"Yes," said Mrs. Langkabel. "They did. They really did, Katie."

When Dr. Ehrlich had finished his drink, he turned to the boy and began to talk again, gesturing with the empty dipper:

"No wonder the wheel-people didn't know what to make of Surd," he said. "They had a right to be puzzled, because a great thing had happened, and the first human being had been born. I doubt if even Surd realized it, but if he really *was* the first human being, as many scholars think to this day, then it was a great moment in the history of mankind, indeed, wasn't it, Albert?"

"Yes, sir," said Albert. Then he added: "I'll bet Surd didn't die, though, like they all thought he would."

Dr. Ehrlich laughed and put his hand on the boy's head. "Oh, no, Albert; that didn't happen. No, indeed. Surd managed to live somehow and to grow up to be a man."

"What did Surd look like then, Dr. Ehrlich?"

"Well," said Dr. Ehrlich slowly, "at a glance he looked a great deal like the other wheel-people. Certainly his back wasn't quite straight, and he walked on short twisted legs, just as they did.

His long yellow hair fell down to his shoulders, the same as theirs did. But his blue eyes weren't cold and cruel the way theirs were, and I imagine if anybody could have told the great difference between him and the other wheel-people, it would have been that way.

"The thing which would have puzzled the wheel-people the most, if they had known about it," said Dr. Ehrlich, "was this: Surd didn't have any hard feelings against them at all, even though they had treated him so badly. All he wanted was to make them believe in his new ideas, and he would lie for hours on the rocks wondering how he could ever manage it. Things must have seemed hopeless to him in those days, because if he even tried to come near one of his people, they would either run away in terror or pick up stones and throw them at him. The whole thing looked impossible, didn't it, Albert? But he didn't give up; and then one day as he looked about him and saw how drab and gray the sky and the earth-wheel were, how little color there was, he thought of a way to do what he wanted to do so badly."

To the left a neighbor walked down the lane. He stopped when he saw the old man and waved his hand. "Howdy, Dr. Ehrlich," he called out. "How's Miss Emma getting along?" The old doctor waved back. "Very well," he said. "Very well, indeed, thank you."

When the neighbor had passed, Dr. Ehrlich turned his head and looked once more at the sunset, which seemed to grow in brilliance each minute. "That was one of Cousin Emma's friends," he said. He smiled and shook his head humorously. "I've already met him three times, but I still have no idea what his name is, because Emma never tells a name when she introduces people." He smiled again, sat beside the boy on the top step and clasped his hands around his upraised knee.

But the boy was not interested in these details. "What was it Surd thought of?" he asked.

Dr. Ehrlich said: "It was a crazy sort of an idea, I suppose, or some people would think so, anyway; but to me it's always been the most wonderful thing I've ever heard of." The boy moved closer to him on the step, looking earnestly into his eyes.

"What Surd wanted to do," said the doctor after a moment, "was simple, really, as all wonderful things are, and it was this: He wanted to paint the gray, cheerless sky with colors." The old man paused, smiled and stroked his white beard. He nodded his head slowly, a faraway look in his eyes.

Inside the house Mrs. Evans spoke again: "Poor man! He's certainly had his troubles! I hope Albert doesn't plague him too much. If I had known what I know now, I'd have kept him here with us."

"Albert won't plague him," said Mrs. Langkabel. "Don't think that for a minute. Why, Cousin Albert's talked more to him today than he has the whole three months that he's been here with me."

"From the moment he had his great thought," continued Dr. Ehrlich, "Surd didn't think of anything else, and the first thing he did was to pick out the best place in the sky for his work. It was the spot where the sun-palace passed over the rim of the wheel, just before night came. There was a high mountain there, with a shelf which stuck out a long way over the ocean.

"So Surd made himself some brushes and put them away. Then he looked about for colors to work with, but all he could find were a few dull-colored berries. They didn't look very promising, but they were the best he could do, so he gathered them up, and one morning he set out to do his work. It was well into the afternoon before he got to the top of the mountain and walked across the shelf. It was just as he had thought: the sky was so close at this place that he could stretch out his arms and touch it.

"Then Surd put his berries into hollows in the shelf, each according to its color. He crushed the berries and poured water into the vats. He dipped in his brushes and began to paint the sky, but his colors faded as fast as he put them on. He painted for a long time, not willing to give up even then, but when he had used up all his colors, there was nothing to show for his work. The sky had closed over it and wiped it all out."

The doctor paused in his story and looked at the boy beside him. Albert smiled and moved closer, and the old doctor lifted his arm suddenly and put it about the boy. They sat that way for a few minutes and then the doctor went on with his story:

"When Surd's colors failed him, he knew what it was he had to do next; so he filled his vats with water again and then he pulled out his long, yellow hair. He put the hair into one of the vats, and all at once the water there turned a bright yellow. Then Surd dipped in his brushes and began to paint again, and this time his colors held fast. The yellow streamed across the sky in long, trembling lines that spread out to pale lemon at their edges. Surd looked with joy at what he had done, but almost immediately he began to shake his head, because he wasn't entirely satisfied with his work. 'It needs some red in it,' he said critically. 'It needs a little red.'

"So Surd ripped his body open with a stone and reached upward for his heart. He held it in his hands for a little while and then he put it gently into the second vat. Instantly the water there turned the deepest and most beautiful red you ever saw, my little Albert, and when Surd touched the red with his brushes there came a soft, humming sound. Then Surd painted the sky with red, and again his color held fast. He mixed the red and the yellow together so well that it looked, after a moment, as if they would never be separated again." Dr. Ehrlich was silent for a while, leaning back against the steps with his eyes closed, and during the silence Albert heard his mother's voice once more:

"Did Dr. Ehrlich have a family in the old country, Emma?"

"That's the most terrible part of all!" said Mrs. Langkabel. "I said to myself, 'I won't tell Katie *that* part of the story even if she asks me to!' . . . It was all so senseless. Cousin Albert and his family never hurt anybody in their whole lives." She sighed deeply. "Well, anyway, it's all over now; and I for one can't understand how Cousin Albert has stood it as well as he has. If it was me, I'd have given up and gone crazy long ago."

The old man opened his eyes, sat upright and continued his story: "And so Surd stood there on the rocky shelf looking at what he had made. 'Who would have thought that all that bright color was in me?' he said in surprise. He lifted his arms high above his head and began to sing, and he had a right to, if ever a man did, but after a little while he stopped singing and shook his head stubbornly. The picture still was not quite right, and he knew it. 'What it needs now, is blue,' he said. 'It would be perfect if it had some blue in it.'

"He sat down on the rocky shelf and began to cry in a weak voice, because he knew very well that if he did what he *must* do to make his sunset perfect, he would never be able to see his work in all its beauty. He would not even have that pleasure before he died. Then he looked up and saw that the sun-palace was directly over his head. Soon it would pass over the rim of the wheel, soon the earth would be dark and cold again, and he must hurry.

"It was then that Surd found the courage he needed. He got up, walked over to his third vat, and took out his mild, blue eyes. He dropped his eyes into the water, picked up his brushes and began to paint the sky with a color which was bluer than any sapphire you ever saw; and again his color held fast. The blue mixed with the red and the yellow in rich and delicate shades never seen before. Color flooded the sky from north to south and upward and downward. Surd painted quickly, and when the blue was all used up, he fell down exhausted, his blind eye-sockets turned eagerly toward the first sunset."

The old man's voice became very gentle. "After awhile the great, pagan gods looked down from the sky, and they were very much upset when they saw that somebody had defaced their property and left it alive and flaming with colors, just as it is at this instant, my little Albert."

Dr. Ehrlich and the boy turned their heads at the same moment and looked at the sunset before them. It had reached its greatest brilliance, and across the western sky there were long lines of purple, gold and crimson. The sunset seemed to reach up with its lavenders and greens as high as the very top of space itself, and even the clouds which were in the east were pearl-like and rosy from beneath.

It was the doctor who first lowered his eyes. He smiled,

touched the boy's head and spoke softly. "Oh, yes, little Albert, there was a great commotion when the gods looked down and saw what Surd had done. They were furious and puzzled at the same time, but when they saw Surd lying on the rocky shelf, they realized what had taken place, and they sent a messenger for him. That is how Surd happened to be brought into the presence of the great pagan gods themselves, if we are to believe the stories that his followers on the earth-wheel told their grand-children and great-grandchildren later on."

The old doctor stretched out his legs and sighed. "I often think," he continued, "how small and helpless Surd must have seemed in such a company; but he wasn't afraid of them in the least, my little Albert, and he wouldn't wipe his sunset off the sky no matter how much they threatened him. He only shook his head at their threats and answered, 'What pain can you think of that I haven't already known?' Then he raised himself upward and spoke again: 'It may be, when the people on the earth-wheel understand my sunset, that they will repudiate their hate and cruelty and injustice, as I have done; it may be that they will understand at last what I wanted to tell them, and that they will believe in mercy and kindness and love, as I believe in those things.'

"So when the gods saw they couldn't do anything with him, they killed him, thinking to be rid of him and his sunset that way. To be on the safe side, they ground his body between two stones and scattered his dust to the winds, so that it wouldn't defile the sun-palace again, and we come to the end of our story."

Dr. Ehrlich laughed in a tender, half-ashamed way. He took out his pipe and filled it, packing the tobacco in with his thin, brown fingers, catching up the shreds which hung over the bowl and tapping them in lightly. When he had lighted his pipe he smiled, put his arm closer about the boy and looked at the sky once more.

"Well, little Albert," he said at length, "those are the bare facts, but the story doesn't really end at this place after all. This is the kind of story which only begins when all the facts are known." The doctor narrowed his eyes thoughtfully. "It's true the story might have ended at this place if the pagan gods, instead of scattering Surd's dust, had sealed it up somewhere in space, but they didn't think of that, as we have already seen."

Dr. Ehrlich drew on his pipe, making a faint, sucking sound. "Oh, yes," he said, "the pagan gods made a mistake when they scattered Surd's dust, because his dust was blown about by the winds and some of it settled on the earth-wheel again. Some of it settled on our own earth, too, although it was only the tiniest pinpoint in space in those old days. . . . You see, Albert, the gods didn't realize that Surd's spirit was a thing which would not pass away when he died. His spirit was in his dust, too, and since that time, whenever a grain of it touches a man, there is always something inside him which is a little like the first sunset. These are Surd's true followers. They are the beautiful people of the earth and they confirm with their lives or their works, each according to his particular talent, Surd's message of beauty and mercy and love."

The old doctor bent forward and rested his face in his cupped hands. When he spoke again, he spoke slowly, as if he were putting into words for the first time things which he had long pondered in secret. "Sometimes," he began after a moment, "it happens that a man is so worthy of the trust or is touched so deeply with Surd's dust that he becomes as great as Surd himself was. These, the great ones, are not alone Surd's followers; they are his children, and their mission is to lead the world from brutality and hate back to peace and dignity again."

The boy was quiet for a time, turning these matters over in his mind. "Are you one of Surd's children?" he asked.

"No," said the old man sadly. "I wasn't selected. I wasn't honored so highly. I am only one of those who believe."

Mrs. Langkabel and Mrs. Evans came onto the porch at that moment. Mrs. Evans had her son's cap and coat in her hands. It was time for them to go home. Dr. Ehrlich got up from the steps when he saw them. He said that he would get their automobile from behind the barn, where he had parked it, and would drive it through the lane and leave it in front of the house for their greater convenience.

Mrs. Evans stood looking at his retreating figure. She shook her head sadly. "The things you've told me today don't seem believable, do they? Why, they're enough to make you lose faith in everything and simply give up in despair. Personally, I don't see how he's stood what he has. I couldn't. I know that."

"That part's a mystery to me, too," said Mrs. Langkabel. "Sometimes I think he draws comfort and hope from things we don't know anything about."

The boy pulled away from his mother suddenly and ran toward the barn, in the direction the old man had taken. He was so young that the fissures in his mind had not as yet closed up, and the deep, primitive parts of his being were not shut off from his consciousness. He understood the story the old man had told him that afternoon with his whole body, and he accepted its inconsistencies without criticism. In some ways it seemed more real, more sensible to him than dozens of other things which he accepted every day as truth; more believable, even, than the cruelties he had heard his mother and Mrs. Langkabel talking about.

Dr. Ehrlich was standing beside the barn, as if he knew all the time that the boy would come, and was waiting for him. Albert spoke when he got his breath again, his eyes fixed earnestly on the old doctor's face.

"Is Surd's dust still blowing about the world?"

"Yes," said the old man. "Oh, yes. You may be sure of that."

"How do you know? How can you tell for sure?"

Dr. Ehrlich said: "I think you'll be sure, too, when I finish the story and tell you the part I saved for the end. You see, it happened this way, Albert: Before Surd died, he said a thing which the gods didn't believe at the time, but which came true. He said that the sunset was to be the symbol of the things he believed in and that it would be against the sky as long as beauty and gentleness and love lasted among men. When those things died, his sunset would die with them, and fade out of the sky."

"I'll bet they laughed at Surd for saying it," said the boy seriously. "I'll bet they thought he was trying to fool them."

"Yes," said Dr. Ehrlich, "I imagine they did; but you may be

sure Surd didn't care whether they made fun of him or not, because he was thinking at that moment how hard life was in a
world of intolerance and cruelty, and how unhappy he had been.
He knew that his followers wouldn't have an easy time of it
either, and these were the things that concerned him the most.
So he was determined that his sunset should come back every
day at the time the sun-palace passed over the rim of space, and
shine out in the western sky, for then his children could look at
it when they were feeling weak and helpless and know they
weren't all alone in the world."

The boy thought a moment, shaping his next question carefully: "When we were sitting on the steps," he began, "you said
sometimes a man is touched so with Surd's dust that he acts like
Surd himself did, and leads the world back to what Surd believed
in." He stopped speaking for a time and stood with his brows
puckered a little. When he spoke again his voice came rapidly.
"Is one of Surd's children living in the world now, Dr. Ehrlich?
Do you believe there's a man like that in our world this very
minute?"

Dr. Ehrlich rubbed his eyes as if he were very tired. "Yes,"
he said. "Yes, I believe that. I don't know who he is or where
he is, my little Albert, but he is there. I know that in my heart.
He is in the world somewhere." The old doctor lowered his hand
and let it hang wearily at his side. "Yes, I believe that. If I didn't
believe it, I wouldn't have courage enough to live." He stopped
speaking suddenly and smiled, his lips turned up in an odd,
quizzical way. "Do I sound too sentimental?" he asked. "Do
you consider me a little silly? Are you ashamed of me?"

The boy shook his head.

Dr. Ehrlich leaned against the barn door, looking down at
his namesake with tired eyes. "It is a strange thing," he said, "but
a man may shout out his hatred without shame and feel that he
is both intelligent and dignified when he does it, but if he dares
to say that he has a spirit, then he must do it apologetically, in
whispers, and his friends are embarrassed at the spectacle." He
lifted his hands helplessly and laughed in a mild, self-deprecatory
way. "It is a strange situation, indeed, but it's something you'll

find out for yourself when you're older." Then his eyes wavered and he looked at the ground, turning over the littered straw with his foot.

When he raised his eyes again there was a pleading look in them. "Yes," he said softly. "Yes, I believe there is someone, somewhere in the world, who will lead us back to peace and kindness again. I believe that because I must: There are people who can live in a world from which all beauty and tenderness and hope have gone, but I am not one of them."

Then the boy held out his arms and walked toward his new friend blindly. Dr. Ehrlich dropped to his knees and took the boy in his arms, and for a few minutes they clung to each other without speaking.

Later, the doctor drove the car through the lane and left it in front of the house where Mrs. Langkabel and Mrs. Evans were waiting. At that moment the neighbor who had passed earlier in the afternoon came back from his errand. He had an old horse collar over one of his shoulders, and he turned when he saw Mrs. Langkabel, waved, and walked toward her.

Albert and the old doctor looked at each other, nodded and smiled knowingly, since the same thought was in both their minds. The doctor bent down and said, "I think I'm going to meet him again."

"Maybe she'll tell his name this time," said Albert.

The old doctor shrugged humorously. "Wait!" he whispered. "I know Cousin Emma too well. You'll see."

Mrs. Langkabel had already begun the introductions. She spoke first to Mrs. Evans. "I want you to meet a neighbor of mine," she said. "He lives on the Reedyville Road and raises the finest onions in Pearl County." Then she turned to the stranger. "This is a lady I've known for a long time. We used to go to high school together when we were girls. She and her son came out to spend Sunday afternoon with me and my cousin from the old country."

Dr. Ehrlich spoke quickly to the boy. "You see?" he whispered, "I was right about Cousin Emma." He raised his shoulders in mock despair and shook his head humorously. "Oh, well—I'm resigned now. I'll never know that gentleman's name as long as I live."

The boy took a step forward, turned and glanced at the doctor over his shoulder. He winked mysteriously and pursed out his lips as if to say: "Just wait! Just watch *me* find out his name!" Then he walked toward the stranger with his hand extended. "Howdy-do, Mr. Onions," he said gravely; "I'm glad to meet you."

The farmer's jaw dropped in surprise and he drew back so quickly that the old horse collar almost fell from his shoulders. "Now, listen, Sonny!" he began patiently. "*Onions* is what I raise for a living. It ain't my name. My name's *Barber*, like Miss Emma just told you." He shook his head sadly and turned to Dr. Ehrlich. "Chillun get more book-learnin' than they did when you and me was boys, but they don't seem to get no *apter*, do they, Doc?"

Albert and the old doctor began to laugh at the same instant, their arms about each other. Later, he and Mrs. Langkabel stood at the gate and watched while Mrs. Evans drove away down the country road, passed a bend and was suddenly lost to sight. Mrs. Evans drove slowly, guiding the car between the bumpy ruts. "Emma was telling me all about Dr. Ehrlich while you two went walking," she said. "You might not realize it, being so young, but he's one of the most famous men in the whole world. You must always remember this day, Albert, and some day you can tell your own little boy about how you met him."

She yawned, tired out from her visit and anxious to be in her own home again. "It's been a real nice visit, hasn't it, son?"

"Yes'm," he said.

The colors of the sky were fading now, soon it would be dark again. At the side of the road were tangles of blackberry vines and wild okra bushes. Bullbats were out, darting ghostlike through the air and making now and then their thin, cheeping sound. Everything was tranquil and very quiet. There was only the chirping of crickets and a scurrying of small animals among the vines.

The boy sat back in the seat and watched the puffs of red

dust which rose from in front of the car and floated in long lines across the fields, toward the western sky, thinking of the story that Dr. Ehrlich had told him. He knew, then, that he loved the old doctor in some strange way which he had never known before. It was not the way that he loved his mother or his father, or even the way he felt about Mr. Vernon Baker, the milkman, who took him to ride in his cart. It was something else entirely. It was deeper and different and it was at once passionate and impersonal.

He straightened up suddenly, thinking these things, and caught his breath, his eyes wide with surprise. It seemed to him at that moment that he had stumbled upon something of the greatest importance. He stretched out his legs and looked at them for a time; then he stared curiously at his hands, as if he had never seen them before. All at once he leaned out of the automobile and tried to catch the settling dust in his hands. "Touch me, Surd!" he said under his breath. "Make me one of your children!" His eyes had a faraway look in them and they were half closed, as Dr. Ehrlich's had been, and his lips turned up with the distinctive, quizzical expression which he had seen on the old doctor's face.

His mother, seeing what he was doing, spoke quickly, her voice sharp and frightened. "Sit farther back on the seat, Albert!" she said. "You'll hurt yourself, if you aren't careful." Then she laughed with relief, softly. "Heavens and earth," she said. "I never saw a boy who could find so much trouble to get into."

The boy sat back against the seat, his legs stiff and straight before him, but his eyes were still remote and his thoughts still far away. He had not, before this moment, thought of himself as having any identity apart from the reflected identities of his father and mother, nor had he considered an existence apart from them, outside the circle of protection they provided him; but he knew, now, that he was something in his own right as well. He was individual and separate and himself, a part of time and space, just as other people were. He was a living link which joined those who had lived before him with those who would inhabit the earth long after he, too, had died, with the dependencies and the responsibilities that such a relationship inevitably brought with it. He was all these things, and yet he was different from all others. He was uniquely himself, Albert Evans, with decisions and judgments which he must make for himself alone.

After a moment he turned his head and looked again at the shadowy fields, at the red, dusty road and the fading sunset; then, suddenly he straightened his knees and leaned forward a little. "Touch me! Touch me!" he repeated stubbornly. "Touch me! Make me one of your children!"

1938

YOU AND YOUR SISTER

*W*HEN the 'phone rang, Doris came to the kitchenette door, a spoon and two forks in her hand. "Is it Mildred calling up about the dress they spoiled at the cleaners?" she asked.

Newton made a sour, slapping motion with his hand. "Wait!" he said. "Can't you wait a minute?" He lifted the receiver and said hello, and instantly a heavy, male voice at the other end of the line came reverberating through the earpiece with the eerie rise and fall of an old phonograph playing in an empty tomb.

"Hello, yourself," said the ghostlike, metallic voice, "and see how you like it! This is old Joe Bushwick from Dallas. Remember me? Well, here I am back in the big city for my fall buying trip. I meant to come by the store to see you today, but I got tied up."

Newton held the receiver farther from his head and delicately vibrated his ear with his little finger. "Old Joe *Bushwick!*" he repeated. "That's fine! That's really a treat!"

He twisted his neck and looked at his wife, lifting his eyebrows in the questioning gesture she knew so well. From her place beside the door, Doris had heard everything which Joe had said. She nodded, and shaped the word dinner with her lips, pointing to the telephone. "Hold on a minute, Joe," said Newton. "My wife wants to tell me something. Just a minute now."

He put his hand over the mouthpiece and Doris said in a whisper, "Ask him to dinner, you dope! Go on and ask him!" Her voice took on a tragic note and she added: "You can't get out of asking him after the nice way he took the three of us out when he was here last time."

Newton turned back to the 'phone. "Look here, Joe," he began briskly. "Doris wants you to come to dinner tonight. Nothing fancy. Just a little home gathering."

397

"*Tonight?*" repeated Joe, as if swept off his feet with surprise, the hollow sound of his voice beating against the wall like heat waves above a boardwalk in August. Then recovering almost instantly he added: "Why, sure I will if it doesn't put Doris and you out too much. If you're really sure it won't, nothing would suit me better than a good home-cooked meal."

"Give me the 'phone," said Doris impatiently. She took the receiver, straightened her hair with her free hand, and said: "Now, you come right over, Joe Bushwick. I was talking to Newton about you just the other day and recalling that wonderful evening the four of us had last time you were here. Of course Newton and I knew it was really Mildred you wanted to take out, but we enjoyed it too."

"Think nothing about it," said Joe, but his voice had suddenly become a little wary.

"It's all settled then," said Doris. "We'll expect you around seven. That'll give you an hour and a half." She glanced at her husband, winked and added: "Mildred often speaks of you too. She's a girl that appreciates everything so much."

"My God!" said Newton softly. "Did you have to drag that in?"

From the receiver there came a burst of chilling, sepulchral laughter. "I heard the little lady married and moved to Boston since I was here last," said Joe. "Give her my congratulations when you write."

"Where did you hear a thing like that?" asked Doris in surprise. "Why, Mildred's still right here in town. She's having dinner with us tonight, too. I expect her along any minute; but I won't tell her you're coming too. I wouldn't give a thousand dollars to miss the look on her face when you come in the door unexpectedly."

"My God!" said Newton. "Do you think he's out looking for dames? Do you think a guy don't know how to get women for himself without you throwing them at his head?"

Joe's exuberance seemed to have died suddenly. His voice was now subdued and cautious. "I may have to go home a little early, after all," he said. "I been up late every night this week and I'm feeling—well, you know."

"Go home whenever you feel like it," said Doris. "We all want you to feel at home with us. We'll just have a quiet evening together." She hung up the 'phone and said: "I guess it could have been worse than Joe Bushwick. It might have been somebody peculiar that you went to school with in Jersey."

"My God!" said Newton, raising his hands upward. "Why punish him with that sour God-damned sister of yours?"

"Shut up," said Doris absently. "I've got to call her now and tell her to hurry over."

Newton held his head tragically in his hands, groaned and went to the bathroom. When he came back, Doris had finished her call. She looked at him for a moment, bit her lip and said: "I just got time to bake an apple pie for that jug-head. That's what people in Dallas eat for dinner, don't they?"

She went to the kitchenette and worked energetically, humming a tune under her breath. She could hear her husband moving about in the living room getting out the glasses and emptying ash trays, but she paid little attention to him. She had finished her pie and was ready to put it into the oven when the bell rang. "There he is now," she said to herself, "and I look a sight. Everything came out just right, didn't it?"

But it wasn't Joe, after all. It was Mildred dressed in her sister's best and trailing behind her the perfume which Doris and Newton had given her that Christmas. The sisters looked appraisingly at each other. "You got your make-up on too low," said Doris.

"Relax," said Newton. "He hasn't got here yet. And for God sake don't dispute everything he says. You don't make a guy fall for you by tearing him down."

"It's not me who's always disputing people," said Mildred gently. "It's you who's always disputing people and making yourself disagreeable."

"You see?" said Newton to nobody in particular. "You get my point?"

When Mildred had taken off her coat and put down her bag, she went into the kitchenette to help her sister, but they need not have hurried so, for at 7:30 Joe had not come; neither had he telephoned nor shown up at eight. At nine, the dinner being spoiled anyway, they sat down to the table. Newton was becoming a little concerned, but Mildred, more adjusted to disappointment, apparently, was entirely philosophical. "There's no sense in crying over spilled milk," she said brightly. "Maybe Mr. Bushwick got hit by a cab or something."

Doris laughed bitterly. "*That* one get hit?" she asked. "Him? Oh, no!"

When the telephone finally rang at ten, everybody jumped. Newton answered it, and at once the pulsing volume of sound beat through the defective receiver. "I just had a terrible experience," said Joe in a thick, fumbling voice. "It was really terrible, and what happened to me shouldn't happen to a dog."

He went on to explain that since he had had more than an hour between his first call and the time he was invited for dinner, he had decided to take a quick look at Radio City. So he had gone down some stairs and through a big door, and the first thing he knew, there he was at the post office.

"He's drunk," said Doris casually. "He can't talk straight."

"So then I wander around a long time," continued Joe in his blurred, lurching voice, "trying to find my way out; and so I passed this underground street with stores on both sides, but the stores were closed by that time. Well, I went up one level and down another without meeting anybody, but no matter what I did, or what turning I took, I always came back to the post office."

"Is that where you got the skinful?" asked Doris. "Right there at the special delivery window?"

"It *couldn't* have been the post office," said Mildred in her gentlest voice. "The post office is downtown some place. I know where the post office is."

"So there I was, lost and wandering around until a few minutes ago," said Joe. "Then finally I saw a little door and banged on it, and an old man with hair growing out of his ears let me out through a cigar store."

"It's a new one," said Doris. "It's an excuse I never heard before. I got to remember that one."

"Where are you now, Joe?" asked Newton.

"I don't know for sure," said Joe; "but it's some place at the edge of a river."

Mildred laughed gaily, as if she had been waiting all the time to catch him in some obvious error. "Now, that can't be true, either," she said, "because Radio City doesn't go as far as the river."

"That was a bad experience and no denying it," said Newton sympathetically, "but look here: Why don't you come over for a sandwich and a glass of beer anyway? You must be hungry, being shut up all evening."

"No," said Joe. "No, thanks, Newton. I appreciate that, but I already had my dinner." Then, as if he had revealed too much, he added hastily: "I got something to eat after I escaped from the post office." There was a silence, and then Joe added hesitantly: "Well, good-bye, Newton. Maybe I'll see you next time I'm in town; and in the meantime thank Doris for the trouble she went to."

"I baked him a pie," said Doris. "The jug-head!"

Newton hung up the receiver, yawned and began unlacing his shoes. "The mistake you made," he said to his wife, "was telling him that Mildred was still in town. That's where you slipped up."

Doris went to her sister to help her with her coat. "It doesn't make any difference," she said. "Joe Bushwick isn't worth your little finger."

Newton shook his head sadly. "You and your sister!" he said. "You and your God-damned sour sister!"

"People always get drunk at the last minute and don't show up in this town," said Mildred haughtily, from the depths of her individual experience. "Either that, or they say 'yes' and then don't come."

1938

TRANSCRIBED ALBUM OF
FAMILIAR MUSIC

*A*LFRED N. WAGSTAFF: Mr. Challett rang for me and said, "Cancel my four o'clock appointment. I just talked with my son and he's on his way to see me now." The appointment he referred to was with that feature writer from *Power*, the Magazine of Big Business, who's doing an article on him for the Anniversary Issue. I tried to make the cancellation, but I could not, and when the gentleman in question arrived, I went to the reception room to explain the situation. I offered to make another appointment for the next afternoon, but this reporter yawned, lit a cigarette and said he'd wait, having nothing further to do that day.

I could have given him much material if I had cared to do so, because I know Martin L. Challett from the ground up. That's to be expected, I suppose, since I've been his confidential secretary for so many years. Naturally, Mr. Challett has no idea that I see through him so clearly, but then important people never do consider such possibilities, do they? They like to think that while they can estimate others correctly, they, themselves, are shrouded in mystery.

I went back to my own office and stood there, screened by the filing cabinets. Through a crack in the door beyond, I saw Mr. Challett take out his son's letter, the letter that had disappointed him so deeply, and read it again. When he had finished, he put it down angrily and said, "The young idiot! Who is he to upset the plans I've made for him? Most young men would be glad to have such an indulgent father! Most young men—"

He stopped, never finishing the sentence, and pushed the buzzer for me. I answered, and he said, "When my son calls, send him in at once."

"Yes, sir," I said.

"I don't want to be disturbed while he's here. Take all phone calls at your own desk."

"Yes, sir," I said. "Yes, indeed, Mr. Challett."

I went back to my own office, but I continued to watch him. Presently he frowned, swayed back in his chair and rested his feet on the bottom drawer of his desk: the old desk which has traveled with him from obscurity to great wealth, for he is a rich man now in the wide sense of the word. Not merely well-to-do!—Rich!

After awhile, he laced his fingers across his vest and his face set into that look of cautious impassivity which has become his distinctive expression. "Cautious impassivity," is really a quotation. It's what his wife used to say about him when she was frightened and hysterical. "I can stand anything," she would cry out, as she wandered from room to room; "anything at all, Mr. Wagstaff, except that cold look of cautious impassivity he has."

JUDGE ENOS WHITESIDES: When I was a boy, the Challetts were considered to be shiftless and eccentric people—dependent, most of the time, on the charity of others for their living. Martin's father was a loud-mouthed, arrogant man who liked to think of himself as a liberal and an intellectual. He made no effort to hide the contempt he felt for those less intelligent than himself, and that was everybody. He considered himself a sort of preacher, too; a man with a message for the world; and each Saturday afternoon he spoke in the public square to an audience of farmers, who laughed at him. His particular hate was the Salvation Army, who, he said, were trying to upset the economic structure of the world; and once when he called for volunteers to burn their headquarters, the police had to arrest him and put him in jail for a time.

Martin's mother was known in town by her maiden name, Jessie May Easton. Occasionally she put on amateur plays for the local societies, and she really had talent for that sort of thing, too. The trouble was, she wasn't dependable, because nobody could tell when one of her depressed spells would come over her, and when that happened, she would throw up her job, refuse to see the committees, or listen to reason. She was an untidy woman at best, but when she was in one of her moods, she did nothing at all about the house. She would sit in her kitchen at such times and rock back and forth. "The world lost a great actress, when it lost me!" she would say. "A great actress! Oh, a very great actress, indeed!"

That takes care of the parents, and brings us down to Martin, himself, doesn't it? I'll commence on Martin by saying that he was a boy whom Horatio Alger would have admired. He was clean, neat, ambitious, and honest in the obvious ways. He carried a paper route in the mornings; he worked in the drug store on Saturdays and Sundays, when he was out of school; then, too, he shined shoes at the barber shop several afternoons a week and picked up some extra money that way.

They subscribed to several magazines and out-of-town papers at the barber shop, and Martin brought home all the old copies, so that he could read at leisure about the lives of the rich. He read every word he could find on the subject, and he cut out and pasted the juicier items in an old ledger which he kept under his mattress. I know these things about him because I was probably the only friend he had in those days, and even we were not close.

Once, when his father was out of town on a preaching trip, Martin asked me to come to his house for supper, and I did so. He got out his book of clippings at once and read aloud from it. I remember three of the stories to this day. The first concerned an old lady who had the hoofs of her horses studded with diamonds; the second was about a dinner-party in Newport for a pet monkey, who, it appeared, had bitten two of the guests when they tried to stroke him—the writer of the story being of the opinion that the monkey had thus shown a more highly developed critical sense than his mistress. The third item, which seemed to me at the time the most fascinating of all, had to do with a bachelor dinner at which naked chorus girls rose out of an enormous pie which the waiters had wheeled in and set before the drunken guests.

As Martin read these treasures of his aloud, his face was flushed and his eyes shone with excitement; and after each story had been finished, and the page turned, he would lift his head, nod, and stare at the wall, as if dedicating himself each time to a secret purpose of his own.

Later, when we went downstairs to see if supper was ready, we found Mrs. Challett sitting alone in the kitchen between a stack of dirty dishes and the unlit stove. She said there was nothing to eat in the house, and when Martin asked her for money, so that he could go to the store and buy groceries, she rocked back and forth and said she'd already spent the money her husband had left with her. She had bought American Beauty roses, she explained, and, sure enough, there were roses all over the place. "But they were such a pretty color," she said in a whimpering voice; "and cheap at the price they charged, too."

She got up from the rocker and began puttering about the kitchen, glancing at her son reproachfully. There was no occasion to worry about the money, she explained, because she had cleverly stopped at the Charity Aid Society and asked for help. They had promised to send groceries that very afternoon, and as soon as they came, she'd start supper. "They should be here any minute," she said petulantly. "I can't imagine what's keeping them."

The groceries came a little later, and with them the ladies who had donated them. They set to work at once to clean up the littered rooms and to instruct Mrs. Challett in the blessings of thrift and her responsibilities as a housewife. For a time Martin stood in the doorway listening to the ladies, and then, as if overcome with such shame that he could no longer endure it, he turned suddenly and walked away.

He stopped at the alley gate and stood there frowning. I joined him a moment later, and there, together in the twilight, he confessed his ambitions to me. He said that he had determined to build up a fortune so big that it would make the combined wealth of his home town look trivial by comparison; and when that was accomplished, he would move in a social world so far above anything the people here in town knew that they would have no comprehension of it when they, in turn, read in their Sunday papers about his box at the opera, his dinner parties or his yacht.

"Making that much money won't be as easy as it sounds," I said cautiously. "How are you going to do it?"

"Why don't you go home?" he said. "That's the least you can do now."

I remembered that scene when I read of his marriage to Miss Nellie Van Vleck some years later. He was about twenty-five at the time, and she was at least eight years older. The yellow journals of the day referred to her as "The Van Vleck Old Maid." There were even cartoons showing her as an old hen setting on a nest of money bags.

Oh, yes, I can see the pathetic side of the picture as well as you can! I can even feel pity for Martin Challett, in a way, no matter how much sorrow he's caused in the world. I've thought of him a great deal lately, and, strange as it may seem to us now, I've come to the conclusion that he was the true ideal of his period—an ideal whose absurdity he made plain by exaggeration; but perhaps the ideal of our own time, the ideal which we accept now with such earnestness, will seem equally strange to others in the generations that follow us.

NELLIE VAN VLECK CHALLETT: Even when I was a young woman, the newspapers referred to me as an old maid, and I think they were justified in doing so, because that is what I always was. They were incorrect, though, in depicting me as homely and dried-up: Actually, I was rather plump in those days, and insofar as looks were concerned, I was as attractive as any of the other girls in my set. Certainly, there were several men who wanted to marry me. I could even have had my choice of a title or two, but that idea displeased my father. He despised fortune hunters— an expression which was common in my day—and he was determined that I should marry what he referred to as a "red-blooded, old-line American," or nothing at all: a man with power and drive in him, who could be relied upon to keep my fortune intact and to make one of his own, as well.

Martin Challett was my father's ideal, and so we married.

He was a handsome man when I first met him, and, when he cared to, he could be charming. For a time I loved him as deeply as I'm capable of loving anybody; I even deluded myself into believing that he loved me a little in return, which shows you again how inexperienced I was, for I know, now, that as a woman I was never of the slightest importance to him. For all my father's caution, I might just as well have taken one of the titles. In that event, everything would have been aboveboard, and when my husband deceived me with an actress in Paris, or with one of the peasant maids in the village, it would have been done with caution, tact, and even, perhaps, with graciousness.

But if Martin never loved me, he did have a feeling of friendliness toward me at times, particularly in the early days of our marriage. Sometimes he talked about himself and his early life in Madison Bluffs, and once when we were lying together in the dark, he confessed his ambitions, and defined the philosophy that guided him. What he told me explained both his snobbishness and his desire for wealth, although it did not make him a more lovable character.

The accumulation of money was easy enough for a man of his instincts; the acquisition of social ease, which he considered so important, was not possible for him. He must have seen quickly that the old patterns were ineradicable, and the knowledge of his limitations both angered and shamed him, I'm sure. He would always be clumsy and resentful in the presence of those who were, in his mind, so plainly *not* his betters, and he knew it. He would always have that dry-mouthed, unreasoning desire to run away and hide, just as he had often hidden from the midwestern church ladies when they came to leave supplies and to admonish his mother in thrift.

Robert, my son, was born in the second year of my marriage. I saw instantly why the child was so important to my husband; I knew by instinct that he meant to realize through him the juvenile triumphs which he had been unable to claim in his own right. He did not deny these things when I mentioned them to him; instead, he became excited, a strange, unreal look in his eyes, saying, in substance, that Robert would never feel shame or insecurity, as he had felt those things; that he would grow up naturally in a rich man's world, the equal from birth of those fabulous ones whom his father had envied so desperately as a boy.

I listened in astonishment, and then said, "But the things you imagine never existed except in the minds of cheap journalists and comic strip artists. Never at all. Never at any time. Dullness, yes! Stupidity, yes! Vulgarity, yes! But the romance and the glamour you believe in were never there. You may take my word for it."

After that, I knew how to revenge myself for the cruelties my husband had made me suffer, and that is why I taught Robert to despise everything his father desired. I have been successful in my efforts, and that knowledge is now my sole pleasure.

I think these things over and over, here at this sanitarium which is so expensive and so private. There's nothing particularly secret about what I've told you. My doctor has heard it over and over, and in greater detail, too. He says that I should forget the past, that I should interest myself in new things; but I am an old woman now, and I find his advice difficult to take.

And, oh, another thing before you go: You know, of course, that my son is marrying that notorious woman who's always getting manhandled by the police and having her name in the papers, do you not? I clip all the cartoons about her that I can find, and some of them are quite amusing. If you come to visit me again, perhaps I'll show them to you. No, I did nothing to arrange the match. That was not necessary. I've known for a long time that it would be Jennie Jablonski, or somebody very much like her.

ROBERT VAN VLECK CHALLETT: When I arrived for my appointment, Mr. Wagstaff said that my father was waiting, and asked me to go in. I did so, and my father stood up and said abruptly, "I find this new, noble attitude of yours hard to understand."

"I didn't expect you to understand it," I said.

He frowned and stared at me from under his eyebrows, then said in a more placating voice, "There's no need of your making a martyr of yourself. All I ever asked of you is that you behave yourself like any normal son of a rich father should and enjoy what I've accumulated for you over the years."

I smiled, shook my head and sat in the big chair before his desk. "I find that a sickening prospect, I'm afraid," I said.

"Travel!" he said. "Enjoy yourself in the fashionable places of the world! Sow your wild oats as widely as you please! That's all I ever asked, all I ever expected of you. Take this Polish peasant woman with you, if that's the way your taste runs, but don't be stupid enough to let her trap you into marriage."

He walked to the window and stared down at the street. "Keep the fashionable friends you have and cultivate even more important ones!" he said slowly. "Enjoy the life I've created for you, son!"

"I can think of nothing more tiresome than such a life," I said.

He looked at me oddly and started to speak, then, changing his mind, he stared down at his hands. After a moment, I said as politely as I could: "You've been very generous, Father, and I appreciate it; but as I told you in my letter, it won't be necessary for you to continue my allowance, now that I'm of age and have finished my education."

"You're a colossal damn fool!" he said angrily.

"Perhaps I am," I said. "At any rate I want you to understand that I have my standards, too. You see, Father, I'm no longer willing to play a walk-on in your compulsion neurosis."

"You'll starve to death," he said. "You'll come running to me quick enough when you're hungry."

"I don't think so," I said. "In fact, I have a job already. I'm starting in as a common laborer, and as soon as I'm making enough to support a wife, Miss Jablonski and I will be married."

He stared at me in that overwhelming way he has, but I'm no longer afraid of him, and I think he realizes that now. I got my hat and coat and moved toward the door. I wanted to tell him that he was the emblem of everything I despised in life, but I did not. What would have been the use? He wouldn't have understood what I was talking about.

MARTIN L. CHALLETT: When my son had gone, I sat for a time at my desk thinking how little I'd known of his real character, and how quickly it had hardened into its individual pattern. I had a feeling of rage inside me, but I would not let it come out. Rage can be a weapon like any other, but it must be controlled, to be effective.

It was all his mother's doing, and I know that now. But why does she hate me so? What did she expect out of marriage, anyway? I treated her well enough, and I never used one penny of her dirty money: As a matter of fact, I increased it for her, and she's worth a good deal more now than she was when I married her—unless the psychoanalysts have got it away from her by this time.

My thoughts ran in this direction for a while, and then, having another idea, I rang for Wagstaff. When he answered, I said, "Bring me the information on Jennie Jablonski. I'd like to go over it again. He brought the folder, and I examined once more the facts which my private detectives had gathered. All at once I closed the file, took off my glasses and leaned back in my chair, knowing at that moment that I'd do nothing at all to stop the marriage.

I had met Miss Jablonski once or twice at labor meetings, and when I talked to her, she had raised her voice a little, as if anybody as stupid as myself must also be deaf. Well, I may not be bright according to some standards, but I didn't live with my wife all those years not to know that La Jablonski's belly-ache is not caused by the injustices that others suffer, as she imagines, but by the more personal injustice which she herself suffered when she was born so unattractive that no man ever looked at her until my son came along and saw that she was the nearest thing to his mother that he could reasonably expect to find.

I got up and moved to the window, knowing clearly that despite her modern, unconventional earnestness, Miss Jablonski is a conventional woman who will want a home and a houseful of children. (Her mother had fourteen children, according to my information!) She'll justify her impulses on the most complex grounds possible, you may be sure of that; but she'll have her children one right after the other, and nothing will stop her. Soon, no doubt, I'll be the grandfather of a family who were raised in an atmosphere of brave conversation and petty want—children who'll hate poverty as I hated it; who'll long for wealth and power as I longed for those things.

I walked up and down excitedly, knowing my plan was not defeated, after all: that its consummation was merely delayed a generation. I would start making money again, more thoroughly than ever before, and when my grandchildren were ready to take it, there'd be a fortune waiting for them that would stagger the imagination of the world.

I thought, then, of my boyhood dreams of the rich, and saw how childish those ideas really were. My grandchildren will not find it necessary to make a display of themselves, for they will be able to buy everything, and everybody will know it. They will have all the rare and fine things of the world. They will be intimate with princes and kings; and most of all, they will be Challetts, every one of them—all bearing my blood and my name!

A little later, Wagstaff rapped and came in. He said that the reporter from *Power* was still waiting in the reception room, and asked if I cared to see him. I nodded, and when the reporter came into my office, I apologized for having kept him waiting; but he said that was perfectly all right—that he'd improved the time by having an informal chat with my son.

I said, "I understand you've also been making inquiries of my wife. I'm told that you've even been in Madison Bluffs, getting material there."

"Yes," he said. "That's quite correct."

I said, "What would you like from me? I'll tell you anything you want to know"; and he answered, "Suppose we start by discussing your son Robert. What's your reaction to his marriage to the Jablonski woman?"

I said, "It seems to me that the generations move in a monotonous pattern, always a little different on the surface, always the same underneath. Does that answer your question?"

1938

THE SLATE

GRADY had a rash on his scalp that spring, and his mother stood at the dividing fence discussing his condition with her neighbor, Mrs. Webster. She wondered unhappily if it were worthwhile to continue sending the boy to Dr. Cromwell, the doctor who handled the company business under contract, since his condition, as anybody could see for himself, was not improved.

Mrs. Webster was of the opinion that Dr. Cromwell was capable enough at simple problems in medicine, such as cutting off a leg or probing for a bullet, but that he was entirely inadequate before the more complex ailments of man. He was particularly bad when it came to rashes and eruptions, she said positively, and that was a thing which she had always told others with the completest candor.

The screen door of the Webster cottage creaked on its hinges and slammed shut with a bang and Mrs. Webster, twisting her neck sidewise, watched her daughter Mamie lumber to the end of the back porch and empty a pan of dishwater in the weeds. Mamie Webster was a strong, clumsy girl of sixteen, and her mother regarded her now with heavy and habitual disapproval.

"Fix your stockings!" she said fretfully. "And brush that loose hair out of your eyes! How do you expect to catch a fellow for yourself when you go around looking like a tinker's slut?"

The theme of her daughter's unattractiveness was one which Mrs. Webster never quite exhausted. Mamie, as usual, pretended that she did not hear. She yawned placidly and came to the fence, the wet dishpan dripping grease and water against her legs. She stood leaning against the pickets and looked into space, saying nothing.

Mrs. Webster went on with her interrupted conversation. "No, sir," she continued heatedly. "I wouldn't even send a dog I

413

thought anything of to Dr. Cromwell for tetter, ringworm or rashes of any sort." Suddenly she moved closer to Grady and examined his scalp thoroughly. "If this boy was *mine*," she said at length, half closing her eyes and holding him away from her as if he were a collector's item, "I'd send him right off to Dr. Eldridge, dead wife or no dead wife, slate or no slate. Personally, I never saw anything so crazy about the doctor. It looks to me like he was only grieving more than ordinary."

Grady pulled away from Mrs. Webster and glanced up at his mother, waiting for her to veto the idea; but she only raised her left hand and held it flat against her cheek. "I don't know," she said doubtfully. "I don't know what's the best thing to do."

Everybody in town knew the stories that were being told about Dr. Eldridge, except, perhaps, the doctor himself. He had married in his late forties, and his devotion to his wife, who had been a school teacher when he met her, had caused the town much amusement during the three years they lived together. Then, unexpectedly, tragedy had struck, and Mrs. Eldridge drowned while bathing with friends at Crown Point. The situation was commonplace enough, and the doctor's grief at the death of his greatly loved wife was understandable. That was all natural and to be expected, as everyone agreed; it was his behavior afterwards which gave rise to the whispered stories about him.

At first he had refused to believe that she was dead and he had worked over her without rest for a long time, trying to bring breath into her body once more. At the end of the third day he collapsed and they put him to bed, his exhausted hands lying quietly on the counterpane at last. "Do what you please with her body," he said, "but I will have no part in it." Then, turning slowly on his side, he wept.

They buried her that afternoon while he was still asleep. Afterwards he refused to discuss her death with his friends, and when the Reverend Hamber called to pray with him, to counsel him to bow in humility before the stern will of God, Dr. Eldridge said: "I find you a little presumptuous, I'm afraid.

How dare you offer me sympathy? How can you possibly know what I have lost?"

These things were in the mind of Grady's mother as she stood that day listening to Mrs. Webster's advice. "I don't know," she repeated. "Anyway, I don't think Grady would go, even if I told him to."

Mamie Webster spoke for the first time. "If Grady won't go of his own free will and accord," she said, "I'll take him for you, Mrs. Dorney. I'm not scared of the doctor's wife or of his slate, either." She glanced down at the eight-year-old boy with quiet ferocity, nodding her head a couple of times. "I'll see that he gets there, all right," she said. "Don't worry about that."

"Maybe that's really the best thing to do," said Mrs. Dorney after a moment. "Nobody ever denied that Dr. Eldridge was a good *doctor*, even if he does hold traffic with spirits." Then, as if she had reached the end of her endurance, she gave her son an impatient shove and said, "Go see him! Go with Mamie right this minute! I'm tired of looking at that bothersome head!"

Mamie went toward her own house, saying over her shoulder: "Wait a minute till I change my clothes. I won't be gone no time at all." When she returned, she had on her Sunday dress and her new shoes. She had combed out the front section of her hair, but the back of her head remained as tangled and untidy as it had been originally. Her face was excessively powdered and she had sprinkled herself with cologne. She approached the dividing fence slowly, a little self-conscious in all her finery.

Mrs. Dorney said, "There, Mamie! Take his hand so he can't run away!"

"Come on!" said Mamie. "Come on, cry baby!"

"I'm not scared to go there," said Grady. "I'm not even thinking about that slate. I'm not thinking about ghosts, either."

"You're not scared," said Mamie. "Oh, no! I can see that!" She closed the gate behind them and gave him a jerk forward.

Later, on the road to the doctor's office, Grady abandoned his pose of contemptuous bravery. He spoke breathlessly now, half running to keep abreast of Mamie Webster. "Is it really true that he keeps a slate under his pillow?" he asked. "Is it, Mamie? Is it?"

"I wouldn't be surprised," said Mamie in an affected voice. "I wouldn't put anything silly past a man."

"Does his wife really come back from her grave and write messages on the slate like everybody says?" Grady insisted.

"Maybe she does," said Mamie. "Maybe she don't. How do I know?"

"People say that he looks at the slate every night and every morning, and if there's a message on it from his wife he always does what she tells him to without asking any questions. Do you believe it, Mamie? Do you?"

"If it's not true, then most of the folks in this town tell lies all day long," said Mamie. All at once she seemed annoyed at the boy and she jerked his arm roughly. "Talk! Talk!" she said. "Chatter! Chatter! . . . That's all boys or men, either, know how to do!"

They walked in silence after that and presently they came to the bungalow which served Dr. Eldridge both as an office and as a home. The Negro woman who kept house for him opened the door when they knocked, and they went into the reception room and sat down. To the left was the bedroom, and through the half-open door a chest of drawers, a mirror and a portion of the bed itself were visible. Grady tugged at Mamie's sleeve and pointed to the bed excitedly, but she pretended that she did not know what was in his mind.

"Sit up!" she said sternly. "Sit up on your chair; and don't give Dr. Eldridge no trouble, if you know what's good for you."

Dr. Eldridge, who had few patients these days, came out of his office a moment later. It would be difficult to imagine a less sinister figure. He was thin and not very tall. His hair was turning gray at the sides, and there was a patient, uncomprehending expression in his mild, gentle eyes. Seeing that the bedroom door had been left open, he went there first and closed it, and when he turned once more and faced his visitors he had managed somehow to bring himself back to the practical world of reality.

"Yes?" he asked, speaking to Mamie. "You came to consult me professionally?"

An astonishing change came over Mamie with the doctor's

entrance, and Grady, staring at her in surprise, his jaws relaxed
a little, was of the opinion that she had suddenly lost the last of
her wits. She giggled, scraped her foot across the floor and rolled
her eyes alarmingly. "It's not *me* that needs treatment," she
screamed. "It's Mrs. Dorney's little boy who came for treatment."

She continued to laugh shrilly and to roll her eyes, pressing her
crushed handkerchief against her mouth as if the doctor's mistake were too witty to be endured. She lowered her lids and
opened them rapidly, glancing sidewise and coquettishly at the
doctor, but when she had recovered sufficiently she said: "Dr.
Cromwell's been treating him, but he didn't do him no good at
all, so I told Mrs. Dorney that she ought to send him to you.
'Dr. Eldridge is a perfectly wonderful man in every respect,' I
said to her, 'and if he can't cure Grady's rash you might as well
give up and say that *nobody* can cure it!'" She spoke more softly
now, looking provocatively at the doctor through half-closed
eyes.

For a moment Dr. Eldridge stared thoughtfully at the girl and
then he seemed to dismiss her from his mind. He came to the
boy and put his arm about him. "Come in, Grady," he said.
"We'll have a look at that scalp of yours in my office." He
opened the door and stood aside while the boy preceded him.
"There," he said. "Sit in the chair by the window where the
light is better."

All his vagueness had left him now, and he seemed very thorough, very efficient. He bent above the boy and whistled softly,
eager to be at work again. He patted the child reassuringly and
said: "It's my guess that everybody in town except me has already prescribed for that scalp of yours. Tell me: Did your
mother put on it everything the neighbors suggested?" He sat
on the window ledge and lit a cigarette, shaking his head gently
from side to side.

Suddenly Grady's fears were all gone. He looked straight into
the doctor's eyes and smiled. "Yes, sir," he said, as if he and Dr.
Eldridge shared the ultimate riddle of women. "Yes, sir, that's
what she did, all right."

"You're suffering from a bad case of too much attention," said the doctor. He drew deeply on his cigarette, exhaled and continued: "Your scalp will clear up of its own accord in a few days if your mother will leave it alone that long." He turned toward his desk, saying: "Here! I'll write her a note and explain the situation." He stopped, stroked his chin and pursed out his lips humorously. "No," he went on, "I'd better prescribe something after all." He winked at the boy as if they were conspirators together, and said: "The salve I'm going to give you won't help your head in the slightest degree. Its sole purpose is to keep your mother's mind occupied. Do we understand each other, Grady?"

He came closer to the child and looked down at him affectionately. "Tell your mother that she isn't to put anything else on your head while you're using my salve—particularly no more soap and water. Tell her if she does, certain obscure chemical reactions will instantly take place, and her fine-looking young son will explode before her eyes like a cannon cracker." He laughed again and touched the boy's shoulder; and turning toward the anteroom where he compounded his own prescriptions, he added: "I'll fix the ointment for you now."

Grady waited by the desk for a time, thinking about Dr. Eldridge and staring idly out of the window; then wondering what Mamie was doing, he returned to the reception room. To his surprise, she was nowhere in sight, and he wondered if she had tired of waiting and had returned home alone;. but seeing that the door to the bedroom was open once more, he approached and looked inside, and there, before his eyes, was Mamie Webster standing over the doctor's bed. She had a large, clothbound slate in her hands and when she heard the shocked, involuntary sound the boy made, she returned it quickly to its place beneath the pillow, smoothing out the sheet and counterpane. A moment later she closed the bedroom door, stuck out her heavy jaw and said: "You say one word to Dr. Eldridge or anybody else and I'll—"

She had got out of the bedroom just in time, for the doctor returned with the ointment before she could finish her sentence. He handed the jar to Mamie, saying gravely, "The directions are written on the label. They're quite simple." Inexplicably his cheerful, professional manner had deserted him, and he looked down at the floor, the lost uncomprehending expression once more in his eyes.

"Mrs. Dorney didn't send no money," said Mamie nervously; "but if you'll tell her what she owes you, she'll take care of it, she says."

"The money," repeated Dr. Eldridge vaguely. "Of course. I beg your pardon for forgetting." He reached absently into his pocket and put a fifty-cent piece in the boy's palm. "I'll try not to forget again," he said. "My wife usually handles these details for me but she went to Crown Point for the afternoon with some friends. If I didn't know what an expert swimmer she is, I'd be getting a little worried about her." He passed his hands over his eyes, bowed stiffly and turned away, having already forgotten Mamie Webster and the patient she had brought.

When they were on the road once more, Mamie spoke defensively: "All right, tattletale! Tell everybody in Williston what you saw! What do I care? I'll say I didn't do it, and everybody will believe me, because I'm grown up and you're not."

"He really keeps a slate under his pillow like they say," said Grady. "That part's the truth, isn't it, Mamie?"

"Yes," she said. "It's the God's truth. And what's more, there's a slate pencil tied to it with a string, if you've got to know."

"That makes it easier for his wife when she writes her messages," said Grady. "It saves her the trouble of looking for the pencil every time she comes."

Suddenly he stopped in the road, caught at Mamie's hand and pulled her around so that she faced him. He stared at her a moment, an odd, intent expression in his eyes. "Was there anything written on the slate?" he asked. "Was there, Mamie?"

Mamie, her alarm at being caught red-handed having abated somewhat, decided to compromise. "Listen!" she began. "If I swear to tell the truth, will you swear never to repeat what you hear?"

"Yes," said Grady, "I swear."

"All right, then," said Mamie: "There wasn't anything written on the slate when I took it from under the pillow and looked at it."

The precise phrasing of her reply puzzled the boy. He knew she was holding something back, being so familiar with her character, but he could not decide what it was; then, remembering that she had had the pencil in her hand when he discovered her bending above the slate, he understood in a moment of intuition precisely what she had done.

"You wrote something on it *yourself!*" he said. "What was it you wrote on the slate, Mamie?"

Her eyes wavered and she glanced down. She thrust her rough, manlike hands behind her and her face and neck turned red slowly. "Let me alone," she said. "Why can't people mind their own business and let me alone?"

"What did you write on the slate?" he insisted. "You better tell me, because if you don't keep your promise, I don't have to keep mine, either. I'll tell everybody in town what I saw you do, and the first one I tell will be your mother."

She turned away in confusion and hid her face in her hands. "I can't say it right out," she said after a time. "I just couldn't! I'd be too ashamed."

"Write it on the ground," said Grady. "You can rub it out as soon as I read it."

Mamie hesitated a little longer, but squatting by the roadside at last, she picked up a twig and wrote laboriously in the dust:

> When loanley or looking for
> good company
> comunercate right away with
> Miss Mamie L. Webster
> here in town.

For a time the boy and the gawky, unattractive girl knelt beside the road staring at each other; then Mamie rose upward on her heavy thighs, thrust out her foot and obliterated what she had written. "Now you know as much as I do," she said sullenly. "Are you satisfied?"

The boy said: "Do you think he'll do it, Mamie? Do you?"

"Why not?" she said reasonably. "Don't he always do what his wife tells him?"

At that moment Grady had a clear picture of how Mrs. Eldridge had looked in life: She had been gay and provocative and gentle, and half the men in Williston had been in love with her at the time she married the doctor. She had been soft and gracious and lovely—the very opposite of Mamie Webster in everything. It was then he knew that Mamie had revealed herself without purpose, that she had accomplished nothing, and with the detached brutality of children, he shook his head slowly and spoke:

"He won't do it, not even if he does think his wife asked him to. You're too big and greasy-looking."

But Mamie seized his hand more firmly, jerking him along so rapidly that he was running every few steps to keep abreast of her. "Talk! Talk!" she said bitterly. "Chatter! Chatter! It's all boys or men know how to do!"

1939

THE WILLOW FIELDS

*W*HEN she answered the bell and saw her sister there at the door, Mrs. Niven drew back in dismay and laughed softly. "I declare, Agnes," she said; "I was just on my way to visit Nettie Rodney upstairs. A minute later and you wouldn't have found me in." Then, her hand still grasping the knob, she explained about Nettie, and why she didn't like to break the appointment with her.

Mrs. Rodney, it appeared, had been widowed only a few weeks before, so naturally she was still heartsick and lonely. Then, too, she had no people of her own to turn to in her sorrow—no children, either, and that made things harder, Mrs. Niven thought. "So I run up for a visit every afternoon about this time," she went on, "and Nettie makes tea, and we talk—or rather Nettie talks, and I listen."

The sisters stood in the small vestibule, sighing and shaking their heads. They were much alike in appearance, both of them being bony, solidly built women who seemed capable of turning even the heaviest mattress with one quick, efficient flip of their wrists.

"But why don't you come along with me?" Mrs. Niven asked suddenly. "Nettie will be glad to have somebody new to talk to. She talks about her husband mostly, and I've heard it all so many times."

And so, shoving their durable busts before them, the sisters went into the hall and ascended the fragile, uncarpeted stairs. Nettie Rodney, hearing the noise of their feet, came to her own landing and peered down the stairwell. "You're a fine one, Dora Niven," she called out gaily. "I was ready to ring up the police and get out a search warrant to find you."

She was plump and middle-aged, and as she watched the heads

of her visitors rise higher and higher toward her, she jerked her body from side to side with the coquettish, sudden gestures of a robin. She was wearing a bright print dress with short sleeves, and the powdered flesh of her forearms, as she bent forward and rested her elbows on the stair-rail, had the fluted, bluish-white appearance of a plucked hen. Her hair had recently been bleached yellow and elaborately waved. Her lips, cheeks and fingernails were an indiscriminate scarlet.

Dora said, when they were inside Mrs. Rodney's apartment: "This is my sister Mrs. Agnes Nicolson. She lives in Jackson Heights, and she dropped in unexpectedly just a few minutes ago; so I brought her along with me, knowing you wouldn't mind."

"I hope it wasn't an imposition," said Agnes, "seeing that you've just sustained a loss. What I mean is, people in mourning generally want to be by themselves until—" She paused in confusion, realizing at that instant that Mrs. Rodney was most plainly not in mourning. Nettie, feeling that an explanation was expected of her, hesitated and then said, "Fred didn't believe in making a show of your feelings."

"Fred was her husband," said Dora unnecessarily.

Nettie jumped up from her chair and placed one finger against her crimson lips. "The water!" she said in a high, vivacious voice. "It's boiling away on the stove!" She hurried to her kitchen, and a moment later the sisters heard her arranging cups and saucers on a tray.

"She doesn't have to worry about money the way some widows do," said Dora solemnly, "because Fred left her comfortably off." She lowered her voice and listened, then realizing that Nettie would be busy for the next few minutes, she recited the salient facts of Mr. Rodney's past in a hollow, hushed voice. He had had a good job with an insurance company, and he had been in the same position for many years. He had been a real family man, not caring about outside company and hardly drinking at all, or throwing his money to the winds, the way many did. Nettie had always given in to him and pampered him in little ways. Maybe that was a mistake—tying yourself so close to a man, no matter what good qualities he had. Maybe it would have been better if she'd gone out and made friends of her own. Maybe if she had done that she wouldn't feel his loss so terribly now.

"Why, she seems real gay and unconcerned to me," said Agnes. "I would never call her a grief-stricken woman."

"It's all show," said Dora. "She's taking his death very hard, but of course she's got to keep going as best she can."

At that moment their hostess returned with the tea, and Agnes changed the conversation abruptly. She said: "I see they're showing 'Commandos from the Sky' in this neighborhood. I saw it last week. It's a good picture, I thought."

Nettie put down the cups and saucers and turned quickly. "Now, that's a coincidence," she said: "Your mentioning moving pictures, I mean. . . . You see, Fred was crazy about them. It was the only thing that interested him much; that and reading the papers. He read three different ones after he got home at night."

She opened her compact and examined her make-up; then, sighing inaudibly, she went back for the teapot and the sugar. When she returned, she poured tea for her guests with complete absorption, her toe tapping nervously against the rug.

"I always thought Fred missed his calling when he went into insurance," she said. "A man with so much appeal for the ladies, and with such a handsome face and fine figure, should have been on the stage. He joked about it when I brought it up, and said he'd only make a fool of himself, because he didn't know the first thing about acting. And so I used to tell him, 'But you don't have to know anything about acting. A good director could teach you all the tricks and movements in no time.'"

Agnes, who had pictured Mr. Rodney as another type of man entirely, spoke in surprise: "Was your husband as good-looking as all that? I didn't realize."

Nettie smiled and nodded toward a table which stood against the wall, a table entirely bare except for a photograph which had plainly been posed and tinted by someone who believed with his whole being in the camera as a medium of artistic expression.

Agnes straightened up and twisted her head, examining the photograph with concentrated care. The face which stared back at her from the expensive frame was that of a plump, middle-aged man whose features were small, glum and unobtrusive. His hair was thin but still dark, and it had been plastered fiercely to his skull, with two small almost circular curls on either side of the part. His eyes were fixed and somehow intolerant behind the glasses he wore, and his lips pursed slightly, as if he had contemplated making a suggestion or two to the photographer, but had thought better of it.

"You see?" said Nettie. "You see what I mean?"

Then, as if her words had evoked thoughts too near the surface, emotions too powerful to be easily controlled, she passed the sugar and cream needlessly, repeating under her breath all the things which Fred had said about showing your grief in public. Dora and her sister glanced at each other, and then, staring again at the elaborate, tinted photograph, they smiled cautiously and shook their heads.

Agnes was the first to break the silence. "Where did you find such a nice frame?" she asked. "It's real leather, isn't it?"

"I got it after he died," said Nettie. "I looked and looked until I found that shade of green. It isn't exactly right, but it was the closest I could come to what I really wanted. Green was always his favorite color. I mean that real bright shade of green— the color of grass in spring, or of willow trees coming out." She leaned forward with eagerness now, and her words came in a rush, as if she could no longer keep them bottled up in herself.

"Now, here's something I wouldn't tell just anybody, for fear they'd laugh, or think it sounded crazy, but Fred had a peculiar notion in his head, and he used to talk about it sometime. I suppose it wasn't so much a *notion* as it was a sort of *picture*, if you know what I mean. . . . Anyway, the thing that bothered him at times was whether he'd really seen the picture, or whether it was something he'd made up in his mind."

Agnes put down her cup with a small clatter. "What was it, Mrs. Rodney?" she asked excitedly. "What kind of a picture did he see?"

"It was a place out in the country," said Nettie, "and the main thing about it was the fact that it was so untroubled and silent. There was a white farmhouse and a sign which read: THE WIL-LOW FIELDS; and all about the house there were sloping meadows so green that you couldn't believe your eyes. There was a stream of water running through the fields, with clumps of willow trees growing along its banks. It was all so strange, and yet it was real too in a way. He could see it so plainly, and if he told me about it once, he told me about it a hundred times."

Agnes, who had expected something more dramatic, said in a vigorous, practical voice: "Maybe he really did see such a place. When he was a little boy, perhaps, before you two met."

Nettie shook her head instantly, as if she had long anticipated this solution and was prepared for it. "No," she said. "No, it couldn't have been that way. You see, Fred was born right here in New York City and his mother told him, when he asked her about it, that he'd never left the city at all when he was young— not even to go to Brooklyn."

"I think it was something he imagined in his mind," said Dora. "What else could it have been?"

Nettie leaned back in her chair and pleated her dress with her white, nervous fingers. "Anyway," she said, "Fred believed that such a place existed somewhere. He meant to go look for it some day, after he'd retired from business and had more time."

She got up suddenly and went to the kitchen. She returned with fresh cream and a pitcher of hot water, and when she had refilled the teapot and taken her seat again, Agnes said: "Your husband really fell in love with that place, didn't he? It must have made a great impression on his mind."

Nettie did not speak at once, but after she had replenished the cups, she nodded twice and answered, making her voice as casual as she could: "Yes, that's very true." She leaned back in her chair and rested her forehead against her palm. She felt herself sinking, despite her will, into the despair which seemed always to wait for her. With determination she straightened up again and forced her lips to smile. Afterwards she talked rapidly, compulsively, going over and over the trivial details of her trivial life. She talked on and on, her shallow eyes desperate and staring, her plucked, powdered forearms digging into the upholstery of her chair; but at last her guests rose to leave, and standing there on the landing once more, she watched until they were out of sight, knowing at that moment that her whole day had been lived through in anticipation of this casual visit.

When she heard Mrs. Niven's door close, she came back into her own apartment and stood before the photograph in its green frame, moving it forward a little so that the late sunlight brought out its details more clearly; then she carried the dishes out, washed them and put them away. When that task was done, there was nothing to do until she cooked her supper; afterwards there would be nothing to do until it was time for her to go to bed.

Without thought, with no definite plan in her mind, she went into her bedroom and put on the dress she had bought a few days before. It was made of some soft, clinging material; it was years too young for her, and its color was an intense, clamorous green. Her dyed yellow hair, arranged so elaborately above the green of the dress, gave her the appearance of a rumpled and ornate buttercup.

Later, she tried to read, but she could not; and pressing her palms flatly against her cheeks she went to the window and looked down at the street, watching the dense, five-o'clock crowd hurrying to their individual and unknown destinations. There were so many people in the world, she thought—so many people, and she meant nothing to any of them. "But they mean nothing to me, either," she said aloud. "Nothing at all." She found this thought too dreadful to face, and moving back into the room, she stretched out on her sofa, her hands locked and tense between her bulging knees, her bright green dress outlining the plump curve of her body.

She had not slept well since her husband's death, but now she had a feeling of drowsiness, as if she wished to escape, somehow, from the shrill, relentless thoughts which beset her mind. She turned on her back and adjusted the pillows against her head, thinking vaguely of Mrs. Niven and Agnes Nicolson. She won-

dered if she had been indiscreet in speaking so freely to them—
if, after all, she had not made herself absurd. She was not sure,
but Fred would know, if he were alive, and he would tell her at
once.

She sighed and turned slowly on the couch. The sounds from
the street seemed farther and farther away, and a moment later
even the familiar room became blurred and remote. Then,
strangely, although she was not in the least surprised, she found
the farmhouse which Fred had looked for, and at once she
thought: "It was not a dream after all. May God forgive me for
having doubted him." She looked about her thoughtfully, speaking softly to herself. "There is the sign outside the house," she
said. "There are the wide, green fields and the willows growing
in clumps along the stream."

She turned slowly, staring with a sense of incredulous delight,
and at that instant she saw her husband plainly. He was standing
alone, at the edge of the farthest field, and he looked precisely
as he had when she first met him. She started forward in her
eagerness, and stretching her arms wide, she ran toward him,
without effort, through all that sea of bright young green. She
felt there was something both definitive and overwhelming which
she should say to him, but she could not remember what it was.
She could only cry out, "Fred! Fred!" in a thin, tremulous voice;
but when she reached the place where he was standing, and
lifted her hands to touch his face, she awoke from her dream
with a nervous start, shuddered and sat up straight on the sofa,
thinking that she would never be able to move again. She sat
there as if dazed for a long time, her hands pressed tightly
against her face,

It was then she remembered a conversation with her husband
many years ago. "Even if you did find the willow fields again,"
she had said, "you'd probably be so old and tired out that you
wouldn't care whether you went there or not. That's the way
things usually work out in this world."

"I'd still want to go there," he had said, "no matter how old
or tired I was at the time. I'd go there all right, no matter what

the circumstances were—even if I had to come back from the grave to do it."

"No, no, Fred!" she had answered. "You mustn't say such things, even in fun. They're sacrilegious!" But he had only laughed his odd, individual laugh and continued stubbornly: "I'd do it though, just as sure as you're a foot high."

It was dark in the living-room now, but she did not turn on the lights. There were no sounds from the street at all, and even the small, intimate noises of the house itself had ceased. In this complete, waiting stillness she could hear the sound her own breath made, the tiny, scratching sound of her stockings as they pressed together. She got up from the couch, and for a time she stood in the center of the room in complete and waiting passivity; but when she could bear her thoughts no longer, she turned and went to the bedroom which she and her husband had shared for so many years, to the chest of drawers which still held his intimate belongings.

His shirts were arranged neatly in rows, just as he had left them. From one of the shirts she took a piece of rough, grayish cardboard which the launderer had put there to hold it firm; and then, her mouth tight with her desperation, she found a pencil and printed boldly on the surface of the board: THE WILLOW FIELDS.

Without pausing to consider, her eyes wide and frightened at the audacity of the thing she meant to do, she opened the door of her apartment and fixed the sign there with a thumb tack. She drew back against the wall, but she left the door open a little so that nothing would impede his progress when he came back to her. She patted her curls into place and rearranged her silly, bright green dress seductively. "Here I am," she said softly. "Here, by the door."

She waited there in the dark for a long time, her breath coming irregularly in thin, quick rushes, her puckered, dead-white hands making small, meaningless gestures. Then, realizing that her throat was dry and constricted, she started for the bathroom to get a glass of water. She recognized the stuffed chair, the smoking-stand and the big, metal lamp as she passed and fumbled them for an instant; but when her hands touched the photograph on the polished table, she trembled so that she sank slowly to the floor. In the darkness she rested her yellow, elaborately curled head against the edge of the table. "Here I am," she said. "Here."

She got up after awhile and went to the bathroom. She turned on the light above the basin, examining her rouged, harassed face in the mirror. Automatically she fumbled for her compact, but such a feeling of distaste came over her at that instant that she never completed the gesture. Instead, she leaned back against the towel rack, stared at her own reflection, and wept. "Old woman!" she cried fiercely. "Old woman! Old woman!"

She could no longer endure the sight of her own face and she walked quickly away from the mirror; but when she came into the living-room again, and stood there in indecision, as if she could no longer recall the purposes which impelled her, her knees collapsed beneath her and she fell forward against the rug, knowing clearly at that moment that no matter how senseless her husband's death seemed, nor how greatly she longed for his return, he would not come back to her.

Then, slowly, she turned on her face and gave way completely to grief, but even in that bitter moment of realization she found excuses for him, for she said to herself over and over: "But why should he? Why should he come back to a silly, impossible old woman like me?"

1943

I BROKE MY BACK ON A ROSEBUD

*T*HIS is a story which Corporal Curtain tells to those who will listen, and this is the way he told it to me:

I'm talking about the last war, remember—not about this new, fancy one. . . . Say, how old do you take me to be? All right. Go on. Go on and say sixty. It won't hurt my feelings any. But you'll be wrong if you think that, because I was forty-eight years old on my last birthday.

Okay. Okay. So I'm forty-eight on my last birthday, and that makes me twenty-four in 1919, now don't it? And you want to know something else? My birthday falls on the eleventh of November—Armistice Day—remember that far back? I was luckier than most, I used to say to myself, because I went through the fighting and didn't get a scratch. Didn't get gassed, either. Didn't even get flu or trench-feet. Didn't get anything, see?

Then, after it was all over, comes this parade in New York City, up Fifth Avenue, and as we marched along, I kept thinking that my army days were about over—that it wouldn't be long before I was on the outside. And so we paraded up the avenue at attention, according to regulations. People stood on both sides of the pavement, waving flags and cheering, but I didn't pay them any mind. I was too busy checking off each landmark as we went by. "That's Fourteenth Street ahead," I'd think; or, "There's Madison Square to the right, as big as life and right on schedule." So finally we got into the public library neighborhood, and I knew we'd be passing the reviewing stand before long.

There was some sort of commotion taking place near the south side of the library steps. I looked in that direction, without really turning my head, and there, standing on a pedestal above the crowd, between the front feet of one of the stone lions, was a good-looking woman. A pink basket was hung around her neck on a wide, pink ribbon; and what's more, the pink basket was full of pink rosebuds. Not the stems and leaves, too, mind you—just the pink heads. . . . And every once in a while she'd show all her pretty teeth, blow a kiss to the troops and sing out, "Welcome home to each and every one!" Then with a little twitch which started at her ankles and ended in a shake of her yellow curls, she'd reach in her pink basket and toss a pink rosebud to the boys.

Now listen carefully to me, because here comes the pay-off. . . . When my platoon was almost flush with the stone lion and the dame standing there above the heads of everybody else, I cut my glance up and around a little—and there she was, looking straight into my eyes. So she reached in her silk basket, picked out a fat rosebud, all for me, and tossed it in my direction. "Welcome back!" she called out, while people on the sidewalk looked at her and clapped their hands. "Welcome back to the United States of America!"

I felt the rosebud hit me on the chest, and I saw it bounce off; and the next thing I knew, there was something soft and sliding under my foot, like a big, pink eyeball. I tried to get my balance back, but I couldn't; and then I was lying flat on my back, right in the middle of the street, with the men of my company detouring around me. I didn't feel pain anywhere—the only thing was, I couldn't get up when I tried. So first they carried me into a store. After that an ambulance took me to the hospital, but it wasn't until a couple of days later that I knew, for certain, my back was broke. . . . You know the rest, I imagine. Somebody must have told you already that I've been lying on a board since 1919. Figure it out for yourself. That's a quarter of a century. Well, that's the way it is, and there's nothing I can do to change it.

Pull down the shade a little, will you, fellow? The sun's in my eyes.

All right! All right, let's get on with the story. . . . Anybody would think I'd be downhearted, knowing I had a fractured spine, but I wasn't. Well, not right away. I kept saying to myself, "Look at the discoveries doctors are making these days. Somebody is sure to find out what to do for me." And so I lived on hope for ten years or more, and every time something new came up, why, I'd let 'em do it to me first, saying to myself that this time everything was going to be all right; but it never was. The Government took good care of me, and sometimes when visitors came, the doctors would point to me and say, "This is Corporal Curtain. He sets us all an example in fortitude."

Hope dies hard in a man, but it does die finally. . . . Am I telling you something new? Am I telling you something you haven't heard before? I don't know how hope died in me, but one morning I woke up wise to myself. I knew, then, what the doctors had known all along, and that was, I'd never be any better, no matter what they did for me. That's when I started to see the woman's face again. I'd close my eyes and try to shut it out, but I couldn't. I cursed her and damned her from morning to night, like a crazy man. "Why wasn't she home, where she belonged, cooking her husband some dinner?" I'd say. "Why did she have to show herself off like she did?"

I'd known from the beginning, you see, that she didn't come out that morning to look at the soldiers. She came out to have the soldiers look at her. . . . And she didn't throw me a rosebud because I was a returning hero in her eyes. Oh, no! Not that one! She did it so people could see how nice she *looked* throwing a rosebud! That was the worst thought of all, and when it came to me, I'd close my eyes and lay my head deep in the pillow.

Lift my neck up some and give me a drink of water, will you? My throat's dry. . . .

Now, here's a thing I never figured out to my satisfaction: You'd think hate would last longer than hope, but it didn't work out like that. Not with me, anyway. And so after a year or two I wasn't able to see her face any more. I didn't blame her for anything, either. I leaned over backwards to be fair and reasonable. She couldn't know that I was going to slip and fall, now could she? How could anybody anticipate such a thing? It was probably something which had never happened to a man before in the whole history of the world, so why hold her responsible?

Then I had another thought, and it was this: Maybe the woman was an instrument in the hands of God. Maybe I was being punished for something I did once, but couldn't remember. So I said to myself, "If that's the way it is, that's the way it's going to be, and I've got to accept it." So you see? First I hoped, and then I hated—but at last I was resigned.

Then a year or so later I saw things in another light, and now I laugh to myself when I think back. Can you figure out what changed me? I've already given you a hint or two. You can't? Okay. I'll tell you before long, but let me lead up to it gradual. Let me tell you first about the man who wrote a piece about me in the newspapers.

It was Richard Emery Simms, the famous columnist, and the story was printed all over the country, in I don't know how many papers. A lot of people read about my case, and it wasn't long afterwards before some of the boys I knew in the old outfit, who had forgot me years ago, started writing me letters, or even coming to see me here at the hospital.

Now, hardly a day passes without somebody dropping in—strangers or otherwise. The boys from my old outfit talk about themselves for the most part. I guess they figure that since I never had a real life of my own, I'd be glad to hear about theirs. They tell me who they married, and how many kids they got. They tell me everything that's happened to them since we saw each other last—what they had hoped to get out of their lives, and what they had really got.

So one morning a fellow named Jamie Ethridge (he used to be a sergeant in the old second platoon) came to pay me a visit. He talked about his troubles even more than the others. All he had ever asked was a little peace and security, he said. Once he thought that he had it, too, and then something had gone wrong somehow. He had hoped so much, he said. He had tried so hard, and then something had happened, although he didn't know how or why. I quit listening to him about that time, and my mind went back to my own troubles.

At first, what happened to me seemed like an accident without sense, then it seemed like something planned for me alone. All at once I knew both ideas were wrong, and I've been a changed man from that minute on. This may sound silly to you. If it does, that's all right with me, too! But now I think of that woman as something made out of paper and wires. Something curled and painted pink for the people. Something that lives right there in the library, with the romances and poems. . . . And every once in awhile the authorities get her out, dust her off, and send her out for the world to see—like a beauty contest winner with Miss Universal Dream across her belly.

When that thought came into my head I started to laugh in earnest, while Sergeant Ethridge looked at me and wondered what had happened. . . . You see, I used to think that no other man was in my particular fix. That was my mistake, and I know better now. Oh, no, fellow! I'm not the only man who broke his back on a rosebud. Not by a long shot. Sometimes it seems to me that everybody in my generation done the same thing one way or another. "I'm not the only one," I say to people now. "There's many another. Oh, many and many a one."

Light me a cigarette and put it between my lips, will you, bud?

1943

IT'S YOUR HARD LUCK

THERE was a late spring that year, and only now, in June, had the trees come fully into leaf. Mist hung over the paths, and as we entered the park together it swirled and drifted reluctantly before our steady, advancing feet. We walked that morning with arms interlocked past the benches and the animal cages, pausing only to watch the rapid, hungry seals; we walked past the little cafe and through the culvert which led west, and when we came to our particular seat under the trees, against the solid rock itself, we laughed for no reason at all and sat down. Before us was the triangle of shrubs we knew well; beyond, there were benches so placed on the curving path that only their backs were visible to us.

Mally sighed and looked about her. "It all seems so freshly made and pretty this morning," she said. "So very pretty and so vague."

The two men who sat on a bench to our right went on with their talk. One of the men was petulant and untidy, and although it was warm he wore a muffler and an overcoat. The other was a well-washed, adolescent sailor with a starched cap set precisely on the back of his limp, flaxen hair. He was obviously on leave, for his uniform was so white, his shoes so polished and neat, that you knew at once that some fretful superior officer had inspected them only an hour or so before.

"What's the matter with this park?" asked the young sailor. "They told me you could meet girls here. I don't see any."

He turned his body with one quick movement, peering about him with intense, speculative eyes. The gesture stretched his tight, immaculate uniform more closely to his flesh, bringing sharply into relief the flat precision of his shoulder bones, the young, stringy muscles of his thighs, the small, plump thimble of his sex.

"They'll be along directly," said the man. "It's something you can be sure of."

The sun broke through at that moment, and with it the heavy pigeons flew down from the sycamore trees. They stood warily in the path before the sailor and his companion, not daring as yet to venture too near, and gazed at them sidewise with an expectant, thoughtful stupidity.

"I know plenty about military life," said the man finally. "I ought to, God knows, because I put in two years during the last war. But it wasn't in the navy. It was in the army. I can't say I got along well, but I wasn't as dumb as they tried to make out later."

Suddenly the sailor shoved his thin, wiry legs toward the pigeons. "Go on, beat it!" he said. "We haven't got anything for you!"

The pigeons fell backward in alarm and lifted upward a little, their wings anchoring them above the path, their tail feathers spread wide for balance and sucked inward, like the tight, protective tails of shrimp.

"As a matter of fact," continued the veteran, "I wasn't dumb at all. My trouble was I didn't do things like others, and not doing things like others don't get you far in the army."

The sailor relaxed and yawned. "I do things the way everybody else does them," he said in a bored voice.

The pigeons settled on the path once more, but nearer the curb this time; and then, as if the ground beneath them had fallen away, they rose upward with a rush and flew through the trees and the triangle of shrubs before us. We saw, then, that while we had been listening to the sailor and his companion a stranger had taken his seat on the curved line of benches to our left, and Mally, watching the pigeons wheel and flutter above him, said: "It's somebody they know well; somebody they were expecting."

From where we were only the stranger's back and head were visible. He wore a peaked cap so unusual in design, so eccentric in appearance, that it was, obviously, the outer symbol of some deepseated crotchet in the mind of its owner. It was a dull, bird-like brown and it fitted tightly against the stranger's fragile, rounded skull. For a moment the man sat quietly, ignoring as best he could the rumbling voices of the pigeons above him; but at last he jerked back his neck and said in an intense, piping voice: "Let me alone. I want nothing to do with you."

He had a bag of grain in his hands, and an instant before the pigeons discovered him and circled excitedly above his head he had apparently been trying to make three ragged, shivering sparrows come forward and accept the food which he had brought for them; but they were too frail, too timid to claim what was rightfully theirs, and they remained in safety beside the curb, blowing out their feathers and cocking their shrewd, nervous heads from side to side. At that moment the pigeons descended in a shifting mass of color and pecked at the grain with their precise, flexible necks, crowding the sparrows from the path and onto the grass itself. When the last kernel was eaten, the pigeons looked up at their benefactor and made their expectant, oily noises; and since he threw them no more food they lifted once more and settled with a sliding motion upon his peaked cap, his shoulders, and even upon his tense, out-thrust arm. Then the sailor and his friend went on with their talk.

"This will give you an idea of what I mean," said the old soldier. "They said I could never do anything right, but after the fighting around Soissons they changed their tune a little. So they decided to make a corporal out of me. So I got my warrant in due time and the supply sergeant issued me some chevrons to sew on my sleeves."

The stranger made a sudden, threatening gesture at the pigeons and said: "Go away. Nobody invited you, did they? Don't you know when you're not wanted?" But the pigeons merely fluttered beyond the reach of his arms and peered at him contemptuously, but without malice.

"So when the time came to sew on my chevrons," continued the veteran, "I didn't put them on with the point toward the shoulders, which was according to regulations, but the other way round—with the point aimed at the elbow. And so the sergeant called me in when he saw how I'd sewed on my chevrons and said to me, 'How does it happen you put your chevrons on up-side down?' And I said, 'It depends on what you call upside down. If I was in the British army it wouldn't be considered upside down at all. What we do would be upside down.'"

"'But you're not in the British army,' he said to me, 'and you never were.' 'That doesn't change the situation one way or the other,' I said. So then he got mad and shouted out, 'It looks like anybody would know how to sew on chevrons without even being told!' And then I said, 'Not necessarily so.'" The old soldier spat moodily across the path and became silent.

Beyond the triangle of shrubs, the man in the peaked cap stared with distaste at the pigeons, making threatening gestures in their direction with his rolled newspaper; then, believing perhaps that he had intimidated them, he poured more grain into his palm and tossed it where the sparrows were huddled together on the grass. "Take it," he said. "Don't let them get this away from you too." But with the movement of his arm the pigeons dipped downward, pushing the sparrows away from the lawn, forcing them back, with their bulk, to the place where the shrubs began. The stranger became excited when he saw what had happened. "Stand up for your rights, you fools!" he called out in his shrill, piping voice. "If the pigeons push you, push them too!"

But the alarmed sparrows flew up and sat among the branches of the shrubs, shivering and swaying back and forth.

When the last kernel of grain was eaten the pigeons swarmed over the stranger once more. This time he sat quietly, making no move to dislodge them; then, angrily, he emptied the bag of grain in the path and said: "I don't care which of you gets it! What concern is it of mine?"

He shook himself and got up from the bench—and we saw him plainly for the first time. He was a small man indeed, hardly four feet tall. His back was straight enough, but his chest curved forward in a plump arc, like the breast of a bird, and as if to heighten the illusion, he wore a gray suède vest which fitted precisely beneath his throat. For the rest, he was dressed in varying shades of brown, and the tails of his eccentric, old-fashioned coat lay neatly behind him, like folded wings.

"Why waste my time on you?" he said grandly. "Really, you are beneath my contempt!"

Then, as he approached us on his thin, dried-out legs, I understood why he envied and hated pigeons, why he loved and despised sparrows; for he was not, as I had so ingenuously thought, the frailest of men: he was, instead, the strongest of birds. He passed our bench proudly and walked toward the culvert, while the endless tale of the old soldier came to our ears once more.

"They broke me from corporal and put me back in the ranks," he was saying. "I tried to explain things to the top sergeant, but he wouldn't even listen to me. 'If the shape of your mind is different from regulations, it's your hard luck,' he said, 'and not mine.' "

The sailor glanced earnestly at his nails and lit a cigarette. "I do things like everybody else," he said. "What's the sense of acting any other way?"

Above us, where the boulders were, there came a burst of forced, sudden laughter. Instantly the young sailor reset his cap and smoothed down his white, immaculate uniform; and without a word of explanation to his companion, as if leave-taking were an act beyond his will, an experience too complex for him to attempt, he vaulted the bench and began climbing the boulder, at whose top the young girls awaited him.

The veteran seemed not at all surprised at the abrupt departure of his acquaintance. He merely rubbed his chin for a moment and then, wanting to finish his story, he turned toward us, but we pretended not to see him, since there was little point in our hearing the end of a story which we already knew. Instead, we focused our eyes on the man in the peaked cap, watching him as he walked jerkily down the path.

Already the pigeons had devoured the food which he had scattered, and now they flew in a cloud above his head. They would not leave him alone, no matter how greatly he threatened them. They merely rose upward beyond the reach of his arm and anchored themselves in the air, gazing at him with vacant affection. Their rolling voices were liquid and flattering in their throats, but their wings, fanning against the air, made a thin, contemptuous sound.

"'It's your hard luck!'" continued the old soldier. "That's what the sergeant said to me. 'If you're not like everybody else, it's your hard luck! And now get the hell out of here!'"

1943

THE BORAX BOTTLE

*T*HAT Sunday afternoon we sat on the shady, east porch of the Kent bungalow and gossiped, but with no real interest, about the people of Reedyville. Finally Mrs. Kent shook back her bracelets, picked up a palmetto fan and waved it languidly beneath her nose, her white, fluffy hair lifting upward in the breeze. "I don't know when we've had such a hot spell," she said in a resigned voice, "or one that's lasted so long, either."

There was a silence, and then I spoke idly: "How did you and Dr. Kent happen to fall in love, Miss Cordie? Did it come in a blinding flash, or was it something that developed over the years?"

"It developed gradually," said Dr. Kent. "Very gradually, I'd say. I suppose it couldn't have happened otherwise: You see, Cordie and I have known each other all our lives."

Behind us, inside the house, there was a sound of tiptoeing, and Mrs. Kent, turning her neck a little, called out over her shoulder: "Who is it? Who is moving about in the living-room?" There was a deep sigh and then the voice of the Kents' cook came from beside the door. "It's me," she said with unexpected bitterness. "It's nobody but old sneaking Mamie. I'm eavesdroppin' again. You know I do it ever' time I get the chance. I try not to, but it don't seem to do no good."

"Don't feel so badly about it," said Mrs. Kent. "It doesn't really matter. Eavesdrop to your heart's content, Mamie."

"Yassum," said Mamie, drawing the word out. "Yassum."

Dr. Kent glanced at his wife as if she were a perpetual source of astonishment to him, and then, turning to me, he continued: "I fell in love with Cordie gradually. I couldn't put my finger on any particular moment and say it happened then to save my life."

"That may be your individual experience," said Mrs. Kent,

"but as far as I'm concerned, love came to me in what the novel writers used to call 'a quick moment of revelation.' In fact, I made up my mind to marry you the afternoon you had your experience with the borax bottle." She took a long sip from the glass beside her, and turning to me she added: "It's quite a gruesome little story; perhaps you'd like to hear it, Clark. It has its amusing side, too. There's an element of pure terror in it, and it has always seemed to me that terror is the basis of all true comedy."

Dr. Kent straightened and looked about him. "Cordie!" he said. "You know very well you can't tell a story as intimate as that one!"

Mrs. Kent reached out and patted his hand reassuringly. "Why not?" she asked with an innocence which was completely false. She picked up her fan, waved it languidly back and forth, and continued: "When I look back over the years, I can see how the incident shaped the entire course of my life. It seems to me now that it has a deeper significance than the total significance of its parts: like a story by somebody really important—Chekov, for instance."

She rocked in silence for a moment, reviewing her material and arranging it properly in her sharp, neat mind; and when she began to speak again, you would have thought that she had abandoned her original theme. "Dr. Kent and I aren't related by blood at all," she said. "I used to think so when we were children, and to this day I don't see how we escaped, since the Kents and the Overtons have so many kinsmen in common. Anyway, the two families were forever visiting back and forth. It was a custom for the Kents to eat Sunday dinner with us, and to spend the afternoon at our house; and it was on a Sunday afternoon in summer, not unlike the one today, that little Frankie Kent had his terrible ordeal."

Dr. Kent knocked out his pipe against the edge of the porch and said: "Can you hear all right, Mamie? If you can't, Miss Cordie will gladly raise her voice a little more."

"Oh, leave poor Mamie alone," said Mrs. Kent mildly. "She's

known you as long as I have, and nothing I'm going to say will surprise her in the slightest degree."

"I speck I've knowed Dr. Frank longer than you," said Mamie. "I was just about raised on the Kent place, and don't forget that I'm older than you is."

Mrs. Kent seemed to have forgotten about the heat. All at once she sat up straight in her chair, a bright, interested expression in her eyes, and said: "I was about six years old at that time, and I used to despise Frankie Kent above all living creatures. He was two years older than I was, and a more objectionable little boy I never expect to meet! He was forever ridiculing me because I happened to be a girl, and for that reason of no importance whatever in his world. It seemed to me that he was even more disagreeable than usual that Sunday afternoon, and finally my mother, hearing us quarreling in the library, called out, 'Why don't you take our little visitor into the garden and play with him there, Cordelia?'

"I asked Frank if that's what he'd like to do, but he stuck out his lip even farther, shrugged and walked away. Naturally I followed him, being a sort of hostess for my mother at the time, and when we got to the old peach tree we stopped and stood there glumly. 'There's a dirt dauber nest under the eaves of the carriage house,' I said after awhile. 'Would you like me to show it to you?'"

Mrs. Kent laughed suddenly like a little girl, her ear pendants swinging back and forth. "It seems that my charm and my social graces were effective even in those days. At any rate, Frankie Kent *did* respond to the suggestion—in his own repulsive fashion, of course. He grunted, spat into the canna bed and said he supposed he might as well, since there was nothing else to do at our house.

"And so it happened that we stood and watched the wasps building their home; then Frank got one of my father's fishing poles and began poking at the busy, earnest workers. I tried to tell him that it wasn't quite the correct thing to do, because there's nothing in all the world so vindictive as an aroused dirt dauber; but little Frank, keeping in character to the very end, wouldn't listen to me. He explained that I didn't know how to handle a dirt dauber, being a girl and so scary about everything. To illustrate his point, he gave rather a detailed impersonation of how I walked and talked, taking little mincing steps across the grass, squealing and drawing back before imaginary snakes and caterpillars. Naturally a dirt dauber had no respect for such a creature, he said. But it was altogether different where boys were concerned, particularly an intrepid little boy like himself. When a dirt dauber realized he was doing business with that type, he behaved himself very well indeed."

She laughed gaily, her plump shoulders shaking a little. "And so Frankie continued his dissertation on the natural superiority of boys over girls, illustrating each point, as he made it, with little jabs at the dirt daubers' nest. They were getting pretty wrought up by this time, you may be sure, and a swarm of them came boiling out from under the eaves."

"When I was a little girl," said Mamie, "Dr. Frank had him a peashooter, and ever'time I went to the back fence to empty the dishpan for Mamma, he peppered my laigs. It got so I used to dodge and shake ever'time anybody spoke his name out loud, and Mamma had to give me a switching before I'd go to the woodshed and get kindling. It's a God's wonder I didn't get me a nervous breakdown, like Mrs. Stockbridge done after lightning hit her bedpost three times running. I declare, I just don't see how such a mean little boy turned out to be such a nice kind man."

Dr. Kent bent over his pipe, loosening its crust with his pen-knife. "Shut up, Mamie!" he said mildly. "I have no control over my wife, as everybody knows, but remember I can always *fire* you."

Mamie gave her thin, delighted laugh. "Yassuh," she said with spurious meekness. "Whatever you say, Dr. Frank."

"I think by this time that we've pretty well established Frank's character as a boy of eight," said Mrs. Kent, "so let's get back to the dirt daubers. It wasn't long before they linked up cause and effect, and a dozen or so of them zoomed downward in Frank's direction. He dropped the pole when he saw them coming and ran back of the chicken house, where I was hiding. For a time it looked as though he had outwitted his enemies, and then the dirt dauber who had flown up the leg of his loose, linen trousers went to work, and Frankie sank down to his knees, groaning and rolling about on the grass.

"He told me that he'd been stung on the leg, but I didn't believe that story for an instant. After all, I've got eyes, and I'd seen the clutching gesture he'd made when he fell. But it wasn't precisely a lie that he'd told: it was more of a euphemism. You know—like 'a natural son' or 'an unkissed bride.' "

Mamie had not been able to follow Mrs. Kent's elaborate but restrained explanation, and now she asked: "Where was it he got bit? You know I can't take in big words."

"Now, Mamie," said Mrs. Kent. "Don't embarrass me before our guest. Use your imagination."

"I am," said Mamie. "Still I don't see."

"Very well, then," continued Mrs. Kent. "Let's put it another way." She pressed her finger tips against her temples, looked up and smiled brightly. "When I was a young lady, there was a story going the rounds which was considered very daring. It seems that a bride was reproaching her husband for something he'd done, and telling him how *she* would have acted under similar circumstances, when the groom said: 'Perhaps so, my dear. But there's a slight difference between you and me.' At that the little bride sighed and rolled her eyes. 'I know it,' she said, 'and I thank the Lord for the variation!' . . . Now, do you understand, Mamie?"

Mamie laughed explosively and slapped her leg. "Oh, my good Lord!" she said. "Oh, my good Lord up in heaven!"

"Shut up, Mamie!" said Dr. Kent. "Quit gloating."

"And so little Frank twisted about on the grass for a time," continued Mrs. Kent, "but when the pain subsided, he got up and went back to the house. I followed him faithfully, as I wouldn't have missed anything for the world. The grownups were in the front parlor, and the story Frank told them about his mishap was a little edited, to put it mildly. Anyway, the fact that he had been stung by a bee, or something, did emerge, and my grandmother, who was visiting us that summer, and who loved to prescribe for the ailments of others, said promptly: 'Borax water is the best thing of all for the sting of an insect. I keep a supply of it on hand for family emergencies, and if the little boy will go to the bathroom on the back porch, he'll find it in the cutglass bottle."

Dr. Kent spoke directly to me: "I believe she's going to tell the story after all. I've been waiting to see how far she was prepared to go."

"Of course I'm going to tell it," said Mrs. Kent cheerfully. "You can tell things about children with the completest propriety. Then, too, this story has a moral attached, as I've already hinted, and a good moral has made many a bad story respectable before this, my dear."

Dr. Kent closed his knife and put it in his pocket. "I think I'll go have a look at the chrysanthemums," he said with a carelessness which misled nobody. "There should be a few buds on them by this time."

Mrs. Kent and Mamie laughed at the same instant. "Po' Dr. Frank," said Mamie, doubling up with mirth. "You got him bothered this time and no two ways about it. You ought not to chaw the po' man thataway, Miss Cordie."

"If anybody should be embarrassed, I'm the one," said Mrs. Kent, "because what I did later on would be considered terrible in any generation. In my own day, it was too shocking to be credible. You see, when Frank went into the bathroom and locked the door, I skipped innocently around the house and hid in the big pantry on the back porch."

"I bet you went there to peek at him," said Mamie shrewdly. "I bet that's just what you done."

"Yes," said Miss Cordie. "That was my purpose. I'd like to say now that I was sorry afterwards, but the fact remains that I wasn't. At any rate, there was a knot hole high up in the dividing wall, and I'd already discovered that by standing on a pile of trunks I had an excellent view of the bathroom. It had been a hall bedroom originally, but my father had had a zinc tub built against one wall, with a drain to let out the waste. There was no plumbing at all such as we have in bathrooms today, and when anybody took a bath, water had to be brought from the kitchen by the bucketful. There was a bowl and pitcher painted with morning glories, and a cake of scented soap on an ornamental stand for those who merely wanted to wash their faces."

Mrs. Kent sighed and lifted her plump, ringed hands. "I offer no excuses for my conduct. I merely state what I did. My parents would have considered me a completely depraved little girl if they had found out, and yet I know I was nothing of the sort. It wasn't pruriency that impelled me: it was simple curiosity. Nobody ever told children the truth in those days, so I decided to discover things for myself. I was entirely objective, and the things I learned at the knot hole were of neither greater nor less importance than the things my governess taught me.

"And so I stood on the trunks and watched little Frankie with the liveliest interest. The borax bottle held about a pint, and being made of cutglass, it was rather heavy to handle. He stood undecided for a time, trying to decide which was the best way to apply the water. First, he tilted the bottle and tried to pour it, but that only wet his clothing and didn't work at all well; then he tried dabbing the water on with his finger, but that wasn't successful either. At last he went the limit, and after looking guiltily around the room, he inserted his wounded member into the bottle itself. That seemed to be the ideal method, and when he felt the cool water taking the sting away, he sat on the edge of the tub, a peaceful expression spreading over his face.

"He sat there in complete serenity for five minutes or better, and then someone rapped abruptly on the bathroom door. The sound was so unexpected, so disturbing, that I started and almost fell off the trunks. The rapping was repeated, and this time the voice of Frankie's mother came through the partition. 'Your father is driving us over to Aunt Hester's for a call,' she said. 'Hurry up! We're all waiting for you!'

"Frankie jumped up nervously when the first rap sounded, trying to detach himself from the bottle, but he'd failed to take into account the inescapable fact that a sting has a tendency to swell, and to his dismay the bottle clung to him stubbornly. He waited a moment and then tried again, but with no success whatever—and all the time his mother was rapping on the panel or rattling the door knob. 'Frankie!' she said, losing patience with him. 'If you don't unlock that door, I'm going to summon your father! Really, I can't understand why you're behaving so strangely! At least you might be courteous enough to answer your own mother when she's addressing you!' "

Mamie let out a long, excited squeal. "Po' little boy!" she gasped. "Po' little boy, with that old bottle dangling on him that way!"

"It was a trying situation for me, too," said Mrs. Kent. "Naturally, I didn't want to give myself away, but I was dying to suggest a method of escape to Frankie. And so I stood there on the pile of trunks and twisted my feet nervously, not knowing what to do. The situation became even more nerve-racking when Mrs. Kent called her husband. He had a peppery temper, and Frankie was always afraid of him. When Mrs. Kent explained the situation, he shook the knob and said sternly, 'Come out of there, young man! Come out this instant!'

"At the sound of his father's voice, Frankie became even more frightened than he had been, if that's possible. He walked up and down in the room, tugging desperately at the bottle, but with no success. Then he had a thought, and he tried to stick the bottle inside his trousers; but that was manifestly impossible, and it was no real solution, anyway."

Mamie caught her breath sharply and made a quavering noise with her lips. "Oh, my good Lord!" she said. "Oh, my good Lord up in heaven!"

"The knob shook with greater violence now," continued Mrs. Kent, "and the lock gave a little under the pressure of old Mr. Kent's shoulder. 'You'd better answer me!' he shouted. 'If you're not out of there in two minutes, I'm coming in and get you!' "

"Answer your papa, boy!" said Mamie shrilly. "Better answer him quick, or he'll sho' do what he say!"

"At that instant Frankie stood completely still," continued Mrs. Kent, "a haunted, terrible look on his face. Then he turned and picked up the heavy window stick, holding the bottle against the side of the tub. "When I saw he was going to break the bottle, I couldn't stand it any more. 'No!' I whispered hoarsely. 'No! No! Don't break the bottle whatever you do! Get it off with soap and water! Soap and water, idiot!'

"I've never forgotten the expression on his face when he heard my voice from above but couldn't decide where it came from. 'I'm here at the knot hole,' I said as loud as I dared. 'It's me—Cordie! . . . Take it off with soap and water—the way you do a ring!'"

Mamie groaned and covered her face with her hands. "Do like little Cordie tell you to do!" she said in an anguished voice. "That's the onliest out you got now! But don't you break that bottle, boy! Don't do that, no matter what else you do!"

"Outside in the hall Frankie's father had worked himself up into a fine rage," continued Miss Cordie. "He pounded on the panels of the door, or pressed against the door with his shoulders. The screws which held the lock in place were beginning to give way, and slivers of wood fell to the floor. 'Soap and water!' I said desperately. 'Hurry! Hurry! Oh, please hurry!'

"Then Frankie poured water into the bowl with the morning glories on it and tried the soapsuds method, and sure enough, after the third or fourth tug, the bottle came away easily. He got his clothes arranged and the bottle back in its place just a second or so before the lock gave way and the assembled Kent and Overton families crowded into the bathroom. Seeing that his son was completely safe, Mr. Kent's manner changed a little. 'Why didn't you answer your mother and myself?' he asked sternly. 'We were worried to death about you.'"

Mamie bent forward and clutched her knees. Her muffled scream contained both horror and relief. "My! My!" she said. "Oh, my merciful Father up on high! I was scared up to the last minute that they was gwiner catch him."

"Frankie's mother came over to her son, turning him so that he faced the light squarely," said Miss Cordie. "She examined him with love, curiosity and considerable suspicion; then, speaking directly to her husband, she said: 'I'm afraid boys are beyond my comprehension. From the scared look in Frankie's eyes, and the way he's trembling, you'd almost think something had *happened* to him.

"It was the last straw for Frank, after all the indignities he'd suffered that day, and I knew exactly how he felt. He pulled away from his elders, his mouth twisted with the astonished bitterness you see so often in children; then, suddenly, he threw himself on the floor and cried out his rage and humiliation, kicking at the bathtub with his heels. My own mother stared at him in complete bewilderment. 'You're going to have trouble raising that boy, Amelia,' she said. 'I believe he's inherited the Gowers' nervous temperament—going into a tantrum like that over an innocent, well-meant rebuke.' "

Mrs. Kent shook her head and smiled, as if repudiating the world's lack of perception. "And now for the little moral I promised, if you can really call it that," she went on. "At any rate, Frankie's conduct that afternoon, and his predicament afterwards, which was so largely a result of that conduct, made the problems which confront boys much easier for me to understand. Girls have their peculiar problems too, and nobody knew it better than I, since I was always a thoughtful, unhappy child; but the difference between the basic problems of boys and the basic problems of girls is the difference between the active and the passive voice, if you still remember your grammar, and that's an enormous difference indeed."

Mamie, who rarely listened to the philosophical asides of her mistress, rocked back and forth in the living-room, her chair creaking in three different places, on three different notes.

Mrs. Kent said: "Nobody wants to grow up, really, and the way we achieve it, it seems to me, is by deluding ourselves, little by little, through dressing up in mother's clothes, or making houses out of blocks. Then we find to our surprise that we've left childhood behind us somehow, and our play has become reality indeed. I watched my own children growing up, and I noticed that adolescent girls are rarely taken in by the roles they're expected to play—that among themselves they make no effort at all to maintain the illusions. It's quite different with boys. They observe their standards with great seriousness, and there must be no letdown whatever, not even with their own kind. So Frank's attitudes at eight were merely the usual practice poses. They bore the same relationship to his character as it finally developed that the comic-strip narrative bears to real life. I could elaborate on all this, and would dearly love to do so, but Mamie's already bored, and if I don't stop, I'm afraid she'll find me too tiresome even to *eavesdrop* on in future."

Mamie paused in her rocking and said, "But that don't explain why you wanted to marry Dr. Frank, and no other gentleman, now do it? How come that happen, Miss Cordie?"

Mrs. Kent laughed softly in remembrance, her ear pendants swinging merrily, her bracelets clashing against one another and making a small, tinkling sound. "Oh, that!" she said. "That's the simplest part of all to understand! You recall what he did when he could neither pour nor dab on the borax water, don't you? Well, that was the instinctive reaction of the romantic to frustration, and I must have realized, even at six, that he'd always try to solve his difficulties that way. So when I came out of the pantry, and stopped in front of the hall mirror to straighten my hair ribbon and to compose my face into its customary expression of vapid innocence, I said to myself, 'Frankie Kent needs somebody practical like me to keep him out of trouble, and when I grow up, I'm going to marry him.' "

For a time she rocked back and forth in silence, and then, waving her hand, she called out gaily: "Frank! Frank! It's all over! You can come back now and sit with us!"

Dr. Kent returned slowly from the chrysanthemum bed. He sat on the top step and filled his pipe. "If you must tell these intimate, family secrets," he said, "a fiction writer like Clark McBride is the ideal person to confess to. At least you can be sure who he's going to tell afterwards, and that's merely the American reading public." He raised his eyes and glanced reproachfully at his wife, but seeing her gentle, amused face, he laughed in spite of himself and we all laughed with him.

Mamie got up regretfully. "I better be getting along towards home. I pledged myself to come to four o'clock prayer meeting, and I don't want to come trompin' in the church late."

Mrs. Kent picked up her fan and waved it lazily back and forth. "Ask your pastor to pray for cool weather, won't you, Mamie?" She rocked back and forth for a time, her white, silky hair lifting upward in the breeze from her fan. "I don't know *when* we've had such a hot spell," she said absently, "or one that's lasted so long, either."

1943

DIRTY EMMA

*I*N WILLISTON, when I was a boy, there was a woman known to everyone by the cruel but accurate name of Dirty Emma. The expression had become so familiar with usage that even the Friendly Society—a group of ladies banded together for the fostering of kindness—were conscious of no lack of charity when they openly used it in addressing her. Often she was seen on the streets of the town, moving timidly from place to place or resting in the shade of a china-berry tree, her matted hair hanging about her eyes in confusion, her skirts fouled with burrs and caked with mud at the hems.

All agreed that she was an eyesore and a public disgrace. It was even said that she stole at times, but if she did, nobody bothered to bring her to justice, for her station in life was so low, her appearance so wild and degraded, that others felt they could not in fairness demand the same standards of her that they demanded of themselves. Thus it was that the position of Dirty Emma lay somewhere between that of the Negro, who was so innocent in outlook, so ignorant of the subtleties of good and evil, and that of the barnyard animal, to whom the laws of decency and morality did not, in the eyes of God, apply at all.

The Friendly Society often discussed her as a problem, knowing as they did that she lived miserably with a man who beat her. Mrs. Oscar Blake, perhaps, would say: "I saw Dirty Emma at the meat market this morning. She didn't speak a word—just stood there at the counter begging with her eyes and looking more than ever like an old wet sheep until the butcher filled her apron with beef bones. Her face was a sight this time. Her lip was split and one eye was so puffed out that she couldn't open it at all. After she'd gone, the butcher said with a wink, 'It looks like Tom Gunnerson's on the warpath again, now don't it?' "

Most of the ladies sighed and folded their hands, but old Mrs. Cobb said indignantly: "There's a law against wife beating in this State. People ought to see that it's enforced, if you ask me."

"The butcher told me a funny thing later on," continued Mrs. Blake. "He said that after Tom had treated her real cruel, Dirty Emma always came down the next morning to beg beef bones for soup, so that she'd have something hot and nourishing for him to sober up on. He said it looked like the worse Tom treated her, the more she did to please him."

"She's not really married to Tom Gunnerson," said Mrs. Opal Nesmith in an uncertain voice, as if knowing in advance that she would not be believed. "She lives with him in open concubinage, or so I've always been told."

The ladies pondered this familiar bit of information once more, and then they once more rejected it as absurd, persisting stubbornly in their belief that Emma's union was both regular and blessed, since, in the cynical and disenchanted minds of the pure, the distasteful and the legality of the marriage bed are so closely associated.

One clear, crisp morning in late winter, my mother decided to transplant her hyacinth bulbs from their old place near the porch to a new bed against the fence, where they could be seen to better advantage. She was proud of her hyacinths, and each spring when they were in bloom they were admired by people passing our house. In theory, at least, I was helping with the transfer; actually, all I did was to sit on the steps and watch as she dug up the bulbs and separated them, according to the color of their flowers, into small, neat piles.

Later, I looked up and saw Dirty Emma approaching our gate. That day she was wearing a pair of Tom's old shoes which were run over at the heels and which she had laced up raggedly with common twine. Her skin had that yellowish, dense look of ditch water seen in sunlight; her nails were broken and caked with grime, and even her lips and her eyeballs seemed soiled.

My mother, following my glance, turned her neck and smiled absently, as if Emma were her oldest and dearest friend, and they had parted only an hour before. Emma nodded, blinked her eyes and spoke timidly: "I seen them blossoming last year when I passed by, and I said to myself at the time that I never seen flowers set out prettier."

My mother rocked back and forth on her heels and laughed with pleasure. "Oh, did you really think so?" she asked gaily. She went on to explain that the hyacinth was her favorite flower. She didn't know why, but perhaps the old story of Apollo and Hyacinthus had a great deal to do with it. "Do you remember it from your own childhood?" she asked.

"No," said Emma thoughtfully. "No, ma'am, I never heard that story."

My mother had been a school teacher before her marriage and she had never lost her desire to impart knowledge. She put down her trowel, sat beside me on the steps, and began softly: "Long ago in ancient Greece the god Apollo worshiped a boy named Hyacinthus, the most beautiful mortal on the whole face of the earth. Now, things of this sort never run smoothly, as we all know, and so it happened that Zephyrus, who was really the West Wind, also admired Hyacinthus, and when he realized the boy preferred Apollo to himself, he planned to take his revenge.

"One day as Apollo and his friend played quoits together, Zephyrus seized the discus which Apollo had thrown and hurled it back in such a fashion that it struck Hyacinthus on the forehead. It was plain to all that the boy was going to die, and when Apollo realized it too, his grief was terrible to see. He wept, tore his robes and cried out: 'Thou diest, Hyacinthus, robbed of thy youth by me! Would I could die for thee!'

"But Apollo could not do this, for he was a god, and the gods are immortal; and so he decreed that a flower as lovely as Hyacinthus himself should spring up from the blood of his dying friend, and it happened that way. Then the great god Apollo bent in humility before the perfection of the flower and marked it with the words, 'Ai! Ai!' which mean 'Alas! Alas!' in our language. . . . And so it happens each spring when hyacinths bloom once more that the grief of Apollo and the beauty of Hyacinthus are renewed and made plain for all to see."

There was a silence, and then Emma spoke timidly: "What happened to the West Wind, Mrs. Gavin? Did he get punished for what he done to that poor boy?"

My mother laughed a little and went back to her bulbs. "Why, really, I don't know," she said. "It's a point I never considered before."

Emma put her elbows on the fence and glanced sideways at the bulbs; then, shaking back her limp, oily hair, she sighed and turned away. Somehow, my mother knew the thought in her mind, for she said quickly: "You'd like one of the bulbs for your own, wouldn't you?" Emma could not bring herself to answer; she could only hang her head, as if abashed at such presumptuousness on her part, and shuffle her feet in the dirt.

"Which color would you prefer?" continued my mother in a casual voice. "I have several shades of both pink and purple; then there's a sort of bluish color, and one that's pure white."

Emma raised her head desperately and looked into my mother's eyes for the first time that morning. She said: "I'd like one of the white ones, if you're sure it ain't putting you out none."

My mother went to the fence and placed a plump, handsome bulb in Emma's hand. She explained in detail how to plant and care for the flower. She said that if Emma put it in a pot and kept it indoors, it would bloom long before spring came. Emma said over and over, as if she were not really listening: "Yes, ma'am; yes, ma'am, I sure will"; and when the instructions were finished, she turned and walked rapidly away, her greasy old skirt pulling up sharply in front and trailing in the dirt behind.

She held the bulb lightly in her hand, as if it were alive, and as she walked past the log pond, in the direction of her house, she spoke aloud in a thin, delighted voice: "Mrs. Gavin didn't have to tell me how to plant and care for you," she said, "because I already know. You wait and see. You won't have no complaints at the treatment you get."

When she reached the sagging, unpainted old shack where she lived—a place which had long since been abandoned by others as unfit for habitation—she paused outside and listened;

then, hearing no sound from within, she went below the slabpit for leaf mold and moss. She selected, sighed, and discarded, her lips puffed out thoughtfully, her eyes fixed and intense, but after she had collected what she needed for her purpose, she came back to her house, punched drainage holes in a tomato can, and prepared a bed for her flower.

She had hardly finished before she heard Tom shuffling up the path. He was a man in his early thirties, perhaps ten years younger than Emma herself. He was rapidly growing bald, but as if to counterbalance the loss, reddish hair grew in thick, tight coils on his forearms and erupted shaggily above the throat line of his undershirt. He was powerful physically and completely mature. Mentally, he was perhaps average. Emotionally, he was a child of six, with all the petulant and ingenuous cruelty of the boy and with none of his defenselessness.

Emma peered anxiously through the shack's one window, but she saw at once that he was in a good humor. He would not even mind if his dinner was a little late, for he had a new funny paper under his arm, and as she watched him, she saw him sit down on the steps and begin to spell it out. His literary ideal was the blonde member of the Katzenjammer team, and in a moment Emma heard him laughing loudly and slapping his leg at the irresistible antics of his favorite. Perhaps those boys who never grow up do, on occasion, become Peter Pan, as we have been taught; more often they become Tom Gunnerson.

Emma turned and surveyed the mean, bare shack before her. It consisted of one room and a lean-to, which served both as a kitchen and as a woodshed. It was almost bare of furniture and its walls were plastered with newspapers and patched with bits of tin. It was incredibly dirty. Suddenly she felt depressed and a little apologetic. She picked up the can which contained her bulb and put it behind the stove, where it would be both dark and warm. "I don't know why I took so much trouble to plant you right," she said, "because I'll bet you haven't got any idea whatsoever of coming up."

Nevertheless, the knowledge of the bulb lying there so close to her, gave her a sense of excitement, and she examined it once more, to see that everything was in order, before she finally called Tom to his dinner. Each morning afterwards, as soon as Tom was safely out of the shack, she went to examine her plant, not really believing that it would grow. "I want you to know I won't hold it against you, even if you don't come up," she said craftily, "so just suit yourself about it. Come up, if you want to; stay down there, if you want to. But don't come up to do me a favor, no matter what you do."

Then one day she saw the first spearhead of green thrusting upward from the dirt. At once she moved the can to a shelf beside the window, examining it with a sense of incredulous delight. She laughed, nodded her head and said: "Do you know what you look like? You look like the little green tongue of a kitten sticking out. You really do, for a fact." All at once her excitement left her. She sat down on the bed and brushed her hair out of her eyes. "But you won't bloom," she said cautiously. "I know that just as well as you do."

The plant grew steadily, and soon a tight bud formed in the center of its protective sheath of green. When she saw the hard, brilliant bud for the first time, Emma stood still in the center of the shack and spoke with a carelessness she did not feel: "All right! Maybe you really are going to blossom, but that's nothing to brag about. Anyway, I bet you won't turn out white when your time comes." She went to the door and paused, then, speaking over her shoulder, she continued indifferently, as if to mislead the jealous and evil spirits who envied her: "But if you're not white, after all, it won't matter to me in the least. To tell you the truth, I wish now I'd asked Mrs. Gavin for a purple one."

Then even this last anxiety was dissipated and the bud opened into a hyacinth as perfectly formed and as white as any she had ever seen. The miracle, or so she took it to be, left her shaken and almost at the point of tears. "Well!" she said. "Well, I never!" She raised her arms in the air and shook her head with amazement, for she felt that she had been through some revealing and shattering experience, one whose implications she did not perfectly understand; then she went outside and sat on a box in the sunlight, throwing her apron over her head.

A few nights later, having money in his pockets once more, Tom went to town and got drunk. He came home late, and Emma heard him muttering to himself as he stumbled up the path. The hyacinth was in full bloom now, and Emma glanced at it nervously, wondering if it would not be wiser to put it some place beyond the reach of his whirling, drunken fists; but she waited too long, and as she sat there in indecision, the door opened and Tom stood before her.

He was in one of his petulant moods, and when she saw his face, she approached fawningly and stroked his arm. "Come sit here by the stove," she said. "I saved your supper. I'll warm it up in no time." She hurried about the house, as if to divert with movement the direction of his thoughts, but Tom saw through her intention and sighed, following her with his eyes.

"What kind of life is this for a man?" he asked in a despairing voice. He staggered and steadied himself against the door. "Every hand is against me and always has been. Even when I was a boy at home the others got everything and I got what was left." The wrongs he had suffered itched eternally in his mind, unforgiven and forever unresolved, and his face twisted with bitterness as he remembered anew the old and unavenged insults he had endured. He sat solidly on the bed and unbuttoned his jumper coat, allowing the thick, reddish hair of his throat to boil upward stiffly like crimped and raveling rope.

"There's good blood in my veins," he continued; "blood as good as any in this here land. And what have I got to show for it? I got nothing to show for it but poverty and injustice and a filthy slut no other man would look at twice."

Emma spoke patiently: "Let me take your shoes off for you. You can't sleep all night with shoes on. It might stop the movement of your blood."

He sat tractably as she approached him, but when she was within range of his arm, he bent forward and hit her with his heavy, opened palm. "Clean this place out!" he shouted. "It's dirtier than a pigeon run!" Blood flowed from her nose and from the old split in her lip which never seemed to heal completely. She backed away from him and stood braced against the wall, her shoulders sagging, her eyes lowered abjectly.

The people of Williston predicted that some day Tom Gunnerson would kill old Emma and that he would hang for it. In this they underestimated both the prudence of his temperament and the high refinement of his skill. There was not the slightest chance that he would kill her, for he had perfected his technique over a long period, and he was as familiar with the strains her body could stand as an engineer is with the stresses of the common arch.

He beat her now with a formal and discreet fury. After he had finished, he walked to the kitchen and washed his hands and face, thinking once more of injustice and how cruelly the world had used him; then, raising his eyes, he caught sight of the hyacinth on its shelf. He went to it at once and held the pot balanced in his hands; and with a disavowing gesture, as if some tiny pocket of fretfulness remained unexpressed within him, he twisted off the flowering spike of the plant and threw it to the floor, obliterating it slowly with his sliding, brutal shoe.

Emma, from her place beside the stove, where she had fallen, drew in her breath like some tormented old animal. "You didn't have no call to do that," she said miserably. She bent forward from her haunches and trembled. "No," she said. "No, you didn't."

"Keep this place clean, like I told you to a thousand times!" said Tom. "It's dirtier than a hog wallow!"

Later, he stretched out on the bed, yawned, scratched himself, and went to sleep at once. When she heard his heavy breathing, Emma pulled a chair to the bedside and stared at him with a most minute and flattering care, as if she had never seen him before. Her mind filled slowly with sadness and with a sense of inexpressible loss. It seemed to her that the finished span of her sorry and ridiculous life opened outward before her, with finality beyond her power either to affirm or reject. It was at this instant that the thought first came into her consciousness, and she looked about her wildly, and shuddered, shaking her head in helpless denial of what she knew to be inescapable. "No!" she said, "Oh, no!"

Then, not quite believing in the actuality of her intention, she locked the kitchen door and shuttered the window so that it could not be opened from the inside. When she had completed these tasks, she lifted the lamp and held it high above her head, examining the walls, the floor, and even the ceiling of the shack with a thoughtful, impersonal glance. Later, moving backward a little, she pursed out her lips, sucked them in, and threw the lamp suddenly against the wall. She waited long enough to see the kerosene explode, catch fire and spread; then, smiling to herself, as if she knew a most charming secret, one which she could never be coaxed into telling, she locked the door and stood outside in the dark, hearing the flames as they crackled, sighed and moved steadily across the walls.

She waited beside the door for a time, a still, transfixed look on her face, before she turned and moved off down the path. Later, after the roof had fallen in, she went to the log pond and sat on a cypress stump. It was there that others found her. When she saw the crowd, she showed them her beaten face and touched her nose lightly with the back of her hand. "Tom ran me out of the house and locked the door," she said. She shivered, as if suddenly cold, and covered her ears, swaying back and forth in the glare from the burning cabin. "He was drunk at the time. I guess he upset the lamp."

Nobody doubted her story; nobody questioned her further.

She disappeared from town a few days later, and afterwards she was rarely seen in Williston. It was said that she wandered about the countryside alone, begging her food from others and sleeping wherever she could find shelter. Once she stopped at our back gate and stared at the house. My mother called to her, but she hurried to the corner, hesitated, and looked back over her shoulder. Then my mother put food in a paper bag and left it on the fence post, and after a time Emma approached and took it, like an alarmed and mistrustful old animal.

Occasionally a farmer coming to town reported having seen

her. "There she was sitting alongside the road," he would usually
say. "She had her hands clapped over her ears, like there was
something she didn't want to hear, and when she seen me coming
toward her, she jumped up and loped away across the fields."

Many months later, a half-grown Negro boy came to our
house with a message for my mother. It seemed that while he and
his sister were picking berries near Sour Water Swamp, they had
found Dirty Emma lying sick and helpless in a clump of bushes.
Not knowing what else to do with her, they had borrowed a
wheelbarrow and had taken her to the Negro quarters, where
she now was. "She won't let nobody fetch the doctor for her,"
he said, "leastways, not till she see you first. She keep saying,
'Go get me Mrs. Gavin. She the one I want to talk to.' She
mighty sick, and I think, please, ma'am, you better hurry. Ever'-
body say she can't last the day out." My mother asked me to
come with her and we went at once.

Emma was lying on a pallet in the long shade of a cedar tree.
The quarters themselves, usually so noisy, so bursting with excitement and sound, seemed completely deserted. Since this was
an affair which concerned white people, and the Negroes were
determined to have nothing to do with it, every shade was drawn,
every door and window closed. There was not even a child or a
dog outside, and after the boy had finished his errand, he, too,
disappeared into one of the silent houses.

We approached the pallet and stood there, listening for a time
to her harsh, labored breathing. We were startled, despite ourselves, at the changes in her appearance. Her eyes were rolled
backward in their purple sockets; her body was blotched and
dried out, as if mummified imperfectly in its own dirt, and her
hair, which had been cropped close to her skull, was matted
with grass seeds and bits of straw.

My mother spoke after a moment, and Emma, at the sound of
her voice, rolled her head from side to side. "I got a black sin
on my soul," she said. "I want to tell it before I die." Then, lying
back on the pallet, her face burning with fever, her voice com-

ing weakly, as if each word that she used exhausted her more, she told us the things which I have already told you.

When she had finished, she closed her eyes and sighed, plucking feebly at her dress. "That night of the fire, I knew the very second Tom woke and jumped up," she added, "because I heard his shoes hit the planking. The next thing, he was at the door shaking the knob. 'Emma!' he kept saying. 'Emma, let me out of here!' He threw his shoulders against the door, but he couldn't break it down, so he went to the kitchen and tried the door there. He couldn't get out that way either, and I heard him stumbling about and calling to me. 'Emma!' he kept saying. 'Emma! Emma!' But I wouldn't let him out, no matter how loud he called."

"So he came back to the bedroom and tried to open the shutter. When he couldn't move it, and knew for certain what was going to happen to him, he put his mouth to the little crack between the window and the wall. And you want to know what he done then, Mrs. Gavin? . . . He screamed. 'Emma! Emma! Emma!' he kept saying over and over. That was when I covered my ears and walked down the path, but I couldn't shut out that sound, even with my ears covered up."

I went to the porch for a basin of water, and when I returned, my mother bathed Emma's hands and face with a wet cloth. "I think God has more perception than we give Him credit for," she said. "He understands why you did it. Try not to worry so. I think He will forgive you."

There was a silence, and then I spoke for the first time. "Everybody knew how mean Tom Gunnerson was, and I don't believe a soul in town would blame you for killing him, not after the brutal way he treated you."

Emma raised her hands weakly and attempted to sit up, bewildered that her motive had been so greatly misunderstood. Then, with many pauses, as if she sought from her meager vocabulary the precise words for her purpose, this dying old woman made clear to my mother and myself both her individual system of esthetics, and the peculiar standard of values by which she governed her life.

"If the people of Williston think they made up the name Dirty Emma, they're way off the track," she said, "because I been called that all my life. Now, Mamma used to wash me as much and put fresh clothes on me as often as she did the others at home. She even put my hair up in curlers a time or two, but when the papers were off, my hair wasn't crimped and pretty the way you'd expect it to be. It just hung down limp and dirty-looking, like it is now. You could wash me with hot water and soap until you were tired out, and still I looked dirty. My stockings fell down when everybody else's stayed up, and I could put on a clean dress, sit in the front room doing nothing, and still look dirty. So everybody called me Dirty Emma from the beginning, no matter whether I was really clean at the time or not. At first I used to cry and hide under the house when they said it, but afterwards, all I could think of was, 'Well, it's the truth. That's what I am, for a fact.' So finally I gave up and quit trying."

She was growing feebler, but she talked on and on, reciting for others the simple alphabet of her humility. She explained that she had neither felt resentment against Tom for the manner in which he had treated her, nor blamed him afterwards in her heart. She had accepted these things as her due, she said, since she was so clearly what she was, and could understand how greatly she had provoked him. But the hyacinth had been something else entirely, for it had not been dirty in the least. On the contrary, she had considered it as clean and pretty as anything in this world can ever expect to be. It was fully open at the time of its destruction, she explained, and it was so fragrant that you could smell it plainly as you came up the path.

"He didn't have no call to harm a thing like that, now did he, Mrs. Gavin?" she asked anxiously. "Twisting off its neck the way he did, and then tromping it to pieces with his foot. That was a cruel thing to do, and I said so at the time; and as I lay there by the stove, I kept thinking to myself, 'You ought to be punished for doing such a hateful thing. You ought to be taught a real good lesson, and that's a fact!'" She turned her head away, overcome by the things she remembered, and cried harshly against her pillow.

She had reached the end of her story. She had made the confession which she felt that she must make, and now she was no longer interested in us. There was a long silence, and then, moving one infirm and feverish arm across the pallet, she said, with no interest at all in her voice, "You can send for the doctor now, if that will comfort your mind any." My mother said, "Emma, is there anything you want? Anything special that I can do for you?" Emma said no, there was not, or if there was, she could not remember it at the moment.

She died that same afternoon, and they buried her later in the company graveyard beside the railroad tracks. Afterwards, I thought of her a great deal, and for a time I even dreamed of her now and then. I knew that my mother thought of her too, but neither of us mentioned her name for a long time; and then, months later, when we sat in the living room before the open fire one night, my mother turned to me and said softly, as if unconsciously speaking her thoughts out loud: "You know, Jamie, the classic Greeks would have understood old Emma from the beginning."

My father laughed, put down his newspaper and said: "Make for the hills, children! Your unfortunate mother is on the *Greeks* again!"

My mother laughed a little too. She was sewing on school dresses for my sisters, and for a time she worked in silence; then, biting off a thread, she spoke quietly to my sisters and myself: "There are two kinds of crimes against humanity, children, and the Greeks, who saw things so much more clearly than we do, knew this well. First, there was the obvious crime, the crime which even the dullest understood and knew how to punish."

She held the dress closer to the light, examined the buttonhole she had just completed, and then said: "The other kind of crime was more difficult to detect, and often it was so cunning in its seeming innocence that even the gods, themselves, were misled. That was why they created three terrifying old women, and assigned to them the task of rooting out and punishing these other crimes. They called these old women The Furies, and that was an appropriate name indeed, for they were without mercy in fulfilling their mission."

She searched in her sewing-box for her strawberry-shaped emery bag, and when she had found it, she continued: "When I think of Emma now, I see her with the lamp held above her head, at the instant she moved back a step and hurled it against the wall. I see her in this pose because I've come to think of her as one of The Furies themselves, a creature dedicated to the avengeance of those subtle crimes against mankind which pass unnoticed—those most terrible crimes of all, since men, as individuals, are so often unaware that they have been wronged."

She got up and put away her sewing; then, bending above my father, she laughed softly, kissed his forehead and said: "And now I think I shall go to bed, if my handsome but illiterate lord will accompany me."

1944

SEND IN YOUR ANSWER

$\mathcal{A}$ GONG with a plump, muffled sound struck four times on four separate notes, and "Heart Throbs of Our Day" was on the air. First, there were a few bars from Beethoven's Ninth Symphony to set the mood, to indicate to the frivolous that this was a program of earnestness and dignity; then, against the background of the receding music, a vibrant tenor voice said: "And now for Mr. Allen Underwood Paul, the well-known novelist, lecturer and radio personality, and his famous program, 'Heart Throbs of Our Day.'" He paused, and the theme, which had almost sunk to nothingness, flared up and died away once more.

"Yes," continued the tenor, "the makers of Minnits, the celebrated remedy compounded to cure headaches and the nausea which so often accompanies a headache, take pleasure at this time in presenting 'Heart Throbs of Our Day.' In a moment Allen Underwood Paul will speak to you personally, but first an important word from our special announcer, John Locksmith, regarding Minnits."

Instantly, a rich baritone voice with a faint hiss in it, said: "Friends, do you suffer from headaches and the nausea which so often accompanies a headache? Of course you do. We all do at times. But to you, the countless victims of a nagging, exhausting headache, we offer a message of hope. Why not go to your druggist at once and ask for Minnits by name? Say, 'I want Minnits! Minnits, please!'" He continued rapidly, pointing out that Minnits were compounded of rare ingredients, found hitherto in only the most expensive prescriptions. It was senseless to endure a headache when Minnits were easily obtainable, at all drug stores, in three sizes: the ten cent size, the twenty-five cent size, and the large, economical family size which sold for one dollar.

He finished his plea with a recorded testimonial in the form of a drama:

CHILD: "Mummy, why don't you play with me anymore, like Shirley's Mummy plays with her? Why do you lie in a dark room with a wet towel around your head?"

MOTHER: "Mummy has a headache and the nausea which so often accompanies a headache, dear. Please go outside and play by yourself."

CHILD: "I think you should take Minnits, Mummy, like everybody else does; so I went to the corner drug store and bought a large, economical, family size box of that remarkable headache remedy. Now, you can take Minnits and be' like Shirley's Mummy. Now, you can be bright and cheerful, and your old self again."

MOTHER: "Thank you, my darling. Of course I'll take Minnits, as you advise. It was stupid of me not to have had any in the house when my headache struck." (Sound effect of spoon against glass and of water being swallowed.)

CHILD: "Always remember, Minnits save the day!"

MOTHER (she is fully recovered—her old bright and cheerful self again): "Yes, indeed! Minnits save the day! I won't forget it again!"

The commercial lasted exactly two minutes. When it had ended, Allen Underwood Paul himself spoke. His voice was clipped, brisk and very nearly British: "Friends, in this great city of ours, little unnoticed dramas of little unnoticed people daily unfold themselves before our eyes: dramas which we, in the hurry and bustle of life, are prone to pass over or to ignore. Now, as you know, 'Heart Throbs of Our Day' presents a true story of real life each week at this time for the makers of Minnits. This week I have chosen a story which I hope our great audience of Minnits users everywhere will find as intriguing as I did."

He paused significantly and then said: "A few months ago, as some of you will remember, there was an item in the papers regarding a certain man—a man whom I shall refer to on this program as Mr. George F. This gentleman was found dead in his modest apartment under suspicious circumstances, but after a proper investigation had been made, it was determined that death was due to natural causes. When pressed for the exact cause of death, the doctor who performed the autopsy said, 'In my opinion, this man died of grief: in other words, of that romantic ailment our grandfathers called a broken heart.'

"This, in itself, was enough to intrigue anyone's interest, but there was another factor in the case, a factor of equal fascination. You see, the dead man left a most remarkable message in his room, one which adds piquancy to our drama, and at the proper time you will hear that message read by John Locksmith. Then, at the conclusion of our story, it will be our purpose to ask you, the Great American Jury of Public Opinion, to determine why Mr. George F. wrote that intriguing message, and what, if anything, he meant by it. So, in order to help you form your opinion, we have summoned four people who knew Mr. George F. at different stages of his career. Listen carefully to their testimony. You will find it rewarding. . . . First, let us hear from a witness who knew Mr. George F. during his formative years. Mr. Locksmith, the first witness, please!"

Mr. Locksmith's rich and hissing baritone rang out instantly: "Calling Mrs. Hattie M. Peterson! Will Mrs. Peterson take the stand?" Mrs. Peterson did so, and Mr. Paul began his examination without delay. "You are appearing on this broadcast as a special guest of the makers of Minnits, I understand. You reside in a City in the Midwest, do you not?"

"That's right. I live in Kansas City, Mis—"

Mr. Paul interrupted her. "Please! Please!" he cried out. You could not see him, but you knew from his voice that he had closed his eyes and had pressed his palms desperately against his temples. When he had recovered a little, he said with exasperated gravity: "No names of people, places or products are mentioned on this program, Madam! This is necessary through reasons of policy."

It was a rule, he said, which applied not only to Mrs. Peterson, but to the other witnesses as well. He asked if the matter were now clearly understood. The witnesses said that it was, and Mr.

SEND IN YOUR ANSWER   471

Paul replied patiently: "Thank you. Thank you for your co-
operation." Then, turning back to his first witness, he continued:
"I understand you grew up in the same town with Mr. George F.
Am I correct in my assumption?"

Mrs. Peterson said, "George lived right across the street from
us. I knew the whole family well. I saw them every day."

"Yes," said Mr. Paul. "Go on, please. Were they prosperous
people? Were they well off? Were they poor?"

"I guess they were comfortably well off. George's father was
Passenger Agent for one of the railroads and made a good salary.
His mother gave singing lessons, but she did that free, as a
service to others."

"Now, tell us something about the home life of George F.
Were his parents happy together? What things interested them?"

"They took a prominent part in civic matters, like beautifying
the parks and raising money for hospitals. George was their only
child. Yes, sir, I'd say they were happy as a family."

Later, under Mr. Paul's prompting, she described Mr. F.'s appearance as a boy, the house he lived in, his character and his
particular temperament. He had been called Socrates by his
schoolmates, she said. That was because he was interested in deep
subjects, and was such a reader. It was history and poetry and
psychology that he read—subjects of that kind. Then, too, the
whole family had a liking for music, and when Mr. F. senior
had a vacation, they all went away somewhere to hear concerts.
"I guess they all rode free," she said. "On railroad passes."

"From what you have said, Mrs. Peterson, I take it the boy
was quite bright in his studies. Correct me, please, if I'm in error."

"I don't know whether he was especially bright, or just
studious," said Mrs. Peterson. "Anyway, he did stand at the head
of his class. He graduated first when he finished high school, too,
and at the exercises he read an essay. It was entitled 'The Basic
Nobility of Man,' and everybody kept applauding and bringing
him back to bow. One of the papers published it the following
Sunday, and people predicted that George would go far, with
all that talent."

When she had finished, Mrs. Peterson stepped down from the

witness box, disappointed, on the whole, with this, her initial experience on a national hookup. She had promised Mrs. Rosenberg and Mrs. McGovern, her closest friends back home, to mention their names over the air at least once, so that all those millions of listeners would know they existed; she had even promised her husband to work in a plug or so for his stationery and notions store. And she had done none of these things, for Mr. Paul, she felt, had thwarted her at every turn.

She was walking away, back to her original seat, when John Locksmith's voice rang out gaily: "Now, now, Mrs. Peterson! Surely you did not think we'd let such a charming lady escape so easily, did you? Here's a special gift for you: a generous-size guest-package of Minnits for your personal use." There was a burst of controlled applause from the audience. When it had lasted the precise number of seconds called for in the script, Mr. Locksmith stopped it and summoned the second witness, a Mr. Otto Wall.

Mr. Paul went to work at once, and the facts he desired to establish came rapidly to light: Mr. Wall resided in a City in the Southern Section of the United States, he said. He had met George F. during the First World War. They had both been attached to a field hospital as ambulance drivers, at that time. He had got to know George F. quite well.

"Just a moment," said Mr. Paul. "Let's try to fill in some of the gaps between the time Mrs. Peterson left him reading his essay and the time you knew him in France. Can you help out?"

"Yes, I think I can. George often talked about himself. I know his mother died right after he finished high school, and that fall he entered—well, a Famous Eastern University. He got his sheepskin in due time, but before he could go back for his Master's degree, his father died too, and there wasn't any money left. That was in 1917, the year war was declared, so George enlisted. He said he picked a non-combat unit because he couldn't reconcile killing others with his moral principles. Then, too, he thought that aiding the helpless and saving the wounded was a practical way of serving humanity in general. He told me these things one night in the dark near a town called Pont-a-Mousson."

Mr. Wall coughed nervously and then continued his story. People might be surprised to hear it, he thought, but George F. had made a fine record as a driver. In fact, he had become something of a legend with the combat troops, for he seemed to have neither regard for his comfort nor fear for his personal safety. As an example, the drivers weren't expected to go up to the line, but George had done that over and over. He was a big, powerfully built man, and you could often see him, only a little behind the advancing troops themselves, searching through the wheatfields or the underbrush for the wounded. When he found them, he gave them first aid. If there were no stretcher-bearers to be had, he even carried them to safety on his back."

"How did the combat troops react to all this?"

"They thought he was a little cracked in the head, if you know what I mean. But everybody liked him, and everybody respected him, particularly after he was decorated for bravery before the regiment."

"You said a moment ago that George F. was considered a little —well, a little eccentric. Will you explain this a little?"

"He was always talking about justice, the common man and things like that. He maintained that the average man was naturally kind, unselfish and brave; that when he went wrong, it was only because his leaders had betrayed him or exploited his goodness. I guess his trouble was that he said aloud, before others, the things you expect to read in private, in a book."

"The men found this talk embarrassing, perhaps?"

"Some of them did. Most of them kidded him."

"Did he resent this joking at his expense?"

"He didn't even know they were making fun of him. George was always serious."

"I understand your association with George F. was continued in the United States, after the war was over. Will you tell us something of that period too?"

Mr. Wall explained that both he and George F. had gone to work for a Nationally Known Manufacturer of Plumbing Fix-tures: Mr. Wall as a salesman, George in the accounting department. George had promptly fallen in love with one of the stenographers, a Miss Bernice Oliver.

"Please!" said Mr. Paul in a voice which was at once humorous and despairing. "No names on this program! Just use the lady's initials."

There was a moment's pause and then Mr. Wall continued: "And so George fell in love with this Miss B.O. and she seemed to like him, too—"

"Refer to the young lady as Miss O., please," said Mr. Paul coldly. "I think that will suffice."

"Well, anyway, they got married," said Mr. Wall, "and set up housekeeping; and that's about all I know. I got another job and left town about that time. I never saw George F. again."

"You mentioned earlier on the program that George F. was decorated for bravery. What decoration was that?"

"It was the Congressional Medal of Honor."

"But no such decoration turned up among the dead man's effects," said Mr. Paul in a surprised voice. "Do you know what became of that medal?"

"No, I don't."

Mr. Wall accepted his gift package of Minnits and stepped down, feeling that he had made an excellent impression. It was something, after all, to be brought all the way to New York, with all expenses paid, to appear on a broadcast as famous as "Heart Throbs of Our Day." One never knew what might result from such an appearance. Perhaps he, himself, would be sought out by the national advertisers and offered a position on the air. That would be wonderful, for Mr. Paul was said to earn more than one hundred thousand dollars annually.

Mr. Paul said: "In a short time you will hear from our third witness, who has an intriguing story to tell, but first, a friendly suggestion from John Locksmith regarding Minnits." Mr. Locksmith picked up his cue smoothly: To people of discrimination, Minnits represent the last word in headache relief, he said. Millions of happy, satisfied users daily attested its worth. He believed, frankly, that everyone should be told about Minnits, the wonder-remedy: that quick-acting, easy-dissolving headache remedy endorsed by medical men everywhere. His plea ended with another transcribed drama, the scene this time being the busy office of a big executive.

BIG EXECUTIVE (answering phone): "Cartright speaking. No, I can't come, Chalmers. I have a headache, a terrible headache. Yes, I know we'll lose the Excelsior account as a result, but it can't be helped. That Acme crowd have licked us this time."

He hangs up the phone just as a hearty but respectful male voice speaks at his elbow: "Beg pardon, Mr. Cartright, but I couldn't help overhearing your conversation, so I took the liberty of bringing you a Minnits. I'm never without them, for you can never tell when a headache will strike. Now, if you'll take one with this sip of water I have here for you, you'll soon agree that there's nothing like Minnits for quick-acting headache relief."

The big executive takes his Minnits with a grunt, a gurgle and a satisfied smacking of the lips. He is well instantly. He picks up the phone and says: "Get me Chalmers right away! . . . Hello, Chalmers, this is Cartright again. I'll be right over. Hold that Excelsior crowd in line until I get there. I'll show them what a fight is, if that's what they're looking for! . . . My headache? Oh, that's a thing of the past. You see, I took a Minnits, and Minnits save the day!"

He chuckles happily, hangs up the receiver and turns to his secretary, a Miss Forsythe. He says: "There's a quick-thinking man in our shipping department, an intelligent man with gumption enough to carry Minnits. See that he gets a raise of ten dollars a week at once."

The commercial was over at last, but there still remained a presentation ceremony to be worked through, for it appeared that the four million readers of *Loudspeaker*, the Magazine of Radio, had voted "Heart Throbs of Our Day" the most distinguished program on the air. The editors of *Loudspeaker*, obeying the verdict of their subscribers, took this opportunity to award a statuette commemorating the poll. Mr. Paul accepted for the makers of Minnits, promising *Loudspeaker* and its readers that "Heart Throbs of Our Day" would maintain the same uncompromising standard of refinement, the same stern level of good taste, that it had in the past.

Afterwards, the third witness was summoned, identified, and seated for examination. She was a Miss Elaine Marlowe, an actress. She had appeared in many dramatic successes in the past, she said, but at the moment she was recouping her energies between engagements. Some years ago, when she had been nothing but a child, she had worked for the same firm which had employed Mr. George F., so naturally she had got to know him. Her voice was low and dramatic, with many unexpected pauses. Listening, you could almost hear a coach whispering somewhere behind the soundness of her technique: "Timing! Always timing! Never forget that timing is the essence of good acting, Miss Marlowe!"

"Now, tell us of the remarkable theft which took place in the office, and the part which George F. played in it later," said Mr. Paul.

"Well," said Miss Marlowe huskily, "this large sum of money disappeared, and it looked as if Mr. George F. had taken it. He said that he had not, although he knew who the real thief was. Later the police questioned him too, but even then he wouldn't name the true criminal."

"Did he give a reason for such an eccentric attitude?"

"He said the real culprit must confess of his own accord, for the sake of his moral integrity; but nobody believed him, naturally, and so he was arrested and stood trial."

"Now, tell me, Miss Marlowe, did anybody come forward later and confess to the crime?"

Miss Marlowe seemed startled out of her dramatic pattern of controlled emotion for a moment. She laughed suddenly and her voice went an octave higher. "Don't be silly!" she said.

She went on to describe the trial and the sentence afterwards. George F. had served his term. He had come out without bitterness, as if what had happened to him was of little importance. His wife had divorced him by that time, and later he found it difficult to start his life over again. She went on and on, squeezing from the story the last drop of hysteria, tearing from it the final tatter of melodrama. When she paused for breath, Mr. Paul interrupted quickly:

"Did you believe in the innocence of George F., Miss Marlowe?"

"Yes, I did. I believed him with my heart, despite the evidence against him. You see I—I loved him."

She had rehearsed this scene over and over with her publicity manager, and they both hoped that the big Broadway producers would be listening to her performance. It was a marvelous opportunity to prove her ability, to establish her once more in the theater. It was an unexpected audition which had miraculously fallen into her lap just when her fortune was lowest, and she meant to make the most of it.

"Yes—I loved him," she repeated simply. "He was like an angel from another world! He was so good—so fine! Oh, I loved him so, Mr. Paul!" Her voice was husky, low and torn with emotion.

"Please," said Mr. Paul. "Please try to control yourself."

"But I loved him! Oh, I loved him so greatly, Mr. Paul!"

"Tell us something of his life after he left prison," said Mr. Paul; "something of his daily routine."

Miss Marlowe ignored him. "A short time ago you asked what became of his medal," she continued, "so I'll tell you now what became of it! He sold it to buy bread. He was hungry and friendless and abandoned by a world which had once honored him, you see. Oh, the terrible irony of such a situation! He had to sell his medal in order to have the bare necessities of life for a few days more. It was to a wealthy collector of military decorations that he sold it—a man who could not comprehend its value as a symbol of courage, patriotism and devotion to duty; a man who wanted it only to complete his collection."

She was sobbing now, and after a moment Mr. Paul spoke with a spurious gentleness: "I'm afraid you misunderstand the purpose of our investigation. Our program this week is concerned with the history of Mr. George F., not with your emotions."

Miss Marlowe, knowing that she had only a short time left, let herself go in earnest. "Where are you now, Greatheart?" she cried out. "Can you hear my voice, there beyond the stars? Can you feel my love mounting upward toward you. Come back to one who loves you, George! Come back to me! Back—"

"Mr. Locksmith, please assist the witness to her seat," said Mr. Paul with cold exasperation. "I'm afraid she's too distraught to go on with her story."

"I loved him! I loved him!" said Miss Marlowe proudly. "I am not ashamed to confess my love." She was sobbing now without restraint, and she moved reluctantly from the microphone, her voice dying gradually away. The episode of the medal was something which neither she nor her manager had anticipated, but having turned up as it had, she felt that she had made the most of it. On the whole, she was pleased with the soundness of her performance, although there was one small thing which continued to bother her, for she kept wondering curiously which of her fellow-employees, remembered now so dimly, had really been Mr. George F. Mr. Locksmith assisted her to her chair and gave her a glass of water, but in the excitement he forgot to present her with her guest package of Minnits, which somehow seemed a pity.

The final witness, a man named Alfred Marks, took the stand quickly. He explained that there was a group of men who met in Central Park to play checkers, and that George F. had been one of them. That was about all he knew, he said, except that George had lived in a cheap apartment somewhere on the west side, near the river.

"Did he seem depressed when you first knew him, Mr. Marks?"

"No, sir. He was always cheerful. It was just like the other witnesses said: He talked a lot about the dignity and nobility of mankind—that sort of thing."

"How did he make a living—or do you know that?"

"He took orders for Christmas cards and calendars. He also made fancy boxes which he sold to decorators. He could have lived better than he did, I thought, but he was always giving away his money to people he considered less fortunate than himself."

Mr. Paul said: "Now, tell our great audience of Minnits users about the visit Mr. George F. paid you one night. Tell it as you told it to me last week, or as nearly as you can."

"Well, you see we got to know each other pretty well, and I went over to his place a few times, and so one night I asked him to my place. We played checkers awhile, and then I said there was a program I wanted to hear, and so I turned on the radio. It was one of those confession programs where people tell their troubles and ask what to do, if you know what I mean."

At that instant Mr. Paul broke one of his own inflexible rules, for he said quickly: "The program was 'Tell Me Your Troubles' —Dr. Christopher's program advertising Vimpep, the whole wheat breakfast cereal, wasn't it?"

"That's right. It was."

"And how did George F. react to that particular program?"

"He reacted in a peculiar way, Mr. Paul, if you know what I mean. At first he couldn't believe that real people would shame themselves that way. So I told him they were real people, all right, and asked where he'd been all these years, but I didn't know at the time he'd been in prison. So then he wanted to know why people were willing to do such a vulgar thing, and I said I guessed it made them feel important to have all that attention paid to them, or at least that's the way I always sized it up, if you know what I mean."

"Did he say anything else you remember?"

"He said the whole thing was cheap and degrading, so I told him he must be the only one who thought that, because the program won the *Loudspeaker* popular poll—that was last year, Mr. Paul—and people liked it well enough. Then he wanted to know what purpose it served. I started laughing about that time, but good-natured, like he was a little boy I was talking to, and I said I didn't know what purpose it served, but it seemed to be a very good way to sell a whole wheat cereal. After that, he didn't speak for a time—just sat there thinking, with a peculiar look in his face; but finally he said: 'My life has been based on a false premise. Will you accept my apologies?' Then, a little later, he got his hat and left."

Mr. Paul chuckled softly. When he spoke, you understood

why he had had no objection to having this particular program identified plainly: "So Mr. George F. considered 'Tell Me Your Troubles' cheap and degrading, did he? Well, we mustn't tell Dr. Christopher that. He's a sensitive man, you know." He waited until the laughter of the studio audience had abated somewhat and then he continued: "Now, tell us, Mr. Marks, when you next saw George F."

Mr. Marks said: "I didn't see him again until a month or two later; then one day I happened to be in the neighborhood where he lived and I stopped by his place, thinking maybe he was sick, since he didn't come to the park to play checkers anymore; but I couldn't get an answer to my ring, so the janitor opened the door for me—and there he was, lying dead on a studio couch. The note was on the table, where the police found it later, and I guess that's about all I know."

After the witness was rewarded and dismissed, Mr. Paul said: "As Minnits users everywhere know, it is customary at this point for me to sum up the evidence. Now, I think I'm correct in saying that Mr. George F. was a man of good moral character, despite the cloud of suspicion which hung over his head regarding the theft. He was trustworthy, sober, unselfish and kind. He possessed strong altruistic traits and unusual courage; but he was also impractical, idealistic and lacking in common sense: In other words, a good but unworldly man—one badly handicapped for success in the great struggle of life." Then, pausing a little, he added solemnly: "And now we come to the message found on the dead man's table: the message which I promised Mr. Locksmith would read to you.—Mr. Locksmith, read the message, please!"

The Beethoven theme came up softly, subordinating itself to Mr. Locksmith's voice. "Man never had anything except dignity," he read slowly, "and now he has lost even that." He repeated the message for the dull, pausing a little between words, and when he had finished, Mr. Paul took over again.

"Friends," he began briskly, "you have heard the story of Mr. George F., and the message he left behind him. Now, we ask you, the Great American Jury of Public Opinion, to send in your answer explaining what, if anything, he meant by his cryptic words. Address your answer to Allen Underwood Paul in care of this station, but be sure to accompany it with a box top from a package of Minnits—preferably one from the large, economical family-size package. For the best and most original answer, the makers of Minnits will award a five hundred dollar war bond. So send in your answer at once. Who knows? You may be the lucky winner." He paused a second or two and then said, "And now for a final friendly word from John Locksmith regarding Minnits."

Instantly there was the sound of trumpets blowing in triumph, and as they died away, John Locksmith's ripe, hissing voice said: "Friends, the sound you have just heard is the makers of Minnits blowing their own horn! And why shouldn't they? You see, we believe that when we have a product as wonderful as Minnits, the whole world should be told about it." He went on to discuss some of the great turning points in history. He said that one of them had occurred some years ago in a chemist's shop in Syracuse, New York, for it was on that day that the first quick-acting, easy-dissolving, handy-packaged Minnits was carefully compounded from its rare ingredients. There was another little transcribed drama, this time concerning a girl who was left out of everything, since she was so often troubled with nagging, uncomfortable headaches. But one day a stranger on a bus told her about Minnits, and she had bought a package at once. Her life since that day was full and complete, for she was now invited everywhere and her telephone rang all day long.

Time was running short and in a few seconds "Heart Throbs of Our Day" must go off the air. Mr. Locksmith, realizing this, spoke his last message rapidly: "Friends," he said, "have you, at this very moment, a headache and the nausea which so often accompanies a headache? If you have, go at once to your drug store and ask for Minnits by name. Say, 'I want Minnits! Give me Minnits, please, for Minnits save the day!'"

1944

SHE TALKS GOOD NOW

$\mathcal{M}$R. ROSEN, a methodical man, circled the path twice before he found a place which suited him: and that was a wide, flat stone beneath a willow tree, against a bank which sloped upward to the terraced walk above. Before him was a small brook; beyond that, an insipid lawn which had been a lake before the authorities filled it in. He seated himself, opened his book and leaned against the bank, his cigarettes, his spectacles-case and his other small belongings arranged beside him. Later, he was conscious of somebody standing on the path before him, of a soft, surprised voice saying: "Look-a-dere, little Ermie! A white gennelman done taken our seat! What you speck we gwiner do now, sweetheart?"

He turned and looked up, closing his book on his index finger. Before him stood a massive woman in a white, thickly starched uniform such as nurses wear; and against the texture and strength of this heavy material her confined flesh strained outward. Her black, broad face was good-natured and without guile, and as Mr. Rosen examined her, she laughed, stooped ponderously and said: "Honey, what make you hide behinst Lula's skirt? This white gennelman don't aim to bother nobody. He didn't have no way of knowin' that this was our regular restin' place, now did he? So come on out and show him how pretty you is."

A three-year-old girl, dressed in a pink, elaborate frock, peeped from behind her nurse's sheltering bulk. "This here is little Ermie," said Lula proudly. "Now, ain't she the sweetest thing in this big city of New York, New York?"

Mr. Rosen agreed, got up and began assembling his belongings.

"Oh, he fixin' to give us our seat back," said Lula with spurious surprise. "Ain't that a nice thing to do, honey? He say he druther sit on that little rock over there, 'cause that rock is sized right to fit him, but not near big enough for ole spread-out Lula." She laughed good-naturedly and raised her arms in the air, and instantly the little girl duplicated the laugh and the gesture with a fidelity which was startling. Lula bent down, as if she could no longer control her affection, and lifted the child in her arms. "My baby," she said. "She like to do ever'thing the way Lula do it."

Mr. Rosen, who had intended moving to a bench on the terrace above, found himself settling down, instead, on the small, flat stone which Lula had selected for him—drawn there, somehow, through the sheer force of the woman's genial, overwhelming personality. When he glanced up again, he saw that Lula had opened a week-end case and had taken from it a bathing cap and a pair of coveralls. She undressed the child and adjusted the coverall deftly. "Now, stand still a minute longer," she said, "till I get this ole rubber cap fixed right, 'cause I don't want your pretty curls to get muddy this time." When everything was arranged to her satisfaction, she held the child at arm's length and then said: "Now, go play in the branch and get as dirty as you want to."

The child ran eagerly toward the brook, and when she reached it, she knelt beside the sluggish, rather dirty water, clapping her hands and laughing with pleasure. "Ain't she sweet," said Lula, almost bursting with love and pride. "Ain't she the sweetest thing in this wide world."

"A most attractive child indeed. What is her name?"

"Her name's Ermintrude," said Lula; "but it was a crazy way to name my baby, so I call her Ermie."

Mr. Rosen filled his pipe, struck a match and nodded. The child was plainly not the Ermintrude type, and never would be.

"Maybe you heard tell of her mamma and papa," continued Lula, " 'cause they mighty well known people. Her papa's Professor Reginald Ainsworth, and he take an interest in the Greeks, and them ole dead people. Always goin' around diggin' up buried towns, and fumblin' with bones. He and his lady been out of town all summer long—in Mexico, some place; but they got to come home pretty soon now, and go back to teachin' at the

University. Yes, *suh,* the Professor's a smart man, and no two ways about that. They tell me he was ready to go to college when he was twelve years old, and done so; and what's more, he come out first in his classes. I heard once what they called him, but I completely forgot."

"A prodigy, perhaps," said Mr. Rosen.

"That's it," said Lula. "It's the word I heard him named; but ever'body say no matter how smart he is, he ain't nowhere near as smart as his good lady. She was a little English prodigy, and come from the city of London; but they managed to meet up, one way or another, and marry. Her name's Kate Hopperly Ainsworth, and she speak ever' language there is, or nerabout. She's wrote I don't know how many books, on one subject or another. She's a great one for grammar and always talking proper, too." Lula paused and stared thoughtfully across the lawn. "The Professor and his lady are sho finicky people," she said after a moment. "With them, ever'thing got to be cut and dried, and accordin' to the way the book say do it."

"I suppose you've been the child's nurse for a long time?"

"No, suh, I haven't. Fact is, I been Ermie's nurse only 'bout three weeks now. Befo' that time they had a nurse that was trained in college. You see, ever'body figgered since the Professor and his wife was *both* so smart, any child they had was bound to be as smart as they was, if not smarter. That's why they tried so hard to make something out of Ermie, I expect.

"Why, when the Professor got home from the University, he used to go in for an hour and talk deep things to that baby lyin' there in her little cradle; then, after he done left, his lady would come in and read to her in Greek and other languages too, I expect. I was cookin' for the Ainsworths at the time, but for some reason or other, wouldn't nobody let me come *near* Ermie; and then one day that ole college nurse taken sick, and they had to ride her to the hospital for treatment. The Professor and his wife was in Mexico long before that, so it left me and Ermie alone in the house, and that's when we really got together."

Ermie had taken off her shoes and stockings and was wading

in the brook, but hearing her name mentioned, she turned and waved. At once Lula shook her finger and said: "Quit spreadin' them stories about me! I didn't put no conjur on that nurse woman, and you better quit sayin' so, you ole mean Miss Ermintrude, you!" She bent forward from her bulging thighs and laughed gaily, rolling her eyes from side to side. The child laughed with her, bending forward as her nurse had done, rolling her eyes in an identical manner.

"And did the little girl become a prodigy, too, with all that training?" asked Mr. Rosen after a moment.

Lula glanced at the child and lowered her voice. "That's the trouble," she said gravely. "You put your finger on something that time. Oh, they tried hard enough to make her one, like I told you, but it wouldn't work out, 'cause my baby's got a mind of her own, and nobody can make her do nothin' she don't want to do. Fact is, the Professor and Mrs. Ainsworth got mighty scared toward the end, 'cause they thought there was something bad the matter with Ermie, and they taken her to all sorts of doctors. Trouble was, Ermie was almost three years old, and she never had spoke a word in her life. They was afraid there was somethin' bad the matter with her little brain. I was the onliest one that wasn't worried, and I knowed all along what ailed her, 'cause Ermie was just like me: You see, we ain't apt, and don't want to be!" Then, attracting the child's attention, she called out: "We ain't so bright, is we, sugar?"

Ermie shook her curls and danced up and down.

"We don't *need* to be bright," said Lula, exploding with mirth once more. "We're *pretty!*"

Then, lowering her voice, she continued: " 'Course Ermie didn't talk none! There wasn't nothin' she wanted to say! Ever'body used such big words around her, she didn't know what was goin' on half the time. Here I am, a grown woman forty years old, and iffen I couldn't understand that high English, how come a little girl can understand it?"

Mr. Rosen admitted that this was a point reasonably taken, and added: "And can the little girl talk now?"

"Talk!" said Lula in astonishment. " 'Course she can talk now!

Ermie can talk as good as anybody, when she wants to, but it's got to be somethin' she likes to hear herself sayin'.' "

At that moment there came a shrill, frightened sound from Ermintrude, and she ran forward blindly, her arms stretched before her. Without raising her eyes from the child, Lula said: "She's seen a policeman. It's the onliest thing she skeered of now. Somebody tole her a policeman will lock her up in jail and feed her bread and water." She bent forward, making soft, reassuring noises, and lifted the child to her lap. "Where he at?" she asked. "Where that policeman at?"

But the little girl only trembled and pressed herself closer to Lula's breast. Lula shaded her eyes and squinted across the brook. A stout, somewhat dispirited policeman was walking at the far edge of the lawn, and when he reached the path that led to an ornamental bridge to the right, he paused, scratched himself thoughtfully and looked upward. "I see him!" said Lula. "I see him now!"

Then, stroking the child's curls, she added: "That policeman ain't aimin' to bother you, baby; but if he try to, I'll bust him down so quick he'll think a truck hit him, and furthermore wish it had!" The little girl lifted her head and stared solemnly at her nurse, but she was still trembling a little. "It's exactly what I'll do," said Lula. "I'll bust him down one time right after another, and I'll step my foot on his ole fat, red neck." She pressed her lips to the child's forehead. "You ain't got nothing to be scared of, honey, because when I finish doin' all I said, I speck I'll hit him with a rock, too."

But the little girl was not entirely reassured, and Lula continued soothingly: "A little later on, I'll hold him down and you can tromple him till he so scared he don't know *what* to do. And pretty soon, when you trompled him as much as he can stand, he'll begin to cry and take on. 'Mamma! Mamma!' he keep sayin'. 'Come here quick and pull Miss Ermintrude offen me!' "

Suddenly the child laughed and scrambled from her nurse's lap. She stuck out her jaw and strode up and down, muttering to herself and making ferocious gestures; and when, a little later, she returned to the brook to play, she paused every few steps, examined the horizon for policemen, and stamped on the turf with her foot.

"That's right," said Lula. "That's the way to do it. Whup him good, so the next time he sees you in the park, he'll remember who you is, and run the other way." She closed her eyes and leaned against the bank. "My baby," she said dreamily. . . . "She's my lamb, that's what she is."

Mr. Rosen said, "When do you expect the family back?"

Lula sat up and pulled thoughtfully at her lip. "Well, sir," she began, "the Professor and lady are due next Monday morning, but that nurse woman don't get out of the hospital till Thursday of the same week." She lowered her voice, hesitated, and glanced about her cautiously. "I been thinking about that nurse," she said, "and how to keep her from takin' Ermie away from me; and so I cooked me up a scheme, and I expect it gwiner work out fine."

She paused to collect her thoughts and then said: "Now, I already told you how ever'body was worried to death because Ermie couldn't talk, and how they thought she might be deaf and dumb, or worse, even, than that. Remember? Well, just as soon as I got her to myself, I learned her to talk in no time at all. She talks good now, like I told you, but her mamma and papa don't know that; and so I learned her a little welcome speech to say as a surprise when they come in the door." Then, raising her voice an octave higher, she called out: "Honey, come here a minnit. This gennelman wants to hear your welcome speech."

The child came at once and stood in the path. She put her hands on her hips and spread her legs in a manner which Lula, herself, affected, pursing her lips and rolling her eyes from side to side. When she spoke, her voice was so like that of her nurse in timbre, accent and phrasing, that, if you turned your head away, you could not be sure which of the two was speaking.

"Welcome back, dear Mommer and Popper," she began. "I hopes you had a fine time down there where you been at, 'cause Lula and me sho had us one fine time here in the city. Now, ain't you all surprised to hear me talkin' good? Well, sir, it was Lula what learned me. She done it all by herself, as sho as God made little apples. So why don't you jus' let Lula be my nurse from now on, and keep learnin' me like she started out to do?"

Lula laughed with pride and slapped her thigh, and, after the child had returned to her play, she said: "When the Professor and his lady hear Ermie jabberin' away like that, I expect they gwiner fire that other nurse, like Ermie asked them to. They gwiner say, 'Lula, you take care of Ermie from now on, 'cause we know there's a heap mo' you could learn her, iffen you had mo' time to do it in.' That's exactly what they gwiner say, and I know it just as sho as I'm settin' on this rock."

She turned with an eager gesture, her starched uniform crackling and straining at its seams, confident that Mr. Rosen would confirm her hopes. But he would not look at her immediately, fixing his gaze, instead, on the ornamental bridge and the piled boulders beyond. He was mistrustful of her plan, and, frankly, he did not think it would work at all, for in his mind's eye, at that instant, there was a clear picture of both the scientific professor and his austere English wife—the lady who spoke so many languages, who laid such stress on the essentials of grammar, the purity of diction.

"Don't you think they gwiner be surprised?" asked Lula once more. "Don't you think they gwiner let me *keep* Ermie?"

Mr. Rosen glanced at his watch, buttoned his jacket and prepared to make his departure; then, realizing that an answer was expected from him, he sighed and said that at least Lula could be certain of one thing: The Professor and his wife were going to be *surprised*.

1944

I'M CRYING WITH RELIEF

JERRY GOLDFARB and her friend Grace Palumbo met occasionally in front of the building where they both worked and walked together to the subway. Often they prolonged their walk in order to stretch their legs, or merely to discuss what they'd done since they'd seen each other last.

One day they turned into the subway entrance at Twenty-third Street, and, still talking together, descended the stairs. They had opened their purses, and had each taken out a coin, when Jerry hesitated in front of the turnstiles, drew back and said, "Oh, no! No! I saw a terrible thing happen in this station not long ago, and I can't bear the thought of taking the train here again!"

"I'd just as soon walk to Twenty-eighth Street and take the subway there," said Grace. "I'm not tired."

"Let's walk up to Twenty-eighth, then," said Jerry. "I know you'll agree with me, Grace, that I'm not a nervous type girl usually, but what I saw was really something awful, or I wouldn't be acting the way I am."

They went up the stairs, and when they were near the top, Grace said: "Why don't you tell me about it while we walk along slow. Maybe telling about it will get it off your mind."

Jerry lifted her handbag and held it tightly against her thin, bony chest, inching herself sideways through the crowd at the head of the stairs. "It happened two-three weeks ago," she said, "during the time you were laid up with the grippe; and so I walked into this Twenty-third Street station, just like we did today, and went down to the platform. At first, I thought there wasn't anybody but me there, because a train had just pulled out, and then I spotted this shabby-looking little middle-aged man standing there by one of the pillars and talking to himself. You know, Grace: just standing there and mumbling, sort of; and passing his hands over his face every now and then, like he wanted to rub off his features. And so there was a strange look in this man's eyes, and when he turned and stared at me, it scared me a little, and I walked away and pretended to fix my hair in the mirror over the peanut vending machine. But I was watching him all the time in the mirror, and I breathed a sigh when two fellows and a girl came through the turnstiles, and over near where I was."

"I know that type fellow," said Grace. "You see people like him in the subway every day, only sometimes it's old women crying."

"Just about that time, an old lady came up to this fellow and asked him what the matter was, and if he was sick, could she be of help."

"That was wrong," said Grace promptly. "It's better not to notice people like that. Noticing them only brings on conversation, and don't really do any good."

"I guess you're right," said Jerry. "Anyway, this fellow didn't answer, and so the old lady said was it money he needed, and opened her purse, only he wouldn't take anything from her. I don't know why, but the old lady talking to him seemed to start him off worse than ever, and he began to tell a hard luck story in a loud voice, so everybody on the platform heard him. It was something to make your blood run cold, and believe me, Grace, the things that happened to that man shouldn't happen to anybody in the world."

"What did he say, Jerry? Do you remember any of it now?"

"I remember it, all right, but I don't want to repeat it. I don't want to even think about it again, it was so depressing."

"What happened then, Jerry?"

"Well, the station began to fill up with people, but this man went on talking, telling his troubles, and saying he didn't have anything to live for, and would be better off dead; and about that time a local was coming into the station, and all of a sudden this man ran to the far end of the platform, where there weren't so many people gathered; and so the old lady screamed and said, 'Look out! Stop him, somebody! He's going to jump!' "

Grace moved her hands nervously and twisted her gloves into a ball. "My goodness!" she said. "Did he do it?"

"Yes, he did. A man tried to catch hold of him, but he was too late; and so this man jumped in front of the train that was just coming into the station."

Grace covered her eyes and stopped at the edge of the sidewalk at Twenty-sixth Street. She sighed and crossed herself quickly.

"I told you it was terrible, didn't I?" said Jerry. "Well, it really was. You see, I was bending over the platform when he jumped, and I saw the train hit him and go over his body. I can still hear that bumping sound the train made, and the screeching of the brakes jammed on suddenly. Some of the passengers stayed to see them take him from under the train, but I couldn't bear that thought. I just ran up the steps and over to Lexington Avenue, and took a bus. I was trembling all the way home, and people kept looking at me."

"I don't blame you for not wanting to go into the Twenty-third Street subway again," said Grace. "I wouldn't either, if I'd seen what you saw." She smoothed out her gloves and sighed, and for a moment the girls walked in silence.

"I couldn't get over that experience," said Jerry with an odd primness in her voice. "I kept wondering what they'd done with the poor man finally, and I talked about it at home so much that Mamma said, 'If it bothers you, why don't you call up that Donnelly boy you went to high school with, and ask him. He's on the police force now, or so his mother told me at the New Method Bakery the other day. I'll bet he can find out the information for you.' And so I did 'phone Lester Donnelly a few days ago, and sure enough he told me all the police knew.

"He gave me the man's name, and said he was still alive when they got him from under the train and took him to a hospital. He said the police records didn't show final disposition of the case, but maybe they'd tell me at the hospital, if I called up and asked.

"At first I thought I'd 'phone, like Lester suggested, and then I thought, no, it would be better if I went there in person and asked; so yesterday at lunch hour I walked over there and got the information I wanted. I said a friend of mine had seen the accident, and we thought at home that maybe it was Mamma's cousin that we hadn't seen for a long time, and the description of the man was the same. So this man at the hospital looked in the files and said no, the man hadn't died like I thought. In fact, he said the man was resting as comfortably as could be expected, and was making progress, considering that he had lost both legs, and was blinded for life; and of course there was still this terrible gash in his head. Then the man at the hospital put the file back in the cabinet and said in a strange voice, 'If this man is really your mother's cousin, then your family must be made out of pig iron, because he's going to get perfectly well, and be out of the hospital before long.'"

Grace Palumbo, who wept as spontaneously as others sweated, paused at the entrance to the Twenty-eighth Street station and leaned her face against the metal wall beside the stairs. She dabbed at her eyes with her handkerchief, and said: "I'm crying with relief, Jerry! I thought all along that the poor man died!"

1944

THE STATIC SISTERS

*W*HEN Mrs. Furness, in her pinched widowhood, opened her home to the public, it was her most earnest wish that her establishment conform precisely to the pattern of the formal town home, that it seem not a boarding-house at all, but the exclusive residence of gentlefolk. Often she pondered how best to achieve this simulation of privacy, this illusion of ladies and gentlemen gathered together in her home for a hushed and perpetual house party. To achieve this end, she kept her windows shuttered both summer and winter, and for a time she considered removing the chairs from her front porch, so that her lodgers could not loll there and be seen from the street; but at last she saw that her purpose was to be achieved in another and a more unexpected manner, and the day the Clayton girls arrived and made arrangements to live in her house was the day she knew clearly that she had achieved her intentions.

The young women came with their boxes, their trunks and their treasured mementos of the past, announcing that they would remain for the summer only. Actually, they were never to leave, and in the end it almost seemed as if Mrs. Furness had been widowed and ruined financially in anticipation of a need the Clayton girls would some day have for an unimpeachable place of shelter.

When her new guests were settled in their apartment, Mrs. Furness went downstairs to confer with her cook. "Hannah," she began, trying to stifle the satisfaction in her voice, "Miss Adeline Clayton and her sister Miss Leila Clayton are going to be with us for several weeks. Of course I needn't tell you who they are, or what they represent, for you understand these things as well as I do." She raised her arms and reset the hairpins at the nape of her neck, her bosom lifting upward in a triumphant curve.

"They are distinguished but impoverished gentlewomen, like myself," she went on; "but in their case there is, fortunately, something left to live on, and even if there were not, their connections in the State would see that they lacked for no essential comfort."

"Yassum," said Hannah. "I knows very well who the young ladies is. And now tell me this, Mrs. Furness: Where we gwiner seat 'em in the dining room?"

This was a problem which Mrs. Furness had not as yet considered, and she stood in puzzlement for a time, her hands pressed anxiously together, as if the Clayton girls could not be expected to mingle with their inferiors except on those fixed and public occasions when bazaars were opened or hospitals dedicated; occasions when, by appointment, reporters were present to chronicle their nods of approval, to record for the masses their official, tedious graciousness.

At last she decided to set her little rosewood table in the alcove where she normally kept her ferns and begonias, and it was here that the Clayton girls dined alone, but not in silence, for they talked interminably, and often at the same time; and since their arrival coincided with the development of radio, with the earphone and the crystal set, it was inevitable that the other boarders, after listening to their muffled and irritating chatter, called them in private the Static Sisters.

When their dinner was finished that first evening, the girls came instinctively to the front porch and seated themselves in rocking chairs. They were of average height, and their coloring and their general appearance was similar, but the elder Miss Clayton was cursed with clumsy thighs and a thick waist, and her legs, when they could be glimpsed through her summer dresses, had the stuffed, shapeless look of a highwayman's weapon.

She had, in fact, inherited the Weatherby figure, and she knew that well; but she accepted her cross with fortitude, or even perhaps with pride, for the defects she bore on her person had been borne as well by two celebrated bishops, a Supreme Court justice, and a president of the United States. Then, too, she took consolation in the knowledge that from the waist up she was at least proportionate; and, as everybody knew, she had been given as compensation for her figure the lovely shoulders and the beautiful face of the Cameron women.

Miss Leila Clayton, who was twenty-six and therefore two years younger than her sister, had also been both handicapped and rewarded, for she had not only received by descent the slender, graceful figure of the Lankesters, but, by some prankish twist of heredity, Nature had set in the middle of her pretty, rather delicate face, the jutting, aquiline nose of her celebrated Indian forefather, a nose which, while appropriate enough to a warlike chieftain with a scalplock, could hardly be thought of as an asset to a young lady of refinement and fashion.

She had been conscious of the nose for as long as she could remember, and in many ways it had shamed her and cruelly shaped her character, for when she was a child still toddling about, long before the compensating blessing of the Lankester grace had manifested itself, each member of the family upon seeing her for the first time had lifted his hands and exclaimed, half-laughingly, half in horror: "Tuscaloosa's nose! Oh, good heavens and earth, the child has inherited Tuscaloosa's nose!"

And so the Clayton girls, sitting on Mrs. Furness' porch, beneath the splendor of her blossoming coral vine, discussed their handicaps and their blessings, debating interminably the sources from which each had acquired her eyes, her hair, her hands, or her throat. Hearing them, one would have got the impression that nothing they had belonged personally to them, that each feature, each mannerism, each trait of character, even, had been borrowed for their lifetime from the vast grab bag of the past.

"Look, Adeline!" said Leila after a moment's silence. "Look at that odd old woman crossing the street! She reminds me of the music teacher we had that winter we spent in Washington with Aunt Frances and Uncle Hillary. She has the same walk and the same stiff gestures. Do you remember her at all?"

"Her name was Miss Geneva Gentry," said Adeline, "and she was the sister of Senator Gentry. Oh, yes, I remember her well.

She carried a common alarm clock with her when she visited her pupils."

"I know," said Leila. "She carried it openly through the streets, her middle finger hooked in the metal ring. She always put it on the piano when we were taking our lessons, so we could see how quickly time was passing and how little we were accomplishing."

Adeline smiled and shook her head gently. "No, Leila—not on the piano! She put it on a marble-top table beside the piano. She was afraid it might scratch the piano, if you'll think back a little."

"We always jumped when the alarm went off," continued Leila, "and pretended it had startled us, but of course it hadn't in the least."

Adeline sighed and lay back in her chair. "Do you remember, years later, when we made our debut in Washington and asked Aunt Frances about her? Do you remember she told us that the poor old thing had been hit by a street car and killed instantly?"

"I remember," said Leila. "I remember very well, indeed. It seemed such a peculiar way to die: being struck by a street car, I mean. I think, though, you're wrong about her dying instantly. As I remember it, she was alive when the ambulance came, but died later in the hospital." She glanced thoughtfully at her hands, and then, as if the street car were the final association in the chain of associations which had preceded it, she went on in a low, intense voice: "Adeline, do you remember how we used to cross pins and put them on the rails, so when the car ran over the two pins, it crushed them flat and turned them into one little pair of doll's scissors?"

Adeline said: "Why, of course I do. I remember it all perfectly."

And thus it was that the sisters recalled the past with both a jealous attention to detail and a stylized precision of form, for, like children who want everything repeated the way they first heard it, the girls did not deviate from the first drafts of their memories, preserving with patience even the small inaccuracies of the original versions.

✦

Barricade, the ancestral home of the Claytons, was so rich in associations that the Historical Society bought it at length from its threadbare heirs and made of it a memorial to the past, with, during the height of the tourist season, young ladies in crinolines who draped themselves against the pillars, or moved languidly, with one hand stretched forward, across the lawns. Its location, its very existence, was intimately connected with the first Clayton to appear in America. He was a certain Sir Randal Clayton, a captain in DeSoto's army, and Mrs. Furness, both as a member of the Historical Society and as Secretary of the Association for the Preservation of State Shrines, was almost as interested in him and the plantation home which had housed his descendants, as were Adeline and Leila themselves.

The girls breakfasted late, and Mrs. Furness, as a compliment to them, served them personally in their bedroom. At nine o'clock one of the maids would appear with the trays and place them on a serving table beside the bed, with Mrs. Furness bending critically above each dish as it was uncovered and occasionally rejecting one with a cry of astonishment and a wave of her puckered, old-woman hands. She would usually have coffee, or even eat a hot biscuit and quince jelly while her distinguished guests dined robustly on spoonbread, eggs, and slices of tender Virginia ham; and somehow before the meal was finished, the conversation invariably turned to Barricade and the early splendors of the Claytons.

Adeline, perhaps, would say: "Sir Randal was a soldier of fortune, I'm afraid. You see, certain oddities of temperament made it impossible for him to live in England any longer, and that is how he happened to be in Spain at the time DeSoto was equipping his final expedition to the New World." She sighed, sipped daintily from her cup, and added: "Does this explain the unusual circumstance of an Englishman who was also a captain of Spain?"

"Yes," said Mrs. Furness. "Very completely, my dear."

"DeSoto had already plundered the Incas," said Adeline, "but he was greedy for more, and he believed the Indians of Florida had wealth which made that of the Peruvians seem trivial by

comparison. And so his party landed in 1539, on the west coast
of Florida, and worked its way inland." Thus step by step the
sisters followed the expedition until it reached the country where
Tuscaloosa ruled. "He was a great chief indeed," said Leila. "He
was a man of imposing stature, with a countenance singularly
handsome, but severe."

"Nevertheless, he received DeSoto with pomp, to the playing
of many flutes," said Adeline. "His warriors stood behind him
in the forest, the trees casting designs of light and shadow on
their half-naked bodies. Over the head of Tuscaloosa there was
stretched a deer-skin umbrella painted in stripes of different colors. Some say he received his guests in full war paint, in a
mantle of rich marten skins and a diadem of brilliant feathers."
She closed her eyes, seeing again in her mind the barbaric magnificence of the scene. "The Indians had never seen armor, or
firearms, or even horses," she went on. "The Spaniards knew
this quite well, and hoping to impress Tuscaloosa with their
power, they fired their muskets, paraded their troops, and
pranced their glittering, Arabian stallions before his eyes."

Later, when the Spaniards were moving westward, a scouting
party became separated from the main body of troops, and finding themselves menaced by hostile Indians, they had erected a
barricade atop an oddly shaped knoll near the bend of a river.
There they had been attacked and destroyed, with the exception
of Captain Clayton, and he, it appeared, had been wounded and
taken prisoner; but his life had been spared after all, for Leetamahachee, the daughter of Tuscaloosa himself, had implored her
father to preserve him and give him to her as a husband. Her
wish had been granted, and the handsome Englishman settled
down to spend the remainder of his life with his Indian wife,
a woman who resembled her father strikingly both in temperament and physique.

Adeline nodded, pushed back her tray, and continued: "Many
years later, Sir Randal's youngest son, a boy in his early twenties
at the time, made his way to the settlement at St. Augustine, and
was well received by the Spaniards. He arrived in time for the
sacking of the town by Sir Francis Drake, and when he made

himself known as the son of Randal Clayton, Drake carried him back to England, where people referred to him as an Indian prince. He married, had a number of children, and was widowed early; but he never forgot the place of his birth, and in 1608, when he was a man in his late thirties, he gathered his children together and sailed for Virginia with the first colonists, the distinction being that while the others journeyed to a new world, he returned to his old home."

And so the story went. Being aggressive, the Claytons had played important parts in the development of America; being acquisitive, they had accumulated money; being amative, they had left their descendants everywhere. From Virginia, they had spread south and west, to the Carolinas, to Georgia, and even to the settlements at Biloxi and Mobile, for like eels traveling from their inland ponds and rivers to the exact spot on the floor of the ocean where they had been spawned, the Claytons, too, made the long journey to the place of their origin. At last one of them found the knoll at the bend of the river, just as it was indicated on the crude map which Sir Randal had made for the guidance of his son more than two hundred years before, and later on another of his descendants built the great plantation home which he named Barricade.

At this point, Mrs. Furness began gathering the breakfast things together. "There's a monograph by a certain Professor Pomfrey in the library of the Historical Society," she said. "In it, he doubts that Tuscaloosa had a daughter named Leetamahachee, or if he did, that she married a white man. He's plainly quite an impossible little man, and I don't recommend that you bother with his book."

Leila raised her hand and unconsciously touched her nose; then, realizing what she had done, she turned her head a little and blushed. "But that's silly!" she said in confusion. "I never heard a statement that was so obviously absurd!"

Mrs. Furness glanced at her watch, jumped up and exclaimed: "It's almost ten o'clock!" She hurried to the hall and called down the stairwell to her maids: "Louise! Melinda! Carry Lou! The breakfast trays! The morning's half gone!"

Afterwards the girls seated themselves at their writing desks, for they kept up a tireless correspondence with members of their family they had not seen in years, had never actually liked, and never wished to meet again. They wrote steadily for a while, and then Leila raised her head and stared at her reflection in the mirror above the mantel.

As she grew older, as her face broadened and her neck thickened, her nose did not seem so inappropriate as it once had. She had never cut her hair, feeling that the style would not suit her; instead, she wore it pulled back tightly from her forehead and coiled low on her neck. Somehow, her face seemed to irritate her, for she frowned, put down her pen and said: "I'm not in the mood for writing letters. I'm nervous and upset today." She went to the window and stood there, playing anxiously with the curtain cord.

Across the street, the little Howard girls were performing a duet with difficulty. It was "Ripples of the Alabama," and Leila, speaking over her shoulder, said: "Adeline, do you remember we played that same piece years ago?"

Adeline nodded and smiled, the Cameron dimples showing plainly. She came at once to the window and stood there on her thick, clumsy legs, one hand pressed against the lacy foam of her pinkish negligee, the other resting on her sister's shoulder. She seemed to grow more girlish as she grew older. Her pink, relaxed face was entirely unlined, and her gray hair was elaborately arranged in tiny curls, with bows of sapphire velvet at either side to match her wide-open, brilliant eyes. There was something soft and defenseless about her, particularly when she laughed and lowered her head a little, as she did at this moment.

"We tried and tried," she said, "but we could never get the ripples to come out right. We practiced on Grandmother's old duet-stool, remember? The one Mamma sold later on for such a fabulous price."

"It was really two stools joined together," said Leila, "with two fan-shaped backs which were carved ornately with Cupids and garlands of flowers. The stools were connected in three places with cross-pieces whose panels depicted little scenes in the career of Venus."

"The legs ended in claws which grasped crystal balls," said Adeline eagerly. "The seat and the cross-pieces were of polished satinwood, but the rest of it was gilt. I can remember to this day how the carving hurt my shoulder blades."

"It was sold after Papa's death," said Leila, "the year we had so little to live on. A gentleman from one of the big museums came to look at some of our pieces. He mentioned a duet-stool while talking to Mamma, and said he'd simply combed the country for one, but without success. And then Mamma said, 'Sir, you need look no farther. There's one in our attic that you're welcome to.'"

"Not in the attic," said Adeline. "She said in the carriage house. You've forgotten that Mamma never put small pieces in the attic."

"It was the attic," said Leila. "I must insist on the point because I went with her to look for it, and was present when she found it."

"Perhaps so," said Adeline doubtfully. "Anyway, the man's eyes fairly popped out of their sockets when he saw it, even though it was so badly tarnished, and needed repairs. He said it was probably the only one left in the world, and Mamma laughed for the first time in weeks and said she was sure of it, because nobody but us would have preserved such a monstrosity."

Thus the Static Sisters recalled the past in a sort of operatic recitative for two, a duet in which each knew her cues, and returned at once to her partner the exact wording of a memorized text. Their world had become a small one indeed, but it was one both rich and reassuring, for everything they encountered in it was either similar to the past they remembered or differed from it in a remarkable way. They were content, then, to talk and compare and remember—rocking away the years from the ending of one war to the beginning of another.

Outside their bedroom, against the weathered red brick of the house itself, there was a curved balcony of wrought iron where the girls had made a garden of sweet alyssum, phlox, and petunias. They had planted morning glories and cypress vine as well, and had trained the tendrils up the fluted, iron columns and through the involved design of the grille work that decorated the ceiling-pieces and the balustrade. They liked to recline there during the long, sultry afternoons of summer while they chatted and digested their heavy luncheons in a sort of drowsy seclusion. Adeline was fond of crossword puzzles and she would often bring out her book and work at it diligently while Leila, seated beside her, played solitaire.

Sometimes, as she laid out the cards, she wondered why she and her sister were interested only in games where two things, through the exercise of skill, could be combined into one, but the thought was so elusive that she could not hold on to it and it slipped at once through her mind.

Adeline, who was turning the pages of a magazine, paused before a photograph and said: "I consider General MacArthur a most distinguished-looking man. Do you suppose he's connected with our family? . . . Let's see, now: There are the MacArthurs of Virginia who are related to us through the Lankesters, and there are the Kentucky and Georgia McArthurs, but they spell their name another way."

Leila did not reply, and Adeline glanced at her reproachfully. Of late her sister had been behaving strangely, she thought, and she wondered what it was that disturbed her. Surely it was nothing in her daily life, for that was precisely what it had always been. "Leila! Leila!" she said in gentle exasperation. "I believe you're dozing in your chair!"

Leila frowned and shoved the cards from her with a quick, impatient gesture. "Let's go downstairs where we can at least see people," she said. "I can't stand it here any longer."

Later, they came onto the wide, front porch and deployed themselves side by side, as they always did, one of them bending forward, one of them leaning back against her cushions, their chairs arranged at an oblique angle to the street with such precision of alignment that one might well suspect some desperate and unacknowledged need in the tableau they chose for themselves.

Adeline maintained that she was susceptible to drafts, and for that reason, no matter how warm the weather was, she sat with a shawl draped cunningly across her lap, while Leila, on the pretext that her eyes were sensitive to light, concealed her nose behind the black, lacy veils she affected. "Adeline," she said after a moment, "do you remember Maggie and Milly Jesperson, the Siamese twins who were born on a farm near Barricade? They were joined together at the hip by some sort of fleshy ligament, and the doctors said they could never be separated because they shared certain organs in common."

"They were older than we were," said Adeline. "When we were young girls, they were almost grown, and their parents put them in a circus. I remember how we both cried. You wanted to go to the Jesperson farm and forbid it, but Papa laughed when you told him, and he pinched your cheek. He said you concerned yourself needlessly, because Maggie and Milly didn't mind being a freak in the least. He said they were proud of it, and that being joined together was their one claim to distinction."

Leila frowned and closed her eyes, wondering what claim she and her sister had to distinction. They, too, were joined together in a way, she thought—not by a ligament of flesh, but by the more cruel ligament of the past. She felt these things rather than thought them; then, as if they were too painful to be endured, even in the confused and unspoken state in which they existed in her mind, she reached up and broke a spray from the coral vine, turning it slowly in her hands, and thinking: "All our lives Adeline and I have waited for something to begin, but whatever it was we waited for, it passed somehow as we sat here on the porch."

All at once, one of the things which had troubled her became clear; she knew at last in consciousness what she had felt for a long time in the fumbling recesses of her brain, and that was the reason why she and Adeline arranged themselves with such fussy exactitude on the porch, for it seemed to her now that they grouped themselves there as if they were the panels of a stereoscopic slide, as if the pose were a scheme to deceive the eye of the passer-by into seeing them, by tricks of focus or the refraction of light, not as two weak and ridiculous creatures, but as one strong, composite one: an irresistible woman who had Adeline's perfection of face and her own perfection of figure.

"But why?" she thought. "Why should this be so important?"

The answer eluded her; then, curiously, her mind went back to the party given for Adeline on her tenth birthday. It was the time that Cousin Cecil Clayton, noted in the family for his wit, had posed the little girls and examined their faces and their figures with mock-seriousness, exclaiming at length: "Somebody should put these girls in a kettle and melt them down. If he did, the result would be two remarkable creatures, and one of them would be so ravishing that the world would be at her feet."

She recalled the scene to Adeline, but her sister laughed, waved her hands gaily and said: "He also remarked that the other girl would be too horrible to contemplate, if you remember."

"He didn't actually remark it," said Leila. "He implied it. That's why it was considered so witty, and why the other guests laughed as they did."

"At any rate," said Adeline, "the thing that made the greatest impression on my mind that day was the way you hurled yourself at him when he said it, biting and clawing and screaming with rage. Mamma made you apologize, and sent you up to your room. You missed the refreshments, remember? Really, you behaved dreadfully that day."

Leila said: "I always hated Cousin Cecil. I hate him at this very moment."

She moved nervously in her chair, wondering what the strange, oppressive feeling was that she felt in her breast; the odd, excited humming in her ears. She felt as if she were about to understand something both terrible and important for her sister and herself, something which it was better, at this late period of their lives, that neither of them knew. She fought it down for a time, and then since she was frightened and needed the reassurance of speech, she turned to Adeline and spoke at random; but even then her unconscious wish betrayed her, and the automatic cabinet of her mind found and brought to memory the one association which was to make everything clear to her at last.

"Adeline," she began, "do you remember the bulb we found

when we were children and planted in a pot in the cellar? We forgot about it for several weeks, and when we came back to it, the stalk had grown to the ceiling and then turned down again, being too heavy to support itself."

"We looked at it every day after that," said Adeline, "and wondered what the plant would turn out to be. Sometimes Mamma came with us, but she joked and predicted it wouldn't bloom at all. She was wrong about it, though, and the plant did bloom in a way."

"There were two tiny, pink buds at the very tip of the stalk," said Leila, "and when we saw them that first time, we all laughed and said: 'Why, they're nothing but common gladiolas!' I suppose we'd known it all along, really, but wouldn't admit it to ourselves." She lowered her eyes suddenly and examined a crack in her thumb nail, thinking: "It may be Adeline and I are so interested in the past because Papa and Mamma were alive then, and protected us from the outside world. Everything was arranged for us in those days, and everything was secure. Perhaps we believe that if we talk about the past, we can make it exist again."

She was conscious of her sister talking once more, and she half turned in her chair and listened. Adeline was saying in a soft, vivacious voice: "I remember how Mamma stood there that morning with an arm around each of us and remarked laughingly: 'Just think! Only two pale, shriveled little buds at the end of all that growth and foliage.'"

At that instant, as if the final barrier of resistance had broken, Leila understood the secret of the union between herself and her sister; knowing clearly that, while together they were secure, honored, and invincible, apart from the other, each was merely half a woman, a being without strength and with no defenses against the menacing world at all.

For a moment she stared strangely at her sister, and then she said: "Adeline, this is all there will ever be for us. Come inside and close the door." She walked quickly across the porch and into the hall, and a moment later Adeline heard her running up the stairs, her heels making a clatter on the polished wood.

She did not come down to dinner that evening, and Adeline dined alone in the alcove. Afterwards, she waited for her sister on the porch, rocking to and fro and peering through the twilight at the activity of the street. Then, at last, Leila did come and sit quietly in her regular chair.

"Look, Leila!" said Adeline as if nothing at all had happened. "Mr. Howard has discarded that old panama hat he wears! Do you remember the panama Papa once had? Mamma tried for years to make him stop wearing it, because it really was disreputable, but he'd just smile at her and say: 'Have you forgotten I paid a hundred dollars for that hat in New Orleans, on our honeymoon? A good panama never wears out, my dear! The clerk who sold it to me, guaranteed it for a lifetime.' Do you remember that battered old hat, Leila? Can you visualize it now?"

She waited for her sister's answer, but Leila raised her head and stared steadily at the horizon above the trees, saying nothing at all. Then Adeline bent forward timidly, put one hand on her sister's knee, and said: "Leila! Leila! I don't understand you at all, any more! Why don't you answer me? Have I offended you in any way?"

"I remember," said Leila after a moment. "I remember very well indeed."

1944